A SON OF THE REVOLUTION

Phillipe's head was dizzy with the "subversive" teachings of that firebrand, Rousseau . . . and the response of William Pitt the Elder, speaking to a fellow member of the British Parliament, only served to inflame Phillipe further:

"The gentleman tells us that America is obstinate; that America is almost in open rebellion. Sir, I rejoice that America has resisted!

"The gentleman asks when were the colonies emancipated. But I desire to know when they were made slaves! They are subjects of this kingdom, equally bound by its laws and equally participating in the constitution of this free country.

"THE AMERICANS ARE THE SONS, NOT THE BASTARDS, OF ENGLAND!"

But the English King, "German George," had other ideas. And Phillipe found himself plunged into a maelstrom of events—including a blazing battlefield struggle that would bring him face to face with his hated half-brother, Roger . . . a tempestuous romance with the daughter of an American revolutionary . . . and a series of exhilarating encounters with a little band of radicals and patriots who authored one of the most revered documents of all time: The U.S. Constitution!

THE BASTARD . . . FIRST IN THE EXCITING SERIES OF AMERICAN BICENTENNIAL NOVELS

The American Bicentennial Series

With all the color and sweep of American history itself, The American Bicentennial Series is a mighty eight-volume saga of heroism and dedication, patriotism and valor, shining spirit and abiding faith.

Here is the story of our nation—and an amazing family living in the turbulent times that began the American nation.

This magnificent American Bicentennial Series of novels is more than absorbing, entertaining reading . . . it is a resounding re-affirmation of the greatness of America.

Volume 1   THE BASTARD

Volume 2   THE REBELS

Volume 3   THE SEEKERS

Volume 4   THE FURIES

Volume 5   THE TITANS

Volume 6   THE WARRIORS

THE BASTARD

•

JOHN JAKES

THE AMERICAN BICENTENNIAL SERIES • *Volume I*

PYRAMID BOOKS ▲ NEW YORK

THE BASTARD

A PYRAMID BOOK

PRODUCED BY LYLE KENYON ENGEL

Pyramid edition published October 1974
Twenty-ninth Printing, April 1977

Library of Congress Catalog Card Number: 74-11927

Printed in the United States of America

Pyramid Books are published by Pyramid Publications (Harcourt Brace Jovanovich, Inc.). Its trademarks, consisting of the word "Pyramid" and the portrayal of a pyramid, are registered in the United States Patent Office.

PYRAMID PUBLICATIONS
(Harcourt Brace Jovanovich, Inc.)
757 Third Avenue, New York, N.Y. 10017

The eight novels in this series, carrying the story of an American family forward from its beginning in Revolutionary times to the two-hundredth anniversary of the Republic, could only be dedicated, book by book, to the eight Americans I love best of all. And so, Rachel, this is for you.

"The *gentleman* tells us that America is obstinate; that America is almost in open rebellion. Sir, I rejoice that America has resisted . . .

"The gentleman asks when were the colonies emancipated. But I desire to know when they were made slaves . . .

"They are subjects of this kingdom, equally entitled with yourselves to all the natural rights of mankind, and the peculiar privileges of Englishmen; equally bound by its laws, and equally participating in the constitution of this free country. The Americans are the sons, not the bastards, of England."

1766:
William Pitt the Elder,
before Parliament,
in support of repeal
of the Stamp Act.

Contents

Book One

Fortune's Whirlwind

Chapter I	The Beating	17
Chapter II	Behind the Madonna	41
Chapter III	Blood in the Snow	61
Chapter IV	Kentland	77
Chapter V	A Game of Love	98
Chapter VI	"A Perfect Member of the Mob-ility"	121
Chapter VII	Brother Against Brother	139
Chapter VIII	Trap	154
Chapter IX	Flight	169

Book Two

The House of Sholto and Sons

Chapter I	Swords at St. Paul's	181
Chapter II	The Black Miracle	205
Chapter III	Mr. Burke and Dr. Franklin	227
Chapter IV	The Wizard of Craven Street	242
Chapter V	The One-Eyed Man	256
Chapter VI	The Bristol Coach	276
Chapter VII	To an Unknown Shore	293

Book Three

Liberty Tree

Chapter I	The Secret Room	317
Chapter II	Mistress Anne	340
Chapter III	September Fire	367
Chapter IV	Night of the Axe	405
Chapter V	Decision	427
Chapter VI	The Sergeant	456
Chapter VII	Betrayal	476
Chapter VIII	Journey to Darkness	497

Book Four

The Road From Concord Bridge

Chapter I	The Letter	519
Chapter II	A Death in Philadelphia	540
Chapter III	Alicia	558
Chapter IV	Too Much for the Whistle	576
Chapter V	Alarm at Midnight	596
Chapter VI	"God Damn It, They Are Firing Ball!"	613

The Bastard

Book One

Fortune's Whirlwind

CHAPTER I

The Beating

i

THE WOMAN'S FACE BURNED, glowed as though illuminated by a shaft of sunlight falling from a high cathedral window. But the woman was no madonna, unanimated, beatific. Her face showed violent emotion.

He fought to turn away from the searing brilliance, but he could neither run nor move. The old, strangling dread began to tighten his throat—

The woman stared at him, accusing. Her black eyes shone nearly as bright as the highlights in her black hair where it crowned her forehead and cascaded on either side of her oval face. Behind her was darkness, nothing but darkness. It intensified the frightening radiance of her face, emphasized the whiteness of her teeth. Unlike most women of her years—she was three less than forty; he knew every dreadful detail—by some miracle of inherited health, her mouth was free of gaps and brown rot.

He struggled to hide from the face and could not even avert his head. The dread quickened. He heard his own strident breathing. It grew louder, because he knew she would speak to him—

And she did, the words frightening as always, frightening because he could never be certain whether she spoke from love or rage.

"Don't try to run. I told you—*don't*. You will *listen*."

Run. God, as if he could! He was held in that vast

17

darkness where her face burned so fiercely; and her eyes—

"There will be no Latin. Do you hear? *No Latin*! You will study English. The reading and writing of your own language, and English. And how to figure sums—something I never learned. But I had no need of it, acting in Paris. You will. There's a different role for you, Phillipe. A great role, never forget that—"

Like coals on the hearth of a winter midnight, her eyes were fire, hypnotic. But they held no warmth. He was all cold sweat, terror, crippled immobility—

"I'll tell you what the role is when I feel the time is proper. Till then, you must obey me and learn English as your second tongue—and also such things as how much an English pound is worth. That way, you'll be ready to take what belongs to you. Let the fools around here chatter about the glory of France. The greatest empire the world's known since Rome lies across the water—where you must go one day, to claim what's yours. So let the little church boys learn their Latin from that bigot priest and his helper!"

Stabbing out, disembodied white things, white claws, her hands reached at him. Closed on his upper arms. She shook him, shaken herself with the ferocity of her passion.

Trying to deny her, negate her, he was able at last to turn his head from side to side. The effort required all his strength. But she would not release him. Her face floated closer, wrenching into the ugliness that brought the old, silent scream climbing into his throat.

"You will learn your English from Girard!" she cried. "From good, decent books—none of those filthy, blasphemous things he hides in his cupboard. Do you hear me, Phillipe?"

He tried to speak but his throat somehow remained

clogged. Nothing but a feeble hiss of air came out between his teeth.

She shook him harder, then harder still, as a wind from the limitless dark tossed her lustrous hair. The wind added its keen to the rising shrillness of her voice; its blowing and buffeting seemed to shimmer the burning image of her face like a candle-flame in a gale—

"Do you hear what I say, Phillipe? *Do you hear me?*"

At last he brought forth sound: a howling, animal cry of fear and pain—

The wind-roar broke off like an interrupted thunderclap. He tore himself from the clutching hands, fled through the darkness. Away from the white claws. The face. The eyes—

But the darkness to which he fled was without substance. His legs churned on emptiness, as he fell, and fell, and *fell*—

This time the sound from his throat was a scream for mercy.

ii

He awoke sweating. Sweating and—after a moment's realization that it was over—enraged.

The dream came on him from time to time. He should be used to it. But he wasn't. Always, the dream brought unaccountable terror.

In those first muzzy moments, his anger turned to shame. He rubbed his eyes to rid himself of sleepiness. The roughness of his knuckles against his eyelids was a reassurance.

His body was slick with sweat. Yet at the same time he was cold in the garret room above the inn. He knuckled his eyes harder. A little more of his drowsiness sloughed away. And more of the fear. He tried to laugh but made only a rough, croaking sound.

The dream's details were essentially the same on

every occasion. Her face. Her eyes. Her hands. Her
implied accusations, couched in the long, jumbled
harangue. He'd heard bits of it before, often. In sleep.
And awake too.

She always insisted that England was the rising star in
the world's constellation of powers, and now he wondered again whether she said that because she had been
treated so shabbily by her own people.

She always insisted that he was better—much better—than any of those among whom they lived.

But she refused to say precisely why. Whenever he
pressed her for specifics, she would only smile—how
haughtily she could smile!—and reply:

"In good time, Phillipe. In good time."

The garret smelled of straw, and his own sweat. He
rolled on his side, toward the little round garret window
that looked out onto the basalt hillside touched now with
the glint of starlight. Under his left arm, the stiff corners
of book spines jabbed him through the prickly wool of
the knee-length shirt that he merely tucked into his
breeches when it was time for the day's work to start.

Uncomfortable, he tugged the precious, carefully hidden books from under his body—the books whose contents he understood so poorly; the dangerous books
Girard had been slipping to him for more than a year
now, always with the caution that he keep them concealed.

One of the volumes, by an Englishman named Locke
whom Girard much admired, had been helpful in
Phillipe's study of the second language he had learned.
But *Two Treatises of Government* also puzzled and confused him in many places. As did the other two books.

The first was a slim volume called *Le Contract social*.
By a Swiss writer Girard called one of the *philosophes,*
whenever he didn't refer to him with a wry smile as the
mad Master Jean Jacques. The largest and bulkiest book
was one of Girard's two most cherished possessions.

The first volume of something called *L'En-cyclopedie*—a compendium of the world's knowledge to date. Mind-numbing essays on everything from politics to the nature and construction of the heavens. Two more of those admired *philosophes,* a thinker named Diderot and a scientist named d'Alembert, had assembled the vast work, Girard said.

The first two volumes of the work had been suppressed the moment they went on sale because, as Girard put it, quoting with acerbity some official of the French government, the compendium "tended to destroy the royal authority, to encourage a spirit of independence and revolt and to erect the foundations of error, the corruption of manners, irreligion and impiety." Somehow a few copies had been privately circulated before the official suppression. Girard had been lucky enough to get hold of one of each of the initial volumes.

As Phillipe buried the books underneath the straw, his mind turned back to the dream. Perhaps he deserved it, as punishment. On every possible occasion when more legitimate works—safer works—were not under study, Girard patiently tried to explain some of the vast, hard-to-grasp ideas Phillipe could read but could not fully understand. Voltaire. Montesquieu. The mad Rousseau. They were all represented in that precious big book Phillipe slid on top of the other two and hid with straw. They were all, Girard maintained smugly, unarguably great. They were all rattling the world to its foundations—

And turning Phillipe into one corrupted by error?

If she only knew! How often would the dreams come then?

Probably never, he reflected with a small, weary smile. Very likely she wouldn't let him sleep but would lecture, lecture, lecture—

All three books safely out of sight, he relaxed a little.

Breathed more slowly and deeply, for the first time since waking up. He sniffed the damp mist of fall drifting down from the Puy de Dome in the north. The tang of the autumn night was a kind of tonic, restoring his senses but shoving him hard into reality again—the reality in which he always doubted the dream and all it contained.

Another cold, difficult winter would soon wrap around the Velay plain and freeze the Allier, which flowed northward to join the Loire. The dreary days would pass, and he would shiver and work and sleep his life away at a moldering inn that no longer attracted many customers.

He stuck a straw between his teeth and chewed the end absently. He was supposed to believe there was some marvelous, shining future waiting for him? In *England*? The homeland of France's traditional enemies?

He bit on the straw and let the corners of his mouth wrench up in another sour smile.

The very idea was laughable.

But it was also an explanation of why he had no friends his own age. Though he hardly believed the shrilled promises of the dream and the daytime harangues that carried the same promises, he knew he sometime acted as if he believed them completely. Others sensed that unconscious arrogance—

God, he could make no sense of it. Especially not now. He was sleepy again, wanting to escape into dreamless rest. He was totally exhausted. He lay back on the straw, bumping the hidden books before he wriggled and got comfortable. He pulled up the ragged blanket that stank of smoke and age.

A splendid future? For *him*? Who was he, after all? A tavern boy, nothing more.

And yet, when her face came to him in the frequent dream—when she hectored him—he *would* wonder just a little, as he started wondering again now, whether there was something in what she said.

"*In good time, Phillipe.*"

Was there something not yet revealed? Something waiting—as winter was waiting—to descend at its appointed moment? Something mysterious and exciting?

He didn't know. But of one thing he was utterly certain.

He feared and detested the dream. He hated being afraid of the savagery in the eyes of his own mother.

iii

Ramshackle, its wood sign creaking in the ceaseless wind of Auvergne, Les Trois Chevres clung to a hillside above a narrow road some three kilometers below the hamlet of Chavaniac. Four persons lived at the inn, tending the common-room fire, sweeping the rooms and changing the bedding, cooking the meals and serving the wine. They drew a meager living from the occasional coachloads of gentry bound farther south or heading eastward, toward the dangerous Alpine passes to the sunshine of Italy, which he imagined, in his most realistic moods, that he would never see.

Such a mood was on Phillipe Charboneau in the misty dawn following the nightmare. He felt he would probably spend his whole lifetime in the rocky country that was the only homeland he could remember.

With eyes fully open and his mind turning to the cheese to be fetched for the coming week, he displayed no sign that he believed the promises his mother shrilled at him in the dream. No sign, that is, except a certain lift of the shoulders and a touch of a swagger when he walked.

Of course, a short but strongly built boy of seventeen could be expected to stretch and swagger some. There were wild, powerful juices flowing at that age.

Phillipe's mother, Marie, ran the inn. It had belonged to her now-dead father, who was buried, as befitted a good Catholic, in the churchyard at Chavaniac. Years ago, Marie had run away to Paris to act in the theaters, and found herself automatically excommunicated from the Mother Church.

Phillipe helped her with the place, as did the hired girl, Charlotte, a buxom wench with a ripe mouth and wide hips. Charlotte's people lived a kilometer farther south. Her father, a miller, had begotten seventeen children. Unable to keep them all, he'd sent some of the brood to find employment where they could. Under Marie's guidance, Charlotte did most of the cooking.

The fourth resident at Les Trois Chevres was Girard, the tall, thin, razor-nosed man who had wandered by some four years ago, a pack of precious books tied to a stick over his shoulder. He had been persuaded to stay on because, at that time, Marie needed an older, stronger male to help around the place. Coming downstairs to the common room this morning, Phillipe found Girard mopping up sticky wine stains from the one table that had been occupied the night before.

"Good day, Phillipe," Girard greeted, in French. "We don't exactly have a bustling trade again this morning. May I suggest another lesson?"

"All right," Phillipe answered. "But first I have to go buy more cheese."

"Our sole customer of last night ate it all, did he?"

Phillipe nodded.

"He was a scrawny sort for a traveling tinker," Girard observed. "On the other hand—" He clinked sous down in his greasy apron. "Who am I to question the man's choice of vocations? He paid."

"Is my mother up yet?" Phillipe asked, starting toward the old, smoke-blackened door to the kitchen. Beyond it, he smelled a fragrant pine log burning on the hearth. "I heard no sound from her room," he added.

"I imagine she's still sleeping—why not? Our tinker took the road early." Girard rolled his tongue in his cheek. "I believe the charming Mademoiselle Charlotte's back there, however. Take care that she doesn't attack you." One of his bright blue eyes closed in a huge wink. "It continues to be evident that she'd like nothing better."

Phillipe flushed. The subject Girard hinted at excited him. He understood what men and women did together. But in actual practice, it still remained a mystery. He stopped a pace from the kitchen door. Yes, he distinctly heard Charlotte humming. And for some reason—his ill-concealed excitement, or nervousness, or both—he didn't want to face her just now.

Girard perched on a corner of a table, amused. He was an oddly built man of about thirty. He reminded Phillipe of a long-legged bird. Origins unknown —destination and ambition in life, if any, also unknown—Girard seemed content to do menial work and teach Phillipe his lessons, orthodox and otherwise. Fortunately, master and pupil liked each other.

"Go on, go on!" Girard grinned, waving. "A warm bun and the ample charms of Mademoiselle Charlotte await. What else could a chap want on a nippy morning?"

But Phillipe shook his head. "I think I'll go after the cheese first. Give me the money, please."

Girard fished the coins from his leather apron, mocking him:

"Your virtue's admirable, my boy. Eschew temptations of the flesh! Cling to the joys of the soul and the intellect! After all, are we not privileged to be living in the greatest of all ages of man? The age of reason?"

"So you keep saying. I wouldn't know."

"Oh, we're grumpy this morning."

"Well—" Phillipe apologized with a smile. "I had a bad dream, that's all."

"Not because of Monsieur Diderot and company, I trust."

Phillipe shook his head. "But there are some more questions I want to ask you, Girard. Half of that business about politics, I just can't understand."

"But that's the purpose of education! To *begin* to understand! Then to *want* to understand!"

"I know, you've said that before. I got a little of what some of those writers were talking about. Enough to tell me that what they're saying doesn't—doesn't sound *right*, somehow. All that about kings no longer having God's authority to run other people's lives—"

Girard's emphatic nod cut him off. "Exactly."

"But we've always had kings!"

"Always is not forever, Phillipe. There is absolutely nothing inherent in the structure of the universe which dictates that any free man should be expected to obey authority unless he wishes to—for his own benefit, and by his own consent. Even the best of kings rules by tradition, not right. And a man must make up his own mind as to whether he's willing to be ruled by the authority in question."

"Yes, I got that much."

"Our mad Swiss was even more blunt about it. He once observed that if God wished to speak to Monsieur Jean Jacques, He should not go through Moses." Girard paused. "Scandalous stuff I'm teaching you, eh?" he said with a twinkling eye.

"Confusing, mostly."

"Well, save your questions until we devote a little attention to something more conventional. When you return we'll try an English play. There are witches in it, and old Scottish kings who murder one another. You'll find it stimulating, I think. Learning ought not to be dull,

though God knows it is the way the priest peddle it."
With mock seriousness, he concluded, "I consider it not
just my job but my sacred obligation to sweeten your
preparation all I can, my young friend."

At the inn door, Phillipe turned. "Preparation for
what?"

"That, dear pupil, is for madame the actress to tell
you."

Phillipe frowned. "Why do you always speak of her
as madame?"

"For one thing, she insists upon it."

"But she has no husband. I've no father that I know
about."

"Nevertheless, I consider your mother a lady. But
then"—Girard shrugged, smiling again—"when she's in
a bad mood, she herself calls me an unconventional, not
to say dangerous, fellow. And she's not the only one!
Pity I can't force myself to stick to sums and English
where you're concerned. I can't because you're a bright
lad. So before you keep on pestering me with questions,
remember what I've told you before. Some of my
philosophical ideas could land you in serious trouble
one day. Consider that the warning of a friend. Now
hurry along for the cheese, eh? Or I can't guarantee
you'll be safe from Mademoiselle Charlotte!"

iv

So, on a gray November morning in the year 1770,
Phillipe Charboneau left Les Trois Chevres. He had
never, as a matter of record, seen a single goat on the
premises, let alone the three for whom Marie's father
had named the establishment.

He set off up the rock-strewn road in the direction of
Chavaniac. As the morning mist lifted gradually, the sun
came out. Far on the north horizon he glimpsed the
rounded gray hump of the Puy de Dome, a peak, so

Girard had informed him, that was surrounded with pits which had once belched fire and smoke. Small extinct volcanos, said the itinerant scholar.

Phillipe walked rapidly. On the hillsides above him, dark pines soughed in the wind blowing across the Velay hills. The air of Auvergne could shiver the bone in the fall and winter months. The inn was seldom warm this time of year, except when you stood directly at the fireside.

He wondered what it would be like to dwell in a splendid, comfortable chateau like the one near Chavaniac. The Motier family—rich, of the nobility —lived there, his mother said, usually hinting whenever the chateau was mentioned that he would experience a similar sort of life one day. In the stinging wind, Phillipe was more convinced than ever that she was only wishing aloud.

His old wool coat offered little protection from the cold. He was thoroughly chilled by the time he turned up a track through the rocks and emerged on a sort of natural terrace overlooking the road. Here stood the hovel and pens of du Pleis, the goatherd. Higher still, behind a screen of pines, bells clanked.

A fat, slovenly boy about Phillipe's age emerged from the hovel, scratching his crotch. The boy had powerful shoulders, and several teeth were missing. Phillipe's eyes narrowed a little at the sight of him.

"Well," said the boy, "look who graces us with his presence today."

Phillipe tried to keep his voice steady: "I've come for the week's cheese, Auguste. Where's your father?"

"In bed snoring drunk, as a matter of fact." Auguste grinned. But the grin, like the mealy dark eyes, carried no cordiality. The boy executed a mock bow. "Permit me to serve you instead. Sir."

Phillipe's chin lifted and his face grew harder. "Enough, Auguste. Let's stick to business—" He took out the coins, just as another, taller boy came outside. He carried a wicker-covered wine jug.

The new boy belched. "Oh. Company, Auguste?"

"My cousin Bertram," Auguste explained to Phillipe, who was studying the older boy. Bertram bore a faint scar on his chin. From knife fighting? He wore his hair long, not clubbed with a cheap ribbon at the nape of his neck, like Phillipe's. Bertram had dull, yellowish eyes, and he swayed a little as Auguste went on:

"This is Phillipe Charboneau, Bertram. A noted inn-keeper from down the road. And far better than any of us. The little lord, some people call him."

"A lord of the horse turds is what he looks like," Bertram joked, lifting the jug to drink.

"Oh, no!" Straight-faced, Auguste advanced on Phillipe, who suddenly smelled the boy's foul breath. "Though his mother's place isn't prosperous enough to have even a single horse in its stable, he's a very fine person. True, he's a bastard, and that's no secret. But his mother brags and boasts to everyone in the neighborhood that he'll leave us one day to claim some fabulous inheritance. Yes, one day he'll brush off the dirt of Auvergne—"

Auguste swooped a hand down, straightened and sprinkled dirt on Phillipe's sleeve.

"Don't laugh, Bertram!" Auguste said, maintaining his false seriousness. "We have it straight from his own mother! When she lowers herself to speak to lesser folk, that is." He squinted at Phillipe. "Which brings up a point, my little lord. At the time my own mother died— just last Easter, it was—and yours came up to buy cheese, she didn't say so much as one word in sympathy." He sprinkled a little more dirt on Phillipe's arm. "Not a word!"

Tense now, Phillipe sensed the hatred. Bertram shuffled toward him, swinging the jug. Phillipe knew that what fat Auguste said was probably true. But he felt compelled to defend Marie:

"Perhaps she wasn't feeling well, Auguste. That's it, I recall it now. At Eastertime, she—"

"Was feeling no different than usual," Auguste sneered. To Bertram: "She was an actress on the Paris stage. I've heard what that means, haven't you?"

Bertram grinned. "Of course. Actresses will lie down and open themselves for any cock with cash."

"And for that she's not allowed inside a Catholic church!" Auguste exclaimed, hateful glee on his suet-colored face. "Very unusual for such a woman to be the mother of a lord, wouldn't you say?"

Bertram licked a corner of his mouth. "Oh, I don't know. I hear most of the really grand ladies at the court are whores—"

"Damn you," Phillipe blurted suddenly, "I'll have the cheese and no more of your filthy talk!" He flung the coins on the ground.

Auguste glanced at Bertram, who seemed to understand the silent signal. Bertram set the wicker jug at his feet. The cousins started advancing again.

"You've got it wrong, little lord," Auguste said. "We'll have your money. And perhaps some of your skin in the bargain—!" His right foot whipped out, a hard, bruising kick to Phillipe's leg.

Off balance, Phillipe fisted his right hand, shot it toward Auguste's face. The fat boy ducked. A blur on Phillipe's left indicated Bertram circling him. The taller boy yanked the ribbon-tied tail of Phillipe's dark hair.

Phillipe's head snapped back. But he didn't yell. Bertram grabbed both his ears from behind, then gave him a boot in the buttocks.

The blow rocked Phillipe forward, right into Auguste's lifting knee. The knee drove into his groin. Phillipe cried out, doubling. Bertram struck him from behind, on the neck. The ground tilted—

A moment after Phillipe sprawled, Bertram kneeled on his belly. Auguste started to kick him.

Phillipe writhed, fought, struck out with both fists. But most of the time he missed. Auguste's boot pounded his legs, his ribs, his shoulders. Again. Again—

In the middle of the beating, one of Phillipe's punches did land squarely. Bertram's nose squirted blood onto Phillipe's coat. The older boy spat out filthy words, grabbed his victim's ears and began to hammer his head on the ground.

Phillipe's head filled with the strange sound of the heavy breathing of his two tormentors, the distorted ring of the goat bells from up beyond the pines. They beat him for three or four minutes. But he didn't yell again.

From inside the hovel, a querulous man's voice asked a question, then repeated it. The man sounded angry.

Auguste scooped up Phillipe's money. Bertram lurched to his feet, picked up the jug, brought the neck to his bloodied mouth and drank. Groaning, Phillipe staggered up, barely able to walk a straight line.

Auguste kicked him in the buttocks one last time, driving him down the track toward the road. The fat boy shouted after him:

"Don't come back here till your whoring mother can speak to her neighbors in a civil way, understand?"

Phillipe stumbled on, the sharp north wind stinging his cheeks. His whole body throbbed. He considered it an accomplishment just to stay on his feet.

v

Exhausted and ashamed of his inability to hold his own against Auguste and his cousin, Phillipe stumbled back to the inn along the lonely, wind-raked road. His sense of humiliation made him steal past the tavern perched on the hillside—he was grateful no one was looking out to see him—and seek the sanctuary of the empty stable behind the main building.

Hand over bruised hand, he pulled himself up the ladder to the loft and burrowed into the old straw, letting the blessed dark blot out the pain—

"Phillipe? Phillipe, is that you?"

The voice pulled him from the depths of unconsciousness. He rolled over, blinking, and saw a white oval—a face. Beyond, he glimpsed misted stars through cracks in the timbers of the loft. Down on the stable floor, a lantern gleamed.

"Sweet Mother of the Lord, Phillipe! Madame Marie's been out of her mind all day, worrying about your unexplained absence!"

"Charlotte—" He could barely pronounce her name. His various aches, though not unbearable, remained more than a little bothersome. And waking up—remembering—was not a pleasant experience.

Charlotte climbed off the ladder and knelt beside him in the straw. He licked the inside of his mouth; it failed to help the dryness. Charlotte swayed a little, braced on her knees and palms. He thought he smelled wine on her. Probably filched from the inn's cellar—

And it seemed to him no accident that Charlotte's position revealed her bare breasts all white where her soiled blouse fell away. For a moment, he thought she was ready to giggle. Her eyes seemed to glow with a jolly, vulpine pleasure. But her touch of his cheek was solicitous.

"Oh, my dear, what happened to you?"

"I had an accident," he said in a raspy voice. "Fell, that's all."

"Down ten mountainsides, from the look of you! I don't believe it for a minute." The girl stroked his cheek again; he was uncomfortably aware of the lingering nature of her caress. Nor could he overlook the feel of her fingertips. She must have been in the kitchen. She hadn't wiped off all the lard.

"Who beat you, Phillipe? Brigands? Since when have poor boys become their game?"

"Not brigands—" Each word cost him energy. But he managed to sit up, groaning between clenched teeth. "Listen, Charlotte, never mind. I came back and wanted to sleep so I crawled in here."

She began to finger his arm. A light, suggestive tickling. Ye gods, was *that* what she had on her mind? At a time like this? He was too stiff and sore, end to end, to be much excited.

But for her part, Charlotte was closing like a huntress.

"Poor Phillipe. Poor, dear Phillipe." He caught a flash of her white leg as she hitched up her skirt to descend the ladder again. "You need a little wine."

"No, honestly, I don't really—"

"Yes, wait, you just let me help you, Phillipe. I've some wine hidden in one of the horse stalls."

So she was stealing from the inn supplies, he thought, hardly caring. He had an impulse to totter down the ladder after her, and flee. But he didn't. Wine might not taste bad. Might help revive him—

Charlotte made rustling sounds in the stall below. Then Phillipe's eyes popped open—a second after the yellow light of the lantern went out. From the ladder, he heard a single delighted little syllable—

My God. She *was* giggling.

Feeling trapped, he started to roll over and rise to his knees. Aches exploded all over his body. He groaned and leaned back, trying to forget the humiliation and hatred the pain produced—the residue of the morning. Once more Charlotte uttered that strange, pleased sound as she maneuvered from the ladder to the loft.

This time, she didn't even try for grace as she tumbled out next to him—permitting him, in the process, an ample feel of her breasts against his forearm. She pressed the bottle into his hand and didn't take her own hand away. Because his cut lower lip had swollen, he still spoke thickly:

"How did you find me?"

"Well—"

She stretched out beside him with a cheerful little wriggle of her shoulders. She turned onto her side, facing him, so that his arm nestled between her breasts. He shifted his arm. She immediately moved closer. The wench was not sober, he realized with a sudden sense of confusion.

She ran her palm over his forehead, said abruptly, "Are you warm? You feel all icy."

"Yes, I'm warm. Very warm."

"That's a dreadful lie, your teeth are clicking!"

"My teeth are cold but I'm warm everywhere else. I asked you—"

"Drink some wine. That'll help."

She practically forced the mouth of the bottle to his lips. The inn's wine was poor and sourish. He coughed and spluttered getting it down. But when it reached his stomach, it did indeed warm him a little, and quickly.

Charlotte hitched her hip against him. Though he was conscious of aches in his belly and groin, he was suddenly conscious of something else. A reaction in his loins. Unexpected; startling. And—*God help me,* he thought with some panic—not entirely unpleasant.

But he still felt like some cornered fox.

"To answer your question," Charlotte explained in a whisper, "we don't have a single customer tonight. Not one! The worrying in the kitchen got so tiresome—your mother and Girard saying this happened, or that happened—I just got thoroughly sick of it and crept out here for a drink from the bottle I keep put away. Isn't that lucky?"

Her laugh this time was throaty. That alarming, exciting hand strayed to his collar, teasing his neck. He didn't even feel the lard residue because he was feeling too much that was surprising elsewhere. *What in heaven's name was happening?*

He tried to sound gruff: "Who gets the rest of what you steal? Your family?"

"No, I drink it all! Drink it—and have the loveliest dreams of—a certain young man—"

"I don't believe that."

"The dreams? Oh, yes! They are lovely!" She leaned her head in closer so that her curls tickled his cheek, accelerating the peculiar transformations taking place in his body. "What a pity they stay dreams and nothing else—"

"I mean I don't believe you about the wine, Charlotte."

"Well, I do take *some* home." She brushed his cheek with her lips, the kiss a soft, quick, smacking sound. "You will keep my secret, won't you? Please?"

He answered with a confused monosyllable. But it seemed sufficient to make her happy—and even more interested in his welfare, or something else. She burrowed closer.

"Phillipe, you're freezing."

"No, sincerely, I'm p-p-perfectly—"

"You need more wine!"

His protest ended in a gulp as she forced it on him. The strong-smelling stuff ran down his chin. Gasping for air, he asked:

"Charlotte—you didn't finish—how did you find—?"

"Oh, yes, that. Well, when I came in, I heard you thrashing and muttering in your sleep. Are you still hurt-

ing so much?" One of her hands slipped across his hip.
"Can you move at all?"

"Uh—yes, I can move. In fact I should go inside
and—"

"Oh, no!" she cried softly, pushing his chest with both
hands. "Not until the chill passes. If you go out in the
air, you might catch a fever. You need more wine!"

This time he hardly resisted at all. The sour stuff
tasted better by the moment. It was relaxing him—except in a certain critical area over which he no longer
seemed to have any control, thanks to Charlotte's constant wriggling and stirring and pressing and touching.
In the darkness, she seemed to be equipped with
numerous extra hands, many more hands than were
customary for a normally built human being. They were
all over him. But after the first shock of fingers straying
down his stomach and hesitating an instant, he got so
caught up in this peculiar, half-fearful, half-exciting encounter that the torment of the beating quite vanished
from his mind.

"My turn," she giggled, prying the bottle from his
faintly trembling hand. She drank. Somehow the bottle
slipped, thudded to the dirt floor of the stable.

"Oh dear," Charlotte sighed. "Whatever will we do to
warm you now?"

"Charlotte, thank you, but I'm sufficiently warm—"

"No, your poor sweet hands are still like ice!"

She's tipsy, he thought. His head buzzed. She wasn't
the only one.

"We *must* do something for your hands. A warm
place—"

She seized them, pressed them between her breasts.
He now felt his bruises hardly at all. But he felt the other
sensations with mysterious and mounting ferocity.

"Goodness no, that's *still* not good enough! Oh,
you'll think me too forward, but—in the interests of
your health, you sweet boy—"

Giggle. Then she somehow got her skirt up—guided his hands to a place new and warm, furred and mind-numbing.

"Ah—better," she purred. His hands seemed to have absolutely no control because she was doing certain equally new and amazing things with them. All at once she kissed him on the ear. Strange heats burst inside him, little fires, as she tickled his earlobe with her tongue.

"Love warms the blood too, Phillipe, did you know that? Unless you hurt so much—"

"I ache, I was stoutly beaten, Charlotte. I don't think we—"

"Oh, don't tell me! You don't care for girls?"

"Actually, I haven't been thinking much about that tonight—"

"Well, *think!*" Another kiss on his ear. "You darling boy—you'll feel so much better afterward. I promise!"

And before he knew it, her mouth came down on his, and he tasted the wine of her tongue. In some miraculous, crazy way he no longer ached—from the blows, that is.

"Oh, I'm just *suffocating*," Charlotte gasped.

A moment later, with another of those mental explosions, he comprehended the bareness of her breasts against the hairs of his arm, not to mention her fingers at the waist of his breeches.

Then the breeches were gone. And the mystery unfolded itself at last in the eagerness of her body.

"Here, here, dear Phillipe. Here—no, not quite —there, that's better—oh, you *are* warmer. I can feel you're warmer already! Oh thank goodness, the treatment's working—!"

"God, yes," he croaked, and let every other consideration go except the heat of her mouth and the strange, wondrous rhythm that began from the almost unbearably pleasant joining of their bodies. Charlotte seized the back of his neck and held fast. Somewhere a door opened and closed.

The rhythm quickened. The girl's hands worked up and down his back. He could feel her broken, work-blunted nails. The scratching only made him breathe more and more frantically. Uncontrollable surgings began in the depths of him, then roared outward in what his addled mind crazily decided was a most consuming, astonishing and remarkable cure for bruises and bad memories.

vi

They drowsed pleasurably, arms intertwined. Then, without any warning, light blazed below. He heard something kicked over—the blown-out lantern?

"Phillipe? *Charlotte?*"

Rousing, Phillipe made a noise. Charlotte tried to shush him. A moment later he heard his mother's voice ordering them down.

Feeling trapped, he pulled up his breeches hastily. Charlotte was going, "Oh! Oh!" softly, fearfully. He touched her hand to reassure her. But her eyes looked stricken, her cheeks dead white in the glow of the other lantern at the foot of the ladder.

Phillipe climbed down first. He stepped off the bottom rung and groaned. The pain was back.

Charlotte joined him, smoothing her skirt, which appeared to be on sideways; the tie straggled down her left hip. Obviously terrified of the glaring woman with the lantern, she began, "Please, Madame Charboneau, let me say—"

"Be quiet, you little slut."

Charlotte started to cry. Phillipe's mother lifted the lantern higher, fixing her eyes on her son.

"My God, did you get caught in a rock slide? Or did she rake you like that?"

Marie Charboneau was a handsome woman with a wide mouth, a fine, aristocratic nose, and the dark hair and eyes of Auvergne that her son had inherited. As Charlotte continued sniffling, Marie addressed her quietly:

"Go inside and tell Girard he's to give you wages for the week. And escort you home tonight. Don't come back."

"I'm not good enough for Phillipe, is that it?" the sobbing girl burst out. "What a noble attitude for a woman like you! A woman who can't even get past a church door because—"

Marie's slap was swift and vicious. Charlotte cried out and stumbled back, terrified, one hand at her cheek.

"You will leave," Marie said.

"Look, Mama, that's not fair," Phillipe said. "She was only trying to comfort me because I'd been in a fight—"

But even as he spoke, a shadow flitted past him; and Charlotte was gone. Crying or cursing, he couldn't tell which.

Marie Charboneau studied her son.

"Is this the first time with her?"

"Yes."

"With anyone?"

"Yes. For God's sake, Mama, I'm seventeen! There's no crime in—"

"Who beat you?" Marie interrupted.

As matter-of-factly as he could, but omitting all reference to the slurs against her, he explained. Then he looked straight into her eyes.

"I want to know why they call me a little lord. I've heard it before—and always with a sneer. I want to know what's wrong with a girl like Charlotte. She was kind, I was hurting, she brought me wine—"

"To trap you," Marie said.

"That's no explanation. What if I said I wanted to marry Charlotte? Boys in Auvergne are sometimes fathers at fourteen!"

Marie replied, "Phillipe, you will come inside. There are things I must tell you now, before you mire yourself in trouble and error."

Turning, her lantern held high and her step somehow assured, she walked out of the stable. In a turmoil, he followed her—to learn whatever secrets she had at last decided to reveal.

CHAPTER II

Behind the Madonna

i

"I WANT TO TELL you of your father," said Marie Charboneau, in the stillness of the large, sparsely furnished room she occupied at the head of the stairs. She kept the room spotless. Or rather insisted that Charlotte do so, in the hope that an overflow of guests might require its rental. That happened perhaps once a year. In a good year.

Phillipe thought briefly of Charlotte; she was gone now, with Girard. He recalled the indescribable sensations of their coupling; swallowed, his cheeks warm.

His mother was obviously awaiting his response to her statement. He perched on a little stool at the foot of her high bed, tried a small smile.

"I always assumed I had one, Mama."

Marie did not smile in return. More soberly, Phillipe continued, "I imagined he might have been English, too, since you speak so highly of that country. But I don't know how a French woman could meet a man from a land that's always been our foe."

She stepped toward a dark corner where the glow of the single candle burning on her washstand barely penetrated. In that corner were clustered the room's only ornamentations. On the wall, two small, crudely done miniatures of an elderly, fierce-eyed man—his grandfather, Paul Charboneau—and his grandmother, a tiny woman, Marie had told him once. But even at the age at which she had been painted, the woman possessed that dark, lustrous hair that her daughter, and her grandson, had inherited. The portraits had been done by an itinerant artist who could only afford bed and board by bartering a few days of his time and mediocre talent.

Just beyond the miniatures was an oversized niche containing a Madonna and two small votive lights in amber glass. Although his mother had long ago been barred from Holy Church by her choice of profession, the statue had occupied its place in her room for as long as Phillipe could remember. He had never seen her praying before it, however.

Now she moved the Madonna aside. From the darkness behind, she lifted a small, leather-bound casket with nailed corner pieces of mellow yellowing brass.

"It was not difficult for me to meet an Englishman when I was twenty, and playing Moliere on the Rue des Fosses-St. Germain." He kept staring at the cracking leather of the casket as she went on, "Do you recall the coach that stopped here in August?"

He certainly did. "Four very elegant and nasty English. Gold thread on their coats. Powder in their hair. And all of them not more than a year or two older than I am. But each one had two servants of his own—and they were almost as foul-mouthed as their masters. I'd have hit a couple of them for the way they talked about Charl—things here, except they were spending a lot. Girard and I spoke about them afterward. How they ordered everyone about as if it were their right. Girard said that before many more years go by, the nobility will no longer be allowed to behave that way."

Annoyed, his mother sat near the foot of the bed and leaned toward him. "Girard is engaged to teach you mathematics and English speech—"

"I know both tolerably well already."

"—*not* to fill your mind with his radical rot. Those young gentlemen are of a class to which you will belong one day." As if to emphasize the point, she set the casket firmly on the duck-feather comforter. Then her features softened a little.

"Besides, not all men of noble birth are as ill-mannered as those four. But do you know why their coach stopped here for the night? Where they were bound?"

"Over the Alps to Rome, I heard them boasting."

"On the island of Britain, it is the custom for wealthy and titled young men to take what's called the Grand Tour after finishing their university education. They visit Paris, Berlin, Rome—the great capitals. The museums, the theaters. That was how I met your father. In Paris, when I was twenty and he was just a year older. He came to the Comedie-Francaise, where I was playing. He didn't watch from the pit, with the drunken fops who baited the players loudly while soldiers stood by, their bayonets ready in case of a riot. Your father sat in one of the rows provided for the gentry right on stage. He didn't jeer or joke or indulge in the kind of nasty games that enraged too many of our hot-tempered company and got them clapped in prison at For-l'Eveque, courtesy of the Chamber of Police.

"When I withstood the rage of my father—your grandfather—at age nineteen, and went to Paris, and apprenticed to a company, I knew that play-actors were not considered persons with rights. I knew the risks. Jail at the pleasure of any drunken duke in the audience, who could hurl the vilest insults without reprisal but call for the arrest of any hapless actor goaded into answering with a taunt in kind. I also knew about the immediate barring from the Church—"

Her tone had grown bitter. Outside, the night wind began to creak the eaves, a melancholy sound.

"I cared about none of that because I'd had enough of

this place. I felt that to stay here would be to waste my life. Despite the perils—the low status of men and women of the theater—I was convinced that in Paris I had a chance at something better. I went to jail twice myself for refusing to let ugly fools with titles sleep with me at their pleasure—did I ever mention that?"

Held fascinated by this tunneling back toward his own dimly perceived beginnings, Phillipe could only shake his head. Marie spoke again:

"But then came that glorious night when your father visited the playhouse and sat on the stage, watching me. I ruined half my lines because he was so handsome and seemed to look at no one else. At that moment, I knew again that the filthy jails, the scorn of the priests, my father's anger and my mother's broken heart were all worth it. He was on the Grand Tour, you see. More than seventeen years ago—and one year before the great war started. Before France and England began brawling all over Europe, and in the Americas too. I think I fell in love with your father on sight. He remained in Paris for nearly two months while the rest of his friends went on to Rome. It was the happiest time of my life. I wanted nothing more than to bear his child. And I did. I bore you."

"What—what was his name, Mama?"

"*Is*, Phillipe. His name is James Amberly. His title is sixth Duke of Kentland. It's because of him that you must not throw yourself after cheap little strumpets like Charlotte. Noblemen's children—even bastard sons —can marry well, if they've the money. Your father is alive today, in England. He cares about you. He writes me letters inquiring after your welfare. That's why I have prepared you to speak his language far better than I ever learned to. I believe he'll want to see you someday. And you must be ready. Because, Phillipe—"

Marie's roughened hands, perhaps soft long ago when they flitted a stage fan in Paris, clasped tightly around the leather casket. She lifted it like some kind of offering.

"Your father intends for you to inherit a substantial part of his fortune."

ii

Outside, the wind groaned louder around the inn. Phillipe walked to the window, unprepared for all he'd heard, and shaken to the center of his being.

He pushed the shutter out and hunted for stars, for any sign of the world remaining stable. But the northern wind had brought heavy mist rolling down. The stars were gone. Cold dampness touched his face.

He turned back to Marie. She slumped a little, as if at last relieved of a burden.

"I thought," he said slowly, "that when boys like Auguste teased me—called me a little lord—it was only their stupid joking."

She shook her head. "I'm afraid I am responsible for some of that. Now and then, when I'm feeling blue, I indulge myself in a glass too many in the village. Sometimes things slip. I don't think the fools around here have ever believed what I've hinted at, though. I'm sure they consider any comments about you just more of what they refer to as my 'airs.' "

"An English lord!" he exclaimed, unable to keep from clapping his hands. He wished Auguste could hear; how stupefied he'd look!

Phillipe rushed to the bed, sat close beside his mother, all eagerness. "You say his name's Amberly?"

"But the family title is Kentland. They own a splendid estate and have many important connections at the court of George III. Your father served in the military when the war broke out in fifty-four. He rode at the great battle of Minden in fifty-nine."

Phillipe nodded. He'd heard of Minden, one of the historic clashes between the alliance of France and Austria on one hand, and Prussia, Hanover and Britain on the other. Marie continued:

"But for all that, Phillipe, he was—and is—a mild man. Kindly. At Minden he took a saber in the side. A bad wound. It happened when the men in his unit, the Tenth Dragoons, charged of their own accord after their cowardly commander, Lord Sack-something, refused to commit his horsemen to the battle even though he'd been ordered three times. After the battle, your father was forced to return to England. His letters say the wound still troubles him."

"Is he married? I mean—he never married you, did he? Even secretly?"

She shook her head. "Both of us understood, during those two months in Paris, that it wouldn't be possible. In fact, he didn't so much as kiss me till he'd explained that he could never marry any woman except the one already chosen for him. I didn't care. I was full of the joy of being with him. And despite the reputation of actors as willful children who never grow up, I understood the realities very well. I came from nothing. From the dirt of Auvergne. And in the eyes of the magistrates and the prelates, I was no better than a street harlot. So what chance had I for marriage? As I say—it didn't matter. Your father, being a decent man, is dutiful to his wife. But he has always cared for me in a special way—"

Slowly, then, she opened the casket.

By the dim glow of the candle, Phillipe saw ribbon-tied letters. Written in French. Marie pulled one from the packet.

"I will not show you all of them. But this one's important. It's the only reason I came back to this hateful place after Paris. To wait. To raise you properly—"

She dropped the finely inked parchment into her lap

and seized his shoulders, her black eyes brimming with
tears that mingled sorrow and happiness.

"I tell you again—it is no shame to be a nobleman's
bastard. Your father loves you like any son. And this
very letter is the proof!"

iii

They talked almost until morning. Marie's revelations
helped Phillipe to understand various matters that had
been puzzles before: her fury over a possible liaison
with Charlotte, her haughtiness toward others up and
down the valley.

He had long imagined that he might have been
fathered by some foreigner—perhaps even a runaway
soldier who'd somehow happened along during the turmoil of the Seven Years' War. But an English lord! She
had every right to put on airs! And no wonder she never
reprimanded him for his occasional unconscious swaggering.

As she filled in details of the story during the long
hours before dawn, Marie made it clear that she had
loved this James Amberly, Lord Kentland, freely, completely—but with no claim on him. Phillipe realized the
depth of that love when she told him that, after Amberly's departure from Paris, she had made a conscious
decision to return to Auvergne even though she
suspected she was already pregnant.

"I knew I would have a son," she said. "I knew—and
I came back to this dismal place for that child's sake.
You see, James promised me that he would acknowledge our child at the proper time, in order to leave
him a portion of his inheritance. So I returned and made
peace with my father as best I could—"

She gestured in a sad way, pointing to the cracked
miniature of the old man hanging near the niche.

"A week after you were born, I wrote—in French, which of course your father reads well—that his son had come into the world. Since then, he has sent money faithfully each year."

"Money?" Phillipe repeated, thunderstruck. "For me?"

"For us. The equivalent of ten sterling pounds. A handsome sum these days. Enough to let us get along even when no coaches roll through for days at a time. Enough to enable me to hire a tutor when I could find one. Girard was heaven-sent."

"So the reason for the English lessons is to help me when I eventually meet my father?"

"Yes. It may be many years before that happens. I may be long buried. But this will guarantee that it happens. This will carry you out of this accursed land for the rest of your life."

She lifted the letter again, carefully unfolding the crackling parchment so that he could read.

The letter was dated in December of 1754, one year after his birth.

> *My beloved Marie,*
>
> *I have spent a substantial sum to ensure that the courier bearing this missive reaches you despite the outbreak of hostilities. This is the letter which I promised you in Paris, and it is dispatched with all my faith and devotion. I rejoice in the birth of our son, whom you have named Phillipe. I wished to send you my assurances concerning his future long before this. But, in candor, my wife encountered difficulties, and indeed nearly perished, in the delivering of our newly born son, Roger.*

Phillipe glanced up, frowning. "He has another boy? Born after I was?"

"Of course. The hereditary title must be continued. Read the rest."

> *Because of the aforementioned difficulties, the learned physicians inform me that my wife shall never again in her lifetime be able to accomplish woman's natural role. This makes it all the more imperative, my dearest, that I fulfill my pledge to you. By the witnessing below, this letter becomes a legal document. My two friends have signed in confidence, thus testifying that my natural son Phillipe is hereby acknowledged by me, and, upon my death, shall receive, in accordance with the laws of this realm, an equal share in my estate, save for Kentland itself—*

Again Phillipe's dark head bobbed up. "Kentland?"

"That is also the name of the family residence. Go on, finish and I'll tell you the rest."

> *—which, by custom, must pass to my legitimate son's eldest male issue. I declare in sight of Almighty God and the presence of my two worthy friends, who shall add their names below mine, that this is my true and irrevocable intent, the whole declaration being freely made by my own choice. Because, dearest Marie, even though I cannot honorably write the details of it here, you are fully aware of the lifelong devotion of him who shall remain*
>
> *Ever yours,*
> *Jas. Amberly*
> *Duke of Kentland*

Below the signature appeared two other, unfamiliar ones. Phillipe stared at his father's name for a long mo-

ment. Then, exhilarated, he jumped up. In his haste he
brushed the parchment against the bedpost. A corner of
the brittle letter broke away, making his mother exclaim:

"Be careful with it!"

She seized the letter with urgency, yet with delicacy
too, and began to re-fold it along the old creases.

"This is your passage to freedom and position,
Phillipe. As you read, the woman he married could bear
no more than one child—the son he named Roger.
You've half your father's wealth. Half!"

Carefully, she slipped the letter back into the ribboned packet, returned the packet to the casket, the
casket to the Madonna's niche. She straightened the statue so that it once more concealed the box.

"Now," she said, "let me explain how it's possible for
that half to be yours."

Briefly, she outlined her knowledge of English
inheritance law, which she had made it her business to
learn.

Lord Kentland, she told him, could not will his title to
a bastard. Nor could his home, his landed properties go
to any save the eldest son of his son Roger, who was
thus prevented from disposing of same and squandering
the proceeds while he lived. By means of intricate legal
arrangements, Roger, in effect, would become the
lifetime tenant of the estate, unable to sell or mortgage it
except by means of a troublesome and costly procedure
involving special dispensation from the English Parliament. In this way, great family land holdings were
preserved.

"The remainder of your father's wealth," Marie continued, "principally money—of which he has a great
deal—is divided in equal shares between his children.
You see what that means? Thanks to his letter, you are
acknowledged. There is only one other heir—and so
half the money automatically falls to you. Believe me,

you will be a rich man. The finest drawing rooms will be open to you. Not to mention a choice of wives! Perhaps you can marry in England. A titled lady might not have you. But a prosperous merchant's daughter is another case entirely. Your father has written that the mercantile classes are coming into great power in their own right. What father of a girl who stood to inherit—oh, say a tannery—wouldn't relish the addition of half a duke's income?"

Phillipe turned cold at the last remark. Perhaps it was the lateness of the hour. Or his increasing weariness. But he sounded quarrelsome when he said:

"Mama, I've no wish to marry some woman just because her father owns a leatherworks!"

That angered her. "An example, nothing else! Do you miss my point altogether? I have given my life—*all* of my life, here in this place I despise—so that you might go where you want in the world. Away from Auvergne. To walk among gentlemen of wealth, and be one yourself! I don't care who you take up with so long as it's a woman who is your equal. Since you will be a person of station in your own right, your marriage must advance your fortunes even further."

He rebelled against the callous way she put forth the idea. But he kept silent this time, because her eyes were so intense. She gripped his shoulders hard.

"Remember this above everything, Phillipe. The greatest crime a human being can commit is to allow himself to be humbled into poverty, into obscurity, into—" She let go of his arm, swept the room with a gesture at once damning and sad. "This. I committed that crime so that you will never need to. Swear that you won't, Phillipe. Swear!"

He seemed to be staring at a woman he did not know. A woman of agate eyes, a woman full of grief and hatred. He was afraid of her.

"Yes. I swear."

At once, she softened, hugging him to her breast. "Then it's time we slept, my little lord. It has a good sound, doesn't it? And now you know it's the truth."

Motherly again, she comforted him as she led him toward the door.

"I suppose I should have told you years ago, but I saw no reason. As I said, you may well wait a very long time until James Amberly dies. But you won't wait in vain. That's why you mustn't squander your future by entangling yourself with a penniless peasant girl. Perhaps I acted in haste, sending Charlotte away. But it's done and I feel better for it. Go to sleep now. Only don't forget the oath you swore."

As if he ever could!

He lay in the garret with gray light already beginning to break outside, his dazzled mind playing with details of the story as if they were wondrous toys. In imagination he saw himself dressed in a gold-frogged waistcoat, a splendid, beautiful lady on his arm. They were passing through a crowded street, receiving the cheers of a crowd. He recognized a face—Auguste—and spat on his boots. Auguste did not dare to react.

He finally drifted to sleep thinking of what his mother had described as the greatest crime a human being can commit. For him, Marie Charboneau had committed that crime.

For her, he never would.

iv

"So," remarked Girard, picking his teeth, "now you know. The scholar is not a noble humanitarian but has remained here these four years because he's been paid. Actually it hasn't been a bad bargain. I am basically out of step with the world. I study the wrong things—and

frequently believe them! If I loafed around Paris, for example, I'd probably wind up drinking too much, proclaim my libertarian views—and get clapped in prison
for it. Or worse. I've told you how Master Jean Jacques
has been hounded from country to country—and he has
an international reputation! Important friends, like
Diderot. Imagine how a common fellow like me would
be treated!"

Girard and his pupil sat at the top of the rock escarp-
ment overlooking the inn and the winding road. Several
days had passed since the revelations in Marie's room.
She had obviously communicated the fact of the talk to
Girard. He had behaved in a somewhat more relaxed
way ever since.

It was a stunningly bright morning, all the mist burned
from the tumbled hills. But Phillipe still felt winter's bite
in the stiff wind. The backs of his hands were numb
from gripping the little book they'd been studying, the
play about the misadventures of a Scottish king called
Macbeth. At his feet, shielded from the wind by his
boots, were Girard's three precious volumes. Phillipe
had carefully smuggled them from the garret up to the
site of instruction, in the hope that Girard would be
willing to amplify some of the puzzling ideas the books
contained.

But for the past hour, the tutor had insisted on fulfilling his regular obligation to Marie. Phillipe had read
aloud from the play, while Girard corrected his pronunciation of the familiar words.

"Don't ask me about the unfamiliar ones—sweet
William's Elizabethan cant. How should I know what
that means? The play's an antique. And fashions
change, in everything from metaphors to monarchies."

"Yes, but it's still English."

"And truthfully, you don't speak it badly after four
years of practice—though I admit that for the first two,

I just about gave up. Today, however, if you crossed the Channel, they'd recognize you for a foreigner. But you could communicate well."

At the lesson's conclusion, Phillipe asked, "Have you ever been to England, Girard?"

"Yes. I prefer not to discuss the circumstances."

Phillipe pointed at the topmost volume stacked behind his heels. "Is that where you found this book by Monsieur Locke?"

"No, I purchased that in Paris. But visiting Monsieur Locke's homeland was, at least in part, almost like a holy pilgrimage." The bright blue eyes gleamed with mirth. "Provided an unholy chap like myself is permitted such an experience. You mentioned a day or two ago that you had some questions about Locke—?"

Phillipe sighed. "I've forgotten half of them already. His English is hard for me to follow. Too deep. I read some passages two and three times before I got the notion that he didn't believe kings ruled by God's will."

"And so they don't. Among men who gave death blows to the theory of a king's divine right to hold a throne, Locke was one of the foremost. If you'll study him a little more closely, you'll discover he actually put forth one of the ideas for which Monsieur Rousseau is receiving much credit."

"You mean that business about some kind of contract?"

Girard nodded, turning the tip of his boot toward the stack where gold letters stamped on the binding of a slim volume spelled out *Le Contract social*.

"Locke actually espoused the contract theory as part of his justification of constitutional monarchy. Stated that a king's role was one of steward, not tyrant—and that the ultimate test of a government was whether the subjects were happy and prosperous. If so, the ruler should be obeyed. If not, he should be booted out."

"So the best kind of king is one of those"—Phillipe fumbled for the term—"enlightened what?"

"Despots. Enlightened despots. Yes, that's a popular theory. But even those who give it credence do so with reservations. Here, pass me *L'Encyclopedie*."

Phillipe did, and Girard leafed through until he found the passage he wanted. He showed Phillipe the page.

"Have you read this?"

"No."

"Well, Monsieur Diderot is no flame-eyed revolutionary. Yet he recognizes the dangers inherent in having a hereditary king—even a good one. Pay attention—"

Girard cleared his throat, began quoting from the page:

" 'It has sometimes been said that the happiest government was that of the just and enlightened despot. It is a very reckless assertion. It could easily happen that the will of this absolute master was in contradiction with the will of his subjects. Then, despite all his justice and all his enlightenment, he would be wrong to deprive them of their rights even in their own interests.' ".

Phillipe shook his head. "But if there are to be no kings at all, who does have the authority in this world?"

Quickly Girard flipped pages. "This is Diderot too. 'There is no true sovereign, there can be no true legislator, but the people.' "

"You mean kings rule by their consent."

"By *our* consent. Who are the people if not you and me and even poor, love-crazed Mademoiselle Charl—come, don't pull such a face! Is it really such an astonishing idea?"

"Yes. I can see it leading to all sorts of trouble. Fighting—"

"And why not?" Girard exclaimed. "Once, man swallowed every opinion or order that was handed

him—" The scholar spat. "So much for the age of faith.
Then, slowly, and with greater acceleration in the last
hundred years, man began to perceive the power of his
own reason. His power to ask *why*. To find logical
answers in every area of human endeavor. Once un-
leashed, such a force can't be halted. I venture to say
that by the time your titled father passes to whatever
waits on the other side of the grave—oblivion, is my
opinion—the world may be radically changed, thanks in
part to these fellows—our mad Jean Jacques most of
all."

Pointing to the gold-stamped book, Phillipe said,
"But honestly, a lot of that seems just gibberish."

"That must be overlooked! Rousseau has fired the
world's imagination. Who can say why some writers
can, and others can't? But he has! I understand he's very
popular on the other side of the Atlantic, for instance. I
agree, a lot of his notions are drivel. Or rehashes of what
others have said before. Yet from time to time, he puts
down with masterful precision some of the most astute
statements on the subject of government and men's
freedoms I have ever encountered."

Phillipe squinted into the bright wind, his thoughts,
and hence his words, coming slowly:

"It seems to me he doesn't like *any* kind of government."

"Quite true. He considers them all evil and unnatural.
He recognizes, however, that unlimited freedom, no
matter how desirable, simply won't work. So, he com-
promises."

"The contract idea again?"

"Yes, but carried even further. Here, the book—"

The man's obvious delight made Phillipe smile;
Girard was like an infant with a shiny new play-bauble
as he hurried through *Le Contract social*, hunting the
section he wanted. Turning pages, he explained:

"Master Jean Jacques actually distilled much of the

political thinking of the past hundred years. He states that not only does no man in a government hold power by personal right, but that he has no authority independent of those he governs. Ah, yes—"

He read:

" 'I have demonstrated that the depositories of the executive power are not the masters of the people, but its officers. That the people may establish or remove them as it pleases. That for these officers there is no question of contracting, but only of obeying. That in undertaking the functions which the state imposes on them, they only fulfill their duty as citizens, with no right of any kind to dispute the terms—' "

Phillipe whistled. "No wonder he's notorious."

With a shrug, Girard closed the book. "I repeat, much of the man's work strikes me as idiotic. His novels especially. Silly romantic fancies! But on politics—ah, on politics—!" He kissed the tips of his fingers.

"I'm still surprised he hasn't been arrested," Phillipe said.

"Well, for one thing, the time's right for his ideas. More and more people are coming to realize that we are all born in a natural state of freedom—and that power is therefore *not* something which descends in selective rays of light from heaven, to touch only a few of the especially appointed. Such as our good King Louis XV up in Paris—" Girard grimaced. "Or the Hanoverian farmer who holds the throne of England. *They* don't care for the notion that power and authority are the results of contracts between the people and the rulers—or that the people may break those contracts at any time."

Mock-serious, he tucked the Rousseau work into his capacious side pocket. "Oh, it's dangerous stuff."

"I wonder."

"What?"

"Maybe it's just a lot of words. Soap bubbles—"

Girard started to sputter. Phillipe continued quickly:

"I mean—one of the things I really wanted to ask you was—has any of this actually changed anything?"

"*Changed* anything!" Girard rolled his eyes. "My dear pupil! It's stirring new winds all over the world. Have you ever heard travelers at the inn mention the former British Prime Minister? Monsieur Pitt?"

"Yes. With curses, mostly."

"Of course! The Great Commoner, as his people affectionately called him, directed England's effort in the late, unlamented Seven Years' War—and stole most of France's territory in the New World in the bargain. A few years ago, the ministers of King George attempted to levy various niggling taxes—in such forms as an official stamp on all legal documents, for example. These taxes were to be levied only in Britain's colonies in America. And Pitt himself—already an earl—actually stood up in Parliament and challenged the king's right to enact such a tax! He proclaimed injustice being done to England's sons across the water. And he helped get the stamp tax repealed! How's that for being a steward of the people? At the same time, there was an Irishman in Parliament—a Colonel Barre, if I recall. He likewise praised the colonists for refusing to pay the taxes because they had no representation in London. He termed the contentious Americans 'sons of liberty.' Don't tell your mother, but I like that touch. Phillipe, do you realize that a hundred years ago, both of those spokesmen for ordinary people might well have had their heads on the block?"

"I'll take your word for it."

Smiling briefly, the tutor went on. "It amounts to this. *Because* of books like the ones you've been struggling to understand, there's a test of wills coming in the world. The people against the rulers. It's reached England already. It will reach France one day."

"Well," said Phillipe, a little smugly, "my

mother—and father—chose the side I'm to be on, I guess."

Now it was Girard's turn to squint into the sunlight, unhappily. "For the sake of your future—and your mother's ambitions—I trust it is not the wrong one."

"Do you seriously think it could be?"

Girard stared at him. "Shall I answer as your paid tutor? The fellow hired only to instruct you from non-controversial texts?"

"No," Phillipe answered, oddly chilled. "As yourself."

"Very well. Although this may be envy talking, I don't believe I'd be comfortable belonging to a titled family just now. As I suggested, the British have always loved their liberties a little more fiercely than most Europeans. And done relatively more to secure those liberties—at the expense of their kings and their nobility. When intellectuals such as our mad Master Jean Jacques thunder that contracts between governors and the governed may be broken by the will of the people, should the governors grow too autocratic—and when British statesmen stand up, question the propriety of laws written by a king's own ministers, and take the part of a king's defiant subjects—well, I shall only observe again that there are strong winds blowing. Who knows what they may sweep away? Or whom?"

Phillipe asked, "In a contest like that, Girard, which side would you be on?"

"Isn't it obvious? The side to which I was born. My father was a farmer in Brittany. He was stabbed to death by the saber of a French hussar when the hussar 'requisitioned' our only milk cow for his troops. In the name, and by the authority, of King Louis. My father refused, so he was killed. If it were in my power, I would forever shatter the contract with a king who would permit that kind of murder."

Girard's expression had grown melancholy. What he had just revealed was the first—and last—bit of autobiography Phillipe Charboneau ever heard from the tutor. Now Girard went on:

"Yes, gentlemen such as Monsieur Rousseau are subtly nudging common folk to the realization that, together, they can simply say, '*We are finished with you!*' to any monarch who serves them ill."

"But I still can't imagine a thing like that would really happen."

"Why? Because you don't want to? Because it might spoil your splendid future?"

Irritated, Phillipe shot back, "Yes! Here, I've finished with your books."

Girard took the other two volumes, said quietly, "The point is, Phillipe, they haven't finished with you. Whether it pleases you or not." He sighed. "Ah, but let's not quarrel over words. When I started giving you these books months ago, I only meant to shed a little more light into a bright young mind—"

"And instead, you've got me thinking the world's going to be blown apart."

"Well, it's true. There are whispers of it—no, much more than whispers—from those same British colonies I mentioned. And the Commoner—and others in King George's own government—applaud! Doesn't that tell you *anything?*"

Phillipe overcame his annoyance, grinned. "It tells me I'm lucky I'm going to be rich. I'll have money enough to build a big house with safe, thick walls."

But Girard did not smile back.

"Since I am fond of you, Phillipe, let us devoutly hope there are walls wealth can build thick enough to withstand the winds that may rise to a gale before you're very much older."

CHAPTER III

Blood in the Snow

i

AT NOVEMBER'S END, word circulated in the neighborhood that old du Pleis the goatherd had died. His son, Auguste, disappeared. The hovel up the track was abandoned. And Phillipe was spared further encounters with his now-vanished enemy.

Since the beating, he hadn't gone back to the hillside terrace, walking instead the full three kilometers to Chavaniac to replenish the inn's supply of cheese. But each time, as he passed the point where the track turned upward from the road, he still felt an echo of the humiliation—and regret that he hadn't found a means to settle his score with the goatherd's boy.

He walked into the village with considerably more confidence now. His mother's revelations had given him that. He was even able to pass by the tiny Church of Saint-Roch without experiencing more than a touch of the old boyhood fear that the priest would suddenly appear and recognize him as the unredeemed child of the unredeemable actress.

He set out on one such trip to the village on an afternoon a couple of weeks before Christmas. The first furious snowstorm of winter was howling out of the north, driving white crystals into his eyes above the woolen scarf he'd tied over his nose and mouth. He had wrapped rags around his hands and boots. But even so,

he quickly grew numb as he trudged through the
already-drifted snow.

Yet in a curious way, he relished the unremitting fury
of the wind. It reminded him of the winds of which
Girard had spoken. And of other, more fortuitous gales:
the winds of luck, of changing circumstance, that had
suddenly plucked him up and were hurling him toward a
new kind of future. Fortune's wind might be savage, he
decided. But to be seized and swept along by it was
much more exciting than to live forever becalmed.

Leaning into the blizzard, he fought it like a physical
enemy. He was determined to reach the village and
return home in record time, just for the sake of doing it.
Concentrating on making speed, he was totally unprepared for an unexpected sound.

He halted on the snowy road, listening. Had the wind
played tricks?

No. He heard voices crying out.

One was thin; a boy's, perhaps. The others were
lower. Harsh.

Directly ahead, he saw where the storm had not yet
concealed the tracks of a horse. The tracks led off to the
right, into the great, black, wind-tormented pines. The
thin voice sounded again—

From back in those trees!

Phillipe began to run.

Following the cries and the drifted horse tracks, he
quickly passed into the forest. Not much farther on, he
spied a boy defending himself from two ragged attackers.

The boy wore a long-skirted coat and a tricorn hat,
the hat somehow staying on his red head as he darted
from side to side, fending off the lunges of the other two
by means of a sharp-pointed, lancelike weapon that
looked all of seven feet long. In the swirling snow
beyond the struggle, a small, tethered sorrel horse

snorted and whinnied in alarm. Phillipe kept running.

"You little sod!" shouted one of the attackers. The boy had slashed the lance tip from right to left and caught the stouter of the two brigands across the face.

The injured man reeled back, cursing. As he stumbled, he turned. Phillipe saw him head on. Even with a mittened hand clasped to his gashed cheek and a shabby fur hat cocked over his forehead, his face seemed to leap out at Phillipe through the slanting snow.

Auguste.

"Circle him, circle! Grab that damned thing!" the other attacker screamed. Phillipe recognized the voice of cousin Bertram.

The boy—twelve or thirteen at the most—darted to his left, manipulating the lance with trained grace. Bertram ran at him, a knife gripped in his right mitten.

"The hell with holding him for money!" Auguste yelled over the wind. "He's ripped my face to pieces—do the same to him!"

And that was just what Bertram intended, it seemed, as Phillipe ran the last yards to the clearing and shouted, "Here! Stop!"

The cry distracted the boy, whose clubbed red hair was the only patch of color in the gray and white scene. Phillipe saw a face frightened yet determined. But when the boy turned suddenly, he lost his footing.

While the boy slipped and slid, Bertram seized the lance shaft, wrenched it from the boy's grasp and threw it away behind him.

Phillipe ducked as the lance struck pine boughs near his cheek, showering him with snow. Bertram slashed over and down with the dagger. But the boy dove between his legs and the cut missed.

Then Phillipe looked at the closer of the two attackers. Auguste drew his mitten away from his bloody face, gaping. The three-inch wound below one startled

eye glistened pink where the skin had been laid open. As
he recognized Phillipe, his face grew even more ugly.

"You'd have been wiser not to answer his cries for
help, little lord."

Blood spattered on the snow from the point of
Auguste's chin. His red mitten fumbled at his waist, producing a dagger similar to the one Bertram kept stabbing at the intended victim. The boy's tricorn hat had
finally fallen off as he jumped one way, then another
like an acrobat, trying to avoid the slashes.

Hate and hurt in his dark eyes, Auguste charged. The
knife was aimed at Phillipe's belly.

Phillipe had no time to think. He simply reacted,
reaching for the nearest weapon—the lance fallen nearby. He thrust with both hands, hard.

Auguste screamed, unable to check his forward
momentum. His run impaled him on the head of the
lance. Phillipe let go, jumping backward as Auguste fell,
raising powdery clouds of snow.

Blood spurted from all around the vibrating lance.
The fabric of Auguste's coat had been driven into his
wound. Bertram checked a lunge, goggling at his fallen
cousin. Auguste writhed onto his side, staining the im-
maculate snow a bright scarlet.

"Christ preserve us," Bertram quavered. "*Cousin?*"

Then he glanced at Phillipe with raging yellow eyes.
The red-haired boy ran to the little sorrel, opened a
sheath and drew an immense pistol.

Bertram pointed at the unmoving body. "Murderer.
You killed him!"

With audacity Phillipe could hardly believe, the
young boy showed Bertram the muzzle of his pistol.

"You'll find yourself in a similar condition if you're
ever seen near Chavaniac again. My aunts told me
Auguste du Pleis had taken to thievery after his father

died. But I didn't assume that included snatching rabbit hunters."

Phillipe stared at unblinking hazel eyes in the freckled, young-old face. The boy's voice sounded assured. Though he was three or four years younger than Phillipe, and slightly built, he handled weapons—the lance and now the pistol—with perfect familiarity.

The boy took a step toward Bertram.

"Don't you understand me? Get away from here or I'll shoot you. I'm giving you a chance. Take it."

All at once Bertram read the lesson of the pistol's eye. A moment later he was gone, boots thudding away into the wind-bent pines. Then not even that sound remained.

Phillipe moved shakily toward Auguste. "Is he really—?"

"I'd say so," the boy interrupted, planting a boot on Auguste's neck. "An officer doesn't carry a spontoon into battle for show. They're killing instruments."

With no trace of emotion, the boy twisted the gory head of the lance until it came free of Auguste's belly. Then he indicated the pistol he'd thrust into his belt.

"It's lucky those two knew nothing of firearms. I couldn't have got a ball off in this damp. The powder would have flashed in the—here! Stop looking so nervous! I've scared the other one off. We won't see him again. And you killed this one in my defense. Let's drag him deeper in the woods. When he's found next spring, not a person around here will know how he died—or care."

Despite the boy's words, Phillipe had started to shake with reaction to the struggle. He had slain another human being. And apparently the red-haired boy was not the least upset.

The boy tossed the spontoon aside. He reached down for Auguste's collar, then glanced at Phillipe with a touch of irritation.

"Look, will you help me?"

Phillipe wiped snow from his eyelids. "Yes. Yes, I will. But—how old are you?"

"Thirteen, if that matters."

"You handle weapons like a soldier."

"Well, I've been up to Paris for two years now. I only came back for Christmas, to visit my aunts and my grandmother. In the city, I've been schooled in the use of swords and pistols by an old officer who's one of the best. De Margelay's his name. When spring comes, I'll be a cadet in the Black Musketeers."

Again that stare of annoyance when Phillipe didn't respond. "Surely you've heard of the regiment that guards King Louis!"

Phillipe shook his head. "I don't know about such things. My mother keeps an inn near here. The Three Goats."

"Ah! I've ridden by it."

"Why did those two attack you? Hope of ransom?"

"Undoubtedly. It's no secret that I returned home for the holy days. I was searching so hard for rabbit tracks, they took me by complete surprise. But you won't be punished for killing this one. I can assure you of it. In fact, what happened makes us blood comrades. In the military, there's no stronger tie. Now come on, let's move him."

Phillipe's shock and fear were lessening moment by moment. He and the boy hid the body in a drift some distance from the clearing. The young soldier kicked snow over Auguste's ghastly face. Then he resettled his tricorn on his head and asked:

"Were you headed home?"

"No, to the village."

"Then mount Sirocco with me. Two can ride as easily as one. No objections, please—I insist!"

It struck Phillipe that the youth wasn't accustomed to having anyone go against his wishes. Remarkable. Espe-

cially for a thirteen-year-old. Without a word, he
followed the red-haired boy back toward the stamping
sorrel.

ii

"The crime was theirs, not yours," the boy shouted
over the roar of the wind, while the sorrel pounded
through the snow toward the village. "Any soldier has
the right to kill his enemy in battle."

"I'll try to remember that," Phillipe yelled, hanging
onto the boy's waist with one hand and gripping the
spontoon across his shoulder with the other. But his
mind still swam with ugly visions of Auguste bleeding.

Snow stung his face. Ahead, he discerned the first of
the cottages at the end of Chavaniac's single winding
street.

"I must get off soon," Phillipe cried. "I walked to
town to buy cheeses for—wait! Slow down!"

But the boy nicked the sorrel's flank with a spur, and
the horse bore them up the short cobbled street, soon
leaving it behind. The boy turned the sorrel's head
westward.

"Where are we going?" Phillipe demanded.

"To my home. It's just ahead. There'll be a warm fire,
and some wine, and I can show you a trick or two with
the lance. You've had no training in arms, have you?"

"None. My father was a soldier, though."

The remark came out unbidden as the sorrel plowed
through drifts beneath the limbs of bare, creaking trees.
All at once Phillipe knew where he was. But he didn't
believe it.

"So was mine," the boy shouted in reply. "He fell at
Minden in fifty-nine. Hit by a fragment of a ball from a
British cannon. What was your father's regiment?"

"I can't remember." The sorrel bore them past the
facade of an immense, blockhouse-like chateau at whose

corners two towers rose. "He's no longer with our family, you see."

"Can you remember your own name?" the boy asked, amused.

"Phillipe Charboneau."

"You must call me Gil. The whole of my name is too tedious to pronounce."

"Tell me anyway."

"Marie Joseph Paul Yves Roch Gilbert du Motier. And since my father's death, Marquis de Lafayette. See, I warned you! Make it just Gil and Phillipe. Fellow soldiers," he finished, turning the sorrel into a spacious stable behind the chateau—

Which belonged to the Motier family. Richest in the neighborhood. Each hour, it seemed, the winds of fortune were blowing him in new and astonishing directions.

iii

The relatively calm air inside the dark, dung-smelling stable came as a relief. Gil nosed the sorrel into a stall and leaped from the saddle. Then the young marquis took the spontoon from Phillipe's hand, knelt and began rubbing at some dried blood still visible on the head.

"As to the story we must tell," he said, never glancing up from the work, "you discovered me at the roadside. Floundering in the snow and hunting for Sirocco, who stumbled, fell, unhorsed me, then ran off. After some delay, and with your assistance, I finally located the animal."

Gil looked up. "Agreed?"

Held by the steadiness of those young-old hazel eyes, Phillipe murmured, "Agreed."

Light flared from the far end of the stable. An old groom with a lantern hobbled toward them. He spoke with a clicking of wood false teeth:

"So late home, my lord! How was the hunting?"

"Poor," Gil replied. "Except that I found a new comrade. Give Sirocco an extra ration of oats, please." He took Phillipe's elbow with perfect authority and steered him out of the stable. They crossed the yard through the whipping snow, then entered the chateau, where new wonders awaited.

iv

"I don't believe the tale for a minute," said Girard, much later that night. He was warming his stockinged feet at the fire in the common room. "You stole the cheeses, Phillipe."

"I tell you I didn't! His aunts gave them to me. Saint-Nectaire. The most expensive kind!"

With a flourish, he slapped coins down on the table. "Go on, count. You'll find every last sou I took with me."

Girard fingered the coins. "We thought you'd fallen victim to brigands. But it turns out that it was only a marquis."

Despite the teasing, Girard's blue eyes couldn't conceal a certain admiration. As for Marie, she was jubilant, using a cheese knife to slash through the wrapping cloth with almost sensual joy. She slipped a piece into her mouth, chewed, exclaimed:

"Saint-Nectaire it is! I had some only once before in my life. Phillipe, how did you get on with the marquis? Easily?"

"Yes, very. And I don't think he was being kind just because I helped save—save his horse. We're friends now. I'm to visit him again tomorrow. And as many times as I wish before he returns to Paris after the holidays. His mother died last spring, you know," Phillipe added with the slightly condescending tone of one privileged to reveal a bit of gossip. "In Paris, he's to be a cadet of the Black Musketeers."

They said nothing. With outright loftiness, he informed them, "The regiment which guards the king himself!"

Flash went the blade, deep into the cheese. Marie wielded the knife almost as if she were striking an old enemy.

"You see, Girard? They got along famously because my son was born to that sort of life. Blood tells! In the end, a man finds his rightful place."

Sampling a morsel of the cheese, Girard glanced at Phillipe. The latter was too excited by memories of the splendid chateau, the incredible gilt-decorated rooms, the kindly aunts, to notice the dismay in the eyes of the lank scholar.

v

Long after the fire had gone out and they'd locked the inn for the night, Phillipe lay shivering, trying to sleep. He was kept from it by recurring memories of Auguste's blood staining the snow bright red.

Again and again, he recalled Gil's reassurances. Gradually, the worry about discovery—punishment—diminished. But he was still disturbed by one aspect of the personality of his new friend the Marquis de Lafayette: the casual way Gil took a life—and hid the deed.

Did the nobility consider another human life worthless when their own lives were threatened? Did they dispose of their victims secure in the knowledge that their position would shield them from reprisals? Did his father, James Amberly, behave the same way? If so, Phillipe could well understand Girard's approval of rebellion against such high-handed actions.

Troubled, he drifted into chilly drowsiness. His mind

turned to the things he might learn from Gil before the young marquis returned to Paris. On balance, perhaps the day had been more good than bad.

I must forget the dead boy the way Gil forgot him, he thought, close to sleep. *I must remember what is the greatest crime of all. That is the only crime I must never commit.*

vi

In the days that followed, Phillipe—with his mother's blessing and encouragement—became almost a daily visitor at Chateau Chavaniac.

Gil's aunts and his feeble, elderly grandmother treated him with polite kindness. And there were so many exciting things to do, and see, and learn, that Phillipe never noticed how the aunts now and again glanced at one another; how they smiled in wordless amusement when Phillipe upset a wine glass or tramped across a luxurious carpet in snow-covered boots.

Gil proudly showed off his military uniform. It was scarlet and gold, with a blue mantle that bore a cross encircled by a ring of fire, the devices sewn in silver thread.

In the stable yard, where the snowbanks glared white in the winter sunlight, Gil demonstrated the rudiments of self-defense with a sword. Of course they didn't use real swords, only stout sticks. But Gil didn't seem to mind demonstrating thrusts and parries with the beginner's implements from which he'd graduated long ago.

Then, two days before the holiday commemorating the birth of Christ, Gil took Phillipe down to the frozen lagoon near the chateau. From oiled cloth, he unwrapped his most prized possession.

"My military tutor bought it in Paris, for my birthday," he explained. "They're damned hard to come by, you know."

He thrust the shimmering walnut-stocked musket into Phillipe's hands.

"It's the finest military weapon in the world. Brown Bess. See, even the barrel's brown. They treat the metal with a secret preservative."

The incredible gun was more than five feet long. Phillipe held it gingerly, awed, as Gil produced a cartridge box from his pocket and initiated his friend into the step-by-step ritual that preceded a shot.

"Most of King George's redcoats can load and fire in fifteen seconds," he commented. "That's why, militarily, the French hate Georgie *and* his muskets."

In less than an hour of teaching, Phillipe learned how to pour powder into the muzzle, drop in the ball and ramrod the crumpled paper which held the powder.

Next—lift the firing-pan frizzen. Bat the barrel with the heel of a hand, to send a little powder through the touchhole—

With the Brown Bess at his shoulder for the first shot, he nearly blundered. Gil cried out, "Don't keep your eyes open! In a bad wind you could go blind from a flareback from the touchhole. Just hold it tight, aim in the general direction you want to fire, shut your eyes and pull the trigger."

Phillipe followed instructions. The thunderous impact knocked him flat. A pine branch across the lagoon cracked and fell.

"Not bad at all," Gil nodded, smiling.

Phillipe stood up, dusting off snow and shaking his head. "Gil, I don't understand how a soldier can win a battle with his eyes closed."

"When a thousand British infantrymen close their eyes and fire together, they can destroy anything standing in front of them. If we had such muskets, we could rule the world. Lacking them, we've nearly lost it. Try another shot." He smiled across the sun-gleaming brown barrel. "You hold her as though born to it. Must be the blood of that soldier father of yours."

Phillipe smiled back, friendship and his secret both serving to warm the bitter day.

vii

But as quickly as it had begun, the friendship ended with Gil's return to Paris.

The return was signalled on the eve of the New Year, 1771, by the *clop-clop* of a horse climbing to the inn door. Marie peeked out, clasped her hands excitedly.

"God save us, Phillipe, it's your friend the marquis! And this place isn't even swept properly—*Girard!*"

Her cry brought the gangling man from the back of the inn, just as Gil entered, afternoon sunlight making his red hair shine beneath the tricorn hat.

Flustered, Marie curtseyed. Girard sighed and began to swish the broom over the floor. Phillipe rushed forward to welcome his friend.

"I expected to see you later this afternoon at the chateau!"

"But my grandfather wants me back in Paris two days hence. The coach is departing in an hour. Here, I've brought you a gift. I've been saving it for the last day we spent together."

"My lord," said Marie, "may I offer you a little wine?" Phillipe winced. Her expression was almost fawning.

Gil waved the offer aside courteously. "Thank you, no. I must ride back almost immediately. There's only time enough to present this to Phillipe."

He held out a long, slender package wrapped in oiled cloth.

"In token of our friendship. Perhaps you'll find it more enjoyable to practice with than a stick."

Touched, Phillipe laid the parcel on one of the

scarred tables, carefully undid the wrapping. A bar of winter light falling between the shutters lit the slightly curved steel of the blade, the warm brass of the cast hilt.

"Dear Lord, what a beautiful sword!" Marie breathed.

Phillipe could only agree. The hilt had a bird's-head pommel and a single knuckle-bow and quillon. The grip was ribbed. Picking up the amazing gift, Phillipe discovered a second, separately wrapped parcel beneath it. Even Girard expressed admiration for its contents: a scabbard of rich leather, tipped and throated in brass.

"There's a staple and strap for carrying it," Gil pointed out, obviously enjoying his role of benefactor. "Now you have a briquet like any good French grenadier."

"I don't deserve such a splendid present, Gil."

"But you do! I think you have the natural abilities of a fighting man, should you choose to develop them."

"But—I have nothing to give you in return."

The hazel eyes seemed to brighten a moment. Gil's reply, though seemingly casual, communicated clearly.

"You have given me a great deal, Phillipe. Companionship during what would otherwise have been a typically dull visit with my dear aunts and grandmother. And the pleasure of teaching some fundamentals to an apt pupil. Now I must go back to being the pupil."

"I hope to have the honor to meet you in Paris one day," Phillipe said.

"If not Paris, then somewhere, I have a feeling. A battlefield? Well, who can say? But comrades in arms always keep encountering one another. That's a truth old soldiers know with certainty."

With a last, piercing look—the renewed swearing of secrecy—he stepped forward and seized Phillipe in an embrace. It was affectionate, yet correct. It left the older boy with tears in his eyes.

"God grant His favor to you all," Gil said, waving as he departed. Outside, he mounted Sirocco and hammered away north through the snowdrifts toward Chavaniac.

"He embraced you like an equal!" Girard exclaimed.

"I told you my son's breeding was recognizable to any man with wits," Marie countered.

"But—comrades in arms? That's a peculiar term for a friendship between boys."

Phillipe closed his fingers around the ribbed hilt-grip of the shining sword. "It's because I helped him find the sorrel in that snowstorm. It's just his way of speaking. Everything in military terms."

"Um," was Girard's reply. Phillipe turned away from the blue eyes that had grown just a shade curious—and skeptical.

"Shut the door, it's freezing in here!" he said loudly.

To his astonishment, Girard did.

viii

The year 1771 brought more of the buffetings of fortune—and this time, the winds were bitter ones.

As touches of green began to peep between the basalt slabs of the hillsides of Auvergne, a courier on horseback galloped to the inn. Refreshing himself with food and wine, he informed Marie Charboneau haughtily that he had been hired to ride all the way from Paris to this godforsaken province to deliver *this*—

He proffered a rolled pouch, ribboned and sealed with maroon wax. Into the wax, a sigil had been impressed.

Marie retired to the kitchen to open the pouch. Though he hadn't been told, Phillipe suspected the sigil belonged to his father. He guessed it from the way she touched the wax with faintly trembling fingers, then from the courier's remark about the pouch having been forwarded across the Channel.

Phillipe was busy hustling up more wine for the irritable messenger when Marie screamed his name, piercingly.

He found her white-faced beside the kitchen hearth. She pressed a letter into his hand. Written in French, he noted. But not in Amberly's masculine hand.

"It's from your father's wife," Marie whispered. "He's fallen ill. They fear for his life."

Phillipe read the brief letter, whose cold tone suggested that it had been penned by James Amberly's wife on demand of her husband. Phillipe's dark eyes grew somber by the time he'd finished.

"She says the old wound from Minden has poisoned his system."

"And he wants to see you. In case he di—"

But Marie could not speak the word. She rubbed fiercely at one eye, fighting tears.

All at once Phillipe noticed something else. A packet of notes lying on the trestle table. Franc notes. More than he'd ever seen in his life.

Suddenly Marie Charboneau was all composure, decision:

"That money is ample for our passage to Paris, then by ship to England. We'll leave immediately. Surely Girard will keep the inn for us—"

She rushed to her son, wrapped her arms around him, pulled him close.

"Oh, Phillipe, didn't I promise? I've lived for this moment!"

Then he felt the terrible tremors of the sobbing she could no longer control.

"But I don't want him to die. *I don't want him to die!*"

CHAPTER IV

Kentland

i

THE COASTING VESSEL, a lugger out of Calais, slid into the harbor of Dover in bright April sunshine.

Phillipe gripped the rail, staring in awe at the white chalk cliffs rising behind the piers and the clutter of small Channel vessels anchored nearby. Gulls wheeled overhead, crying stridently. The air carried the salt tang of open water.

Phillipe had seen so many new sights and wonders in the past fortnight, he could hardly remember them all. Especially now. He felt a tinge of dread because he was entering his father's country both as a stranger and as a traditional enemy: a Frenchman.

Beyond that, Marie had not weathered the journey well. During the one night they had spent in the splendid, teeming city of Paris, she had been confined to her bed at a shabby inn on a side street. Phillipe had wanted to roam the great metropolis, see as much as possible before the coach departed for the seacoast. Instead, he'd sat the whole night on a stool beside the bed where Marie lay wracked with cramps and a fever.

Perhaps the cause was the strain of the trip. Or—the thought struck him for the first time that night in Paris—perhaps the hard years in Auvergne had drained away her health and vitality.

He saw further evidence that this might be true when the lugger put out from Calais. Complaining of dizziness, Marie went below. She vomited twice during the night crossing, much to the displeasure of the French crew, who provided a mop for Phillipe to clean up the mess personally.

He gave his most careful attention to the cheap second-hand trunk they'd bought in Chavaniac before departure. He mopped it thoroughly, even though the work—and the smell—was sickening.

Marie lay in a cramped bunk, even more pale than when she'd received news of Amberly's illness. She alternately implored God to stop the churning of the waves—the Channel was rough that night—and expressed her shame and humiliation to her son.

He finished cleaning up the ancient trunk and stared at it a moment. The trunk contained what little they owned that was of any value. Save for the inn, of course. That had been left in the care of Girard.

Marie's few articles of good clothing were packed in the trunk. Her precious casket of letters. And Phillipe's sword.

Why he'd brought the weapon he could not fully explain. But somehow, he wanted it with him in the land of the enemy—

Now he leaned on the lugger rail, squinting up past the gulls to a strange, tall tower on the chalk cliff. His confidence of the preceding months was all but gone.

He saw figures bustling on the quays. Englishmen. Would his limited knowledge of their language serve him well enough? He and his mother still had a long way to travel to reach his father's bedside. No instructions had been provided in the letter written by Lady Jane Amberly. Perhaps that was deliberate. He looked again at the cliff tower, strangely forbidding, as the sails were hauled in and the lugger's master screamed obscene instructions to his crew scampering around the deck.

The mate, a man with a gold hoop in one ear, noted Phillipe's rapt expression and clapped a hand on the boy's shoulder. He said in French:

"Busy place, eh? You'll get accustomed to it. The captain would probably have my balls for saying this, but I don't find the English a bad sort. After all, there's a lot of old French blood running in the veins of these squires and farmers."

The mate then proceeded to point out some of the structures high on the cliff, including the Norman keep and the strange, tall tower. Of the latter he said:

"There were two Roman lighthouses up there long ago, not just the one. Their fires guided the galleys of the legions into the harbor. And Caesar's troops fathered plenty of bastards before they pulled out. So whatever your business in England, my lad, don't let the locals put you down. Their ancestors came from all over Europe and God knows where else. Besides, we're at peace with them. For the present."

As he started aft, he added, "I'll be glad to help you and your mother find the coach. Shame the sailing wracked her so. She's a handsome woman. I'd court her myself if I didn't have two wives already."

Phillipe laughed, feeling a little less apprehensive. He went below.

He found his mother sitting in the gloom beside the shabby trunk. Her white hands were knotted in her lap. He closed his own hand on top of hers. How cold her flesh felt!

"The mate said he'll assist us in finding the overland coach, Mama."

Marie said nothing, staring at nothing. Phillipe was alarmed again. Distantly, he heard the lugger's anchor splash into the water.

ii

The mate led them up from the quay into town. He carried the trunk on his muscular shoulder as though it contained nothing at all. In the yard of a large, busy inn, he tried to decipher the English of a notice board that listed the departure times of various "flying waggons" bound for towns with unfamiliar names.

"Flying waggon is intended to be a compliment to the speed of the public coaches." The mate grinned. "But I understand that's nothing but the typical lie of any advertisement. Bah, I can't read that ungodly script! I'll ask inside. What's the name of the village you want?"

"Tonbridge," Phillipe said. "It's supposed to lie on a river west of here."

The man with the gold ear hoop disappeared, returning shortly to report that they wanted the coastal coach, via Folkestone, departing in midafternoon.

The mate kept them company while they waited, stating that he'd only squander money on unworthy, immoral pastimes if he went off by himself. He was a jolly, generous man, and even bought them lunch—dark bread and some ale—at a public house called The Cinque Ports.

Then he saw them aboard the imposing coach, whose driver kept yelling, "Diligence for Folkestone, m'lords. Express diligence, departing at once!"

The mate had helped them change some of their francs for British money. Now he picked the correct fare out of Phillipe's hand and paid the agent. He waved farewell as the diligence rolled out of the yard.

Five of the other six persons packed inside the coach chatted in English as the vehicle lurched westward. Phillipe and Marie sat hunched in one corner, saying nothing and trying to avoid stares of curiosity. Among the passengers was a cleric, who read his Testament in silence. But a fat, wigged gentleman in claret velvet talked enough for two men.

Apparently he had some connection with the weaving industry. He complained about the refusal of the "damned colonials" to import British goods—in protest against some of those taxes of which Girard had spoken, if Phillipe understood correctly.

"But damme, we've the King's Friends in power now!" the fat gentleman sputtered. "North shall bring those rebellious dogs to heel. Eh, what do you say?"

The merchant's mousy wife said she agreed. Oh yes, definitely. The fat man became all smiles and smugness. Dust boiled into the coach windows as it lurched along the rough but supposedly modern highway leading southwest along the coast.

iii

They arrived in Folkestone late at night, and Phillipe engaged a room. His English proved sufficient to the task, even though his pronunciation did elicit a momentary look of surprise.

The landlord treated his French guests with reasonable courtesy, however, and at dawn he helped Phillipe hoist the trunk into the luggage boot of another coach. Shortly after sunup, Marie and her son were bouncing northwestward, through a land most pleasant to gaze upon. Gentle downs, green with spring, unrolled vistas of tiny villages set among hop fields and orchards whose pink and white blossoms sent a sweet smell into the coach. Marie even remarked on the welcome warmth of the sun.

Phillipe got up nerve to ask an elderly lady what the district was called. She replied with a smile, "Kent, sir. The land of cherries and apples and the prettiest girls in the Empire!"

Near the edge of a great forest called The Weald, the coach broke an axle. They lost four hours while the coach guard, leaving his blunderbuss with the driver for protection of the passengers, trudged to the nearest town. He returned with a replacement part and two young wheelwrights, who performed the repairs. Finally, on the night of Phillipe and Marie's third day in England, the coach rolled across a river bridge into the village of Tonbridge, a small, quiet place in the valley of the Medway.

They found lodging upstairs at Wolfe's Triumph, an inn evidently renamed to honor the heroic general who had smashed the French at Quebec. In Auvergne, the general's name was jeered and cursed.

The inn's owner was a short, middle-aged man with protruding upper teeth. Phillipe went downstairs to find him late in the evening. Marie was already in bed. Not asleep, but unmoving. As if the trip had proved too great a strain.

A fragrant beech fire roared in the inn's inglenook. The spring night outside had grown chilly. A crowd of Tonbridge men packed the tables, drinking and gossiping about local happenings. Most of the men were fair, ruddy-faced, in sharp contrast to Phillipe's dark hair and eyes. But he was growing accustomed to drawing stares.

As Phillipe approached, the innkeeper turned from an ale cask. He handed two mugs to a plump serving girl, who switched her behind and smiled at Phillipe as she walked off.

"Well, young visitor," said the proprietor, "may I serve you something?"

"No, thank you. I am not thirsty." Phillipe was careful to speak each English word clearly. But the answer was a lie. He felt too insecure about the future to squander one precious coin.

"Too bad," said the older man. "I meant the first one to be a compliment of the house."

"Why—in that case, I'll accept. With thanks."

"That woman who arrived with you—is she your mother?"

Phillipe nodded.

"Is she quite well?"

"She's tired, that's all. We've come a long way."

"Across the Channel. You're French, aren't you?" The man drew a frothing mug from the cask, replacing the bung with a quick, deft movement, so that very little spilled. "Good English ale," he said, handing Phillipe the mug. "I don't hold with serving gin to younger folk. It's the ruination of thousands of little 'uns up in London."

Phillipe sipped, trying to hide his initial dislike of the amber brew. "Mmm. Very good. To answer your question—" He dashed foam off his lip with his sleeve. "I am French. But I have a relative who lives near here. My mother and I need to find his house so we may go see him."

"Well, sir, Mr. Fox knows most if not all of those in the neighborhood. What's the name of this relative?"

"Amberly."

At the nearby tables, conversation stopped. Eyes stared through the smoke rising from clay pipes held in suddenly rigid hands. A log fell in the great walk-in hearth.

Mr. Fox picked at a protruding upper tooth with one cracked nail. "Amberly, eh? Is that a fact?" Someone snickered.

The landlord surveyed Phillipe's shabby clothes. Then he asked: "You mean you have kinfolk serving the Amberlys, don't you?"

"No, sir. I'm related to the family itself. How far is their house from this town?"

"If you mean their estate, lad—only us ordinary folk live in measly houses—" Laughter in the room. "Not far. A mile up the river. The Duke lies ill, did you know that?"

"Yes. Is there someone I could pay to take a message saying we've come?"

"My boy Clarence, I suppose." Mr. Fox sounded both amused and skeptical. "But in the morning, eh?"

At the appointed time, Phillipe paid a ha'penny and waited. By noon, his hope was failing. But then Mr. Fox came clattering up the stairs to knock and announce:

"Clarence has returned! Lady Amberly is sending a cart for you and your mother at three this afternoon."

Mr. Fox was, without a doubt, dumbfounded.

iv

The cart clacked along the towpath beside the clear-running Medway. On the banks, green willows drooped their branches into the river. Phillipe and Marie sat in the cart's rear seat. They were dressed in their finest. And Phillipe was conscious of just how threadbare that was.

The elderly carter, by contrast, wore clothing far more elegant. Orange hose; a frogged coat of yellow velvet. Castoffs, perhaps. But rich garments nevertheless.

Shortly after they left the village, Marie asked, "Can you tell me anything of the Duke's illness?"

The old fellow hesitated. "Well, 'tis really Lady Jane's role to speak for conditions in the household. But I will say Dr. Bleeker's much in evidence. I understand he bleeds the Duke regular. The Duke's bedroom is kept dark. He's never seen out of it. A shame, a terrible shame!" the man exploded suddenly. "Him having so many friends at court, I mean, and being talked about for an assistant secretary's post, now that Lord North's prime minister. For days, we've been expecting His Lordship to call personally. We had no word of other visitors," he finished, pointedly.

No, Phillipe thought, *I'm sure my father's wife would not announce our unwelcome arrival too widely.*

The cart horse ambled around a green hillock. The driver volunteered another bit of information:

"There is much turmoil at Kentland, you must understand. Lady Jane engaged the famous Mr. Capability Brown to redo all the landscaping just before her husband fell ill. No matter how important you think your business may be, I'd advise you to make your visit brief."

Coloring, Marie started to retort. Seated beside her, Phillipe shook his head. The carter did not see the woman's mouth and eyes narrow down.

Hatred? Apprehension?

Or both?

But she accepted her son's guidance. He suddenly felt much older.

The carter jogged up the pony. The towpath curved around another hillock. Marie let out a soft cry.

Kentland overlooked the river Medway with serene authority. The old, yellow Tudor brick of the vast, two-story main house shone mellow in the sunshine. The house was situated at the center of a grassy parkland alive with scurrying figures. Men carrying small trees with the roots wrapped, or turning the earth with spades. Phillipe was awed by the immense, rambling place. He counted six outbuildings as the cart rolled up the long drive.

The carter let them off at the front door and drove away without looking back.

v

Afterward, Phillipe decided that every detail of their reception had been planned to intimidate them.

The intimidation began with the delay after his knock. The door did not open for several minutes.

Eventually a footman in powdered wig, white stockings and satin livery answered. He turned away without waiting for them to state their identities. Apparently he already knew.

The footman led them to a vast, airy room on the southern side of the house. There, great windows with tall mirrors between them opened onto green expanses leading down to the river. The drawing room boasted carved doorframes, a chimney-piece painted in brilliant white, and chairs and tripod tables of gilt wood with needleworked cushions.

In one of these chairs directly beneath a huge crystal chandelier sat a woman of about Marie's age. She did not rise as the footman ushered the visitors in.

An austere, graying man lounged beside an open window where the scarlet damask curtains blew gently. He had a prim mouth, indifferent eyes. He wore black, with only white cuffs showing.

But it was the woman who riveted Marie's attention, and that of her son. She had gray eyes and rather sunken-looking cheeks. But obvious beauty could not be completely hidden by her masklike expression. Blue tinting powder in her wig caught random sunlight. The powder matched the rich blue of her long gown with Turkish sleeves.

Marie did not wilt under the impact of the woman's stare. Standing squarely, like a peasant ready to bargain, she announced in accented English:

"I am Marie Charboneau. I have brought my son, Phillipe."

Lady Jane Amberly inclined her head slightly. Her quick inspection of Phillipe said a good deal concerning her feelings about having Amberly's bastard in her drawing room. She addressed Marie.

"I was not certain you would be able to converse in our language. Since you can, we may conclude our business with greater dispatch. I will not offer refreshments since this is not a social occasion. I wrote you only at my husband's insistence."

Perhaps Marie drew on some reserve of inner strength. Or on her training as an actress long ago. Either way, she sounded fully as haughty as Lady Jane when she answered:

"A correction please, my lady. I am not here primarily for business, as you term it. I am here first of all because your husband wishes to see his son."

"Since I wrote you, circumstances have changed. That may not be possible."

The damask curtains stirred again. Phillipe felt a sudden, inexplicable chill. The gentleman in black stepped forward with an air of authority.

"Lady Jane is quite correct. The Duke's wound is severely inflamed. Poisonous. The suffering drains him of sense and energy. He is seldom awake."

Once more the blue-tinted wig inclined just a little. Lady Jane sounded weary, as if each word were an obnoxious duty:

"Dr. Bleeker is one of the most respected physicians in London. He is staying at Kentland to attend my husband. I do not wish the Duke to die, but the possibility exists. We must all accept it. And behave accordingly."

Phillipe studied the black-garbed doctor, thinking, *From London? The expense must be staggering—*

Silence, then, save for the rustle of the curtains, the tinkle of the chandelier and a shout from one of the small army of gardeners laboring outside.

Finally Marie challenged the silence:

"Does James know his son is here, my lady?"

"He was informed shortly after your message arrived this morning. He was awake briefly at that time."

"Then in spite of his perilous condition, I ask that we be taken to him without delay."

"Permission for that," said Dr. Bleeker, "I cannot grant. The doors of the Duke's bedroom are expressly closed to all but those few whom I personally admit. At the moment, a good friend and spiritual adviser to this family, Bishop Francis, is with him. Praying while he sleeps."

"The face of his son might be better medicine than prayers!" Marie said.

"As to this young man being my husband's son"—Lady Jane's gray eyes touched on Phillipe again and dismissed him—"I have no evidence."

"But I have a letter, my lady. A letter from your husband granting Phillipe his rightful share of James Amberly's estate!"

Suddenly Lady Jane rose. "I will have no loud voices in this house, madame. I fulfilled my husband's request. Reluctantly, but I fulfilled it. That is all I intend to do. If there comes an appropriate time for this boy you claim is the Duke's illegitimate son to see my husband, well and good. If not—" She shrugged.

"I *claim* nothing!" Marie retorted. "Nothing except the truth."

"*Will you in the name of God lower your voice and speak in a seemly fashion?* Don't you understand? You are intruders! Having stretched my conscience to its limits and told him you've come, I will not have him disturbed further unless Dr. Bleeker approves."

Bleeker said, "For the immediate future, the prospect is doubtful."

Marie looked shaken. "Then we will retire to the inn at Tonbridge—"

Lady Jane's eyelids flickered, hooding her gray pupils

as she frowned at the physician. For his part, Bleeker acted amused. Marie's labored English had brought the name out as *Town-breedge*. Phillipe felt a raw impulse to use his fist to eradicate the doctor's supercilious expression.

As Lady Jane controlled her brief show of anger, Marie concluded in a somewhat stronger voice:

"But we will not leave until my son has met with his father."

Lady Jane said softly, "To wait might not be prudent."

Marie caught her breath. Like her son, she sensed the threat that seemed to hover just beneath the surface of the remark. The breeze whispered at the windows. The moving curtains of scarlet damask created slowly changing patterns of sun and shadow that seemed somehow sinister. Phillipe felt cold.

Was there a threat in what Lady Jane had said? Or was his reaction only a product of his own imagination, as he confronted a tense and difficult situation—?

He managed to say, "I'm not certain I entirely understand your meaning, my lady."

"Oh—" A delicate shrug of Lady Jane's shoulder; a false, waxen smile instantly in place. The gray eyes were all at once bland, unreadable. "I only meant I am aware that your funds must be severely limited. Even considering what my husband sent you."

Was that all she'd meant? Somehow, Phillipe doubted it—

Dr. Bleeker broke the silence: "And I must repeat, the wait may be not only lengthy, but entirely fruitless." He turned his shoulder to them, in dismissal, staring outside with a languid expression.

"The decision is of course yours," Lady Jane said to Marie. "I should, however, like to examine the letter which you say you possess." Her voice had an unmistakable catch in it. Phillipe felt a point scored.

She knows from my face that I'm his son, he thought. She *knows* the letter exists. *And she's afraid.*

There was brief, vengeful pleasure in the realization. By what right did this elegant woman continue to stare at Marie Charboneau as if demanding obedience from a servant?

He heard Marie reply, "I do not have it, madame. It is put safely away."

"Then at some future time you will certainly permit me to see it. Verify its doubtful authenticity—"

"There is nothing doubtful about—" Phillipe began loudly, only to be interrupted by a commotion of voices.

He spun around, angry again. The laughter of the new arrivals told him that Lady Jane's words about the grave situation at Kentland were at least in part a sham; a sham to intimidate the peasant woman and her peasant son.

A young man of around Phillipe's age burst into the drawing room, holding the hand of a girl of perhaps nineteen. Or, more accurately, he dragged her along after him. The pair stopped suddenly. The young man exclaimed:

"Why, God save us! The French visitors? My supposed half-brother—what, what?"

Phillipe could only gape. At first glance, the young man might have been a subtly distorted mirror portrait of himself.

Yes, the mouth was thinner. The shoulders wider. And the new arrival stood half a head taller, even though he was at the moment affecting a somewhat limp posture. But the resemblance was still marked.

Not in terms of costume, of course. In contrast to Phillipe's plain garb, the boy was dressed in a long, checkered coat much like a dressing gown. His outfit was completed by loose Dutchman's breeches and shoes of pink satin. He clutched a tall, varnished walking stick with a huge silver head. The carry-cord was looped around one wrist.

The young man's wig was stuck through with pearl-headed pins. Phillipe had never seen such a peculiar figure. Only much later did he learn that the apparel was, according to the lights of the macaronis—youthful noblemen who adopted the latest fads and aped the sputtering "What, what?" of the king—conservative.

For perhaps a heartbeat's time, Phillipe was tempted to burst out laughing at the young man's bizarre appearance and studied pose of boredom. But two things checked the mirth—the first being the total lack of any softening humor in the boy's eyes. Focused on Phillipe, those eyes belied the pearl pins and pink shoes and limp wrist draped over the stick head. They were ugly eyes—

Ugly as the small, purplish birthmark Phillipe saw at the outer end of the young man's left eyebrow.

The mark was shaped roughly like a U, and tilted, so the bottom pointed toward the left earlobe. Then Phillipe noticed a cloven place in the mark's lower curve. He decided the mark didn't resemble a letter so much as a broken hoof.

No more than a thumbnail's height in all, the mark was still livid, disfiguring. Phillipe recalled the words in his father's letter about the difficulties Lady Jane had encountered bearing Amberly's legitimate son. Phillipe had no doubt about who the young man was—or why he stared with such open animosity.

The scene held a moment more—as the girl drew Phillipe's attention. She was beautiful, so softly beautiful, in fact, that he almost gasped aloud at his first close look at her.

She was about the same height as her companion, but slimmer. High, full breasts were accented by her military-style riding costume. The double-breasted coat was dark blue, faced with white. A froth of white cravat showed at her throat. She wore no wig, her tawny hair bound in back by a simple ribbon. She tapped a crop against her full skirt, from under whose hem peeped the polished toes of masculine jackboots.

The girl's sky-blue eyes engaged Phillipe's with frank interest. And without the obvious dislike with which the boy continued to regard him.

Slowly, then, with a curling little smile, the girl glanced away—

But not before Phillipe's startled senses caught a similarity between her gaze and Charlotte's. Like Charlotte, she was a creature of the flesh, some instinct told him. But she was not common. A whore at heart, perhaps. But a gilded one—

Obviously the two young people had been outdoors, engaging in some strenuous activity such as horseback riding. The young man gave off an aroma of sweat as he swaggered toward Phillipe, hitting the floor with the ferrule of his stick at each step, *rap, rap.* His grin remained lopsided, relaxed—unlike his eyes. The girl pretended disinterest, half-turning from the two young men. But she continued to watch in an oblique way, a faint sheen of perspiration glowing on her upper lip.

Rap, rap, rap—

The young man stopped two paces in front of Phillipe. Stared. The lopsided grin straightened out; disappeared, leaving his mouth stark with distaste.

With unmistakable reluctance, Lady Jane at last broke the prolonged tension:

"May I present my son, Roger, and his fiance, Alicia, daughter of the Earl of Parkhurst?"

Roger whipped up his stick. Phillipe had to step back a pace, quickly, to avoid being struck by the tip. He didn't miss the flicker of pleasure in Roger's eyes. Roger pointed the stick at Marie.

"This is the Charboneau woman?"

"Yes, that's correct. I've forgotten her boy's name."

Rage boiled inside Phillipe as Marie burst out, "You know his name is Phillipe."

Studying Phillipe through tawny lashes, Alicia Parkhurst remarked, "I do think there's a resemblance."

Lady Jane's gray eyes went to flint. Roger saw his mother's fury, and as if some unseen signal had passed between them, whirled on the girl, slamming the stick's ferrule on the floor.

"None! None at all!"

"Oh, but Roger my sweet, use your eyes!"

Roger's mouth wrenched. His color darkened as he went to Alicia in three swift strides. The mark at his eyebrow seemed more black than purple as his voice savaged her:

"Mine are perfectly clear, Alicia dearest. Yours, however—well, one would almost think you'd been indulging your excessive fondness for claret. You're babbling."

The girl's face turned pink. Her shoulders trembled. Her expression changed from anger to humiliation, then to fear as Roger lifted his free hand to tweak the point of her chin. Not lightly, Phillipe saw. He hurt her. The girl's eyes blazed again as Roger said:

"Pray be silent, Alicia, while we conclude this tiresome private matter."

Shut out, intimidated, the girl seemed on the point of attacking him; her fingers around her riding crop had gone dead white.

But under the impact of Roger's furious stare, she wilted. Though still angry, she turned her back. What had made her surrender? Phillipe wondered. Fright? Or something more?

Rap—

Rap—

RAP—

Very slowly, in control again, Roger Amberly returned to stand before Phillipe, feigning a smile.

"No," he sighed, "no resemblance. Except one. We smell about the same. But then, I've been for a frisky ride, what—?" He jabbed lightly at Phillipe's armpit with the heavy silver head of his stick.

Phillipe's hands flashed out. He jerked the stick so hard, the carry-loop broke. He flung the stick without looking. It skittered and clacked across the floor, landing at Dr. Bleeker's feet.

"Don't prod me like some animal," Phillipe said.

The birthmark over Roger's eye darkened as he lunged forward. "You filthy French clod, how dare you touch a hand to anything of mi—"

"*Roger.*"

Lady Jane's voice, steel, brought her son up in midstride. A blood vessel stood out in Roger's throat. He took another step forward but Lady Jane intercepted him.

"Roger—you will not. I will handle this."

He obeyed her. But not easily. Balked, he glared at Phillipe—and over Roger's shoulder, Phillipe thought he saw Alicia Parkhurst's eyes brighten with a moment's delight. It was quickly masked as Roger stormed toward Bleeker, snatched up his stick in a sudden wild arc. The stick's ferrule struck a small porcelain vase on one of the tripod tables, shattering it.

Once more Lady Jane stared at her son. A last piece of the vase clinked to the floor. Roger let out a long, heavy breath, as if something in him had been given release. With mingled dread and curiosity, Phillipe speculated as to whether the boy's marked face was somehow a sign of a deeper, more damaging mark on his mind— From the hard birth, perhaps?

Lady Jane addressed Marie in a toneless voice:

"Be so good as to take yourself and this brawling boor out of my house."

"There's some doubt about who is the brawling boor," Phillipe said. Roger's eyes narrowed, hateful.

"I will leave," Marie replied. "But I will stay in the village until Phillipe stands at the bedside of James Amberly and is recognized as his son."

"On both counts, madame," said Lady Jane with that impeccable control, "there is much doubt about the outcome."

"I have his witnessed letter! You cannot destroy the truth of that!"

Marie wheeled and walked away. Face hot, Phillipe started to follow, only to have Roger dart forward:

"Hold one moment!"

Phillipe turned, waiting.

Roger was younger, he had decided. But by no means lacking in physical strength. Roger held his stick in one hand, fingering—almost caressing—the heavy, scrolled silver head.

"Under the law," Roger said with venom, "I could have you maimed for attacking me."

"If that's so, then your laws are as worthless as you."

Roger stiffened, hand dropping from the silver head that winked deadly bright in a shifting gleam of sunlight. Phillipe expected an attack, tried to ready himself—then grew aware of Lady Jane again warning her son off with those strong gray eyes.

The corners of his mouth tight, Roger said, "But I won't call the law down, my little French bastard. If there's any punishing to be done, I'll do it. Thoroughly and well!"

Swallowing his fear of this crazed young man with the rampaging temper, Phillipe retorted, "Perhaps there'll come a time when we can test the truth of that boast."

"If you stay in Tonbridge long, I'm certain of it."

All at once Lady Jane was between them again, a hand on her son's arm.

"This is not a London cockpit! I will have that remembered."

Dr. Bleeker took out a tiny snuff case. "Shall I summon assistance to have the boy removed, my lady?"

"Oh, no! Such boldness shouldn't be punished!"

Phillipe and everyone else swung around, startled by Alicia Parkhurst's merry little laugh. The girl let her sky-blue eyes linger on Phillipe—

Admiringly? Or was that merely hopeful self-deception?

Still smiling, she addressed her husband-to-be:

"I wouldn't venture to be too bold, Roger—"

"Shut your mouth."

Alicia rolled with the verbal blow, hardly blinked. She was afraid of Roger, that Phillipe sensed quite clearly. Yet she would not be easily humiliated. Under her lilting words, there was malice:

"But I mean it, dear Roger. The boy appears a match for your own hot temper. And brother against brother—that would be shameful."

Her head came up, defiantly. "Striking him would be like striking yourself. He does have your good looks, after all. Perhaps he's even a shade handsomer, I can't quite decide—" She was daring them—any of them—to deny her right to speak.

"Can you, Lady Jane?" she asked. "You, Dr. Bleeker?"

Phillipe both admired her courage and deplored her foolhardiness. Lady Jane now looked nearly as wrathful as her son, though she said nothing. Parkhurst must be a name fully as illustrious and powerful as Amberly, he thought.

But insult for insult—cruelty for cruelty—the atmosphere in this breezy, sunlit room was all at once too foul and dangerous to be borne. He stalked toward Marie at the doorway, aware of a smoky, sidelong glance of speculation from Alicia.

As he reached Marie's side, she spoke, implacable:

"We will wait in the village. As long as necessary."

"At your peril," said Roger.

Hearing Lady Jane's sibilant burst of breath as she tried to still her son, Phillipe concentrated on taking Marie's arm and leading her out of that room of enraged faces. Still half-blind with anger himself, he seemed to see but one image: Alicia Parkhurst's sky-colored eyes, vivid and intense in the moment he passed by her—

Lady Jane's voice was raised behind them. It did no good. Roger shouted anyway:

"Your son will be dead before anyone calls him my lawful brother, you French harlot!"

Phillipe swung around, making a guttural sound. Marie's hand on his arm restrained him. Fighting his anger, he stumbled after her.

He didn't know whether the encounter had been a victory or a defeat. But there was no doubt that new perils had developed in the confrontation. As if to convince the world—and himself—that he wasn't afraid, he slammed the front door thunderously on the way out.

CHAPTER V

A Game of Love

i

THAT NIGHT, back at Wolfe's Triumph, Phillipe expressed a worry that had troubled him ever since the stormy confrontation at Kentland.

"How long can we wait?" he asked Marie. "Lady Jane was right— our money won't last indefinitely."

"Then we will find a way to get more."

Phillipe couldn't see his mother's face when she answered. He was lying on the truckle, pulled from underneath the higher bed into which he could hear her settling. Downstairs, the sounds of laughter and friendly argumentation emphasized again just how isolated and vulnerable they were in this alien land. Vulnerable especially to the temper of Roger Amberly—

But his mother's reply seemed to take no account of that. After a moment she went on, "We will not leave this place till your father has seen you, and you have seen him. No matter what it costs us." With a sharp exhalation of breath, she blew out the candle on the stand beside the bed.

Hands locked under his neck in the darkness, Phillipe reckoned that it had cost a good deal already.

After leaving the Amberly house, he and Marie had found no cart waiting to return them to Tonbridge. So they walked—not a long walk, at least not for him. Despite the attempted humiliation by Lady Jane and her son, he could take pleasure from the fact that she had not quite been able to conceal her fear of Marie Charboneau's presence—or his.

But Marie had made the trip to Tonbridge with difficulty. She grew short of breath, asking often that they pause and rest. In the low-slanting light of late afternoon, her face had an unhealthy pallor that disturbed Phillipe considerably.

In the sultry darkness of the room at Mr. Fox's establishment, he voiced his concern:

"Are you positive you're well enough to stay here for some length of time, Mama?"

"Why do you ask that, Phillipe? Because the boy threatened you?"

"No!" he burst out. "I'm not afraid of him—he's probably all bluff." In truth, he didn't completely believe either statement. He finished, "It's you I'm worried about."

"I am stronger than she is! You'll see. Now go to sleep."

Over the noise from below-stairs, Phillipe heard a faroff rumble. The first thunder of a spring storm. Coming from the north, the great city of London. Blue-white light flashed across the sky outside the open window.

Lightning flashes filled his uneasy dreams.

And an enraged face branded with a purplish mark.

And a vase shattering—

And the sky-blue eyes of an aristocratic girl.

ii

Next morning, early, a knocking at the door roused him.

He clambered up from the truckle bed, aware that the sleeve of his coarse nightshirt was damp with rain. A shutter banged in the chilly breeze.

As he stumbled over to close it, he glimpsed the river

winding near the High Street, all gray in a mist of morning. Tiles and thatching on the roofs of cottages in the village glistened from the storm that had drenched Tonbridge all night long.

Directly below the window, he saw a team of matched grays standing in the mud. The team was hitched to a splendid gilt-and-blue private coach with a coat of arms on its door. Two men huddled on the rear step while the driver complained about the sudden end of the fine weather. One of the men at the back of the coach picked at mud spatters on his white stockings and wondered rhetorically how long they might be forced to wait.

The knocking sounded again, waking Marie. She came muttering up from sleep, as though still partially in the grip of a bad dream. Phillipe touched her arm to calm her. Her dark eyes opened wide, suddenly full of fear as the knocking was repeated a third time, loudly.

As Phillipe strode to the door, he glanced at the trunk, wondering whether he should quickly unwrap his sword. But he decided to go ahead and slip the door latch, blocking the opening with his body.

A moment later, sounding relieved, he said to Marie, "No danger. It's only the landlord's boy."

Young Clarence Fox, a towhead with teeth equally as protuberant as his father's said in a hushed voice:

"You have visitors below. They want to speak to you private. My father and I are to stay in the kitchen. They ask you and your mother to come down as quick as possible. You'd better do it, because Father can't afford to anger the most important folk around here."

Tense, Phillipe asked, "Who are the visitors? People from Kentland?"

"Lady Jane herself. And some churchman wearing purple. My father treated 'em plenty polite."

Marie was sitting up, covering her threadbare nightgown with the comforter. Her dark eyes were clear and alert now. Her faint smile showed satisfaction.

Phillipe took his cue from that. "Go down and say we'll attend them as soon as my mother is dressed, Clarence."

As he shut the door, Marie laughed. It took no words to explain why. Lady Jane Amberly would not have bothered to seek them out if there was no validity to Marie's claim.

iii

But the brief period of exhilaration vanished the moment Phillipe and his mother went down to the common room.

Mr. Fox and Clarence had indeed retired, leaving a wedge of cheese and two apples on a serving board at the table where Lady Jane sat motionless. The hood of her pearl-gray cloak was pulled up over the powdery pile of her hair. Her hands were clasped tightly atop the handle of an umbrella of waxed silk.

Fox had built a small fire in the inglenook. Silhouetted against the flames was an obese man of middle age. Wearing purple, as Clarence had reported.

The man turned as Marie preceded her son into the room. The man's full moon of a face matched Jane Amberly's for severity. Small blue eyes that scrutinized the arrivals seemed to lack any emotion, save a remote distaste. But perhaps Phillipe was deceived by the flickering light of the fire—

All at once the man licked his thick, already moist lips and smiled an unctuous smile. Thready purple veins showed in his fleshy nose. Still, he radiated affluence, importance, authority. And once in place, his smile never wavered.

Marie maintained the pretense of politeness:

"I am sorry for the delay, my lady. I was not yet awake when the boy knocked."

Lady Jane offered no similar courtesy, coming to the

point at once. "Last night, madame, I reflected for several hours on the unpleasantness which took place at Kentland. I then sought counsel from Bishop Francis."

She indicated the obese man standing at the hearth with hands clasped behind his back. So this was the prelate supposedly praying for James Amberly. Phillipe thought the man looked more acquainted with the ways of the flesh than with those of holiness.

With an air of sympathy, the bishop spoke in a deep, honeyed voice:

"And I naturally advised Lady Amberly to bring the matter to a speedy and amiable conclusion—for both your sakes. Affairs at Kentland are troubled enough, as I'm sure you understand." A tiny pursing of the bowed lips. "If you are truly concerned for the welfare of the Duke—as well as your own—you will be receptive to my lady's proposal."

"I am concerned for his welfare but also for that of his son," Marie shot back with a sharp gesture at Phillipe.

"Yes, yes, of course, but don't you mean his *alleged* son?" Bishop Francis asked with the merest flicker of his eyelids. "The matter *is* in dispute—"

"Not as far as we're concerned," Phillipe said.

Lady Jane lifted one gloved hand from the head of her umbrella. "Please. Let us come to the solution without quarreling over the problem itself." To Marie: "You must realize that your presence places additional strain on our entire household. I have come here in the hope of persuading you to leave, thereby removing the extra burden. At the good bishop's suggestion, I am prepared to make a favorable reaction to my request worth your while."

Instantly, Phillipe suspected the game. So did Marie. Her cheeks turned chalky white. But her acting ability helped her keep control.

She walked to a chair near Lady Jane, sat down

gracefully. Her dark eyes met the other woman's; held. Bishop Francis continued to smile sympathetically. But the little blue seeds of his eyes showed worry. He already sensed resistance.

"You have come to make us an offer of money?" Marie asked.

"Entirely and solely for the sake of forestalling further unpleasantness, my dear lady," said the bishop.

Marie whipped around to face him. "No. To ensure that my son will have no share in his father's estate, should the Duke's illness prove fatal."

Lady Jane maintained her composure with effort. "Madame, your crudeness is an affront."

"Does the truth affront those of your class, my lady? What a pity."

Lady Jane stood up. Bishop Francis stepped away from the hearth, raising one fat pink hand. His voice oozed conciliation:

"Let us have no un-Christian words when a man's immortal soul lies threatened." He walked toward Marie, fingers unconsciously stroking the purple folds draped across his large stomach. "The offer is most generous. Remove yourself and your boy from Tonbridge within a reasonable time—a day or two—and my lady is prepared to turn into your hands the sum of fifty pounds. Why, do you realize how much that is?" His smile was touched with irony. "Some of our village curates survive comfortably on two or three pounds a year."

All of Marie's theatrical talents focused in her contemptuous laugh.

Lady Jane looked as if she'd been struck in the face. Bishop Francis' eyebrows shot up. Folds of fat appeared between the lines in his forehead. Marie said:

"A mere fifty pounds? For a young man who's the rightful heir to part of James Amberly's fortune?"

"Oh, but my dear woman, we have no proof the Duke

fathered him!" Francis said. "None whatsoever."

"Then I'll show you the proof!" Marie cried, running upstairs.

In moments she was back, carrying the brass-cornered casket. Phillipe had withdrawn to a place several tables removed from Lady Jane's. From that vantage point he watched Bishop Francis inspect the casket with eager curiosity. Like his mouth, the bishop's eyes looked moist.

All at once Francis noticed Phillipe's scowl. The prelate turned back to the fire, sighing and daintily rubbing at one eyelid with a sausagelike middle finger.

Lady Jane was breathing faster. Even though the bishop smiled again, his pendulous lips glistening in the firelight, Phillipe felt an inexplicable sense of danger.

Marie set the casket on a table and opened it. From the packet she took out the topmost document.

"This is written in the Duke's own hand. And witnessed by two friends, for the sake of legality. The letter promises Phillipe his portion under English law. Since James has only one other male issue, that portion is half. Not fifty pounds. Half!"

Bishop Francis extended his right hand. "Would you be so good as to let me examine the document?"

Defiantly, Marie started to give him the folded letter. Phillipe saw Lady Jane glance from the letter to the fireplace. He ran forward and snatched the letter out of his mother's hand:

"I'll show it to him."

Phillipe unfolded the document carefully, held it top and bottom. Bishop Francis lowered his extended hand, all expression gone from his suet face for a moment. Then, hunching forward, he scanned the letter. He said to Lady Jane:

"My knowledge of French is no longer what it was in

my student days. But I recognize the handwriting as your husband's. And the letter is indeed witnessed."

Phillipe carried the valuable possession back to the casket, folded it away and shut the lid. Bishop Francis fingered his jowl thoughtfully.

"In view of those facts, my lady," he said, "perhaps we might show a larger measure of Christian generosity. Obviously this woman and her son are not well off. A hundred pounds—?"

"Half and nothing less!" Marie exclaimed.

The tip of the bishop's tongue roved over his lower lip. He looked almost grief-stricken. "You reject my lady's offer?"

"Completely!"

Abruptly, Lady Jane made a quick gesture of disgust. She started out, her gray eyes venomous. At the doorway, she turned.

"Madame, you are attempting to deprive my son of his full inheritance—exactly as you have deprived me of my husband's affections for years. I cannot predict what will befall the Duke as a result of his illness. But regardless of the outcome, Roger will receive his full share of the estate—now or later. I nearly gave my life to bring my son into this world. His welfare has always been my paramount concern, because he is the only child I could ever bear. For almost a year after his birth, we were not even certain that he would survive—indeed, the midwives and the physician who attended my confinement had some suspicion that at birth he was harmed in some unknown way. When he did survive, and grow, I thanked the Almighty, and vowed he would receive my constant attention all his life. So I do not take any threat to his future lightly. Be warned."

And she stormed out, straight to the coach, where the footmen sprang down into the mud to open the door.

Bishop Francis paused a moment, a gross figure

against the gray morning mist. His smile remained sad.

"Madame—young master—permit me to speak as one whose holy charge and duty it is to be sensitive to the situations of all human beings, regardless of their station. For your own sake—your own safety!—do not, I beg you, challenge the power of this family. To do so for any prolonged period would be extremely ill advised. And I would be saddened by what must surely be the inevitable consequences. Heed me—and reconsider."

Marie said, "No."

With a sigh and a shake of his head, Bishop Francis left in a swirl of purple. Phillipe couldn't decide whether the churchman was sincere—or a wily charlatan.

After the lavish coach had pulled away, Marie pressed her palms against the sides of the casket. She was jubilant.

"Do you realize what all of that signified, Phillipe? The claim is valid! She knows it! We will wait to see the Duke, no matter what happens. We're not dirt to be kicked aside as she pleases—or bought off for a pittance!"

Phillipe said nothing. In principle, he agreed. But he hoped it was not a foolhardy decision.

Distantly in the stillness, he thought he heard the Amberly coach thundering out of Tonbridge. He resigned himself to more waiting.

Among those who were now clearly enemies.

iv

That same day, Phillipe drafted a short letter to Girard. He wrote that they would be delayed longer than expected, and requested that Girard continue management of the inn as best he could. Mr. Fox helped dispatch the letter via coach post.

Phillipe had no idea what the next move in the game would be. He was convinced that Lady Jane would somehow keep track of their continuing presence. And indeed, it wasn't long until he had another proof of their peril.

Two days had passed. To fill the hours, he'd taken to helping young Clarence with chores around the inn. It was from Clarence that he received confirmation that he and Marie were being spied upon.

"A groom from Kentland stopped this morning," Clarence reported.

"What did he want?"

"He asked my father whether a French woman was still staying here. A French woman and her son."

"Is that all?"

Clarence gnawed his lip a moment. "No. The groom said that if anyone from Kentland caught the son alone anyplace, they'd break his head for sport."

Down on his knees scrubbing the grease-spattered stones of the kitchen hearth, Phillipe ignored the look that hoped for an explanation. Once again he realized he and Marie were pitted against powerful antagonists in a strange and silent war. Who would surrender first?

More important, when would they face the next direct attack?

v

As the sweet month of May filled Kent with the green of tree buds bursting open and the colorful splash of flowers blooming in cottage gardens, Phillipe, despite the open and implied threats, began to roam the countryside. The wandering filled the time when he wasn't helping Clarence pitchfork straw or polish tables; it filled the emptiness in which no word, no sign was received from Kentland. The war held static, as if the opposition forces were pondering basic strategies very carefully.

Tactics, however, were a different matter. Those were all too clear—and menacing.

On an early morning tramp in the direction of his father's estate, Phillipe encountered three grubbily dressed servants trudging toward the village with hampers. Though they wore no livery, he guessed at once that they must be from Kentland. Instant recognition showed on their faces.

He stood immobile at the edge of the towpath, watching the three come to a halt a few yards off.

"Why—'tis the French bastard!" sneered the youngest of the trio. "Still daring to show his dial in daylight!"

One of his companions crouched down quickly, snatched a stone, hurled it hard.

Phillipe didn't dodge swiftly enough. The stone struck his forehead, left a stinging gash that bled.

Growling under his breath, Phillipe started to charge the servants—and only checked when he saw two of them go for bigger rocks and the third drop his hamper and reach into his boot for a skinning knife.

The blade flashed in the low-slanting sun. Confronting bullies was one thing. But dashing unarmed toward suicide was quite another. What if he were seriously wounded? Even killed by these nobodies? Though it galled him to hesitate, he knew he shouldn't risk the danger of his mother being left with a dead or injured son on her hands. Not when she had poured so much of her strength and hope into bringing them this far—

He thumbed his nose at the trio and gave them a good, obscene cursing in French as he turned his back.

In response, he heard laughter, jeers, English oaths fully as blue as his own. His face reddened as he quickened his step and angled for some trees on the side of the path away from the river. He knew what he was doing was right. But it was still humiliating.

Trying to pelt him with stones, the servants gave

chase. But only for a short distance. Once into the woods, he eluded them easily. He negotiated his way back to Tonbridge over the downs, stopping only to wash the blood off his forehead in a brook.

All the way to Wolfe's Triumph, the taunts tormented him.

He kept reminding himself that he must keep his eye on the larger purpose. It had taken more courage to flee than might have been required to attack the servants and jam their insults back down their ignorant throats.

Or so he rationalized, to ease his conscience.

When Marie asked him about the clotted cut over his eye, he gave her an evasive answer. He'd tripped, sprawled out, that's all. No use letting her know of the new evidence of their continuing danger—

But he was damned if he'd let intimidation from the Amberly household deter him from wandering wherever he pleased. He would not—could not—surrender that completely.

So if anything, the aborted attack only made his ramblings bolder and more frequent.

One bright afternoon he took another long stroll beside the Medway, then sat down to rest at the edge of a large, shadowy grove on the summit of what the locals called Quarry Hill. Seeing no one, menacing or otherwise, in the vicinity, he yawned, leaned back and dozed off.

Hoofbeats wakened him.

Below, on the towpath, a rider reined in. A splendid, glistening black stallion pointed its muzzle up the hillside. He scrambled to his feet, alarmed until he saw tawny hair flash in the sun—

It was Alicia Parkhurst.

She had evidently recognized him asleep against the tree trunk. Phillipe's forehead felt warm all at once.

He walked forward as the girl dismounted, holding the black's reins with one hand. She looked down the hill, then swept the horizon with a glance, as if to make certain she was not being observed. She wore the same fashionable riding costume in which he'd first seen her, and again he noticed the way it emphasized the swelling fullness of her breasts.

"Good afternoon, Master Frenchman," she said with a coquettish nod. "I've never spied you on Quarry Hill before."

"Oh," he grinned, "have you looked?"

She feigned annoyance. "You have a saucy tongue."

"My apologies. Do you ride this way often?"

"Not as often as I'd like. Every few days—if I'm lucky."

"Well, I've never stopped here before. But I've seen enough of Tonbridge to last awhile. So I've been exploring. May I ask whether there's any news of my father?"

Alicia Parkhurst shook her head. "The situation's little changed. That ghoul Bleeker lets more and more blood. But still the Duke seldom wakens. They do fear for his life."

Phillipe swallowed hard. "I thank you for that much information—they've sent us no further word." He decided to avoid the subject of the attempted bribe.

"Nevertheless," Alicia said, "Lady Jane is very much aware that you are both still here."

"Yes, I've learned she has—informants, keeping track. I ran into what I presume were three of them on the towpath some days ago."

"But you haven't seen Roger," she countered; it was more of an assertion than a question.

"No, not so far."

"Because Lady Jane is restraining him. He'd like nothing better than to ride to Tonbridge and thrash you—for a start. You do realize how dangerous he can be?"

Phillipe's eyes looked bleak as he nodded. "He has what you could call a fragile temper, doesn't he?"

"And you upset him so, that first day. You positively drove him to the limit!"

He wanted to comment that she'd had some hand in that too. But he refrained, asking instead:

"Why is his mother keeping him leashed? I can't imagine it's because she's concerned about my well-being."

"Certainly not. I think she's convinced you'll give up waiting and go away eventually."

"She's wrong. I intend to see my father."

"I knew you were determined the first minute I looked at you. So did Roger, I believe. Perhaps that's what prodded him into that awful display at Kentland."

Again Phillipe held back a comment. Alicia's brilliant blue eyes slid obliquely across his face. Her next words, couched as a request, were really more of a subtle command:

"Will you walk with me back in the trees where it's cooler? I love to ride hard but it tires the poor horse—" She stroked the animal's neck, but looked at Phillipe. "I can't linger too long. I'm really not ever supposed to ride about the countryside unescorted. But Kentland's so tiresomely gloomy—and I reach the point at which I'll gladly bear Lady Jane's criticism in return for a little freedom—"

She walked under the low-hanging branches, leading the black. Phillipe followed. Alicia seemed to relax the moment they were safely concealed in the green darkness at the heart of the grove.

"You're staying with the family for an extended period?" he inquired.

"A month or two—into the early summer, at least."

"Are you making plans for the wedding to Roger?"

"Of course. We're to be married next year. It's the way large estates are made larger in England. The Amberly lands added to those of my father will leave an inheritance of increased size to my children. Provided—"

Smiling in a sly way, she tied the sweating stallion's rein to a branch.

"—provided I can induce—or should I say—seduce?—Roger to carry out his duty. The dear boy has his father's occasionally hot temper—you share some of that, don't you—?"

"I hope not to the degree Roger does."

"—but I do believe he also inherited some of his mother's coolness toward more—intimate pursuits."

She didn't look at Phillipe as she said it, bending instead to touch a patch of emerald moss growing near a gnarled root. The leaves in the grove rustled. For a moment, Phillipe was both stirred and shocked to discover that aristocratic young English ladies would even allude to the subject of sex. The revelation brought to mind one of Mr. Fox's recent diatribes against the loose morals of the nobility. Mr. Fox was of the relatively new, Methodist persuasion.

Deciding to explore his discovery a little further, Phillipe picked up the conversation with, "Intimate pursuits, you said—are you well acquainted with such pursuits, Miss Parkhurst?"

The sky-blue eyes took on a smoky look. "What is your opinion?"

His cheeks felt flushed. He managed to shrug. "I'm not sure. I'm no expert on English manners. Or English girls—what they do and don't do. However"—he kept his gaze unblinking, a half-smile on his lips—"I do believe that with your eyes and certain other little—mannerisms—you want to make it seem that you're quite experienced. Maybe that too is the fashion here—?"

"La, how bold you are!" she said with a bright laugh. "Such perception! How old are you, Master Frenchman?"

"Eighteen soon."

"I'm nineteen."

"That accounts for the look of experience," he joked. Then, more soberly: "How old is Roger?"

"A year younger than you. He should have a splendid career—if he doesn't fall into some silly quarrel over cards or a bear-baiting wager and get himself killed. Lady Jane worries about that constantly. She's quite protective—"

"So I've noticed."

"—which I believe is the reason she has imposed her will and forbidden Roger to look for you in Tonbridge. Thus far, she's been successful. I think she's the only person on earth of whom Roger is honestly afraid."

Phillipe plucked a blade of grass, ran it absently between his index and middle finger. "Tell me more about your future with Roger, Miss Parkhurst. What kind of career are you counting on for him?"

"Oh, first I imagine he'll serve in the army. Purchase a commission, of course. One can't achieve high rank quickly any other way. The army is a good steppingstone to a political career, so afterward, I imagine we'll live in London. No doubt Roger will enter one of the ministries. Those in politics have many avenues for increasing their fortunes. The closer they can position themselves to His Majesty, the more numerous become the avenues. I look forward to a fine, prosperous life—"

Phillipe's curt laugh made her scowl for the first time.

"What do you find so amusing?"

"You seem to have forgotten how Roger humiliated you the day we met. Hurt you, in fact."

Her lips set. "I haven't forgotten. But larger considerations make it prudent to show no public distress."

"Larger concerns." He nodded. "Roger's future. Roger's fortune—"

"Exactly." The word hung between them, flat, final. Then, with another of those smoky looks at Phillipe,

Alicia seated herself against the trunk of a beech, gracefully settling her skirts. She sighed what sounded like a contrived sigh, remarking:

"Of course, even when Roger and I are married, I shall have to find lovers."

Phillipe laughed again. "That's the fashion too? One husband isn't enough?"

She brushed back a lock of hair, laughing with him. "Poor ignorant foreigner—!" she teased, patting the ground next to her riding skirt.

He sat down beside her, then felt annoyed that he'd obeyed her pantomimed command so promptly. Despite many differences, he saw traces of Lady Jane in Alicia, foremost being her unspoken assumption that, because of her position, her whims would always be gratified.

Still, he couldn't deny that she was lovely.

Alicia leaned her head against the bark and closed her eyes, musing on:

"Among our class, Master Frenchman, marriage has little if any relation to more diverting pastimes. Except on those occasions when an heir must be gotten, of course. Oh, I shouldn't say that categorically. Much depends on the quality of the husband."

Edging a bit closer to her, he asked, "What are your feelings about Roger's quality?"

"Didn't I hint at it? He's cold with a woman. I've yet to discover his—quality."

Her voice lent a shade of vulgar meaning to the final word. Phillipe felt warmer than ever. And aware again of Alicia Parkhurst's skill in sensual games. He asked:

"Would you like to?"

"What a frivolous question!" She ran her pink tongue over the edge of her teeth. "Shouldn't the wise person sample an apple before buying the bushel?"

She was leading him down a contradictory path all at once, a path that had little to do with the other one winding, presumably, to wealth and position as the spouse of the next Duke of Kentland.

"Then—" Phillipe's gesture was wholly French, eloquent. "Why not sample, Miss Parkhurst?"

"Heavens, I've already told you that he hesitates to touch me! Besides, it's really quite impossible on a practical basis. I mean—watched day and night at Kentland by gossiping servants—"

Another wistful sigh; artifice. Layer on layer of artifice—it had been born into her, he supposed; and more of it taught as she grew. Yet her behavior both unsettled and excited him.

"I rather suppose," she concluded, "that at best, Roger will be a crude lover. Unsure of himself, and therefore crude and rough. Only seeking to be done quickly—satisfy himself—never sensitive to the desires of "—a small catch of breath; the sky-blue eyes pinned him—"a partner. Tell me something, Master Frenchman." She inclined her head nearer to him. "Would you hesitate to touch me?"

"No." A pause. "Not if I wanted to."

"Ah, wicked!" she laughed. "Venomously wicked!" There was a hint of anger in the way she tapped his cheek. It reminded him of Roger's use of the silver-headed stick. He closed his fingers on Alicia's wrist, gently but firmly thrust her hand away.

With a pretty pout, she pretended hurt. He let her go.

"I expected better manners from you," she told him.

"It will take some of my father's money to polish off the rough edges."

"Then you and your mother do intend to press the claim?"

"To the finish."

"Well, you're liable to cause no end of difficulty— and you'd better stay out of Roger's way if Lady Jane's leash ever snaps—"

She left off rubbing her wrist when she saw Phillipe

was paying no attention. He was looking directly into her eyes. The smile of the genteel harlot teased at him again.

"But we've quite lost the drift of our conversation—"

"I believe you said I disappointed you."

"Yes. You're a lord's bastard—and a Frenchman to boot. I was entertaining the notion that you might be quite unlike your half-brother in the way you behaved toward a woman. Gentler—yet at the same time more impassioned. We're told that the French are experts in matters of love."

All at once, Alicia's physical presence and the intimacy of the rustling grove started a deep, now-familiar reaction in him. He was infuriated by the mannered way in which this haughty girl toyed with him, playing her romantic word games. At the same time, he was tempted.

In no more than seconds, he succumbed:

"Were you also thinking of indulging yourself in the novelty of finding out?"

For the first time, she was taken aback, pink-faced. The subject changed instantly.

" 'Indulging yourself.' There's yet another pretty turn of phrase. You speak our language surprisingly well."

"I had a special teacher, because I knew I'd be coming here to claim the inheritance."

Alicia touched his wrist. The feel of her warm fingertips excited him even more. She, too, hesitated only a moment.

"Have you had special teachers in Cupid's disciplines as well?"

"A few."

He placed his own free hand on top of hers, nervous, yet somehow compelled. Her own grip tightened just a little. He looked into those remarkably blue eyes.

"And you?"

"Oh, yes—many."

Something told him she was lying. But he only said, "Miss Parkhurst—"

"My name is Alicia."

"The conversation's wandered a long way down an unfamiliar path—"

"Shall we turn back, Master Frenchman?"

From her expression, her tone, her touch that brought him to stiffness, her meaning was unmistakably clear.

"It depends on the reasons for going on. I don't want to be used as a means for you to strike back at Roger for what he did to you at Kentland."

Her quick intake of breath said he'd struck the mark again. She started to pull her hand away, ready to rise and leave, angered. He caught her fingers, felt their heat once more, refused to release her as he finished:

"That is—if it's the only reason."

For a moment her eyes darted past his shoulder, full of the fear of chance discovery. Then she looked back to his face. Their gazes locked, held a long moment. A lark trilled somewhere at the edge of the grove. The stallion stamped. Slowly, she leaned her face toward his.

"No," she whispered. "It isn't—"

Phillipe kissed her. Hesitantly at first. Her warm, sweet breath cascaded over him. All at once his hands were on her shoulders, pulling her close. Her lips parted. Her kiss became eager, hungry. He thought his tongue tasted wine; through his mind fleeted a memory of Roger scoring her for an excessive fondness for claret—

They tumbled over onto the grass, arms twined, kissing. They began to let their hands explore. Very shortly, he discovered that young ladies of the English nobility wore silk drawers beneath their underpetticoats. Not to mention scarlet garters elaborately trimmed with lace.

The greenish darkness had turned steamy as a jungle. After much fumbling and struggling, Alicia's shoulders were bare; then her breasts. He bent to kiss the soft valley between. He moved his head to one side, kissed again. She uttered a small cry of surprised pleasure. Was she, then, mostly artifice and little, if any, experience—?

The play of hands and mouths grew more intense. Soon he was crouching above her, gazing down at her tumbled beauty through the green haze that seemed to surround them. Her upper lip was moist with perspiration. Her garments all a-tangle around her slim hips— the silken drawers had been cast aside—showed him a delicate golden place above her white stockings and her garters.

She looked at him with wide, almost alarmed eyes. She started to speak. He laid his fingers gently on her lips.

"Shall I stop, Alicia?"

"What's fair for me is fair for you. Only—only if you're just attacking Roger—"

"I've forgotten all about Roger," he said, and wrapped his arms around her so violently that her head accidently struck the tree trunk.

She let out a low exclamation of pain, then another, sharper one a moment later when he forced his entrance. The lark rilled. The stallion clopped his hoofs. The green darkness seemed to light and glow with a fire that might have been kindled within Phillipe's own flesh—

At first, it was awkward; her body was still not prepared for him, although it had already received him. And something said over and over that, despite her talk of it, she'd never had a lover. That excited him even more. He kissed her eyelids, her cheeks, stroked her back—

Until finally the awkwardness passed in favor of a matched steadiness whose speed increased and increased like their breathing until she was hugging him convulsively and crying softly for him to press her even harder.

She clung to his neck with both arms, driving herself as close as she could to meet flesh with flesh. He

gasped—and her answer was a strident, lingering moan
of joy that slowly faded under the lark's singing.

vi

Dressed, reasonably composed and ready to ride
away on the rested horse, Alicia looked at him differently. She tried to smile and play the courtesan but
her eyes betrayed her.

He asked quietly whether he'd in any way hurt her.

"No," she murmured. "Oh dear God—no. I—" A little gasp when she tried to laugh. Another brush at a
stray lock of tawny hair. "—I found my answers about
Frenchmen, too. And I think, I do think the Amberlys
have finally met an adversary worthy of them."

"What a strange way to form a judgment," he teased.

She shook her head. "Not really—" All pretense
seemed stripped away as she leaned forward to let their
mouths touch quickly, passionately.

He experienced strange feelings. He knew she was
still a creature of skills and deceptions. Yet he hadn't
the heart to force her to admit whether she had ever lain
with a man before. He wasn't sure—but asking was a
cruelty he couldn't perform. A half-hour ago, yes. But
not now.

Nor did he care much whether, at the start, she'd been
goaded into this game of love by a desire to secretly
spite the man who had hurt her.

"I want to see you again, Alicia."

"I don't know—"

"While the spring lasts—while I'm here—I want to
see you."

"It will be so difficult—" She mounted, steadying the
restless black. "I told you how I'm watched."

"You must find ways to get around that. Dammit,
you must! Unless you were lying to me, and just wanted
to revenge yourself—"

Her voice turned husky:

"No!"

"Then come to Quarry Hill when you can. I'll be here as often as I can. You can do it if you want to badly enough."

"I suppose," she said, sounding uncertain. Their eyes met again. "I meant to say I suppose I can do it. I'll try. I want to come again, Phillipe, even though I think having met you could prove—very dangerous."

"For whom?"

"Both of us."

"Tomorrow? The same time?"

"I don't know for certain."

"I'll be here."

"But if it's not possible for me to leave Kentland—"

"Then I'll be here the next day. And the next." His voice was low. He was as shaken as she was, because he too sensed that they were plunging into something far more entangling than a casual liaison—

"All right," she said suddenly, leaning down again to caress his cheek. "At the first possible moment."

She wheeled her black stallion away, cropping him savagely all the way down the hillside.

CHAPTER VI

"A Perfect Member of the Mob-ility"

i

THE END OF MAY brought a spate of changes to the south of England—and to Phillipe, who was growing aware that he was not the same person who had stepped so hesitantly off the lugger at Dover.

He fretted about the dwindling supply of money Marie kept hoarded in her casket. Even at Mr. Fox's modest rates for bed and board, it would not last much longer.

On top of that, every few days Clarence reported that some servant or other from Kentland dropped by the hostelry—and did not depart without making an inquiry about the French woman and her son.

Though Phillipe still had not explained the reason for this unusual interest, he had gained Clarence's confidence to the point of convincing the boy that it was important Clarence keep him informed about the watchers. So Clarence kept a wary eye out, and an ear open. Phillipe had hoped the spying would stop. Apparently that was not to happen.

Blended with the anxiety these circumstances produced was the hope and the joy he felt each morning at the prospect of perhaps meeting Alicia.

Assignations had proved difficult, as she'd predicted. Somehow, though, the protracted periods of waiting be-

tween their furtive meetings on Quarry Hill only intensified his emotions—and the shattering satisfaction when
a rendezvous did take place.

After that first tempestuous afternoon, he'd gone to
the hill four days in a row—and no sign of her.

The third and fourth days were agony. On the fifth,
he slipped back to the grove convinced he would never
see her again, save perhaps at Kentland—and there she
was, tearfully clinging to him, overflowing sweet, sad
apologies.

She would never be able to ride off alone oftener than
every three or four days, she told him after they made
love. However, she believed she had found a system to
at least minimize the potential danger to herself—and,
she quickly reassured Phillipe, to him.

By paying close attention to household gossip—
closer attention than she usually paid, she was frank to
say—she could pick up hints of plans for the next day or
the day after. Would Roger be off hunting? Lady Jane
entertaining the bishop between prayers? When such
situations developed, Alicia would now employ the services of a girl named Betsy.

Betsy was the one lady's maid Alicia had brought
with her from home. She felt she could trust the
girl—particularly when a few extra coins were slipped
from hand to hand.

After Alicia had outlined her plan, she and Phillipe
searched and found a felled oak with many rotted places
in its lightning-blasted trunk. Phillipe scooped out one
such place, which was designated the message spot.
Here Betsy, sent on some fictitious errand, would leave
a slip of paper with a crudely printed word or two on
it—*Tuesday twilight*—so Phillipe might better know
when to expect the tawny-haired girl.

After their third rendezvous, Phillipe noticed that
she looked drawn, weary. He questioned her about
whether the strain of outwitting and eluding dozens of

people, from Lady Jane and Roger down to the pantry
and stable help, was too taxing.

"Taxing, yes," she replied. "But worth it, my darling.
And after all, haven't you told me I do exceeding well at
games?"

She kissed him with lips parted. But not before he saw
the shadow in her eyes, the shadow that said she was
meeting him at the price of raw nerves.

One mellow evening when she brought a bottle of her
favorite claret in a hamper—she drank twice as much of
it as Phillipe—she speculated aloud that it might be
amusing to let Roger know she'd acquired a lover.

Her eyes twinkled with hard merriment as she said it.
Then she saw Phillipe's scowl, touched him.

"Though you know I wouldn't—ever."

"That first time, Alicia—"

"Yes?"

"You did let me make love to you because he hurt
you, isn't that right?"

"You know me too intimately, Master Frenchman!"

"But you did."

"Partly." Her voice was thickened by the wine. "Only
partly—" She kissed him.

The suppressed streak of cruelty in Alicia was an
aspect of her personality he intensely disliked. But it
was an aspect that dwindled to insignificance alongside
the overpowering reactions she produced in him, mind
and body, when he was away from her, anticipating
their next stolen moments together.

The message-tree system worked reasonably well. Yet
there remained occasions when he would wait hours
past the appointed time, then trudge back to Tonbridge
when she failed to arrive. On those lonely walks, he experienced what he realized must be one of the first signs
of full manhood. He knew the full meaning of sorrow.

During one such frustrated return to Wolfe's Triumph,
he came close to losing his life.

In the mist of early evening, he was passing a copse when a blunderbuss blasted. He dropped instinctively, flattening in the tall grass—

Balls hissed through the tops of the nearby grass stalks, spending themselves. A bad shot, he decided. With a weapon of too short a range.

Still—

Who had fired?

Hunters? Yes; he heard them hallooing in the copse as he raised himself cautiously to hands and knees.

Rooks cawed their way into the sky's yellow haze, flushed from the thicket by the shot. Phillipe remained still, presently saw four riders emerge from the trees and canter away toward Kentland. As the figures vanished, he identified the livery of the Amberlys.

He doubted the attempt had been deliberate. He had seen no one following him earlier, and he was always careful on his walks now, surveying in all directions as he moved. More than likely the servants had spotted him by chance while pursuing the bird among the trees.

But the very fact that they'd fire at all said much about Roger Amberly's feelings. How pleased the Duke's son would be if there were a report of a fortuitous accident—!

Phillipe reported nothing of the incident to his mother or Alicia. But his apprehension deepened.

There was another change in him as well. His conscious decision to keep the affair hidden from Marie. He didn't want to flaunt the conquest of the heiress of Parkhurst, drag it into the open for his mother to examine as another twisted proof that her son rightfully belonged among his so-called betters.

When Marie asked questions about his frequent walking trips, he gave evasive answers. Excuses: Boredom: no work to be done at Wolfe's Triumph. The deception was but one more signal that his feelings for Alicia were growing more serious than he'd ever intended.

It was, all in all, a May of changes.

Thunderous weather struck the Kentish countryside. Swift-flying spring stormclouds blackened the sky. The world did not glow. That seemed appropriate, because he knew his time with Alicia would pass all too soon.

ii

"Alicia?"

She answered with a sleepy murmur. They were deep in a dell they'd found, two days after the first of June.

They lay together on a mossy bank, Alicia with her bodice unfastened, Phillipe with his head resting between the pink-tipped hills of her breasts. Across the dell, bluebells nodded in the oppressive air. High up in the sheltering trees, raindrops patted tentatively on leaves just beginning to stir in the wind. Thunder boomed in the north.

When he didn't speak immediately in reply to her murmur, she stroked his forehead, as if to soothe away the hesitation she sensed. He rolled onto his stomach, touched the coral tip of her left breast and watched it rise. At last he said:

"Lovers shouldn't have secrets, isn't that so?"

"That's so." She pressed his caressing fingers against her body. "Secrets are only for husbands and wives. I'm not even wed to Roger yet, and think of the bagful I've hidden from him."

Completely true. By now there was no intimacy Phillipe and Alicia had not practiced.

"Go on, speak your mind," the girl urged softly.

"All right. Do you know what I thought of you that first day we met?"

"Tell me."

"I thought you were a fine lady—and a proper slut."

"What a horridly truthful young man you are, Phillipe! Of course you're perfectly right. Earls' daughters are taught to practice feminine wiles. How do you think I got Roger to agree to the match our parents arranged? Still, isn't knowing the art of love a good thing—for lovers?"

"For lovers," he agreed. "But what about those who fall in love?"

She sat up as thunder echoed along the river valley. "You mustn't say such things, Phillipe."

There was no reproof in her remark. Only sadness. She avoided his gaze. He pulled her head around gently, stared into her eyes.

"You mustn't," she insisted. "We have no chance together."

"What if Lady Amberly was finally forced to acknowledge my father's pledge?"

"It will be a long time happening—if it ever does. You see how skillfully she resists. Letting you sit and sit, wait and wait, cooped up in the village—"

"Damme, how I hate her for that!" he exploded, jumping up. "Then other times, I have doubts—"

"About what?"

"Doubts that I don't know my proper place."

"Lady Jane would concur with that opinion," Alicia told him, though not with any malice. She tried to gesture him back to her side. But he stalked across the dell, scowling. She let her hand fall back to her side.

A moment later she began to lace her bodice. The mood was broken; they had strayed onto perilous ground.

"In my opinion, Phillipe, the reason you feel doubt is just because you're still trying to decide who and what you are. I'll admit my own feelings are tangled, now that we've started—well, you understand. I don't care for Roger, although I should, since I'll marry him. I love to be here with you like this, although I shouldn't."

Phillipe went back to her, kneeling and closing his hand on hers. "Alicia—"

"What, dear?"

"I've wondered since the beginning whether you've said similar things to other lovers."

Her blue eyes never blinked. "And I've wondered when you might ask me that."

"Is there an answer?"

"Yes—never. You were and are the first. Do you wonder I've been shaken so? And risk these rides—the stares and questions afterward? You don't know what you've done to me, Phillipe. Now I have nights when I can't sleep at all. Nights when I lie weeping and dreaming it was all different. When I wish to God I could board a ship and run off—perhaps all the way across the ocean, to live with a family like the Trumbulls and never have you torment me again."

He asked her who the Trumbulls might be. She explained that her mother's sister—Aunt Sue, she called her—had married and emigrated to the American colonies. Aunt Sue's husband, one Tobias Trumbull, had become exceedingly wealthy as the owner of the largest ropewalk in Philadelphia City. He lived in a fine house, endorsed the policies of George III and his ministers and was altogether a right-thinking Tory gentleman.

"There, at least," she concluded, "I'd be safe from what's happened. Something I never imagined would happen at all. For as I told you, anything beyond meeting this way is quite impossible. I am not strong enough to follow any course except the one planned for me. Marriage with Roger."

"Remember what I told you that first time? You could do whatever you wanted—if you wanted it badly enough."

"Badly enough? Oh yes, there's the problem—!"

Then she flung her arms around his neck, clinging to him and crying. It was a facet of her personality he'd never seen before. It touched him. Made him—yes, why not admit it?—love her all the more.

The rain began to drip through the leaves. She broke away, ready to ride back to Kentland. The parting lent urgency to his sudden question:

"Tell me one thing. Are they tricking us? Is my father really so ill?"

"Oh, yes. That doctor with his bleeding basin seldom leaves his side."

"Then if you care for me at all, help me this much. Use your skills to persuade Lady Amberly to relent just a little. My mother's nearly out of her mind with worry. She feels we're being deceived."

"Not deceived," Alicia said, adjusting the ribbon in her hair. "Fought. On very genteel terms. But fought nevertheless. Lady Jane is particularly afraid of you. I understand why. I told you a moment ago—you haven't decided what you want to become. A proper nobleman's bastard. Or a man who spits on noblemen."

"That's beside the point. Can't you persuade her to let my mother see the Duke for even a moment?"

Alicia pondered. "I can try. It must be discreetly done. A seed planted one day, then nourished little by little. She's not an evil woman. Only protective of what she considers is rightfully hers—"

"Like my mother."

"—and it is possible she might bend to a suggestion from her future daughter-in-law."

Alicia's eyes grew somber. "But it would have to be arranged for an occasion when Roger's away. That might happen quite soon, however."

"How so?"

"Lady Jane's leash is wearing thin. She realizes it. Roger storms about in a perfect rage most of the time. And whenever he talks about going to Tonbridge, there's a fearful row. Even behind locked doors, he and Lady Jane practically shake the house. I know she's trying desperately to persuade him to take a holiday in

London. You see, it's as I said—she does fear you. Not only because of the claim but because of the harm you might do to her legitimate son. Yes"—she nodded suddenly—"what you suggest could be possible."

"Please do what you can. We're nearly out of money."

She lifted her face to the wind stirring the leaves. The afternoon had grown heavy with stillness before the storm. "And time. Time's our enemy, Phillipe. Sweet Christ, I sometimes wish you'd never come here! Forcing me to a choice I want to make and can't—!"

She turned and ran.

"*Alicia!*"

The cry died away. He was left alone in the dell as the rain slashed down through the treetops suddenly.

For a moment he felt thoroughly miserable. He suspected some of her motives one instant, and the next cursed the system that had locked her into a preordained future. But despite the torment, he couldn't deny it—he loved her.

From the edge of the trees, he watched the mounted figure receding into the black-clouded distance. He trudged back to Tonbridge feeling utterly alone.

iii

Alicia's seed, planted on his behalf, took three weeks to mature.

One afternoon on Quarry Hill, he found a note in the message tree telling him to come that night to a different spot—a willow grove along the river between Tonbridge and Kentland. Wary over the possibility of a trap, Phillipe nevertheless kept the appointment—though he surveyed the grove carefully before setting foot into it.

Alicia was waiting. She had only moments to report that Lady Jane had won out. In a day or two, Roger, at his mother's absolute insistence, would be off to town—London—to select items for a new fall wardrobe and learn the latest gossip in the coffee houses.

Further, Lady Jane did show small signs of yielding.

But Alicia had to exert pressure carefully, she said. She must not seem too unlike herself; not show too much interest in the welfare of the claimant and his mother. She'd positioned the suggestion as a possible means of ridding Kentland of the presence of Marie and her son. Once having seen the Duke lying comatose, she argued, the unwelcome visitors might realize their wait was hopeless.

For his mother's sake, Phillipe was encouraged. For his own—just the opposite. Alicia had all but admitted falling in love with him. Yet she was still protecting herself with exquisite care.

On a showery Saturday, the arrogant old cart driver appeared at Wolfe's Triumph. Lady Amberly requested their presence at the estate, he said.

She personally met them at the door and ushered them to the stair leading up to the second floor. Of Alicia there was no sign. But she had done her work, as Lady Jane's remark to Marie testified:

"Though it should not, my conscience began to bother me. I wondered whether you thought I was perhaps not telling you the truth. This visit will put your mind to rest on that score, certainly."

Marie's cheeks showed patches of scarlet. She looked as if she wanted to run up the steps. Following the two women, Phillipe was conscious of footmen below staring scornfully.

At the head of the stairs, a maid waited with a candle. She led them down a dim corridor that had a dank, unhealthy reek. Near the corridor's end, a shadow seemed to dissolve out of the wall. Phillipe recognized Dr. Bleeker, in black as always.

The physician eyed the visitors with disapproval. Standing in front of carved double doors, he said:

"You may not enter, only look at him from here. I've granted that much at the request of Lady Amberly. I wouldn't have done so on my own."

Marie's right hand dug into Phillipe's wrist as Bleeker opened one of the doors.

At first all Phillipe could see were the flames of two candles flanking the great bed in the draped and darkened room. The air gusting out smelled even more foul, a mingling of smoke and sweat and the bitter tang of some balm. Marie let out a low cry, took a step forward.

Bleeker shot out his black sleeve as a barrier. Marie's hand flew to her mouth. Lady Jane turned away, gazing at rain-washed leaded windows at the end of the hall.

The candles flanking the bed quivered a little. At last Phillipe discerned a white face on a pillow. He might have been looking at an older version of himself.

Then came the sound—an incoherent muttering from the man lying in the stifling room. Details leaped out. A trace of saliva trickling from the corner of James Amberly's mouth; the glitter of sweat on his waxen forehead. Phillipe's legs felt weak.

Marie grasped Bleeker's arm. "Please let me go near him. Just for a moment!"

"I forbid it absolutely. You see his pathetic condition. Even when awake, his mind is not his own."

Marie stared into the room again. In a moment, Bleeker shut the door.

"I trust we have extended ourselves sufficiently for your convenience, madame."

Marie didn't hear. She was weeping. Phillipe wanted to strike the insufferable doctor. He went to his mother instead, anxious to take her out of this place of sickness and horror. *We shouldn't have come,* he thought. *It's worse for her to see him this way than not at all.*

Quickly, he hurried Marie toward the stairs. She was trembling but she'd gotten her sobbing under control.

He would never dare tell her that he had arranged the viewing. He'd hoped that the sight of James Amberly would lift her spirits. The effect was exactly the reverse. And he was to blame.

As fast as he could, he helped her down the staircase and across the foyer. They were but halfway to the front door, Marie still clutching at him, when Lady Jane spoke from behind:

"Now that you have gotten your desire, madame, I trust you'll trouble us no further. Leave England. Do you hear what I say?—*leave England.* He cannot answer you. He cannot speak to your claim. I am the Duke's voice now. And while I live, I will deny the contents of that letter with all my power. Finally—you know quite well how my son feels concerning this alleged claim—and the claimant." Her glance at Phillipe was pointed. He shivered. "I cannot forever guarantee to hold my son's natural instincts in check. Good day."

A footman had glided forward to open the door, as if to hasten their departure. Looking back at Lady Jane, Phillipe felt rain spatter his neck. He heard the noise of a coach rattling up the drive. *Now* he understood why Alicia's seed had fallen on fertile ground.

Lady Jane had summoned them not out of kindness or conscience but out of a desire to intimidate them even further—this time with the threat of direct intervention by Roger.

Phillipe suspected the threat might be a bluff. But it would be rash to accept that assumption completely.

In any case, Amberly's helplessness, Lady Jane's determination and the absent heir's vengeful temper were now openly ranged against them—and would defeat them. That was the message the encounter had been meant to convey. It did no good for Phillipe to remind himself that he and Alicia had actually been responsible for Lady Jane gaining her desired end by suggesting the strategy to her. The point was, she had seized on it eagerly.

And when Marie stumbled on the steps leading down to the drive, Phillipe knew how well the strategy had succeeded.

He couldn't catch her in time. She landed on her knees in the mud. He helped her up, filled with humiliation and rage.

iv

Marie's skirt was filthy with spattered mud. As Phillipe lifted her to her feet, he saw a splendid coach-and-four arriving, its wheels throwing off more mud as the liveried driver braked and reined in the white horses.

Astonished, the senior footman called into the house, "My lady—unexpected visitors!" He darted down the steps to assist the liveried postilion just opening the gilded door.

Leaning on her son, Marie seemed to be regaining her composure. For his part, Phillipe was fascinated by the sight of a plump, wigged gentleman alighting from the coach. The only word for his apparel was magnificent, from the buckles on his shoes and the ribbons fastening his breeches at the knees, to the ruby-and-emerald-studded hilt of his sword and the intricate frogging around the golden buttons of his plum-colored coat.

The footman, the coach driver and the postilion gave Phillipe and his mother angry looks, because they still stood near the coach's right front wheel—at the foot of the steps up to the front door.

Lady Jane appeared in the doorway. "My lord, we've been anticipating your arrival for weeks. But we finally assumed that matters of state prevented a visit. We're not prepared—"

"I realize my presence is long overdue," answered the

new arrival, pausing on the coach step. "And I cannot stay long—indeed, you can see my journey was made in extreme haste, without my customary full retinue. But I seized the moment because I am anxious to extend my sympathies and learn of my good friend the Duke's condition."

The coach driver whirled on Phillipe and Marie. "Stand aside, if you please."

His clothes daubed with mud, his emotions still chaotic because of the grim scene upstairs, Phillipe glared at the new arrival. The man remained on the coach step, only a twitch of his pink lips revealing momentary displeasure. The bedraggled woman and her son effectively blocked his way to the stone steps.

"Stand aside!" the driver demanded.

Phillipe said, "Why?"

"My lord, excuse these ill-mannered foreigners—" Lady Jane began.

Now the new arrival looked faintly amused. He lifted one ringed hand to stay the angry servants, stepped carefully down into the mud and around a puddle, confronting Phillipe face to face.

The man might have been a cousin to Bishop Francis in the general shape of face and figure. But his countenance was different in one way: it lacked oozing piety. Indeed, it had a certain merry charm. Yet the eyes were not those of a light-minded man. They met Phillipe's in a direct, challenging way.

"Why stand aside, sir? Because these good people believe some small deference is due the Prime Minister of England."

The senior footman seized Phillipe's arm. "You ignorant sod, this is Lord North!"

Savagely, Phillipe threw off the footman's hand. "And I should therefore step aside?"

The second most powerful man in the British Empire

looked mildly astonished. But he managed to maintain a surface geniality.

"Yes, sir, that is essentially the reason."

"Well, I don't give a damn who you are," Phillipe shot back, too overwrought to let reason exert a calming influence. Stunned and furious, Lady Jane was rigid in the doorway. The Prime Minister said to her:

"I detect a trace of the French in his accent. Do you suppose we have here a disciple of the infamous Rousseau?"

"I've read him, yes," Phillipe said.

"The pernicious Locke too, I suppose?"

"Yes."

Lord North sighed. "Well, we may thank the Almighty that the former no longer graces our realm, but has taken himself and his mad ideas back to the continent—while the latter is at least forever buried. Would the same could be said of his writings!"

"I find nothing wrong with the writings of either man, my lord."

"Oh-ho!" exclaimed North, warming as if to an oration. "I suppose we shall be informed next that you are also a pupil-in-correspondence with that horned devil, Adams? It must be so, since one mischievous idea only lures its believer toward more and more of them! Tell me, young sir, are you truly one of those who holds that the countryman, let us say, has the same rights as the king? That the power of the former matches that of the latter?"

Phillipe managed to screw up his nerve to reply, "If a king oppresses people, then the countryman should throw the king over. And has the right."

Lord North became less amused. "Lady Amberly, you have indeed attracted a perfect member of the mobility, as we call the rabble over in our rebellious province of Massachusetts Bay."

He turned to Phillipe once more, hectoring him now.

"Though I do not make a habit of discoursing with commoners in the rain, my young friend, I must advise you of one fact. Englishmen enjoy the fullest liberties of any race under the sun. But liberties are not license. And those who question the natural order of society do so at their peril. As the members of that infamous Boston mob-ility are learning! Wherever you caught this wicked disease of false libertarianism, purge yourself of it before you come to disaster. Now, if you will be so kind as to remove yourself from my path, I will get on with the business of my visit."

But Phillipe still refused to budge.

Lord North flushed in anger. Finally, though, manners won out. He stepped around Phillipe with such elegant contempt that the servants snickered openly in approval.

Phillipe saw Girard's face in memory, shouted at the broad back ascending the stairs:

"By what right does one man call himself better than another? Or rule another? Kings rule because the people *let* them!"

North turned and peered down, this time with open hostility.

"Young man, I fear the noxious doctrines of Locke and Rousseau have mortally infected your soul. You'll come to no good end."

And with that, the Prime Minister vanished inside.

The door closed on Lady Jane's hasty apologies and angry denunciations of Phillipe.

Pushing back his tricorn hat with its decoration of white Tory roses, the coach driver exclaimed, "By God, I've never witnessed such audacity. Lucky for you, my little sport, that Lord North is a mild-tempered gentleman."

"And a puppet of your German king!" Phillipe sneered. Even as he guided Marie away from the coach, he was aware of the postilion slipping up behind him. "I've heard what they say in the public house. King George hoists the hoop and North jumps through."

"Speak the name of him who said that and his tongue'll be out 'fore midnight!" vowed the coachman. He reached high to the seat and snaked down a coiled whip. "Anyone who repeats it deserves something only a mite less harsh." He uncoiled the whip with a single snap.

Phillipe wasn't averse to a fight. But he realized that he was outnumbered by the driver and the circling postilion. In a clumsy fray in the mud, Marie might be a chance victim. So he suppressed his anger and urged her down the drive, while the coachman played with his whip and called them obscene names.

Finally, out of range of the jeers, Phillipe slowed up. "Lean on me, Mama. The mud makes for hard walking."

Her face shone with pride. "Before God, Phillipe, you have a real fire in you!"

"Only when we're treated as nothing. I really don't have any desire to start brawls and bring down trouble. But why are we less than they are?"

"That's always been the order of things, as the man told you. Imagine—the Prime Minister himself! I don't blame you for anger. But use it wisely. To gain your ends, not endanger your life."

She seemed almost her old self again, even though she held his arm for support as they made their way along the towpath that had become a quagmire. She added another bit of advice:

"Remember, you must take your place among people of that class, not alienate them."

Phillipe shrugged. "Evidently I'm already consigned to—what did he call it?—the mob-ility. But who's the 'horned devil, Adams?' I'll have to ask Mr. Fox. He seems well up on political affairs."

As they trudged along through the rain, he was swept again by a mood of discouragement. He recalled the blunderbuss firing from the copse, Lady Jane's warning that she might not be able to hold Roger at bay much longer. He found himself saying:

"Perhaps all this is useless, Mama. My father can't speak on my behalf—and even leaving Roger out of it, we both know Lady Amberly could hire whole armies of lawyers to argue against the claim. Should we go back to Auvergne?"

Her face turned bleak. "No. Not as long as I own that letter."

But as they tramped the towpath, muddy and tired, Phillipe began to wonder whether his mother was leading him—or pushing him—toward a destination where he would never be welcome and would never fit.

CHAPTER VII

Brother Against Brother

i

"MR. FOX," SAID Phillipe two mornings later, "I must speak to you about the arrangements for our quarters. My mother and I have nearly come to the end of our money."

"Then, sir," answered the graying owner of Wolfe's Triumph, "I must let your quarters to others. Much as I'd like to extend you charity, I can't."

The two stood in the yard of the inn, near the arched gate through which the coach for London had departed only a few moments earlier. The yard smelled ripe from horse droppings.

Mr. Fox negotiated his way around several such fragrant mounds and dropped onto a bench against the inn wall, to rest. Inside, Clarence could be heard saucing one of the serving girls. Overhead, the morning sky was blue and sultry.

"It's necessary that my mother and I stay on—" Phillipe began.

"That may be. But I ask you in all candor, is it safe?"

Standing in the sunlight, Phillipe still felt a brief chill. "I can't let that influence the decision, Mr. Fox."

The innkeeper's lined face looked startled. "But aren't you aware that you're the talk—and in some quarters, the scandal—of the neighborhood? Because of the way you braced the Prime Minister himself? With what I understand are dangerous liberal opinions? You're fortunate his lordship's of an even humor, or God knows what obscure law he'd have invoked against you."

Fox peered at him shrewdly. "You have some hold on the Amberlys, don't you? It makes the family loathe you, yet tolerate your presence. I know you claimed to be related—"

"I am."

"I'd like to know how."

Phillipe glanced up at the closed shutters of the room where Marie was still sleeping. The homely, toothy inn proprietor sensed his uneasiness, laid a kindly hand on his arm.

"Come, lad, I've no great affection for the Amberlys myself. I'll keep your answer private, I promise."

The reassuring touch of the man's hand somehow drained Phillipe of his tensions. It was a relief to step from the already hot sun, slump on the bench beside Fox and, for better or worse, share the secret that dominated his life:

"James Amberly is my father, although he never married my mother. The Duke summoned us, before his illness grew so serious that he can't speak to anyone. Lady Jane hates me because the Duke promised me part of his fortune."

Mr. Fox let out a long, low whistle. "That explanation never so much as popped into my head. Yet it accounts for everything that's been puzzling me. Lady Jane condescending to call here—on two foreigners who speak imperfect English. The endless parade of servants dropping in to inquire about you—well, well! Bastardy in the Amberly woodwork. Imagine that!"

When he got over his surprise, the landlord asked, "Have you anything to substantiate this claim of yours?"

"A letter, written by my father. My mother keeps it

hidden away. I think Lady Amberly knows the letter's genuine. She may despise me, but I don't believe she's quite ready to take action against me." He hoped it was the truth. Roger, of course, was another factor entirely.

"I trust that's right—for your sake." Fox scraped a grimy nail against one of his protruding teeth. "You're staying in the hope your father will recover, then?"

"Yes, and receive us, and say the claim will be honored."

"I can understand that. Still, it doesn't get 'round the subject on which we began."

"I could work for you," Phillipe said. "Not just a little, as I've been doing, but all the time. All day long and into the night. Just don't turn us out now, Mr. Fox!"

The older man pondered a moment. "I'd have to move you to my smallest room—"

"Even the stable if you'll let us stay!"

Fox was amused at the seriousness of Phillipe's expression. "No, the small room will do. As I suggested, Lady Jane's no favorite of mine."

"Mr. Fox, I can't thank you enough!"

"No thanks necessary. I'll get my due in hard work."

Phillipe frowned. "There's only one thing—"

"Sir?"

"By staying here, are we in any way exposing you to risk?"

"Lady Jane," he returned emphatically, "would not dare overstep that far. The laws of England are a right good tangle these days. A poor child's hand can be lopped off for pinching a cherry tart, for instance. But mostly, the laws are good. They protect Englishmen. During his ministry, Mr. Pitt remarked that even the King himself couldn't set foot inside the humblest cottage in order to violate the owner's liberties. And thank God. Such principles are the strength and glory of this country. Also the reason why our cousins over in the colonies are so exercised by His Majesty's ministers," he added wryly.

That brought to mind Lord North's reference to "the mob-ility." Phillipe asked Fox about it, and the innkeeper proved knowledgeable on the subject:

"The nub of it is, the colonists consider themselves Englishmen just like me. They want the same rights. German George sees it different. He's determined to have all the power in his hands. The Hanoverians on the throne before him were lazy, profligate men. So when the King was very small, his mother drummed one idea into his head. '*Be* a king, Georgie!' As a result, he's had one prime minister after another. And he's kept searching for others even more willowy and pliant—the ideal being a man who'd execute the King's policies without question. In North, he's found him. And North's packing the government with his own kind.

"I think George would stamp on the rights of people in these very isles, if he thought he could. But he does appreciate the consequences that might ensue. Englishmen fight when they feel something's unjust."

As an example, Mr. Fox cited mobs burning turnpike gates across the land in protest over the high road tolls levied by this or that nobleman who had secured control of a turnpike.

"Some Americans are protesting their grievances in much the same fashion," Fox went on. "But that, George will not allow."

"The Prime Minister said I sounded like a pupil of someone called Adams. Who is he?"

"The longest, sharpest thorn in the side of His Majesty. Samuel's his first name, I believe. Said to be the most adamant and reckless of those who've opposed the King's policies in the Royal Province of Massachusetts."

Then Mr. Fox went on to sketch some of the events

that had produced increasing hostility between George III and his colonial subjects over the past few years.

The trouble had really started at the end of the Seven Years' War. The financially exhausted government had reached the perfectly logical conclusion that, since British troops had defended and secured the safety of the American colonies during the struggle that had raged from India to Canada, it was only right that the colonies begin paying a proper share of the war debt.

Various taxes had been levied on the Americans by a succession of pliant and accommodating ministers. Mr. Fox referred to a sugar tax, then a tax in the form of royal stamps ordered to appear on various colonial documents. Phillipe recalled Girard's mentioning the latter.

The taxes raised the question of whether the King's government in London had the right to impose such levies on the colonies without their consent.

"The crux of their complaint is that they have no voice in Parliament. Therefore they reserve to themselves the right to say what's taxed internally and what isn't."

Colonial protests, Fox explained, ultimately forced revocation of the stamp tax. But then, Chancellor of the Exchequer Townshend—"Champagne Charley," Fox called him with pious distaste—put through a program of new taxes on all glass, lead, paints, paper and tea imported into America.

"And do you know what happened then, lad? The good Englishmen of the colonies got together and said, 'Be damned to your merchandise! We don't need it.' Trade dropped off like a stone falling into a chasm. There were other, more violent protests—attitudes aren't all that clear-cut, you see. Many American subjects of the King want only fairness. Agreement to the principle that they alone control internal taxation. A good example of that position is one of their trade representatives who's in London right now. A learned man called Doctor Franklin. Others, though—especially the Massachusetts crowd—hate the whole idea of a king telling 'em what to do. Adams is reputed to be the worst of the Boston hotheads. He created so much mischief in sixty-eight, royal troops were sent in to garrison the place.

"Surprisingly, though, when the colonies stopped importing, the loudest squeals came from this side of the water. From the merchants of London and the other cities. And they're influential enough to be listened to—so when North took office last year, he threw out Champagne Charley's duties. All except the one on tea. That was kept merely to show America the King does have the power to tax, and the colonials had best not forget it.

"Things seemed to be getting back to normal till Adams and his friends stirred the pot again. The Boston mob provoked the troops one winter night. There was a street riot. Five colonials shot down in the snow. Altogether, it's a troubled land. On one side, good Englishmen totally loyal to the King. In the middle, others still loyal but arguing for fair dealing. And the rest—radicals like Adams—crying that even redress of grievances isn't enough.

"That dangerous man may actually want complete freedom from the Crown's authority! Of course he'll never get it, short of fighting. Because King George *is* a strong-willed man in spite of that soft Dutchman's face of his. He'll have his way. That's why he keeps the soldiers in Boston-town. That's why he chooses an accommodating fellow like North for prime minister.

"It's a curious thing," concluded Mr. Fox, rising, "but travelers bringing news from London say the colonials by and large believe the King to be their friend. Their difficulties, they think, spring from the character of his high-handed ministers. But it's not the ministers who arrange things, it's His Majesty. For some reason, the Americans don't understand that."

"What's your opinion of the right and wrong, Mr. Fox?"

After a pause, the other answered, "I suppose it might be fair to allow the colonists a certain say in how they're taxed. Beyond that, I draw a line. Even Pitt drew it. The King is the king. If the Americans refuse to bend to the reasonable exercise of his will, they must be punished.

"Ah, but I've dawdled too long. Time we got on with more practical things." He pointed to the horse turds littering the yard. "Such as shoveling."

Phillipe got to work cleaning up the dung. He had enjoyed listening to Fox. And he would have liked to discuss the theories expressed in the books Girard had given him. Especially the notion of the contract between men and their monarchs, the contract that could be broken if the rulers proved too autocratic.

Phillipe really didn't know where he stood on the whole complex of questions. His outburst at North had been more personal anger than moral conviction. He really didn't want to be classed with the "mob-ility." If he could negotiate the perils implicit in the confrontation with the Amberly family, he would much prefer to be well-dressed, well-fed, rich and secure.

At least that was the state of his thinking on this sunlit morning in June 1771, while he was shoveling up horse manure.

ii

The Kentish summer turned steamy, June melting into July, then August.

Phillipe's secret meetings with Alicia Parkhurst continued, though less frequently, because Mr. Fox kept him busy at Wolfe's Triumph. He and Marie had moved into a single tiny, airless room. Marie worked in the kitchen. The activity didn't seem to lessen her general despondency. She spoke little, even to her son.

The summer heat and the waiting grew oppressive. Phillipe's only respites were the occasional nights he could arrange to slip away to Quarry Hill. But even those became less than satisfactory.

Alicia brought occasional reports that Amberly was no better. And she began to act distant, guarded. Phillipe picked up unsettling hints that she was reverting to her old self, hiding deeper emotions that might threaten her future.

As they lay together after one particularly long and ardent period of lovemaking, Alicia reached out through the darkness of the dell to fondle him with a kind of callous intimacy. He couldn't see her face. But her amusement was unmistakable—and her speech slightly thickened; when he'd kissed her at the start, he'd smelled claret again.

"If only Roger knew how this sweet, strong machine pleasures me. His expression would be priceless, I think."

Phillipe pulled away, upset. It was the gilded whore talking. He gripped her shoulder.

"You promised you'd never tell him."

Fireflies glowed golden in the dark. She sounded annoyed as she answered, "Why, not unless you abuse me in an ungentlemanly way. As you're doing now."

He let go, tried to kiss her to make amends. She permitted it. But she wouldn't abandon her original subject.

"Roger thinks he's such a perfect master of his world. The condition only grows worse after he's strutted around London awhile—"

"He's back, then?"

She nodded. "I really think it would be charming to shatter his illusions. But don't worry, my dear. I meant what I said before. We'll keep the secret. I was only teasing you."

Still, the remarks troubled him for days afterward—until other events intruded with devastating abruptness.

Phillipe was serving a platter of mutton to evening diners. He was out of sorts; he'd gone to the message tree four days in a row and found not so much as a note. He presumed Roger's presence had sharply curtailed Alicia's freedom. He fervently hoped there was no other reason for her silence.

All at once, he overheard a remark by one man in a coarsely dressed group at a corner table:

"—given wages and told to leave for the rest of the day. I guess Amberly will never have the pleasure of seeing the fine greenery we've been laying out according to Mr. Capability's plan."

Phillipe turned cold. He approached the table.

"Sir? What's this you speak about at Kentland?"

"The black wreath hung on the door," said the laborer. "We were told his lordship died shortly after noon."

The platter dropped from Phillipe's shaking hands. Some of the juices spattered the laborer's breeches. But Phillipe paid no attention to the cursing as he streaked toward the kitchen to find Marie.

iii

They ran down the now-familiar towpath through summer darkness pricked by heat lightning along the northwest horizon. Marie seemed obsessed with one thought, which she kept repeating aloud:

"We were not told. She wouldn't lower herself to tell us!"

As they dashed up the long drive, Phillipe noted that most of Kentland's windows showed lights, as if the household were in a state of commotion. A death wreath did indeed hang on the great door. Marie broke into tears at the sight of it.

Phillipe hammered the door. The senior footman answered, recognized him, said:

"This household is in mourning. Private mourning."

"I am entitled to see him!" Marie sobbed.

"Be quiet, you vulgar slattern," snarled the footman, starting to close the door. Phillipe's anger quickened. But before he could move, Marie hurled past him, a fist striking the footman's cheek.

"I will see his body! *Let me in!*"

Her hysteria drove all concerns but one from Phillipe's mind—the desire to spare her humiliation. He seized her arm, tried to pull her back.

"Mama, I know how you feel. But there are certain courtesies to the dead—you mustn't carry on this way. Let's go back to Tonbridge. We'll come tomorrow, when you're feeling—"

"Let go! He was your *father*! I have a *right* to see him!"

All at once the footman vanished. The door swung inward. Phillipe caught his breath at the sudden sight of Lady Jane Amberly.

The Duke's wife was dressed in black. She seemed to tower against a background of shocked faces—the horrified servants. Then Roger appeared, crossing the foyer, equally somber in a black suit much like that worn by the physician Bleeker.

Roger's face was wrathful in the light of the candles illuminating the doorway. The hoof-shaped mark at his left eyebrow looked nearly as black as his clothes. He carried his varnished walking stick. Its huge silver head reflected the candle flames in glittering highlights. At the sight of Phillipe, he shook visibly. But not from fear.

Gripping the edge of the door with one pale hand, Lady Jane said, "Madame, you exceed the bounds of all decency. Leave at once! And take this information with you—my husband woke briefly before he died, He charged me to care for his son. His *legitimate* son. He never mentioned your name, nor that of your boy. You have no claim on us. The matter is closed."

The horizon lit with white light. Roger's face glowered over his mother's shoulder like a branded skull.

"If they won't walk away, I'll see they crawl away—" he began.

Lady Jane's stern eyes and upraised arm held him back. Then she started to shut the door.

Stunned, Phillipe inadvertently relaxed his grip on Marie. He realized his error too late. With another cry, she threw herself at Lady Jane and would have knocked her down if Roger hadn't stepped quickly in front of his mother to shield her.

"*Leave this house, you French scum!*" he screamed, and struck Marie in the side with the silver head of his stick.

Marie stumbled back. Roger Amberly wore no wig tonight. His hair was virtually the color of Phillipe's, contrasting with his white face, accenting the death's-head pallor of his cheeks. This came as a blurred impression while Phillipe tried to catch his mother as she fell.

He wasn't quick enough. Marie sprawled on the top step and exclaimed in pain.

That sound drove through Phillipe like a knife. He grabbed Roger's throat with both hands and dragged him outside.

Roger rammed the silver head of his stick against Phillipe's chin. Phillipe let go, staggered back, his foot missing the top step. He flailed, then tumbled all the way down to the drive.

Dizzy, he heard Roger's shoes clatter on the stone. Two male servants shouldered past Lady Jane, to help their master. Roger whirled on them, the brandished stick a blurred arc.

"Stay back, all of you! *I said stay back!*"

The servants hesitated, withdrew past Lady Jane as

Roger leaped down the steps, loomed over his dazed half-brother, almost cooing:

"No one shall give the bastard his comeuppance but me—"

Face twisting with savage glee, Roger whipped his arm up. Frantically, Phillipe rolled aside. Holding the stick by its ferrule end, Roger sought to smash the huge silver knob down on Phillipe's head.

Roger's blow struck the ground instead, missing Phillipe by inches. He scrambled up, listening to the sibilant, almost deranged sound of Roger's violent breathing. Lady Jane cried out for her son to be careful, not to injure himself on a worthless nobody—

Roger paid no attention. Neither did Phillipe, circling away from his antagonist. In the yellow candlelight spilling from the house, half of Roger's face took on a jaundiced, poisoned color.

"I'll kill you for tormenting my mother," he said, taking a firmer grip on the stick. Then his voice dropped lower. "And for Alicia. Oh, yes—she's told me. Flaunted you! Her little French lover—"

Panting for breath, Phillipe tried to assimilate what he'd just heard. One of his worst fears had been realized. Alicia had revealed the liaison—but why? *Why, when she'd promised—?*

Roger kept circling, poking at him with the silver stick head. "You're afraid of me, aren't you?"

Thrust.

"I can see it in your face, bastard. You're afraid—"

Thrust.

"Well, by God, *you have good cause!*"

Abruptly he grasped the stick with both hands, club-fashion, and brought it whipping down toward Phillipe's head.

Phillipe tried to dodge. The silver head glanced off his temple, bringing immediate dizziness. Lady Jane cried

out again—some caution or warning, Phillipe didn't
know. He was trying to outmaneuver Roger's foot in the
uncertain light. But the kick caught him in the groin,
doubled him over, dropped him to his knees.

He heard the warning hiss of air, stabbed both hands
upward, deflected the stick blow that would have
smashed his skull.

Then four hands gripped the stick, wrestling for it as
Phillipe lurched to his feet.

Roger was mouthing incoherent obscenities now. But
he was strong. Phillipe couldn't break his grip by jerking
or twisting. The two figures swayed back and forth.

Roger drove his knee into Phillipe's genitals again. As
Phillipe reeled and let go, Roger spat in his face, then
swung the stick in a sideways arc. Phillipe ducked;
ducked again, as the winking head whipped back the
other way.

The spittle sticky on his face, Phillipe rolled his right
shoulder down and bowled into Roger full force. He
crashed his half-brother to the ground, kneeled on his
throat. Roger squealed and clawed at Phillipe's eyes, his
cheeks purpling till they were almost the hue of the
cloven mark—

But Phillipe got hold of the stick.

With one hand he seized Roger's right arm. With the
other, he brought the stick down head first on Roger's
pinned fingers. He struck the open palm once, twice,
then again, again, the silver head hammering, each blow
bringing the release of more hatred and frustration.

Smash.

SMASH—

Marie shrilled his name in warning. He twisted his
head around, saw servants with branched candlesticks—and one with an ancient saber—boiling down
the steps. Marie's streaked face shone like a coin in the
windwhipped glare of the candles. Concern for her son

had brought her back to reality. She tugged at him while Roger writhed on the ground, gripping his right wrist with his left hand. Spittle foamed on his lips—

The skin of Roger's right palm was broken. The fingers were bloody and oddly angled. *God help me,* Phillipe thought in terror, *what have I done?*

One of the footmen almost caught him. Phillipe tore away, ran with Marie down the driveway full speed. Two servants gave chase. Over his shoulder, Phillipe saw the antique saber flash—

Then he heard Lady Jane call out:

"Let them go! See to my son first, all of you. Do you hear me? *See to my son!*"

With oaths of disgust, the pair of pursuers fell back. Phillipe and Marie dashed on through the darkness.

When they reached the junction with the towpath, Phillipe looked back.

At the door of Kentland, candlesticks still bobbed and fluttered. He thought he could make out the bent, pain-wracked figure of Roger being helped inside. He urged Marie to run faster, away from the sight of the great door closing, the entrance darkening to black.

Fear swallowed him as they fled to Tonbridge.

iv

"I would say the situation for you is very desperate." Mr. Fox spoke with sad frankness, having heard Phillipe's gasped-out story.

Noting the appearance of Marie and her son when they stumbled back to Wolfe's Triumph, Mr. Fox had immediately hurried them into the kitchen and sent Clarence out, along with the serving girls. Now he brought them a tankard of ale each and blocked the door to the common room with his back.

Phillipe gulped the ale. It did little to wash away the taste of fright and ruin.

"You say Lady Jane's son struck first?" Fox asked.

"He did. He struck my mother cruelly hard."

"But they have witnesses, and you have none. They have status—and you have none. For your own safety, you must leave Tonbridge at the earliest opportunity."

"For the coast?"

"No, they'll expect you to go to Dover. Go to London instead. Lose yourselves in the town awhile. It won't be easy, but it's better than surrendering your lives."

"In God's name, how can we get to London?" Phillipe stormed, the tankard still shaking in his hands.

Mr. Fox tried to remain calm. "On the diligence that leaves at half past eight o'clock tomorrow."

"But we have no money!" exclaimed Marie.

"I will advance you some, though I can ill afford it. Let's hope morning won't be too late. Perhaps not, if young Roger's the paramount concern right now. I'm sure Lady Jane is convinced she can have you taken any time she wishes. Otherwise, she wouldn't have let you go."

"I think I destroyed his hand," Phillipe said, unsteadily. "I didn't mean to do it. But he was attacking me—he'd have killed me if he could—"

Because of Alicia.

And he'd trusted her! To repay that trust, she had bragged about their affair!

Mr. Fox's steady voice interrupted his confused thoughts. "I'll put Clarence on watch, to alert us in case of surprise visitors. Try to get some sleep if you can. And if French folk pray to the deity, I'd suggest a prayer asking that confusion at Kentland and assistance for Roger spare you the attention of the Amberlys for another twelve hours."

But it was not to be. The Amberly coach arrived at the inn at half past seven in the morning.

CHAPTER VIII

Trap

i

AT THE APPEARANCE of the Amberly coach, Mr. Fox came racing to their cramped room to warn them.

Marie started when she heard the news. She nearly dropped the brass-cornered casket which she'd been about to pack into the open trunk. Phillipe heard horses stamp, a coach door slam.

"Who's in the coach?" he asked, already reaching for Gil's wrapped sword.

Fear chalked Mr. Fox's face as voices sounded down below. "I didn't wait to see or inquire! Put down that damned sword and run for the back stairs. If you hide in the stable, perhaps I can convince 'em you've gone. Quickly, *quickly!*" He pushed Marie.

Phillipe left the sword. As he rushed out of the room, he thought about going back long enough to hide the casket; it lay in full view on the bed. But he didn't because Mr. Fox was in such a state of agitation.

Fox hurried them down the rickety steps and out across the rear yard. The morning sky showed unbroken gray clouds. As Mr. Fox gestured frantically from the stable door, a whiff of a breeze sprang up, bringing the first patters of rain.

The landlord rolled the creaky door aside, pointed to the dim interior where green flies buzzed over the straw.

"Go in the last stall. Don't make a sound, in case they search. Don't even draw a loud breath till I come back to tell you it's safe." He rolled the door shut and left them in darkness.

Phillipe led the way to the hiding place Fox had mentioned. They crouched behind the splintered partition. His initial alarm had begun to fade, replaced once more by anger. He squatted with his back to the partition, staring at Marie's face, a face he hardly recognized.

She looked beaten. Gone was the strength that had tautened every line of her features when she first drew the casket from behind the Madonna in Auvergne. Her dark eyes avoided Phillipe's. Veins stood out as she clasped her hands together.

Praying?

But he knew of no gods mighty enough to protect them from the wrath of people like the Amberlys.

Overhead, rain drummed the roof thatching. The sound was counterpointed by Marie's strident breathing. A dismal voice deep inside him said, She's surrendered. To illness. To strain. To fear of the Amberly money, position, power—

With a terrifying creak, the stable door rolled open.

Phillipe searched the stall for a weapon. A stone. A bit of wood. He saw nothing. Footsteps scurried in their direction.

Marie cowered visibly. Phillipe resigned himself to fighting with his hands—

Suddenly Clarence appeared at the end of the partition. Popeyed with astonishment, he reported, "The coach brought only that fat churchman. He wishes to see you. In Father's room—he said it must be private. He pledged no harm to either of you. Father's greatly relieved. But he asks you to hurry, so as not to anger the visitor."

All at once Phillipe began to feel a little more confident. He helped Marie to her feet, guided her out of the stable and across the yard through the showering rain.

They climbed the rear stairs again, to the commodious sitting room Mr. Fox reserved for himself. Seated in an armchair next to a chipped deal table on which a single candle burned, Bishop Francis awaited them, his porcine hands folded in his lap, his moon face piously sad. Of Mr. Fox there was no sign.

Clarence went out and closed the door. The prelate's small blue eyes studied mother and son a moment. Then, in that syrupy voice, he said:

"I beseech you to cooperate with me in making this meeting as brief as possible. Grave spiritual matters require my presence at Kentland. Let me, then, go immediately to why I have come here."

He adjusted a fold of his robe. "Around midnight, I was awakened and made aware of grievous news. The tragic, untimely death of Lady Jane's husband. I proceeded to the estate with all due speed—sending prayers ahead. On arrival, I learned how sorely such prayers were needed. I found circumstances that compound an already tragic situation. Young Roger was being treated by Dr. Bleeker. His mangled hand may never straighten again."

At the conclusion of the mournful pronouncement, the bishop's tiny eyes flicked momentarily to Phillipe. More compassionate than condemning—

Unless the bishop was trying to gull them. Phillipe was suspicious. Perhaps from tiredness, tension—

"Roger has no one but himself to blame for what happened," Phillipe said. "He struck my mother."

Bishop Francis raised his hand. "Such a remark is unnecessary. Did not our blessed Savior forgive, no matter what the sin or its cause? Following His precepts, my purpose is not to wrangle over who is guilty. As I believe I remarked on my previous visit, the Church must play the role of conciliator. Peace maker. Binder of wounds. That is my mission—in addition to enumerating certain distasteful but unfortunately relevant facts."

Phillipe's distrust mounted. It wasn't rational; but it was there nevertheless, gnawing in his mind.

"I arrived at Kentland to discover young Roger raving and screaming in his bed. Oh, a most heart-rending sight! Despite the young man's pain, he made his intentions quite clear. He wished to pursue you—" He indicated Phillipe. "When Dr. Bleeker categorically stated that Roger's injuries made such action impossible, and I interjected that the action would be morally reprehensible, Roger still threatened to employ surrogates—armed servants—to carry out his desire to shatter one of God's prime commandments—"

"In other words," Phillipe interrupted, "he wants to kill me or have me killed."

"Sad to say, you are correct."

"That's nothing new."

The bishop ignored the bitter comment. "Only with prayers and fervent persuasion at the bedside did I manage to turn him from that course."

Phillipe trembled a little, hearing the mellow pulpit voice speak of murder. Francis went on:

"I could not stand by and permit such bloodshed! But from a practical standpoint—and this is the part distressful to my soul—Roger would, of course, be safe from reprisals."

"Safe?" Marie burst out. "He could kill my son and not be punished?"

"Not even accused or troubled by an inquiry—under the secular law. Believe me, madame, striking at the Amberlys, you have struck very high. Such a family is all but invulnerable. No one in the neighborhood—no one in the realm, I venture to say—would concern himself about your son's death. As the sparrow falls, God's eye is upon it. But not, alas, the eyes of a magistrate. However—" Francis hitched forward slightly, his lips and forehead beginning to glisten. "My intercession and prayers showed Roger Amberly and, more importantly, his mother the moral folly of Roger's desire. True, my restraints may be no more than temporary—"

Phillipe spoke with a clarity that matched the cold rage he felt inside:

"Let me understand you, bishop. You're telling us that because I'm low-born, and Roger a nobleman, he can have me murdered and not be punished?"

"That is the unhappy fact, yes."

In that case, Phillipe thought, then Girard was right. It was indeed time for storm winds to blow away the rotten structure of the aristocracy.

Said the bishop: "After winning Roger's assurance that he would not act in haste—and seeing him finally asleep with some of Bleeker's laudanum—I took counsel with Lady Amberly. As you might suspect, her situation has become intolerably tormenting—"

"No more tormenting than ours!" exclaimed Marie.

"Yes, yes, madame, I fully appreciate your state of stress," he soothed. "But do remember—Lady Jane has not only lost her husband, she has seen her son possibly maimed for life. She is not the sort to accept all that lightly. But she *is*, we may say with thanks, at heart a Christian woman. Able, ultimately, to overcome her natural instincts and listen to a higher voice—a higher doctrine than the doctrine of Cain."

Sweet, flowing words. Almost hypnotic—

And yet Phillipe kept sensing a trap being set behind the pious, blubbery face.

"In short," Francis concluded, "after much soulful struggling, I wrung a concession from Lady Jane. She is prepared to let the past be forgotten—provided you both agree, finally and unequivocally, to certain terms—"

Phillipe almost laughed aloud. He had suspected before that he and his mother had in their possession the

means to force a victory. Now the bishop's words
assured him of it. Relishing the realization, he got a jolt
when he heard Marie say:

"Go on."

"In the coach, dear woman, I have a pouch containing notes in the amount of two thousand pounds
sterling. Lady Amberly has reluctantly agreed to that
sum—and no action against you—" The blue seed eyes
focused on Marie, picking up reflections of the candle in
their depths. "—*if!*—if you and your son will renounce
all claims upon the family and return to France. Permanently."

"Two thousand—?" Stunned, Marie was unable to
finish the sentence.

"I beg you to accept the offer!" Francis struggled to
his feet like some purple mountain rising from a tremor-
ing earth. The sausage-fingered hands spread in pleading eloquence. "It's not only a just settlement
but—realistically speaking—handsome. Handsome indeed! Lady Jane is anxious to bring an end to the
disputation, the turmoil. Join her in that endeavor! I
can see the sad ravages of this wrangling in your face,
madame—the toll it has taken. Why harm yourself further? Why risk your safety or your son's? Depart, and
you can live in modest comfort for the remainder of
your days! I plead as much for your welfare as for Lady
Jane's—accept!"

"No," said Phillipe.

Marie glanced sharply at her son. Bishop Francis bit
his lower lip, teeth sinking deep into the wet pink flesh
for a fraction of time. Then he recovered, his melancholy seeming to deepen.

"Oh, God's wounds, sir!—is this another Cain who
confronts me? I've wrestled one already tonight!
Haven't I explained the alternative to acceptance—?"

"Yes, but the facts are no different than when we first
knocked at the door of Kentland. Amberly was my

father, the letter is legal, she knows it and apparently she'll do anything to see that Roger takes the whole inheritance. What if I wait another few hours? Will her price go higher?" Phillipe said contemptuously. "It can't be high enough unless it's the amount full due—half!"

Abruptly Francis faced away, concentrating on Marie:

"Madame, you are my last hope. I come here with the best of motives—and find Satan's imps of greed and error have preceded me. Talk to your son, madame. Open his eyes!"

Looking worn out, Marie said, "We can at least consider the offer, Phillipe—"

"Yes, yes, madame! That's being sensible. Besides"—Francis turned back to Phillipe, the skirt of his purple gown belling—"if you wait, as you put it, for the price to go higher, there is no guarantee you will be alive to receive the payment. May I be forgiven in Heaven for alluding to such a grim reality, but it's the truth."

Marie gave a small, humbled nod. To his horror, Phillipe saw that the bishop—and the Amberlys—had broken through her defenses at last.

His jaw set. "Mama—"

"Don't you understand what the good bishop's saying, Phillipe? I won't risk your life!"

"And by accepting, you will save and enrich your own!" the churchman exhorted. "Roger will recover. Lady Jane may waver. I cannot constantly, constantly be in attendance, urging restraint—" He pressed his palm against his eyes suddenly, as if seized by a dizzy spell. And in that moment of postured overstatement, Phillipe knew there *must* be a trap.

"Be damned to Roger and his threats!" he shouted. "I'm not afraid of him."

"But I am," Marie Charboneau said wearily.

She faced the bishop, her shoulders slumping. Phillipe started to argue. She was quicker.

"Two thousand pounds will last many years—we will accept the offer."

"Mama, listen! You're selling out everything you wanted, everything you—"

"I will not sacrifice your life. We will accept the offer."

Heaving a long sigh, Bishop Francis intoned, "Blessed be God's holy name. Wisdom and virtue have prevailed."

ii

Phillipe stared at the prelate's round face. The jowls shone with dozens of tiny diamonds of sweat. The battle of words had been an exertion. He thought bitterly, *No, power has prevailed.*

Showing more animation, the bishop seemed to collect himself.

"I will go down to the coach and bring you the money. I ask only the opportunity to read the document at the heart of the dispute. You'll recall that when I tried to examine it before, I was not permitted to touch it." The blue eyes avoided Phillipe's on that point. "Thus I saw only that the handwriting appeared to be the Duke's, and that the letter was duly witnessed. Before bringing this matter to its happy conclusion, it would be poor stewardship if I did not assure myself of the letter's contents."

Marie gave a forlorn little nod. "Fetch it, Phillipe."

"I don't see why that's necessary, Mama. Lady Jane knows the contents of—"

"Fetch it," Marie said, her voice hoarse, her eyes exhausted.

He wanted to refuse. He didn't. The will to fight had

gone out of his mother. Nothing he could say or do would overcome her fear for his safety.

He left Mr. Fox's sitting room and returned shortly with the casket. Bishop Francis was removing a tie cord from a pouch that contained a thick packet of notes. As he did so, he said:

"On Christian as well as material grounds, madame, I could not be more pleased. This sum will indeed keep you in comfort many, many years—" For the first time, the unctuous smile Phillipe remembered from the first interview tugged up the corners of his mouth. "A moment more and we're done. The letter—"

His right hand lifted, palm up. Phillipe saw sweat-diamonds glistening on the fat and in the deep folds. Again he was deviled by his conviction about a trap. Swiftly, he looked to Marie. Tried to explain, plead, warn with a glance—

She didn't see. Or did, and chose to ignore it. She turned away.

Swallowing, Phillipe opened the casket. He removed the folded letter carefully, handed it to Bishop Francis.

"Thank you, my son."

The bishop inclined his head to study the French script. He held the letter in two hands, blinking abruptly—squinting—as if having difficulty with his eyesight. He lowered the letter to waist level, his concentration still fixed. A bead of sweat ran down from his left ear. Phillipe's mind screamed a wild warning—

He shook his head, angry. *What was happening to him?* Bishop Francis was still reading. Nothing was amiss.

The bishop held the letter only by its right margin now. He turned his flabby body toward the deal table, as if to provide more illumination on the document—

The bishop's right hand kept moving.

Toward the light.

Toward the candle—

"Mama!" Phillipe shouted. In that wasted instant, Francis thrust a corner of the document into the candle flame.

Francis still smiled. But his eyes were triumphant.

For a harrowing moment, Phillipe was too startled to move. He was mesmerized by that vicious smile. By the thread of smoke rising. By the faint crackling. He drove himself forward, dropping the casket—

But Marie, her eyes wild as any harridan's, was quicker. And more savage; she had fallen all the way into the snare.

She seized the bishop's right wrist with both hands, jerking the fat arm toward her. Charring at the edges, the letter came out of the flame. Francis' left hand, an un-Christian fist, rose with startling speed. He smashed the side of Marie's head, knocking her over—

Ugly-faced, Francis started to kick her as she went down. Phillipe leaped on him from behind, digging his fingers—his nails—into the folds of white fat at the nape of the bishop's neck. Francis shrieked like a woman.

His right hand opened. The letter fluttered toward the floor, still afire. On hands and knees, Marie had presence enough to reach for the burning document, slap out the glowing edges even though she gasped in pain doing it.

"You stinking, hypocritical bag of pus!" Phillipe howled, whirling the bishop around by the shoulder and hammering his fist into the veined nose. The fat man staggered, upsetting the armchair, then the deal table and the candle. The candle winked out.

The light of the rainy sky filtering through the shutters turned the bishop's face gray as rotten meat. He reeled clumsily along the wall, mouthing one filthy oath after another. Outside, Phillipe heard hallooing coachmen, wheels creaking, hoofs clopping away.

Francis wiped a sleeve across his bleeding nose. Gone

was all pretense of piety. The small blue eyes glittered like a snake's.

"Impious whoreson!" he spat. "Hell take you for striking a man of the cloth!"

"As it's taken you already," Phillipe retorted. "She sent you here, didn't she? But never for the purpose you pretended. She sent you with tricks and sweet words to get the letter and destroy it—because we'd never suspect that of a man who pretends to serve God. It nearly worked the first time, so she sent you back again—*get out of here before I break your damned neck!*"

Face contorted, the bishop suddenly comprehended the rage that turned Phillipe white. A terrified look flashed over the bishop's face. He bolted for the door.

Phillipe took two steps after him, reached down and seized the pouch of money. He threw it after the retreating churchman.

Snuffling, his robes stained with blood and mucus, Francis picked up the pouch and disappeared down the stairs. Moments later, Marie and her son heard the sounds of a second coach departing.

Phillipe went to his mother's side. She was unfolding the burned document. The lower edge, including the last few letters of the right-hand witnessing signature, crinkled to black ash and fell away. A section of the upper edge was likewise destroyed. But the central message remained intact.

Boots clattered on the stair. Mr. Fox burst in on them:

"You young madman! What did you do to the bishop?"

"Hit him," Phillipe growled, righting the overturned chair and sinking down in it, fingers against his temples.

"In God's name, lad, why?"

"The only purpose of his visit was treachery. He pretended to make a settlement with us—just the way he did on the first occasion. He claimed to be protecting me from Roger's revenge. All the time, he wanted nothing but that letter. You can see where he tried to burn it."

Fox shuddered. "Then the Amberlys are desperate indeed."

"He offered us money," Phillipe raged. "Two thousand pounds if we'd go away—"

"And I agreed!" Marie said. "I *agreed!* I never dreamed they could buy a holy man."

Sadly, Fox shook his head. "Madame, I've tried to give you some notion of the reach of that family. There is nothing they cannot order, or cause to have done. They'll probably have this place burned to the ground because I've harbored you," he added in a rare moment of self-pity. He stalked to the window, clouted the shutters open to reveal the roofs of Tonbridge under a slanting gray shower.

Phillipe rushed to his side. "Mr. Fox, you've showed us only kindness. We'll leave at once."

"Easier said than accomplished," replied the older man, staring miserably out over the village. "Didn't you hear the other coach? The one for London—departing right on schedule? And," he finished after a moment, "there's not another till tomorrow morning, same time."

He rubbed his eyes, then looked chagrined.

"I'm sorry I turned on you, lad. I won't worry about losing this place till it happens. What must concern us is your welfare. I wonder if you dare risk waiting for the next coach?"

The late summer rain pattered in the silence. From the High Street came the ringing of a bell and the cry of a baker's boy hawking buns. Finally, Phillipe said:

"No, I think we'd best go immediately."

"Go where?"

"The country. We can hide in the woods. That way, if they come hunting, you can prove we've gone."

"Phillipe's right, Mr. Fox," Marie agreed. "We can't let your generosity bring you to harm."

Fox licked one of his protruding upper teeth. Then a certain determination sparkled his glance again.

"I appreciate that, madame. On the other hand, is it fit that a piece of real estate take precedence over human lives? I can compromise my cowardice one more day, I think. I prefer that to feeling like a hypocrite at the Methodist meeting."

He tried to give them a show of cheer; an encouraging smile. Phillipe realized how great the effort must be.

"If you want to chance it," Fox said, "I'll offer you the same fine quarters you enjoyed earlier. I mean the stable. Should anyone come inquiring, I'll say you left the inn this morning—which will be true. Then you can slip aboard the coach at half past eight tomorrow—my offer of fare still standing."

Marie Charboneau flung her arms around old Fox's neck, hugging him and weeping her thanks in French. The landlord looked acutely embarrassed.

Phillipe said, "I think we'd best pack the trunk and haul it to the stable with no further delay."

iii

Clarence brought them bowls of cold porridge and two mugs of ale an hour later. Then he rolled the door shut and sealed them in again.

Phillipe was already wishing they hadn't stayed. The place grew oppressive with its smell of moldy straw and horse droppings. He watched a spider weaving a web in the corner of the stall. He thought of Jane Amberly, Duchess of Kentland. And wondered whether the poor and powerless of the world were always at the mercy of those in authority.

Somehow, there should be another way.

Again he recalled Girard's talk of the storm winds sweeping the world. No breath of them seemed to reach Kent. Then where did they blow, cleansing the evil of those who manipulated men's lives to their own ends?

A small sound from Marie broke into his thoughts. She looked waxen, leaning back against the side of the stall with her eyes closed.

She put down the ale without drinking. She hadn't touched the lumpy porridge, either. "I am sorry for this, Phillipe. My ambition for you has led us into a game we had no chance of winning."

He touched her hand. "Perhaps there's still a way when we reach London." He tried to sound optimistic; inside, he was anything but that. "We might find a charitable, decent lawyer to help us press the case. We could offer such a man a portion of what we finally recover."

Marie stared at him a long moment. "I'm glad there is still some hope in you. Those people have all but destroyed mine."

He clasped his fingers tighter around her cold flesh. "I swore you an oath, remember?"

Eyes still closed, she gave a faint, embittered nod. The rain kept up its beat on the roof.

Phillipe felt troubled again. In attempting to reassure Marie with false words, he came to the unanswerable question again. Did he really want to become like the Amberlys? *Did he?*

Tormented by the dilemma, and chilled to drowsiness by the dampness of the stable, he roused abruptly when the door creaked. Mr. Fox appeared.

"A hired boy brought a message—"

"Summoning me to an ambush, no doubt."

"It's possible," Mr. Fox agreed.

"What's the message?"

"There is a lady waiting in a willow grove a half-mile

up the river. Her name wasn't mentioned. But she claims she must see you—it's most urgent."

"Who hired the boy? The lady?"

"No, some servant girl from Kentland. She met the boy delivering milk at the edge of the village, and—"

Phillipe scrambled up, clutched Fox's arm. "Did the boy tell you the name of the servant wench, by chance?"

"I believe it was—yes, Betsy. That's it, Betsy."

"And what did you say to the boy?"

"Exactly what we agreed. That you'd left the inn. He didn't care one way or another. He'd already been paid, and he was all in a rush to get back to his milk pails—here! You're not going?"

"Yes, I must."

Phillipe turned to speak to Marie, saw she'd fallen asleep. As he started for the stable door, Fox cautioned him:

"By your own words, you could be walking into their trap."

"I realize. I'll be careful. When my mother wakes up, tell her I'll be back in good time—"

"Go through the trees along the shore, then," Fox shouted after him. "For God's sake stay off the towpath!"

The words faded as Phillipe ran through the gray morning, toward the Medway and the one person he hoped would be waiting there.

CHAPTER IX

Flight

i

HE KNEW THE LOCATION of the grove well enough, having met Alicia there once before. Taking Mr. Fox's advice, he avoided the towpath, running instead among the trees on the riverbank below.

He jumped little inlets where the Medway had cut into the lush banks, moving so fast that his chest began to hurt. At the same time, he kept an eye on the towpath in case a cart should appear—or pursuers dispatched from the estate, perhaps.

The supple willow branches lashed his cheeks as he rushed along. He saw the grove ahead. Nearby, the towpath curved away from the river, toward the green hillock from whose far side he'd first glimpsed his father's estate.

The willows in the grove grew close together. But in the gray-and-green of the stormy summer day, he thought he detected a black horse moving behind the screen of overhanging branches. That reassured him a little, though he remained wary of surprise attack.

He leaped a last channel, pushing at the living, green-leafed curtain—

"Alicia?"

"Here."

He plunged into the dim heart of the grove. Rain

began to pelt again. The towering willows offered protection.

He came on her suddenly, waiting beside her splendid black stallion. She wore the same familiar riding costume. But her tawny hair was disarrayed, the ribbon at the nape of her neck half undone. Her cheeks were flushed. And one was marked with a nasty blue-black bruise.

She saw him notice it immediately, smiled in a forlorn way.

"A small remembrance from my intended. It's of no importance. Phillipe, I can stay only a few moments. This time I literally had to creep out of the house like a thief—after sending Betsy ahead. I only managed it because all the attention's on the bishop and"—sudden fear on her face—"plans for you." Tearful, she looked into his eyes. "Oh, Phillipe—what possessed you to attack Francis?"

"The pious bastard tried to trick us. On Lady Jane's orders, I imagine. He tried to burn my father's letter."

"The coach brought him back to Kentland in a perfect rage. Face all bloodied—and his language! Foul enough to make a fishmonger blush. You've got to leave Tonbridge, and quickly. That's why I had to see you. Warn you."

Bitterness twisted his mouth. "Salving your conscience for telling Roger about me?"

She turned pale. "How did you know?"

"He told me the night he attacked me."

"I don't imagine you'll soon forgive me—"

"No."

"It did happen by accident. At dinner. I drank too much claret—"

"A habit of yours, it seems," he said, harsh. Then he regretted it. He could understand a little about why she had to dull her senses so often.

For her part, Alicia was quick to answer him:

"He provoked me in the extreme, Phillipe! It was right after he returned from London. He began boasting of an orange girl he'd dallied with. He met her one night at the theater—"

"So you, in turn, had to cut him down with an account of your own amusements? I really wonder if you weren't planning to do that from the start."

She nodded, as if tired. "Perhaps I was. Perhaps—even despite my promise to you. Well—" She fingered the blotched bruise. "I got my reward. Roger saw to it—in private."

"And you're going to marry a monster like that?"

"Yes," she answered, a whisper. "There are —disagreeable parts to any bargain."

"Christ in heaven! That's not a bargain. That's sentencing yourself to—"

"Don't, Phillipe. It was settled long ago. Long before Quarry Hill—"

She touched his cheek. Her hand was warm. And capable of arousing memories, emotions, that quelled some of his anger.

"But what we shared was far more than amusement, my darling. Don't you know that by now? If it wasn't so, would I risk coming to tell you that Roger's up, and readying his plans to dispose of you? His hand's all wrapped in batting, like a mitten. My God, I've never seen him so angry—like a madman. This very minute, he's organizing some of the household men. To send them after you and your mother. At the very least they'll attack you and take the letter. At worst, they may kill you. I tell you he's completely out of his head!—you destroyed his hand, even Bleeker admits that. I—"

She hesitated, turning away. Never before had he seen so much as a trace of shame on her face. Now he saw it.

"—I know I'm partly responsible for what happened. Because I drank too much—and refused to bear his bragging."

Phillipe still wondered whether her regret was wholly honest. There was no pleasure in Alicia's blue eyes. Yet he could vividly imagine its presence when she'd flung the truth of her liaison at her intended husband.

He cared for her. Deeply. But he knew, with a sadness, that his original impression of her was still, in part, valid. There was a whore in her.

True, the whore was elegant and soft-eyed. But underneath, calculating. And with the quick temper of her kind.

He rubbed the shiny flank of the restless black horse. The animal turned its head to nip. Phillipe stroked the stallion's muzzle to calm him, saying:

"That's done with. Obviously I'd better be concerned about the present. My mother and I plan to leave Tonbridge in the morning, by the London coach."

"You don't dare delay that long! Believe me! Get out of the village. Hide in the fields. Along the river on the other side of Tonbridge—anywhere—but hide."

He shook his head in disgust. "They're ready to kill me—when they should be making preparations to bury my father? What a despicable lot they are."

"You've pushed them too far. As to preparations for the burial—"

A peculiar stiffness seemed to freeze her features. She turned away again, gazing down between the overhanging leaves at the Medway dappled with raindrop rings.

"—those can wait awhile," she finished. "Until the more important business is accomplished."

He puzzled about the change in her expression a moment ago. He'd learned to recognize when she was concealing something. But his emotions made him forget that. Almost against his will, he slipped his hands around her waist and up her back. He pulled her close to savor her warmth; the sweet breath he'd known so intimately.

Very softly, he said, "I wish you could come away

with me, Alicia."

"In spite of the grief I've caused, telling Roger?"

"God help me—yes."

The blue eyes brimmed with tears. She bent her head into his shoulder. He stroked her tawny hair while she cried.

"I—I wish I could too. But I've told you I'm not strong enough for that. I'm what I was born and taught to be. The Alicia who drinks too heavily, and spills out secrets that should stay hidden. I will be Roger's wife next year."

He sounded bitter again: "I realize I have far less to offer. No inheritance except on a piece of parchment they mean to destroy. No pack of servants to call up to do murder at my bidding—"

"*Please!*"

She wrenched away, in agony.

"You knew what I was from the beginning, Phillipe. Do you realize how much I've thought about leaving everything to be with you? How close I am even now? So close it terrifies me! That's what you've done. That's how you've shaken and changed me."

"But not enough." Rage passing again, he drew her close. "Not enough."

His own eyes had grown blurred with tears. He fought them back as he lifted her chin, gazed at her a long moment before kissing her. Alicia clung to him with all her strength, bending his head into an almost painful embrace.

He didn't want to shatter the suspended moment. All the realities—the danger from Roger Amberly; the soft rustling of the willow leaves in the rain; his mother waiting back in the village—had faded to the background.

But one by one, those realities claimed his mind. He broke the embrace gently.

"I loved you, Alicia. Nothing that happens can ever change the truth of that."

"*Loved*, Master Frenchman?" Once more she tried to smile through the weeping. This time, she almost brought it off. Her shoulders lifted, though the jauntiness was still false and forced. "Can't we keep it in the present tense? Do you think a woman—even a woman like me—can ever forget the first man she really cared about? Or gave herself to? I love you and I always will. I swear I'll feel you close even when I'm with another man, for all the rest of my life. If I've never spoken the truth before, I swear by Almighty God I'm speaking it now. Be thankful we had the summer. Now go—before I decide to come with you."

Whirling, she dashed to her horse and mounted, pulling the rein so fiercely the black whinnied against the bite of the bit. She ducked under the branches and drove the stallion up the slope through the willows to the towpath, and out of sight.

Phillipe touched his face. Wet. With tears. And rain. The shower was driving hard enough to penetrate the trees—

As he walked out of the grove, he marked down one more score against the Amberlys of the world. They offered what he could not. The property and position that, in the end, had lost him a woman with whom he might have spent the rest of his life, knowing her weaknesses but loving her uncontrollably in spite of them.

ii

Less than an hour after Phillipe Charboneau crept back into the village of Tonbridge, he and his mother had left it for the last time.

Walking through clover meadows still damp with the morning showers, their plan was to strike north-westward, toward the hamlet of Ide Hill. At Phillipe's belt hung a tied kerchief with five shillings and some bread inside; the landlord's way of helping their journey.

Mr. Fox had apologized for the smallness of the gift, then issued warnings about the dangers to which they must be alert. Highwaymen on the public roads. Fees to be paid at the turnpike tollhouses if they went that way—or dodged, if they didn't. Suspicious country folk who might recognize them as foreigners and, very likely, fugitives of some kind.

Mr. Fox had advised that they might filch apples from orchards and find creeks with sweet, drinkable water, but they would be wise to avoid towns of any size until a week's walking, give or take a day or two, brought them near the city of London. Because of the necessity to travel swiftly and lightly, living off the land, the trunk was left behind at Wolfe's Triumph. Phillipe carried Gil's wrapped sword, Marie the small leather casket. They took nothing else.

By the time they neared Quarry Hill, Marie already looked weary. Despite the anguished memories the hill held, Phillipe decided to wait there until dark before pushing on, both for Marie's sake and to give them the cover of night.

The showers had cleared. A peaceful blue late afternoon sky replaced the earlier gray. Crickets began to harp noisily in the fields.

"We must go faster till we reach the hill," he urged, aware of their high visibility in an empty pastoral landscape. Marie countered with a question about the identity of the woman who had sent for him.

Phillipe kept his face expressionless. "I didn't realize Mr. Fox had told you—"

"Certainly. Who was she?"

He answered with an elaborate lie. It was a kitchen wench from Kentland. She knew one of Mr. Fox's serving girls. Phillipe had met her when she'd come to the inn to visit. Embellishing the falsehood, he added that he'd even passed some hours strolling with the young lady out in the country during the summer.

Being a kindly girl, he finished, this morning she'd arranged to warn him of Roger's planned action, at some personal risk.

Face wan, eyes remote as they trudged through the fields, Marie Charboneau accepted the explanation without question. But she said in a hollow voice:

"There was another girl. A beautiful girl—with the young man, the first day we went to Kentland. Remember?"

He kept his face impassive, scanning the horizon in the lowering light. A speck moved on a distant road snaking across the top of the hill. Only a farmer's cart, he realized a moment later, relieved.

Marie went on with her toneless reverie:

"She was the kind I wanted you to marry. Rich and beautiful and of good station. I had such hopes of a good marriage."

To try to cheer her, he smiled. "I'll make a match like that yet. My claim still stands." He tapped the casket which she crooked in her arm protectively.

They reached Quarry Hill as sunset came on. Settled on the damp ground well back among the trees, Phillipe broke the coarse, crumbly bread Mr. Fox had given them. He handed the larger half to Marie. She was shivering. She'd brought only a plain woolen cloak to wear over her already muddied clothing. He could hear her teeth chatter when she tried to bite the bread.

He sat beside her, pulled her head close in against his shoulder, to let the warmth of his body reach her if it would. And suddenly, he felt the strange reversal of their roles, a reversal that had come about without his realizing it.

She was the child now, and he the adult, her strength. He helped steady her hand as she brought the bread to her mouth. She chewed it slowly, like an old woman.

In the distance he heard the sound of horses, traveling fast.

He left her and slipped to the edge of the trees.

Below, in the red light of the August evening, half a dozen men rode in the direction of Tonbridge. He recognized their liveries. The sunset flashed on the belled muzzle of a blunderbuss carried by the leading rider. As he watched them pass, his stomach began to ache.

When the horsemen disappeared, he crept back into the woods to find Marie dozing. He touched her forehead. Warm.

He sat awake most of the night, feeling like a speck—nothing—beneath the twinkling summer stars.

Yet if he were nothing, why did he feel so much fear? And so much hate?

Book Two

The House of Sholto and Sons

CHAPTER I

Swords at St. Paul's

i

THE GREAT CITY of London stank and chimed and glittered.

And as he first observed it with feverish eyes in the mellow light of early September, Phillipe Charboneau thought he'd never viewed anything half so marvelous and awesome.

They had approached through the southern sections, coming at last into the tumult of Southwark. Phillipe's fair command of English gained them the information that to reach the Old City, they must cross the Thames River. As they were doing now, near sunset, by the Westminster Bridge.

All around, crowds jostled; iron-tired coaches rumbled; and the great river below, alive with barges plied by shouting watermen, mingled its tang with the more pungent aromas of those passing to and fro on the bridge.

Marie walked listlessly. Her eyes were half-closed. Phillipe carried both the casket and the wrapped sword. Their money was long gone, spent carefully for tart cider or sugared buns, at small, poor inns they'd felt free to visit only after dark.

But now the long, exhausting journey on foot seemed to fade behind the panorama spreading in front of Phillipe's astonished eyes.

London. A sprawl, a hurlyburly of wood and brick
buildings of all conceivable styles, shapes and heights,
bordering the river upstream and down for what
appeared to be two or three miles. Splendid church
domes shone dull gold in the autumn light, despite the
pall of smoke accumulating from thousands of rooftop
chimney pots. One dome in particular, eastward around
the curve of the Thames, glowed with special
magnificence.

Phillipe stopped a pair of boys. Both carried short
brushes fully as black as their cheeks and ragged
clothing. He inquired about the imposing dome in the
distance.

"Country lout, not to know Master Wren's greatest
church!" jeered one of the boys, giving a wink to his
companion. "St. Paul's! 'Ware you don't get sold a piece
of the river!"

The sweeps were hidden suddenly behind a sedan
chair whose liveried carriers jostled Phillipe and his
mother out of the way. Inside the chair, a wigged
gentleman fondled the brocaded breasts of a woman
who laughed and slapped his wrist lightly with a sequinned domino on a stick.

"Mama—" Phillipe was forced to speak loudly because of the incessant din. Church bells predominated,
clanging and chiming from all quarters of the stained
sunset sky. "We'll have to sleep where we can again
tonight. There's a great church yonder. If we make for
it, perhaps we can find shelter."

Marie's lips barely moved, the only sign she'd heard
him.

Soon they reached the end of the bridge. Phillipe
discovered that negotiating their way to the landmark
dome had all at once become impossible. They were
plunged into streets that took abrupt turnings. Buildings
hid the skyline. Creaking wrought-metal shop signs effectively shut out the little remaining daylight.

The cobbled streets were perilously narrow, too. A drainage channel ran down the center of most of them. After a few minutes on such thoroughfares, Phillipe began to make sense of the patterns of foot traffic.

Those more elegantly dressed, or more robust, or armed with swords or sticks, kept to the sides of the street closest to the walls. Shabbier, less bold pedestrians made their way down the middle, walking as best they could through and around the mess in the drainage channels—fruit peels and vegetable garbage, human turds and puddles of urine, even an occasional rotting cat carcass.

But the head as well as the feet had an occupation—to stay wary, and dodge and duck when a bone or a heap of refuse came sailing down from above without so much as a cry of warning.

Phillipe's hair soon stank from being pelted with soggy garbage. Yet so alive and exhilarating was the spectacle around him that he learned the lesson without great anger. He started to keep sharp watch, and congratulated himself when the contents of a pot for human waste came showering down—and he pulled his mother safely out of the way.

Of all the sensations driving in upon him in one magnificent blur, the greatest, perhaps, was that of continual noise.

Stage coaches and wagons creaked and clanked in nearby streets. Young boys hawked newspapers, bellowing through tin horns. Rag pickers and post collectors rang handbells to announce their presence. Link boys with torches already lighted against the descending darkness shouted for those ahead to make way.

When this happened, Phillipe and Marie had to fight for space along the wall, bumped here by a barber prancing along with a load of wig boxes, there by an old toothless apple woman shoving ancient-looking fruit at them with a plea that they buy. Then the linkboys would pass, preceding a sedan chair from whose windows there looked out yet another finely dressed member of the gentry, safe about the turmoil and the filth.

A cadaverous young man with yellow skin and foul breath thrust a sheaf of printed sheets under Phillipe's nose, fairly screaming, "New songs for sale! Latest ballads and amusements of the town!"

When Phillipe tried to back away, the balladeer clutched him. Phillipe broke into French, with gestures of noncomprehension. The vendor spat an obscene word, turned away and, grinning instantly again, accosted the next potential customer.

Phillipe and Marie struggled on. He was afraid they might be going in the wrong direction now. He approached two women at a corner. Their backs were to him as he said:

"Pardon, but is this the way to St. Paul's church?"

He expected young faces. To his horror, he saw old ones, all white paste and rouge. One of the women grabbed at his trousers, began to shamelessly manipulate his penis so hard that he quickly came to erection. The stringy-haired slut whispered, "Ye'll not get a fancy fuck in that place, young sir. But step up the way a bit and we'll accommodate ye. We'll put yer auntie into the trade, too, if yer's pressed for a livelihood—"

Once more Phillipe resorted to French and helpless gestures as a defensive weapon. The tactic incurred curses even more flamboyant than those of the song vendor. Up the lane from the corner, Phillipe glimpsed a pair of hulking men lounging in the shadows. He suspected that something more than a "fancy fuck" awaited anyone foolish enough to accept the invitation of the two sisters of the street. He and his mother hurried away.

As darkness deepened, merchants shuttered their shops. Other windows began to glow. Coffee houses, taverns, eating establishments. They had passed into a section he was told was indeed the Old City, dating to Roman times. The crowds thinned out. Phillipe grew more wary.

And more lost.

He and Marie wandered through a square of elegant brick homes, then along several more lanes to a broad avenue where huge market wagons groaned in from the country with fragrant loads of melons and cabbages and apples. The wagons lighted sparks with their iron tires. Another cart passed, full of butchered cow quarters crawling with flies.

Finally, unable to catch so much as a glimpse of the great dome above the rooftops, Phillipe accosted an old gentleman standing on a ladder at a lantern post in another square.

"Which way to St. Paul's?" he shouted, dodging drops of hot oil that came sputtering down from the fresh-lit wick inside the box.

"That way," waved the old gentleman, climbing down and looking annoyed because Phillipe acted confused by the generality of the instructions. *That way* was a dozen streets, or a hundred; who could tell in this incredible urban maze?

"Keep straight on the way ye're going!" the lamplighter barked. "Ye'll know the place from the immoral songs, and the beggars. I'd sooner visit hell at night."

Grumping, he lugged his ladder to the next lantern post. Such lighting devices, Phillipe noticed, were located only in areas like this one—tree-filled squares surrounded by prosperous homes. Once back in the narrow lanes and stews, light vanished, save for that of the ubiquitous linkboys preceding their masters, who walked or rode in chairs.

Phillipe pressed on—eastward, if he reckoned directions properly now that the sun had dropped out of sight. He was stinking dirty, and dizzy from fever, lack of food, or both. Marie was no more than a voiceless weight clinging to his arm. Yet he was continually excited by it all. By the wagon noise which, if anything, increased after dark. By the yells and bawdy laughter from the taprooms and coffee houses. By the occasional cries that might have been pleasure—or pain. He even caught the sound of two distant pistol shots.

How many hours he and his mother wandered, he had no idea. He heard loud bells chime to the number of eleven when they finally turned a corner and saw a wide paved area. At its far side towered the magnificent architecture of the church he'd glimpsed from the bridge.

St. Paul's Yard, sure enough. On the ground near numerous shuttered stalls, booths and business establishments ringing the open area lay a host of cripples and semi-invalids. Some rose to surround him and stretch out their hands— "A farthing, gentle sir. Remember the poor and save them from the curse of prison!"

Phillipe pushed a path through a half-dozen of these remarkably agile wrecks of all ages and degrees of uncleanliness. He stepped between Marie and one scabrous, slimy hand that pawed at them. He made threatening gestures. The beggars retreated, spitting at his feet, cursing him. He helped Marie up the great stone steps of the church to the doors, pulled at one of the rings.

The church was locked for the night.

He turned and surveyed the Yard. One lantern shed feeble light on a couple of seated balladeers. They passed a gin bottle back and forth between choruses featuring the most blasphemous, scatological quatrains Phillipe had ever heard.

The air had grown chill. The din of London receded. He realized how friendly a background the noise had become during the time they'd walked the mazy streets.

Coach wheels grumbled and halloos rang only occasionally now, from far off. Other than the lanterns of the beggars, lights were few. A linkboy's brand winked like a firefly down some distant lane, then vanished.

And out in a darkened section of the Yard, Phillipe heard a shuffling that prickled his scalp.

He helped Marie sit down against one of the porch pillars. She mumbled an incoherent syllable or two. Phillipe rubbed her forehead. Burning. His own wasn't much cooler. His belly, though long accustomed to the pains of shrinkage, hurt again. His mouth was dry. The reek of his own body offended him.

He was glad to see Marie already dozing. Her torn woolen cloak provided her only protection against the night air. Again he heard a *shuffle-shuffle* of rag-wrapped feet—and sibilant voices.

The beggars.

He smelled them before he saw them. They advanced slowly up the steps in the darkness, stinking phantoms festooned with rags. He heard quavery old voices. Younger ones, too. *Shuffle-shuffle* went the feet as they came on.

Abruptly, one voice became audible:

"—leetle box. Could be jewelry. Also a long bundle. Might be a sword, General."

"An' the poor need 'em things more than the strangers do, ain't that so?"

"True, General, true," another man replied. Phillipe heard a raspy laugh.

The balladeers had extinguished their lantern and gone to sleep. St. Paul's Yard was silent.

Inside the church, there might be protection, other human beings. Out here, there were only human predators, chuckling and shuffling up the stone stairs as Phillipe fumbled to unwrap Gil's sword while there was still time.

ii

He counted eight or nine surrounding him in a half-circle. They looked shaggy because of their torn garments. The gleam of the stars above the rooftops revealed little more than their shapes. But here and there, a detail stood out. The glisten of a pustular sore on a cheek; the paleness of light-colored facings on the old uniform coat of the one who styled himself the General.

Phillipe could see nothing of this man's features. He was of good size, though. The top of his head gleamed faintly silver. A dirty wig. Stolen, probably. The wig hung low over his left ear, lending the General's head a peculiar, cocked look.

Metal winked in the General's right hand. A sword? But so short—

Then Phillipe realized the blade was broken off halfway to the hilt. A wicked weapon.

His breath hissed between his teeth as he let the wrappings of his own sword fall between his feet. He kicked them behind him, waiting to see how the game would play out. One of the beggars fluttered a hand in his direction.

" 'E's got a proper sword indeed, General. One we might fence for a nice sum."

"Here, sir!" the General announced, advancing up another step and flourishing his broken weapon. "Will you surrender 'at prize to me army of poor? We're only a hop and a step away from debtor's chains in the Fleet, don't ye realize? 'Em valuables, sold off, will keep me troopers warm an' cozy till Christmas or better."

"Get away," Phillipe warned, sidestepping nearer the pillar where his mother dozed. Marie muttered in the night's cold. Phillipe feared for her exposed position.

But he was glad the fever screened out the reality of the immediate situation. He repeated his warning:

"*Get away!*"

"Funny sound to his talk, ain't they, General?" asked one of the others. "Ha' we caught ourselves some Frenchified rat what swum the Channel?"

"Even more reason for surrendering to 'is Majesty's sojers," allowed the General, moving up one more step. He was now just two down from Phillipe. "Hand us 'em things an' there'll be no military reprisals 'gainst that old lady with you."

Two of the raggy phantoms at the right of the ring— Phillipe's left—suddenly scampered up the stairs, hands shooting out for the casket in Marie's lap.

Phillipe had no chance to recall even the rudiments Gil had taught him with sticks. He had time only to pivot and bring his sword arm hacking down.

The blade bit to bone. One of the pair shrieked and dropped to his knees, wrist half severed.

"Then it's no terms!" cried the General, sounding almost happy. "Attack, men—*attack!*"

The command was wholly unnecessary. With the exception of the injured beggar who fled down the stairs wailing oaths, the rest advanced as one. The ring closed with the General at the center, so close Phillipe could smell his unbelievably putrid breath.

Phillipe whipped the sword up to block a downward stroke of the General's blade. Metal rang. Sparks flew.

Hands caught at Phillipe's legs, his ankles, tripping him off balance. He fell on the stairs, head striking stone. A beggar stamped on his belly. The General gouged at his eyes with the broken end of his sword.

Despite the pain in his middle, Phillipe managed to wrench his head aside. The General's blade raked more sparks from the stair. Phillipe thrust out with his right arm, took satisfaction when Gil's sword slid through

rags to a thigh. Another beggar howled and scrambled
away.

But the rest piled onto Phillipe, sitting on his legs, his
abdomen. The General kneeled next to his head.

One rough-nailed hand caught Phillipe's hair, lifted,
then smacked his head down on the stair. The other beggars spread-eagled him, pinned his right arm out and
began to scratch and claw his wrist. Phillipe's fingers
opened. He lost the sword.

The General's crooked wig loomed, clearly defined by
a sudden wash of ruddy light behind him. "Cut both
their shitting throats!" the General panted, driving the
end of his blade at Phillipe's neck. Simultaneously,
another voice shouted from the foot of the stairs:

"Let be, Esau! It's none of our affair!"

Phillipe wrenched his head again, violently hard. The
General's blade gashed the left side of his throat, a fiery
track of pain. At the same time, Phillipe heard a loud,
solid thwack.

The General fell on Phillipe, struck from the rear. A
frayed epaulette tickled Phillipe's nose as he fought out
from under the burden.

The General rolled off, staggered to hands and knees,
his lowered head weaving from side to side. His wig,
even further askew, hung down over his left eyebrow.

"Bleeding balls of the martyrs, who be hitting me?"
he groaned. More weight lifted from Phillipe's arms and
legs; the beggars jumping up, scattering down toward
the Yard—

Through blurred eyes, Phillipe glimpsed two sturdy
figures. One, on the stairs, lashed about with a heavy
stick, knocking a head here, a shin there.

The other man down in the Yard took no part. He
was a motionless silhouette against the source of the
ruddy light—a linkboy's torch.

The attacker with the swinging stick thudded and

thwacked the beggars, bawling, "You scum would pick the very linen off Christ on the cross!" He bashed one slow-moving fellow in the side of the head. The man went down in a floundering heap.

Phillipe sat up, a little more clear-headed. Suddenly a noise drew his attention toward Marie.

The General had managed to hold onto his broken blade, shifting it to his left hand as he crouched and reached for the casket. Phillipe saw his own sword being carried off by a beggar whose tatters fluttered as he ran.

Ignoring the warm, sticky wash leaking down his neck into his collar, Phillipe lurched after the thief. He caught him in the Yard and tackled him around the middle.

A-tumble, they rolled back toward the bottom of the stairs. Phillipe used his fist to bludgeon the back of the man's head, heard teeth crack on the paving stones. Then he was on his feet with Gil's sword secure in his sweaty right hand.

The big stranger had caught two more of the hapless beggars and was trouncing them in turn. Mere boys, Phillipe saw by the guttering torch. But he felt no pity—nor had he time for any. The General, one hand clutching his half-sword, the other Marie's casket, was pelting down the steps toward the sanctuary of the darkness beyond the torchlight.

Phillipe drove himself into a run, caught up with the older man and killed him with one sword stroke through the back.

The General crashed onto his belly. The side of his face flattened against the pavement. His mouth flopped open as his bowels emptied, a terrible stench.

The big stranger on the steps paused to search for more enemies; saw none. He jogged down toward Phillipe, slapping his stick against his tight breeches while his companion and the linkboy approached to bend and stare at the General.

Phillipe retrieved the casket. Unbroken, he saw with relief. The stranger who hadn't fought said thickly to the other:

"Now there's murder done, Esau. To whom do we explain that?"

"To no one, Hosea. Because no one cares. Vermin squashed, that's all. They're a ruination of the neighborhood anyway. The good fathers locked up safely inside Paul's can decide what to do with the body in the morning. Let them be thankful decent citizens are protecting their holy sanctuary."

"But the boy—"

"Our linkboy saw nothing. Heard nothing." The big young man with clubbed hair swung toward the shabbily dressed carrier of the torch. "Did you, now?"

"No, Mr. Sholto. I've your money in my pocket to assure I didn't."

"Then let's go home," mumbled the other stranger, still with that slightly thickened speech. He bore a strong resemblance to his companion with the stick. He had the same wide shoulders and heavy, squarish jaw, though he looked to be a year or so younger. Perhaps twenty-one or twenty-two. Rather petulantly, he added, "You'd have us rescuing half the poor in London, I suppose."

"Only those unjustly preyed upon, Hosea."

The young man with the stick approached Phillipe. He had a blunt jaw, a broad nose, thick brows—and a suddenly amiable grin. "I heard the hullabaloo as we rounded yon corner, sir. I saw you put up a nice fight, considering the way they outnumbered you. I am Mr. Esau Sholto. This somewhat tipsy gentleman's my brother, Hosea. He's a good boy, but not of a temperament for street brawling."

"I'm grateful to both of you," Phillipe said. "I think they'd have killed us." He bent down and wiped Gil's blade on the patched back of the General's filthy uniform.

For a moment he glanced at the hideous wound left by his blade. Perhaps because of his feverish condition, or his exhaustion, he felt nothing. He'd changed a great deal since the woods where he'd accidentally killed Gil's would-be kidnapper. Well, so be it. That, apparently, was the price of survival.

Clutching casket and sword, he saw Mr. Esau Sholto flick a speck of dirt from the lacy ruffle at his throat as the latter said:

"Yes, sir, they would have killed you. For that reason, sensible folk stay shuttered indoors at night. Save when one brother must go with another to see he doesn't wager away the family business at the new quinze table in White's public rooms. Were you sleeping by yonder pillar?"

Phillipe nodded. "We came to town this afternoon. A church seemed a good place—"

"No, not any London church or street, after dark," advised Esau Sholto. "But you've learned that lesson, eh? Your speech isn't regular English. Do you come from France?"

Phillipe knew he must be careful. "Originally—some months ago. Then last week, we decided to journey up from—" he hedged the rest— "from the south."

His vision began to swim. He saw a double head on Mr. Esau Sholto's burly shoulders. He blinked away the illusion as Hosea thrust himself between them.

"Good God, Esau, will you have us chatter all night on top of a fresh corpse? Even the scruffy singers who were sleeping yonder have more sense than you. They ran off."

Esau laid a hand on his brother's shoulder. "We'd not have met any trouble at all, I wager, if it had been my kind of evening."

Hosea snorted. "Spring—Vauxhall Gardens open —an hour of that dreadful orchestra music—and home to bed, early and bored."

"Hosea, you are a narrow young man, thinking only of gaming and skirts. If you weren't my brother you'd be a thoroughly detestable fellow. As it is, I find you merely half-detestable. Do the Sunday sermons never bore past your ears?"

"Well, I'm usually dozing, so—"

"How many times has our father read the story of the Samaritan aloud?"

"Thousands," Hosea Sholto sighed. "To savor the King's English—"

"*And* drum some moral precepts into your thick skull. He's failed miserably."

Hosea took the rebuke in embarrassed silence. Esau asked Phillipe, "Have you some means of employment in town?"

"No, sir. But I expect I can find some. You've been of great help, don't trouble yourself furth—"

"I'll trouble myself as long as I please, thank you! Permit me to give you another quick piece of advice. Sleep somewhere else tonight. Far from here. The beggars of St. Paul's are a curious brotherhood. They remember faces. Even voices. They *never* forget grievances. It's the way of the ruined, gin-crazed poor. If you run into some of them again, it won't go easy with you. Or that woman you were protecting. Who is she?"

"My mother."

"Still sleeping," Esau said, sounding surprised.

"She's not well."

Hosea rolled his eyes toward the stars as Mr. Esau Sholto dug thick fingers into his waistcoat pocket.

"Perhaps I can spare a coin for lodging tomorrow night. I don't know a respectable landlord who'd admit you this late. I suggest you and your mother go back west, out toward Mayfair where the beggars seldom rove—"

All at once, St. Paul's Yard began to reverberate with

the heavy clang of bells. Hosea stamped one buckled shoe. "Damme, Esau, it's twelve of the clock already."

"All right, all right, coming!" Esau extended two copper pieces to Phillipe. "Here, and good fortune to you. Let's hope other nights in London prove more hospitable than this one's been. There's work for industrious youngsters—"

"Younger in years, maybe," Hosea grumbled. "Look at his eyes. Living to four-and-twenty hasn't given you a corner on keen observation, you know."

With a tolerant chuckle, Mr. Esau Sholto dropped the coppers into Phillipe's hand. Somehow he lacked the power to close his fist. All at once his teeth were clacking. Waves of weakness, then nausea, wiped out his strength. He lurched forward.

Phillipe crashed against Esau Sholto, dropping the casket, the sword, the money. The coppers rang on the paving stones as he slipped to his knees at Esau's feet.

"Here!" exclaimed the big young man. "His mother's not the only one in bad health, it seems." Phillipe felt a callused palm on his cheek. "Why, his head's hot as the bottom of a kettle."

Phillipe mumbled apologies, tried to stand, couldn't. Esau's voice seemed to echo from a far distance:

"And that slash on his neck badly needs dressing—"

"Oh, damme, I suppose you'll summon the most expensive physician in London!" Hosea complained. Phillipe's skull rang and hummed. He saw only a blurred glow, as if the linkboy's torch had been lost in fog. He scrabbled blindly till one hand bumped Marie's casket.

"And why not?" Esau Sholto retorted. "You won at cards for a change. We've plenty of empty rooms. You go fetch the woman, you mean-souled wretch. Be quick, or I'll give you the kind of knocking I gave those beggars!"

Hosea's voice retreated: "Dear God, what would I be without you for a conscience?"

"A sot, flat broke, afflicted of the whore's pox—not to mention detestable."

Big hands supported Phillipe under his arms. He let the foggy orange delirium give way to the dark of unconsciousness.

iii

A beamed ceiling, dark with age. Beneath his head, a feather pillow of amazing softness.

He felt other sensations. The scratch of some kind of wool garment against his legs. A nightshirt? The thickness of a plaster dressing on his neck, where the General's broken blade had gashed.

The bed was a place of incredible warmth and comfort, thanks to the feather-filled blanket. But the bedframe vibrated occasionally from heavy thudding somewhere below.

He smelled something hot and fragrant, focused on a china cup held in the tiny hand of a small, mobcapped woman whose face was a crisscross of wrinkles.

"Can you drink this?" the woman asked. "Esau said you speak English although you're French—do you understand me?"

He nodded, astonished that he found himself in such luxurious circumstances.

"I doubt you've eaten in a while," she said.

He shook his head to agree.

"That's the reason we'll begin gently, with some black Bohea."

She cradled the back of his head with one hand, held the cup to his lips. He gulped, then spluttered. The woman laughed.

"Slowly, slowly!"

Thus, still feverish, Phillipe was initiated to his first taste of a beverage that, later, came to symbolize the essence of the haven he'd found. A haven whose full nature and identity he did not yet know.

He drank more of the strong tea, thanked the woman, said, "My mother was with me—"

"She's asleep on the other side of that wall. She'll mend with rest, I think. I bore Mr. Sholto five children. But only my two sons lived. The three little girls died early. Since we bought this house for a sizable brood, we've no lack of space."

The little woman said all this without a hint of pity for herself. As she left his bedside, she added:

"My son Esau has his father's good sense. Hosea is a good boy too, but he drinks too much. In fact Mr. Sholto caned him six times for being so reluctant to help last night. Hosea apologizes. Now try to sleep if you can."

With that she vanished, closing the door behind her.

Phillipe drifted back to drowsiness against the pillow, marveling at the comfort, at how safe he felt. Most miraculous of all was the renewed realization that the world was not entirely populated by Amberlys.

The occasional thudding continued below. Speculating on the cause of it—such a tame problem for a change—he slept.

iv

Mrs. Emma Sholto would not let him get up, except to use the chamber pot, for three days.

Big-shouldered Esau appeared a few times, wearing black-smeared breeches and an equally stained jerkin over a full-sleeved shirt. And Hosea visited too, once, rather sheepishly. He was equally black-stained and smeared.

Hosea stated that he hoped the visitors were receiving good care and recovering their strength. Then he said with a guilty smile:

"Esau keeps reminding me I've no capacity for port.

You do understand I was somewhat drunk in the churchyard?"

"You really didn't show much sign of it." Phillipe smiled back.

Hosea looked chagrined. "Some fall down. Some puke up their guts. But I walk around like a perfectly normal fellow—paying no attention to anyone but myself. I got Mr. Sholto's cane across the ass several times, by way of chastisement."

"Your mother mentioned that."

"I also got extra evening work, which I suppose is good. I won't squander so much of what I earn at the clubs. We'll produce our new editions more speedily. I'm not altogether certain whether Mr. Sholto's insistence that I work more hours is chiefly in the interest of punishment or profit."

Phillipe hitched higher in the bed. The plaster aside his neck itched. "Editions? Do you mean books?"

"What else? Don't you recognize this hellish black paste?" He displayed his smeared hands. "It takes hours to scrub it from under the fingernails. I thought you'd have heard the press thumping, too."

"I did, but I couldn't identify the sound."

"We work downstairs, live upstairs. This is Sholto and Sons, Printers and Stationers, of Sweet's Lane. Only a few paces from where we found you. Well—I'm under orders not to tire you out. Just wanted to make amends for the other evening—"

Phillipe grinned. "Not necessary."

With a wave and a smile, Hosea left.

Reflecting on his new circumstances, Phillipe again drifted into deep, relaxed sleep.

v

On the evening of Phillipe's fourth day in the Sholto household, the patriarch himself appeared for the first time. At least if the man had looked in before, Phillipe hadn't been aware of it.

In truth, he probably wouldn't have known if a coach thundered through the room. He had been luxuriating in sleep and security.

Mr. Sholto was a small person, lacking the breadth of shoulder of his sons. Both of them appeared with their father, standing behind him as he took the only chair in the modestly furnished bedroom.

Mr. Sholto's most prominent features were his over-sized stomach, all out of proportion to the rest of him, his stern brown eyes and his aroma of ink.

The printer subjected Phillipe to a careful scrutiny, as if totting up his impressions before starting a conversation. His tiny, wrinkled wife appeared with a tray. Crisp-crusted mutton pie, a roast apple, a cup of the inevitable Bohea.

"Well, sir, I am Solomon Sholto," said the gray-haired man at last, as Phillipe dug into the mutton pie with ferocious hunger. "You are French, I understand. You have a mother in our next bedroom, and both of you were beset by the ungodly rascals who loiter at St. Paul's after dark. That's most of what I know. Are you well enough to tell me anything more?"

"First, Mr. Sholto, that we'll be in your debt forever for your kindness. I wish we could repay you."

"Who has asked for payment? We do our duty to our fellow men, according to the precepts of the Scriptures." The brown eyes darted momentarily to Hosea, who had wandered to the far corner of the bed, perching there until his father glanced his way. Immediately he stood up. He clasped his inky hands together, first at his waist, then behind him. Leaning against the wall, big Esau covered a smirk with one black-nailed hand.

"Your mother has wakened once or twice," Mr. Sholto said. "But the fever still claims her. And so far, we don't know your names."

"Mine's Phillipe Charboneau, sir. Of the province of Auvergne."

"A long way from London," the elder Sholto observed. "What brings you to the city?"

Phillipe hesitated, the teacup at his lips; he was already beginning to like the strange, strong brew.

"Come, sir," Mr. Sholto chided firmly. "Enlighten us! French people don't simply pop up from nowhere. Unless you're an escaped murderer destined for hemp out on Tyburn Road, you've nothing to fear."

Phillipe thought a moment, then said carefully, "We came to England because of an inheritance."

"Somehow connected with that box you guarded so well?" Esau wanted to know.

"Yes, it—where is the casket?" he asked abruptly.

"Safe in the wardrobe in your mother's room," Mrs. Emma Sholto assured him.

"Along with that French sword," Hosea put in. "I'd give a deal to be able to hang that elegant sticker at my hip next time I visit White's."

"You and the fleshpots of St. James's Street," grumbled Solomon Sholto, "will not become reacquainted for quite some time. Would God that those infernal dens would shut all their rooms to the merchant classes, not just their subscription rooms. But extra presswork will serve the same temporary purpose. And allow time for reflection on the sins of drunkenness and vanity, which permit no thought for the well-being of others."

Hosea cringed. Esau again looked amused, only this time he let the amusement become a guffaw. Solomon Sholto silenced him with a glare equally as stern as the one he'd thrown Hosea. Then he continued to Phillipe:

"We do not pry into the belongings of our guests, you may be certain. So whatever's in the leather box, only you know."

But his straightforward gaze as he hunched over, one

ink-stained hand on his knee, indicated that he would
very much like the information.

Phillipe glanced from face to face. Esau. Hosea. The
small, strong wife. And finally the heavy-bellied head of
the household—

Danger seemed remote. He offered a hint to test that
conclusion:

"My mother and I fled from a village in Kent because
we incurred the wrath of a great family. My life was
threatened. We thought we'd be safer in the city
crowds."

Mr. Sholto said nothing, merely continued to stare.
Warmed by the food and by these plain, open faces,
Phillipe felt resistance and suspicion melt. It was a relief
to speak.

He told them most of it, omitting only the primary
reason for the fateful struggle with Roger—Alicia.

At the end, he leaned back on the pillow with his
hands around the still-warm teacup, awaiting a reaction.

"*Amberly!*" Mr. Sholto exclaimed with sudden
animation, hopping up and pacing the plank floor. "I
don't wonder you fled from that high-handed Tory
crowd. This house is of a different persuasion. The Whig
persuasion, which does not fully approve of the an-
tidemocratic policies of the King or his puppet
ministers—that little clique of King's Friends. From all
I know of Whitehall gossip, your father would have been
welcomed to that group with enthusiasm, had he not suffered an untimely death."

"My mother speaks nothing but good of James Amberly," Phillipe protested. "It was the same with the
landlord and several others in Tonbridge."

"Yes, well—the dead are the dead. Why haggle over
their politics? I rather admire your audacity in challenging such a family. But I sense you have discovered what
I could have told you merely from knowing the Duchess
of Kentland's reputation. You waged a lost battle from

the start. Nor would you be any more successful here, I expect. For every twisty-tongued lawyer you could buy, they could buy a baker's twelve, plus judges, magistrates—and thugs of every ilk, if that became necessary. When a woman like the Duchess wishes to refuse your claim, it *will* be refused, fair means or foul. Babies from the wrong sides of noble blankets can be found on every street in London. Some very few are lucky. Press their causes to successful ends. But most fail. For your own safety and peace of mind—as well as your mother's—I'd advise you to give up your quest, find a means to earn enough money to pay your way back to France, and forget the whole matter. Above all, say absolutely nothing about your claim—and your origins—outside this house. You'll never become rich, but you'll live longer."

Emma Sholto rested a tiny hand on her husband's shoulder. "He's tiring, Solomon."

"Nonsense, he's a stout young man."

"Still, I insist we let him go to sleep."

Garrumphing, Mr. Solomon Sholto pushed the chair back to its place. He herded his sons toward the door. Both stared at Phillipe with new appreciation.

After the printer's wife had gone, Esau and Hosea lingered in the hall while the elder Sholto paused in the doorway.

"Should you decide to follow my advice, young man, and wish to do honest labor to accumulate that passage money back to France, we might be able to make a place for you here."

"I wouldn't want special favors, Mr. Sholto."

"None given, sir! You'd be in for hard work, I guarantee."

"Don't London craftsmen keep apprentices to help them?"

"Aye, and I've had two. Both have run off. I am demanding, but not cruel. The lads, however, considered me the latter. I wouldn't tolerate the swilling of gin by ten-year-old boys. Where they came by the stuff, I preferred not to know. Stole it? Killed for it?" He shrugged unhappily. "They were already so hardened before I took them on, they reminded me more of ancient dwarfs than children hopeful of learning a trade."

"Bad sorts, both of 'em," Esau agreed.

Phillipe broke in to say that the Methodist landlord of Wolfe's Triumph had mentioned the evils of gin drinking among the London lower classes.

"Then," said Mr. Sholto, "there's a point at which I, a High Churchman, and your friend of a Dissenting sect, may agree. But it's no wonder boys like that must besot themselves early in order to survive. They're brutalized from age seven or eight on up. With long hours. Backbreaking labor suitable only for grown men. The abuses of inhumane masters. I don't blame a lad who's known nothing but brutality and poverty for learning to drink, and drink hard, almost as soon as he can walk. For that reason, I did not order pursuit of either of the runaways—you realize there are severe punishments for the crime? Fingers or toes may be cut off. The two boys I lost one after another will be punished enough before their days run out all too soon. Ah, but I'm chattering on—Mrs. Emma will have after me in earnest. You've heard we have an opportunity here. Esau could teach you the fundamentals, I imagine—"

"Right quickly," Esau grinned.

"And it's a noble trade, because it promulgates that which neither kings nor armies can put down. The free traffic of the ideas of men's minds."

A small, protesting voice sounded from down the hall.

"Yes, Emma, yes—a moment more!" He looked at Phillipe. "To put it plain, we would welcome your assistance. Especially since some in the firm prefer virgins' sighs to vellum bindings. The offer is open."

The door closing hid the three—including Hosea, who had turned all red again.

vi

The next day, Phillipe made his way to Marie's room. He told her of the printer's advice, finishing, "I think I'd best accept Mr. Sholto's offer."

Marie protested instantly: "No! I will not let you give up the claim!"

"Just for a time," he said, with quiet authority. Inside his mind, a faint voice mocked him:

Or do you really mean forever?

Marie started to argue again, then looked closely at her son's face. It seemed older, showing the understanding of hard lessons recently learned. She put her head back on the pillow and turned away.

Phillipe left the room with a sense of sadness. Yet he was excited by a fresh sense of purpose, too. A purpose born of plain, homely kindness, of black tea—and the new world of presses and books waiting for him downstairs.

CHAPTER II

The Black Miracle

i

THE BUSINESS establishment of Mr. Solomon Sholto was divided into two sections. The smaller, occupying the front part of the main floor, opened onto the clatter of Sweet's Lane. This was the stationer's shop, where Mrs. Emma presided over the sale of an assortment of drawing and memorandum books, fine Amsterdam Black writing ink, quills, sealing wax and sand.

During the preceding year Mr. Sholto had expanded the shop with a new service—a lending library. Several similar libraries had become popular in recent years because, as Mr. Sholto explained it, only the rich could readily plunk down two guineas for a personal copy of a monumental literary achievement such as *The Dramatick Works of Wm. Shakespeare, Corrected and Illustrated by Samuel Johnson,* which ran to eight annotated volumes with deluxe Turkish leather binding.

Mr. Sholto bemoaned the popularity of "frivolous" fictional tales such as Defoe's *Moll Flanders,* Fielding's *Tom Jones* and Johnson's moralizing fable, *Rasselas.* But he was quick to recognize the commercial appeal of such works. As a result, his lending shelves had expanded to fill two walls of the tiny shop and were crowded with all manner of novels, as well as nonfiction. Phillipe was captivated by some of the lurid fiction titles. *Delicate Distress. Married Victim. Adventures of an Actress.*

But he had little time for reading. Mr. Sholto was, as promised, a demanding taskmaster. He kept Phillipe busy in the noisier part of the business, in the back.

Here, two tall, wooden flat-bed presses sat on platforms flanking a central work area. On these premises Mr. Sholto and his sons did the production work for their clients—booksellers in the Strand, Ludgate Street, Paternoster Row. Sholto's churned out editions on individual contract to each seller.

Mr. Sholto and his sons divided the labor according to the skills of each. Esau, who looked the least graceful because of his size, proved to have hands of amazing speed and dexterity. These hands plucked the metal type letter by letter, then locked it into the large chase. The chase held a form of four pages. Mr. Sholto had invested in presses of some size, to be able to print that many pages at one time.

The father and his other, more easily bemused son were responsible for operating the two machines. Mr. Sholto was faster and more expert. But Hosea knew what he was doing. When Phillipe would lug one of the astonishingly heavy chases over to him, Hosea would lift it as if it weighed nothing.

Hosea would then seat the chase in the coffin, which sat on the rails of the horizontal carriage. He would place a dampened sheet of paper between the tympan and frisket hinged to the coffin, then snap his fingers for Phillipe to be at his work.

To the new employee fell the task of inking a pair of leather balls. The balls were used to apply the ink to the waiting type. Though the balls had handles, it was messy work. Phillipe's leather apron, as well as his face, hands and forearms, was constantly sticky and smeared.

On his first few tries, Phillipe failed to press hard enough, leaving several lines of type uninked. But all three Sholtos were patient. They sensed Phillipe's eagerness to learn. Within a couple of days he had the hang of it and could ink a form neatly with no difficulty.

As soon as Phillipe finished the routine at one press, he frequently needed to run to the other to perform the same job. Hosea, meantime, would clamp the sheet between tympan and frisket, and fold both down so that the paper showed through the frisket in four page-sized cutout sections. These cutouts permitted the paper to come in contact with the inked metal.

Next Hosea would slide the coffin under the massive vertical head of the press. Hauling on the screw lever lowered a four-inch-thick piece of hardwood on top of the closed coffin. The leverage thus applied brought the thick platen down with sufficient pressure to leave an impression on the paper.

Finally, the platen was raised, the coffin pulled back along the rails and the finished four pages removed as a single sheet and set aside to dry. A new sheet was inserted in the coffin and the process was repeated, with re-inkings as necessary, until the right number of sheets had been run.

Handling his chores on both presses, each of which creaked and thunked outrageously, kept Phillipe running from one platform to the other virtually all the time.

But in spare moments, he was also assigned the task of washing the ink from each form once Hosea or Mr. Sholto had finished with it. To do this, Phillipe used a foul-smelling alkali solution that not only removed the ink from metal—and his knuckles—but left his hands raw by the end of the long day. The print shop operated from before daylight till after sunset every day except Sunday.

As the winter of 1771 approached, Phillipe grew

fairly skilled at his job. His hands became swift and adept with the leather balls. His arms strengthened from carrying big stacks of dried sheets printed on both sides. The sheets were taken away by the apprentice who worked for Mr. Sholto's bookbinder. Sholto had long ago decided that he could produce books more quickly by subcontracting the sheet cutting, the sewing of the binding and the mounting of the leather-covered boards.

What gave Phillipe the energy to endure the always tiring, often confusing weeks was his interest in, and admiration for, the process of which he'd become a small part. It struck him as downright amazing that so many black-inked pages, precisely alike, could be produced at such speed by the rattling presses.

One noon, the elder Sholto noticed the way Phillipe's eye kept straying to a stack of finished sheets, even while he paused to munch sections of an ink-smeared orange. Sholto came down from his press platform and waved at the stack:

"Gad, Phillipe, you look as though you were in church! That's only a small reprinting of the *Wild* novel, which is certainly one of Mr. Fielding's lesser works."

"But to see words duplicated so easily—it really is like a miracle. In Auvergne, if you wanted a chair, the furniture maker carved and glued it with his hands, one chair at a time."

"Machines are the coming thing. All over England, factories spin cloth—spit out iron bars. The age of handwork is gone."

Wiping his fingers on his apron, Mr. Sholto accepted a wedge of orange Phillipe offered.

"Despite the way I complain about the trashiness of so many books, I love the business. Reading's the means by which the lowest man can lift himself from a state of ignorance. You see how popular my little loan library up front has become. The masses are hungry for words and

more words. Whether the words be for diversion or
enlightenment, printing them, as I've said before, is a
profession of which a man can feel rightly proud."

Popping a piece of orange into his mouth, Phillipe
could only nod in agreement. Ideas multiplied me-
chanically, for all to share, certainly had to be one of
those new winds sweeping the world. And he was
delighted to be at the heart of the gale.

ii

During her first weeks in the Sholto household, Marie
seemed to recover some of her health. Color returned to
her cheeks. She even showed a certain animation when
Hosea and Esau discussed affairs of the town at supper.

But she said nothing about the Amberlys, not even to
her son. Phillipe didn't mind. He was too occupied with
the exciting, tiring work downstairs even to think about
the casket and the letter. It was Hosea who first brought
the subject up again.

The family was gathered in the upstairs sitting room,
an hour before the customary nine o'clock household
bedtime. Mr. Sholto was reading a *Gazette*, a penny
paper containing, among other items, the latest bad
news about the great East India Trading Company. The
company's mismanaged affairs had caused its stock to
take another alarming dip, he reported. He was thankful
he owned no shares. The household did not use the
products imported by the firm. Mrs. Emma served
cheaper tea smuggled in from Holland. It was sold
everywhere.

The printer's wife sat doing embroidery while
Phillipe, already yawning, sprawled at his mother's feet,
listening to big Esau run through some melodic country
dances on the flute he played with considerable skill.

Hosea, who had excused himself to visit the jakes, walked back in to say:

"Phillipe, I've been making some inquiries in the coffee and chocolate houses—"

"Concerning which gambling establishments are the most lenient with credit?" asked his father.

Hosea flushed. "No, sir. About the man responsible for bringing our lively helper to England."

Esau took the flute from his lips. Emma Sholto frowned. Solomon Sholto folded the penny sheet into his lap. Only Marie failed to respond. She continued to stare into space as if still entranced by the music.

Hosea sensed the tension generated by his remark, and quickly defended himself: "I thought there might be some interest in what's been said about the Duke's passing."

That lifted Marie's head slightly. Phillipe saw remembered hurt in her eyes.

Speaking rapidly, Hosea continued, "The curious thing is—nothing's been said."

Mr. Sholto exclaimed, "What?"

"That's right. As far as I can discover, no word of Amberly's death has come up to town."

"You're not exactly in the circles that would be the first to know," observed Esau.

"Yes, but the public rooms are always full of gossip about the leading peers of the realm. No one's breathed a word. I—I thought it puzzling," he finished lamely.

Emma Sholto said, "Perhaps the Amberlys have retired to a long period of private grief. Perhaps they prefer to say nothing of the death outside the immediate family until a suitable mourning period is over. Loss of a loved one can affect an entire household for months, you know."

Mr. Sholto put one hand over his eyes. Was he recalling his three dead infant daughters? Phillipe wondered with a touch of sadness.

In response to Hosea's obvious embarrassment, Marie said, "You needn't worry about mentioning him in my presence. The kindness Phillipe and I have found in this house has healed the wounds of the past."

Phillipe was pleased at that. Whether his mother did or did not mean what she said—and he felt she didn't, fully—the sentiment was correct. Marie went on:

"The presence of my son and I taxed Lady Jane to the extreme. Perhaps the death did indeed affect her mind. They shut the Duke up in a foul, airless room while he ailed. I wouldn't wonder they've chosen the same kind of solitude for themselves. They're peculiar, twisted people."

Somehow Phillipe wasn't entirely satisfied with the explanation. But he could offer none better. He yawned behind his hand, anxious to retire. He thought the matter closed until he heard Marie say softly:

"However, Hosea, if any word should come to you on your rounds, I would welcome hearing it."

Scowling, Phillipe stared at his hands reddened by the alkali solution. The past was past. Why couldn't she let it go?

Esau noticed his expression, promptly took up his flute and began another country dance. Marie was soon lost in her private reverie.

Seeing what? Phillipe wondered sourly. Himself? Still as the little lord?

Well, he had other ideas now. He had already begun to formulate the first tentative plans for a possible future. A future far more realistic than that which had dragged them to England, and to grief.

iii

As October waned, the first brief snowflakes fell on the great city of bells. But immediately, the weather turned pleasant again. Phillipe and his mother began to go out and see the sights with the family.

On a Sabbath afternoon all flamed with sunlight falling through the coloring leaves, they strolled St. James's Park. On another unusually warm Sunday, after the printer and his wife had, as usual, worshiped at St. Paul's, they took a short barge trip down the Thames to view the Tower, whose history Mr. Sholto could describe in gory detail.

At one point on the return upriver, two elderly female passengers and their male escort paused next to Hosea, who was lounging against the rail and staring at the sky in a bemused fashion. Suddenly, with scandalized expressions, the ladies pointed to the water between the barge and the stately Parliament buildings on the north bank.

"Whoever it is, he should be prosecuted for profaning the Sabbath with vigorous activity!" declared one of the thin-lipped women.

As Hosea turned to follow the accusing fingers, the second lady gasped, "I believe his shoulders are entirely unclothed!"

The gentleman peered. "Perhaps the rest of him, too."

"Scandalous!" said the first woman.

Hosea smiled in a languid way. "He's traveling in the river—we're traveling on it. What's the difference?"

"If you don't know, then you are obviously an irreligious person," the first woman snapped. Hosea looked nonplused.

Along with a number of other passengers, Mr. Sholto and his party crowded around the outraged trio. Phillipe looked past the printer to see a most curious and unexpected sight: something which at first glance resembled a small white whale paddling and splashing downstream.

Only after he shielded his eyes against the sun's glare

did the peculiar aquatic specimen take on definition. It was a man—and not a young one—swimming vigorously. On the embankment, a band of urchins followed the swimmer's progress, whistling and offering merrily obscene encouragement.

"It would serve the fellow right if he drowned!" the first woman said.

"Charity, Aunt Eunice, charity!" the man said. "It might be that he's suffering some mental lapse. There is nothing more pathetic than a gentleman of middle age who vainly attempts to behave like a youth. Don't scorn such derangement. Pity it."

At this, Mr. Sholto chuckled. "You're off the mark, sir. The gentleman is far from deranged. To the contrary—he's a scientist and diplomat of the first rank. Keen of mind. And he swims the Thames often."

"Damme, yes!" Hosea exclaimed with a snap of his fingers. "I thought I recognized him." He took no notice when one of the ladies appeared faint after he cursed.

"But—but the chap looks sixty years old!" the male escort sputtered.

"Very nearly," Sholto nodded. "He has a rugged constitution, however." The printer cupped a hand to his mouth and hailed, "Franklin! Ho, Dr. Franklin—over here!"

The racket made by the swimmer's youthful admirers on the embankment prevented him from hearing. He continued downriver, his thrashing arms and legs churning up water that sparkled in the sunshine.

One of the narrow-lipped ladies whirled on Mr. Sholto.

"Do you mean to say that is *the* Dr. Franklin? The godless wizard from the colonies?"

"I don't believe your adjectives are entirely correct, madam. 'Godless?' Perhaps. Certainly he doesn't observe the Sabbath as strictly as some of us." Mr. Sholto harrumphed for emphasis. "But 'wizard'? I think not. Rather, call him a genius. Of international repute."

"You seem well acquainted with him," the woman sniffed; it was far from a compliment.

"Yes, we take coffee together when my schedule permits. And he does visit my bookshop on occasion—when *his* duties as business agent for the Massachusetts colony don't keep him running from one ministerial office to another—"

"Genius or not," the woman retorted, "I have read something about his tamperings with the divine mysteries of nature. 'The modern Prometheus,' isn't that what he's called in some quarters?"

"Aye, so the philosopher Kant christened him."

"I still say anyone who meddles with the heavenly fire is santanically inspired!"

Annoyed, Mr. Sholto replied, "Then you are merely displaying your ignorance, my good woman. Of all the scientific thinkers of the modern world, it was that very Dr. Franklin—" his hand shot toward the bow, and the diminishing glitter of water marking the swimmer's passage.—"who brought the study of what scholars term 'electricity' out of the province of superstition and into full respectability. Furthermore—"

Mrs. Emma tapped her husband's elbow. "Solomon, please."

"No!" exclaimed the printer. "I will not have a friend vilified. Are you not aware, my dear ladies, that 'Franklin' is the most famous American name in the civilized world? Are you not aware that our own Royal Society awarded him its highest honor, the Copley medal, for his *Experiments and Observations on Electricity* in fifty-two? He proved that lightning contains the same electrical forces which had previously been observed in laboratories at the University of Leyden and elsewh—"

But the trio of outraged puritans had turned their backs.

At first Mr. Sholto looked furious. Then, after his wife patted his arm several more times, he sighed, resigned. He gestured Phillipe, Marie and his family to another section of the deck, to prevent further friction.

Phillipe craned for one more view of the swimmer. He stared in fascination at the tiny figure still splashing down the great river.

"Solomon, that was not polite," Mrs. Emma chided.

"I know, but I can't abide stupidity. Franklin may not hold much brief for any sort of church, but he's no more devil than I am!" Catching Hosea's start of a smile, Sholto added, "No remarks from you, sir."

Marie wandered to the rail, indifferent to the conversation. Phillipe remained intrigued.

"And he's an American, you say?"

"Indeed. Nor was I exaggerating about his reputation. He's known all the way to the court of Imperial Russia. Do you know how he started his career? As a printer!"

Sholto's pride was obvious. Warming to his subject, he went on, "When he and his son performed their experiment at Philadelphia, and published the results, Franklin was immediately hailed throughout the world as a scientist of the first rank. But there's hardly a field of man's knowledge to which he hasn't added some improvement. When he couldn't find the proper type of spectacles to suit his weakening eyesight, he invented them. He was dissatisfied with the street lighting in his home city, so he created a better fixture. When his rooms got too cold, he built the famous Pennsylvania stove. And as deputy master of the colonial postal network, he overhauled the entire system, making it possible for a letter to travel from Philadelphia to Boston in two or three weeks instead of six or eight. Do you wonder I feel privileged to be his acquaintance?"

Phillipe looked thoughtfully past the stern of the barge. "I don't know a thing about those scientific subjects. But yes, I can see why you'd admire him. It's plain he has an independent spirit. I'd like to meet a man like that. One who won't let himself be trod on by others—"

Solomon Sholto raised a cautioning hand. "Don't get the wrong idea. Dr. Franklin is a loyal Englishman. His own natural son William—"

"Must you bring up such indelicate subjects on Sunday?" sighed Mrs. Emma.

"Well, Franklin makes no secret that his first-born's a bastard. By a woman whose name I've never heard him speak—" Belatedly, Sholto caught his wife's glance at Phillipe and with some show of embarrassment exclaimed, "But he loves his son no less for that. If anything, he loves him the more! William Franklin's the royal governor of the New Jersey colony, Phillipe. So don't go thinking his father is the Crown's enemy. A stiff partisan of colonial rights, yes—but within the law."

Phillipe wished again that he might have the chance to meet such a free-thinking gentleman face to face. He was ready to ask about the possibility when a yell from one of the watermen signaled their approach to the pier. In the rush attending debarkation, he had no chance to discuss the subject further. But the famous American was much in his thoughts in succeeding days.

In the lending library he located a copy of Franklin's study on electricity, which included an account of the celebrated "Philadelphia experiment." Phillipe was confused by a great part of the material, knowing nothing of the theoretical background or terminology. He did get the impression that considerable danger must have been involved when the doctor and his illegitimate son sent their kite aloft in a violent thunderstorm, then waited for the "heavenly fire" to travel down the string to a metal key.

Mr. Sholto confirmed the danger. So potent was the force which Franklin believed was contained in lightning, he had literally risked instant death performing the experiment. Fortunately, when he touched the key at the critical moment, he felt no more than a repeated tingling in hand and arm—the "electrick spark" that gave him international fame instead of an ignominious grave.

With such knowledge to be gained from it, London remained a constantly unfolding series of wonders and diversions for Phillipe. He spent another free afternoon strolling the far western reaches of the town with Esau. There, on the site of the great May fairs of the years past, fine new residences of the nobility were beginning to rise below the Tyburn Road. Esau discoursed on the new Georgian architectural style, which he much admired.

And one weekday evening, over Mr. Sholto's protests about trivial amusements, Hosea was permitted to take Phillipe and his mother to the gallery at Drury Lane. They watched a performance of a lively farce called *High Life Below Stairs*. Marie clapped and laughed with such animation that Phillipe felt she might be starting to free herself from the grip of the past.

Afterward, Hosea apologized for having chosen a play in which the great Mr. Garrick appeared only to speak the prologue instead of playing a leading role. But Marie was thrilled just to have seen the famous actor whose name had been well known in Paris when she performed there.

At Christmas, the family gathered for a festive dinner of roast mutton and many side dishes, all capped by plum pudding. Mr. Sholto matter-of-factly presented a gift to each of their boarders. Phillipe received a new shirt of white wool, Marie a set of tortoise combs. She wept happily at the table, and later was prevailed on to perform a lively dance in the sitting room, while Esau piped on his flute.

Outside, snow drifted down in Sweet's Lane. The bells of St. Paul's clanged in the lowering darkness of Christmas Day. Phillipe felt stuffed, warm and content.

But he realized it was time to begin giving serious consideration to the future. The few shillings Mr. Sholto paid him for his work in the print shop were beginning to accumulate in a kerchief he kept under his pillow. He needed to broach the subject of a return to Auvergne. He hoped to discourage Marie from going back to a life of managing a dilapidated wayside inn.

He had a better plan. Or should it be termed a dream? Either way, it filled most of his waking thoughts. To give it room to grow, he asked Hosea after the turn of the New Year whether he had yet heard anything about Amberly's death.

Hosea answered, "No, nothing."

Phillipe actually felt relieved. There was no doubt they would have to begin again. But why automatically back in France? Why not in another part of the world?

He had been borrowing books from the lending shelves in the front shop, where Marie helped Mrs. Emma from time to time. Late at night, he had begun reading about the American colonies.

iv

In early February, a spell of bitter weather struck London. Mr. Sholto fell ill with a wracking cough, then fever. With the printing staff reduced to three, Phillipe worked even longer hours.

Esau still handled the typesetting because his hands were so skillful. But Phillipe took on new duties in addition to inking, washing the metal and lugging the finished sheets out to the binder's cart. Under Hosea's guidance, he began to operate the other press.

As with the ink balls, he was clumsy at first. He misaligned sheets between the tympan and frisket. He didn't lever the platen down far enough to produce the right weight and resulting good impression. But the mistakes were quickly corrected. And despite the elder Sholto's eternal remonstrances that Hosea was of light temperament, the young man proved a good and patient teacher. Phillipe's blood began to throb with the beat of the press.

Thunk, roll the coffin under the upright head. *Squeal,* pull the lever to tighten down the weight. *Squeak,* screw it up again. *Thunk,* retract the coffin and whip out the inked sheet. Then do it faster next time—

He no longer thought about the letter in the casket. He thought only occasionally about Alicia Parkhurst. Although her memory would never totally leave him, in the reality of his new life he recalled their love affair as if it were a dream. Full of pain and sweetness while it lasted. But ultimately unreal.

The rhythm of the flat-bed press created a new pattern to his days, a mounting hope. He gave voice to that hope one twilight late in February.

"No, Solomon! I forbid it!" Mrs. Emma cried, rushing down the stairs after her husband. The elder Sholto had appeared in his nightshirt, coughing and looking abnormally pale. "You're not well yet!"

"Cease, woman! If you want food on your table, I must look to the welfare of my business."

He closed the stair door with a bang, hiding his wife's dismayed face.

Sholto raised his eyebrows at the sight of Phillipe, smudged black from forehead to waist. Phillipe was tugging the lever to lower the platen for another impression.

"So we've a new hand on the press, do we?"

"And a mighty swift one he's turning out to be," Esau

called from the type cases. His hands kept flying, independent of anything else.

"What's the work?" Sholto inquired, coming up the steps to Phillipe's press as the latter slipped a new, dampened sheet into place.

"A reprinting for Bemis in the Strand," Hosea informed his father from the other side of the room.

"It looks interesting," Phillipe said. "Written by a Mr. Dickinson of the Pennsylvania colony."

Mr. Sholto nodded. "It's a very lucid discourse on the position of the colonists in regard to taxes. A position supported by quite a few leading Americans—including Dr. Franklin."

"I'd have guessed that from what little I know about him," Phillipe nodded.

"Dickinson's book is already four years old. But it continues to sell nicely. He's a lawyer, by the way. Trained right here at the Inns of Court. He struck the proper tone in his arguments. Many in Lords and Commons heartily approved of his sentiments and his reasoning."

"Then I'll have to read what he says when I have time."

"Phillipe's gobbling up the library—every available piece of material on the colonies," Hosea said. "Good *or* bad."

"Nothing wrong with that," Sholto said to Phillipe, "so long as you understand that many who have taken up the quill to write about America have never been west of Charing Cross."

Phillipe said, "I've noticed that some of the books on the subject are fifty and sixty years old."

"And most of 'em paint a false, visionary picture of instant wealth for the hardy man who will but set foot on those shores. It's true in isolated cases. But as much depends on the man as on the country. For a more realistic picture, you'd do well to look through another monograph of Franklin's. One which he also wrote in the fifties. It brought him nearly as much recognition here and in Europe as the electrical discourse. By combining mathematics with sharp social insights, he produced a truly brilliant study of the potential for growth in the Americas."

"What's the name of the work?"

"*Observations Concerning the Increase of Mankind and Peopling of Countries.*" Sholto glanced at his elder son. "We own two copies in the front, do we not?"

"We did," Esau answered. "Both are gone. One fell to rags, and someone never returned the other." To Phillipe: "The book hardly came in but it was taken right out again."

"Perhaps we can turn up another copy. In any case, Phillipe, I think a realistic appraisal of the colonies is this. They do seem to be raising a new sort of person over there. Tougher. A mite more independent than those of us who've stayed home. And the land *is* bounteous. The southern colonies are rich from agriculture, the northern ones from commerce—you've heard how the merchants here exerted pressures on Parliament to repeal the obnoxious taxes about which Lawyer Dickinson was writing?"

Phillipe said he had.

"When the colonial trade fell off, all Britain suffered. That's proof the Americans are prospering. Becoming important to the Empire economically. For the time being, things are relatively calm over there. If that situation continues, I'm sure a good life—even riches—can be won. But not without diligence."

The printer stifled another cough and squinted at Phillipe. "Why does the subject interest you so much?"

"I've been thinking that one of the colonies might be a good place for my mother and me to settle."

"Ah—" Sholto smiled. "My guess was correct. But what trade would you follow?"

"Why, the one you and your sons have taught so well. You said your friend the doctor prospered in the printing business—"

"Hardly the word for it. He grew rich. First he ran a widely read newspaper. Then, with an eye on the commercial success being enjoyed by annual almanacs, he started his own. When he couldn't hire a suitable philomath for his publication—"

"A suitable what, sir?"

"Philomath. Resident astrologer. Predictor of the weather—giver of sage advice. Every almanac must have its philomath. Franklin couldn't find a scrivener capable of turning out work up to his standards, so he dreamed up Richard Saunders—and proceeded to write all of Poor Richard's pronouncements himself. Practically put the competing almanacs out of business, too. Poor Richard's aphorisms are universally quoted."

Hosea said, "The one I'm fondest of is 'Neither a fortress nor a maid will hold out long after they begin to parley.' "

"That is the one I would expect you to be fondest of," charged Mr. Sholto. "You conveniently forget many that are relevant to improving a person's character."

Esau nudged his brother with cheerful malice. " 'Experience keeps a dear school, yet fools will learn at no other.' "

Hosea turned pink. Mr. Sholto couldn't hide a faint smile. Phillipe spoke:

"All you're saying suggests there are a great many printing houses in the colonies—"

"Thriving ones. A lively book trade, too. The very Bemis for whom we're producing the Dickinson reprint supplies various American retailers with the latest titles by ship. Franklin says New York, Philadelphia and that troublesome Boston are particularly good markets. I also understand there are a great many penny papers and gazettes. Some support the Crown, others the radicals. No, there'd be no shortage of work for a young man handy at the press."

The upstairs door opened. Mrs. Emma appeared, carrying a cup of tea. She delivered it to her husband with a solicitous glance but no further advice or protests.

When his wife had disappeared into the stationer's shop, Sholto sipped tea, then remarked, "Never let a good woman know how much you depend on her. Spoils 'em—gives 'em a sense of excess authority. Now where were we? Ah yes, employment in the colonies. Have you discussed the idea with your mother?"

"Not yet."

"Do you feel you'd meet resistance?"

"Yes. A little or a lot, depending on her mood. I've had a hard time reading her mood lately."

"My wife and I also. Your mother's the soul of politeness. She works hard, helping up front. But even though she never talks about the original undertaking that led you here, I have a feeling she broods on it privately a great deal."

Phillipe's hands, hard and calloused by now, clamped on the lever handle, pulled, then released.

"That's what bothers me, sir. I hope she's still not clinging to some dream of gaining the inheritance. I'd sooner steer a course for a harbor that can be reached. And strange as it sounds, I think we might be better off to try the long voyage to the colonies, rather than go back to France. Life had nothing to offer there except false hope. You can't serve that at suppertime."

"Agreed. Your course sounds sensible. When I'm over this accursed sickness, perhaps I can assist your endeavor. Introduce you to an American or two. We have 'em for visitors at the shop now and then—"

"I'd really like to meet your friend the doctor."

"Capital idea—but as you've heard before, he's not been by in many a month. Too much to do looking after the interests of his constituents. If we can't put you in touch with him, we'll try someone else. At least you could see whether you think your temper would match that of the Americans. Also whether you would be willing to undertake the attendant extra risks involved in going there."

Phillipe frowned. "What extra risks, Mr. Sholto?"

"The problem Lawyer Dickinson argued has not been settled by any means. Only hid away for a time. It will be settled eventually. In peace, or with open trouble. Read those essays," he finished, pointing at the press. "Between the lines!"

As he started across the room to inspect Hosea's work, he added, "Dickinson and Franklin are men of reason. They openly and frequently avow their allegiance to His Majesty. But they are men of principle as well. I doubt such men will ever submit to what they consider tyranny. Weigh that— and all its possible consequences—before you decide."

v

So as the presses piled up the sheets during the gray, wintry days, Phillipe inquired further into the American character by means of the collection of essays first published in early 1768 under the general title *Letters From a Farmer in Pennsylvania to the Inhabitants of the British Colonies.*

The land-owning, law-practicing Pennsylvania aristocrat had been replying with firm but reasoned pen to the Townshend taxes. Dickinson conceded Parliament's authority to regulate American overseas trade. But he emphatically denied Parliament's right to tax within the thirteen colonies for the purposes of swelling the Crown's treasury.

He declared Townshend's duties—now already repealed save for the one on tea—as illegal. He hinted that such taxes must not be allowed for another reason. They might set precedents for a host of other levies, regulations and impositions of foreign rule.

To Phillipe, Dickinson emerged as a man implicitly loyal to King George. One passage read: "Let us behave like dutiful children who have received unmerited blows from a beloved parent. Let us complain to our parent; but let our complaints speak at the same time the language of affliction and veneration."

On the other hand, as Mr. Sholto had said, Dickinson also had steadfast loyalties to what he believed was right. How such men would stand in the event of any further clashes of king's law and private conscience, the essays did not make clear.

Phillipe read the material with reasonable ease because of the expanded command of the language that his work for Sholto had given him. Thinking it over, he decided he was a definite partisan of Lawyer Dickinson and his American brethren, if only because they seemed opposed to the sort of high-handed behavior that had brought the visit to Kentland to such a tragic outcome.

If Dickinson fairly represented Americans, then Phillipe could only believe, with mounting excitement, that perhaps he belonged over there among them.

vi

By early March, Solomon Sholto recovered his health. Activity in the printing room returned to its original, pleasantly brisk pace. Feelings of hatred for the Amberlys began to trouble Phillipe less and less. The colonies were hardly out of his thoughts. He was convinced that he and his mother should emigrate.

What remained was to convince Marie. Somehow, he hesitated to bring up the subject. Perhaps for fear of refusal, he admitted to himself.

But one sunny day in April 1772, when a balmy breeze began to melt the last gray snow and send it rushing down the street channels, two unexpected visitors to Sweet's Lane took the decision about approaching Marie out of his hands.

CHAPTER III

Mr. Burke and Dr. Franklin

i

"WIPE THAT BLACK mess from your hands, lad, and come up front at once!"

Startled, Phillipe nearly dropped the leather ink ball. Interruptions of the workday were rare; Mr. Sholto not only preached but practiced diligence. Yet there he was at the door leading to the shop, gesturing with some urgency. When Phillipe glanced at Hosea, the latter shrugged, equally baffled.

Phillipe grabbed a rag and cleaned his hands as best he could. Then he hurried to the doorway, where Sholto enlightened him a little further:

"I promised to introduce you to a colonial, didn't I? Well, Franklin's come by, out of the blue! In company with another of my good friends. Quickly, quickly!—we don't want to take too much time away from the press."

Phillipe followed the printer into the front shop. Two soberly dressed gentlemen were conversing with Mrs. Emma. Marie, busy dusting the bookshelves with a feather whisk, gave her son a surprised stare as he entered. Following Mr. Sholto, Phillipe didn't stop for an explanation.

The younger of the two visitors, a ruddy-cheeked man in his early forties, was speaking to Sholto's wife in lilting English that Phillipe later discovered was a hallmark of the man's Dublin origins:

"—we've missed your good husband's occasional presence at the Turk's Head. The Whig party is coming back to life over the coffee cups." The man turned to acknowledge the printer's arrival. "Even irascible Johnson, who thinks the first Whig was the Devil himself, has inquired after you, Solomon."

"Illness and work have kept me away," Sholto said. "When health prevails and profits are secure—*then* there's time for idling with friends."

But it was the other visitor at whom Phillipe stared in awe. The "godless wizard"; the internationally hailed genius, the lusty Thames swimmer—

Dr. Benjamin Franklin was a stout man almost twenty years older than his companion. He had jowls, receding gray hair, a paunch and keen eyes. Spectacles enhanced his sagacious expression. At once, Phillipe noticed a peculiarity about the lenses. The lower halves seemed to be of a different thickness from the upper. Could the spectacles be the invention to which Sholto had referred?

Franklin said to the printer, "I agree about work, Solomon. Hundreds and hundreds of times have I agreed!" He smiled. "Poor Richard said the same thing endlessly—whenever, in fact, I ran out of witty words for him. I long ago concluded that I have written overmuch concerning the virtues of thrift and labor. I'm supposed to be the very model of a dull, parsimonious drudge—and gad, how the reputation lingers! Let me so much as crack one jest among most Britons and eyebrows fly to heaven. But you know, my friend, I enjoy the presence of maidens and Madeira as well as the next."

"Better than the next," Sholto smiled.

"Keep my secret, Solomon. Meantime, let me

echo Edmund. You have been too long away from our gatherings."

"And you from Sweet's Lane, Benjamin."

"Thank you. My sentiments also."

"There *are* other attractions at the Turk's Head besides political chatter," advised the Irishman, his eye merry.

"Quite so," Franklin agreed. "Doctor Goldsmith's been favoring us with readings from his new comedy. He hopes you'll land the printing commission after Garrack gets the play on. I predict it will be a solid hit. Very popular in the playhouses on our side of the Atlantic as well."

Sholto called a halt to the pleasantries by clearing his throat and glancing at Phillipe.

Both visitors focused their attention on the younger man. Phillipe was also aware of his mother watching him closely. He hated to have his speculations about America revealed to her in this fashion. But he saw little he could do about it.

A mussel seller pushing a barrow went by in Sweet's Lane, crying his wares as Sholto said, "This young man is a guest in my household. A sort of unofficial apprentice. His name is Phillipe Charboneau. His mother, Madame Charboneau, is there behind you."

The two gentlemen offered cordial greetings. Marie executed a stiff curtsy, still obviously confused. Phillipe didn't miss the way the older visitor adjusted his spectacles and boldly took note of Marie's still-shapely figure.

Sholto said to Phillipe, "Mr. Burke is an orator and pamphleteer of outstanding skill. Also a member of Commons from the pocket borough of Wendover. Doctor Franklin, I've already told you about. Phillipe shows an aptitude for the printing trade, Benjamin. He's most anxious to talk with you—and to read your *Ob-*

servations Concerning the Increase of Mankind. Our two copies, alas, are gone."

"Then come by my lodgings at Number Seven in Craven Street, young man—of an evening, preferably—and we'll accomplish both objectives. May I ask, however, the reason for your interest in my paper on population in America?"

Aware of Marie watching, Phillipe hesitated a second. Sholto answered instead:

"For various reasons, Phillipe's considering going there, rather than returning to his home in France."

Marie's intake of breath was sharp and sudden. Phillipe glanced her way long enough to see the anger in her dark eyes. He was caught off guard by Dr. Franklin's robust voice:

"Good for you! The opportunities are virtually unlimited. Particularly for an ambitious young fellow who can ply a press. Before I rose to my present position of eminence—" the twinkle in Franklin's eyes disclaimed any seriousness in the words. "—I was a printer myself. Philadelphia."

Phillipe nodded. "Mr. Sholto told me."

"I actually learned the trade in Boston, as an apprenticed boy. Never regretted it, either. I arrived in Philadelphia at age sixteen with absolutely nothing to my name but one Dutch dollar, a few copper pennies—and considerable hope. Thanks to printing, before too many years were out I was living well—and even making a modest mark in the world."

"Faith—'modest!' " Burke grinned. "The doctor's a man of parts, Mr. Charboneau. Inventor. Scientist. Founder of hospitals. Organizer of a society aiming to do away with the obnoxious slave trade—"

"He doesn't want to hear about me, Edmund," Franklin said. "He wants to hear about the colonies. Am I right, young man?"

"You are, sir. And I'll take you up on your offer to call in Craven Street."

"Excellent. I warn you—I may reminisce. I frequently wish I could go home, instead of wandering through the unspeakable maze of British politics. I formerly represented the commercial interests of Pennsylvania. Now it's Massachusetts Bay—but it's all the same kind of wrangling. And I had to leave my dear wife, Deborah, behind. She has an absolute horror of sea travel. Sometimes it's a lonely life," he concluded, with another glance at Marie.

Franklin's sighed complaint didn't match his lively eye. Marie wasn't interested.

"How much have you told the boy about America, Solomon?" Franklin asked finally.

"What little I've picked up from you. That there's hardly a city street corner where a hawker isn't peddling some broadside or penny sheet—"

"Did you also tell him that many of the publications are scurrilous and radical?" asked Burke in a tart tone.

"Who's to blame for that, Edmund?" Franklin retorted. "The longer His Majesty insists upon imposing unjust laws on Englishmen, the oftener the radicals like Adams and his engraver friend Revere will cobble together their inflammatory broadsides. The fault lies on your side of the Atlantic, not ours."

Edmund Burke returned a dismal nod. "You know I agree. Haven't I stood up in Commons many a time to plead for checking the excesses of the ministers? My position is conciliation. The government simply can't go on acting like a brutal father punishing a child."

Dr. Franklin smiled, raised a plump hand. "Edmund, you needn't impress me with your Irish oratory. I know your good intentions. I also know you're in the minority—a steadily dwindling group that can no longer even count on Mr. Pitt's full support."

Burke agreed: " 'Twas a double tragedy when we lost him to the peerage, then to his mental disorder."

"And now," Franklin returned, "the King and his supporters have the votes, in both the Commons and the Lords, to do exactly as they wish, provided they can keep the British merchant class content and prospering. Even though there's a temporary stand-off, I am very fearful the government may again soon take up the same willful course that led to the massacre from which Adams made so much capital."

"There was a massacre solely because the Boston mobs provoked the troops!" Burke insisted.

"Damme, let's not argue like enemies, Edmund! We hold the same basic position, after all. And we both know one important fact which most of my countrymen do not. That it's really the King, not the toadying ministers, chiefly responsible for the vile taxes lying at the center of the trouble."

"Here, Benjamin!" Sholto said, dismayed. "That's a change of heart, isn't it?"

Franklin smiled sourly. "Many things change as a result of eavesdropping and maneuvering on the back stairs of Whitehall. Daily, I grow less and less enchanted with His Majesty—"

"Well, those taxes you mentioned may plague you again," Burke warned. "Have you heard the latest clack about the East India Company?"

"No, I haven't."

"It's rumored that because their fortunes have sunk so low, they may try to manipulate passage of a bill to give them a monopoly on the tea trade overseas."

"They'll do so at their peril." The keen eyes behind the peculiar spectacles showed a ferocity Phillipe found surprising in a man of such benign appearance.

Abruptly, Franklin turned his attention away from Burke. "I am supposed to paint you a cheerful picture, Mr. Charboneau. And here we are daubing out a gloomy

one. But there's some sunlight among the thunderheads
after all. Come by Craven Street and I'll show it to
you."

"I look forward to it, Doctor."

"The colonies really have no desire to create problems, you see. The future tranquility of America rests
solely in the hands of King George."

"Nonsense!" Burke protested. "Your friend Adams,
for one, is anxious to provoke trouble. He can't wait to
manipulate his mobs again, in order to feed the fire of
his personal ambitions."

"Adams may run to excess on occasion," Franklin
granted. "But if we do not share the same means, we
share the same principles. We crave peace and harmony
above all things save one." He paused a moment. "Our
rights as Englishmen. I would have that warning repeated from the Turk's Head to your farmer king's own
private cabbage patch. Yet I fear none will listen, except
for a few good men like you, Edmund."

At that, Burke merely looked glum.

Phillipe noticed Marie watching him across Burke's
shoulder and hastily averted his eyes. He realized that
before the day was out, he would have to confront her.

Franklin became more animated again, producing a
fobbed silver watch from his waistcoat pocket. Showing
Burke the painted dial, he said, "I've an appointment
shortly with the Secretary of State for the American
Department. I must beg leave to go along."

"I'll go as well," Burke said, "now that we've concluded our main business—inquiring after Solomon's
health."

As the two visitors started for the door, the Irishman
added, "Rush orders or no, Solomon, your friends will
be expecting you for coffee or chocolate at the Turk's
Head within a fortnight. Uninterrupted work creates
sour dispositions—"

"And wealthy printers." Dr. Franklin grinned. "Mr. Charboneau, don't fail to call."

"I won't, I promise. And thank you."

The two men disappeared down Sweet's Lane, trailed by half a dozen urchins who suddenly materialized to importune them for gin money. Before the men and the noisy children had passed out of sight, Marie bore down on her son with a vengeful look in her eye.

"What is this plan you discuss with strangers when you haven't so much as mentioned it to me?"

Phillipe didn't flinch from the glare. "I intended to speak to you about it soon, Mama."

Solomon Sholto said, "Your son wanted to investigate the idea first, Madame Charboneau."

Marie's fists clenched. "To labor like a nobody in some foreign land where everything's in a turmoil—is *that* your proposal?"

In an attempt to rescue Phillipe, Sholto stepped between mother and son. "Madame, I remind you that we are in the midst of a working day. I appreciate that you and your son have matters of consequence to discuss. But pray do so later, when I'm not paying for it."

With effort, Marie suppressed a retort. The front bell tinkled. Two bonneted ladies entered. Mrs. Emma bustled forward, saying much too loudly:

"Good day, Mrs. Chillworth! Come for the newest novels? Madame Charboneau will help you find them—"

For a moment Phillipe feared that his mother would explode with anger. But she didn't. Seconds passed. Mr. Sholto cleared his throat.

With a final glance at Phillipe that promised an accounting later, Marie turned and stalked off to aid the new customers.

Another welcome diversion, albeit one that made Mrs. Emma exclaim aloud, was a sudden crash from the back. Hosea bellowed, "Oh, God damn and blast!"

Phillipe and Mr. Sholto dashed into the printing room. They found Hosea furiously kicking one leg of his press. The thick, all-important platen had split through the center.

At his type case, Esau was smirking. "Too much pressure on the lever, dear brother. Where was your mind? Up some doxy's skirt?"

"We shall take all day replacing it!" Mr. Sholto fumed, purple in the cheeks.

But as Phillipe followed the owner up the steps to where Hosea was swearing and rubbing his toe, he realized that no delays of any kind could prevent an inevitable—and inevitably unpleasant—confrontation with Marie.

ii

Mr. Sholto had to send all the way across the Thames to Southwark for a replacement platen. The part didn't arrive until well after dark. Installation took two hours. The family's customary eight o'clock supper was delayed. Phillipe was tired and edgy when he finally followed Sholto and his sons upstairs shortly after St. Paul's rang ten.

Marie was waiting for him.

"We will not eat until I have spoken with you, Phillipe."

He checked his temper with great effort. "All right. But at least we needn't disturb the household. We'll go for a walk."

"Careful of the streets at this hour," Mr. Sholto advised, moving on toward the kitchen, from which drifted aromas of steaming tea and new-baked bread. Phillipe nodded absently.

Marie fetched a shawl from her room. They walked down the outside stairs into darkness that had become thick with fog. Their feet rang hollow on the cobbles of Sweet's Lane. Phillipe was hardly conscious of which way they were going. His mother didn't speak. The tension mounted. Suddenly Marie slipped in the slime of the drainage channel.

He reached for her arm. She shook off his hand angrily. Then the outburst came:

"Your mind's been affected! You're ready for that asylum they call Bedlam! How can you even entertain the idea of traveling to another country when there's wealth—position—power waiting for you in this one?"

He could no longer treat the subject tactfully. "Mama, that's an illusion! Have you forgotten the trouble at Kentland? We've no chance of pressing the claim successfully."

Marie seethed; he could hear it in her rapid breathing. "What has turned you into a coward, Phillipe?"

He wheeled on her. "Nothing! I'm trying to look at the future like a grown man, not a bemused child!"

"I won't listen to—"

"You will! Do you propose that we live on charity all our lives? Clinging to the hope that some miracle will happen? The Duchess of Kentland won't permit miracles! And what's left for us in Auvergne?"

"Therefore—" He'd never heard such awful bitterness in her voice. "Therefore you intend to waste your life as a printer's boy? You, who swore an oath that you wouldn't let yourself be humbled into obscurity?"

Phillipe winced inwardly at that. Guilt lay heavy on him a moment. Marie was expert at striking at the most sensitive part of his defenses.

"I hadn't definitely decided to propose that we sail to America," he hedged. "It seemed worth looking into, that's all. Printing is a worthy occupation—"

"Being a tradesman is *worthy*? Faugh!"

"Dr. Franklin did well at it. His writings made him

more than welcome among the nobility—"

"Oh, yes, I remember all the talk on the river trip. A genius!" Her tone grew cutting. "Are you a genius, my son?"

"No, no, of course not, I—"

"But you *are* a nobleman," she argued, as their clacking footfalls carried them deeper into the mist that beaded cold on his cheeks. "Even your American *genius* can't claim that. It comes down to this, Phillipe. If you refuse to press your claim, then I've lived for nothing."

Phillipe's spine crawled. She no longer spoke with fiery conviction. She ranted, on the edge of hysteria:

"Will you do that to me, Phillipe? Will you destroy me after I've surrendered my whole life for you?"

"Mama, you know I'd never willingly hurt you. I love you too much. But you must be realistic—"

"Exactly. *Exactly!* Why do you think I've hoarded every shilling we earn helping the Sholtos? To buy passage back across the Channel?" Her harsh laugh unnerved him even more. "No. Oh, no. I've been making secret plans of my own, Phillipe. When we have enough money, we'll find a lawyer here in London. One who can help us use the letter to advantage—"

Phillipe's voice was edged with irritation: "But I still plan to accept Franklin's invitation. Talk to him. Talking can't hurt—"

He realized Marie hadn't heard a word. She was caught up in her own wild monologue:

"—because I've no intention of sailing to a land peopled by tradesmen and farmers and those—those hideous red Indians everyone prattles about. I've no intention of leaving England until you have your full and rightful share of—"

"In God's name, woman, *let it die!*"

Die die die die rang the echo in the slowly swirling fog.

He hadn't meant to shout. Or call her by any other

name than the one he'd used since childhood.

But he had done both. In an eerie way, that told him something new about their relationship.

His shout had cowed her a little. She spoke less stridently:

"Phillipe, what's happened to you? Don't you still have a desire to be like your father?"

He thought briefly of Lady Jane, of Alicia and, with hatred, of Roger. "Only sometimes," was the most honest answer he could give.

Marie Charboneau began to cry then. Short, anguished sobs that tore at Phillipe's heart. Miserable, angry with her as well as with himself, he lifted his head suddenly.

He'd heard another sound.

It came again, in counterpoint to her sobbing.

Shuffle-shuffle-shuffle.

The sound prickled his scalp and turned his palms to ice. It came from their left, but the source was invisible in the fog.

Then a second set of footsteps blended in. This time from the right.

Phillipe realized they must have wandered near St. Paul's Yard. There was a feeling of open space. High up, he glimpsed very faint lights in the murk. The small windows under the church dome. He groped for Marie's arm.

"Mama, I think we'd best turn back—"

Abruptly, an unfamiliar voice barked out, "I tell ye it's him! I knew when he yelled."

That voice came from the left, where the shuffling grew louder. Another responded from the right:

"Then old Jemmy weren't daft, saying 'e thought 'e'd seen 'em along Sweet's Lane. Let's find out fer sure—"

A lantern shutter clacked open. A sulfurous yellow flare lit the mist close by. Phillipe leaped back in alarm.

The lantern light revealed a graybeard with browned gums and one cocked eye. The apparition exclaimed, "Him, all right!"

Phillipe didn't recognize the hideous, leering face. But he wouldn't have known the face of any of those who had attacked him that first night on the church stairs.

Holding the lantern high, the beggar seized Phillipe's forearm with his other grimy hand. His one good eye glared. A second rag-festooned creature appeared behind him. A woman; a crone. Her sagging dugs were partially revealed by torn places in her filthy blouse.

The crone's mouth was just as toothless as the man's. Her eyes shone as she extended her hand, palm upward. The fingers wiggled suggestively.

"A penny to buy a posy for the General's grave?"

Phillipe stepped in front of the frightened Marie, tried to shake off the man's clutch as the crone shrilled:

"Just a penny. That's not much for a lad who works in a fine bookshop. Old Jemmy, he saw sharp. He recognized you!"

"Let go, damn you!" Phillipe pried harder at the dirty hand holding him. Suddenly the man with the crazed eye dropped his lantern, shot out both hands and closed them on Phillipe's throat.

"Can't buy a flower for a good man's grave?" he screamed. "You owe him! *You killed him!*"

Savagely, Phillipe drove his fist into the beggar's belly. One punch was enough to tear the broken nails from his throat. He practically jerked Marie off her feet, dragging her away as the old man and the crone began to shrill together:

"Murderer! *Murderer!*"

Their feeble shuffling followed Phillipe and Marie a short distance down Sweet's Lane, then faded.

Out of breath, they reached the sanctuary of the rickety stairs ascending to the Sholtos' second floor.

They clattered up. Only the closing of the door behind them stilled Phillipe's hammering heart.

The beggars had really presented no serious physical threat. He'd been startled, that's all. Gotten alarmed all out of proportion to the cause.

Yet he was still shivering. He thought that somewhere out in the fog, he could still hear voices crying, "*Murderer—*"

Marie went to her room without speaking.

iii

Phillipe slept badly that night. In the morning he described the incident to Esau. The big-shouldered young man shrugged it off.

"It was only an attempt to bully you into giving them drink money. Do you really think they care when one of their own dies? The man you cut down—the General—was probably stripped and left to rot naked five minutes after Hosea and I brought you home."

Trying to take reassurance from the words, Phillipe was still troubled. The beggars knew where he lived. What if someone else came searching for him? Inquiring of the street people about a French boy?

Of course there hadn't been so much as a hint of any pursuit since the flight from Tonbridge. But he couldn't shake off the new worry.

Esau grinned at him. "Look here, stop scowling! Go ink Hosea's type or I won't be able to pick up my flute till midnight!"

Phillipe nodded, started to work. Yet the anxiety lingered with him most of the day.

He didn't mention his fear to Marie. In fact he avoided her. He didn't want to reopen the discussion—the argument—about their future until he'd hit on some way to persuade her that further involvement with the Amberlys was not worth the risk and was futile to boot.

By the next day, a warm but windy harbinger of spring, he had thrown off some of his apprehension. Though the gray sky threatened storms, he made up his mind to walk to Craven Street that very evening. He hoped he'd find Franklin home.

Marie retired early. Thus he was spared the need to tell her where he was going. He told the Sholtos, however. Once more they repeated their warnings about the unsafe streets. Out of range of observation by his father, Hosea slipped Phillipe a cheap dirk to stick in his boot.

"Don't ask me where I got the bloody thing—or how I use it. Just take it."

Phillipe thanked him and set out.

Thunder rumbled as he proceeded down the Strand. He glanced behind frequently but saw no sign of anyone following him. He located Craven Street, which led south to the river, without incident.

Going up the steps of the house at Number 7, he dismissed his anxiety about the beggars as foolish. By the end of the week, he was to discover that was a grave mistake. But as the night sky glared white and a thunderclap pealed and fat raindrops began to spatter down, he had no inkling.

CHAPTER IV

The Wizard of Craven Street

i

EVEN AS PHILLIPE LET the door knocker fall, lightning blazed again, raising white shimmers on the Thames, churning only a few steps further south of the brick residence. All at once the wind turned chill. The rain slanted harder. He huddled close to the building until someone answered.

A woman. Of middle age, but still attractive. She raised a candle in a holder as she peered at Phillipe from the gloomy foyer.

"Yes?"

"Good evening. Is this the house of Dr. Franklin?"

"No, it's the house of Widow Stevenson. But he lets rooms from me." The woman glanced past Phillipe to the dark doorways on the other side of the rain-swept street. Her eyes suspicious, she asked, "Are you a friend?"

"An acquaintance. Dr. Franklin gave me leave to call. My name is Phillipe Charboneau. If the doctor's at home, I'd be obliged if you'd announce me."

Mrs. Stevenson's suspicion seemed to moderate. She stepped back, motioned him in. "Very well. But I'm afraid you'll be interrupting the doctor's air bath."

"His what?"

Phillipe's words were muffled by more thunder. Mrs.

Stevenson didn't hear. Turning toward an open door
on one side of the foyer, she continued:

"Normally he takes his air bath first thing in the
morning. Today, early appointments prevented it." At
the entrance to a well-furnished parlor bright with
lamplight, the woman called, "Polly. Polly, my dear—"

In a moment, a pert, pretty girl appeared. She was
about Phillipe's own age.

"Benjamin has a caller," said the older woman.
"Mister—?"

"Charboneau."

"My daughter will show you up."

Phillipe thanked her, moved aside to let the girl pre-
cede him with the candle. Thunder boomed, then faded
as they climbed the carpeted stairs. In the lull of silence,
Phillipe heard someone singing behind a door on the
second floor. He recognized the voice. Franklin's—accompanied by music unlike any he had ever
heard before. Shimmering, almost eerie notes. The
melody itself was plaintive; the words equally so:

> *Of their Chloes and Phyllises poets may prate—*
> *I sing my plain country Joan.*

"Oh," exclaimed the girl named Polly, "he's playing!"

"It sounds to me like he's singing."

"Well, of course—that too. What a foolish remark."

"Excuse me," Phillipe snapped. "I was told he was
taking something called an air bath."

> *Now twelve years my wife—still the joy of my life—*
> *Blest day that I made her my own,*
> *My dear friends—*
> *Blest day that I made her my own.*

"Dr. Franklin can do all three at once!" responded
the girl, her eyes positively sparkling in the candle's

bobbing glow. "He's very accomplished on the fiddle, the harp—*and* his armonica." Her gesture indicated it was this last, unfamiliar instrument upon which Franklin was performing now. "He invented the armonica in this very house. Sometimes I sit with him and listen for hours." Young Polly Stevenson sounded smitten.

As they continued up the stairs, the strange, ethereally sweet notes grew louder. Franklin sang with gusto, yet with unmistakable feeling:

> *Some faults have we all, and so may my Joan—*
> *But then, they're exceedingly small.*
> *And now I'm used to 'em, they're just like my own—*
> *I scarcely can see 'em at all,*
> *My dear friends.*
> *Blest day that I made her my own*

"He made up that song about his Philadelphia wife years ago," Polly declared as they reached the landing. "It's the only one he sings that I don't care for."

Phillipe readily understood why. Admiration had given way to jealousy in the girl's eyes. She knocked. The vigorous voice pealed on:

> *Were the finest young princess, with millions*
>   *in purse*
> *To be had in exchange for my Joan,*
> *She could not be a better wife—might be a worse—*
> *So I'd stick to my Joggy alone,*
> *My dear friends—*

Polly rapped louder. "Dr. Franklin! If you please!"

> *I'd cling to my lovely old Joan.*

The last high notes melted to silence beneath the distant roar of the storm. Polly's third knock finally produced a response:

"That you, Polly my girl?"

"Yes. You have a caller."

"Male or female?"

"The former. A young man. He says he knows you."

"Then he may come in at once. But you stay out—I'm still bathing."

Polly giggled. She stood aside for Phillipe to enter. As he walked into the spacious sitting room, bright-eyed Polly was on tiptoe, craning for a view of the apartment's occupant. Phillipe turned to close the door, catching her. She looked acutely embarrassed. When he pivoted back in response to a boomed-out greeting—"Charboneau! Good evening to you!"—he instantly appreciated why.

Never in his days had Phillipe beheld such a bizarre combination of sights as in that chamber lit with lamps whose flames were shielded with chimneys. For good reason. All three windows overlooking Craven Street were wide open. The curtains blew, rain gusted in—and so did the wind, exceedingly chilly. The pages of a book lying open on a reading desk fluttered and snapped in the miniature gale.

But Benjamin Franklin appeared perfectly comfortable, seated on a bench near the opposite wall, in front of a totally incomprehensible device Phillipe took to be the source of the odd musical sounds. Franklin beamed cheerily.

"Have a chair. Help yourself to that Madeira. I'll be finished with my air bath in just a few moments."

He continued to smile with perfect aplomb, despite the fact that he was totally nude except for his spectacles.

Now just as embarrassed as Polly had been, but for a different reason, Phillipe made for the sideboard, and the decanter. He poured half a glass, sipped it hastily as Franklin rose, stretched, took several vigorous steps in one direction, then several the opposite way.

"Glad you fulfilled your promise, Mr. Charboneau. Please excuse my appearance. I've always believed fresh air has a salubrious effect on a man's health and longevity. Winter or summer, I throw open the windows and take the air in this fashion one hour per day—come, come! Don't look flustered. Is there any need for false prudery among gentlemen?"

"Well—ah—" Phillipe chucked down the Madeira, which hit his stomach with a sudden exploding warmth. He struggled for words. "No. *No!* But I've never walked into a room before and seen—seen—a device like that—"

Somewhat wildly, he pointed past Franklin's bare paunch to the peculiar instrument against the wall.

"My armonica? Performances on musically tuned glasses are all the rage over here, I found. I merely improved on the primitive arrangement generally in use. Here, I'll give you a demonstration—"

A mantel clock chimed the half-hour. "Ah, but time's up. Your momentary indulgence—"

He disappeared into a dark adjoining room, returned clad in a much-worn dressing gown and old slippers of yellowed lambswool. He bustled from window to window, closing the shutters and latching them. Then he crossed to his armonica, while Phillipe, now less nervous, poured another tot of Madeira.

He walked over to the bench at which Franklin had seated himself. He was beginning to notice other details of the room: books and portfolios of papers stacked everywhere; on the mantel, a trio of miniature oils in expensive gold frames. The central portrait was that of a plain-faced, even homely woman. She was flanked by a young, bright-eyed boy and a charming little girl. Franklin's children? Phillipe wondered briefly whether the young man was the bastard governor, William.

Franklin's fingers ranging over the armonica captured Phillipe's attention again. The high, shimmering notes faded away as cracks in the shutters admitted lightning glare. Thunder rocked the house. Phillipe bent forward to look while Franklin explained:

"Until the advent of my little creation, performers on
the musical glasses simply had to arrange their vessels
helter-skelter—and seldom within easy reach. I
approached the problem a bit more scientifically, that's
all."

He indicated the closely spaced glass hemispheres
containing varying amounts of water. Each hemisphere
resembled the bowl of a wineglass, but with a hole in
place of a stem. Each hole fitted onto a peg on a spindle
which, as Dr. Franklin demonstrated, moved back and
forth at the touch of a foot treadle. Thus, certain glasses
could be brought closer to the performer, or moved
away. So precisely arranged were the hemispheres, not a
drop of water spilled when the shaft changed position.

"Thirty-seven hand-blown glasses from three to nine
inches—ranging through three octaves—and originally
tuned with the aid of a harpsichord. Using a diamond, I
engraved the note's letter on each glass."

Phillipe saw that when Franklin pointed it out. The
older man moistened his fingertips in a bowl of water on
a taboret beside the bench. Then he began to touch the
rims of different hemispheres while operating the pedal.
A surprisingly lovely tune rang forth, complete with
simple chords that swelled and diminished as Franklin
varied the finger pressure.

In mid-phrase, he laughed and turned back to the
amazed younger man.

"That's enough musicology for the evening, I think.
You're more interested in America. Sit down again, and
let's have another glass of Madeira."

As a result of the two he'd drunk, Phillipe was
already hearing a slight buzz. His eyes were a bit blurry,
too. But he accepted the full glass Franklin poured and
took the chair offered.

Franklin selected an even larger goblet for himself.
He filled it to the brim, then relaxed in a second chair in
front of jammed bookshelves, facing his visitor.

"I do recall I am supposed to give you a copy of my population essay before you depart. But tell me, Mr. Charboneau—where's your home? France, to guess from your accent."

"That's right, sir. My mother and I came to England from Auvergne."

"On business? To visit relatives? What?"

Phillipe was about to blurt that he was the son of a member of the nobility. He checked the impulse. Franklin might not be friendly with all the peers of the realm—and very likely not with the so-called King's Friends, among whom the late Duke had been numbered. Still, he wasn't eager to have the story of his origins too widely circulated, especially not since the unsettling incident with the beggars. So he answered:

"Business, I suppose you'd call it. My mother was never married to my father, who was an Englishman of—good station." He saw Franklin's eyes dart quickly to the boy's framed portrait; unabashed affection showed before the doctor returned his attention to the goblet he was warming between his palms. Phillipe continued, "When my father died, I was supposed to receive an inheritance, but—well, let's say there were complications."

"Some pack of rascally relatives cut you off, eh?"

"You're very quick to get to the heart of it, sir."

Franklin waved. "It's an old story among the supposedly refined upper classes. So now your thoughts turn west across the sea—"

Phillipe nodded. "My mother's against it, of course."

"Handsome woman. Devilishly handsome! Can you persuade her?"

"I think so." It was a hope, not a fact. "Particularly if there's a more solid future than we'd find back in France."

"You couldn't have found better instructors in the fundamentals of printing than old Solomon and his sons.

And the presses in the colonies do grow more numerous
by the year. Commerce expands—that means more
handbills, more advertising sheets. Literacy rises—the
appetite for knowledge and news becomes voracious.
Beyond that, we've a relatively open society over
there—"

Phillipe shook his head, not understanding. Another
intense glare through the shutters preceded a stunning
roll of thunder. Franklin helped himself to more
Madeira before going on:

"In America, a man's free to rise as far and as fast as
his wit and industry permit. The colonies are largely
spared the constraints of the antique European system
of nobility and privilege—with which you hint you've
had some encounter."

The shrewd eyes pinned him from behind the spectacles. Plainly the question was an attempt to draw him
out. But Phillipe kept silent except for another nod.

Without thinking, he'd helped himself to more
Madeira. The buzz in his ears had become pronounced.
He wasn't sure he could tell the Amberly tale coherently
if he wanted to. He was growing dizzy—from the wine,
and from basking in the nearly godlike presence of this
famous man who, in some ways, acted as comfortably
common as his old lambswool slippers.

Seeing he'd get no answer, Franklin resumed, "Yes, a
man can go far in America, no matter how humble his
beginnings. That should continue to be the case unless,
God help us, the Crown alters the course of colonial affairs."

"You discussed that trouble with Mr. Burke at some
length—"

"Because it's seldom out of my mind. The future of
relations between the colonies and the mother country
depends entirely—*entirely*—upon the actions of His
Majesty."

"Can you forecast the next year or so? Will conditions over there be so unsettled that it's foolish to entertain thoughts of a solid future?"

Franklin peered into his goblet in an almost cross-eyed way. He said somberly:

"I hope not. As do most of my countrymen, from the Virginia tidelands to the Maine lobster banks. By living where they do, they have already gambled on *their* futures. I wish I could be more specific, but alas—" A rueful pucker of the mouth. "As a prophet, Poor Richard Saunders is a pious fraud. I do know that Englishmen will not be driven to their knees. To sketch it candidly for you, I would say America in the immediate future represents a unique combination of opportunity and risk. Opportunity to the extent I have already described—in plain terms, the air there is less stifling. On the other hand, German George—and many of his ministers who are supposedly Englishmen!—simply fail to understand the American temper. As you heard me tell Edmund, we seek justice, not enmity. But if they force the issue with their infernal taxes and fiats—that outrageous tea scheme, for example! I investigated Edmund's rumor—the scheme's certainly afloat. Should the high-handed ministers eventually push through a law granting an American monopoly to the half-wrecked East India Company—and should this government go on quartering royal troops among us at our expense—continue burdening us with aggravations and harassments of every devising—little 'innovations,' the wags in Parliament term them—*then*, Mr. Charboneau, you will see thirteen colonies pull and haul together as they have never done."

Silence. The mantel clock ticked against the murmur of the rain. Abruptly Franklin stuck out his lower lip.

"No doubt I'm depressing you. I've certainly depressed myself. More Madeira!"

Before Phillipe knew it, both glasses had been

refilled. He said, "No, I'm not depresh—uh, depressed. I'm heartened. You've been honest. I think I'd welcome the free air in America. Whatever the dangers in the future."

"Good! Remember—I may have overstated the grimness of the outlook. As long as there are no new assaults on our liberties, all may continue in relative calm—"

Franklin had barely spoken the last words when lightning blazed outside—and the loud, strident *dang-dang-dang* of a bell brought the half-tipsy Phillipe leaping out of his chair.

"Damme," Franklin exclaimed, "I must have forgotten to unfasten the wire to the rod—"

He rushed toward the doorway where he'd disappeared before. This time, however, the black room beyond was illuminated by a ghostly light that made Phillipe's scalp crawl.

Franklin noted his visitor's white cheeks, chuckled.

"No need to be alarmed—the house is merely electrified from the storm. Come look."

Dang-dang-dang-dang, the bell shattered the eardrums like some tocsin of judgment. Phillipe swallowed, wobbled as far as the doorway, looked in and observed Franklin silhouetted against a weird white aura glowing around a spot on one wall. *Dang-dang-dang-dang—*

"The natural force contained in the electrical storm makes them ring," the scientist shouted over the clatter. He resembled some white-lit creature of hell as he gestured to a little brass ball dancing in the center of that strange fire. The ball—and the white glow itself—appeared to leap back and forth between two bells mounted to the wall. *Dang-dang-dang-dang—*

"Normally I keep the roof rod grounded—the charge runs harmlessly through a wire into the earth. But on occasion, I connect the rod to the bells for the amusement of visitors."

"Rod?" Phillipe repeated in a blank way.

"The type of rod I devised to prevent lightning from damaging property. See where the wire comes down, suspending that ball by its silk thread?"

Phillipe stumbled forward through the semidarkness, past a table littered with laboratory ware and tin-lined jars. The white glow was lessening. The ball moved more slowly; the bells rang with less stridence. Awed, Phillipe extended his hand toward the dancing sphere of brass.

"For God's sake don't touch it!" Franklin cried, seizing his wrist. "You might be fried where you stand."

Intoxicated and nearly frightened out of his wits, Phillipe took three long steps backward. He managed a weak grin.

"That—that's certainly a diverting demonstration."

By now the ball barely touched the bells. The white glow had all but disappeared. Franklin clapped an arm over Phillipe's shoulder, escorted him back into the sitting room.

"I imagine you'd prefer to be diverted by that book I promised you." He adjusted his spectacles, poked along the shelves, withdrew a slender volume—knocking several others on the floor in the process. Phillipe was relieved that he wasn't the only one feeling the wine.

Franklin handed the book to his guest. "Glean what facts you can from it. Then, since my friend Solomon is lacking a copy, donate it to him with my compliments."

"Dr. Franklin, I thank you most humbly for your time, your friendliness, your—"

"Electrifying discourse?"

Both laughed.

"Please keep me advised of your plans, Mr. Charboneau. Don't be discouraged or deterred by what *might* happen. America is a new, brave land—and her free air makes the risks attendant to emigrating there more than acceptable."

"I thank you again for the advice."

"It costs me nothing! And who knows? It may do the colonies a service by adding a citizen of worth. Truthfully, I can, and would like to be, of more practical help. Should you reach a decision to go, let me know and I'll write you a list of good printing establishments in the major cities. I'll also give you a note of introduction and recommendation."

"Sir, that's unbelievably kind. But I'd hate to trouble you—"

"Trouble me? I can do no less for a marked man."

Phillipe gulped. White spots seemed to dance behind his eyes. *"Marked—?"*

Franklin crooked a finger and walked to a front window. "To visit Craven Street is to be deemed dangerous," he said, pushing a shutter open and pointing. "At the next lightning flash, look across the way."

They waited for several moments. Then the sky glared, clearly illuminating a man lounging in a passageway between houses. The man was dressed as a seaman. A tiny ring in his earlobe glittered while the lightning flickered over Craven Street. Franklin slammed the shutter, his expression sour.

"I'll conduct you out the back way. For your own sake."

"You have spies watching you, Doctor?"

"Almost constantly. Certain members of Parliament even declare I should be hanged. And compared to Mr. Samuel Adams and some of the rest of that Boston crowd, *vis-a-vis* King George I am a moderate! Still want to take up with us Americans, Mr. Charboneau?"

Full of wine and excitement, Phillipe said to the great man, "Yes, I think so."

"I had that feeling shortly after we met. You're the right sort, young man. Yes indeed, the right sort."

The compliment, and another stout clap of Phillipe's shoulder, put him into a state of complete euphoria.

With the precious book tucked inside his clothes, he whistled and hummed all the way back to Sweet's Lane—and didn't realize until he arrived that he'd gotten thoroughly soaked.

But after an experience like tonight's, what did it matter?

ii

He found Hosea drinking a pot of ale in the nearly dark kitchen. All but a few embers had gone out on the hearth. Esau perched on a stool, chin on his chest, snoring. His flute lay beside his right foot.

"Well!" Hosea grinned, tottering up. "The specter from the storm. No robberies?" Phillipe shook his head, tugging off his sodden shirt. "No assaults by wenches?" Phillipe shook his head. "Gad, what a dull evening."

"The most exciting evening of my life, Hosea. The man is—he's a giant!"

Hosea shrugged, weaving as he grabbed Phillipe's arm. "Listen. Himself is tucked up in his nightshirt. I smuggled this ale out of the cellar. Private stock. Join me—"

"No, I want to read."

"Read instead of drink?" Hosea leaned closer, blinking. "You must be drunk." He sniffed. "You are drunk. Pickled in the doctor's well-known Madeira. All right, if that's your pleasure, be unsociable!"

It wasn't a question of sociability, but of consuming eagerness to delve into the book. Phillipe lit a taper beside his bed, pulled off the last of his wet clothes, crawled under the blankets and turned to the first page. Within minutes, Franklin's prose began to light his thoughts almost as that electric display had lit the room at Craven Street.

In carefully structured phrases, and with precise logic, Franklin put forth his case for the coming

greatness of the colonies. At the time he was writing—
the fifties, hadn't someone said?—there were over one
million Englishmen in North America. Yet only about
eighty thousand had emigrated from the mother country
since the start of colonization.

That fact alone established a fundamental difference
between the Old World and the New. In Europe and the
British Isles, population was more or less stable. But
America, with its virtually unlimited land—land beyond
the mountains of the eastern seaboard; land as yet
unexplored except by soldiers and the hardiest
woodsmen—gave families room to grow. The land provided them with sustenance as well. In Franklin's view,
there was hardly any restriction on the number of people
the American continent could support.

In fact, the mind-expanding essay predicted that
America's population would double every twenty to
twenty-five years—and a distant century in the future,
"the greatest number of Englishmen will be on *this* side
of the water."

Dawn's light found Phillipe still reading—drunk now
on the words and their promise, intoxicated by the night
just past, and by the force and vision of the man who
had so patiently spoken with him—

Starting, he heard the dawn church bells. His head
hurt. So did his eyes. He'd soon have to be up and working—a full, long day.

But it didn't matter. Nothing mattered except the
sonorous word that rang and rang in his mind, a thousand times louder and more majestic than Franklin's
electrified bells—

America.

America.

He blew out the taper and drowsed, murmuring the
name.

CHAPTER V

The One-Eyed Man

i

THE FIRST HINT THAT Phillipe and his mother were in danger came disguised as no more than an item of dinner conversation, three evenings after the visit with Franklin.

He was busy spooning the last of Mrs. Emma's delicious lentil soup from his bowl. Talk at the table was animated this evening. But as usual, Marie did not enter in. Whether this was because she felt secretly superior to the Sholto family or because she was still not at ease among English people, Phillipe could never decide.

As Mrs. Emma moved around the table, ladling extra portions of soup into the bowls of the three young men who had worked up their customary ravenous appetites in the press room, she said:

"The strangest person appeared in the shop this afternoon." An aside to Marie: "Just when you'd come up here to light the fire for tea time."

Marie responded with a faint nod. Her glance met Phillipe's briefly, slid away. They hadn't discussed their differences since the night the beggars accosted them in the fog. He'd been anxious to tell her about his remarkable evening at Craven Street, but thus far he'd lacked the opportunity—

Or was it the courage? They had been alone several times. But on each occasion, Marie's morose behavior quelled his enthusiasm.

He was growing concerned about her health again. She was wan, too silent all day long. He knew she was probably worried about their future, which would have to be decided eventually. But she seemed to be retreating into herself—as if, that way, the issue could be sidestepped altogether.

He heard Esau ask, "What was so strange about the visitor, Mother?"

"For one thing, he had a positively frightening phiz. Particularly his eyes. No, that should be singular. Eye. One was covered with a greasy patch of old leather. But the other had a distinctly mean glare. He was a tall chap. Imposing—though I've seldom seen cheeks so pitted with the marks of the pox. He kept darting glances every which way. As if he were ill at ease in a bookshop."

"How was he dressed? Was he a gentleman?" Esau wanted to know.

"A flash gentleman! Ill-assorted clothes. Old mended breeches. Jackboots. His coat, very dirty, might have been shot silk of bright orange—once."

"Orange was the macaroni color ten years ago," Hosea put in. "Today a gentleman dresses in more restrained hues."

Chuckling, Esau reached for his tankard of ale. "Naturally you speak from hope, not personal experience." Hosea scowled.

Mrs. Emma ignored the banter, seated herself next to her husband and continued, "Well, I certainly have little knowledge about high fashion. But it was obvious this person wanted to look like a gentleman but couldn't quite bring it off. His sword had a very fancy French knot. He didn't appear wealthy enough to have bought it new."

"From your description," said Mr. Sholto, "it sounds

like he might have bought it on a coach road. At pistol point."

His wife replied, "That's exactly how he struck me, Solomon! A thief in stolen finery."

"Well, maybe some victim gave him books instead of rings, and he acquired a taste for literature," Hosea said between mouthfuls of bread. "I can't exactly see why such a fellow's worthy of so much discussion."

Mrs. Emma gestured helplessly. "He—he frightened me, that's all. His beetling stare. His darted looks at every cranny and closed door."

"Did he say anything ill-mannered?" Esau inquired.

"No. No, but—"

"Then for once I agree with Hosea. What's the fuss?"

"Well, it occurred to me that perhaps our store was being examined for possible robbery!" Mrs. Emma exclaimed. "The man did not belong here!"

Sholto asked, "How long did he stay?"

"Oh, ten minutes, perhaps. He spent most of his time at the bookshelves, taking down one volume and studying several different pages a long while. I finally got up nerve enough to speak to him a second time. I greeted him when he came in, of course. I got a hawkish flash from his good eye, and a bare nod. On the second occasion, he snapped the book shut and said he was searching for some diverting, fictional adventure. But the volume he'd been examining didn't measure up. With that, he walked out."

It was one of those rare occasions when Solomon Sholto laughed aloud. "Emma, Emma, you are a dear nervous wren. Some gutter peacock leafs through a novel and you're alarmed—"

"But you still don't understand! The book to which he'd devoted so much attention was Mr. Chambers' *Cyclopaedia Britannica*. I'm positive the fellow couldn't read! And if not, what was he doing loitering in our shop?"

Phillipe lowered his spoon back into the bowl and sat stock still. He didn't so much as flicker an eyelash to reveal one possible answer.

Mr. Sholto pondered his wife's information and, after a modest belch, said, "Then it might be as you say. Maybe he was looking us over with robbery in mind. Puzzling, since any flash gentleman would have to fall quite low indeed to think about robbing a bookseller's. Looting one of the new mansions out in Mayfair would be much more lucrative. However, there's no accounting for the peculiarity of persons in London. Any big city attracts some strange ones. We'll lock up tight. Hosea, you put your pallet in the press room for a few nights, just in case."

Hosea grumbled that he'd planned to be out late a couple of evenings during the week.

His father replied blandly, "That is why you may put your pallet in the press room instead. Guard duty will keep you out of your unsavory haunts—and perhaps prevent a misadventure. I'd just as soon not lose my book stocks to some deranged captain who's been temporarily forced off the highway."

But after four nights of Hosea sleeping downstairs, and no robbery, nor even a reappearance of the peculiar stranger, the household relaxed and forgot him.

All except Phillipe.

ii

Mrs. Emma's fiftieth birthday fell on the last Saturday in April. The evening before, Mr. Sholto made a surprise announcement at supper. He would close his doors at three the following afternoon. Having hired a four-wheeled post chaise, he planned to drive them all out to Vauxhall Gardens, which had just opened for the season.

At the gardens they would eat a picnic supper and enjoy the music, while avoiding what he termed "the more salacious entertainments which I understand take place in the bowers and along the dark walks."

Mrs. Emma hugged him. Esau looked delighted. Even Marie showed some animation at the prospect of an outing; Mr. Sholto had made a point that she and her son were invited.

So, the next night, Phillipe Charboneau again glimpsed a world he was trying to forget.

The spring dusk smelled of thawed earth and the perfumes of the finely dressed folk dining in lantern-lit pavilions scattered around the vast pleasure park. Ladies in brocaded gowns and gentlemen in suits with sequinned buttons filled the twilight with much laughter and loud talk.

Admission to the park had cost Mr. Sholto a shilling per person. Mrs. Emma had therefore insisted on preparing her own birthday meal—which, Mr. Sholto privately revealed to his sons and Phillipe, he had planned for her to do all along, generosity having its limits.

Ignoring the food and drink available for sale on the grounds, they chose an open stretch of lawn from which they could hear the musical performance, spread blankets like many others around them were doing and enjoyed a splendid supper featuring minced chicken and two newly bought bottles of claret. The lilting strains of a string orchestra drifted from the far part of the grounds. And as full darkness settled, the garden walks livened with the scurrying footfalls of men and maids, not to mention other, occasionally sensual sounds. The only illumination came from the pavilions and from a few glowing lanterns hung from trees.

Soon Hosea began to display signs of impatience.

"May I have leave to wander a while, father? I don't have the ear for Mr. Handel's airs that Esau does."

"Yes, I suppose. But don't be gone longer than half

an hour. I'm told those dim walks are dangerous places after the concert ends."

A moment or so later, Phillipe jumped up and announced that he wanted to walk too. The spring air, the sweet music, the muted laughter of lovers wandering the mazy paths had brought disturbing memories of Alicia Parkhurst. He hoped a little activity would dispel them.

He started off down the sloping lawn in the direction Hosea had taken. His mother, busy helping Mrs. Emma close the hampers, left her work and caught up with him.

"Look well at the places where the genteel folk are spending the evening, Phillipe." Her voice was low, but full of the intensity he remembered from Auvergne. "That's where you belong. And that's what you'll throw away if you keep entertaining this foolish dream of going to America. I promise you one thing. I'll never let you do it so long as I draw a breath."

She turned her back, leaving the soft steel of her words to twist in his mind.

Well, she'd given him the answer he'd wondered about ever since their first argument. The lines of battle had been laid out. She'd only been awaiting the proper moment to deliver the first salvo.

Unhappily, Phillipe hurried down the slope to catch up with Hosea.

The two young men circled a large pavilion. Under its lanterns, a bewigged young macaroni was heartily puking all over the gown of his female companion. Other ladies and gentlemen in the party squealed in exaggerated shock. But several applauded drunkenly.

Phillipe hurried on by, wishing Marie could view the coarse scene. *That* was the world she wanted him to join?

Granted, it had its attractions. But sweet Christ, how could she overlook its darker side so easily? Those people lived with the assumption that any behavior, no matter how gross, could be excused—even approved—because of their wealth and position. Did Marie honestly prefer such standards over the simple decencies they'd found in an ordinary household like that of the Sholtos?

Of course, he realized his sweeping judgments were just that—and consequently, in certain instances, unfair. Hadn't Mr. Fox assured him that his own father did not conform to the pattern?

Still, Phillipe had conceived a hatred of all noblemen and their frivolous, painted women. He knew it was partly because he hadn't been good enough for one such woman, and because he'd threatened another—to the point where she retaliated through her son. But as he and Hosea ambled, trying to explain away the reasons for the hatred did little good. The hatred remained.

Shortly, Hosea was no longer content merely to amble. He literally hopped from one foot to the other, excited by something he'd spotted behind them. Phillipe came out of his reverie, heard feminine laughter.

"Shopgirls!" Hosea hissed. "Two of 'em—and damned pert looking. Come on, let's follow."

Phillipe grinned. "I didn't think you slipped away from your father just to study the botanical plantings."

"Stop gabbing or we'll lose 'em, Phillipe!"

Tempted, Phillipe finally shook his head. "You go if you want. I'll meet you back where we saw that young beau amusing his friends by throwing up. Then your father won't suspect we've done anything but stroll."

Hosea needed no further prodding. He ran off after the two flirts, who had disappeared around one of the many turnings the path took between high hedges.

Phillipe wandered on. He inhaled the night air, watched the clear stars, listened to a nearby nightingale singing in harmony with the violas and cellos and French horns of the orchestra. No matter how he resisted, memories of Alicia flooded his mind.

Head down and pensive, he wandered deeper into the unlighted sections of the gardens. He failed to hear the footsteps until they were very close behind him.

All at once the back of his neck prickled. He realized that some solitary walker was approaching with unusual speed. He turned.

The glow of distant lanterns filtered across the tops of the hedges. Silhouetted against the faint light was a tall man. Phillipe could see nothing more.

The man reached him in three long steps.

"I have a present for you, sir," said the shadow-figure, who seemed to be rummaging in his right-hand pocket. "The one to whom you gave a ruined hand gives you this in return—"

The vague light between the hedges flashed on the barrel of a pocket pistol.

Phillipe only had time to fling himself forward and down as the pistol crashed. A spurt of fire showed him the hem of the killer's dirty coat. Once it had been a vivid color. Orange—

The pistol ball hissed through the leaves directly behind the spot where Phillipe had been standing a moment before. On his knees, he grappled at the man's jackbooted legs. He knew the identity of his attacker now, even though tonight the man wore no sword.

The man cursed, pulled back, aimed a knee at Phillipe's jaw. Phillipe let go, wrenched his head out of the way, seized the heel of the viciously flying boot and heaved upward.

The man tumbled, dropping his pistol. His left hand dove into his coat for another.

Phillipe attacked, clumsily, but with power. He jumped on the bigger man's belly, driving his knee down hard, then again. At the same time he struck at the attacker's face.

The man slammed his head to one side, dodging the

blow. Phillipe's fingers raked something leathery. An eye patch, he was certain.

On the far side of the hedge, he heard feminine cries of fright. The killer's left hand was coming up. For one dreadful instant the dim light again glared on a pistol barrel pointed directly at Phillipe's forehead.

He beat both fists against the man's wrist an instant before the attacker triggered the pistol. The cock fell; the powder flashed; the gun exploded. Phillipe wrenched aside, felt the sharp sting as the ball grazed his left temple. Only his fists, striking the attacker's wrist and angling the ball high and to the side, had saved his life.

The killer beat at the side of Phillipe's head with the butt of his empty weapon. One dizzying blow. Another—accompanied by blasphemous curses. Phillipe lunged backward, managed to gain his feet. He tried to jump in and stamp on the bigger man's throat. But by then, the outcries from nearby sections of the gardens had begun to multiply. Boots hammered the paths—

"Hallo, who shot?"

"Over this way!"

"No, to the left!"

The killer sprang up, kicked Phillipe's shin. The hard blow brought more pain. Off balance, he crashed into the hedge. The whole left side of his head was wet with running blood. He was certain the killer would come at him again.

Instead, the tall man hesitated, as if listening to the approaching runners. Then he ran himself, six steps taking him out of sight around a curve of the path. The hedges hid the belling skirt of his dirty coat of orange shot silk.

iii

Panic and shock overwhelmed Phillipe as two men arrived from the direction opposite that which the one-eyed man had taken in flight.

"Here's the fray, Amos," yelled one of the arrivals, skidding to a halt and plucking something from the path. "Or what's left of it. A pistol. And the victim—or the cause?"

The man confronted Phillipe. "Who are you, sir? What happened here?"

About to blurt an answer, Phillipe's panic got the better of him. He snatched the pistol from the astonished man's hand and bolted off in the direction the killer had gone.

"Here, stop! The watch must look into this, sir. You must make explanation—!"

A foreigner make explanation of attempted murder by a thug employed by the Amberly family? He wanted none of that!

As he ran blindly through the pathways, he felt much as he had when he and his mother fled from Tonbridge. His hatred seethed because he knew again that he was a nobody, to be disposed of at their pleasure. How long had the search been going on while he foolishly thought himself secure at Sholto's?

A young couple barred the path ahead. " 'Ware his gun!" the affrighted young man yelled as Phillipe raced by them, accidentally bumping the girl. She began to scream:

"*Blood! He's messed me with blood!*"

Her scream shrilled up the scale, hysterical. Now that same blood was running into Phillipe's left eye. He plunged right, then right again, trying to find his way out of the warren of hedges, alert to the sounds of people searching for the cause of the commotion. Finally, he broke into the open. Off to his left he thought he recognized a pavilion near the lawn where they'd taken supper.

Moments later, he found the Sholtos and Marie.

They were all on their feet, wondering at the outcries and alarms. Marie let out a low scream at the sight of his bloodied face. Sholto exclaimed, "We heard two pistols discharge—"

"Both aimed at me," Phillipe panted. "By the one-eyed captain. But the Amberlys hired him."

At that, Marie seemed about to swoon. Mrs. Emma supported her. Phillipe threw his coat aside as Solomon Sholto demanded to know what had become of Hosea.

Pulling off his shirt and using it to wipe the blood from his face, Phillipe told them the younger son had gone off by himself. As he flung the shirt away, Mr. Sholto snapped, "Find him, Esau. And let's hide this."

Phillipe felt the pistol tugged out of his belt where he'd thrust it while he ran. He didn't even remember. "Bring Hosea to the chaise with all speed," Mr. Sholto called after his son. Then he bent to conceal the pocket pistol in his wife's hamper.

Next he picked up Phillipe's coat, draped it around the younger man's shoulders. "Everyone to the carriage—and quickly. In case we're stopped, we'll tell them the lad drank too much, fell and hurt himself—here, let's go to the left. Around that milling mob near the path."

They walked rapidly in a group, Phillipe in the center. Mr. Sholto's head swiveled constantly, surveying the situation. People dashed to and fro. Back in the hedges from which Phillipe had escaped, torches and lanterns bobbed. Mr. Sholto's nervous excitement showed in his almost nonstop speech:

"The devil who fired on you may still be lurking—we mustn't linger. But the park's crowded—and thievery's common—practically a robbery a night. We may be able to get away. We don't want to be questioned—"

Phillipe's eyes blurred. The lanterns in a nearby pavilion swam and grew hazy. He managed to say, "No, because I can't tell anyone the truth."

"Are you positive the man was sent by the Amberlys?" Sholto asked.

"Roger Amberly. He wasn't mentioned by name. But the man said my—my *present*, as he called it, came from the one to whom I gave a ruined hand."

He could barely gasp out the final word. His head ached violently. He felt blood running again, staining the coat Mr. Sholto had wrapped around his shoulders. The printer cautioned him in a whisper:

"The gate watchman's eying us—" Loudly: "A casualty of the perfidious gin bottle, sir. The young scoundrel fell and cut his head. We must get him back to town—to a physician, then to a state of sobriety!" Sholto's smile was feeble and nervous.

But the guard seemed more interested in another subject: "Why all the lights and hallooing?"

"There's been a robbery, I think."

"Something new," said the guard, with sour amusement. "Pass on."

Phillipe's step was unsteady. He heard Mr. Sholto say, "The chaise is just ahead." But he never really saw it. He was only dimly aware of climbing inside.

Hours seemed to pass before he heard voices he recognized as belonging to the brothers. Mr. Sholto whipped up the hired team. The chaise clattered away from the lights and clamor in Vauxhall Gardens.

"Safe, thank heaven!" Mrs. Emma exclaimed.

Barely conscious and feeling sick to his stomach, Phillipe knew despairingly that the safety was illusory. Somewhere under the stars Phillipe could hardly see, the one-eyed man was still alive.

iv

St. Paul's tolled one in the morning.

Near the lamp on the Sholtos' kitchen table, the dismantled weapon gleamed. A turn-off pocket pistol, its center-mounted box lock and the screw-on barrel lying separately.

Solomon Sholto had ordered the serving of a third bottle of birthday claret he had left behind when they went on their outing. Phillipe drank a little, feeling better physically. His head was wrapped in a clean linen bandage. The graze was not deep. It had clotted soon after Mrs. Emma cleansed it.

Hosea poked the coals in the kitchen hearth. The poker clanged loudly as he hung it up. Esau scowled an uncharacteristic scowl.

"You are *certain* the attack was made with a purpose?" Mr. Sholto inquired.

Phillipe sighed, nodded. "There's only one person in the world who could accuse me of destroying his hand. Roger, or his mother, or both of them, hired that one-eyed fellow. He probably searched a long time in London before he located me. Through the beggars around the church, I don't doubt." Phillipe covered his eyes. "I fought so damned clumsily. If I'd killed him, that might have been the end of it."

Big Esau snorted. "Stop that. We're ordinary folk, not soldiers. And men like that captain are skilled in the arts of murder. They strike by surprise, to protect their own cowardly hides. You said he ran as soon as the risk of capture presented itself."

Marie put down her wine, some of the old fire showing in her dark eyes. "The very fact they sought us, Phillipe, proves that they fear your claim."

Sick of hearing about the claim, he shook his head angrily. The starkness of his face, which hardly resembled a boy's any longer, made her catch her breath.

"They can strike down the claim by manipulating the law, Mama. It's me Roger wanted, in payment for what I did to him. And there's no use asking the law's help to catch the one-eyed captain. If he were to be locked away, the Amberlys would only hire another like him—and another—until the work's done."

Looking upset, Mrs. Emma asked, "Then what do you propose to do, Phillipe?"

"Leave here. And quickly. We're not safe in London, any more than we were safe in Kent. I was a fool to think otherwise."

"But we can't go running again—!" Marie began.

"We can and we will," he said. For her benefit, he added harshly, "The captain or his successor might strike this house next. I will not repay the kindness of the Sholtos by exposing them to that kind of peril. Doing it once to Mr. Fox was enough."

Solomon Sholto scratched his chin, which was already beginning to sprout next morning's beard. "A speedy departure is probably wise. I'm speaking for your sake more than ours, Phillipe—even though I appreciate your consideration more than I can say. Let us assume the Amberlys and their agent anticipate that you will flee the town. Where will they expect you to go?"

"Where they probably expected us to go before—and no doubt discovered we didn't. One of the Channel ports."

"Which could be watched," Esau said.

Phillipe nodded. "If Roger's as anxious for vengeance as it seems, he may have hired many more pairs of eyes than one. So—"

He barely paused. The decision had come to him only a moment before; inevitable.

"—we will go the other direction. Take our chances on finding passage to the colonies."

He saw rage light Marie's eyes again. Before she could speak he slammed his palm down hard on the table. The dismantled sections of the pistol rattled.

"Mama, there is no other way. Auvergne will be

dangerous to reach. And what's left there anyway, except a dilapidated inn? You must listen to me now. It's my life they're after. And my right to save it the best way I know how."

He regretted speaking to her that way. But he felt there was no choice. Every moment spent in London was another moment spent in jeopardy.

Esau nodded his agreement with Phillipe's decision. "The best coaching service in all England runs west to the port of Bristol. You can be away in the morning from the One Bell in the Strand."

"I have no idea what ship passage will cost," Phillipe said. "Maybe I can work for it. Earn it for the both of us. I've probably saved enough to pay for the coach. But before we leave, I must get to Dr. Franklin's house."

"Hardly seems like the time for a social call—" Hosea began.

"That's not the purpose. When I visited him before—"

"You went to call on that American?" Marie interrupted. "When?"

"Some days ago. Of an evening. You were asleep—"

"You said nothing about it. Nothing."

"I intended to. Each time I got close to it, I stopped short—because I assumed you wouldn't even listen to what he told me."

"About those barbarous colonies? You're right."

"There are big, growing cities in America, Mama! And Dr. Franklin promised that if we decided to go, he'd write a list of printing houses where I could apply for work. Also give me a letter of recommendation—"

Contemptuous, Marie was about to answer when Esau said:

"Damn decent of him."

Solomon Sholto shook his head. "No—just typical of his generous nature. Phillipe, you will be busy enough packing your belongings. Esau, you and Hosea go to Craven Street instead. Rouse the doctor. Explain the situation—"

"But please don't mention the Amberlys," Phillipe cautioned. "I hinted at the problem to Franklin but I didn't go into detail."

Esau nodded as his father said, "Speed back as quickly as you can. Start immediately."

As the brothers struggled into their coats, Phillipe received a fresh shock. Marie was watching him. For a moment it seemed as though her eyes brimmed with genuine hatred. Then the emotion—if it was actually there—dulled; her expression became one of slack-lipped resignation.

Her lips and cheeks were drained of color. She glanced away—brushed at a strand of loose hair with a vague, almost pathetic gesture. He could barely bring himself to look at her. He knew how she must be suffering— watching her one dream smashed beyond all repair.

Well, he'd lived with that kind of thing too; he'd lost Alicia and survived. She could learn to live with her ruined dreams, now that their lives were at stake.

One day she might come to understand that the decision forced on him tonight was made for both their sakes. One day she might accept—and forgive him.

Strangely calm, he realized he might as well go the rest of the way.

"While Hosea and Esau call at Franklin's, I'll borrow a quill and paper, if I may. I want to write a letter to Girard."

"Girard?" Mrs. Emma repeated.

"The man who's minding the inn for us. The place will become his—to keep or sell, as he chooses. We won't be going back to Auvergne for a long time. If ever."

Marie refused to look at him.

"I'll find the writing things," Sholto said. He turned to his sons. "On your way, on your way!—and take your sticks. Watch for anyone lurking. We want no more attacks by that vicious captain tonight. Your mother's had quite enough excitement for one birthday."

"For a lifetime of 'em, sir!" said his wife.

V

Exhausted almost beyond feeling, Phillipe still managed to complete the letter, sand it and wax it shut. Mr. Sholto promised to post it.

Phillipe leaned back and covered his weary eyes. He reflected ironically that once again they would be setting out with no more than the clothes on their backs—Marie's casket, the securely wrapped sword —and one dream of fortune now exchanged for another.

Mrs. Sholto packed them a small hamper of food as Phillipe dressed just before daylight. The elder Sholto once again dispatched his sons, who had come back from Craven Street. This time they were to survey the yard of the One Bell in the Strand, to see whether, by remotest chance, the one-eyed man had been noticed in the vicinity.

The One Bell was a major coach departure point. But only one of many. The captain could not be expected to survey them all personally, even if he suspected that Phillipe and his mother might resort to immediate flight. Still, Mr. Sholto advised the precaution.

When the sons came back with the Bristol coach schedule—the first departed at seven—they reported no obviously suspicious persons on the premises they'd scouted. But Esau did remind Phillipe of his own words—that there was no way of telling how many watchers—or of what identity—the Amberlys' agent might employ.

As the family set out on foot together from Sweet's Lane—Mrs. Emma having insisted she would not be frightened out of seeing them off—it was just past six by the great bells. The narrow, twisting streets were still almost empty.

Esau pressed a pouch into Phillipe's hand. "The doctor sends you his commendation on your decision. He also expressed his hope that the list and letter will help secure you at least an apprentice's job at a good printing house."

"I'm sorry you had to waken him," Phillipe said.

Hosea grinned. "Oh, we didn't waken him."

Esau cleared his throat. "Dr. Franklin was—ah—entertaining."

"A damned smart-looking young flirt named Polly. His landlady's daughter," Hosea said. "Really, it was quite a scene. Franklin in his dressing gown—the wench in a filmy bed dress that would scandalize our dear mother. The doctor was ostensibly amusing the girl with tunes on a fiddle. But there was plenty of Madeira in evidence. I wonder if the old reprobate wasn't doing a little fiddling of a different kind—"

"Stop sounding so jealous," Esau said. "Dr. Franklin's relations with ladies other than his wife are entirely platonic."

"Or so he pretends in public," replied Hosea with a knowing smirk.

Annoyed, Esau changed the subject: "Have you any idea what your final destination will be, Phillipe?"

"Whatever the destination of the first available ship." Puzzled, he pointed to a second, smaller pouch Esau had taken from his pocket. "What's that?"

"As you asked, I didn't reveal the reasons behind your abrupt decision. Nor mention the name you wanted kept secret. But I did suggest that you had been threatened with harm. Franklin immediately gave me five pounds to help secure your passage—and cursed the air blue in the process."

Astonished, Phillipe asked, "Why?"

"You said yourself—you hinted to him that you'd encountered some trouble with persons of high station. Persons against whom you had no defense. He abominates that sort of thing. Also, he has a good opinion of you—and your ability to fit in where you're going. Yes, he was most flattering. Said he judged you to be strong, determined, intelligent—and now, obviously capable of quick action when circumstances demand it."

Gil said I had the makings of a soldier, Phillipe thought wearily.

Mama harped that I was a little lord. To Franklin I'm a printer's boy of determined character—just what the hell's it to be?

Then, with a kind of cold, weary insight, he imagined that the truth was closest of all to this: he would know what he was only afterward, when he'd seen how it had all come out.

"By the way," Esau added as they trudged along, "Franklin's not giving you a gift in perpetuity. He specifically charged me to tell you he expects the loan to be repaid one of these days. From the profits of your own printing house. He'll be back in America eventually—and will make a point of collecting. He was smiling when he said it. But he wasn't joking. I'd consider that another compliment."

"Franklin's estimate of my abilities, and of opportunities in America, may both be overrated. By his own admission it's not a peaceful country these days,"

"More peaceful than London—at least for you," Hosea put in. "Have a care. We're almost to the Strand."

He ran ahead, jumping over two bawds snoring dead drunk against a wall At the corner Hosea looked right and left. Then he gestured the rest of them to follow.

Phillipe began to feel a little excitement mingled with a sense of relief at being able to escape so quickly. The sun was starting to slant down between the rickety tenements now. The spring air was sweet and cool, tanged with the scents of the river and the smoke from London's chimney pots. A bit more confidently, he tucked Dr. Franklin's purse of money in a pocket and the pouch of papers in his belt under his coat.

Hosea ran back along the shops of the Strand to inform them, "The express is already loading. A four-horse coach—and it's packed. You'll be lucky to find places on top. Better hurry."

They did, even Marie managing to keep up.

In the noisy, clattering yard of the One Bell, Mr. Sholto helped Phillipe pay the double fare. Eyeing the crowd, Hosea and Esau assisted Marie in her climb to the top, and an uncomfortable seat on the flat roof. She would have only the rails for handholds.

Phillipe noticed that the interior of the coach was indeed jammed with passengers: a large family; two black-clad parsons. He prepared to climb up the wheel spokes before all the room was taken by a third passenger mounting the other side—a hulking blackamoor in a sateen coat and breeches. Evidently the black was the servant of a portly gentleman rudely squeezing inside the coach proper, over the protests of the others.

Mrs. Emma gave Phillipe a quick, forceful hug. She was crying, incapable of speech.

The sons, then stern-eyed Mr. Sholto shook his hand.

"I pray the Almighty protects you. And grants you a better welcome in the new land than you found in this one," the printer said.

Not looking back, Phillipe climbed the wheel to the roof of the coach.

CHAPTER VI

The Bristol Coach

i

SHOUTS FROM THE DRIVER and a blast from the guard's brass horn warned of imminent departure. The guard hung his horn over his shoulder by a lanyard, hoisted himself and his blunderbuss up into position.

Phillipe settled cross-legged on the roof of the coach. He slid the wrapped sword beneath his thighs and deposited the precious casket in the diamond-shaped space between his legs. The blackamoor, whose tricorn hat contrasted strangely with his apparel and the gold hoop that hung from the pierced lobe of his right ear, shifted a little to make more room. Phillipe nodded in polite acknowledgment.

The blackamoor broke into a big grin, displaying a huge expanse of even white teeth. The man thumped his chest with an immense fist.

"I be Lucas, sar," he said in peculiarly accented English. "We ride a long way to the sea town, so we hang on tight, yes?"

"I think you're right," Phillipe replied with amiable casualness. "The roads are probably none too smooth—Mama, hold onto the side rails!"

Marie sat with her knees tucked up near her chin, her hands locked around them. The hands looked white, bloodless.

276

And her lips were moving.

Phillipe's stomach tightened up. He leaned forward, touched her hand. She didn't respond. She was speaking French in a monotone. Her eyes stared past him at the morning sky and saw nothing.

Then he caught some of her words.

"—and when this coach arrives at their door, I'll tell them, 'This is the little lord. Treat him as he deserves. It's his birthright.'"

Terrified, Phillipe shook Marie's arm, said in French, "Mama, we're not going to Kentland. This is the coach to Bristol. For God's sake look at me!"

Slowly, as if returning with difficulty from contemplation of some remote landscape of the mind, she appeared to take notice of the surroundings. Bleak lines showed on her face.

"You must hold on to the rails or you'll fall," he warned, noticing that the Sholto family had all seen the peculiar expression on his mother's face. They watched her with obvious concern. A scrawny man whose greasy clubbed hair shone in the sunlight also gave Phillipe a curious stare as he turned his bay horse out of the One Bell's yard and clattered away up the Strand.

"Please," Phillipe pleaded, trying to pry his mother's hands apart. "You must hold on!"

Her eyes focused on his face. She said in French, "What difference does it make now?"

The driver uncoiled his short whip, gathered up the traces of the four impatient horses. Phillipe reached over, seized the man's shoulder:

"Wait! I must get my mother down inside."

The driver growled, "We've a schedule to keep. We should have left ten minutes ago. Besides, there's no room below."

"I'll make room," Phillipe said, already slipping over the side and skittering down the wheel spokes.

He yanked the coach door open, face to face with one

of the children in the traveling family, a bonneted little
girl, perched on her father's knee. Smiling, she was offering her small hoop to the portly man opposite. He in
turn registered his dislike of children in general, and this
one in particular, with an expression of pompous annoyance.

Phillipe said, "I beg your pardon, ladies and
gentlemen. My mother's not feeling well. Is there space
inside here, out of the wind?"

"No," said one of the parsons on the far side of the
coach. "But we'll make some. Stay seated, Andrew," he
added to his companion. "We'll take turns riding on
top." He opened the door on his side and stepped out.

While the driver continued to grumble, Phillipe
helped his mother down again. He settled her where
the churchman had been seated, placed the casket in her
lap. She clutched it protectively. Then she began to
mumble in French again. Phillipe heard the words *little
lord* as he shut the door, clambered up and resumed his
place along with the blackamoor and the shovel-hatted
parson, who was already clutching the hat to his head
with one hand while he gripped his testament with the
other.

The driver flashed Phillipe a glare, muttering,
"Damned cheeky foreigner." He uncoiled the whip,
cracked it over the heads of his horses. With a jolt the
coach rolled forward. The parson dropped his testament
and seized the rail only just in time to keep from being
toppled off.

The coach clattered away from the One Bell. Phillipe
waved at the Sholtos as their figures diminished and
then disappeared altogether. He could think of nothing
except his mother down below. Had the decision to
make for Bristol, and the colonies, finally undone her?
Unconsciously he tightened his hand on the rail, cursing
the Amberlys and cursing himself. The blackamoor
stared in astonishment.

Phillipe paid no attention. Why couldn't his mother recognize that they were going to a place that might afford them safety, and a fresh start?

He knew the answer. It was not their ultimate destination that was at fault. He suspected she would have acted the same way if they'd returned to Les Trois Chevres. She had harbored her dream too long, to the exclusion of all others. Its destruction was in turn destroying her.

The morning wind blowing over the coach roof forced him to squint into the jumbled distance of streets and buildings. But he saw only Marie—her lips moving; her eyes vacant; her hands gripping the casket like claws.

He was desperately afraid for her sanity.

ii

Westward, the crowded streets and lanes became occasional cottages and gardens—then open country, as the coach took the post road to Bristol.

The spring sun beat against Phillipe's back, making him sweat heavily. But the enforced concentration required to hold his place on top of the swaying, jolting coach helped push the worries about his mother to the back of his mind.

Lucas, the blackamoor, sat dozing, apparently quite at home with this risky mode of travel. The parson had tugged his shovel hat down next to his ears, and now used one hand to hold his open testament practically under his nose. How the cleric managed to read with all the bumps, the racket of hoof and wheel and driver's whip, and the blowing dust that clouded over them, visibly soiling the white lappets of the parson's collar, Phillipe couldn't imagine.

In an hour, though, he'd grown accustomed to swaying and bouncing and holding on. He even managed to relax a little. The sun's warmth helped cheer him, as did

occasional friendly waves from farmers laboring in the
hay fields or maneuvering their vegetable carts to the
road's shoulder to permit passage of the speeding coach.
The rolling, sunlit countryside brought Phillipe a sense
of freedom, security—and direction—he hadn't enjoyed
since the encounter at Vauxhall Gardens. He'd be sore
and aching when they reached Bristol tomorrow. But if
that was the worst that happened, he could be thankful.

He grew aware of the whites of the blackamoor's
eyes. When had the big man wakened? Phillipe hadn't
noticed. Lucas was watching the road behind them. The
wrinkles on the broad ebony forehead made it clear the
blackamoor had spotted something unusual.

"Man on a horse, sar," Lucas pointed. "Not there a
while ago."

As the black man tapped the driver's shoulder,
Phillipe twisted his head around—and exhaled hard.

The rider was pacing the coach perhaps a quarter-
mile behind. Phillipe could make out only essentials
through the dust churning up from the rear wheels. The
rider was scrawny, his mount a powerful bay. Phillipe
remembered seeing such a horseman depart from the
One Bell a few minutes ahead of the coach.

"Could be a gentleman jus' riding," Lucas shouted to
his companions. "Or could be a road captain."

The driver preferred to take no chances. He immediately whipped up his horses.

"In the latter event," yelled the parson, "I will for
once be thankful for the poverty of clerics. A highwayman would want nothing of mine."

Lucas surveyed the landscape skimming by on either
side.

Thickets and low hills now. Not a sign of a farmstead,
nor any other riders or wagons anywhere ahead.

The blackamoor growled, "Been robbed once before,
on the Oxford coach. Sometimes, the captains don' ride
alone. That happen, everybody certain to be poor after."

Alarmed, Phillipe thought of the talk he'd heard about highwaymen in London. Captured ones were summarily hanged from Tyburn Tree. But that didn't seem to discourage extensive practice of the profession. They were a desperate lot.

Phillipe turned around again. The rider on the bay was galloping to keep pace with the speeding coach. His hand came up. Suddenly an explosion split the morning air, louder than the thunder of the wheels.

From beech thickets flanking the post road just ahead, two other horsemen appeared, spurring to the road's center to block passage of the coach. Now it was no longer a question of outrunning a single rider.

The one behind had fired the warning shot. Both men ahead rode expertly, without gripping the reins. Between them they held four long-barreled pistols.

The coach guard flung the blunderbuss to his shoulder, then let it drop—because the driver was already kicking at the brake and hauling on the traces, unwilling to press his luck against a trio.

Phillipe's eyes riveted on the rider who had come out from the left side of the road. He sat very tall in his saddle, the silver side plates and butt caps on his pistols flashing in the sunlight. Even through the billowing dust, Phillipe could see that the highwayman wore a leather patch over one eye, jackboots and a dirty coat that had once been bright orange.

iii

Shrill questions and cries of alarm rose from inside the coach as it swayed to a halt. The guard leaned over the side and yelled:

"Keep still and hand 'em all your valuables and we'll get off safe—if we're lucky."

Phillipe's scalp crawled with sweat. Perched in the

open, he was quite aware that the one-eyed man had spotted him. As the coach settled to rest, the two highwaymen trotted their horses toward it, joined by their companion from behind. He sprang from his saddle, jerked open the left-hand door.

Phillipe sat utterly still. He knew this meeting was not accidental. Perhaps there had been watchers at every coaching inn of importance. His palms grew as sweaty as his forehead. He realized once again the depths of Roger Amberly's animosity.

The one-eyed man gave the driver an empty smile and a salute with one pistol. At close range, the pock marks on his ravaged cheeks stood out clearly.

"Captain Plummer, sir, at your service. We'll trouble your passengers for whatever trinkets they may have. Then you shall be on your way again."

"Everyone out," ordered the scrawny man at the coach door, stowing both of his pistols in his belt. The four barrels of the two others still menaced driver, guard and passengers—sufficient firepower to guarantee success of the enterprise.

The family alighted first, the mother comforting her frightened little daughter. Next came the outraged fat man, then the other parson. Of Marie there was no immediate sign.

But Phillipe was more concerned with Captain Plummer. He brought his horse near the coach and once again smiled his false smile:

"If each one of you ladies and gentlemen obey the orders of my coves in good fashion, we shall have no unhappy accidents." His one glaring eye slid to Phillipe—and the smile froze in place. Phillipe knew full well what was going to happen. At least one "unhappy accident."

When Captain Plummer saw that understanding register on Phillipe's face, his smile became genuine. He wagged a pistol.

"If the passengers on the roof will also alight, please—?"

As the parson began to descend via the wheel spokes, the scrawny man said, "There's one left inside, cap'n. A woman."

Plummer nodded. "Yes, I wondered about that."

Phillipe's cheeks felt fiery. Under his sweated clothes, his heart hammered hard. He knew he had no chance to unwrap Gil's sword. Nor did he have any other weapon at his disposal. But unless he defended himself, he would die, the quickly forgotten victim of yet another highway incident.

Lucas' shiny face looked ferocious as he climbed down. A possible ally there, Phillipe thought, dropping into the dust behind the blackamoor.

"Assist our reluctant passenger," Captain Plummer ordered his scrawny helper.

The man dropped a sack he'd pulled down from his saddle, reached inside the coach toward Marie. For one moment, his body and outstretched right arm blocked the line of sight between Phillipe and Captain Plummer. Phillipe chose the moment because it might be his last chance. He struck for the scrawny man's exposed middle with both fists.

iv

The scrawny man doubled forward, uttering a furious curse. He clawed for the second, undischarged pistol in his belt. Phillipe heard the mother of the little girl shriek—and something else: the sudden clopping of Captain Plummer's horse as the one-eyed man positioned himself to shoot.

Phillipe whirled the dazed man by the shoulders. Captain Plummer's right-hand pistol boomed with a flash and a puff of smoke. Blood splattered Phillipe's cheeks as Plummer's close-range ball blew a hole in the scrawny man's neck.

The man let out a kind of choking sigh, sagging in Phillipe's arms, no longer a shield.

Phillipe released the dead man, leaped away as the passengers yelled and scattered. Plummer roweled his nervous horse viciously to hold him still, pointed his second pistol at Phillipe's head.

A clear target against the side of the coach, Phillipe had no place to run. The dark eye of the pistol muzzle followed him as he threw himself on the ground.

Captain Plummer was a professional. He would not be rushed into the shot for which he had undoubtedly been well compensated. Hitting the dust, Phillipe awaited the explosion, the thud of a ball into his flesh—

But it didn't come. The blunderbuss roared.

Captain Plummer began to swear, his oaths punctuated by groans of effort. Phillipe rolled frantically underneath the coach and out the other side. Just ahead of the horses, the third highwayman toppled from his saddle. A wound in his groin bubbled red.

That man had been the target of the blunderbuss, then. Phillipe ran toward him. Over the lathered backs of the horses he saw what had saved him. The blackamoor had fastened both hands on Captain Plummer's left arm and was holding on ferociously, even as Plummer tried to haul back in the saddle and transfer his still-loaded pistol to his right hand.

But the immense Lucas kept levering the highwayman's left arm down and back. Plummer's mouth worked in obscene rage, spittle on his lips, sweat on his pocked cheeks. With his right hand he hit for Lucas's eyes, to claw them out if he could. Lucas snapped his head back, laughed a big booming laugh that died abruptly as Plummer managed to gouge a thumb into his eyesocket.

Lucas's hold on the highwayman's left arm loosened. Plummer wrenched free and aimed at the nearest target—the black by his stirrup.

Phillipe had reached the fallen man, who was moaning in pain. He snatched up one of the man's pistols. He fired past the bobbing muzzles of the lead coach horses.

With a scream, Captain Plummer arched his back. Phillipe had aimed for the best and biggest target—the man's torso. There, over the left ribs, the shabby orange coat showed an immense black-edged hole from which blood poured.

Lucas pried the pistol out of Plummer's relaxed hand, drew back the cock and fired point blank.

Captain Plummer's leather eyepatch disappeared in a torrent of blood. The sight brought fresh screams and hysterical sobs from the mother and her small girl. The big blackamoor hit Plummer's horse on the flank and sent it bolting toward the trees. The sudden motion flung the highwayman's corpse into the roadside ditch, mercifully hiding the ruin of his head.

Wiping sweat and dust from his cheeks, the blackamoor grinned across the backs of the horses.

"A keen shot, sar."

Phillipe waved weakly, dropped the hot pistol in the dirt. He heard the driver and the guard calling thanks and congratulations. With surprising lack of Christian concern for the dead thieves, even the parsons expressed delight at the outcome.

Phillipe walked back to the right-hand coach door, opened it to look at his mother. He started to speak, couldn't.

Marie huddled in the corner. Her fingers tapped nervously at the old leather of the casket. Her lips moved but produced no sound. Her eyes stared far beyond the wall of the coach. If she'd heard the pistol shots and the screaming, she gave no sign.

Phillipe spoke his mother's name.

Silence.

Slowly he closed the coach door and stumbled to the roadside ditch. There he bent over, violently sick.

v

Presently the journey resumed, Phillipe back in place on the roof with his equally bedraggled companions.

Lucas hummed, striking his palm in rhythm against the sateen of his knee as the coach flashed under low-hanging branches that dappled Phillipe's vision with flickering shadows.

He'd tried to rouse Marie once more before the coach got under way. He had managed to produce a murmur that might have indicated she recognized him. But that was all.

In a way he was glad that she had missed the entire encounter. But her condition continued to frighten him.

He felt totally alone. Only he knew the true reason Captain Plummer and his henchmen had selected this particular coach for plundering. Plummer had planned to earn a double reward. His loot from the passengers, and whatever sum he'd been paid by Phillipe's half-brother.

Phillipe tried to imagine the damage the fight with the silver-headed stick had worked on the young nobleman's hand. It must have been considerable to provoke such retribution. Of course—Phillipe was already familiar with this bitter lesson—Roger would have undertaken his scheme with few fears of paying any penalty. Phillipe only hoped there would be no further pursuit before he was able to secure their passage out of Bristol.

But there was no one to whom he could communicate his anxieties now. Not the driver, whose attitude had become overwhelmingly cordial; not the parsons; no

one. His secrets, and his hatred, were prisoned inside,
where their heat had begun to forge a new Phillipe Charboneau out of the one who had so naively crossed the
Channel only a year ago.

As the coach jounced along, he realized he was near-
ing his nineteenth birthday. He'd lived nearly half a
man's normal life span already. In Auvergne, he had
known virtually nothing of the world. But in the last
twelve months he had learned enough to more than
make up. He only hoped he could put the experience to
some use.

It troubled him deeply that he had now been responsible for the deaths of three human beings—four if he
counted the scrawny fellow he'd thrust into the path of
Captain Plummer's ball.

True, none of the killings was deliberate. All had been
done in self-defense. And his success in each case was,
in fact, the source of an odd, guilty pride.

Still, none of the deaths, not even Plummer's, rested
easy on him. As he clung to the roof rails, beginning to
ache from all the bounces and jolts, he hoped to God he
would never entirely lose that sense of life's value.

If he ever did, he would then have become exactly
like Roger Amberly.

vi

Finally, about an hour after the incident with Captain
Plummer and his men, Phillipe shook off the horror of
the attack and turned his mind to more practical things.

A ship out of Bristol offered not only sanctuary but
hope and opportunity. So the ledger was not entirely
without its credits. He recalled the money Franklin had
advanced and searched for the purse to make certain he
hadn't lost it in his scramblings. He hadn't.

But the pouch containing the list of printing houses
and the letter of introduction was gone from his belt.

Urgently, he bent forward to the driver's shoulder. "Sir—back along the road when we stopped, I lost papers I was carrying."

"Sorry, lad," the man shouted. "Can't turn around. Can't stop except to change horses—I'm fined if we don't keep schedule. Even when the cause is a captain of the road."

"But the papers are valuable. I need them where I'm going."

"Then ye'll have to take another coach back, and try to get off and search," was the answer. An impossible answer, Phillipe knew. Funds were short enough as it was. And he felt he dared not leave Marie alone now that her health had taken such a strange, precarious turn.

He regretted his own stupidity in not taking the time to so much as glance at Franklin's list. Even a few remembered names might have been of assistance when—and if—they reached America. Establishing connections in a new city would be just that much more difficult now.

He smiled a small, bitter smile. Even in failure, Roger Amberly's agents had dealt a blow to his prospects.

But he reminded himself that he was no longer Phillipe Charboneau of Auvergne. He had become someone different; harder, perhaps.

And so he thought, *God damn them all. I will survive.*

vii

The Bristol coach stopped the night at a restful country inn. When Phillipe opened the door to help his mother alight, he was thankful that she seemed aware of her immediate surroundings, and his identity again.

Earlier, when the driver had halted a few minutes at a way station for fresh horses, Phillipe had circulated quietly among the passengers. At that time Marie was

still sitting immobile inside. He told the passengers that
due to recent strains, his mother was not herself. He suggested there was no point in alarming her later with
references to the attack by Captain Plummer. Since
Phillipe and the blackamoor had assumed the temporary
stature of heroes, thanks to boldness and lucky shooting, the others readily agreed.

Even the portly and somewhat pompous man whom
Lucas served grew more friendly. He invited Phillipe to
share his table at the inn that evening.

The portly gentleman was named Hoskins. He lived
in Bristol. He was quick to point out that he did not own
Lucas outright, as a slave—as was the custom in some
of the colonies. The blackamoor was a free member of
the serving class.

"So he can join us, too," Phillipe said as the guard
tooted his horn to signal that the coach was ready to get
under way.

"Oh, no!" Hoskins returned, horrified. "He's still required to eat in the kitchen."

Climbing up the wheel, Phillipe recalled the Irishman
Burke's remark about Dr. Franklin having organized a
colonial society to oppose the institution of slavery. But
he couldn't recall any mention of slavery in the
numerous books and pamphlets he'd devoured. Perhaps
the references had been there and had slipped by him; or
perhaps the propagandists of the colonies preferred to
gloss over the subject. At any rate, the reminder that a
market for human beings existed in America tainted
Franklin's glowing comments somewhat.

At their overnight stop, Phillipe and Marie sat opposite Hoskins. After a filling meal, of which Marie ate
little, the traveling family retired for the night. The parsons withdrew to a private table, presumably to discuss
rarefied theological subjects. The coach driver and the
guard had eaten their suppers on benches near the
cheerful fire. They were already drunk and busy poking

and fingering the rump of the inn's cowlike serving girl.

"Have you and your mother any connections in Bristol?" Hoskins asked eventually.

"No, sir, none." Phillipe glanced at his mother. The fire lit her dark eyes with pinpoints of brilliance, threw patterns of scarlet and shadow on her cheeks. She stared at her mug of ale that had been heated with a poker. She'd managed a few yes and no answers during dinner conversation, but nothing more. Phillipe was terrified in the face of such continuing silent despair.

With effort, he amplified his short answer to Hoskins:

"We're anxious to find a ship for America, though."

Hoskins drank. He was already working on his third or fourth mug. "Oh, then you've connections in the colonies."

Again Phillipe shook his head. "We intend to sail to one of the colonial ports, where I mean to look for work as a printer."

"Which port's your destination?"

"We'll go wherever the first ship goes, probably. Do you know how much it costs for passage, sir? I have five pounds."

Hoskins drank more ale. "Not nearly enough. However—" He belched, wiped his blubbery lips with his sleeve. "Since you defended us so handsomely today, and I take you for a person of good, if humble character, I may confide a secret. I'm carrying a deal of money. Yes, a deal," he emphasized with puffed-up pride, fingering the thickness under his waistcoat. Phillipe had assumed it to be natural fat, not concealed wealth.

" 'M a manufacturer of ironware. Hoskins' kettles and pisspots are the byword in the finest dining places and hostelries in London. Used in many of the very best whorehouses, too—oh. Your pardon, madame. Now I just sold a handsome lot of merchandise this trip. But I also ship to the colonies. Oh, yes, in quantity. And while I'm a loyal Tory—a supporter of His Majesty—I also prefer to see relations with America prosper at any cost. Any cost short of rebellion, that is. I'm glad the King's ministers repealed some of those damned taxes. Might have been necessary, those taxes. But ruinous for trade—ruinous! Urged their repeal myself. Joined with many other important merchants and factory owners. Put the screws on that fat German—"

Hoskins belched even more loudly. Phillipe realized the overweight gentleman was tipsy.

"Beg pardon, His Majesty. Where was I? Oh yes. Colonial trade. Well. In Bristol, one of my first tasks is to immediately hie myself to the wharfs and see what American vessels are in port. For with this—"

Another thump of what had to be a money belt concealed under his clothing.

"—I can finance quite a shipment of Hoskins' finest to our American cousins. Yes. Quite a shipment." Belch.

Phillipe sat silent, letting the fat man ramble on.

"Here's the point, young fellow. I have wide acquaintance with the sailing masters who call at Bristol from Philadephia, New York City and that blasphemous hotbed of treason—" A double belch; a prodigious yawn. "—Boston. So if you care to follow me during my calls on the captains, perhaps I can use my influence to find you a working berth. Only alternative is to sell yourself to the captain for seven years, then hope he can re-sell your indenture contract to some decent gentleman on the other side. Let me see—" A noisy fart"—Madame, beg pardon. Let me see if I can help you get around that unpleasant prospect. I do have influence. I ship large orders. Large! You saved me a deal of money. Grateful. Glad to swing my weight with the captains as best I can. They lose ship's boys all the time, they do. Boys squander their pay on wagers in the cock pits. Dally with whor—prostitutes. Lie drunk when their vessels sail. Shouldn't be hard. Not with a tot of luck. And Hoskins. All the captains know Hoskins. Successful merchant prince. Finest ironware—"

With a gentle *whoosh*, Hoskins settled his lips together, thunked his head against the high back of the bench and began to snore.

Phillipe had already made up his mind to accept the invitation. He would indeed dog Hoskins' every step when he called at the port to arrange his shipment.

Encouraged again, Phillipe slid off the bench. He bent over Marie, slipped an arm around her slumped shoulders, said softly:

"Mama?"

"What?"

"Are you tired now? Do you want to go up to the room and sleep?"

Still gazing at the mug of heated ale, she didn't answer.

A minute went by. Another.

Heartbroken, Phillipe pried her fingers loose one by one. He helped her stand up, all the while speaking to her in a low voice, soothing her as he would a child. She shuffled her feet as she walked, accepting physical direction of her body in a docile way. The parsons watched. Even the driver and his guard stopped their rowdy laughter, to stare with strangely sober expressions.

CHAPTER VII

To an Unknown Shore

i

EIGHT MILES UP THE River Avon from the Bristol Channel, along the brawling, noisy Bristol docks, Phillipe Charboneau discovered that Hoskins was as good as his tipsy word. Under the brilliant blue of a May morning, Phillipe dodged among burly handlers loading and unloading cargo as he followed the portly ironmaker along the tar-reeking pier.

A thicket of masts stood against the sky. Great hulls creaked in their berths. Ropes and pulleys racketed, off-loading a bewildering array of goods from the newest arrivals in port.

They passed men bent beneath the weight of huge sacks of fragrant African cocoa beans. Phillipe saw a factor's agent slash open a canvas bale to inspect a bundle of light brown leaves the size of elephants' ears. Hoskins informed him that was tobacco in its native state, fresh from the tidewater plantations in America's southern colonies.

Hailing another factor of his acquaintance, Hoskins got permission to pluck a sample from a small mountain of stalks, each of which bore dozens of tubular and slightly curved yellow fruits. He handed the sweet-smelling sample to Phillipe, who immediately picked up Hoskins' cue that it was "passing tasty," and started to bite into it.

Hoskins puffed up with shock. "Wait, you must skin it first! Have you never seen a West Indies banana?"

"Banana? No. I've never even heard the word."

"Well, then, Hoskins is giving you a liberal education in world commerce, damme if he isn't."

To which Phillipe could only nod enthusiastic agreement, though it was well nigh impossible for him to assimilate every detail of the busy wharf scene.

Strutting along, Hoskins made inquiries of several clerks and seamen. He seemed to be on familiar terms with many of them. At last he informed Phillipe:

"Excellent luck! One of the more reliable captains docked two days ago. Will Caleb out of Boston. I've shipped goods with him before. A God-fearing man who can be relied upon not to be grogged to the eyeballs during a squall. Profit is too precious a commodity to be risked with a sot. Come on, sir, a little more lively! That's Caleb's vessel second one down. We'll see whether I can strike a bargain."

Bustling ahead with a step surprisingly brisk for one of his girth, Hoskins led the way to the foot of the gangplank running up to the ship. She was three-masted, some eighty feet long and perhaps a quarter of that across. She bore the gilt-painted name *Eclipse*.

At the rail, watching a line of handlers loading large canvas-covered chests aboard, was a hawkish, white-haired man of fifty or so. He had thin lips and a face tanned and roughened by exposure to the elements. He wore a plain coat of dark blue wool.

Hoskins hailed him: "Good morning, Captain Caleb! Are you bound back for Boston?"

"Good morning, Hoskins," answered the sea captain, with a compression of his lips that passed for a smile. "I am that—when the hold's full."

"What are you carrying, sir?"

Captain Caleb replied that he had so far negotiated to

freight fifty chests of green Hyson tea and a quantity of
Lancashire fustian in assorted colors. He added:

"But I've room for more."

"Then by all means let's discuss an arrangement."

As he waved Hoskins aboard, the master of *Eclipse*
glanced at Phillipe with a flash of curiosity. "Step to one
side for Mr. Hoskins!" he shouted to the handlers. "Any
man dropping a chest in the harbor will discover that a
peace-loving captain can still use the cat!"

Hoskins bobbed his head to indicate that Phillipe
should follow, which he did, causing Captain Caleb's
white brows to shoot upward in puzzlement. Caleb
shook the fat man's hand as the latter stepped on deck.

"You've lost Lucas, then? Replaced him with this
young man since last I saw you?"

Hoskins shook his head. "No, sir, Lucas is presently
at the Flagon, attending this young man's mother. She
was not in proper spirits to come knocking about these
piers."

Phillipe wondered how Marie was surviving the wait
at the inn. Though listless, she'd seemed a little more
herself when they arrived in Bristol.

"On the coach trip from London," Hoskins went on,
"this chap, Mr. Phillipe Charboneau, provided
handsome service—as did Lucas—in defending myself
and other passengers from three infernal highwaymen.
Since Mr. Charboneau has small funds, but a great
desire to start a new life in the Americas, I brought him
along in the hope of finding an available berth."

Captain Caleb's eyes displayed innumerable wrinkles
at the corners as he scrutinized Phillipe again. "Well, my
mess boy's felled with a flux. I should leave him
behind—which I won't, since I know the plight of his
widowed mother back in Marblehead. The boy may be
up and about soon or he may not. I might be able to use
a hand and I might not." His glance grew sharper.

"However, I want no hands who are fleeing from the law or the debtor's prison."

"I'm fleeing from nothing like that, sir," Phillipe said as Caleb continued to evaluate his size and probable strength. The half-truth came easily because of the circumstances. "I'm only going toward something —starting with a passage."

Caleb thumbed his wind-roughened chin. "You don't speak pure English. What are you, French?"

Phillipe wanted to reply that the captain didn't speak pure English either, but rather, a strange, nasal version of it. Was that how colonials of Boston talked? Prudence made him simply nod instead.

"How much money can you pay?" Caleb asked.

"I have five pounds."

"For himself *and* his mother," Hoskins emphasized. "As I mentioned, Lucas is keeping watch over the lady right this moment. She is not herself. Certain problems of health—"

At this, Captain Caleb looked even more skeptical. "I'm not taken with sailing a sick woman to Boston. We make a hard crossing. Six, eight weeks, depending on storms and adverse winds."

"She can manage, Captain," Phillipe said. "She's as anxious to be away from England as I am."

"Well, five pounds is hardly sufficient—even if I used you in the mess, helping that Dutch devil Gropius with his so-called cooking."

Hoskins cleared his throat self-importantly. "Captain Caleb, I indicated that Mr. Charboneau performed a brave service, and saved me considerable expense. If you're averse to passengers such as he and his mother, perhaps I should pass along the wharf and seek another vessel for my shipment."

Standing on the gently rolling deck with the shadows of noisy gulls falling through the tangle of spars and lines above, Phillipe felt a tightening in his throat, an emotional response to Hoskins' bluff. He didn't want to lose this chance, even though he was more than a little intimidated by the immense unknown lying to the west along the glitter of the Avon.

"I was planning to ship a deal of kettles," Hoskins sighed. "Yes, a deal. But I want to assist the boy as part of the bargain." He turned to Phillipe. "We'd best make inquiries elsewhere."

"Here, not so hasty!" Caleb exclaimed, seizing Hoskins' arm.

Neither man smiled. But each had a glitter in his eye that signaled the enjoyment of hard bargaining. Caleb said to Phillipe, "You go aft, lad." He was required to point out the direction to the nautical novice. "So you don't interrupt those dock rats doing the loading. Hoskins and I will drop down to my cabin, where I keep a bit of Providence rum for special visitors."

And, slipping an arm around Hoskins' shoulder, he led him away, murmuring, "Now, sir, indicate to me the quantity of iron on which we'll open the discussion—"

They vanished below, leaving Phillipe to pace nervously for almost an hour.

When the two men reappeared, Hoskins was smiling.

"You and your mother are aboard, Mr. Charboneau. In a single, very small and airless cabin, I'm afraid. I couldn't wheedle two from a hard-headed Yankee like Caleb. But I filled his hold for him. We'll load tonight and the pilot will take *Eclipse* down the river on the tide tomorrow. Shall we fetch your mother?"

"Yes, sir, certainly. How can I ever thank you?"

"It's I who have a debt to pay," Hoskins answered as they dodged their way down the plank again. "Thanks to you, I'm less poor than I might have been. Turning over a pound is all in life that matters. Keep that as your maxim in the colonies. Indeed, if you stick to commerce and avoid politics, you'll end up rich instead of hanged."

Thus maintaining his pose of total unconcern for others—a pose his actions of the morning belied —Hoskins strutted away up the wharf. He assumed Phillipe would follow; he did not glance back. Phillipe smiled and tagged after him.

ii

Gray weather greeted the one-hundred-fifty-ton schooner *Eclipse* as she left the western counties of England astern and cracked on canvas, her prow rising and plummeting through an already heavy sea.

The mess boy was still confined to his berth with the flux. Phillipe was put on duty at once. The ship hadn't been away from the mouth of the Bristol Channel two hours before he received six whacks of a stick from the bandy-legged ship's cook.

The Dutchman, named Gropius, spoke only a few words of English, and those mostly obscene. But Gropius' vocabulary and the stick were sufficient to indicate that Phillipe had committed his first error.

Gropius had handed him a kettle of stew to lug to the crew's mess. Phillipe observed aloud that the stew seemed to include a number of recently cooked white slugs. That brought on the howls and the whacking.

Phillipe's anger flared at the first blow. But he accepted the punishment because he realized he was lucky to be sailing for the colonies so soon. He carried the kettle to the mess without protest, rubbed his butt on the way back and decided to say nothing about the weevils in the biscuits or the worms in the potatoes.

Besides, he had plenty to do just learning to negotiate the tilting decks and companionways without spilling the contents of such a kettle, or the tots of rum Captain Caleb allowed his New England crew in the evening.

The first day at sea—the ship rolling and pitching; tackle creaking; canvas snapping; men scrambling aloft to frightening heights as if born to it—brought Phillipe acute nausea and the conviction that he would never be a seaman. And as much as eight more weeks of this lay ahead!

To compound his problems, he was worried about his mother again.

When he'd accompanied her aboard *Eclipse* at sunset before the schooner sailed, he'd tried to ignore the continued listlessness of her movements, the way she spoke only in monosyllables and let her gaze wander up to the tips of the masts without seeing them.

During the second and third days at sea, the weather grew increasingly worse. Phillipe made frequent trips to the rail, to the loud amusement of the sailors. But he managed to recover fairly fast every time. Marie, in contrast, simply lay on her side in the single cramped bunk in their tiny steerage cabin.

Located on the port side of the schooner's berth deck, the cabin was even less appetizing than Hoskins had painted it. For one thing, it was noisy; similar cubicles for the boatswain, the carpenter and the captain's clerk were nearby, along the poorly lit fore-and-aft gangway. For another thing, the cubicle reeked constantly. It reeked of pitch, of the water in the bilges and of other stenches Phillipe didn't care to identify. And seeing anything clearly was almost impossible. A candle in a wrought-iron holder with a hook for securing it into the wood of the bunk provided the only light.

All through the third day, Phillipe looked in on Marie as often as he could. Her position in the bunk seldom changed. She clutched the leather casket to her stomach, her legs drawn up against the now-worthless treasure. Each time Phillipe urged her to eat a bowl of the stew Gropius grudgingly offered, she refused. It was increasingly evident that her precarious mental state and the rolling sea were taking a double toll from her already low reserves of strength.

Two more days, and Phillipe was almost frantic with fear. After dark, he got up his nerve to go to Captain Caleb's quarters in the stern.

He knocked, heard a voice answer above the crash of the waves and the grinding of the hull, bidding him come in.

Caleb's cabin was only about three times the size of Phillipe's. It was sparsely furnished with a built-in bunk, a locker, a small desk bolted to the bulkhead. A small, round table of oak and two chairs were similarly bolted to the decking.

A hanging lantern swung back and forth above the table. Seated there, Caleb glanced up from an open book which Phillipe recognized with some surprise as a Bible.

Caleb gestured to the other chair, then to a platter of biscuits. The swaying lantern threw shifting shadows across the New Englander's face as Phillipe sank wearily into the chair, declining the food.

"Some difficulty, lad?" the captain asked.

"It's my mother, sir. She's not well. Does anyone aboard have medical skill?"

"The first mate, Mr. Soaper, has some simple knowledge. But *Eclipse* is a commercial vessel. We don't often carry passengers. So we can't afford the luxury of a doctor."

Phillipe's face fell. Caleb leaned back, his eyes unblinking.

"I'm aware the hard weather must be troubling the lady, since she hasn't showed herself at table with the mates. Makes me regret you didn't take my warning about a rough crossing more seriously."

"It was important we leave England as soon as possible."

"Because you are running away from some trouble," Caleb said, so quietly he could barely be heard against the smash of the Atlantic on the hull. "I read it in your face the moment Hoskins brought you aboard. I accepted your word that it was otherwise because I wanted Hoskins' cargo."

Phillipe came close to pouring out the entire story to the captain. But didn't. He was just a little afraid that his tale of persecution by the Amberlys might sound like the ravings of a madman. Caleb was tough, practical, independent; a tangled story of a woman who had dreamed of her son becoming a nobleman could hardly interest him.

Besides, that part of Phillipe's life was past. His concern was the immediate moment.

"I felt my mother and I would be better off starting our lives over again in the colonies," he said. "Can we let it go at that, sir?"

"Since the British Isles are now well behind us—yes."

"Now it seems I made the wrong choice."

Caleb touched the page of his Bible without glancing at it. "What man doesn't, almost hourly? Can you tell me what ails your mother?"

He shook his head. "Not exactly. I'm afraid the idea of traveling to a country we know nothing about—a country where we'll be strangers again—has hurt her mind. She won't eat so much as one bite."

"You've tried?"

"Over and over. She just lies in the bunk. I don't know what I can do to help her."

"Say prayers to Almighty God," replied Caleb with perfect seriousness. "There's no way I can turn *Eclipse* back to England."

iii

Seven days onto the Atlantic, Phillipe came to the realization that Marie was in all probability dying.

When the thought struck, his first emotion was renewed guilt. Then came fresh rage at all those he considered responsible. Lady Jane. Roger. Perhaps, in a small way, even Alicia.

But the dominant reaction was guilt. It ate into his mind like some voracious monster.

The mate, Mr. Soaper, examined Marie in the cabin that now smelled sour with her feverish sweat. He stated that unless Phillipe could force her to take nourishment, she would indeed die. Another effort to pour a little broth between her clenched teeth failed.

"Perhaps dying is what she wants," was Soaper's brief and gloomy conclusion.

Phillipe took to staying in the cabin as much as his duties would permit. He hardly knew what hour it was, let alone the day. *Eclipse* continued to run through rough seas. He was able to live with that at last, although he knew he'd never like it.

He slept only for short periods, seated in the corner between bunk and cabin wall, hard planking for his pillow. Even in sleep he was half-awake, alert for changes in his mother's shallow breathing. He woke in the darkness of their tenth night at sea to hear her calling his name.

"Wait, Mama," he said, scrambling up in the black, fetid cabin. "Give me a moment to light the candle—"

"Don't! I know how I must look. I can feel the filth of my body. Come close to me."

On his knees, he crawled to the side of the bunk. He found her hand. It felt almost boneless. And feverishly hot.

"Phillipe—listen to me. I will never see this America of yours."

He wanted to cry then, unashamed tears. But he could not. It was a measure of how much he had changed in two years.

Instead, he stroked her hand, tried to speak in a comforting way:

"Yes you will. If you'll only eat. Help yourself to live!"

"To what purpose? Your father is dead. So is everything I held out as a hope for you. But—I know you made the best choice—the new country—that's what I have been trying to find strength to say before it grew too late."

The limp, fevered fingers fluttered over his face, found his mouth to still his words. She whispered on:

"I hated what's become of us, Phillipe. I hated how it all went wrong because of that accursed family. Worst of all, for a time, I—I hated you for refusing to keep struggling against them. But hating my own flesh—that is a sin. A mortal sin. Only—lately, on this wretched ship, did it come to me that you were right and I was wrong. We had no way to win against them. I should have seen that from—"

She stopped, stricken by a harsh cough.

"—from the first time we entered their house. But the blame is on them, not you. That's—what I have wanted to tell you. To forgive you for—for a crime you never committed—"

"Mama, Mama, what's this talk of crime? We did what was necessary."

"Because I forced us to go to England, where we didn't belong."

"In America, common people are not so helpless. There are no hereditary lords to oppress them—"

"And that's why you are right to make a fresh beginning. You have the youth—the heart for it. I do not. I followed the wrong hope. Saw it—saw it die away. There's nothing left for me—"

"There is, Mama. Life! Please, for God's sake listen. We can be happy again, if you'll only fight this awful defeat that's taken you—"

"I no longer have the strength—or the will. I—can barely make my tongue work even now, when I must. I—made you swear an oath. A wicked, hopeless oath and I know it. You must forget that. I only beg you for a promise—"

"Anything, Mama, if you'll just try to help yourself—"

He realized she wasn't listening. Her voice grew softer, the words more slurred, almost inaudible against the crack of a great canvas sheet wind-whipped somewhere high above.

"—the greatest crime, Phillipe, is still the one of which I spoke in Auvergne. So if you can't take your rightful place in England because of them, at least—at least promise me that in this new land, you'll strive to be a man of position, a—man of wealth. Then someday, perhaps, you can return to England and repay them—"

She cried out stridently:

"Repay them, God damn their arrogant souls—!"

The last word broke off with a sharp exhalation of pain.

"Mama?"

He leaned forward, slid his hand across her cheek, felt her raging fever. Something lost and sad within him said, *God have mercy on this poor woman. She still has the same dream. The words have changed. But not the dream itself.*

Because he loved her, and because it cost him nothing, he said, "I promise."

The waves beat thunderously.

"Mama? Mama, I said I promise—"

Her hand slipped into his, pressed his fingers weakly. She had heard.

She started murmuring in French again. The indecipherable words became a fragment of a melody. She was humming an old, romantic air.

Several times more he tried to break through her delirium. She hummed and laughed, sudden little gasps of delight. Where was she? On the stage in Paris again? With James Amberly? Walking in some chateau of dreams where she was complete mistress, uncowed, unafraid? Her absolution of his guilt poured relief through him suddenly—

He stayed with her most of the night, although he knew it was pointless. She no longer recognized him. She wasn't even aware of his presence.

Inevitably, he thought back over the months that had passed since she first drew the casket from behind the statue of the Madonna. It struck him that, in a larger sense, she might have been right all along. The greatest crime could very well be that of allowing yourself to be humbled into poverty and obscurity.

At the same time, as she understood, events had forced a change in his perspective on the question. He no longer harbored any hope of gaining his inheritance. Nor of striking back at the Amberlys.

He had the hatred for it; the desire. That would never completely leave him. But there were certain practical limitations now. He was sailing toward an unseen shore that would hold more new challenges than he could possibly imagine. And opportunity, too.

Perhaps his mother was only wrong in the means she had chosen to avoid commission of what she considered man's most heinous crime. Through the wearying hours in which he leaned against her bunk and listened to the heartbreaking sounds of delirium—her feverish laughter; snatches of singing—he concluded with a certain coldness that the dream itself might be the right dream after all.

Wealth, status—that was what he wanted from the new land. He would find them. By God he would.

For himself. And for her. Nothing else mattered now. Nothing.

Phillipe Charboneau passed the next twenty hours in the cabin, with little sleep and no thought of food. At the end of that time, the woman of Auvergne was dead.

iv

Captain Will Caleb asked Phillipe about Marie's religious persuasion. He replied with no apology that she had been a beautiful and excellent actress in her youth in Paris—and therefore excluded from her Catholic faith. Captain Caleb said that while he was a Congregationalist, all people were equal in the Maker's eyes. That belief was one reason his own grandfather had fled the English midlands for America. He promised he would try to find an appropriate text for the burial.

v

The late May morning sparkled. *Eclipse* lay becalmed in the bright, windless weather. Fore and aft, to port and to starboard, the Atlantic resembled green glass.

Captain Caleb had turned out his entire crew. His master of sail had supervised the sewing of Marie's body inside a canvas shroud. Just before the last seam was closed, Phillipe returned from below deck. Caleb stepped to his side, white hair gleaming in the noon sunshine.

"Is that what you wish to bury with her?" the captain inquired.

"Yes, I remembered it at the last minute. I think she'd want—"

Suddenly something checked him. He was silent a moment. Then:

"On second thought, I believe I'll keep it. I have nothing else but these few personal letters to remember her by."

And he tucked the leather-bound casket with its long-dulled brass corner plates under his left arm.

vi

"Let not your heart be troubled. Ye believe in God, believe also in me."

Captain Caleb's resonant voice rolled out across the deck between the ranks of the assembled crew. They were clear-eyed, healthy-looking men, colonials every one, except for Gropius, who had not as yet removed his woolen cap. A glare from mate Soaper took care of that.

Phillipe stood beside Caleb at the head of two lines of men. The lines faced inward. Between, the shroud was being carefully lifted by four other sailors.

"In my Father's house are many mansions. If it were not so, I would have told you."

Phillipe felt the beginnings of tears sting his eyes. He glanced from the shroud rising toward the rail to the hard faces of the New England sailors. They were profane men; he'd heard them curse often enough as they clambered aloft in foul weather. They were ignorant men as well; most of them could neither read nor write. Yet in the presence of death they seemed to bear themselves with a certain dignity Phillipe had never seen in England. Could this subtle difference come from breathing what Dr. Franklin had called "the less stifling air?" If so, then Phillipe knew he had indeed made the right choice.

"I go to prepare a place for you. And if I go and prepare a place for you, I will come again, and receive you unto myself, that where I am, there ye may be also. And

whither I go ye know, and the way ye know—"

All at once, the pages of St. John from which Captain Caleb was reading began to snap and flutter. The rice paper whipped over, causing Caleb to lose his place. He riffled back to find the verse. Phillipe noticed the quick shifting of the seamen's eyes. Mate Soaper actually glanced aloft, where the canvas had begun to flap faintly in the new breeze.

"Thomas saith unto him, Lord, we know not whither thou goest—and how can we know the way?"

Phillipe watched as the shroud was lifted high above the rail, slowly tilted forward by rope-galled, tar-blacked hands of surpassing tenderness. Caleb raised his voice a little as the Testament pages snapped again:

"Jesus saith unto him, I am the way, the truth, and the life. No man cometh unto the Father but by me. Amen."

The quartet of seamen released their burden. The shroud fell out of sight. Phillipe heard the splash as it struck the shimmering water. He closed his eyes, praying that his mother would at last find peace on her own unseen shore.

A touch on his shoulder broke the melancholy moment. He raised his head, opened his eyes. Captain Caleb was looking at him with a strange expression on his weatherbeaten face.

"I think a sip of Providence rum might go well," he said gently.

Phillipe followed him below without question. Soaper barked orders and men began to race aloft to prepare for the fair wind's rising.

vii

All sorrow seemed burned out of him as he sat in Caleb's cabin, sipping the strong, sweet rum. The captain contented himself with one of his biscuits.

The casket rested on the table between them. That, and Gil's sword, were the only items of consequence with which he and his mother had begun their journey, the only ones with which he would end this phase of it.

No richer and no poorer, he thought. *But wiser? God in heaven, let us devoutly hope so.*

Concentrating on his biscuit, Caleb asked, "What was the trouble that forced an obviously sick woman to undertake this voyage?"

With no hesitation, Phillipe told him.

He even showed Caleb the letter from James Amberly. After he had finished the narrative, he replaced the letter and closed the casket, saying, "But all that's over."

"Not quite."

Phillipe glanced up sharply.

"That girl of whom you spoke—you said something about her thinking of leaving England, didn't you?"

"Yes, but I don't see—"

"To come with you to America? Where she had relatives?"

"It was only a passing mention, Captain Caleb."

"The point is, lad, the thirteen colonies remain a part of the British Empire. You may not be entirely out of danger yet. Through the girl whom your half-brother is marrying—through her family connections in Philadelphia—the long arm of private or even public justice could reach out eventually. The chance isn't a likely one, I'll admit. But since you were sorely used in England and want to begin with as much in your favor as possible—the Almighty can testify that landing penniless in America, while not unusual, presents huge difficulties—I'd suggest one final separation from that ugly past you described. You have abandoned any hope of claiming part of your father's fortune. Then why not start as a new man entirely? Take a new name? One which would never give you away?"

For the first time in days, Phillipe Charboneau almost smiled. The suggestion was both surprising and exactly right.

"Thank you, Captain," he said. "The idea's excellent. I'll do it."

"Help yourself to the rum," Caleb said as he rose to leave the cabin. "But tell no one that the master of this ship allowed you more than a single cup or I'll have a mutiny. I must be up to the helm—I think we've seen the last of the calm that put us behind schedule. With any luck we can run straight to Boston now. Oh, and one thing more." He paused at the door. "To lose the woman who gives you life in this world is no easy thing. My mother's eighty-seven. Healthy and peppery up in Maine. I hope when she passes I can behave as you did today. You took it as a man."

viii

That night, alone in the stench-ridden cabin for the first time, Phillipe was glad Captain Will Caleb couldn't see him.

He was unable to force himself to lie in the bunk. He took his customary place on the decking instead. He had lost track of time. He heard the ship's bell clang four bells. But of what watch, he didn't know.

He tried to fix his attention on something other than his mother's absence. On the schooner's creaking; on the soft, constant roar of breaking water just beyond the hull planks and the huge rib of rock elm that intruded into one corner of the cubicle. He tried and tried—

Useless.

Unbearable anguish built within him. He heard footfalls in the gangway outside, held back the low, half-uttered cry. The invisible walker hesitated, then moved on.

Just in time.

He wept as he had never wept in his life. Wracking sobs. They lasted five minutes. Ten—

And then he was empty of the capacity to weep any longer. His belly hurt. Something had burned to ash in the center of his being. Burned—and was now forever gone.

Phillipe leaned his forehead on the edge of the bunk and closed his eyes. But no sleep would come all that long, long night.

ix

Near the end of the mid-watch on the morning of the sixth day of July, 1772, Phillipe stumbled up from the berth deck for a breath of air. The ship's bell rang seven times, telling him that in half an hour it would be four A.M. At least he'd learned the system of bells and watches on the voyage, if nothing else.

Stepping out on the deserted deck, he walked toward the bow, away from the men standing watch at the helm, shadow-figures against the quarterdeck's hanging lanterns.

He knew why he'd wakened abruptly from a restless slumber. It was because of the talk the evening before. They should be sighting land soon, the old hands predicted. Perhaps tomorrow—

But it was already tomorrow, wasn't it?

From behind the bowsprit, he peered over the sea at limitless darkness. Slowly he craned his head back. There, at least, was light. Endless stars, thousands upon thousands, dusting the huge arch of heaven and shifting slowly in his vision with the schooner's pitch and roll—

The name. He should do something about the name.

He'd toyed with possibilities, found nothing satisfactory. What if they did sight land tomor—today? Who would he be?

All at once, under the immense canopy of tiny silvered lights, he felt small. Smaller even than on Quarry Hill, the night he and Marie fled from Tonbridge. The vastness of the sky, the sweep of black ocean seemed to press in on him; reduce his size; his hope; his courage—

She was gone. He was alone.

He was *alone*.

And out there somewhere beyond the carved figurehead—a buxom, bare-titted mermaid with painted wooden eyes—an alien country waited—

Suddenly he was almost dizzy with fear.

And why not? Nothing existed any longer to which he could cling. The books he'd read, the kindness of people such as Mr. Fox and the Sholtos and Hoskins, the encouragement of Dr. Franklin—all that was meaningless. Cut away as if it had never been. Lost and gone far behind the ship's faintly phosphorescent wake.

He felt smaller and more forlorn by the moment. He knew nothing of the realities of day-to-day living in these colonies toward which the schooner raced on the night wind. He knew nothing but words and more words—and all of those nearly forgotten. Part of another life, it seemed now. The life of someone who was a total stranger.

Nothing from the past applied to his new situation in this new world. No one could be relied upon because there *was* no one—except himself. Survive alone among these Americans? He who was doubly foreign? Not even able to claim the soil of Britain as his own? The whole of creation, sea of stars and sea of darkness, seemed to laugh with wind and wave at his incredible presumption—

Then, reacting to the fear, he felt ashamed.

He had withstood severe tests up till now. He could withstand more.

He lifted his head. He fought the dread born of the future's uncertainty. He repeated to himself what he had repeated before—

I will survive.

It helped—a little. But the stars and the dark remained vast and forbidding.

Well, by Christ, he thought, *I can be a man outwardly, at least. Never let them see the way I really feel—*

Phillipe knew only smatterings of the Bible. But he was acquainted with the tale of Adam. As he brooded at the bowsprit, his mind fashioned an encouraging little conceit, to help put down the fear—

He was like a man being born in the fashion of Adam, new-sprung into the strangeness of a creation whose details he couldn't possibly guess. All right—he would take control of that creation as befitted a man, not a boy. He *would*, by God—

But who will I be?

The problem kept him awake the rest of the night. Kept his mind occupied, at least—

But deep down, he was still afraid.

x

Just before sunset of that same day, an outcry from the crow's-nest signaled land on the horizon. Caleb's older hands had been right.

He stood at the port rail in the stiff wind as Gropius howled inflammatory curses in Dutch and English about the new mess boy malingering again, even while the regular mess boy still lolled in his bunk.

He ignored the oaths, peering at the greenish-black line, still so very thin and far away, that separated the sky of the mellow summer evening and the white-crested Atlantic. Gulls wheeled and shrieked high above the topmen working aloft.

He held the rail tightly, fairly tasting the salt wind. He felt not only a tingling anticipation, but a coldness in his hands and in his soul. The fear—

At least he had a name now. He'd settled on it during the forenoon watch.

With every tie of consequence severed, his name was his only link to his past existence. And it was a tenuous link at that. But he needed something that belonged to both worlds. Something to help carry him through the gigantic transition rushing to meet him. An old box, a sword, a self-consciously jutting chin and a feigned expression of resolve were not enough.

He had decided to Americanize his given name to Philip. And, to remember at least part of his origins, he had shortened his father's hereditary title to Kent. Philip Kent. He would no longer think of himself, or be called, by any other name. He had already told Captain Caleb.

Thus, self-christened, a new man watched his new homeland rising under the orange-tinted clouds in the west, and wondered what lay ahead for him as *Eclipse* bore into the Nantasket Roads under full canvas.

Book Three
Liberty Tree

CHAPTER I

The Secret Room

i

DURING THE NIGHT, *Eclipse* anchored two miles from the glimmer of Boston light. Before daybreak a pilot came aboard. He took the helm from Caleb and maneuvered the trading vessel through the narrow channel and past the islands dotting the harbor to a berth at Long Wharf.

The early haze of a summer's day promised intense heat. It blurred the hills and the rooftops of the town and the parapets of Castle William, the island fortress out in the harbor. But nothing could blur Philip Kent's sense of anticipation as the lines were snubbed tight and the plank dropped.

Anchored ships lined one side of the teeming pier, ramshackle commercial establishments the other. Philip took a tight hold on casket and sword, about to descend into the confusion of the quay. A hand gripped his shoulder.

"Lad, do y'know where you'll be going now?" Captain Caleb's face was patterned by changing light and shadow as men aloft furled sails between the deck and the sun.

Philip shook his head. "No, sir."

Caleb rolled his tongue in his cheek thoughtfully. "Might have been better after all had you bound yourself to me. With no certain destination—"

"Captain, that makes the possibilities all the more

317

numerous and excit—" He flushed and, despite his best efforts, couldn't conceal a little anger in his voice: "You're laughing at me."

Caleb nodded, and his smile broadened. "No offense meant, Philip. It's just that there's been such a change in you—I'll be flogged if you aren't beginning to sound English already. A few months among these folk and they'll never take you for a Frenchman."

"Because I'm not," Philip replied, embarrassed by his display of temper. Buoyed by the noise and spectacle along the pier, he said eagerly, "I'm like you now. A citizen of the Americas."

"But perhaps we should talk a few minutes about where you could go—"

"Thank you, Captain, no. I'll get along very well."

"So you're determined Mr. Philip Kent will be completely his own man?"

"Completely."

"Although our Mr. Kent is but how old?"

"Strictly speaking, Captain—a couple of days."

"That's right. In a new country, the fact that he's lived eighteen years—"

"Nineteen."

"—doesn't count for much. But this might. Our new gentleman of the Americas lacks even a basic knowledge of the town's geography."

"I'll find my way, sir, don't worry."

Caleb's face said he knew further attempts at persuasion were useless. "You're not only sounding like an Englishman—you're acting like a hard-headed Yankee! Well—" Caleb held out his dark, weathered hand. "Good luck and Godspeed."

Trying to ignore the look of concern that came unbidden into the captain's eyes, Philip shook hands. Then he turned and hurried down the gangway.

Swift movement was necessary. The longer he lingered aboard *Eclipse*, the more he would be forced to acknowledge that Caleb spoke the truth. He was absolutely alone, with no experience to guide him.

But then he reminded himself that, night before last, he'd vowed to turn his solitary condition from a disadvantage to an opportunity to begin anew. Risks and all. So be it. He *was* nineteen years old, and strong, and feeling fit. The sun warmed the back of his neck pleasantly as he pushed and shoved his way up Long Wharf, his entire store of worldly possessions tucked under his arms. Beneath the soles of his boots, the rickety boards that represented his new-found home felt more reassuringly solid every moment.

ii

But by nightfall, he began to think that heeding Captain Caleb's suggestion might have been prudent.

The onslaught of hunger sent him scavenging through a litter heap behind a waterfront tavern. He discovered half a dozen oyster shells, each with a tiny bit of meat clinging to the inside. Scraped loose carefully with his grimy fingernail, the gobbets of oyster served as his first sumptuous meal in his new country. *An event to remember,* he thought ruefully as he pocketed one of the shells and stole away from the crowded tavern.

He trudged down an alleyway hot with twilight shadow. *Oysters from a garbage pile. Something to remember indeed, when I've my own house one day, and silver for fifty guests—and a mantel over which I can hammer pegs to hold Gil's sword in a place of honor.*

The shining vision soon produced negative ones. Bitter memories of the past flooded his mind. Images of Marie, Roger Amberly, the murderous one-eyed man, Alicia. He put them aside as best he could, while thunder rolled over the lamp-lit town. A summer rainstorm was brewing in black clouds that massed above the chimney pots in the northeast.

Not knowing the name of a single thoroughfare or what his position was in relation to the place he'd landed that morning, Philip Kent slept the night in a haystack.

He found the haystack in the tiny yard behind a home on one of Boston's winding streets. On the other side of the warm, fragrant hay, penned pigs squealed miserably in the downpour. He burrowed deep into the stack, one hand curled around the oyster shell he'd kept from the litter heap. He'd discovered the shell had a sharp edge. Almost as keen as that of a knife. A handy weapon, especially for a stranger in a new city—

He awoke well before dawn. He was thoroughly soaked and shaking with the start of a fever.

iii

By midmorning he found his way back to Long Wharf. He had made up his mind to admit his error of launching out hastily on his own, and he planned to seek words of counsel from Captain Caleb.

But the few sailors left aboard *Eclipse* reported that the ship's master had already issued instructions about disposition of the cargo to the mate, Soaper, and departed for his mother's home in Maine.

Grumbling Gropius, looking more than a little hung over from his first night on shore, gave Philip a hunk of weevil-infested bread and a cup of rum before the latter once more turned his unsteady step up the wharf to the town.

He studied passing faces. Some were coarse, some prosperous-looking. Some appeared beneath tricornered military hats. But soon, all began to blur in front of his feverish eyes.

His forehead streamed with sweat. His rain-dampened clothes clung to his body, smelling sour. But he kept on—

And trudged Boston for two days and two nights.

He stole garbage where he could; slept where he could; and, despite the illness that left him weak and short of breath, managed to fix a fair approximation of Boston's geography in his head.

At one taproom where he inquired for work, any kind of work, only to be turned down by the landlord's obese, mustached daughter, he paused long enough to ask about the size of the city.

The fat girl picked something out of her hair and regarded it with curiosity as she said, "Why, the *Gazette* reports we're fifteen thousand souls now. Too damned many of 'em lobsterbacks."

"Lobster what?"

"Redcoats. British soldiers."

"Oh, I see."

"Funny question for you to ask. 'Specially when you want work one minute and look ready to faint away the next. Where do you hail from? You've an odd way of speaking. Like a French mounseer who came here once—"

Too tired to engage in explanations, Philip left.

As he wandered, he began to be more conscious of those lobsterbacks she'd referred to. King George's soldiers wore splendid scarlet coats and white or fawn trousers. Each coat had its own distinctive color for lapel facings and cuffs—buff and yellow and blue and many more.

He'd noticed the soldiers before, of course. But paying closer attention, he saw how some of them moved along the streets with a certain air of authority that drew glares and snide remarks from many an ordinary citizen—although other Bostonians, usually better-dressed ones, treated the troops with politeness, even cordiality.

And the troops were everywhere, from the elm-dotted greensward of an open area identified to him as the

Common, to the shade of a huge old oak tree, the largest of several in Hanover Square, where he watched a group of officers rip down some announcement nailed to the trunk. He saw redcoats from the North End to the double-arched town gate leading to the Neck.

The Neck was a long, narrow strip of land connecting the city with the countryside around it. It was no more than yards across at its narrowest point just outside the imposing brick gate. With the Dorchester Heights across the water to the east and the Charles River on the west, Boston resembled a sort of swollen thumb stuck up from the mainland—and linked to it only by the Neck.

The city's tolling church bells reminded Philip of London. But Boston had its own bustling style and distinct aromas. Predominantly fishy. But spiced by the pigs and cows kept in those small back yards, by rum distilleries and reeking outhouses and, near the water-front, by shipyards and ropewalks that smelled fiercely of pitch.

Ill, Philip lost track of the days. Perhaps two more went by. Perhaps three. He grew filthy and hungry beyond belief. As a result, he found himself more and more the object of suspicious stares from well-dressed pedestrians and gentry on horseback. His inquiries about work—here at a smokehouse, there at a brewery—brought replies that were increasingly curt as his physical appearance worsened. His eyes took on the slightly unfocused glare typical of fever, which didn't help his cause either.

Shaking, teeth chattering, he was wandering somewhere in the city's North End again, just at sunset, when two figures whirled around a corner and crashed into him.

Philip stumbled, fell to hands and knees on the cobbles. His sword and the casket slipped out of his fingers.

He was vaguely aware that the splat of his palms in the mud oozing between the stones of the street had sent droplets of the sticky brown stuff flying—

Straight onto the spotless white breeches of a soldier who now loomed over him.

The man was silhouetted against the ruddy evening sky and the leaded windows of an inn a few steps away. "Damme, Lieutenant Thackery," he said, "the clumsy young bastard dirtied my trousers!"

"Then we shall make him pay for a laundress, Captain." The second man grabbed Philip's collar, dragged him up. "Come round to the headquarters of the Fourteenth West Yorkshires in the morning, boy. Bring sufficient money to—here, hold on!"

He reached forward to grab Philip again. The latter had pulled away to retrieve his two possessions. The lieutenant's fierce grip brought Philip out of his feverish daze—and face to face with eyes that were distinctly unpleasant:

"Pay attention when a King's officer gives you instructions. Unless you prefer to have the order delivered in a more memorable way." The lieutenant's other hand dropped suggestively to the hilt of his dress sword.

Philip glared at the slender officer, then at the beefy captain whose white breeches did indeed display quite a few large mud spots. Something weary and uncaring made Philip utter a low growl and knock the restricting hand away.

"Damme, a scrapper!" cried the heavy captain, careful to back off and let his subordinate handle the altercation. Handle it he did, his mouth tightening, ugly.

Philip heard footfalls coming along the cobbles behind him. But he didn't dare look around. The lieutenant's sword slid from its scabbard and winked in the glow from the nearby tavern.

"He's probably sporting a liberty medal under those stinking clothes," the lieutenant said, flicking Philip's sleeve with the point of his blade. "He's certainly insolent enough to be one of 'em. Do I have leave to thin their ranks slightly, sir?"

The senior officer grumbled assent. But the lieutenant didn't even wait for it, whipping his sword up. The blade caught the late-slanting sunlight, started down on a path that would lay open Philip's face—

Feet planted wide, head ringing, Philip still had presence enough to block the glittering steel by spearing the lieutenant's right wrist with his left hand. Grunting, he held the sword arm off for an instant while his other hand plucked the oyster shell from his belt. He raked the shell's edge down the lieutenant's left cheek.

Howling, Lieutenant Thackery danced back on the slippery cobbles. Blood dripped on his buff lapels. The captain cursed and began to unlimber his own sword as the owner of the footsteps Philip had heard earlier ran up behind him.

The man seized his arm. "Need assistance, youngster?"

Philip stared into the lean, middle-aged face of a black-haired man with flushed cheeks. Philip could do no more than swallow and nod. Lieutenant Thackery was advancing toward them now, sword up, blood pouring down the left side of his jaw.

"Stand out of the way, sir, because I'm going to gut him through. You see what he did to my face—"

"Improved it considerably," remarked the black-haired man. His lilting speech sounded like that of the Irishman, Burke. "What started this, lad?"

"I happened to splash mud on the other one's trousers," Philip gasped out. "An accident—"

"God damn it, sir—move aside!" the lieutenant roared.

The gaunt, black-haired man shook his head. Positioning himself at Philip's elbow, he said, "Sirs, let me remind you of where you are. The Salutation—" he indicated the inn just up the street"—is crowded with my friends. If you truly wish to engage, I can guarantee that a substantial part of the North End will be after your heads before three blows are struck. You've heard the whistles and horns blowing before, haven't you?"

"The whistles and horns of your damned Boston mobs?" the captain fumed. "Indeed we have."

Unruffled, the other said, "Well, I've some ability at summoning them out. I am Will Molineaux, the hardware proprietor." His announcement, as well as his fiery black gaze, was clearly inviting a fight.

The captain swabbed his perspiring face. "*Molineaux?*"

"Yes, sir, the same."

"Leave off, Thackery," the captain ordered the lieutenant. "He's the leader of the whole damned liberty mob in this part of town."

The lieutenant flared, "Sir, I refuse to cower in front of—"

"Leave off, I say! Or you'll have a cut across your throat to match the one on your face."

Swearing bitterly, Lieutenant Thackery rammed his sword back in place. The unnerved captain gestured him to follow up the street.

But Thackery, his uniform cuff pressed to his cheek and already bloody, had to deliver a parting thrust.

"One of these days we'll have laws permitting us to hang you rebel scum!" he shouted.

"No, sirs," Will Molineaux shouted back. "Because we shall see you swinging from Liberty Tree first."

He laughed uproariously as the taunt inspired the fat captain to disappear around a corner, practically running. The bleeding lieutenant vanished into the gloom after him.

The older man turned to Philip. "That captain's a rarity. The King's own quartered in this town are not cowards. Tyrants, yes. Swaggering bullies, frequently.

But not cowards. You did a bold thing, my lad. Some would have truckled."

"I—" Philip had difficulty speaking. His whole body felt afire. The Irishman's features grew distorted, elongated. "—I may have acted out of ignorance, sir. I've only come to Boston city a few days ago."

"And look half-dead from the experience. Where d'ye live, may I ask?"

"Nowhere. I've been seeking lodging—employment. I can find none at all."

"What's your name?"

"Philip Kent."

Molineaux's eyes narrowed. "Are you a runaway bondsman?"

"No, I am not."

"Can you prove that?"

"Just with my word."

Mr. Molineaux studied him a moment longer, then pressed the back of one hand to Philip's forehead. "You're sicker than hell, that's clear. I'm bound up the street to the Salutation. Some gentlemen who convene there are not friends of His Majesty—or His Majesty's military forces. Landlord Campbell holds those sentiments too. So come along and we'll see if he'll give you a bit of sweeper's work. He'll be pleased to do it, is my guess. He'll fancy a fellow who tweaks Tommy's beak the way you did."

Molineaux helped Philip retrieve his belongings and accompanied him to the Salutation's doorway, over which hung a creaking sign painted with the figures of two splendidly dressed gentlemen bowing to one another.

Virtually all those gathered in the cheerful taproom wore old, tar-stained clothing or nautical coats and caps. "A rowdy lot of sailors, hull builders, caulkers and mast-makers," Molineaux commented as he led the unsteady Philip through the smoke to the bar, where a stocky man presided over the kegs. "But a good, freedom-loving lot. Hallo, Campbell."

" 'Evening, Mr. Molineaux."

"Campbell, here's a chap on whom I hope you'll lavish your hospitality. Young Mr. Philip Kent."

Molineaux described the street incident in a rather loud voice. Those at nearby tables listened. At the end, Philip drew a round of applause. Campbell grinned, promised Philip a meal, lodging in the tavern's outbuilding, and a few days of manual work to earn his keep while he looked for other employment.

The tobacco haze and tar and alcohol fumes were making Philip more and more dizzy. But he thanked Campbell, then turned to thank Will Molineaux. He discovered the latter already moving toward a shadowy doorway at the very rear of the taproom.

Molineaux had been joined by a shabbily dressed man of middle years. The man's hands and head trembled with palsy. Where the man had come from, Philip hadn't noticed.

Philip started after them. Campbell caught his arm. "Where you going?"

"Into that back room, to speak my appreciation to the gentleman who—"

Campbell shook his head, no longer smiling. "That's a private chamber, Mr. Kent. Provided so Will and Mr. Adams—" He indicated the palsied fellow disappearing beyond the closing door "—and a few other close friends can confer without disturbance. No one in my employ enters that room unless I send them. Keep that in mind while you're 'round the Salutation. Now do you want to eat or do you want to sleep?"

"As a matter of fact—both."

"Come along then. I'll wake you at sunup and start you working. Even a Son of Liberty must earn his way. I'd say you've joined the organization whether you realized it or no."

With a comradely arm across Philip's shoulder, he conducted him to the kitchen and, soon after, to the welcome sanctuary of a smelly, rickety outbuilding. There, Philip dropped into exhausted sleep on straw, while a milk cow lowed nearby.

iv

What began as a short stay at the tavern on the corner of Salutation Alley and Ship Street lengthened into a week. Then into another. As Philip's natural strength gradually overcame the feverish illness, he sought every possible means to make himself indispensable to the landlord.

He hammered up plank siding to repair the outbuilding where tipsy guests sometimes slept off their revels before tottering home to their wives. He clambered over the roof to nail new shingles onto the Salutation itself, Campbell having idly remarked that during heavy storms, water dripped from the beams near the taproom hearth.

Campbell obviously liked the young man's eager industry. But what held Philip at the Salutation with Campbell's unspoken consent was not merely finding a temporary haven, important as that was. What held him was a realization that had come to him when he woke the first morning after his arrival.

The seedy, palsied fellow glimpsed in company with Will Molineaux bore the name *Adams*.

He'd inquired about the man when Campbell had a moment's leisure. He was told the gentleman's first name was Samuel. So it *was* the same radical politician whom Mr. Fox had described at Tonbridge and Lord North had scorned at Kentland!

At first, Philip could hardly believe that such a frail, badly dressed person could be a serious threat to George III—let alone the fomenter of rebellion.

On the other hand, he supposed it took neither good

looks nor rich apparel to produce a temperament opposed to royal tyranny. Perhaps the requirements were just the opposite: ugliness and poverty. In any case, the frequent visits of Mr. Samuel Adams and like-minded men to the private room at the Salutation fired Philip with curiosity and a determination to get into that room at the first possible chance. So he searched for ways to keep himself busy, reported failure to Campbell after his occasional expeditions to look for work elsewhere—no lies required there—and awaited his opportunity.

It came one afternoon during Philip's third week on the premises. Embarrassed, Campbell confronted his helper with the news that he could think of no other work that needed doing. The opening gambit to politely asking him to move on?

Instead, Philip immediately suggested, "You could let me serve the gentlemen who meet in back, sir."

"*What?*"

"I can be trusted to say nothing about what I hear. And I want very much to meet Mr. Adams."

"For what reason?"

Aware of how incredible it would sound, Philip still brazened ahead: "The Prime Minister of England once told me I behaved like one of his pupils."

Polishing a tankard, Campbell gaped. "The Prime—?" He guffawed. "Oh, you had an audience with him, did you?"

"No, sir, a chance encounter. At my father's home in England."

Campbell squinted at him in the buttery yellow sunshine falling through the leaded windows. "You speak good English, Philip. I think I recognize some French overtones too. But I still find it hard to believe that a lad who arrived penniless in Boston could have encountered that sow-faced North."

"But I did, Mr. Campbell."

"Where do you really come from, Philip? More important—from what are you fleeing? Or should I say *who?*"

"From my father's family," he answered at once, deciding that candor was the only workable course now—and that the chances of being harmed by it were slim. "My father's a nobleman. I'm his son by a woman he never married. He promised me part of his fortune, but when I journeyed to England from my home in France to claim what was mine, my father's family tried to have me killed. I came to America to escape them."

"Why America? Why not back to France?"

"I worked in a London printing house for a time. I got to like the trade, and thought I might have a better chance to pursue it here. And I met a Dr. Franklin—"

"The trade representative for Massachusetts."

Philip nodded. "He convinced me to come to the colonies. He said that in America, people were resisting those who wanted to enslave and oppress others."

Campbell now looked thoroughly astonished. " 'Fore God! The Prime Minister and Ben Franklin too!"

"The doctor was extremely kind to me. I spent a whole evening in his rooms, talking with him about America."

Campbell studied his hands. "You visited his quarters on Marrow Street in London, then."

"No. Craven Street."

Campbell relaxed, nodded. "Of course—Craven Street. I was mixed up." But the words were a shade too casual; Philip knew he had been tested.

He went on, "The doctor really had many good things to say about the freedom here, Mr. Campbell."

"Preserving that freedom requires struggle, Philip. Just as important, it requires secrecy. What is said in that back room would not find favor with Governor Hutchinson. Or the Tory citizens of this town, for that matter. But damned if it doesn't sound like you have good credentials. I joked about it the night you arrived, remember?"

"I surely do."

"But now I really do think you have the makings of a fellow who might wear one of these—"

He tugged a chain from inside his shirt. At the end of the chain, a medal gleamed. Philip bent closer to see the symbols on it: a muscled arm grasping a pole, on top of which perched a peculiar-looking cap. Engraved on the medal were the words *Sons of Liberty*.

The street door opened. Half a dozen redcoats stamped in and headed for a table. Campbell hastily hid the medal, but not his distaste, as the soldiers loudly called for service.

Campbell ordered one of his girls to wait on the soldiers. This done, he scratched his chin and returned his attention to Philip. After a moment of silence, he said:

"All right. I'll risk it once and see what happens. The gentlemen plan to gather this evening. I'll send you in to serve the flip."

V

Later, Philip would look back on that stifling night in late July and consider his entrance to the private room as a passage of great significance in his life. But at the time, his main reactions were immediate excitement and curiosity. If that closely guarded room was the meeting ground of men who had allied themselves against oppression represented by aristocrats such as the Amberlys, then he wanted to know more about such men—and their ideas.

Accompanied by Campbell, he went into the room about eight in the evening. He was carrying a heavy tray of tankards filled with a mixture of rum and beer fresh-heated with a poker.

The room was plainly furnished, windowless. Tonight it contained but five men. Philip had only seen two of them enter the Salutation. Then he noticed a rear alcove, a door in shadows. All five men turned as Campbell and Philip came in.

Will Molineaux saw Philip, gave the landlord a startled look. As Philip set the tankards on the table, Campbell explained quickly:

"I'll vouch for the trustworthiness of this young man, gentlemen. Will knows him too."

"Slightly," Molineaux said, on guard.

"Philip Kent's his name," Campbell went on. "He's newly arrived from England. And Samuel—he encountered Lord North by chance over there. The Prime Minister told him he already behaved as if you personally had taught him his political catechism."

"Indeed, is that so?" returned Samuel Adams. The man's clothing, Philip noticed, was as threadbare and disreputable as before. Food stains, and a smear of what looked to be printer's ink, suggested that he cared nothing for his personal appearance.

Adams fixed Philip with a slate-blue stare. His pale hands shook continually. Now and again his head jerked. Yet those eyes held Philip's' and burned. In a high, quavery voice, Adams asked:

"And how did this remarkable confrontation come about, sir?"

In much the same words he'd used with Campbell, Philip described the circumstances. Adams digested the story with no change in his expression. At the conclusion, he said:

"We always welcome recruits to the cause that must inevitably triumph. From what you say as well as what you don't, I infer you've no love for the English nobility."

"Not for those who treat ordinary folk like property."

"There are no other kind," Adams told him.

A light-haired, exceedingly handsome man in his early thirties, prosperously dressed in dark green velvet, chuckled and turned a long-stemmed clay pipe in fine, slender hands. "You've a foolish consistency sometimes, Samuel. You dismiss our friends like the Earl of Chatham—"

"*Principiis obsta,* Dr. Warren, *principiis obsta!*" Adams retorted, shaking a finger.

The man identified as Warren laughed again, glanced at Philip. "Samuel is constantly quoting Ovid to us. 'Take a stand at the start.' "

Adams' slate-blue eyes shone with that ferocity Philip had already found unsettling. Whatever his personal motives, the man had an unsmiling, almost fanatical air about him—one that did not seem common to the others, who occupied themselves with their tankards as Adams retorted:

"The first appeasement leads only to many more, be assured of that. And at the very moment when we've no issue to stir the citizens of Boston to our purpose—then are delivered two—*two!*—in June—" He swept the gathering with an accusing hand. "You hesitate! It's unforgivable!"

Campbell plucked Philip's sleeve, nodded toward the taproom door, obviously intending for the younger man to leave now that the introduction had been performed. But Adams jumped from his chair, strode toward them with quick, nervous steps.

"No, Campbell. Let him stay. If we hear our remarks abroad tomorrow, we'll know who to blame."

"And who a few members of the mob may wish to visit," Molineaux added with an easy smile. But his undertone of meaning was unmistakable to Philip. Here was another, more critical test of whether he was trustworthy. This one, he had no doubts about passing.

"Come, come—he seems the right sort," a new speaker put in. The man was short, square-jawed, with dark eyes and hair neatly clubbed. He wore plain clothing, considerably less expensive than that of the others.

Dr. Warren smiled. "I'd expect you to say that of a fellow Frenchman, Paul." To Philip: "This is Mr. Revere of North Square. Our resident silversmith—"

"More important," said Adams, "the one man among us who never sniffed the somewhat rarefied air of Harvard Yard. Paul alone has the ear of the huge numbers of artisans and mechanics in town—"

"Because I'm one myself," said the stocky man. He was in his late thirties or early forties, Philip judged. His blunt-fingered hands looked calloused, muscular, testimony to his position as a craftsman. "Mr. Kent, let me welcome you, and suggest that if you're ever in the market for replacement of a fine silver button—"

"I'm afraid I don't have any of those, Mr. Revere."

"You have teeth," Campbell said. "Paul replaces them, too."

"A necessary sideline to feed all the mouths at my table," Revere shrugged. "Mr. Kent, you mentioned your home originally being in France. So was my father's."

"Where, sir?"

"Riaucaud, near Bordeaux. My father's people were Huguenots."

Philip nodded slowly. "We had few in Auvergne. But I know how the Protestant French were persecuted—driven out—"

"Which is why Monsieur Apollos Rivoire emigrated here, apprenticed himself to a goldsmith, and as soon as his first shop on Clark's Wharf began to prosper, changed his name to something more American. I suspect you've already done that?"

"Yes. Our family's name was Charboneau."

"You see?" Revere smiled at the others. "I told you he was all right."

Philip had taken an instant liking to the clear-eyed, forthright artisan, a liking intensified when Revere had the thoughtfulness to add, "You're no doubt confused by all this clack about recent affronts to the cause of Englishmen's rights—"

"I am, Mr. Revere. I'd be grateful for a little explanation."

"The first incident Samuel made reference to involved His Majesty's customs schooner *Gaspee*. In pursuit of smugglers—"

"Real or fancied," said Dr. Warren, with some cynicism.

"—she ran aground on a sandbar below Providence. Now you must understand, sir, that among we coastal colonists, smuggling of Holland tea and similar commodities is a highly respected occupation. But not to be brooked by the *Gaspee*'s most unpopular master, Lieutenant Dudingston. Before his unhappy grounding, he had, in fact, been stopping and searching our ships up and down the coast. Harassing American captains and crews viciously and vindictively. Well, sir, the *Gaspee* aground brought a swift reaction. The high-handed lieutenant and his crew were driven off. Then a group of patriotic citizens burned her to the waterline. As a result, it's been proposed that the offenders be tried in England. *If* they can be brought to justice."

The square-jawed man allowed himself another little smile. "Which is doubtful. Who among those who set the *Gaspee* afire will identify his neighbor?"

Dr. Warren put in, "The second issue Samuel wishes to seize upon is the announcement by the Royal Governor of Massachusetts, Hutchinson, that commencing next year, his salary will be paid not by our Provincial Congress, but by the Crown."

"Two provocations of excellent quality!" Adams cried. "We must exploit them!"

"We are all agreed on that," Warren retorted. "But

the wish doesn't guarantee the deed. Since the last taxes were rescinded—"

"Not their damned tea tax!" Adams said.

Warren went on with forced patience, "Still, the rebellious mood has quieted considerably here. And virtually vanished elsewhere."

"But the June announcements are the most noxious threats against our liberty thus far!" insisted Adams.

Warren gave a weary shrug. "I can only proselytize so many from my surgery, Samuel. And I cannot reach into all the other colonies. As Franklin once observed, the need is to make thirteen clocks strike as one. Not easy."

A heavyset man who had thus far remained silent spoke up:

"I've published articles—yours, Samuel—your cousin John's—Abraham Ware's—in the *Gazette*, and I'll continue to do so. But like Dr. Warren, I fear it isn't enough. The people have simply relaxed with the complacency of prosperity again."

Philip, who had been standing somewhat self-consciously with the serving tray dangling from one hand, perked up at once:

"You're a printer, sir?"

The stout man's nod was brief. "Benjamin Edes. The firm of Edes and Gill, in Dassett Alley behind the State House."

"I learned the printing trade in London—"

"Did you, now?"

"I also learned that it's a worthy, important trade. I told Dr. Franklin it's the one I mean to take up here, if I can."

Adams perked up. "You encountered Benjamin in London?"

"Yes, sir. He welcomed me at his rooms. In Craven Street."

He glanced at Campbell. The landlord smiled, realizing Philip had seen through the little test of veracity.

Philip had decided to say nothing of the lost list and letter. Instead, he told the men, "Dr. Franklin felt I could find work in this country. So if you've ever a need for a devil, Mr. Edes—"

"Constantly," Edes sighed. He ranged his glance up and down Philip, gauging him. "I can't hold 'prentices for long. Most of 'em are frightened of running afoul of the King's justice. It keeps my partner John Gill hovering far in the background, too. You see, I publish not merely a paper, the *Gazette*, but what many Tory citizens label sedition. Samuel, for instance, must cloak his articles under Latin pseudonyms such as Brittanus Americanus. So must some of our other authors. If you've a belly for that sort of risk—" A pointed look toward Campbell. "Perhaps our host didn't err in appointing you to help him serve."

Philip didn't ponder a decision for long.

"When may I come around to talk to you, Mr. Edes?"

The abruptness shocked the other man. But he recovered quickly.

"Why, on the morrow, if that pleases you. Meanwhile, I'm plagued thirsty." He shoved his empty tankard at Philip handle first.

Edes asked the others their pleasure. All wanted refills save for the silversmith. Edes' laughter stirred the tobacco clouds.

"Paul is our sober husband and father," he explained to Philip. "Also the man whose copper engravings illustrate the broadsides we nail up on the Liberty Tree. I suppose we should be thankful he prefers to keep his hand steady."

Revere smiled back. Philip started out.

"Mr. Kent!"

He turned to see Revere facing him.

"Pleasantries aside—what you've heard must indeed go no further. Lives are not yet forfeit in Boston for the kind of talk which takes place in this room. But that time can't be far off. We will protect ourselves at all costs," he finished quietly.

Philip shivered a little under the impact of the silversmith's forthright gaze. "I assure you I'll say nothing," he replied, adding to Edes, "and I'll visit you in the morning, sir."

As he left, he heard the querulous, yet somehow passionate voice of Adams resume:

"The problem is to seize the advantage! Confrontation—conflagration—must surely come. The sooner the citizens understand and *accept* that—"

"You are a manipulator, Samuel," Warren interrupted. "I do not agree that 'conflagration'—your prettified term for open rebellion—for war—is inevitable. Or need be made so by us!"

Philip pulled the door shut.

vi

He paused a moment, gazing out over the black-beamed taproom crowded with noisy North Enders. He noticed two British officers seated in the front corner, finishing platters of meat while they stared with open arrogance at those nearby.

The arrogance was returned with scowls. Philip felt another chill chase down his back. With a single step into the Salutation's rear room, he had plunged far deeper than he'd originally meant to.

True, he'd wanted to meet the radical Adams. But now he was linked to the group by an opportunity to seek work with a printer who spread the propaganda for the American cause.

He noted the British officers again, and felt cowed by the figures of authority, despite his best resolves not to be.

Well, the solution was extremely simple. Leave the Salutation. Never call on Benjamin Edes. Avoid further contact with the men who were, by their own admission, dangerous—

Campbell came through the door, stopped, looked at Philip. The landlord seemed to sense Philip's uncertainty, and his voice bore just a trace of threat:

"I trust you have no regrets about being admitted to that room, young man. It would prove awkward if you did. Molineaux's North End mobs are no longer rampaging quite the way they did a year or so ago, in company with Ebenezer Mackintosh's bullies from the South End. But the warning served inside was not given lightly. Should confidences be violated—even by accident—well, Mr. Adams knows the mob organizers intimately. And he is a determined man."

Philip stared at the bright scarlet coats of the British officers. He remembered his mother, the Amberlys, Girard's books and his talk of new winds blowing—

"Regrets, Mr. Campbell?"

His eyes hardened.

"No, sir. None."

CHAPTER II

Mistress Anne

i

THE PRINTING FIRM of Edes and Gill in Dassett Alley was not particularly prosperous-looking, equipped as it was with but one small flat-bed press in its cramped main-floor room. A few type cases sat nearby. Behind a partition was a tiny, cluttered office from which the stout Mr. Ben Edes oversaw the publishing operation.

As he'd promised to do, Philip called on Mr. Edes at ten the morning following his admittance to the private room behind the Salutation. They soon concluded an agreement for Philip to be a general boy-of-all-work around the shop.

From time to time Edes' son Peter apparently helped out as well. But the boy was small, and Edes wanted an assistant of size and strength. And, he said, "One who won't cower and run off when Governor Hutchinson or some other damned Crown toady makes one of his frequent public denunciations of our sheet."

Before giving his final assent to the arrangement, Edes watched Philip work the press for nearly twenty minutes. At the conclusion of the test, he said, "You've practiced with excellent masters. Come, let's go back to the office and talk wages. Do you have a place to stay?"

Elated, Philip said as he followed Edes, "No, sir. But I'll find one immediately."

"We've an unused room down cellar where we can move in a pallet if you wish—no charge."

"That would be perfect."

"You'll have to catch your meals as you can, in the taverns in the neighborhood."

"No problem there, sir."

"Do you own a trunk? Any possessions you want to store? We can lock 'em in back. Or at my house."

"These—"Philip showed him the casket and wrapped sword"—are all I have."

Settled in the office again, Edes studied him. "Brought 'em along, did you? That's confidence. You came from England with nothing else?"

"Nothing."

"Then tell me what you want in this country. More specifically than you did last evening."

Philip thought a moment. "Frankly, sir, all I can think of at the moment is the chance to start working. Oh, and some new clothes. I'd hope to buy a proper suit from what I save. Without spending all of it, I mean."

"Got any ambitions beyond the job itself?"

"Yes, sir. I think I'd like to put myself in my own printing business eventually."

Edes grinned. "Competing with me already!"

"Well—" Philip nodded. "In a way, I suppose. A man needs to look ahead."

"Understandable, Mr. Kent, perfectly understandable. Let us hope the town of Boston's not burned to the ground in civil disorders or leveled by the King's artillery before you've the capital to take away my trade." He continued more soberly, "As you may have sensed last night, Sam Adams is bent on armed collision with the British government. He's failed in every business venture he's ever attempted. But the man's a positive genius at politics—wheedling here, whispering there, stirring mobs in secret to work his will. His hatred of the Crown isn't all pure idealism, though. Sam's father was ruined in the Land Bank failure a number of years ago. So, as you were warned, you'll be associating with less than respectable men if you join Edes and Gill. Are you still persuaded?"

"I am," Philip replied with an emphatic nod.

Ben Edes looked pleased. He reached for the pull of a desk drawer.

"Then let's have a tot of rum and haggle over the price of your service."

ii

Before many days had gone by, Philip realized that financial success was not the paramount goal sought by the proprietor of Edes and Gill and his seldom-present partner.

True, the establishment did a modest commercial printing business, over and above publishing its little Monday paper, the *Gazette*. In spare hours the press churned out handbills, shop window placards and anything else that might turn a profit. In this last category were several hand-colored copper plate engravings, joint ventures of Revere and Ben Edes.

The two best sellers both dated from 1770. One depicted the still-infamous Boston Massacre. The other was a less sanguinary *View of Part of the Town of Boston in New England, and the British Ships of War Landing Their Troops in the Year 1768. Dedicated to the Earl of Hillsborough.* When Philip asked why a member of the inner councils of the Sons of Liberty would dedicate such a work to any British nobleman, Edes answered, "You wouldn't catch him inscribing it in that fashion today. But Paul's got a houseful of youngsters—and he knows how to sell both sides of the fence to support 'em. His tongue was a good way in his cheek when he wrote those words, Philip. But his eye was on his purse."

Mr. Edes then went on to note that Revere, a self-taught engraver, made no claim to originality as a pictorial artist. All his engravings were "modeled"—stolen was the interpretation Philip put on it—after drawings by others. Revere merely duplicated them on metal with a few embellishments.

"But in working silver, he's entirely original—and many say he has no peer in all the thirteen colonies," Edes added on behalf of his friend.

Despite such frankly money-making ventures as the Revere engravings, however, it was evident that most of Edes' energies were devoted to the *Gazette*. His aim was to make it not only New England's most influential news organ, but the means by which the patriots of Boston town could speak their defiance of the King's edicts and issue their warnings and alarms to a temporarily placid populace.

The *Gazette*'s—or, more correctly, Ben Edes'—political orientation was in fact the prime reason the other partner, John Gill, was seldom on the premises. He did not so much disapprove of Edes' approach as desire to protect his own neck. And, as Edes remarked once, in arguments concerning publishing policy, Gill always lost. "Because I can shout longer and louder every time."

As the summer of 1772 mellowed into clear, crisp autumn, Philip had little time for anything except the exhausting labor Ben Edes demanded. Just as he had at Sholto's, he worked a six-day week, resting only on the Sabbath. He usually spent half of that day sleeping off his tiredness in the small but basically comfortable cellar room Edes had provided for his use.

The printer soon recognized Philip's skill and expanded his duties to include not only inking and operating the press but setting type—a slow process at first. But satisfying once Philip got the hang of it. He would never be as swift as Esau Sholto. But he was competent.

By now Philip was physically grown to manhood. Though not of great height, he was strong and powerful-looking, his shoulders thickly muscled from hauling on the press lever hour after hour. His dark, forthright eyes took in every new sight, every new face—and every word printed by Edes and Gill—with avid interest. Thanks to Sunday afternoon rambles about town, he soon became quite familiar with Boston—and his work acquainted him with the leading citizens involved in defending the cause of Englishmen's rights against the encroachments of the King and Parliament.

Samuel Adams was a frequent visitor to the print shop, usually arriving with sheets of foolscap on which his palsied hand had penned his latest diatribe against the North ministry. In the announcement that the Royal Governor's salary, as well as those of all Massachusetts judges, would soon be coming directly out of England's treasury, Adams had found an issue with which he hoped to excite his countrymen. He wrote about it incessantly. The *Gazette* printed the articles under his various pseudonyms—a continuing indication of the dangers inherent in such literary work.

Another frequent visitor was introduced to Philip as Abraham Ware. A Harvard-trained lawyer, Ware was a small, pot-bellied man with popping, frog-like eyes. He contributed essays almost as inflammatory as those of Adams, but he had only one nom de plume, Patriot.

Revere, the quiet, plainly dressed silversmith of North Square, also called occasionally, bringing bits of news or a crudely engraved political cartoon.

On the second floor of the Edes and Gill building, these men and others met by night. The chamber up there was called the Long Room. Philip was never admitted, even though he was by now a reasonably trusted employee. But Edes didn't mind identifying his nocturnal visitors for his young assistant—

That stout little lawyer from nearby Braintree was

Samuel's cousin John. The handsome, rather dandified man in his early thirties, whom all visitors seemed to treat with special deference, was John Hancock, the merchant prince of Beacon Hill.

Edes said Hancock was no hothead. In fact, he occupied a position of such status that he might have fallen more logically into the Tory camp. Those who supported the King's policies and policymakers were a majority in Boston, albeit a relatively silent, inactive one.

But Hancock had somehow developed a quixotic interest in the ideals espoused by Sam Adams and the others. Then, so Ben Edes explained, in 1768, the Royal Commissioners of Customs had recognized the potential strength Hancock could lend to the cause of the Sons of Liberty. The commissioners had falsely accused him of smuggling Madeira on his sloop *Liberty*. His cargo was impounded.

The strategy backfired. Hancock suffered no financial loss whatsoever—thanks to the convenient and not at all coincidental intervention of one of the famous Boston mobs put together by the cobbler Mackintosh from the South End and hardware merchant Molineaux from the North. The savaging crowd rescued Hancock's Madeira, and from that time on, the wealthy man's devotion to the cause was steadfast. Although he remained less of a firebrand than Adams, he spent considerable personal money underwriting the extra printing expenses—the broadsides, the handbills—that the Sons of Liberty distributed and nailed up surreptitiously all over town.

Hancock, the Adams cousins and Revere—the only non-Harvard man in the group apart from Edes—met at least once a week in the Long Room. Working at the press by the light of whale-oil lamps, Philip could often hear contentious voices raised during those sessions. That of Sam Adams was usually the most strident.

In addition to the Long Room and Campbell's Salutation up north, the Green Dragon on nearby Union Street was another popular meeting spot for the patriots. Philip took many of his meals at the Dragon. He felt that patronizing the place somehow enhanced his association with the cause, even though he was not privileged to share the thinking of its leaders, except as it slipped off the press in the pages of the *Gazette* or in the broadsides run behind locked doors at night.

By early October, the drumfire of propaganda had succeeded in generating a certain amount of public concern about the threat posed by the salaries of the Governor and the judges being paid from England. Adams' next move was to press for the convocation of a town meeting. Its purpose was to establish permanent correspondence committees in Boston, as well as in other Massachusetts villages, to further communicate the position of the Adams group and seek support not only of neighboring communities but of like-minded people in New York, Philadelphia and other colonial cities.

In connection with the committee scheme, Edes dispatched Philip one morning on an urgent errand to the South End. He was to pick up copy from Adams at his home on Purchase Street; copy for a broadside destined for the trunk of the Liberty Tree and other highly visible spots around town.

Hurrying up Purchase Street not far from the Neck, Philip was astonished at the size and splendor of the Adams residence. It was multi-storied, even boasting an observatory on the upper floor.

He imagined the observatory would afford a fine view of the harbor. But he wondered how a man as financially distressed as Adams could maintain such a large home. In conversations at the Dragon and the print shop, Philip had learned that despite a promising start at Harvard, Samuel Adams had subsequently succeeded in mismanaging every single business opportunity life had presented to him.

Adams' father—the Deacon, he was called, because of his strong religious convictions—had indeed lost much money when the British government outlawed the colonial Land Bank he'd organized. But along with resulting lawsuits, son Samuel had inherited the Deacon's thriving brewery-distillery, source of some of the best beer and rum in New England. That firm, having been operated for several years by Mr. Samuel, was now defunct.

Adams' stint as Boston's tax collector had been equally disastrous. When he had stepped down in sixty-five, he was behind in collections to an amount exceeding eight thousand pounds. Governor Hutchinson accused him of malfeasance. Edes said Adams' real problem was "no head for figures—and a tendency to be generous to anyone with a heart-rending story." Philip readily understood how the Royal Governor had become one of Adams' favorite targets.

But after the business debacles, Adams, already into his forties, found his destiny and his lifelong career at last. Politics. Or, as he termed it, "the cause of liberty." At the moment, though, no one in Boston professed to know how he was able to support his family and conduct his busy political life. There were rumors that his younger cousin John, the successful lawyer from Braintree, paid him a dole as a "consultant."

Philip reached the metal fencing outside the Adams house. It became evident that, contrary to his first impression, the property was not being kept up at all. The fence badly needed painting; rust showed everywhere. Behind the fence, weeds that had yellowed in the first frost still stood knee-high.

The front-door knocker was tarnished. And the pretty but fatigued-looking woman who opened the door wore an old dress befitting the poorest-paid servant.

"Is Mr. Adams at home?" Philip asked. "I'm from Edes and Gill—"

"Oh yes, my husband's expecting you," the woman said, shocking her visitor with the revelation of her identity. Her smile was tired. "Step in, won't you? Samuel's in the study upstairs. He's having an early lunch. Would you like to have something with him?"

"No, thank you, I'm to hurry straight back with his manuscript."

The woman started to say something else, but was distracted by the rocketing entrance of a huge New-foundland dog that badly needed bathing. Philip started up the stairs quickly, crunching spilled breadcrumbs under his feet. He noticed cobwebs in the ceiling corners, and scarred woodwork.

Despite the gloomy, run-down atmosphere, Mr. Samuel Adams was humming cheerily beyond the open door of the study near the top of the staircase. Philip walked toward the door. Adams looked up, his palsied head bobbing. His smile broadened. He laid down the quill with which he'd been writing, called out:

"Come in, Kent! Care for a bite of something while I finish up the copy?"

With a trembling hand, he shoved a plate to the corner of his littered desk, nearly upsetting his inkstand. He was wearing hose, breeches, a white long-sleeved blouse stained black in a dozen places. His left shoe was missing its brass buckle.

The politician noticed Philip's expression as the latter stared at the slimy-looking edibles on the plate.

"Raw oysters—good for you! I have an absolute passion for 'em—sure you won't join me?"

"No—no, thanks," said Philip, a little queasy. When he'd been starving in the streets, he'd eaten gobbets of oyster from garbage heaps—and thankfully. This morning he could barely stomach the sight. Another sign his life had changed, he thought, fighting back a sour taste in his throat.

He glanced around the book-lined study as Adams began to scratch with the quill again. Most of the books had titles suggesting their subject was politics. Among them Philip recognized works by Locke and by Rousseau in translation.

Humming again, Adams finished the copy with a flourish, then began to blow on the manuscript.

"Ben Edes tells me you're working out well for him," the older man stated between puffs at the paper.

"I hope so, Mr. Adams. I very much like the job."

"I apologize for my somewhat rude behavior that first evening at the Salutation. But these are dangerous times. We can't be overly careful—"

He handed across the sheet, popped another oyster into his mouth, swallowed with relish. Philip winced.

He studied the copy Adams had given him. It was a strong appeal to Boston's citizens to promote the idea of the correspondence committees. The broadside ended with a warning:

Those who Fail to Adopt the position of the Reasonable and Fair-minded Mr. Adams will Earn our deepest Displeasure.

The signature was one Philip had seen on other pieces in the shop—Joyce Jun'r. He raised his eyebrows at that; the communications of Joyce Junior were usually threatening, even sinister-sounding.

"Is this another of your pen names, Mr. Adams?"

"When a little honest fear must be stirred in the public breast—yes."

"I thought perhaps there really was someone by this name."

"You mean you don't know who Joyce is—or was?"

"No. I've asked Mr. Edes a couple of times. He always breaks out laughing."

Adams' slate-blue eyes sparkled. He laced his hands together, a bit of oyster still clinging to one corner of his mouth. His head continued to bob, but the twined hands shook less visibly. He said:

"Joyce Junior has been a legendary, if unreal, personage around Boston for years. The real Joyce —Cornet George Joyce of the British army—was the chap who captured that damned Charles I. An evil king if ever there was one! Some say Joyce actually wielded the axe that lopped off the King's head, but that part's apocryphal, I believe. On this side of the Atlantic, we call him Junior. And reserve him for tasks or appeals that might be beneath the dignity of more law-abiding citizens. 'Brittanus Americanus,' for example, would never think of calling out a mob. But stout Joyce has, many a time." Once again the slate-blue eyes held a cold brilliance that made Philip shiver.

"I don't doubt we'll be hearing often from the ghost of the good Cornet in the days and months to come," Adams concluded. "Be sure you heed his advices, Mr. Kent, or you'll find yourself in trouble."

Philip matched Adams' smile. "Out of a job, you mean?"

"That's part of it. But only part. No man can remain neutral in the coming struggle."

Despite the surface cordiality, Philip was glad to say a quick good morning and retreat from that cramped, musty little room where the politician hunched over his plate, smacking his lips and lifting oysters to his mouth with a shaking hand. As he hurried to the front door, Philip heard the dog barking furiously, a child wailing—and Mrs. Adams crying out in dismay and frustration somewhere at the back of the house.

Relieved to be on the street again, smelling the fresh harbor wind, Philip thought it was no wonder those in power in England found Adams a dangerous enemy, a man determined to unsettle the future. He might have failed in business, but he would never fail in his current mission—that much, at least, communicated itself in every glance of the almost eerie eyes. Philip felt that by going into the Purchase Street house, he'd stepped into the center of a spider's web. He hoped Edes wouldn't soon send him back again.

iii

On a dark, gloomy morning later in that same month of October, Philip was alone in the shop. He was busy setting type for next Monday's issue of the paper, which would contain yet another piece by Adams proclaiming the value of the committees in promoting colonial unity. The bell over the door jingled. He looked up to see a young woman entering.

She acted unhappy to find Philip the only person present. Throwing back the cowl of her cloak, she pulled foolscap sheets from under the rain-spattered garment and asked:

"May I see Mr. Edes, please?"

"He's gone off to the Green Dragon, miss. Mr. Gill too."

The young woman scrutinized him. "Are you a new apprentice?"

Annoyed by the stare, Philip told her, "I work for Mr. Edes on wages. I am not bound to him."

The girl flushed a little at the sharp reaction. She was an inch or so taller than Philip, though about his age, he judged. Her eyes were brown, her hair chestnut, her mouth generous but firm-looking. Her skin had the lustrous, wholesome color of one who spent time outdoors. He noticed a few freckles on either side of her nose, as well as an ample figure beneath the cloak. Though not dressed with great elegance, the girl carried herself with a certain no-nonsense air that rankled Philip for no clear reason.

"Is there something I can do for you?" he asked finally.

The girl held out the foolscap. "I'm Mistress Ware. This is copy from my father, to be set immediately. He'd have come in person but he's meeting with a client."

Philip took some time to scan the three closely written sheets, noted the Patriot signature and the nature of the message: an appeal to the citizenry to openly support Adams' plan to establish the twenty-one-man Committee of Correspondence for promulgating the "Boston view" to the other colonies—and, as it said near the end, "the World."

He heard the girl give an impatient little sniff, glanced up, found the brown eyes sparkling with irritation:

"I trust the writing has your approval?"

"It seems excellent, yes."

"I'm so pleased. I wasn't aware an ordinary devil approved or disapproved copy. I thought his function was to set and print it, nothing more."

Philip placed the foolscap on a stack of freshly printed handbills, his grin a shade insolent. "But I'm not an ordinary devil, Mistress Ware. May I ask what's annoying you? The dark weather, perhaps?"

Red glowed in her cheeks. "Young women are not accustomed to being so smartly addressed by apprentices!"

Philip's grin hardened. "I told you—I am a free laborer, not an apprentice. But I do believe you knew that when you said it the second time." Then he moderated his tone. "I'll pass the material into Mr. Edes' hands the moment he comes back."

"Thank you." The girl looked embarrassed; Philip's accusation had struck home. She hesitated, then said, "I did address you sharply—"

"And I returned in kind. I apologize."

"So do I. This article's terribly important, you see. The town's buzzing with talk about Mr. Hancock's reluctance to lend his support to the plan for correspondence committees."

"I'm sure your father's usual fine phrasing will help persuade him."

Startled, she asked, "Are you familiar with his writing?"

"Certainly. I read most everything Mr. Edes gives me to set at the font. Some typesetters, I'm told, see only letters, never whole words. I'm not one of them."

"Then I indeed mistook you," the girl said, a little more friendly now. "The apprentices who've worked for Ben Edes before cared for nothing except counting the days till the Sabbath, when they could sleep."

"Well, I do that too. But I came a long way to live in this country. If I plan to make my future here, I should know its affairs."

"A long way?" Mistress Ware countered. "From where?"

"France. Then England. My name is Philip Kent."

Once the opening hostilities had subsided, he'd decided he rather liked the girl's prickly manner and her frank way of speaking. But the friendly overture in the form of his name produced no similar response. Mistress Ware had evidently learned as much about him as she cared to know. She tugged her cowl up over her brown curls and started for the door, saying:

"As soon as the material is proofed, my father would welcome a message to that effect. He may wish to make last-minute corrections. If you will so notify Mr. Edes—"

"Please."

"I beg your pardon?"

" 'If you will so notify Mr. Edes, please,' " Philip said softly but firmly. He was teasing, but not completely.

The girl stood framed in the doorway, the rain slanting down in Dassett Alley behind her. She gave him another of those challenging looks. The cloak shaped to her body showed high breasts; he felt a physical response that had lain dormant months now, except in sweating, unwelcome dreams of Alicia.

Mistress Ware's tart reply put an end to the possibility of getting acquainted:

"I thought I made a mistake about you. I was in error. You have the boorish mentality of an apprentice after all. Good morning."

She whirled and stamped out into the rain.

iv

Benjamin Edes returned shortly after noon. Philip delivered *Patriot's* latest article into his hands, then inquired about the first name of the daughter of the author.

Riffling through the copy, Edes answered absently, "Her name's Anne. Nice-looking girl. But inclined to a sharp tongue."

"So I discovered."

"In my opinion, Abraham's permitted her too free access to his library. A woman should keep to sewing and cooking meals. It'll take some man with backbone and a large fist to wed and bed that one. Anne's nineteen already—well past marriageable age. No regular beaux, to her father's chagrin. He fears she'll turn into a spinster. Too smart for her own good—and failing to fulfill a woman's natural role."

"I can't imagine that someone isn't courting her."

"True, though. Oh, she draws attention from some of the British officers. But she'd as soon spit on them as curtsy. In that respect, she's Abraham's flesh, all right."

A few moments later he handed the foolscap to Philip.

"Stirring, stirring."

"Ware's daughter said he wanted to look it over when it was proofed."

Edes nodded. "As soon as you've set it, take the

galleys to his house in Launder Street. We'll run it on page one, in place of that item about the ropewalk fire. The outcome of the town meeting remains doubtful. Hancock is still balking at the committee idea. Says it's too overt and radical—"

He noticed Philip's distracted look, nudged him. "To work, boy! Don't stand staring at the rain or we'll never get the paper printed."

v

Early next morning, with the sky clearing and a sharp nor'easter hinting of winter, Philip set off with the proof sheets of Patriot's call for support of the Committees of Correspondence.

Following Edes' directions, he located the prosperous-looking two-story home in Launder Street. But he was informed by the cook who answered the door that Lawyer Ware and his daughter had already left on errands. They might be found toward ten o'clock at a place where they frequently stopped, the London Book-Store of Mr. Knox in Cornhill, opposite William's Court.

The moment Philip walked in the door of that establishment, he wondered whether he'd been given wrong information. At first glance, the London Book-Store resembled a salon more than a commercial establishment.

The place was packed. Among the clutter of books, flutes, bread baskets, telescopes and rolls of wallpaper, finely dressed ladies and gentlemen of the town conversed with British officers in friendly, animated fashion. As Philip stood staring, he saw a fat, pink-faced young man speaking with an older officer. The young man wore a silken bandana wrapped around what appeared to be a crippled hand. A memory of Roger Amberly fleeted through Philip's mind.

The fat young man noticed Philip's lost look, bustled over to greet him:

"Something, sir? I am the proprietor, Mr. Knox."

"I'm from Edes and Gill. Hunting Lawyer Ware."

"In the back. Talking with the grenadier captain. I'm afraid the conversation is a bit one-sided. You'll be a welcome distraction."

The fat man waved and hurried back to the officer with whom he'd been speaking, an even fatter colonel of the Royal Regiment of Artillery, resplendent in blue coat with red facings. As Philip moved toward the rear of the store, he heard Knox say enthusiastically:

"I've a new work just in from the continent which contains some interesting theoretical material on the deployment of cannon. Be most interested in your opinion—"

Proceeding past the assorted merchandise displays —and ignoring the amused glances given his poor clothing by some of the chattering ladies and gentlemen and most of the officers—he bore down on the frog-eyed lawyer and his daughter. They were plainly fretting under the attentions of a tall officer in his mid-twenties.

The man's yellow-faced uniform identified him as a member of the grenadier company of the Twenty-ninth Worcestershires. Philip had learned enough about the British troops stationed in Boston to know that the grenadier units were the elite shock troops of every regiment. The men who filled the ranks of such companies were selected for great physical strength and stature. The officer in conversation with the Wares was no exception. Big, long-nosed, not unhandsome, the captain had a scar on his chin and an impeccably powdered wig.

As Philip approached, he heard the captain say:

"—would welcome your permission to call upon your daughter, Mr. Ware. Despite our political differences."

The man's humor was condescending. It produced a

moue from Anne, who was pointedly focusing her attention on a display of vials. A placard announced that they contained *Hill's never-failing cure for the bite of a mad dog*.

Lawyer Ware replied, "As to that, Captain Stark, you don't need my consent so much as the young lady's."

"And the granting of that is an impossibility," Anne said in a cool tone.

The captain couldn't repress his distaste. He said to Ware, "You have no control over your daughter's behavior?"

"Why, of course he does," the girl replied. "My father supplies me with what Mr. Locke called 'a standing rule to live by'—"

"Locke!" the officer exclaimed. "That damned radical—they should have burned his books, and him too!"

The girl shrugged. "In your opinion. I feel he put it well. He meant his remarks for men living under a government, but they apply equally to children living with their parents." Lawyer Ware sighed loudly as his daughter continued, "Once I know the 'standing rule to live by'—the broad rules set down by my government or my father—then I want 'a liberty to follow my own will in all things where that rule prescribes not.' I won't be subject to the 'inconstant, uncertain, unknown arbitrary will of another man.' "

"Is that you speaking?" sneered the officer. "Or Mr. Locke?"

"Some of both, sir."

"By gad, you Whigs are a peppery, windy lot," the captain complained. "I thought Mr. Knox's emporium was considered neutral territory. Politics forgotten in lieu of more pleasant topics—"

Lawyer Ware's eyes seemed to pop even more than usual. "Well, sir, since you've mentioned politics—"

"No, sir, it was your daughter."

Ware ignored him: "—the abridgment of liberties can never be forgotten. Although the King's simple-minded ministers continue to seem unaware of that elemental fact."

Philip had stopped a few steps behind the captain's broad back, awaiting a chance to interrupt. He was struck by the sight of Abraham Ware's daughter. Her opened cloak revealed a simple but well-cut gown of sprigged yellow muslin that Philip found overwhelmingly lovely. The folds of the material couldn't conceal the ample swell of her young breasts.

He wondered whether his reaction was merely general—that is, the same as he would have felt in the presence of any attractive female—or whether it was due to the qualities of this one in particular. Speculation was cut short as Anne Ware noticed him, smiled with startling warmth and brushed past the elegant and powerful Captain Stark.

"It's Mr. Kent from the printing house," she said as she took his arm. "Good morning to you."

"Mistress Anne," he nodded politely, quite aware of her breast against his forearm and the fresh smell of lavender soap she radiated. He couldn't resist a sidelong smile and whisper:

"Your greeting is somewhat different today. For practical reasons?"

Her quick flush admitted guilt. But he didn't mind her strategy of clinging to him as they walked by the huge grenadier. The officer gazed at Philip as if he were something less than dung.

"Your daughter keeps company with mechanics?" remarked Captain Stark to the lawyer.

"That's correct, sir," Anne replied. "By preference."

Disliking the soldier's stare, Philip said, "I trust you have no objections to that, Captain?"

His tone made the grenadier stiffen his shoulders, as

if to emphasize the difference between his overpowering height and Philip's relatively small stature.

"I might, sir, if we were to meet privately, and you were to continue your sarcasm."

The threat in Captain Stark's eyes was not merely the routine arrogance Philip had seen in many of the British troops in town. It was a personal, male reaction to Anne's deliberately insulting attention to Philip. She still gripped his arm as if they were the closest of friends.

Philip's chin lifted. "I wouldn't shrink from that kind of encounter. I've some small skill with a sword."

In response to the bluff, the grenadier's flecked green eyes grew uglier. "Every democrat apes the aristocrat here, it seems. Well, Boston is not a large city. Perhaps I'll indeed have the pleasure of meeting you again."

Cheeks red, Captain Stark bowed to Anne. "Your servant." With another glare at Philip, he stalked off.

Anne released Philip's arm, laughing delightedly. "Insufferable asses! They think their uniforms and their elegant manners make them the catch of the day. Our thanks to you, Mr. Kent. We simply couldn't get rid of him, even with outright rudeness."

Philip said, "I'm happy to make some slight amends for yesterday."

The meaning of that went right by Lawyer Ware. He stuck a pinch of snuff up his nose, inhaled and blinked his frog's eyes. "Annie's run into Stark before. I have it on authority that the man's a whoremaster of the worst sort. Beg pardon, Annie—"

She shrugged, not the least shocked by her father's choice of language. Her reply struck Philip as equally typical of her unusual personality:

"The term is accurate, I imagine. I've heard the same thing. Captain Stark reportedly prides himself on the quantity of his conquests, quality being immaterial. And he has a filthy temper." To Philip, with a genuine smile: "So I do appreciate your playing my little game.

Nothing's ever devastated him quite so completely before."

Somewhat annoyed that he'd been deliberately used, Philip didn't remain annoyed for long. He couldn't. The warmth of Anne Ware's expression pleased him. He found himself glancing down at the scooped neckline of her sprigged yellow gown. How well the color went with her healthy, tanned skin—

Anne noticed where his gaze had wandered. Her brown eyes frosted just a little. She released his arm.

Reaching for his pocket, Philip said in a lowered voice, "I've brought the proofs, Mr. Ware. But this seems the wrong sort of place—"

Ware waved. "Ah, the red-coated fops who hold levee here every morning have nothing on their minds except their Tory lady friends. They'll think I'm reading a brief."

As he accepted the galleys, Ware added, "Annie tells me you pore over everything you set and print for Ben Edes."

"Yes, sir. Because I'm interested in colonial affairs."

Anne had returned to her examination of the display of Hill's mad-dog nostrum. Did she act a bit self-conscious, to be revealed as having talked about him? While Lawyer Ware examined the first galley, Philip went on:

"I was a little surprised by one of the closing lines in your article, Mr. Ware. The one expressing hope that the sword of the parent would never be stained with the blood of his children."

"Adams would have me strike that out," Ware said. "But some sops are needed to satisfy the less intemperate advocates of liberty. Johnny Hancock and Sam's cousin John, for instance. I'd remove the line myself, except for one consideration. We are not yet ready to strike a blow in return."

"Will the colonies ever be ready for that?"

"If the ministerial troops and that truckling Hutchinson don't change their ways, yes."

"When do you think it will happen, Mr. Ware?"

"Hard to say. If not this year, perhaps next. It's what Samuel's counting on—along with some of the rest of us," he added with a steady look that somehow removed all traces of the grotesque or the comical from his appearance.

Ware's statement jibed with the atmosphere that permeated Edes' print shop. Philip had the impression that certain members of the liberty faction would not be satisfied with anything less than open rebellion—were, in fact, striving to manipulate events to achieve that end. Perhaps they were right in doing so. Philip had so far formed no final opinions. He did realize that such a turn would bring a halt to his own ambitions, though.

But such abstract subjects didn't linger long in his mind with Anne Ware nearby.

Her father stumped to the back corner of the Book-Store, muttering phrases in Latin like any good attorney. He hardly attracted a glance from the socializing soldiers and ladies. Philip took the moment to approach Anne.

He indicated the portly Knox up near the front door. "Is that fellow partial to the Tory cause?"

"By no means."

"But he's certainly friendly with the officers. Look at him showing off his books."

Anne Ware's brown eyes grew serious. "Like my father, Henry believes a military confrontation is, if not yet totally inevitable, then certainly possible. Henry's a fox, Mr. Kent. He very cleverly picks the brains of the best officers who stop in here. Encourages them to do so, in fact. He draws them out on the pretext of exchanging opinions about military strategy and tactics. Henry's never served in a military unit. But he wants to be prepared. He's especially interested in the use of artillery. So he allows this place to become more Tory than Whig."

For a moment Philip experienced sharp uncertainty. Surely George III would never permit the situation in the colonies to deteriorate to armed conflict.

And yet, when he recalled the hard-learned lessons of England, the kind of people who held positions of authority there, he was not so sure.

"Mr. Kent?"

Startled, he realized Anne Ware had put her hand on his arm again.

"Yes?"

"I do thank you once more for rescuing me from a most objectionable situation. More important, I want to offer a complete and sincere apology for my own bad behavior yesterday."

Philip smiled, said, "I owe you the same kind. Will you accept it?"

"Of course."

He feigned a frown. "There is one small point—"

Despite herself, she bristled. "Concerning what?"

"You did tell Stark that you kept company with mechanics. Since I fall in that classification, I intend to take advantage of your admission. May I call on you some Sunday? Perhaps for a walk on the Common, or—"

"God's truth," she laughed, "you are without a doubt the most forward printer's boy I've ever met. I've trapped myself, haven't I?"

"Indeed so, Mistress Anne."

She challenged him with her brown eyes. "Depending on degree, Mr. Kent, audacity can be an admirable quality in a man. Or an annoying one."

As he'd done yesterday, she was teasing—but fully so? He couldn't be sure.

"Which is it in my case?"

"Frankly, I haven't as yet decided." She glanced at his clothes. "Do you have a decent suit?"

"No. But I'll get one. I already made up my mind to that."

"Oh? When?"

"After you walked out yesterday," he lied. "Having taken me for an apprentice."

"There is really something unusual here, Mr. Kent," she said. She sounded neither antagonistic nor approving, only speculative.

"Care to expand on that for me, Mistress Ware?"

"Well, for one thing, you spoke to the grenadier as if you considered yourself his equal."

"I am his equal," Philip said. "What's unusual is a woman making that same declaration."

"Oh," she said with a smile, "I thought if the boor had any sort of education at all, the mere mention of John Locke would infuriate him."

"But you were quoting with feeling—and application to yourself."

"So I was. Are we discussing me, sir?"

"I thought it was Locke. I've read some of his writings—"

She looked surprised. "No wonder you took on so about being classed as an ordinary apprentice. What do you think of Mr. Locke's ideas?"

"Sometimes I think what he said was very correct."

"Not all the time?"

Philip frowned. "No. Not all the time. Finish what you started to say. You called my behavior unusual because I took that captain for an equal. Why not? Isn't that one of the central beliefs of your father's group?"

"Yes, but it was more than that. A look, a haughtiness—oh, I can't properly explain it. All smeared with ink, you still carry yourself almost like a lord. Perhaps—" She paused, that challenge in her gaze again. "Perhaps that's why I would be intrigued to have you call. Provided you can indeed afford a proper broadcloth."

He stared her down. "Be assured I'll steal one if I can't."

Her breasts rose sharply as she drew in a breath. Was that heat coloring her cheeks? *Strange, prickly girl*, he thought, feeling physical attraction and something more. He admitted privately that he'd enjoy confronting her with the facts of his origins. How would she treat him then? How would she react? He looked forward to finding out—

"All in order," Lawyer Ware said as he bustled up to them. He pressed the proofs into Philip's hand. Anne said to him:

"Mr. Edes' assistant has asked for permission to call, father."

"Annie," Ware said with another sigh, "that prattle from Locke, Esquire, about a 'standing rule' is all very nice. But ever since your dear mother died, it's been increasingly obvious that I have no voice in such matters. I wish you luck, Mr. Kent. If she takes a mind, my daughter can be quite like gentle Shakespeare's beautiful shrew."

"I'll stand the risk with pleasure, Mr. Ware," Philip answered, touching his forehead to the lawyer and directing a last bold glance at Anne as he turned to go. This time, she didn't seem to mind; she was watching him as if she still didn't know what to make of him.

On that score, he thought, they were decidedly even.

The last thing he heard as he passed through the door of the London Book-Store was the jovial Knox asking two artillery officers about the most effective ranges for mortar fire.

vi

Philip followed the events of November 1772 by means of the stories he set and printed in the *Gazette*.

To the fury of Governor Hutchinson at Province House, Samuel Adams' town meeting convened on the second of the month, established a standing Committee of Correspondence and urged that similar committees be set up all over Massachusetts. Express riders pounding out across Roxbury Neck bore the news to other population centers.

By November's end, the Boston committee had begun to churn out a blizzard of position papers, which the *Gazette* duly summarized.

Adams himself penned a *State of Rights of the Colonists*. Dr. Joseph Warren, perhaps the most popular physician—as well as the most eligible and handsome bachelor—in all the town contributed a *List of Infringements and Violations of Those Rights*. Soon reports began to filter back into Boston that other committees were indeed being set up throughout Massachusetts, as well as in the large cities down the coast.

The men who tramped through the early winter snowfalls to meet up in Edes' Long Room were elated that they had opened permanent communciations with men of like temperament in other colonies. Their excitement brought to mind Warren's quotation of Franklin's remark about thirteen clocks striking as one. If the clocks were not yet chiming in harmony, certainly they were all ticking.

Besides keeping track of political developments, Philip had more personal interests. He hoarded his shillings, visited tailor shops to price merchandise and finally, impatient, asked Edes for an advance against wages that would put him in the printer's debt for nearly half a year.

A few days after the bells in the steeple of Christ's Church had rung the New Year of 1773, he was suitably outfitted in a modest but neat brown suit of broadcloth, his outfit complete with snowy neckcloth, hose and buckled shoes. On a Sunday afternoon of thaw and mellow sunshine, he turned into Launder Street to call the bluff—if bluff it had been—of Mistress Anne Ware.

As he climbed the stoop of the handsome house, a cloud crossed the January sun. In the brief, chilly shadow, he thought of Alicia. He thought of her with sadness—and a question.

Was his interest in the attractive and somehow formidable lawyer's daughter only a convoluted way of circumventing memories of Alicia? Memories that still disturbed him?

Finding no ready answer within himself, he knocked at the Wares' front door.

CHAPTER III

September Fire

i

LOOKING SERENE AND beautiful in a white gown, Anne Ware sat waiting in the parlor to which Lawyer Ware ushered the young caller. The afternoon sunlight slanting through the front bays from Launder Street lit her skin and made it glow like dark amber.

She gave Philip a cordial smile that might have concealed just a tiny bit of amusement at his expense. Philip's new clothing itched. His fidgeting showed it.

"Good afternoon, Mistress Ware," he said. His voice sounded hoarse.

She inclined her head. "Good afternoon, Mr. Kent. Won't you be seated?"

He rushed to one of the chairs with embroidered cushions placed around the room. Lawyer Ware acted almost as nervous as Philip himself, rubbing his hands, shifting his weight from foot to foot and blinking his pop eyes. He hurried to the hall door, saying:

"I'll see whether the tea's ready. We serve nothing stronger in this house on the Lord's day." With that, he vanished.

Dust motes swirled slowly in the sunbeams falling athwart Anne's white lap, where her hands lay folded, composed. She continued to regard Philip with that faintly amused expression.

"Your suit is quite handsome," she said finally. "I did wonder whether you'd keep your vow."

"When the goal's worth gaining—always." Damn, how the girl unsettled him!

Was this merely a charade on her part? A little diversion, to be joked about with friends later? He could almost hear her describing how a bumpkin of a printer's boy had twitched and quivered in her parlor, ill at ease and more than slightly red-faced. The angering thought produced a rash promise. He'd see that tanned and softly rounded body revealed—and submissive to him—before he was done.

Matching her smile as best he could, he asked, "I trust you had a pleasant Sabbath morning?"

"If you call a one-hour prayer and a four-hour sermon pleasant," she sighed. "We're Congregationalists. I think our preachers don't believe in overcoming sin so much as in making the faithful too exhausted to be able to think about it. Do you profess or practice a faith?"

"No, neither. My mother was French. Born Catholic. But because of her—her early career, she was excluded from the rites of the church. She was an actress in Paris," he added, with unmistakable pride.

"An actress! How fascinating. I've begged Papa to let me go see the traveling troupes that play Boston. But such entertainments are considered wicked worldliness in our denomination—"

"I thought you did as you pleased, Mistress Anne."

She colored just a little. "So I do—up to a certain point."

"And what determines that point, may I ask?"

"Prudence. Common sense. You expressed it a moment ago. Is the goal worth gaining?" Her quick glance held a meaning he didn't fully understand. "Is it worth going beyond the prescribed limit? Risking turmoil, disapproval—?"

As if she didn't like the path the conversation was

taking, she veered off: "You mentioned Paris. I thought I detected a touch of an accent in your speech. I recall you said you came to the colonies from France—"

"After some difficult months in England. I was trying to claim an inheritance—"

"Where did you learn the language so well?"

"In Auvergne. My mother hired a tutor. He was the one who introduced me to Locke's writings. And Rousseau's. The preparation was wasted, though. My father was a member of the nobility. But he—" Well, why not admit it? "—he never married my mother. So his family—" Another wary pause "—refused to honor the claim. When they caused trouble for me, I took a ship here to start a new life."

He expected her to mock him with laughter, or at very least with the amusement which came so readily to her brown eyes. So he was unsettled even further when it didn't happen. Instead, she clapped her hands together and cried softly:

"You've just explained the very cloud of mystery I said hovered around you! The way you faced that loutish grenadier—the way you strut a bit—" She extended one hand quickly. The gesture tautened the white fabric across her breasts. "Please, I don't intend that in an insulting way. You have a pride about you that sets you apart. That's good. I'd love to hear more about your adventures in England. How do they color your outlook toward what's happening here? The agitation against the Crown, I mean?"

Quietly, Philip said, "I despise my father's family and everything they stand for. They destroyed my mother's health and peace of mind."

"Was she with you in England?"

"Yes. She died on the ship that brought us to Boston."

"Oh, I'm indeed sorry."

"If I could, Mistress Anne—"

"We can use first names, can't we, Philip?"

A stiff nod. Then: "If I could, I'd go back to England and take everything that's mine. And I'd cause the family pain doing it."

Anne studied his stark face a moment. All trace of her earlier amusement was gone. She asked:

"I don't quite understand. Do you want to be one of them? Or do you simply want to see them brought down? Humiliated?"

"A little of both, I think." It was the most honest answer he could give. And for a moment it produced troubling memories of pledges made to Marie. Pledges now almost completely forgotten.

Anne pondered his reply, said, "Even with your explanation, you're still a puzzle, Philip."

"In what way?"

"You work for Ben Edes, who is certainly no partisan of the aristocracy. Yet you suggest that if given the opportunity, you'd return to England—"

"Oh, there's no real possibility of that. I've made up my mind to find my place here."

"Out of desire? Or necessity?"

"I'll give you the same answer as before. A little of both."

"That kind of position may not be tenable much longer, you know."

"Because of the trouble Mr. Adams keeps predicting? And trying to bring about?"

She nodded. "He's only hastening the inevitable. The people of these colonies are going to have to make a decision. The King is determined to work his will. And for all his questionable methods, I think Mr. Adams is correct about one thing. A small oppression only precedes a larger one. A small nibbling away of liberty will only encourage King George's ministers to take a larger bite. And another, and still another. That's what the Committee of Correspondence is trying to impress on the other colonies—what happens in Boston could very well happen to them. So we must stand together."

She said it all quietly. But she impressed Philip with her seriousness. He thought briefly of Alicia, contrasting Anne Ware's calm-spoken idealism with the frank lack of it displayed by the Earl of Parkhurst's daughter—

A tea tray rattled. Philip looked up to see Lawyer Ware entering, followed by his cook, whom Philip had met at the door on his first visit to Launder Street. The cook was a young, buxom girl with bright red hair and a cheery face. Ware introduced her as Daisy.

The cook put the tray down and began to pour tea into delicate china cups edged with pale blue. When Daisy had finished and retired, Ware hoisted his cup in a small gesture suggesting a toast.

"Will you drink with us to the resistance of tyranny, young man? I should perhaps note that we are drinking smuggled Dutch tea. We'll have none of the damned stuff from England, so long as it still carries that intolerable threepence tax."

Nothing, it seemed, could escape the taint of politics, Philip thought as he raised the steaming cup to his lips, not even a rather awkward Sunday visit in a dark-paneled, comfortable old room from whose chimney piece an oil portrait of a bearded man in severe black stared down.

"I'll drink to your hospitality too, sir," Philip said, and did.

He stayed only half an hour longer. During that time, Lawyer Ware held forth on the various abuses and, as he called them, crimes of the North ministry. At the end of a pause in the diatribe, Philip stood up quickly and announced that he had to leave.

Ware rose in turn. "Your company's been most welcome." He started to the door with Philip. But Anne, rising smoothly from her chair, touched Ware's arm.

"Finish your tea, Papa. I'll see our visitor out."

Sun through the front fanlight lit her eyes and her chestnut hair as she walked with him to the entrance. He felt embarrassed by the entire experience. He didn't have the proper graces or training to hold his own in this kind of social encounter. He had an urge to flee as swiftly as possible, back to more suitable surroundings—the cellar room at Edes'.

Anne said, "I thank you for coming to call, Philip."

"I enjoyed it." His words were forced.

They stood close together for a moment, bodies nearly touching. Where was the shrew Ware had spoken of? he wondered. He saw only the whiteness of Anne's smile—the loveliness of her brown eyes.

She said, "You're welcome to come again."

To his own astonishment, he found himself replying, "Thank you. I will."

And as he set off through the slushy streets under the pale January sun, he felt exhilarated all at once. Ashamed of his earlier desire to run.

But one crucial question remained. What in heaven attracted him to the girl? Beyond the obvious physical excitement produced by too long a period of celibacy?

Anne Ware was aligned on the side of the patriots, of that there was no doubt. She had subtly but unmistakably challenged him as to where he stood. He didn't honestly know.

Well, perhaps that explained it—

Anne Ware was a kind of mirror. One in which he might, with luck, at last discern a clear image of himself.

On top of that, she was poised, intelligent, strong-minded. He was curious as to how she'd come by her independence of thought and action. She wasn't extreme about it—but if personal experience, her father and Edes could be believed, she was still clearly different from the typical young woman of Boston. The curiosity he felt added yet one more dimension of intrigue—

As did the fact that she was damned attractive.

Whistling, he quickened his step. *I'll bed her before it's done, damned if I won't,* he thought.

ii

Philip did not know the precise and complete implications of the word *courting*, a common term in the Americas. But in the months that followed, he gradually assumed that he was involved in the process.

He became a frequent visitor at the house in Launder Street. And the attorney's daughter, in turn, was almost always the bearer of Ware's essays delivered to the *Gazette*.

They walked abroad in Boston a good deal as the winter waned and the mild heat of spring lay over the city. In Sabbath twilight, they would often turn into Hanover Square, where the paper lanterns of the patriots glowed on the huge Liberty oak. The lanterns were constantly torn down by the royal troops or Crown sympathizers. But new ones always appeared to illuminate thinly veiled threats against the Tories from Joyce Jun'r., or broadsides carrying news of the patriot cause.

How the Virginia House of Burgesses had established an eleven-man Correspondence Committee on the Adams model, for instance. That was important, Anne explained, because the more conservative planters of tidewater Virginia did not carry the taint of extreme radicalism that the New Englanders did. When men of property and status—she named *Henry* and *Jefferson* and *Washington* and *Richard Henry Lee*, all unfamiliar—heeded Adams' warnings and set up machinery to maintain communication with Massachusetts, the cause of liberty had been significantly advanced.

Once, as they were strolling at the Common on a late Sunday afternoon, a half-dozen British officers galloped by, racing their splendid horses across the open grass.

One man thundered past, then reined in long enough to look back and verify the identity of Anne and her companion.

Holding his snorting horse in check, Captain Stark did not speak to them. But his glance at Philip said all that was necessary. The flesh around his chin scar looked livid white as he dug in his spurs and galloped off after his hallooing companions. A small, ragged boy who had been sitting against a nearby elm scooped up a stone and flung it after the rider:

"Dirty shitting lobsterback!"

Philip hadn't thought of the grenadier captain since the meeting at the London Book-Store. But today's chance encounter told him Stark had not forgotten their exchange. Nor forgiven Philip's insolence.

As the captain rode out of sight, Anne slipped her arm through Philip's—and smiled. He was immensely pleased. It was the first time, in all the weeks of their strolls and conversations, that she had touched him.

Given extra confidence by that touch, he attempted to kiss her when they returned to the dusky shadows of the stoop at Launder Street. She averted her mouth, so his lips only brushed her cheek. Then she slipped inside with a murmured word of farewell.

The kiss had been a letdown. Eminently unsatisfying. *Damn woman!* he thought as he trudged back to Dassett Alley. *Always in perfect control of the situation.*

Perhaps, he decided wryly, that was why he kept returning to see her.

And would no doubt continue to do so.

iii

"Mr. Kent where is Ben Edes? This must be printed immediately!"

The querulous voice brought Philip out from behind

the press, to see Sam Adams at the door, shaking with
something more than his perpetual palsy.

The man's breath smelled rancid. His threadbare
waistcoat bore numerous wine and food stains. He
looked, in short, as disreputable as ever. And yet he was
a figure of commanding presence as he thrust a sheet into Philip's hand. The ink was still damp.

Outrageous Affront to Englishmen's Liberties! proclaimed the heading of the short composition. Philip
said, "Mr. Edes is up in the Long Room talking with
Mr. Hancock, sir—"

Adams snatched the paper back. "Then they must
both see it personally. The damned rumors were true after all. North's inviting disaster—*and* giving us precisely
what I've hoped for!"

"How, Mr. Adams?" Philip asked as the other scut-
tled for the stairs.

The older man wheeled back, his slate-blue eyes almost maniacal with glee.

"With tea, young man. With their Goddamn tea! A
packet brought the news just this morning. A bill passed
in London not thirty days ago—twenty-seven April to
be exact—granting the rotten East India Company a virtual monopoly in the colonial tea trade. To shore up
the company's foundering finances, the export duties
which East India previously paid in England have been
canceled. And henceforth, no tea may be sold here save
by the exclusively appointed agents of the firm. Even
paying the threepence tax on this side, the company will
be able to undercut the prices of both smuggler's tea and
that sold by law-abiding Tory merchants. *Now* we'll see
the damned conservative businessmen admit I've been
right in saying danger to one citizen—or one colony—is
danger to all."

"But why would they pass such a measure?" Philip
asked. "It's bound to be unpopular."

"They want to test us again! And they have no guilt

whatsoever about using the law to rescue the privileged scoundrels who've manipulated the East India Company into near-bankruptcy. Damme, it's an issue with real teeth—and they'll feel the bite, by God!"

In a transport of delight, Adams clattered up the stairs.

Philip recalled hearing Burke and Franklin discuss a proposed scheme to shore up the trading concern. Now the scheme had become a reality. Whether it would indeed provide Adams and his associates with the clear-cut issue they desired remained to be seen.

With a May breeze blowing through the open front door of Edes and Gill, Philip had trouble getting excited about the turn of events. The warm air, redolent of the salt sea and the green ripening of spring, filled his mind with erotic images of Anne Ware. The images persisted as he went back to the press and listlessly resumed printing a commercial handbill.

But in ten minutes, Ben Edes, Adams and the elegant Hancock came clattering downstairs. Philip was put to work setting type for a broadside that was nailed to the Liberty Tree by sundown.

iv

The heat of early summer brought further intensification of the crisis of colonies against Crown.

In England, Dr. Franklin had somehow come into possession of a packet of letters penned by Governor Hutchinson and the Massachusetts Provincial Secretary, Andrew Oliver, to a member of the North ministry. The letters contained a frank, even brutal appraisal of the character and activities of the Boston radicals.

Franklin sent copies of the letters back to Adams, who was apparently supposed to honor Franklin's original promise to the supplier of the letters that they would be kept confidential.

But that was Franklin's promise, not Adams'. The latter read every one to a secret session of the legislature, then promptly set the Edes and Gill press to work printing the full texts.

The letters revealed and damned Governor Hutchinson as deceitful. They exposed him as a man who was publicly trying to maintain an image of sympathy with the colonists, while at the same time privately advising London to deal with the rebel ringleaders in the only appropriate fashion—harshly. One letter contained the bald assertion that *"there must be some abridgement of what is called English liberty."*

Laboring night after night at the press, with Ware, Warren, Revere and other members of the Long Room group coming and going constantly with new pamphlets, broadsides, articles for the *Gazette*, Philip soon realized that Adams had indeed found sparks he could fan into a blaze.

The Hutchinson letters were kindling. But the real fuel was the tea monopoly.

Governor Hutchinson talked of appointing one of his nephews as the agent and consignee for Boston. Immediately, as Adams had predicted, Tory merchants found themselves economically motivated to add their outcries to those of the liberals. One merchant actually wrote an article for the *Gazette* which said, in part, *"America will be prostrate before a monster that may be able to destroy every branch of our commerce, drain us of all our property and wantonly leave us to perish by the thousands!"* Philip marveled. The temporarily converted Tory sounded almost as rebellious as old Samuel himself.

Anne Ware was exhilarated by what she called this major blunder on the part of King George's ministers.

She predicted to Philip that Adams would orchestrate the issue to a crescendo of protest—and even to open hostilities. The mobs might be roaming Boston again very soon—

But it annoyed Philip considerably that the tea matter was virtually all Anne wanted to talk about when they took their Sabbath walks.

In an attempt to divert her from the constant preoccupation with politics, Philip counted his wages, decided he could afford to spend four shillings and invited Anne to go with him on a Saturday night in late June to view Mrs. Hiller's popular waxworks on Clark's Wharf. Early evening found them outside the stile at the door of the clapboard building, Philip handing the admission of two shillings per person to a ragged boy fidgeting on a stool.

The noise of the wharf faded as they turned the stile and pushed through curtains into the lamplit hall. Elegant duplications of England's kings and queens were ranged on pedestals, the sequins and gold threads and shimmering velvets of their costumes picking up the glow of smoky lamps hung from the ceiling beams. Anne and Philip walked slowly past the first of the curiously lifelike figures whose wax eyes stared unseeing into the lamplight and shadow. There was strong-jawed Arthur of legend, with Excalibur. A handsome Richard Lionheart in crusader's mail. A villainous, humpbacked John. And many more.

But Mrs. Hiller's had only a few customers tonight. Perhaps it was the weather. A muggy mist had settled on the harbor, and the atmosphere was twice as stifling inside. It seemed to affect Anne's mood. She was almost as remote as the frozen image of Queen Elizabeth in her starched white neck ruff. Anne stood staring at the queen, not really seeing her—

"This isn't appealing, is it?" Philip asked finally. He

was sweaty and thoroughly uncomfortable in his good suit. "We needn't stay—"

"Oh, yes, let's see the whole exhibit," Anne responded, though without much enthusiasm, he felt. She pointed. "There's our current monarch. I'm surprised Mrs. Hiller hasn't thrown him off the end of the pier."

Two patrons moved past them in the half-light, casting grotesque shadows on the not too clean floor. Under another lantern, they paused before the pudgy-faced, pink-lipped statue of a young George III. He looked boyish, benign, utterly harmless in a splendid suit of pale blue satin and a neatly powdered wig. The King's cheeks glistened. The wax melting in the heat, perhaps. On the pedestal someone had scrawled an obscene epithet.

Philip shook his head after a long moment of silence. "No, I think we'd better go. Your mind's elsewhere."

She turned, apologetic. "Truly, it is. I'm sorry."

He couldn't resist a little sarcasm: "Shall we stroll up the wharf and discuss tea again?"

"It's poor Mr. Revere I'm concerned about. He dropped in this afternoon with the porringer he repaired for Papa. He looked exhausted. I don't think he spoke ten words."

That, at least, Philip understood. Revere had been to Edes and Gill hardly at all during the preceding month. Early in May, his wife, Sara, had died. Ben Edes said her death had left him devastated.

"Sara Revere shouldn't have borne that last child in December," Anne said. "Isanna came into the world sickly, and my father predicts she won't live long either." She looked at Philip in a peculiar, searching way. "Mrs. Revere was only thirty-six. A year older than my own mother when she died. They say a married woman loses a tooth for every baby. Sara lost many more than that—and life too. That's too high a price to pay for being what the world expects of a woman."

"A wife and mother, you mean?"

Anne nodded. "I want a family of my own. But not at the expense of destroying myself."

"I did get the feeling you took exception to the way a young woman of Boston is supposed to behave." He meant it as a mild joke. The strained expression that came onto her face showed him he'd made an error.

"There's more to living than babies and kitchens and seeing to the furniture!" Anne exclaimed softly. "That's all my mother had. It killed her."

"When—" He hesitated, almost reluctant to ask. "—when was that?"

"In sixty-four."

"I never thought to ask you before, Anne—did you ever have any brothers or sisters?"

"One younger brother, Abraham, Junior. He lived only three months."

"What caused your mother's death?"

Again her eyes seemed to reach through him toward some haunted past.

"The smallpox. There was a terrible epidemic. Almost five thousand people died here in town. Nearly fifty of them from the preventive measure that was supposed to save them. My mother was one of those."

"What kind of preventive measure?"

Running her hand absently along the shabby velvet rope that separated them from the waxworks, she answered, "Back in the year 1721, another epidemic struck. A Dr. Boylston and the Reverend Cotton Mather argued that the only way to save lives was to give prospective victims a light case of the pox by a new method called inoculation. The selectmen of Boston considered that heresy then. But by sixty-four, they were willing to try the idea. My mother took the venom drawn from a pox victim. Took it in the prescribed way—on the point of a needle, directly into a wound cut in her arm. But she developed no light case. She died of it." After a moment, she finished, "Papa never blamed the physicians. The idea was sound. Many more were saved than perished. I think my mother was ready to die. I think she had died long before, really—"

Her voice trailed off as she stroked the rope, staring at Farmer George's bulging wax eyes. Philip felt he might be close to some understanding of this girl's unusual spirit and independence, closer than he'd ever been before. He asked:

"Will you explain that, Anne?"

She looked at him. "Explain what killed her? The same thing that killed Sara Revere. Having the world limit what a woman is allowed to do. Rear babies. Supervise servants. Think no independent thoughts of any consequence—I vowed it would never be the same with me."

"Knowing you, I'd guess it won't."

"But it takes struggle, Philip. Society doesn't change quickly—" Her eyes fixed on his. "Would you like me to show you what destroyed my mother?"

Before he could answer, another female voice boomed out:

"Dear Annie Ware! For heaven's sake—!"

A stout, cheery-faced woman of middle age appeared from the murky shadows at the rear of the hall. Approaching, she clasped Anne's hand between both of her own.

"I haven't seen my favorite pupil in ages. How have you been? Why don't you ever call on me?"

"I do apologize, Mrs. Hiller. It's very nice to see you again." She inclined her head toward Philip. "Let me introduce my friend Mr. Kent. This is Mrs. Hiller, who owns the exhibit—"

Deflated, Philip said, "I should have realized —you've been here before."

"Many times," Mrs. Hiller smiled. "Though generally upstairs, where I conduct my private school for young ladies. Annie excelled in feather and quill work. Embroidery too. But her heart was never in it, I could tell. That's what comes of spending too much time among her father's books!" Behind her smile, the older woman was scolding.

"Yes," Anne said, "Papa's still disappointed that I learned the feminine arts but never do much about practicing them."

"No doubt that will change when you're suitably wed," Mrs. Hiller replied, glancing quickly at Philip. He felt hotter than ever. The stout woman went on, "Too much learning is a hindrance, not a help, in the pantry and the nursery and the drawing room, my dear. Just remember—a man of substance doesn't wed a woman because she has a dominant spirit. The opposite! Wives must be submissive."

Anne sighed. "Then I imagine I'm not destined to marry."

"That could well be your unhappy fate," Mrs. Hiller advised, "*unless* you alter your outlook." But she couldn't conceal her fondness for her former student. Patting Anne's hand again, she said, "Still, you were and are a fine, charming girl. Do come to visit some afternoon, won't you?"

"Yes, I'll try."

"Good. Now if you'll excuse me, I must go see whether that rascal at the stile has sneaked off for a gill of rum again—" Skirts rustling, she hurried up the aisle.

Philip said, "Anne, I wouldn't have brought you here if I'd known you'd seen the exhibit before—"

"Oh, I always enjoy it. And it's been a long while. As Mrs. Hiller said, I most often saw the schoolrooms on the second floor. Poor Papa. I'm afraid he wasted all that money. I detest embroidery!" She smiled. "I hope I haven't spoiled your evening, Philip."

"No. But you've shown me some more mysteries about yourself."

"Mysteries?"

He nodded, began, "Sometimes I think I understand you—"

"Which is more than I can honestly say about you," she teased. "I press and press, and you won't tell me a thing about your time in England."

On guard, he waved: "That's all past. Of no consequence. Let's get some air, shall we?"

They left the waxworks hall. But it was almost as humid on the pier outside. Torches had been lit at dusk. The warm, clammy mist off the ocean still obscured details. Pale yellow faces loomed as they walked; men and women and some youngsters gathered around a balance master performing on a pole nailed to a pair of kegs set far apart. Applause rang out, and a few coins were tossed on a barrel head as the pole walker executed a crisp turn on one foot.

The crowd faded into the mist behind. Far away, a bell buoy clanged. Anne stopped abruptly.

"I asked earlier whether you'd like to see why I've become such a scandalous person."

"It's something that can be shown, then?"

"In a way. We'll have to walk about half a mile up the waterfront—"

"Lead on. While we go, tell me how many different schools you attended. You mentioned grammer school once, didn't you?"

"Yes. And dame school before that. Dame schools are run by women for very young children. From grammar school, boys can enter a university. Girls must go to academies like Mrs. Hiller's. Papa thought he was doing me a service sending me there. His heart was in the proper place. But I learned as much or more from his library—starting with the required books for moral guidance. Mr. Bunyan's works. The Reverend Mather's sermons—"

"Then you graduated to Mr. Locke—and politics?"

"I did. I won't spend my life as my mother spent hers. I'll observe the proprieties when it's necessary. But that doesn't mean I can't think, can't have a role in something besides—besides childbearing that makes all your teeth fall out!"

Philip wanted to laugh. But that anguished tone had come into her voice again. He decided it might be better to let the subject drop until they reached the destination that would supposedly explain something about her free spirit, a spirit that her father clearly could not control beyond a certain limit.

As they walked along through the thick, swirling mist, he lost track of their surroundings. All at once he saw a spot of yellow ahead. The cobbled street ended. He heard water lapping nearby. It was nearly dark. Anne took his arm:

"Careful of the mud. I must stop at the watchman's hut before we go in."

Puzzled, Philip accompanied her toward the yellow blur that brightened to reveal a bent, white-haired man hobbling out of a rickety little shanty. The man raised his lantern.

"Who goes? Speak up!"

"Only me, Elihu."

The man had to be at least seventy. Watering eyes glistened in the lamp's glow. The wrinkled face broke into a smile of cracked teeth and ruined gums.

"Mistress Anne! You've not been here since a year ago—no, more like two. How are you, girl?"

"Fine. Just fine, Elihu."

"And your good father?"

"In excellent health, thank you. Though he still works

too hard. This is a friend—Mr. Kent. May I show him a little of the yard?"

"Why, 'course," the watchman nodded. "I don't care who's supposed to own it—far's I'm concerned, the whole place is still Abner Sawyer's. Send up a yell if you lose your way."

"We won't," Anne smiled. "I know the yard too well."

Taking a firmer grip on Philip's arm, she led him from the hut toward a gate. A huge, crudely painted sign hung between the uprights:

SAWYER SHIP-YARD

Anne stopped just beneath the sign, pointed upward.

"My mother's maiden name was Sawyer. This belonged to her father—all of it. Once."

Slowly she disengaged her hand, walked on with a strange, melancholy expression on her face, as if the past, like the mist, was closing around her.

Philip followed. He passed tall stacks of lumber, great piles of raw logs, saw Anne stop ahead. He came up quickly behind her. She caught his arm again:

"Careful!"

This time she pointed downward. One more step and he'd have tumbled into a rectangular pit that looked nearly as deep as a man. Beyond it, great ghostly U-shaped ribs loomed up like the bones of some primeval monster. Only a moment later did he recognize what looked like the inside of *Eclipse*, minus its hull planking: the keel and ribs of a sailing vessel under construction on one of three timbered ways that inclined toward the unseen water.

"You nearly walked into the saw pit," Anne told him. "One or two men work down there, two more up here.

With crosscut saws they turn logs into sixty-foot planks that'll eventually form the hull for that sloop."

"And your grandfather owned this business?"

She nodded. "He came from England in 1714, indentured to another yard owner. His home was Plymouth. His father and his grandfather before him had worked in the shipyard saw pits. I think that's how the family came to be called Sawyer. English families took names from their work—Carter, Miller, Carpenter—oh, there must be dozens. Even though my grandfather was a landsman, he loved the sea. He loved building ships. But Plymouth had all the yards it needed, so he sailed to America. By the time my mother was born in 1729, he had his dream—his own yard. He was only twenty-five, but he worked very hard to be a success. He was. But he and his wife had no other children except my mother. That was the difficulty—"

She started walking again, the mist swirling around her. They circled the end of the saw pit where crossbeams were planted in the ground to support the long logs to be cut by the saw working back and forth from above and below. Anne wandered toward the skeleton of the vessel on the ways. The huge ribs towered above them as Philip stood at her side, letting her speak because he somehow knew she had to:

"This was my mother's playground from the time she could walk. She loved the place so much, I suppose it was only natural she thought she would own it one day. She never bargained on my grandfather being exactly like most other Englishmen. Disappointed that he didn't have a son. And accepting without question the fact that a woman could never be responsible for this sort of business. Running a yard is man's work—" A somber pause. Then:

"She told me she only asked him about it once. She was fifteen or sixteen. She wanted to know when she could start taking over. Be his assistant. She knew the routine as well as he did. How to scarf the lengths of keel together. Exactly what had to be done to frame up properly. Planking, dubbing, caulking—she knew it all, because she'd helped the men do it. So she asked. She said Grandfather Sawyer never laughed so hard in his life. Laughed till the tears ran on his face. He simply couldn't believe she was serious. He meant no unkindness. He was a man of his times, that's all. But I think he started killing her that very day. Although it's the last thing he would have done on purpose—"

Musing, her voice turned sad:

"Strange, the way people hurt each other. Unknowingly. Because custom says they must. Well—"

With another small shrug, she threw off the mood. "My grandfather's rebuff was a turning point. When my father courted my mother—he was fresh out of Harvard—she married him because she'd already given up her dreams. My grandfather sold the yard to another owner the year before he died in fifty-one. He gave Lawyer Ware and his wife part of the profits. It was a handsome gift. Grandfather never thought twice about refusing my mother the one gift she wanted most—but couldn't have because she was a woman. When I was small, she brought me here time and again, just to watch the workmen. Those were the only times I ever saw her truly happy. When we were leaving to go home, she'd almost always cry a little."

"Did your father know?"

"I'm not sure. If he did, I doubt if it concerned him much. A man's work is a man's, period."

"But why did she marry him if she felt the way she did?"

"She loved him. And—" Bitterness then. "—she realized it was her only course. That a woman would even daydream about taking over this kind of business—she finally understood it was unthinkable. It still is. An establishment like Mrs. Hiller's—well, that's

a bit different. Running a girl's school is accepted. It
falls into a woman's prescribed sphere. My grandfather,
from all I know of him, was a kind, loving man. So is my
father. But they killed my mother all the same."

"So you're going another way. Reading Mr. Locke.
Involving yourself in politics—"

"I'll involve myself in my husband's work, too,
when—" She turned away "—when I know who he is."

"Anne, you're a damned unusual girl."

She laughed. "It has its price. I have no circle of
young female friends my own age. And no gentlemen
who've called more than once or twice—except you,"
she teased. "And you're French, and new to America,
and probably don't know any better! Even
though I attend church dutifully and observe most of the
outward conventions, I am not entirely respectable,
Philip."

At that moment he wanted to reach out and take her
in his arms. He held back, a little in awe even yet. Sensing the awkwardness of the moment, she said:

"It's dark. We'd better go."

They walked away from the eerie ribs of the ship on
the ways. They passed the hut where old Elihu had
fallen asleep beside his lantern, and still Philip kept
silent. She had partially explained herself at last; he understood why Lawyer Ware had sighed when she quoted
Locke at the ill-mannered grenadier.

They left the shipyard and the sign towering into the
mist. As they reached the solid cobblestones, he concluded that a girl like Anne Ware could very well prove
too much for most ordinary men.

But then, had he ever considered himself as ordinary?
he thought with an inward smile.

They walked in easy, companionable silence to her
home, only the distant cry of the watch disturbing the
night—"*Eight o'clock of a foggy evening, eight
o'clock!*" He kept mulling what she'd told him.

Somehow it only increased his fascination with her, his attraction to her, physically and otherwise.

At the steps in Launder Street, she seemed in better spirits, to the point of smiling with real feeling.

"I thank you for the pleasant outing, Philip."

"I apologize again for dragging you somewhere you've been many times before. You should have told me—"

"Not at all. I appreciate how hard you worked for those four shillings. But I have a feeling I talked too much—and too frankly. Are you sure you want to continue associating with a young woman who insists on having thoughts of her own?"

His reply was instantaneous:

"I'm sure."

She laughed, a warm, rich sound. She leaned forward suddenly to give him a gentle kiss on the cheek.

The kiss, prim as it was, left him happier than he'd felt in many a month. He stood on the steps in the mist long after the door closed behind her.

v

The water of the Charles River purled against the bow of the small rowboat. Philip had hired the boat for the afternoon. As he rowed, Anne chattered from her seat in the stern. She wore the gown of yellow sprigged muslin, the one that had first taken his fancy. A wicker hamper rested at her feet.

Gulls wheeled in the mellow September sky as Philip angled the boat toward the grassy hills on the peninsula opposite North Boston. It was a Saturday. With work momentarily slow at the printing house, he'd asked Ben Edes for the afternoon free. He was delighted when Edes consented, because picnicking was not considered a suitable pastime for the Sabbath.

Philip rowed past the neat, sunlit houses and the piers of the little village of Charlestown. The village occupied the southern point of the peninsula. But his eyes were drawn constantly to the green hills beyond. Breed's and Bunker's were the names of two of them.

Only a few white farm buildings dotted the rolling land. Somewhere on those slopes, he planned to make his intentions known to Anne. The demands of his mind and body had grown nearly intolerable during the stifling summer months.

"—and Mr. Adams is certain other ports will be involved too," she was saying. "There's talk that as much as half a million pounds of tea will be shipped to the agents of the East India Company. And that silly ass Hutchinson continues to swear the monopoly scheme will be enforced. It's glorious!"

"Good God, we're back to that again!" he groaned, only partly in jest. "I'm fairly sick of hearing tea, tea, tea!"

"But it's the rallying point we've needed so badly!" she said, brushing back a lock of chestnut hair blowing in the Atlantic breeze. Further out to sea, whitecaps rolled toward the harbor islands. A pair of boys fishing off a Charlestown pier hailed them. Anne waved back, then said in her now-familiar tone of teasing:

"Besides, Philip, what do we have to talk about that's more interesting? That evening at the shipyard, I bored you to death talking about my family—"

"No, you didn't."

"—but we never seem to discuss your side of things. For months, I've kept trying to lure you into telling me more of your mysterious doings in England. All I get in return is silence and portentous looks. Fair's fair. I've revealed everything, yet your past is still locked up tight as a spinster's dowry chest. Don't you think we know each other well enough for confidences by now?"

"We know each other," he replied. "But hardly well

enough." His lingering glance at her breasts, coupled with his sudden, bold smile, brought scarlet into her cheeks.

She patted her hair again. Nervously, he thought. His hope increased that the golden afternoon and the isolation of one of the farmers' hillsides would bring the result he so badly wanted.

Abruptly, Anne touched his hand where it gripped tight on the oar. "I don't mean it the way I think you do. Truly, Philip, I've puzzled over you night after night—"

"Any conclusions?"

"That something haunts you. Drives you."

"And you."

"Yes, but I've explained my—what do the French say?—my black beast. Can yours be so terrible you won't speak of it?"

Resting on the oars, he deliberated. He'd guarded the past overcautiously, perhaps. So, resuming his rowing, he told her.

Not in great detail. But enough. He did omit mention of his involvement with Alicia Parkhurst, and converted the motivation of Roger Amberly's attacks to hints that they had been inspired by Lady Jane. But even the story thus distorted held Anne silent with interest. By the time he beached the rowboat on the northeast point of the peninsula, she was studying him with a new, thoughtful understanding.

"Then I wasn't far off in my chance remark."

"What chance remark?"

"The one about your lordly ways. You really do have some credentials there. I wasn't entirely sure when you said as much the first time you came to our house."

"Yes, I've credentials, as you call them. Useless ones."

"Do you still have the letter from your father?"

"In my mother's casket. I keep it in my room. Worthless too, I suppose."

"But there's a kind of distant hope in your voice when you say that. Did you realize it?"

"No," he lied, clambering out onto the pebbled shore. He took her hand, felt her breast brush his arm as he assisted her from the rowboat. As he reached down for the hamper, she said:

"What is it you want, Philip?"

"You've asked me that before."

"Yes, but you didn't answer. Realistically, anyway. You've escaped the family's reach, surely. You should be moving toward something now, not simply away. So what's the goal to be?"

"Food."

She laughed. "All right. Shall we try Morton's Hill? It's pleasant. But answer my other question, if you will."

As they climbed through the fragrant long grass, he responded at last, "I'd say I want to be a man of property one day. Own my own printing house—"

"Then go back to England and flaunt your position to those people? As you told your mother you would before she died?"

"To be realistic, as you call it, I think that's out of the question."

Half way to the summit of the hill, she touched him again, brought him facing around so that he saw her framed against the late summer green of the hilly pastures, and the church spires, the jumbled rooftops, the harbor masts of Boston across the river. Some of those masts belonged to an English naval squadron.

"Even yet you don't sound certain, Philip."

"Well, then, dammit, maybe I'm not."

"Do you recall what I've said before—echoing Mr. Adams? A time comes to everyone when a choice must be made. A direction must be taken. You can't evade that forever."

He was disconcerted by the firmness with which she spoke; even though their ages were the same, at the moment she seemed the more adult. Perhaps it was because her own direction was already charted.

"Yes, I'm aware that you know where you're going. A husband you can live beside. Not just raising children but working with him to make a success of his trade, his profession—"

"Oh, but that won't come immediately," she said, starting to climb the hill again. "It can't, even if—the proper man should drop from heaven this minute. The future's too uncertain. The questions that obsess Papa and Mr. Adams and the others must be decided before any of us are free to pursue other ends. One of my goals is to see that happen. To help it happen, if I can."

"You really do have conviction about the cause, don't you?"

"Yes. You know I won't retreat from the world like women are supposed to do. And I not only love my father, I respect most of his ideas. Except for the ones concerning the female's role!"

"You seem to have gotten around that obstacle," Philip said, wry. "He lets you have your head—go where you wish—doesn't he?"

"True. The dear man realized that battle was lost a long time ago. Seriously, Philip—when it comes to the law, politics, he's a solid thinker. That's influenced me to place importance where he places it. I've thought matters over for myself, too. Or tried. Resistance is right and proper. I should think all you experienced in England would bring you to the same conclusion. The world *is* changing. People won't permit themselves to be put upon by kings or persons of privilege any longer. You mentioned that tutor you had in France. He knew choice was inevitable, didn't he?"

Philip nodded. "I think so. I'll make mine one of these days."

"Unless you wait too long and have it forced on you by the pressures of the moment. Believe me, I've read enough history in Papa's library to know that chance plays its part. But I think it's better that a man—or a woman—make a choice by his or her own will, not simply be thrust along by events, willy-nilly."

"Anne—" He scanned the shimmering hilltop, the hazed sky beyond, set the hamper in the grass. "I've made one."

"What is it?"

"To tell you I care for you very much." The wind whispered through a moment of silence. "That I want you very much."

Flushing again, she picked up the hamper. "Let's go on to the top. The mutton won't be good if we don't soon—"

"Anne."

He tightened his hold on her forearm, then took her other arm as well. Slowly, he pulled her down beside him in the wind-rustling grass.

He slipped an arm around her shoulder, the excitement in his own flesh relentless now. From the tiny glisten of perspiration on her upper lip he guessed she was experiencing a similar reaction.

"I've waited months for a time like this, Anne."

"Philip, I can't. I mean—"

She stopped as he thrust her backward in the grass, cushioning her with his arm. She didn't resist. But there was a flicker of unhappiness in her brown eyes as he stretched out beside her, brought his face down close to hers and kissed her.

He touched her mouth tenderly, marveling at its soft warmth. Then he raised up on one elbow. She gazed at him, looking almost frightened. Her voice sounded small:

"I knew that if we came here—somehow I knew that we—*oh*."

Giving that strange, almost sad little murmur of surrender, she closed her eyes and lay very still.

He bent close again, stroked the softness of her hair, the sun a fire on the back of his neck. The fire spread through him as he brought his hip against hers.

She still didn't pull away. But there was a resistance, a tension in her that he could feel. Fear?

He kissed her again. This time, her mouth responded. One of her arms stole around his neck. His shirt touched her breasts. She moaned softly, turning against him, clasping him tighter while they kissed with the ardor of the young and the heat of the golden September—

Hidden in the meadow grass, the world lost except for the faraway clank of a cow's bell, they kissed a long time. His mouth caressed her eyelids, the fragrant strands of her hair. The grass was heady with the perfumes of autumn, but no headier than her breath when, at last, her lips parted and he tasted her sweet mouth—

Another surprised little cry deep in her throat told him she'd felt the change in his body. Felt it because they lay so close together, nothing separating them except rumpled clothing. A boatman on the river hailed someone. The sun blazed, showering down gold light to drown them in warmth, to stoke the quick-breathing eagerness of mouths, the tremble of hands exploring—

For Philip there was no holding back. The blood-tide was running too high. He began to tug at the hem of her yellow muslin skirt. He thought she started to draw away, make a sound—perhaps a word of negation—but with the hammer of his own heartbeat so loud in his ears, he couldn't clearly tell.

The skirt came upward. His hands sought her. Warm, private places tingled his fingertips. He felt passion change her body, as his had changed—

The meadow grass rippled in the wind, a whispering. Cries of gulls drifted from the harbor. The hot light poured down as her own hands moved over him—and his grew bolder—

Jolted, he rolled back a second after she pulled away.

She thrust down her skirt as his eyes flared with anger. Sitting up, she brushed off her bodice. She wouldn't look at him.

"For God's sake, Anne, what's the matter?"

"Philip, this was foolish. Foolish and wrong. I shouldn't have come with you. I shouldn't have let you think—oh, dear heaven, please forgive me?"

A hint of tears showed in the corners of her dark eyes. He stood up, his hair ribbon loosened in the tumbling. The ribbon snapped in the breeze as he gazed down at her. He was trembling from fury, from astonishment, from the sudden chilling of the September sun.

"You're denying you want the same thing I do?"

"I—Philip—"

"You can't deny it."

She clasped her hands around her knees, bowed her head. Her voice sounded as he'd never heard it before. Unsure:

"No, I can't. But—"

Abruptly her head came up. The autumnal sunlight caught fire in the tears streaking her cheeks. Yet he still recognized the Anne Ware he'd met on that first day in Mr. Henry Knox's bookshop.

"But I will not have it."

"Oh," he shot back, almost snarling, "a man working his will on you—is that it? Well, by Christ, you'll never get any man to touch you if you insist on—*ah!*"

Angry at himself, he pivoted away. "I'm sorry." He dropped to his knees beside her, took both her hands in his. "From the way you kissed me—Anne, I *felt* what you wanted."

"Yes," she said, unsteadily, "that's true. It's a bright, hot day. We're safe here, we'd never be caught, but— Philip, I've loved no man yet, not that way, not in nineteen years. I—I can't do it so casually."

"Can't because a *man* wants it?"

"I don't blame you for anger—"

He stood up. "I just don't understand."

"—and you'll think me a prude—"

"You don't kiss like a prude. Anything but a prude. Anne—"

"Listen, please *listen!* It was my fault. I was foolish and wicked to lead you on. I didn't mean to do that—" The words spilled out rapidly now, as she dashed tears off her cheeks. "But when the time comes, there must be—there must be some other reason besides the heat of a September afternoon."

Glum, he felt his wrath fading away. He knew all too well what she meant:

"Love."

The grass bent and rustled in the wind. All joy had gone out of the day. Anne's face remained averted:

"Yes. Otherwise, it's like the rutting of a slut and someone who's paid her. Do you understand that, Philip?"

The cries of the gulls rang in the distance, forlorn.

"I do. You want another choice out of me."

"No, I didn't ask for—"

"But it's what you want. What you must have—though you'll forgive me if I can't square the wish with other things you say."

"What things?"

"That talk about your mother, for instance. She married because it was the accepted way. She put herself in bondage. That was also love, wasn't it? You said it was—"

"Yes."

"And she died of it."

"Yes."

"Yet you want that same bondage? From a man? And for yourself too? Is that your much-touted liberty, Anne?"

"For my mother, marriage was—surrendering."

"Which is precisely what you're getting at, isn't it?"

"No. No, there's a difference. I don't know whether I can say it correctly—I'm not saying anything correctly—yes, loving someone is a bondage. But that kind of bondage—to a person, or even to an ideal—you enter it freely. You go *toward* it, you don't use it to escape something—"

"Pardon me, but the difference is pretty Goddamn subtle. How do you decide which kind is which?"

"You—just know. Does it fulfill you, or—or destroy you?"

Too upset to cope with such thoughts for long, he made a sharp gesture. "Well, you may be right. But whatever sort of choice you're after—fulfilling, destroying—running toward, running from—it's one I can't make."

This time her nod was heavy with sadness. "I'm not half clever enough. I think I already knew. And I still said yes to coming here. Realizing what might happen. Wanting—" Her head lifted; her eyes brimmed with sorrow. "—wanting it more than a little."

"Don't lie to me."

"I'm not! It's the truth! But I was terribly wrong to let it go so far—"

Kneeling beside her again, Philip put two fingers on her still-warm mouth. He was troubled and utterly miserable. He concealed it in the protection of a curt laugh:

"Don't score yourself. The error's mine, Mistress Ware. I'd forgotten just how infernally strong a female you are. What positive ideas you have about every sort of human action. You want to be sure of certain things, but to use your words, fair's fair. Don't I get the same privilege?"

"Of course. Of course you do."

"I do apologize for trying to work my will, as they call it. A mere man, demanding—"

"*Stop it, Philip!* I told you that has nothing to do with it."

He knew it didn't; he was ashamed he'd attacked her that way a second time.

To calm the churning of his own emotions, he tried to smile; it was a grimace. "Best we drop it. Here—" He speared the hamper, held it high. "Let's not waste the mutton and good sunshine."

"I—I'm still afraid you're angry—"

"I'm absolutely enraged with you, my girl. And the crazy thing is, that makes me want you all the worse. So badly I ache—damned if I know why. I should row back to Copp's Hill pier and leave you stranded. I guess I won't, though—"

"I'm surprised," she said with a rueful smile.

"Are you? Don't be. There—" He couldn't pretend; he could only speak the painful truth of his own heart. "—there's something in you I admire even when you turn me away. Maybe I admire you *because* you turn me away—I'm plagued if I know enough about women to figure it out! But in your own way, you're tougher than old Adams at his wildest. Come on."

He extended his other hand to assist her. She kept her hands at her sides.

As they started to climb again, he went on, "I wish I could lie to you, Anne. I wish I could pretend I can give you what you say you've got to have. That'd bring everything to a nice, neat solution—"

"But I'd know you were lying—if you were."

"Bet you would at that," he sighed. "Well, anyway, I can't do it. Making promises is impossible."

She stopped and looked at him, her eyes so intense that he felt they reached and wrenched at whatever soul or central essence lay in the depths of his being:

"For now? Or forever?"

His mind swirled with memories of Kentland, of his

mother, of what he could have been—and might yet still be. Damn heaven, what *did* he want?

He said, "Anne—I don't know."

Turning, he stalked on up toward the searing light of the hilltop.

He wished he could lose himself in that fire, be consumed, destroyed, relieved of thinking, of decisions, of trying to unlock the riddles of the whole damned world—and himself—

He managed to calm down and occupy his attention with opening the hamper. In a few moments, Anne joined him. She seated herself beside the cloth he'd spread. Her cheeks were reddened but the tears were gone.

As Philip unpacked the food, he said in an offhand way, "I imagine you'll want me to stop calling after this."

Her smile, though forced, puzzled him until she said:

"That's the last thing I want, Philip. Like these colonies, you'll make choices. One way or another, something will become of you. I'd like to find out what."

She glanced away. "However, the decision is yours."

                                    vi

They passed the remainder of the afternoon in repetitious speculation about the tea crisis and empty pleasantries about the beauties of the early autumn weather. While he rowed her back to Boston in the twilight, neither of them said a word. He left her at the door in Launder Street with a quickly murmured goodbye, and without touching her.

He slept very little that night. The September afternoon had focused the question to unbearable sharpness: What was his ambition? His future? And how much of the choice would be his and how much the result of events he could not control?

Tossing restlessly, he concluded that he must be falling in love with Anne. Nothing else would explain his feeling so forlorn, furious and confused.

vii

Express riders galloping in across Roxbury Neck in late October brought news that a mass meeting in Philadelphia had forced the resignation of the tea agents appointed for that city. A similar meeting was convened locally. But Governor Hutchinson's nephew and two of his sons who had been appointed to the potentially lucrative posts would not relent.

Adams and his followers thundered denunciations of the tea consignees. Called them traitors, enemies of America. To no avail.

Then, on the twenty-seventh of November, *Dartmouth*, the first of three vessels reported on the way to Boston with the hated cargo, was sighted offshore.

The following night, Philip and Benjamin Edes labored almost until dawn. They set, proofed and printed copies of a sheet circulated throughout the town and nailed to the Liberty Tree next morning:

FRIENDS!   BRETHREN!   COUNTRYMEN!

That worst of plagues, the detested tea, shipped for this port by the East India Company, is now arrived in this harbor; the hour of destruction or manly oppositions to the machinations of tyranny stares you in the face. Every friend to his country, to himself, and posterity is now called upon to meet at Faneuil Hall at nine o'clock this day (at which time the bells will ring), to make a united and successful resistance to this last, worst and most destructive measure of administration.

Philip had no idea what Anne Ware thought about the

atmosphere of tension and anger mounting hourly in the city. Since the day in September, he had not visited Launder Street once, and had arranged to be occupied in Edes' back office whenever he spied the girl turning into Dassett Alley on her way to the shop. By now he was not entirely sure whether his reaction came about because he was in love with her, and feared it, or because he wasn't.

The tea ship docking at Griffin's Wharf brought accelerated activity among Edes and his friends. It also provided Philip with welcome diversion from the weeks of painful doubt and introspection, weeks which had still produced no definite answers in his own mind.

viii

He could keep himself physically separated from Anne, it seemed. But he couldn't prevent her from coming to him in other ways. Two nights after *Dartmouth* anchored, he dreamed about her—a heavy, sensual dream in which he glimpsed her naked through mist or smoke.

He groaned, rolled over on the cellar pallet, coughed, smelled the tang of his dream in the damp darkness— *Smoke*?

Instantly his eyes opened. In a panic, he fought free of the sweated blankets. The erection produced by the dream wilted under his sudden fear.

His wool nightshirt flapped around his knees as he stumbled for the stairs. The smoke stench was growing stronger. A splinter stabbed his bare sole as he took the risers two at a time. He was terrified by the roseate light at the head of the stairs. He heard a sound. Crackling—

He burst onto the main floor, dashed past the entrance to Ben Edes' office. Flames shot up from a stack of fresh-printed *Gazettes* near the press.

The fire was not large as yet; the still-damp ink produced the excessive smoke. He leaped for the burning papers, scorched his hands in the process of spilling the sheets off their pallet and away from the vulnerable wooden press.

The leaping fire showed him a fallen pine-knot torch and the front door half-torn from its hinges. The door's outer surface bore the scars of gouging and prying. He'd apparently been sleeping so hard that he hadn't heard the break-in.

"Fire, a fire!" he bawled from the doorway, hoping the hour was not too late.

Relieved, he heard the cry echoed a moment later by other men, some of the loafers hanging around the taverns close to the nearby State House, he suspected. He raced behind the press, seized the bucket of sand kept there for just such emergencies, emptied it on the scattered, burning newspapers with a hurling sweep. That helped—a little.

The voices grew louder in the close confines of Dassett Alley. Philip shouted at figures dimly visible at the door:

"Someone with boots help me stamp this out!"

A tottering tosspot with a red nose and a woolen muffler around his neck was pushed forward by his companions. "And one of you run to Mr. Edes' house and fetch him—quickly!" Philip cried.

By the time Edes arrived in a quarter of an hour, the blaze was well extinguished. A noisy, quarrelsome-sounding crowd now packed the alley, some with torches. Edes had to struggle and shove his way through.

Shivering in his nightshirt, Philip greeted him at the door. Edes surveyed the damage while Philip explained what had happened.

"Sharp work," Edes said finally, fingering the

smashed-in door. "Thank God you saved the press."

"Apparently someone discovered the source of the new broadside hung on the tree."

The printer snorted. "D'you think that's any secret? I've had threats of this—and worse—more times than I can count."

Philip suggested that perhaps some partisan of the Tory cause had worked the damage. But Edes rejected the idea, searching the crowd outside.

"No, lad, the merchants who still kiss Farmer George's ass are too concerned about their own hides—and too scared of the Sons of Liberty—to risk villainy after dark. 'Twould be soldiers, most likely. Come over from the garrison at Castle William. The right honorable King's men."

He spat, turned and began picking up charred sections of the *Gazette*.

"They think they can silence our protests about the tea matter with a little hooliganism. 'Course," he added, managing a smile at last, "they probably got their inspiration from our own organization. We've burned before, when circumstances warranted. Well, we must print again tomorrow. It appears they destroyed about a third of the run—"

"And came close to destroying the only place I have to build a future, damn 'em to hell!" Philip said impulsively.

Ben Edes gave him a keen look of approval. He reached under his shirt, pulled off the chain bearing a medal like the one Campbell had shown. He looped the chain around his startled assistant's neck.

"A little gift, Philip. Wear it proudly. You earned it with what you did tonight. And what you just said."

CHAPTER IV

Night of the Axe

i

"PHILIP, YOU KNOW there's to be action tonight. We need young men. Are you with us? I should warn you—it may be dangerous."

Ben Edes spoke the words shortly after noon on a Thursday, the sixteenth of December. Outside, a thin early winter rain spattered Dassett Alley.

Philip wiped his ink-stained hands on his apron, met the inquiring gaze of the older man; he had no doubt about what sort of "action" Ben Edes referred to. Boston had seethed with talk of nothing else during the nineteen days *Dartmouth* had remained at Griffin's Wharf, her cargo still in her hold. During those same nineteen days, two sister ships, *Eleanor* and *Beaver*, had dropped anchor at the same pier. Both carried more tea.

At public meetings in late November, Samuel Adams had reiterated the demand that all the tea be shipped back to England. Adams' cohorts skillfully controlled the loud, vocal voting—in favor of the patriot resolutions.

But that made no difference to the Royal Governor. Hutchinson issued orders to the Customs authorities who patrolled the harbor that the tea ships could sail only on presentation of official documents to certify that the duty had been paid.

Tomorrow—December seventeenth—would mark

the end of a crucial period. Twenty days after any ship's arrival, Customs men could board her and seize her cargo for non-payment of duties. *Dartmouth's* twenty days expired tomorrow.

In anticipation of that—so Edes had confided to Philip—three or four days ago, Adams had convened a secret session of Committees of Correspondence from Boston and four neighboring towns. The object was to prepare the plan that had to be carried out before the sun rose on the seventeenth—and the tea fell into Crown hands.

"The Governor won't relent?" Philip asked now. "I heard at the Dragon there was to be another last-minute meeting to press for it."

"Aye, there's a meeting. At Old South Church, beginning at three this afternoon. But it's doubtful Hutchinson will change his mind. If he does, several gentlemen I know will be exceedingly disappointed. The Governor obviously realizes trouble's coming. He's fled to his big country place over by Blue Hill in Milton."

"Yes, I heard that too."

"So the tea will be seized unless he permits *Dartmouth* to sail tonight. Which he won't."

"But what about the troops, Mr. Edes? Will they stand for what's been planned?"

"That's the question—and the risk. The soldiers could move in from the island garrison to block us. Worse than that, when we're at Griffin's, we'll be in range of the guns of the English squadron. If that damned Admiral Montague decides to throw a little grape or canister to discourage our—protest, we could be in for it."

"You think they'd damage the tea ships and the wharf?"

"To damage some patriots at the same time? I don't think it's impossible."

Philip shivered. In response, Edes said, "There's no

guaranteeing anything, of course. With the town in its present mood, the lobsters might choose inaction. There's also a question of what orders would be required for the soldiers to act. Orders to shoot us? We plan no harm to any person. Still—" He shrugged. "That's not to say bloody hell couldn't break loose. On purpose or by accident. So you're fairly warned, lad. What's your answer?"

The younger man grinned. "Risk or not, do you think I'd miss it? Especially after they tried to burn us out? Tell me what time and where."

Edes clapped him on the shoulder. "My parlor. We've three groups organizing—one at my home. Lock the shop and be there before sundown. I understand those gathering at Old South will try one final time to force *Dartmouth*'s captain, Francis Rotch, to sail this evening. We'll wait for his refusal—then Sam's signal."

With that, Edes bundled into his surtout of dark gray wool and hurried out of the shop.

Watching him go, Philip noted that Dassett Alley was enjoying more pedestrian traffic than usual this morning. Despite the wretched weather, the Boston streets teemed with people. Almost as if there were a fair, Philip thought wryly. The public mood hardly seemed suitable for a day when a clear and open blow was to be struck against the King's law. Peculiar people, these Americans.

ii

Philip arrived at Ben Edes' home at quarter to five. The rain was beginning to slack off, the clouds to blow away as winter twilight came on. Edes' young son Peter admitted him to the house, conducted him to closed parlor doors.

"I'm not allowed in, except to keep the bowl filled with rum punch," he said unhappily.

The boy knocked. Philip heard muffled voices go silent suddenly.

A moment later the doors slid aside. Edes greeted Philip, gestured him in. He was unprepared for what he saw as Edes shut the doors again.

The room was crowded with young men, all of them unfamiliar. Most were mechanics; artisans, to judge by their clothing. They resumed conversing in lively fashion, joking and posing for one another in ragged costumes that ranged from tattered wool blankets to women's shawls. But the talk seemed too boisterous, as if it concealed each masquerader's apprehension—

The same apprehension Philip felt. Throughout the afternoon, worried-looking strangers had hurried into the shop, hunting Edes. Philip had sent them on to the printer's home.

All at once Philip did recognize one face in the gathering. Revere, the silversmith. He was bundling a blanket under his arm and tucking what appeared to be two wild bird's feathers beneath his coat.

Philip hadn't seen the craftsman of North Square in a month or more. Tonight Revere's dark eyes snapped, alert. His color looked excellent again. Philip reminded himself to remark on the happy reason for the change, if he had the chance.

At the moment Edes was leading him to a polished walnut table in the center of the room. On it were piled a good dozen axes and hatchets. The printer chose one, pressed it into Philip's hand.

"Tonight, my boy, you'll be a noble savage." Edes' smile faded. "Don't be surprised if you're required to use this on something other than tea."

Hefting the weapon, Philip frowned. "Trouble coming?"

"Not sure. The district near the wharf is crawling with tommies. And everyone's lost track of that damn admiral—he may have got wind of this and be readying his guns. But Samuel won't call it off for a piddling reason like that."

Possible bombardment by English sea gunners hardly seemed to deserve the description "piddling." Philip said nothing, however. Edes pointed to a heap of frowsy clothing in the corner.

"Find some costume that suits you. Once we leave Old South, we'll add lampblacking or the ochre to our faces and—lo!—law-abiding townsmen turn into wild Mohawks."

Philip picked up a blanket and cocked an eyebrow as a flea hopped to the back of his sweating hand, then hopped off again.

"Why all this mummery, Mr. Edes? I mean, these outfits will hardly fool anyone—"

"No, but they just might keep you from being recognized if the troops move in and there's a fracas."

Paul Revere walked up, saying, "Some disguises will be more complete than others, Mr. Kent." As Edes moved off and Philip slung the blanket around his shoulders, the silversmith went on, "Look sharp and you may notice gentleman's lace at a cuff or two. Some who support our cause can't afford to risk discovery just yet. But they'll make good Indians nonetheless. And on top of what Ben said, these rags can be shed quickly if we've got to run for it. But come, nothing's happened yet! Let's celebrate while we have a chance."

Smiling, Revere signaled one of the young mechanics, who handed them both cups of rum punch. By now Philip could definitely detect the falseness of the glee turning the room noisy. The bogus Indians were pretending the evening was to be nothing more than a grand party. But it could turn out to be something entirely different.

With the wicked-bladed axe thrust into his belt, he definitely felt like a lawbreaker. He thought glumly of the English men-o'-war riding at anchor. Surely the admiral in command wouldn't be so thick-witted as to order the guns trained on the town. Surely not. But accidents could happen. Tempers could snap—

Trying to forget his tension, Philip hoisted his cup in salute:

"Mr. Revere, I haven't seen you to congratulate you on the happy event in October."

"Why, my thanks, Mr. Kent. A widower with a flock of children can't run a business and a household. Fortune smiled when she directed Miss Rachel Walker my way."

The said Miss Walker, only twenty-seven, had become Revere's second wife less than sixty days earlier. She was not supposed to be a great beauty. But she was called kindly, intelligent, capable. And Edes said that Revere became his old self during the short courtship.

"I was distressed to hear of the death of your youngest child, though," Philip added.

"Your sympathy's appreciated. Poor little Isanna— she wasn't meant to live. But a man can't mourn forever. I've turned my back on past sadness and I take delight in my new and happy state."

"Ben Edes told me you'd made up a clever riddle about the new Mrs. Revere—"

"About her name," the other nodded. "'Take three-fourths of a pain that makes traitors confess—' "

Helping himself to a second cup of punch, Philip said, "That'd be 'rack,' I guess. And three-fourths? R-a-c?"

"With three parts of a place which the wicked don't bless—"

"H-e-l from 'hell'—that makes Rachel—"

"Time to leave!" Ben Edes yelled. "Time, gentlemen!"

Philip and Revere tossed down the rest of their punch, the latter saying, "The next two couplets give the name 'Walker,' and the last two are sheer romantic compliment. But she deserves 'em. So I'll accept an earnest wish that we all live long enough for me to enjoy my first anniversary."

"Gladly given," Philip grinned. "And many more."

His head hummed from the punch. His earlier fear was gone. When he hurried with Edes, Revere and the others down Marlborough Street shortly before five-thirty—no man making the slightest attempt to conceal the disguise he carried—thanks to the liberating effects of the punch, Philip shared the holiday mood. Under a just-showing sickle of moon, he laughed when loungers in doorways applauded and feigned shrieks of terror:

" 'Fore God, it's a Mohawk rising! Look at them tommyhawks shine!"

By the time they neared the corner of Marlborough and Milk streets, darkness was nearly complete. The intersecting streets were packed wall to wall, a larger crowd than Philip had ever seen at one time in Boston. More cheering, more yells of encouragement welcomed Edes and his followers as they shoved their way toward the doors of Old South.

But the crowd whistling and applauding outside was as nothing compared to the huge throng jamming the interior of the church.

Every pew and gallery was filled. Every inch of aisle space was occupied by standees. Edes and his group managed to squeeze into standing room at the very rear. Overhead, the church's chandelier candles flickered.

Philip scanned the restless audience. A man near Edes was whispering, "—oratory's been plenty hot so far. Adams and Quincy and Dr. Warren kept the crowd fired for two hours. But now they're impatient. Already been several motions for adjournment—"

From the pulpit, a man someone identified to Philip as a Mr. Samuel Savage was just gaveling down another such motion:

"I repeat—Captain Rotch has been sent on his way to

His Excellency's home in Milton, and there is no reason to doubt the captain's good faith. Besides, our several towns are very anxious to have full information as to this matter, and are desirous that the meeting should be continued until Rotch returns."

Grumbles and catcalls greeted the statement. Philip's eyes kept ranging over the faces in the high galleries. Suddenly, he recognized two of them. Lawyer Ware and, beside him, Anne.

She was staring at him. He couldn't clearly read her expression. It seemed admiring, yet sorrowful. Perhaps the admiration was to acknowledge his presence, the other emotion more personal—

Another flea crawled down his collar. He scratched, then acknowledged Anne's look with a nod, a tentative smile. She nodded ever so slightly in return.

Studying her fair, bonneted face high up in the crowded rows, he felt a tug of emotion. He wished he could speak to her—

Abruptly, there was commotion at the side doors. A cry went up:

"Rotch is returning! Open the way!"

Everyone began talking at once. Savage hammered them to silence as a pale man in sodden, mud-stained clothing struggled through to a point just below Old South's pulpit. In one of the rows near the front, Philip recognized the back of Sam Adams' unmistakably trembling head. Adams was half-risen in his pew, straining forward to listen.

Revere whispered, "I see you've spotted Sam. He'll give the signal if we're to go."

"Yes, Mr. Edes told me," Philip nodded.

Hammer-hammer-hammer. Finally, the immense crowd quieted.

"Captain Rotch," Savage said to the exhausted-looking man, "have you called upon the Governor?"

For an answer, Rotch gave a tired nod.

"And what is his disposition of the matter?"

The hush was complete. Across the packed pews, Philip heard the master of *Dartmouth* reply, "The same His Excellency indicated several days ago. He is willing to grant anything consistent with the laws and his duty to the King. But he repeated that he cannot give me a pass to sail from the harbor unless my vessel is properly qualified from the Customs House—with the duty paid."

Shouts of "*No, no!*" rang from scattered points in the church. Again Savage banged his gavel for silence.

"In that event," Rotch continued wearily, "I would be free to accede to—to public opinion, and carry the cargo back to England."

"In other words," Savage said, "you are not presently free to sail from the harbor?"

"That is correct."

"But it is the will of the citizens that the tea be returned. Unless you weigh anchor tonight, your vessel is liable to seizure. Therefore, sir, you must sail."

"I cannot possibly do so," Rotch said with a shake of his head. "It would prove my ruin."

From the west gallery, a raucous voice boomed, "Then let's find out how well tea mingles with salt water!"

Yells of assent, clapping, boot-stamping followed the cry. Philip glanced at Anne again, saw her shining face turned toward the pulpit. She and her father looked pleased—as did almost everyone else present.

Savage's gavel thwacked again, and still again, to quiet the clamor as Sam Adams rose from his pew.

Savage recognized him. The crowd quieted once more. The familiar, quavering tones carried clearly in the silence:

"I would remind the audience that Captain Rotch is a good man. He has done all that he could to satisfy the wishes of the citizenry—"

Adams turned a little, partially facing the rear of the church. Revere seemed to be standing almost on tiptoes. Ben Edes looked flushed. Adams' slate-blue eyes glittered with reflections from the smoking chandeliers as he continued:

"No matter what transpires from this hour forward, let it be remembered that no one should attempt to harm the captain, or his property."

Mopping his face with a kerchief, Rotch glanced up, frowned in genuine alarm.

Adams seemed to grow a bit taller, turning more directly toward the back of the hall as he said, "But this meeting can do nothing more to save the country."

Then he lifted his right hand to his waist, and moved it outward in a gesture of resignation.

Philip caught his breath. That must be the signal. The roar from the throat of Ben Edes confirmed it:

"Boston Harbor! We'll brew some harbor tea!"

Men and women surged up from their seats, roaring in approval. Captain Rotch cried, "*Wait—!*" The rest was lost in the tumult.

Revere spun Philip by his shoulder, thrust him in the direction of the doors, as several of the young men around Edes began to utter wild warwhoops. Philip draped the blanket over his shoulders, fastened it with a pin, pulled on a stocking cap he'd tucked into his pocket. Above the shouts and thud of feet in the aisles, he heard the gavel hammering again, a voice exclaiming, "—*meeting is dissolved.*"

Pushed and pummeled, Philip finally reached the outer steps. Under the thin moon, a cold north wind whipped across the rooftops. But it couldn't chill the enthusiasm of the hundreds—perhaps thousands—now gathered in the streets.

"A mob, a mob!" they howled. "Boston Harbor a teapot tonight!"

And over the words shrilled the whooping of the

bogus Indians, busy donning their ragged coats and blankets, thrusting turkey and goose feathers in their hair, daubing each other's faces with lampblack or ochre from hastily opened belt pouches.

Revere decorated Philip's cheeks with several quick streaks of blacking, then passed the pouch in order that Philip could do the same for him.

"Are we proper Mohawks?" the silversmith wanted to know when Philip was finished.

Philip nodded, nearly losing his balance as the mob crowding outward from Old South shoved relentlessly. Off to the right, he heard Ben Edes calling to his group. He started in that direction as Revere yelled behind him, "Then follow Ben to Griffin's Wharf!"

Just as Revere shouted, Old South's bell began to toll the hour of six.

iii

Whooping, Edes' Indians struggled to rally at the head of Milk Street. It was an indication to Philip of how much secret preparation had been made when the crowd opened with fair speed and order to let the crudely disguised men through, then immediately closed in again and began to troop along behind.

As Edes and his followers started for the harbor, people popped out of doorways carrying whale oil lanterns. Before long, Philip could glance over his shoulder and see torches flaring as well. The mob sang, chanted, howled cheerfully obscene oaths against the King, his tea and his taxes—all in all, it was a carnival atmosphere.

Even Edes looked gay, striding along with hatchet in one hand, his cheeks ochre-streaked. He scanned ahead for the other groups supposed to be gathering on Hutchinson Street near Fort Hill—

But Philip was well aware that the partisan mob could

and probably would disappear at the first sign of danger. The Mohawks, not those tramping behind them, would be the ones most easily caught and identified if the British reacted.

By now the effects of the rum punch had completely worn off. Philip felt the gnaw of fear again. So did those around him. There were furtive glances, scowls, teeth nervously chewing underlips because of something the raiders hadn't seen before. Red-uniformed men. Quite a few of them. In tavern doorways. On balconies. Pistols and swords were in evidence.

The watching enlisted men and officers did not draw their weapons or attempt to interfere. Nor did the mob molest them—except verbally. The British gave back a few curses and shaken fists, but nothing more. Perhaps they were awaiting a signal? Philip started to sweat again.

Another hundred Indians waited at the rendezvous point near Fort Hill. The whooping grew even louder as the raiders swept down Hutchinson Street, the distorted shadows of their feathered heads leaping out ahead of them along the walls of buildings. But the first ranks grew quiet suddenly as they swung into the head of Griffin's Wharf. The others following fell silent in turn.

The masts, spars and furled sails of the three tea ships stood out against the emerging white stars. Beyond, in the harbor, all could clearly see the riding lights of the squadron. Were gunners with slow-matches crouched behind the rails—?

By now quite a number of soldiers mingled with the throng following the Indians. Philip saw no muskets. Yet. He scanned nearby rooftops for possible points of attack. Nothing suspicious there—

But in spite of the apparent quiet, his tension grew.

Ben Edes called for his group to follow him aboard the vessel nearest the head of the wharf, Rotch's *Dartmouth*. Other groups charged on down the dock to

Eleanor and *Beaver*, while the dock itself became more and more crowded with the people who had turned out to watch.

Philip saw men race by carrying coils of rope over their arms. And he did indeed notice a lace cuff or two, as Revere had suggested. In moments, Griffin's Wharf grew virtually as bright as day, lanterns and torches by the dozen held aloft to illuminate the spectacle of Edes and his men clambering up *Dartmouth*'s plank to confront an alarmed mate and a man whose uniform identified him as an official of the Customs House.

A total hush had descended on the wharf. Edes' followers gathered behind him as he approached the mate. Philip braced his feet on the gently tilting deck, heard Edes say over the lapping of the water:

"Mr. Hodgdon, it will be to your advantage to stand aside and let this work be done. You know why we are here?"

Mate Hodgdon glanced nervously at the semicircle of torchlit, painted faces.

"Yes. Captain Rotch informed me that something like this might transpire. We will not interfere." *As if it were possible!* Philip thought.

The mate and the gaping Customs House man retired to the quarterdeck. There, together with a few astonished seamen, they watched as Edes spun to his followers.

"Remember—harm no one and nothing but the tea. Now to work!"

A young apprentice near Philip let out an ululating whoop. Edes silenced him with a glare. The carnival mood was gone. Eyes roved nervously toward the lights of the British warships as Philip and the others sped for the hatches and opened them.

Edes organized the activity. Philip soon found himself too busy to worry about danger. He was sent to the rail on the harbor side, as men who had dropped below helped raise the first of the canvas-covered chests by means of a hastily rigged tackle.

The chest was passed along by hand to the rail, and set down. Philip and two others proceeded to hack it open with their axes. When a cut of sufficient length was opened, they lifted the chest, tilted it and let the powdery contents spill over the side. Then they threw the empty chest over too, and went on to the next one.

The strange silence continued. It was punctuated by the heavy breathing of the men, the creak of the tackle, the thump of the chests, the hack of the weapons, the loud *plop* as the empty chests hit the water. Philip and his two associates sneezed repeatedly as the fine Bohea dusted into their nostrils, clogged their eyelids. But they kept working.

The mob on the pier lingered an hour, two. It showed no sign of diminishing. But the number of red military jackets increased. Sweating and breathing hard, Philip could discern the faces of the soldiers as little more than blurs. But here and there, closer to the tea ships, a few did stand out. Incredulous. Or, more often, enraged.

Once more he scanned the roofpeaks. *Was that a Tommy by that chimney—?*

He started to point and cry a warning. Then he realized his imagination had tricked him. The watcher clinging to his high vantage point wore civilian clothes.

The Boston citizens made no effort to bother the officers and soldiers who continued to arrive in twos and threes. Occasional jeers and curses continued to ring out, but the lobsterbacks, still outnumbered, could do little more than return looks of fury and loud promises of reprisals.

The wrecking and emptying of the chests went on for the better part of three hours. At the end of that time, Edes announced, "She's empty. Someone have a count—?"

"Eighty whole chests, thirty-four half-chests," came the reply.

Philip leaned on the rail, stifling another sneeze with his thumb before he thrust the axe back into his belt. In all his life he had never seen such a bizarre sight: the torches; the rapt faces of the silent watchers, friend and enemy; the water all around Griffin's Wharf afloat with ruined chests, some of which sank even as he watched. The firelit surface of the harbor seemed to gleam with a peculiar opaque scum—the tea. One whiff of the cold December air would have convinced anyone that he'd suddenly been plunged into a pot of the stuff—

Halloos from the decks of the other two ships indicated that work had been finished there too. According to accounts in the *Gazette*, the entire three-vessel shipment amounted to three hundred and forty-two full chests. That was a mighty lot of the King's duties ending up in the ocean, Philip reflected.

He honestly didn't know what to make of the whole affair, beginning as it had with a mixture of worry and loud revelry, and ending in this strange, eerie silence, as a few men used brooms to neatly sweep up the spilled tea remaining on the deck. He rubbed sweat from the corners of his eyes, squinted at the squadron lights again. No attack had come. He almost felt let down. The strain of waiting for possible reprisals was nearly as bad as outright hostilities—

Yawning, he watched Mr. Edes salute Mate Hodgdon politely to signal the departure of the exhausted Indians.

Certainly there would be repercussions, he thought as he stumbled down the plank to the pier, his arms aching, his nostrils still tickling. How could it be otherwise? But Adams and the rest had never seemed to care about possible consequences. Thinking back on the attempt to burn out the *Gazette*, Philip decided that perhaps they were right.

But all he really wanted to do now was go back to the

cellar room, throw off the filthy, flea-ridden blanket, wipe the black from his face and sleep.

The crowd was dispersing. Fewer torches and lanterns were visible every moment. Singly and in small groups, the weary tea raiders passed the head of the pier where their group leaders waited to pass out compliments:

"Well done, gentlemen."

"A tidy night's work for liberty."

Edes caught Philip's shoulder as a fife began to shrill farther up the street. "Some of the company are assembling to march to the State House—"

"I'd just as soon go home, sir. I've tweaked the King's nose sufficiently for one evening. I'm worn out."

Edes smiled a thin smile. "Fair enough. Shed the disguise quickly, then. Go your own way—but I suggest the back streets."

Philip nodded, moving on alone as the crowd thinned still more. He turned into the mouth of Hutchinson Street, barely aware of a pair of red-coated officers staring at him from shadows by a wall. He was distracted suddenly by commotion a few doors down: the clatter of a window rising, shouts from the Indians who were just passing in double marching file beneath.

"Sweet Christ, there's the admiral!" one of them pointed. As Edes dashed by, Philip saw a stout man lean from the second-floor window, wig askew. "The yellow dog's been watching from a safe hideout the whole time!"

"Indeed I have, boys," Admiral Montague shouted down. "And you've had a fine, pleasant evening for your Indian caper, haven't you?" A fat finger shook, the voice harsher. "But mind, you've got to pay the fiddler yet."

"Oh, never mind, never mind, squire," another of the ragtag Indians yelled back. "Just come out here, if you please, and we'll settle the bill in two minutes!"

The admiral of the squadron crashed the window down immediately. A second later, the lamp that had been burning in his chamber went out. Raucous laughter rang as the fife resumed, and the marchers continued their parade, in high spirits.

Philip managed a weary smile, started to trudge on. Suddenly he heard faster footfalls behind him.

He turned. Two British officers, hurrying—

The same ones he'd passed a few moments ago?

One of them pointed at him. Then he shoved a woman and her two small boys out of the way. Philip's belly wrenched.

He faced front, quickening his step. The tension and subsequent letdown had lulled him into false security. He'd wasted precious seconds after going by the two watchers without giving them a close look; walked when he should have fled at full speed—

Glancing back a moment ago, he'd glimpsed the face of the soldier who pointed. It was the tall, long-nosed grenadier with the white scar on his chin.

Walking faster, Philip twisted around again. He caught a flash of yellow lapel. Captain Stark shouted for him to hold up.

Philip flung off his cap and stinking blanket, left them lying on the cobbles as he ran. He heard the boots of Stark and his companion clatter in pursuit.

Philip hadn't gone two blocks before he realized he couldn't outrun them. He was too tired.

iv

Desperately, he turned to the right, into an unfamiliar alley. Once more Stark shouted for him to halt. The man's voice sounded peculiarly thick. Had he been drinking?

If so, it didn't seem to lessen the grenadier's steady

pace as he and his comrade rushed to capture their quarry.

Philip's right boot slid out from under him, slicked with some animal's turd into which he'd stepped. He sprawled hard, his chin smacking the ground, snapping his teeth together. He heard and felt a cracking in his mouth. He spit out something that clicked and gleamed white on the stones.

The breath knocked out of him, he struggled to rise. His tongue told him he'd broken off most of an upper front tooth.

He pushed up with both hands, heard Stark cry:

"Down here!"

Turning, Philip saw a glitter at the alley's mouth; Stark drawing his sword.

The other officer protested that he couldn't keep up. A group of citizens with lanterns appeared in Hutchinson Street, hurrying home. Two of these men spotted Stark with his sword drawn; broke away, seized the second officer and began to jostle him. But Stark was too fast. He eluded the others and sprinted on into the alley's darkness.

On his feet, Philip started running hard again. His eyelids itched furiously from the tea. His shoulders hurt. The relentless thud of the grenadier's boots coming on tightened his belly with cold, sick fear. It was only one on one now—but Stark had the advantage of energy and determination.

The alley veered obliquely left. Philip dodged a refuse heap, jumped over a squalling cat whose eyes glowed like gems. Stark's companion was long gone from sight. But the big captain was gaining.

A plank fence loomed on Philip's left. Pretty high, but maybe he could clamber over. He leaped for the top—

But not with enough spring. Cursing, he fought for a handhold, lost it, felt himself falling—

He landed on his spine with a jolt, panting. The

failure to scale the fence had cost him his only margin of safety.

Captain Stark loomed, checking his run. His blade, held out in front of him, gathered the starlight and shimmered.

Stark's chuckle sounded heavy. Philip smelled rum. The captain's eyes were invisible in the pits of shadow under his brows. But his face shone white as a skull in the semi-darkness.

Captain Stark took a step forward. Philip jumped up, backed against the fence.

"I thought I recognized you under that blacking," the grenadier said. "Not only do you insult His Majesty's officers—you flout his laws. I suppose I could haul you up before a magistrate. But I think I prefer more personal justice—"

Again Stark chuckled. This time, it was a laugh of humorless pleasure. He added:

"Especially since I doubt anyone will mourn long for an obvious lawbreaker. And while you're rotting here with the dogs picking over your bones, I'll call on the young lady again. Remember that while you're bleeding to death, eh?"

Without warning, he launched into a formal thrust.

Lightning-quick, his right knee bent as his boot slammed down. His long arm drove the sword forward like a streak of white fire.

Philip calculated his time, ducked at the last possible instant and flung himself forward at the grenadier's boots.

The sword point chunked into the plank fence. Captain Stark swore, pulled the blade free. By then, Philip had his arms wrapped around the man's right leg, pulling him off balance.

Arms windmilling, Captain Stark cursed again. Philip toppled him backward.

But the grenadier was superbly conditioned. Even as

he toppled, he managed to use his left leg to kick Philip's shin, hard. Philip danced away.

Captain Stark scrambled up again, his scarlet-clad shoulders faintly white from the powder knocked loose from his wig. He lunged, simultaneously raised his right arm, then brought it whipping down—

Philip jerked his head aside. The blade glanced his temple, the edge nicking a long cut from hairline to cheek. Blood ran down the left side of Philip's face as he took two hopping steps to the side, managed to free his axe from his belt—

"Slippery little gutter bastard," Stark panted, right arm across his chest, blade ready to chop outward in a lopping horizontal arc. "Bragging and smarting about your swordplay—"

With a sibilant hiss the sword slashed the air. Philip ducked again, running forward bent over, his hand so tight on the axe handle that his fingers hurt. Because he knew the half-drunk Stark meant to kill him, he wasted no time on gentlemanly maneuvering. He darted under the next arc of the sword and swung the axe full force.

The blade chopped through white trousers into Stark's thigh. His left eye blind from blood, Philip barely perceived Stark go stiff. But he heard the grenadier yell in pain.

Stark clutched his red-sopped trousers with one hand, whacked at Philip's neck with the other. Philip ran backward without looking—

Another of those infernal garbage heaps tripped him up. He went down on his back among rotted cabbages and stinking fish carcasses.

The hard-breathing Stark hobbled forward, left hand gripping his thigh wound, right readying the sword for a last direct thrust. The refuse pile was slippery, no footing, no handholds—

Captain Stark had no need to proclaim his advantage, or his satisfaction. Philip could hear pleasure in the incoherent growl building in the grenadier's throat. The rum reek blended with the stink of cabbage and fish. For one awful moment, Philip seemed to stare up at some giant limned against the winter moon showing between the rooftops. Stark drove the blade's point down at an angle toward Philip's exposed throat—

Hacking over from the right with the axe, Philip felt the sword slice the air next to his face. The axe bit Stark's uniform sleeve, cut all the way to the bone. While Stark was bent forward for the finish of the stroke, Philip kicked him in the belly with his right foot.

The grenadier's hand opened. The sword dropped away as the severed muscles of Stark's arm failed him. He moaned, sank to his knees. He turned his head from side to side as if searching for his enemy.

"Lad—" he began—to appeal for mercy? Philip didn't wait to find out. He snatched up the sword and rammed it all the way through Stark's midsection until the point protruded from his backbone.

Stark crumpled slowly onto his side, lips and eyeballs glistening in the starlight. The grenadier let out one hideous grunt of pain between clenched teeth and shuddered, dead.

Numb, Philip listened.

He heard no sound save for some male voices singing drunkenly in the distance. Then a church bell chimed half after nine.

Philip had struck at Stark out of self-defense, not heeding or even thinking of what could happen to him afterward. Now visions of that spilled through his mind with terrifying detail. He dropped to his knees and dug through the garbage till he'd cleared a place in which to hide the gory axe.

Let anyone who discovered Stark think he'd been felled solely with his own sword. By some robber, perhaps.

The same cat he'd encountered before strolled into

sight as Philip heaped slimy cabbage leaves and fish
heads on top of the axe, burying it. The cat licked his
left hand with its rough tongue, pressed its head against
his knuckles and meowed.

That commonplace sound somehow unnerved him
completely. He bolted away, leaving the dead man to the
cat and the darkness.

He could feel the blood drying on his left cheek. He
must be a sight, lampblack and red and half of a tooth
knocked out of his mouth—

He took side streets, pausing now and then to rest and
let the nausea, the dizziness work themselves out. His
teeth were chattering loudly by the time he reached
Dassett Alley.

He dropped the key twice before he got the front door
unlocked. He stumbled downstairs, lit the candle, took a
step toward the basin of icy water and fainted.

CHAPTER V

Decision

i

A DISTANT RAPPING. Repeated—

Philip opened his right eye. The left one took a little longer. Caked blood had sealed the lid.

He squinted at straw near his nose, remembered what had happened. He'd fallen. Some time ago, to judge from the way the candle had burned down to a stub. With a groan, he dragged his knees under his body, pushed up from the floor as the knocking sounded another time. For a moment his eyes glittered with a wild, trapped look.

He knew his crime had been detected. Stark had told the other officer, the one who had fallen behind, that their intended victim worked for Edes the printer. Only that could explain the rapping at the upstairs door—

Philip's head began to clear. He ran his tongue over the broken tooth, waited, breathing softly. Perhaps the nocturnal visitor would leave—

The knock came again.

Philip left the candle burning, climbed the stairs as silently as possible. At the top, he stole toward the shop's rear door.

This time, the knock at the Dassett Alley entrance was accompanied by a voice:

"Philip?"

He whirled, ran up past the press, unlocked the door

427

and jerked it open. A cowled figure shivered in the December wind, a shadow—but not threatening. Familiar.

"Anne!"

Behind her, the moonlit sky looked cold silver. She slipped past him as he knuckled his left eye, trying with that physical act to drive the dull ache from his head. She blended into the shop's darkness as he shut the door and locked it.

He reached for her hand, felt a responding pressure of her fingers as she said:

"I had to see you. I waited until Father and Daisy were both asleep, then crept out of the house—"

"What time is it?"

"A little after three o'clock."

"And you came all the way from Launder Street by yourself? Good God, girl, that's dangerous!"

"Any less dangerous than what you did tonight?" Her voice was husky with emotion. "When I looked down from the gallery at Old South and spied you with Mr. Edes—well, I can't properly describe everything I felt. Surprise. Admiration. The truth about why—why I've been so miserable ever since that afternoon we rowed across the river. Why didn't you come calling again?"

He phrased the answer carefully, so it would carry the truth, yet not hurt her:

"I thought it best not to, that's all. You made your feelings clear. But I couldn't say what you wanted said. I—"

Yes, tell her. The moment demanded no less than complete honesty.

"I still can't. Now I think I should see you back home."

The dim white oval of her face seemed to move in the dark; she was shaking her head. "Not just yet—" She touched his left cheek, gasped softly. "What's that on your face?"

He winced at the pressure of her cool fingers against the clotted gash, drew back. As his eyes adjusted to the faint light filtering up from the cellar, he saw her own widen:

"You're cut! But I heard there was no trouble at Griffin's Wharf! No fighting, nothing—"

"I had an accident running home. I fell."

"So much blood doesn't come from a fall. I want to see it. Where's your room, and some light?"

In her tone he heard the prickly determination that had been one of the first qualities that had attracted him. And her presence—her concern—cheered him. Consequently, he didn't argue. He gripped her still-chilly hand and led her toward the stairs.

She threw back her cowl as they reached the cellar chamber, looked closely at his face. "Dear heaven! That's a sword mark. And you've lost part of a tooth!"

Anne's cheeks had gone pale. The freckles on either side of her nose looked almost black in the dim light.

"The tooth was my own fault. I was running, I fell—Mr. Revere can repair it, I imagine. God knows if anyone can repair the rest of the damage done tonight."

"You don't mean the tea, do you?"

He shook his head, took her hands in his:

"Anne, if I tell you what happened, you must promise to repeat it to no one. Not even your father, do you understand?"

Wide-eyed, she nodded. He released her hands, faced away toward the ledge where Gil's wrapped sword lay, and, in a niche above, Marie's casket.

"There were a few soldiers in the crowd when we sank the tea—"

"So Father reported."

"One was the grenadier Stark. He recognized me. He and another officer chased me. The first one fell behind. But Stark caught me in an alley. With no one watching, he had his chance to do what he's wanted to do since that day at the Book-Store. He'd been drinking a lot, I think—"

"And you fought?"

"Yes. Before it was over, I—I had to kill him."

The dark eyes welled with tears. She rushed to him, bending her head to his chest. "Oh, Philip, what a terrible thing."

"For who?" he asked, a bit ironically.

"You, of course. And the captain. He was a vile man. But death is no light matter."

Absently, he touched her lustrous hair and realized again that she was an inch or so taller. "I've killed men before, Anne. But you're right—there's no joy in it. Just fear afterward. And shock. And knowing it will happen to me someday—in any case, I took a long time answering your knock because I thought I'd been identified. Perhaps by the second officer. I was starting to steal out the back way just as you called my name."

Silence. Anne seemed to be looking at him differently. With a trace of fright in her eyes. Then she drew on that strength she possessed in such amazing degree, and smiled.

"I'm sure you'll be safe. They'll probably think Stark was caught by some of the mob."

"The other officer was."

"There, you see? With Stark's bad reputation, everyone will assume he provoked his own killing."

"Unless Stark did identify me to his companion. There's no way to tell—until someone comes to arrest me."

"Worry about that if it happens. For the moment you're out of danger. Here, sit down and let me clean you up a little. God, you're fearfully smeared with blood. Is there a place where you can safely burn your shirt?"

"Yes."

"Then you must, first thing in the morning."

Pressing his shoulder with soft but forceful hands, she sat him on the stool by the pallet, then hurried to the stand with the basin of water. She unfastened the ties of her cloak, tossed it aside, soaked a towel in the basin.

"Pull your shirt off."

He did, noting her fresh surprise at the sight of the liberty medal hanging on his chest. One hand holding the wrung-out towel, she lifted the medal with the other.

"I didn't know you wore one of these."

"A present from Mr. Edes. For dousing the fire a few weeks ago—*agh!*"

His yelp was a reaction to the sudden cold of the water. Methodically, she scrubbed away the dried blood. Though she tried to do it gently, some pain was inevitable. But he made no further sound. In fact, he began to relax under her ministrations.

Then he grew conscious of an itch under the sole of his right foot.

As Anne worked, dipping and re-dipping the towel into the basin until the water took on a deep scarlet tint, he hauled off the boot. He tilted it—and laughed as a little cascade of black tea poured out.

"I think I should save this! A souvenir of my career as a Red Indian—wait, I know just the thing for it—"

Anne watched with an amused smile as he hobbled upstairs on one bare foot, returned a few moments later after rummaging in the shop. He showed her a small green glass bottle, used to contain the type-cleaning solution. He'd emptied the bottle the previous week and opened a new one, so the bottle in his hand was dry inside.

Carefully, he poured the rest of the tea from his boot into the bottle. The tea formed a layer a half-inch thick in the bottom. He stoppered the bottle and set it on the ledge beside Gil's sword.

"Another Kent family heirloom. To show my grandchildren I attended Mr. Adams' tea party."

Anne directed him back to the stool, began scrubbing his left eyelid. Presently she stood back, surveyed her work, gave a nod.

"Clean at last. Carry the basin out to the alley and empty it while I try to find something to wrap the top of the wound—that's the deepest part."

"Think there'll be a scar?"

"A slight one. But no one will ever be able to say how you came by it." She took hold of his arm, turning him toward the stairway with that crisp, authoritative air that made him chuckle.

As he headed for the rear door, he reminded himself that he should take her home soon. He heard sounds of movement up by the press, where she'd gone to find a clean rag in the supply kept to wipe up excess ink. The night air bit his bare skin as he stepped out under the stars to empty the basin of its red evidence. Going back in, he re-latched the door.

Downstairs again, he resumed his place on the stool while Anne tore a rag in long strips. She wrapped his forehead, covering the worst of the gash, and knotted the bandage at the back. Hands on hips, she stepped away, satisfied.

"You're presentable, at least."

The candle was flickering out. For the first time since her arrival, he was conscious of her femininity, of the swell of her breasts beneath her plain gown of violet silk. He rose and reached into the niche behind the casket as Anne said:

"I've always wanted to see where you stayed, Philip."

He pulled another candle from behind the box. "I'll have a better place one day, I promise you that. Mr. Edes is holding my wages for me. He gives me what little I need for meals when I ask for it. I'm saving the rest. For a shop like this—"

He realized she was staring at something beyond his

shoulder. He turned. The object of her curiosity was the leather-covered casket.

"That must be the place where you store the letter you told me about in September."

Turning away from the niche, he nodded. "But I'm beginning to think I've really put all that behind me, Anne." He touched the fresh candle to the stub, dripped a little wax up on the ledge and planted the new light in place. "When someone tossed that torch into the doorway, I reacted in a way I hadn't before. I was angry as hell. It wasn't only Mr. Edes they were trying to burn out—it was me! It's hard to explain properly, but that night I understood for the first time what Mr. Adams keeps saying. That a threat against one man, or one colony, can have consequences for many others."

Cheeks shining in the candle's glow, Anne sat on the stool, resting her hands on her knees. "Yes, you have it exactly right. We are all threatened—so we're all involved. You've seen how it's spread. At first Boston was the target of most of the King's wrath. Now the repression's reaching out further and further. Tea ships anchoring in other ports—" She paused, then added, "When I saw you at Old South tonight, I did wonder whether you'd come to some decision on the whole issue."

Looking down at the engraved oval of bright metal on his chest, he replied, "It appears I have. I never planned on it. But I felt proud when Mr. Edes said I was fit to wear one of these things. When they organized the tea raid, I hardly hesitated. So—" He smiled, tried to push disturbing thoughts of Marie from his mind. "I am a rebel now, I guess." His eyes clouded; the smile froze in place. "Especially having killed a royal officer."

The girl stood up slowly. Her fingers stirred nervously at her sides. Without taking her eyes from his, she said in a quiet voice:

"One of the things I came to tell you tonight was that if you had made your decision, I had too. Since that trip across the river in September, I've tried to lie to myself. Tried to pretend I didn't feel what I do. As it did to you, something happened to me for the first time. You say I'm strong, but I'm no stronger than—what's inside my heart."

She walked toward him, looking shy, yet radiantly lovely. The implied meaning of her words filled him with surprise and excitement.

"I said I couldn't describe all my thoughts up there in the gallery tonight. I don't think you could guess half of them. But I had to come here and say one thing I've never said to anyone before—"

The color deepened in her cheeks. The sweet lavender scent of her body had grown almost overpowering.

"I want you for a lover, Philip. With no conditions, no promises, no pledges about tomorrow or a fine house, because there's no certainty of any of that after what happened with the tea."

Stunned, Philip protested, "I'm still the same person I was in September, Anne. Not sure—"

"I realize that completely." Her right hand slipped over her shoulder to the back of her gown. "I'll tell you again. No conditions. Even if it should be only this one night, I'd rather have that than nothing."

In the corners of her eyes, tears began to glisten. But she was smiling, too, as she unfastened the closures of the gown, pushed the bodice and sleeves down and her linen shift along with it.

"We have time," she said. "An hour or more before the dawn clocks ring—" She thrust the garments to her waist and ran to him, arms around his neck, mouth seeking his.

Her firm breasts touched his chest. As he slipped his hands to the small of her back, he felt the tips crush to his skin, hardening.

"Anne, Anne—" He stroked her hair, kissed her cheek. "I do care for you—"

"That's enough, then," she breathed. "More than enough for now—"

"I don't want it to be hurtful. You told me you'd never—"

The soft, seeking mouth stopped the rest.

He tasted the sweetness of her tongue as she pressed his back with her palms. She let out a little cry of delight when he pulled her tight against him and she felt his maleness. He'd never fully realized that under her sensible, capable exterior lay this potential for heat and passion—though he might have guessed it, he supposed, from the encounter on the September hillside.

In a way, he was tempted to break off the involvement before it went further. The reason was simple. He cared for her enough to admit that he didn't know how much he cared for her. And that demanded that she not be hurt—physically or in any other way.

Yet the silence and isolation of the cellar room, the candle flickering on the ledge, her kisses and caresses and, most of all, the unguessable future, conspired to overcome his reluctance. They tumbled on the pallet. He bared her body, casting the gown and underthings aside. Then he reached up to pinch the candle out between thumb and forefinger, never feeling the heat.

Anne's hand touched the buckle at his waist. He helped her. He kissed her face, her eyelids, the gentle, warm valley between her breasts. And knew that all of it was still a pledge of sorts—

The darkness turned sweltering as she rolled against him, no longer shy but seeking him—with her hands, then her whole body—

The joining was painful to her; he could tell by the convulsive way she clasped his shoulders. And for him, the end was unsatisfying because it was overly quick, reached just as her flesh began to stir with first reactions. They fell back on the pallet, exhausted, her hair a lavender-scented webbing against his sweated chest. When they separated, she gave a last little cry. Pain or pleasure? He couldn't be certain.

"Dammit, Anne, I know I disappointed you—"

"No. No!"

"Yes. I was too soon. And I hurt you—"

"Isn't—" She still breathed hard. "Isn't it supposed to be that way the first time? The next time I'll know how. I'm not at all experienced yet—" Her laugh was embarrassed, yet totally female in its warmth. Her fingers kept moving on him, lovingly tracing the outline of his right hand where it curled around her naked waist to hold her belly. "Oh, if Papa realized his proper Congregationalist daughter had taken a lover—! But then—" She punctuated the teasing with tender kisses of his throat, his chin. "I've at least had the good sense to become involved with a man of the right political persuasion." She lifted the liberty medal, held it a second, then released it and pressed both hands to his cheeks, kissing him with passion.

They rested a while under two shabby blankets. Presently her exploring hand and wicked, womanly little laugh roused him again. When he took her a second time, she opened herself and clasped him eagerly, without restraint or fear, and responded with a rhythm and ferocity that fully matched his own. The dark of his mind burst alight, lit by a thousand blazing stars, and a thousand more. His body burned, sought—and so did hers.

Together, faster and steadily faster, they surrendered everything, one to the other. And when the last delicious, shuddering moments came on them both simultaneously—moments of impossible, unbearable straining, of sudden, cascading release, of joyful cries and whispers in the slow-cooling aftermath—there was no need for either to murmur an apology.

This time, it had been perfect.

ii

Yawning and whispering and holding hands, they walked through the cold December morning to Launder Street. After an almost prim kiss, he promised to call on Sunday. Eyes aglow, she touched his face a final time and slipped inside.

The memory of her radiance lingered with him as he started back to Dassett Alley, whistling an air in spite of his tiredness. He kicked at a rime of ice in a low place in the street, thrust his chilled hands deep into his pockets and speculated on whether a man ever fully controlled his own destiny. It did not seem so. The encounter with Captain Stark had been an accident. And perhaps Anne Ware might not have given herself if the sword wound hadn't added an extra measure of sympathy and concern to push her across the emotional brink.

Striding along in the dawn with the sky turning opalescent, he could reflect that it had been a night of wonders. With significance for the future in many more ways than he could ever hope to enumerate.

Yet he was oddly content, even smiling as he bent into the northwest wind.

A decision, Anne had called it. A whole series of them, really. Small, casual ones, progressing from incident to incident—

His wrath after the abortive fire. Edes handing him the medal. His resulting impulse to join the tea mob.

The necessity to deal with the grenadier. His unwillingness, at the last moment, to refuse the gift of Anne's love despite his reservations about a permanent future with her.

Well, despite her assurances, he was partially bound

to her now, just as he was bound to the patriot cause. Neither outcome had been foreseen.

His breath formed a plume ahead of him. In the stillness, a watchman called the half-hour after five, and a clear day predicted. He accepted the workings of his destiny without regret.

In fact he slept deeply and blissfully for an hour—until Ben Edes arrived to waken him for the day's work.

iii

Practically at once, Edes inquired about his young assistant's chipped-off tooth, the bandage wrapped around his head, and the remainder of the gash showing below it.

Philip had already decided that the fewer who shared the secret, the better. He said he'd broken his tooth and gotten the wound while escaping from a couple of drunken British officers who had watched the tea thrown in the harbor and had been sufficiently angered to chase him and try to vent their feelings. It was the truth, if not all the truth.

"I outran them," Philip said. "I fell hard, right on my face, then scraped my head dodging around a corner in the dark, that's all."

Edes nodded and accepted the explanation without further question. He left the shop about an hour later. Philip used the opportunity to bring his bloodied shirt up from the cellar, rip it and burn it in the little wood stove that warmed Edes' office.

iv

Anne Ware started coming to the shop with her father's copy again. Occasional speculative looks from Mr. Edes told Philip that perhaps their intimacy was obvious.

Anne always behaved in a ladylike way, of course. But there were moments when she let her hand rest against his as she showed off Patriot's latest indignant phrase. Edes didn't miss the byplay. But he made no comment.

Philip and Anne had no opportunity to be alone in the days that followed. When he called at the house in Launder Street on the Sabbath, Lawyer Ware was usually present, or at least the cook, Daisy O'Brian. The weather was too cold for finding a place to make love out-of-doors. And even though Philip's key would have made use of the cellar room quite easy, Anne didn't want to risk being seen entering the Dassett Alley establishment in daylight, on a Sunday afternoon. As she herself had said, she still had the good sense to respect certain proprieties.

At the same time, her cheeks had taken on a richer color, almost as though the winter could not fade her summer's tan. They both derived a great deal of private pleasure from sharing the secret.

"I think Daisy suspects," Anne whispered merrily, an hour before the new year of 1774 was to be rung in from the steeples of the town. "Have you noticed the way she stares at us?"

Philip turned from the window. Outside, a fluffy white snow drifted down, softening the glow of the lamps in other houses along Launder Street. In the Ware fireplace, beech logs crackled and flamed. Anne's father, who had proposed a toast to the coming year only five minutes ago, now snored like a somnolent frog, his skinny hands folded on his paunch. He kept slipping further and further down in his chair.

Philip had dressed for the evening in his one good broadcloth. He grinned at Anne and replied, "No, I haven't noticed your cook or her staring. All I care to see is you." He picked up his glass of claret and toasted her.

Anne walked to his side, took the goblet from his fingers, sipped from it, then leaned back against him.

Philip glanced at the sleeping lawyer. Ware appeared ready to slide off his chair. He let out a snort but his eyes stayed closed. Philip slipped his arm around Anne's waist.

As they watched the snow fall, Anne went on, "Poor Daisy. She craves a husband in the worst way. Her widower father keeps a farm out beyond Concord. She thought the chances of matrimony were better in town. She's told me she'd even take up with a Tory, if only one would look in her direction. I never realized the true sadness of that kind of longing before we—well, you understand. Oh, Philip! How fine it feels to be close to another person. I'd like for Daisy to make a match—"

She set the goblet on a taboret, turned and laid her hands on either side of his neck. Lawyer Ware snored and bubbled his lips. Anne looked into Philip's eyes.

"I'd like her to be as happy as I am. Even though matrimony is *not* part of the bargain." She kissed him gently on the lips.

Warmed by the wine, he replied, "Yes, but no one said it was out of the question, either."

"I know. But never think you're bound in any way by what happened. I've said it before—the months ahead are too clouded. Too unsure. Let's take only as much as we can, while we can."

She darted one more glance at the slumbering lawyer. Then, eyes sparkling, she asked:

"Have you ever seen the little barn that stands behind the house?"

Keeping a straight face, he said, "Why, I don't believe so, Mistress Ware."

"The former owner put it up. We never use it, because Papa's not the sort to fuss with milking a cow to save a penny. There's a big hay pile in the barn. If you wished, we could welcome the New Year in a more private fashion."

"Anne Ware," he laughed, "you are indeed a scandalous woman."

"No," she said, "one in love." And, taking his hand, she led him to the parlor door.

They paused at the entrance to the kitchen to look in on Daisy. The buxom Irish girl had dozed off after drinking the claret offered by her employer.

"A whole household sleeping!" Anne exclaimed in a whisper. "A fair omen for celebrating seventy-four, wouldn't you say?"

"I would, Mistress Ware. Lead on!"

They stole across the back porch and through the powdery whiteness with an almost conspiratorial delight. On the roof of the tiny barn the snow had accumulated till it looked thick as a breadloaf. Inside, the hay proved warm and comfortable.

Tonight their lovemaking had less of the urgency of the first time. They shared little private amusements with a tenderness and frankness that made Philip ask himself whether marriage to this bright, eager girl might not be as endlessly satisfying as the moment they were sharing now. Alicia Parkhurst seemed an alien figure of the past, less than real.

For her part, Anne now had absolutely no hesitancy about showing physical passion. Though they made love with half their clothes still in place, and laughed about it, she still reached a full, joyous climax just when he did, a moment or two after the bells of Boston began to peal the arrival of the first day of January.

Shortly afterward, however, Philip was again reminded of the tougher, more practical side of her nature. As she smoothed her skirt, she said:

"Has Mr. Knox called to see you yet?"

"The owner of the book-store? No, does he intend to?"

"The other day I told him you might be a candidate for—oh, but it might be better if I let him explain in person."

"Explain what?"

"Henry will make that clear."

"Now see here, woman. You're teasing me again."

"Only a little." She gave him a long, level look. "When you accepted that medal from Ben Edes, you did make one commitment, Philip."

v

The fat Knox arrived at Dassett Alley within a matter of days. He was bundled in a snow-dusted greatcoat, his curly hair unpowdered and his manner businesslike.

"Mr. Kent, are you aware that throughout the town and some areas of the countryside, militia companies are being formed?"

"Militia—? Yes, we've printed stories about it in the paper. Why do you ask?"

Knox stepped closer. "Because, sir, I am recruiting for the Boston Grenadier Company, Captain Pierce commanding. I am one of his lieutenants. Should there be trouble as a result of the tea dispute, we mean to be prepared."

All at once Philip studied the jowly young man with new interest. Knox was obviously well educated, polished. His corpulent figure had a softness that suggested anything except a fighting man. Yet his eyes were keen and determined. He continued:

"We need men for the ranks. Six feet tall if we can find 'em—less than that if we can't. I understand from—certain mutual friends that what you might lack in stature, you make up for in spirit and devotion to our common concern. We drill once a week, and the pay's insignificant. But I feel confident Ben Edes would grant you the time off. If you don't know how to load and shoot a musket, we'll teach you."

Philip realized that Anne's assessment of Knox had to be true. While pretending purposeless amiability toward the British officers who turned his store into an unofficial salon, he was learning their tactical and strategic secrets. Now he was putting them to use. Philip answered:

"I fired a Brown Bess a few times. But that was several years ago."

"The knack will come quickly if it was easy for you the first time." Knox lifted his silk-wrapped hand. "As you may have noticed, handling a musket is impossible for me, thanks to a hunting accident. I suppose," he added with a grin, "that's the reason they turned me into an officer. Oh, I should tell you before you decide that each member of the company is responsible for securing his own musket. They're not easily come by unless you're a rural man who keeps one pegged over the hearth. But we are not overly curious about how a man *acquires* a gun—so long as he gets one. Until he does, he drills with a stick."

Philip stifled a laugh. "A *stick*—!" Instantly, he knew he'd said the wrong thing.

"Be assured, sir, we are not playing children's games. You can and will learn the proper order for loading and firing the weapon, even though you do not have powder and shot or the musket itself. But then when you have them—" Knox's expression showed resolve. "—you will be ready to use them."

A shiver of apprehension chased down Philip's back. The step from orderly mobs destroying tea consignments to organization of military units was a long and significant one. Frowning, he asked the bookseller:

"Do you honestly think that we'll come to open hostilities?"

"Who knows what we can expect when Hutchinson's reports of the tea affair reach England —as they've surely done by now? Our basic position is preparedness. For any eventuality. You were recommended as one who would fit into our unit. If the recommendation was in error—" His unfinished sentence and challenging stare left no doubt about what his opinion would be if Philip responded negatively. The storm winds were

blowing in earnest now, he thought. Buffeting him
along—

"All right, Mr. Knox. I'll join. Provided Mr. Edes
agrees."

Knox clapped him on the shoulder. "You can be certain of it! Once you've taken care of the formality of ob-
taining his permission, come 'round to the store and
we'll arrange the papers."

vi

A few days later, Philip found a couple of spare hours
for personal business. He visited Knox at the Book-
Store to sign the required forms. Then he hurried toward
the North End, where he hoped to see Mr. Revere.

A January thaw had set in. Midmorning sunshine
gilded windowpanes and glittered the ice melting on
rooftops as he turned into North Square. From one end
to the other, the Square teemed with citizens and
tradespeople moving among flimsy stalls put up at sunrise. Several days a week, North Square served as one
of Boston's three chief marketplaces.

Philip pushed by single- and two-horse carts unloading vegetables or firewood fresh from the country, thrust
his way around bargainers buying and selling firkins
of country butter, baskets of fresh-baked gingerbread,
gabbling turkeys. The shoppers were mostly towns-
women with baskets on their arms. They haggled cheerfully with the farmers or their smiling but wary-eyed
agents; some of these last, Philip noted, were black men.
The noise of the market was loud but pleasant. And the
aromas were a banquet: oysters and pickled pork,
mackerel and rye meal, hams and haunches of venison.

Revere's small, peak-roofed house fronted on the
square. Philip was about to descend side steps to the
shop entrance when he noticed a commotion a few
doors down. He shielded his eyes against the sun, saw a

small but rough-looking crowd—men, chiefly—
gesturing and scowling at a second-floor window.
He had no notion of the reason.

He watched a few moments longer, then went on. It
was too fresh and sunny a day for such displays of bad
temper, whatever the cause.

A bell over the door rang to announce his entrance.
From an adjoining room, he heard Revere's voice:

"Right with you—just a moment—"

Philip was content to wait, bedazzled by the profusion
of goods jammed on the shelves, counters, even the floor
of the establishment. Clock faces hung in rows. And
branding irons and sword hilts. Sunlight slanting
through the street-level windows flashed from the blades
in a case of surgeon's instruments.

And he had never seen so much silver in so many different shapes and sizes. Baby rattles and teaspoons,
shoe buckles and chocolate pots, creamers and standing
cups. The sun struck starry highlights from the products
of Revere's metalworking skill.

The craftsman himself appeared a moment later, wiping his hands on his leather apron.

"Mr. Kent! Good day. What brings you to this part of
town?"

"I'm in need of your services, Mr. Revere."

"Well, I've a diversity of those to offer! What's your
choice?" His blunt-fingered hands ranged over a
display. "A baptismal basin? Ah, but nothing's been settled formally with you and Mistress Ware, has it?" The
smith's grin confirmed what Philip already suspected.
He and Anne were the subject of amused gossip among
the group that gathered at Edes and Gill.

Revere picked up a glittering length of silver links. "A
chain for your pet squirrel, then? Or how about a
whistle? An excellent silver whistle—" He blew a piercing blast.

Laughing, Philip held up a hand. "I'm calling on Mr.

Revere the dentist." He opened his mouth, pointed. "I broke this the night we sank the tea."

Revere stepped closer, peered into Philip's mouth. Over the smith's neatly clubbed hair, Philip could see into the darker adjoining room. It was dominated by a brick furnace. The furnace's partially open door revealed glowing coals that gave off pronounced heat and cast a dull red glare on crucibles, an anvil, a heap of damaged silver cups and tankards, and other paraphernalia whose purpose he didn't understand.

"A good tooth lost in a good cause," Revere delcared, straightening up. "I can fit you with a more than satisfactory replacement. Sit you down——" He indicated a peculiar-looking chair amid the clutter. Philip hesitated.

"We need to talk about the price first, Mr. Revere."

"All right. I have a different and much higher set of charges for Tories—don't get much trade from 'em, I confess. How much can you afford?"

Thinking of the sharp bargaining he'd witnessed in the square, Philip put on a doubtful expression. "Oh, no more than a few pence——"

"How few is few? Five?"

"Three would be better."

"Call it four and I'll guarantee to carve you a fine tooth no one will tell from the original. You're lucky you broke a dog tooth—they're easier. The price includes mounting with cement and the finest gold wire for extra permanence. I'll whittle the new one of the very best hippo tusk, too."

He began rummaging through the tiny drawers of a wall cabinet, found a large, curved tooth and displayed it proudly. Then, noting Philip's dumbfounded expression, he asked, "What's wrong?"

"Isn't a hippopotamus an animal?"

"Of course it's an animal. Where else d'you think a man gets a new tooth? The triangular traders bring me tusks from the West Africas regularly. I tried elephant a few times, but it yellows too fast. And sheep's teeth are all snaggled and crooked. Difficult to work. Sit down, sir, and let me put in the wax—"

"Wax?" Philip repeated in a somewhat strangled voice, as Revere thrust him into the chair and forced his head against a pair of pads projecting from an upright rod. Humming, Revere conducted another search under one of his counters, returned with a red chunk of the stuff.

"Open wide, please, Mr. Kent," he instructed, practically yanking Philip's jaws apart. He crouched beside the chair, peered upward at the damaged canine tooth, broke off a bit of the red wax, balled it between thumb and forefinger, then pressed the wax carefully up against the tooth's broken surface.

A moment later he pried the wax out. He carried it to the counter, deposited it in a clay pestle and used a quill pen to scratch some figures on a scrap of paper. The paper too was put in the pestle, which was pushed aside to a place near half a dozen silver pepper pots. Philip wondered how the man could keep all his various business enterprises in order in his mind.

"I'll have the tooth in a week, so drop back then," Revere said.

"Don't you need to take any kind of measurements?"

"I already did." Revere lifted a hand to point to one eye. "The most accurate measuring devices known to man—provided they're used properly. No, sir, we're finished—unless of course you'd like me to clean those teeth up a bit. Only costs an extra pence to make your dental equipment white and sparkling. I use a special dentifrice of my own devising. Several secret ingredients I'm afraid I can't reveal, plus saltpeter, gunpowder, crumbs of white bread, cuttlefish bone, broken crockery—"

Philip gulped. "You mean broken dishes?"

"It's all in how you grind and mix it, Mr. Kent. Does

wonders in attracting the fair sex. But then you don't have that problem, do you?"

"Well—ah—thank you, but I don't believe I can afford—"

"*Paul?*"

A female voice from a curtained door at the rear of the shop spun Revere around and brought Philip out of the chair. He saw a slender, dark-haired young woman in a plain frock and apron, a spot of flour whitening one cheek. She looked alarmed.

"What's the trouble, Rachel?" the smith asked.

"I was just out on the stoop—there's an awful row down the way. I fear a mob's going to do harm to poor Johnny Malcolm."

Instantly, Revere untied his leather apron, flung it aside. "The crazy old wretch will get himself killed with that tongue of his. There's been trouble brewing all morning. Someone out in the square told me a little boy accused Malcolm of upsetting his sled of kindling. Come on, Kent, let's have a look." Grim-faced, he hurried for the door.

Philip followed the smith into the January sunshine. At the house where he'd seen a few people earlier, he now saw a crowd three or four times the size. An angry crowd. Taunts were being exchanged with a cadaverous, white-haired old man who leaned from a second-floor window, brandishing a pistol in one hand and a broad-axe in the other.

Revere and his companion trotted toward the crowd. Philip noticed three men running up from the other direction, carrying a ladder.

"This Malcolm's a friend of yours, Mr. Revere?"

"Far from it. Crazy Johnny's a senile, vile-tempered fool. Likes nothing better than to bait people with his impudent and provocative jibes. Trouble is, he's a flaming Tory. In this neighborhood, that's not safe. The Sons of Liberty got blamed once before when some rowdies chastised him—"

As the two approached the edge of the crowd, the old man with the weapons shrieked down, "Ah, go to Hades, the lot of you! I'll push over that little wart's sled any time I damn please. His father helped drown the King's tea, don't think I don't know that. If I split the sprout's head, I'd get ten shilling sterling from the Governor. Twice that for the rest of you Yankee traitors—!"

The old man's voice was shrill. Spittle flew from his mouth. Philip disliked the fellow on sight. But at the same time, he realized the unfairness of the odds against Malcolm.

Revere shouldered into the crowd. "Let him alone. Let the old lunatic rant—"

Scowling faces swung toward the smith and Philip. "Tend to your cream pots, Revere. He bullied the boy, and he's no high son of liberty, either."

"But he's touched in the head. He can do no one any real harm—"

Revere's argument produced no response except for more yells directed at the old man in the window:

"Have a care with your nasty tongue, John Malcolm!"

"Aye, don't forget you were treated to the tar and feathers once before. If you don't shut up, we'll do it again—properly, this time."

Malcolm howled, "You say I was tarred and feathered and that it wasn't done in a proper manner? Damn you, let me see the man that dares to do it better!" He spat down on the crowd.

A coarse-faced woman cursed and wiped her forehead. That incited the mob to rage. There were cries for the ladder. Before Philip knew it, the ladder was jammed against the front of the house. Two burly men started climbing it, one after another.

"Stay away!" Malcolm screeched. "I'll shoot!"

"He's too daft to aim straight," someone jeered.

"Or load it right," another voice added. "Go get him!"

Revere fought through the press, grabbing arms, shoulders.

"Dammit, if you're friends of liberty, leave off baiting a helpless enemy!"

"Get out of here!" someone bawled. Philip watched Revere stagger from a fist that struck hard into his belly.

Pushing, Philip tried to go to Revere's aid. All around, he saw twisted mouths, vicious eyes, threatening hands. One, raw-knuckled, knocked him in the side of the head. He stumbled. Someone else struck the small of his back, hard.

One of the men on the ladder had already dived through the second-floor window, from which shrill yelps of fright now issued. The sunlight and the blows blinded Philip as he struggled to fight off those who pounded him, slammed boots against his shins. Somewhere near the house, Revere was down, exclaiming in anger. But the mob howled louder:

"Tar and feathers!"

"Tar and feathers for liberty!"

"We'll show the fucking lobster-lover—!"

Suddenly Revere burst through a break in the crowd, staggering. A bruise showed on his forehead. Blood ran from the corner of his mouth. His clothing was dirtied and torn. Men grabbed at him from behind. Revere swung a quick, clumsy punch that drove the leading attacker back, clutching his nose and spitting curses.

Revere reached Philip: "Run for it. They're madmen—"

"Yes, you'd better run, God damn you!" screamed the woman who'd been spit on. "You're no friend of Englishmen's rights, Revere!"

"And you don't understand the meaning of the term!" he shouted back.

Oaths. Another frenzied rush at Revere and Philip. A rock flew. Then more. Philip's ear stung painfully as one of the missiles hit him. All at once the hate-filled faces blurred out of focus and he saw Roger Amberly. A mob of Roger Amberlys, screaming, reaching, threatening— His rage and revulsion matched Revere's.

Equally plain was the smith's humiliation. He didn't want to flee from the crazed crowd. But neither did he want to lose his life in a hopeless struggle. Prudence won out. Dragging Philip by the arm, he dodged a chunk of brick, and the two retreated toward the stoop of the Revere house. A cheer went up from the mob. Almost immediately, there was another—

Disarmed, the pathetic Malcolm was dragged from his front door by the two who had entered to capture him. Malcolm's shrieks sounded incoherent now, mortally terrified—

Rachel Revere was waiting on the stoop. She let out a little exclamation of alarm when she saw her husband bleeding. He thrust her hand aside, watching the mob rampage across North Square, dozens of hands supporting a flailing, wailing Malcolm high in the air.

"Animals," Revere seethed. "God damn animals. To wreck our cause with their savagery—!"

"I thought Mr. Adams sometimes called up mobs," Philip panted, his head still buzzing from the blows he'd taken.

"There's not a man in that pack who wears a liberty medal!" Revere snarled. "All they want is cruel sport."

Philip wondered about the truth of Revere's first remark. The second one certainly seemed true, though. The mob had grown till it numbered hundreds. Shoppers and sellers alike left the stalls to follow, laughing and chattering. The head of the column, and the hapless

Malcolm, were finally out of sight on the far side of the square. It seemed to Philip, squinting into the January sun, that above the hubbub, he heard the old man scream in agony. But he couldn't be sure.

He was sure of one thing. The cheerful morning was ruined.

vii

By nightfall, Crazy Johnny Malcolm's fate was the talk of Boston. Philip sat over supper at the Green Dragon, listening in disgust to a group of apprentices gleefully retelling how the old man had been loaded into a cart, wheeled to a nearby wharf, stripped down to his belt and painted with tar.

Next, feather pillows had been slashed open, the contents emptied over Malcolm's body. Until early afternoon—four hours or more—he was exhibited throughout the town, people in the crowd pulling the cart. He was displayed at the Liberty Tree, then on the Neck. There, somehow, tea was produced. The victim was forced to toast the health of all eleven members of the royal family. Philip could imagine the added pain that had caused. Describing it, the apprentices roared.

But quarts of tea forced down his throat on the Neck hadn't been the end of Malcolm's dark day. There was more parading. To the tree again, and King Street, and Copp's Hill. At these locations, a new element was added. Whips. Malcolm was flogged unmercifully, until the mob wearied at last, and abandoned him.

"A proper sight he was, too." The apprentice chortled, spreading his hands. "The tar an' the whipping took off hunks o' skin this big. First he pissed his pants. Then he yelped a while. But when we finished with him, he looked froze, an' stiff as a log."

Stomach turning over, Philip threw coins on the table and stalked out of the Dragon. The apprentices never even noticed his glare.

Ben Edes was as dismayed as Revere had been. The Malcolm incident, he said, was the kind of thing that only firmed the resolve of the British ministers—and the King—to deal severely with the colonials. What right had animals to be treated as anything else?

Early the next morning, Samuel Adams appeared in person with copy freshly penned for a notice. He too proclaimed outrage. But as Philip started to pull type for the announcement, he pondered the sincerity of Adams' wrath.

Anne had told him quite a lot about the troubled period of the last ten years. Savaging mobs had roamed before—and she knew for a fact that Adams had at least been indirectly involved in their formation. Had Adams adopted his new, more scrupulous attitude out of changed convictions? Or just from the practical realization that violence—for the present—brought no useful end?

Whatever the reason, Adams' words, printed and hammered to the Liberty Tree by sunset, declared the position of the Sons of Liberty:

BRETHREN AND FELLOW CITIZENS

This is to Certify, That the modern Punishment Lately Inflicted on the ignoble John Malcolm was not done by our Order. We reserve that Method for Bringing Villains of greater Consequence to a Sense of Guilt and Infamy.

Joyce Jun'r.
Chairman of the Committee of Tarring *and* Feathering

If any Person be so hardy as to tear this down, they may expect my severest Resentment.

J. jun'r.

For days afterward, Philip continued to speculate about the purity of Adams' motives. In the past, how much blood had been callously scrubbed from the man's conscience, if not actually from his palsied hands?

One conclusion was certain. Governor Hutchinson's denunciations of the cruelty to Malcolm only widened the split between Whig and Tory opinion, hardened attitudes on both sides. In the sanctuary of his Purchase Street study, did Samuel Adams allow himself a smile now that one more branch had been tossed onto the slow-kindling fire?

At least one good result came from the memorable January day, though. As Revere had promised, Philip's partial tooth, carved and polished and fastened in place, could hardly be told from the real thing. Anne said she could only see the difference between the two sections when she came near, starting to kiss him.

And as soon as she closed her eyes, she saw no difference at all.

viii

The Boston Grenadier Company drilled weekly on the Common, in sleet, in bitter wind, in driving snow. Philip found himself one of the shortest members of the group, only eight or ten of whom actually owned muskets. Under Captain Pierce's direction, the rest went through the manual of arms using the already-mentioned sticks—or, in Philip's case, a broom handle Anne Ware happily supplied from the household kitchen.

Standing in the corner of Philip's cellar room, that plain, homely length of wood began to take on a kind of dreadful symbolism as the winter months ran out. Boston received word of impending royal retribution against Dr. Franklin's delivery of the Hutchinson letters into the hands of Sam Adams. Incoming ships in February brought specific information. Franklin had been subjected to a scathing denunciation by the Crown's Solicitor General. The good doctor had been publicly called a man lacking honor—a thief—and had been dismissed from his post as Deputy Postmaster General for the colonies.

Marching and countermarching on the Common as winter snow gave way to March rains, Philip sometimes asked himself another question. What sort of justice would be meted out if the death of Captain Stark was ever traced directly to him? Even Edes' newspaper had reported the "Sensational Fatality" of a Crown officer. But thus far, he had received no hint that he was in any way connected with the crime. As Anne had said hopefully, the trail might end at the point it began. In the alley where Stark died.

As time passed and that assurance began to look like a distinct possibility, he still felt less than calm, though for quite another reason. He'd caught the prevailing mood of Boston. The entire town and surrounding countryside, alive with drilling militia companies, was in a state of steadily increasing apprehension.

What *would* be the Crown's response to the tea affair?

When the air turned warm again and sunlit spring broke across Massachusetts, the answer came—with force more stunning than had ever been anticipated. Except, perhaps, by those few radicals like Adams, who remained convinced that George III was Satan incarnate, and the members of the North ministry his eager acolytes.

As Mr. Edes remarked, the events of spring proved there might be something to that novel metaphysical theory after all.

CHAPTER VI

The Sergeant

i

"I THINK, GENTLEMEN," said Paul Revere as he unfolded the wrapping material, "you'll find this appropriate to the situation. If you do, I'll transfer it to copper at once." He laid his drawing on the table of the Long Room.

Handsome Dr. Warren studied it, nodded somberly. Puffing on his long-stemmed clay pipe, he stepped aside to permit Molineaux and the others to examine the artwork held down by the silversmith's work-roughened hands. April rain pattered at the draped windows.

Philip had never been permitted up here before. It was a measure of the trust he was now accorded by his employer that he was allowed to be present. Squeezed in behind Edes, he looked at the grim symbols Revere had inked: the Phrygian cap, one of the chief emblems of the liberty movement, done large and surrounded by a mourning wreath, the whole bordered with a pattern of skulls and crossbones.

Edes turned to his assistant. "This will be the engraving on the front of our handbill." He nodded toward Adams, who sat at the table's far corner, eyes like blue agates in the lamplight. "Samuel's prose on the reverse. There'll be little sleep for us during the next couple of days and nights, you may count on that."

Dr. Warren raised his pipe to signal Revere. "It's

your intention to ride express with the news and the
handbills, Paul?"

"That's right. I have four other couriers waiting.
Trusted men, every one. We'll start as soon as the press
run's finished. I'll take the south road to New York and
Philadelphia. The others will cover the towns to the west
and north." His calm, open face looked momentarily
rueful. "Though I wish we might be spared the
necessity—" Adams glared. "I'd prefer to stay in North
Square with my engraving work for Mr. Rivington's new
edition of Captain Cook's voyages. However, I know the
hour's much too late for that."

His tone brought headshakes of agreement and a
melting of Adams' brief hostility. Philip had never seen
the Long Room conspirators so grim.

All at once, Adams slapped the table.

"The front as it stands won't do!"

"Why not?" Revere countered.

"We must have a message printed with the drawing.
The other colonies must be shocked—assaulted!—with
the implications of the damnable law. Even though the
law's directed only at us, they must be made to see once
and for all that the intent of the King's ministers is
clear—to dominate and destroy *any* colony daring to
resist."

He licked his lips, stretched out one veined hand to
grasp a quill pen, then quickly inked a line at the lower
margin of Revere's artwork. Philip craned forward to
read it.

The Tree of Liberty Cut to the Root.

Will Molineaux snorted. "That's still an under-
statement, Sam. Hacked down, would be more like
it. But I'm afraid the addition of a slogan won't help this
province one whit."

"You'll discover otherwise, Will, as soon as Paul and
his lads spread the word. The sister colonies will come
to our aid. Rally around us with food, with supplies—"

"I pray God you're right," Dr. Warren sighed. "For if that's not the case, Boston's lost her life from this intolerable act."

"Lost her *life?*" Adams' lips jerked at the corners. "By no means! You know what the eventual outcome will be if the ministers dare to continue sponsoring laws to punish us. You know where that road will lead, as surely as sunrise follows the moon."

Will Molineaux's dark Irish face looked even more troubled. "You mean armed resistance."

"More than that," Adams corrected. "*United* resistance, by all the colonies. Then—independency."

Despite the heat of the lamps, the thick blue of pipe smoke, a sudden chill seemed to overwhelm the Long Room then. Adams had stated a possibility that Philip had never really contemplated before. Separation of America from the mother country—The very mention of it suggested an abyss of uncertainty and peril.

And yet, Philip could see the logic, the inevitability. So could the others, as their faces showed. No one looked happy. But no one looked startled, either. In fact, Molineaux smiled with grudging admiration, murmured:

"I've speculated on who among the group would be the first to speak that word. I imagine you've had it in your mind a long while, eh, Sam?"

Adams' head came to rest a moment. He glanced from face to face. With a small, prim smile, he replied:

"I have. I will accept nothing less."

ii

The Edes and Gill press hammered and clattered for the next seventy-two hours, pouring out the handbills that summarized the dire news from England. Over the objections of the elder Pitt, Burke and a few other conciliators who were shouted down, a new bill had passed Parliament, a bill reflecting the King's personal wish that the province of Massachusetts be punished for destroying the tea, as well as for her long and open rebelliousness against Crown authority in general.

The Boston Port Bill, proclaimed the handbill, forbade the loading or unloading of any cargo in the harbor, effective June 1, 1774. The sole exceptions were military stores and some foodstuffs and fuel supplies given special clearance by the Customs House —relocated to Salem by the same bill. George III would reopen the port only when the duties on the ruined tea, as well as the tea itself, had been paid for in full.

Revere and his couriers sped out across Roxbury Neck, the only route of supply for the town, now that its all-important ocean commerce was to be cut off. Within days, the riders returned bearing communications that allayed the fears of the patriots that the other colonies would be indifferent. Edes' paper circulated the heartening news:

New York's Committee of Fifty-one went on record with its "detestation" of the bill.

The mild Quakers of Philadelphia urged moderation but swore support even to "the last extremity."

The Carolinas pledged rice and money. *They* recognized, Adams crowed, that it could just as easily be the bustling port of Charleston whose sea trade—whose life—was being strangled!

Flocks of sheep appeared on the Neck, driven in from New York, Connecticut and elsewhere, tangible signs that thoughtful men well understood the Port Bill's implications. Throughout Massachusetts, the other Committees of Correspondence began to implement the stockpiling and shipment of foodstuffs for Boston. The supplies were delivered in wagons and carts the public jeeringly called "Lord North's coasters"—wheeled replacements for the coasting ships that would be banned from the harbor anchorages after the first of June.

But an even more severe shock lay in store. Governor Hutchinson announced he would step down, return to England, be replaced by a newly appointed official who bore a triple title: Vice Admiral, Captain-General and Governor-in-Chief of Massachusetts. It was taken as a sure sign of worsening relations between colonists and Crown that the provincial government was to be turned over to a military man, General Thomas Gage.

With him, the last incoming vessels reported, he would bring fresh regiments from Britain. Not to mention warships of His Majesty's fleet to enforce the closing of the port. In hamlets throughout the province, Philip soon learned, the militia companies were organizing and drilling in earnest. And accumulating what muskets, powder and shot they could.

The troubled spring grew even more troubled as the days wore on.

iii

Resplendent in his red uniform jacket, Captain Joseph Pierce called the Boston Grenadier Company to attention.

Up and down the length of Long Wharf, other local units snapped to—including Hancock's Boston Cadets, the merchant himself personally commanding. Fifes began to shrill, drums to beat out riffles and tattoos.

At the head of the wharf, a huge crowd of well-dressed Tories, many seated in carriages, started to applaud and wave handkerchiefs as the brass fieldpieces under the charge of Captain Paddock crashed smoky aerial salutes over the rain-dappled harbor. A nasty day made nastier by this false show of pomp and friendliness, Philip thought.

He was uncomfortable in the uniform procured, like

all those of the Grenadier Company, with Hancock's financial assistance. He felt foolish and damp to boot, clad in a heavy red coat, white trousers and a tall, tapered black bearskin cap with gleaming brass frontplate. He wriggled his nose as the stench of perspiration and wet wool thickened moment by moment.

The rain fell steadily from a gray sky this thirteenth of May, all but hiding the furled topsails of the man-o'-war anchored out in the harbor. By turning his head slightly in that direction, Philip could just make out the cutter being rowed from the fighting ship to the stairs of the wharf. The thwarts were crowded with oarsmen and cloaked officers in tricorn hats. General Gage and staff.

When Henry Knox had issued the orders for the Grenadier Company to muster and join in the official welcome for the man responsible for enforcing the hateful new law, Philip and quite a few others had openly questioned the advisability of such a move. Wouldn't the company's presence demonstrate respect? Loyalty?

Knox was quick to dismiss the complaint:

"Several factors demand our attendance. First, Gage may not be so bad as Sam Adams would like him painted. He's a man of moderate temper, by all accounts. With a fondness for the colonies. His wife was born here. She's a Kemble, from the Jersey state. And while most of us share the current mood of outrage, many would still rather see some method of accommodation worked out between Massachusetts and London. If it can't be done—" He shrugged. "You may all be certain of one thing. Our presence on Long Wharf day after tomorrow will be completely understood by our friends. The joy that will seem to reign will be recognized for what it is—expedient hypocrisy. Mingled, of course," he added with an amused expression, "with the Bostonian's inbred instinct for extending traditional courtesies to any gentleman. Until he proves himself otherwise."

So here they were, miserable in the rain, as General Gage and his staff mounted the wharf stairs, accepted the salutes of the militia officers and proceeded down the line of ranked companies for an inspection.

Gage's broad, middle-aged face showed careful restraint of any emotion. But the expressions of his officers left little doubt about their opinion of the local military. From his place in the second rank, Philip saw eyebrows raised, small scornful smiles exchanged. Philip didn't bother to conceal his reaction.

Gage moved slowly toward the head of the wharf, where the Tory crowd had broken into loud cheering and clapping. A colonel behind Gage noticed Philip's insolent expression, paused and called Knox's attention to Philip's trousers:

"That man's breeches are disreputable, Lieutenant. I see mud spots. In England, he'd be flogged."

"Yes, sir," Knox answered. "But we lack supplies of pipe clay for whitening, sir. And I beg the colonel's permission to remind him this is not England."

The officer's cold stare traveled back from Philip to Knox.

"No, but it shall begin to seem more and more like England as the days pass, be assured of that."

The colonel stalked off. Philip hawked and spat on the ground.

The colonel spun, scanned the ranks. Philip stared straight ahead into the rain. Knox looked dismayed. After a moment, the colonel uttered a controlled curse and continued on.

Members of the Boston Grenadier Company around Philip smirked and growled their approval. One man in the front rank even whistled sharply between his teeth. The break in the colonel's stride showed that he heard the mocking sound. But he did not wheel to confront the offenders again.

As the drums and fifes struck up a martial air, the companies faced around to begin the dreary march to the State House as Gage's honor guard. Knox took the opportunity to fall in beside Philip and complain, "Kent, will it hurt you to behave with military courtesy for one hour?"

"I am not a King's soldier!" Philip said from the corner of his mouth. "And I can promise you that if we ever see action against them, I won't be wearing one of their own damned red coats."

"Nor will any of us," Knox retorted. He was obviously irritated by the continuing coarse comments from the men around Philip. "Sergeant!" he exclaimed suddenly. "Count the cadence for these hay-foots!"

With another glance at his prime troublemaker, he added, "For the moment I am persuaded it would be better if we're never forced to fight. Try to build an army out of an ill-tempered band of apprentices who won't take orders from anyone? I pity the general who's handed *that* assignment."

He strode away to the head of the column.

iv

The colonel's prophecy that Gage would enforce stronger Crown rule in Boston was soon fulfilled. The word "intolerable" started to appear frequently in the *Gazette*'s pages, to describe a new series of Parliamentary decrees.

The Administration of Justice Act almost guaranteed a not-guilty verdict for any Crown official tried for employing violence in putting down an act of rebellion. On the recommendation of the Governor, such an official's trial could be moved to England to ensure "fair" judicial proceedings.

A second act, passed in May, virtually dismantled the Massachusetts provincial government. Judges, sheriffs and even justices of the peace would be Crown-appointed in the future. That meant juries could be packed with Tories, since they were selected by the sheriffs. Finally, in a move designed to rob the radicals of their single most important instrument of political persuasion, the traditional Massachusetts town meetings could only be convened with the Governor's approval—after he had ruled upon the permissibility of all items on a proposed agenda.

Like all the citizens of Boston, Philip and Anne Ware found that each day in the late spring and early summer seemed to bring some new development—or the sight of another man-o'-war bearing down from Nantasket Roads, loaded to the gunwales with more redcoats.

The day after the Port Bill went into effect, the Fourth Infantry—the King's Own—debarked, along with the Forty-third, fresh from Ireland. Up from New York sailed the Royal Welsh Fusiliers. A royal artillery company soon spread its tents on the Common. In all, nearly five thousand military men swelled the population.

And their arrival had a direct effect upon all the colonies, thanks to yet another Parliamentary measure passed in June. Its provisions applied not merely to Massachusetts but to every locale up and down the seaboard where royal troops might be garrisoned.

In private, Adams and the Long Room group gleefully celebrated what they considered to be the King's latest, enormous blunder. But those who were directly affected by the provisions of the Quartering Act were less amused.

"A stinking lobsterback in my own house!" Abraham Ware exclaimed, fairly dancing up and down in front of Philip and Ben Edes one muggy day in late June.

"Imagine!—I am commanded to feed him, to give him a bed, to treat him cordially at all times! Well, the only bed he'll get is in my barn, by God."

"You're not alone, Abraham," Edes told him. "The troops are being jammed into private homes all over Boston. Not to mention the taverns and warehouses. In fact, anywhere their damned officers choose. Has your—ah—guest arrived?"

Ware shook his head. "But I understand I'm on the list for quartering someone from the very next regiment coming in. The Thirty-third. By Jesus, just see if I so much as speak to the swine!"

"Well," said Edes with a rueful smile, "personal inconveniences aside, the Quartering Act's had one good outcome. There's the news of it, just in with Revere—" He gestured, and Ware followed him to the press.

The popeyed lawyer peered down at the type locked into the form. "I can't read your damned lead backwards Edes!" Philip helped out:

"It says that New York and Philadelphia have answered Boston's appeal—and in the fall, there'll be a great congress of representatives from all the colonies. The congress is supposed to decide what's to be done about the Intolerable Acts."

The information partially mollified the little lawyer. But he still left the shop grumbling about being forced to board a British soldier at his own expense. "The moldy hay in the barn is the best meal I'll offer him!" was Ware's pronouncement as he departed.

v

On a blindingly sunny August morning, several hundred citizens—including Anne Ware and, with Ben Edes' permission, her frequent companion these past summer days—crushed into Bromfield's Lane. The crowd was awaiting the opening of the front door of the splendid home belonging to the speaker of the Massachusetts House.

Before the mounting block stood a handsome coach with red and yellow wheels and four chestnut horses. A liveried driver and groom sat on the box. Two black footmen in similar attire waited by the coach door. Four more servants on horseback controlled their mounts prancing nervously at the edge of the crowd. Philip noted the gleam of pistol butts in the holsters of this quartet of outriders.

Anne seized Philip's arm and pointed excitedly. "The door's open. There's Papa!"

The crowd broke into applause and cheering as Ware appeared, engaged in conversation with a fellow lawyer, the soberly dressed John Adams of Braintree. The next man to emerge from the site of the farewell breakfast was almost unrecognizable, so clean and opulent were his claret-colored suit and the snowy ruffles at collar and cuffs. Silver buckles on the shoes of Samuel Adams twinkled in the August light. The golden head of his long cane glittered.

All of these items, Philip knew, had been donated so that Adams might appear fittingly dressed when he attended the great Congress, to be convened at a place called Carpenters' Hall in the Quaker City on the fifth of September. As the *Gazette* had duly reported, only one colony of the thirteen, Georgia, had balked at sending delegates to the meeting, whose express purpose was to agree upon a response to the repressive laws—especially the Quartering Act and the new Quebec Act of early summer. This last had expanded the boundaries of Canada to a distant western river, the Ohio. "Canada," as Philip understood it, now contained land to which speculators in Virginia and Connecticut, as well as Massachusetts, laid claim.

Soon Molineaux, the dandyish Hancock, the smiling

Dr. Warren and others in the party came out to mingle in the crowd. Someone marveled that the Massachusetts contingent, including delegates, servants and outriders, would number close to a hundred men.

While Sam Adams conferred with his cousin John and with Hancock, who was remaining behind, Abraham Ware searched the crowd for his daughter. He located her, waved and fought his way forward. Philip drew aside to let Ware give Anne a farewell hug and a few admonitory whispers. At one of these, Anne's brown eyes flashed with delight as she glanced at Philip.

He experienced one of those rare moments in which he had no doubt about his enjoyment of their relationship. Being with Anne—strolling the town or gossiping in her kitchen about the latest turn of events—had become both natural and automatic. He seldom thought about the nature of their liaison, and he never discussed it. Nor did she. Each had accepted the other's terms. Whenever there was an opportunity for them to discreetly steal time for lovemaking in the Ware barn, they did so with pleasure, and without debate over the significance of the act.

Anne hugged her father one last time. Her face glowed, the freckles along her nose showing dark against the brown sheen of her skin. Philip realized Lawyer Ware was peering at him with a peculiar concentration. Pulling his daughter by the hand, the little man approached Philip to say:

"I've asked Annie to excuse us a moment while we have a personal word."

He released Anne's hand and guided Philip through the crowd applauding Sam Adams' somewhat ostentatious mounting of the coach step. Anne's look seemed to say she had no idea what her father wanted of Philip.

In the midst of the shoving, vocal crowd, Ware found the privacy he sought.

"You know I'll be away at the Congress for several weeks, Philip. And that my daughter and Daisy are alone on Launder Street with that soldier."

"Yes, Anne told me a sergeant was quartered with you now. I haven't met him yet."

"Poor lumpish creature," Ware said. "He's not a bad sort—for a Tommy. But I want to speak to you on another subject. I haven't questioned Annie keeping company with you—even though I'll frankly admit I would be pleased with a suitor of more substantial means and background. Don't take offense! That's a father's natural reaction. Besides, I'm uncertain about your intentions. But as I say, I haven't questioned your association with my daughter—"

"Though you obviously wanted to," Philip said, somewhat irritated.

"Indeed so. However, the truth is, she asked me not to do it."

"Why?"

"Your company gives her pleasure."

"Mr. Ware, I'm very fond of Anne. But—"He structured the falsehood carefully. "—you hit it yourself."

"Hit what?"

"The reason I can't state any—intentions, as you call them. I feel I don't have sufficient money. Or prospects for the future."

Ware digested this with a murmur and a bob of his head. Then:

"In confidence, I can say that Annie has mentioned both reasons. She's also expressed an opinion that neither is genuine. Now don't goggle and swear! Listen! My time's short, and this needs saying. While I gather you have never spoken anything on the subject, Anne's convinced there must be another woman somewhere in your history. Having lived with my own child since her birth, that kind of statement tells me how she really feels about you. Though the struggle goes unmentioned, she's locked in some kind of battle with—whoever or whatever still holds a claim on you. Because she has—" He cleared his throat, obviously ill at ease. "—ah—set her cap for you."

Stunned, Philip looked through the crowd for the blaze of Anne's chestnut hair. He couldn't find her. That she had sensed the tearing in him—the pull of the past, of Alicia—only heightened his appreciation of her sensitivity.

"Ultimately," Ware went on, "a father, of all persons in the world, has the least to say about the disposition of a daughter's life. Outside of royal circles, of course. So I speak to you instead. Asking two things."

The little lawyer's face revealed his concern for his child. "First, in my absence, call frequently at Launder Street. Look after Annie as only a man can. And secondly—whatever your final feelings about marriage—don't hurt her. If there's to be nothing permanent between the two of you, so be it. But when you make your mind up, should the decision be negative, tell her frankly—and quickly."

Ware's hand, surprisingly powerful, locked on Philip's arm. "Because if I thought it was dalliance, with no genuine feeling, I would have you flayed out of your skin. If I couldn't do it myself I would hire it done. I will, if you ever deliberately bring Annie to grief."

In as steady a voice as he could manage, Philip answered, "There'll be no need for that, Mr. Ware. I think too highly of your daughter."

"Fair enough. Come along and let's find her. I must be into the coach for Philadelphia."

vi

Sergeant George Lumden was just under thirty years old. He had mild gray eyes, a large mole in the center of his forehead, crooked teeth. His manner was shy, almost humble.

Lumden had answered the summons of the recruiting drum in his native Warwickshire. The eleventh son of a smithy, he had chosen military life because it offered his only means of escape from poverty. But, as Philip discovered in conversation with the soldier in Ware's kitchen during the last days of August, Lumden was not pleased that the Thirty-third Infantry Regiment had been shipped to Boston.

"There's plenty in the regiment who feel the same way, too. In my case it's personal. I've got a relative—a second cousin—in these colonies."

"Indeed, where?" Daisy O'Brian exclaimed, bringing a heaping plate of hot biscuits to the table and setting them in front of Lumden with a flourish.

The cook's cheeks seemed exceedingly pink, Philip thought. From his vantage point on a hearthside stool where he sat with hands locked around one knee, Daisy looked positively fluttery. She overflowed with gasps and exclamations and too-loud laughter at Lumden's slightest jest or sign of attention.

Philip glanced across to Anne. She was slowly stirring a fragrant kettle of fish-head chowder simmering on a chain over the logs. Anne returned his glance with amused understanding. Neither the enraptured Daisy nor the slump-shouldered Lumden noticed.

Lumden had both of his spatterdashes spread on the table. Using a little brush, he was applying moist white paste from a small jar. His uniform jacket with willow-green facings hung over the back of his chair. His torso, already turning to fat, was clad in woolen underwear that appeared fiendishly heavy for summertime.

"I think the town's known as Hartford," Lumden said in reply to Daisy's question. "I want to visit there—provided all stays calm in Boston. It's my wish that it will. I have never served in combat and, damme, I don't want to," he added, without the slightest embarrassment. "Soldiering's a hard enough life without throwing in the risk of being killed. I mean—just consider! You're damp all the time. Even in summer, you're damp from collar to socks!"

Anne laughed. "I'll agree, Sergeant, those uniforms do look hot."

" 'T'isn't only the sweat," he said. "It's this damned pipe clay. Every inch of white we wear must be clayed day in, day out, or there are hellish penalties." Disgusted, he flung the brush down beside the jar of whitening compound. "When the pipe clay's fresh, you feel soggy because it's wet. When it dries it shrinks the material so tight you're half-strangled—and you sweat all the more. Then there's the damn pewter buttons, each of which must wink and twinkle—" Reaching behind him, he flicked one of the offending buttons. "—or that's another fine or whipping. Or both, if you've a commander like ours."

"Got a tyrant in charge, do you?" Philip asked.

"Yes, sir. The man has the vilest temper I've ever seen. Regiments like the Thirty-third attract such types."

"And other regiments don't?"

"Not so much."

"I don't understand."

"Well, you see, the British army's composed of two sorts of regiments. Royal ones—always in blue facings, surely you've seen those in town—"

The other three nodded almost simultaneously.

"Then there's proprietary regiments like the Thirty-third. Hired to fight by the Crown. A real money-making operation for the nabob who can put one together. He virtually owns it, and even after expenses are met, he can bank on fattening his own fortunes. Take our actual commander. He's a gouty old far. . . —" Blushing, he glanced at Daisy, swallowed. "—Viscount. Name of Coney. He's never marched, never faced fire, never left England. So the man in charge of the regiment here, Lieutenant Colonel Amberly, he's not the real commander at all, if you follow——"

Lumden blinked, noticing the sudden tightness around Philip's mouth.

"Mr. Kent, did I say something to anger you?" He sounded apologetic.

Philip's scalp crawled. The palms of his hands had turned damp. He shook his head.

"Go on, Lumden. Tell me about this lieutenant colonel."

The sergeant scratched his chin, frowned in annoyance when he realized his finger was still smeared with pipe clay. Daisy scampered for a cloth. As Lumden wiped the paste off his jaw, he continued:

"He's the sort you often find commanding a proprietary. Cares nothing about the men—or the profession. Only wants a little experience to put on his record. Bought his commission, of course. Or his father did, I 'spose, that's generally how it works. There's no other way to achieve a high rank quickly. Like I say, Amberly's a bas—uh, a bad-tempered man. He can be plagued cruel. Turn on you in a second! On the other hand, he's not much worse than many I hear about. So maybe I shouldn't complain."

Philip said quietly, "Do you happen to know this Amberly's first name?"

" 'Course. It's Roger. Roger Hook-hand, some of us call him on the sly. He has this crippled right hand——"

Lumden held up his fingers, grotesquely shaped. Philip stared, his throat tight and hot. He jumped up with such suddenness that Daisy started. Lumden again look distressed:

"Ah, I'm sorry! I know it's not decent to mock a man's misfortune. But the lieutenant colonel's infirmities have crimped up something in his soul, damned if they haven't. A bad hand—the mark of a bad birth—"

Lumden touched his forehead near his left eyebrow.
"That's a hell-born combination, I'll tell you. No wonder he's taught himself to use the whip with his left
hand. He enjoys handing out punishment when the
mood's on him—"

"Does this commander of yours ever speak of a
wife?" Philip asked.

"Yes, I've heard tell of one back in England. Mr.
Kent, I've upset you, haven't I? My apologies. But I'm
damned if I know how I—"

Philip spun for the back door, growling, "Never
mind, it's nothing."

"Do you know the commander, is that it—?"

Philip slammed the door and clattered down the stairs
into the mellow August sunshine.

He heard the house door open again. Head down, one
knuckle rubbing against his mouth, he walked to the
relatively cooler shadow inside the little barn. Without
really seeing it, he stared at Lumden's spread-out equipment: his sizable pack, his cartouche, his Brown Bess
with a swordlike length of steel mounted so as to extend
well past the end of the muzzle. He felt rather than
heard Anne enter behind him.

He turned to confront her. The daylight outside set
her chestnut hair aglow.

"The name turned you white, Philip. Is it the same
man you told me about?"

"It can't be anyone else. The first name might be
coincidental, but not the hand and the birthmark."
Searching back, he remembered a statement Alicia had
made and he added, "When I knew him, there was talk
that he'd spend some time in the army. With so many
regiments being sent here, I suppose it's not unthinkable
that he could wind up in Boston."

She glided toward him, touched his hand. "What do
you intend to do?"

Fighting the memories of how Roger Amberly had

been instrumental in arranging his near-murder, Philip said, "I intend to stay out of his way. If he caught sight of me by accident, I imagine he could trump up an arrest. He hated my mother and me enough to want me dead, and I doubt the feeling's lessened very much. He still carries that wrecked hand I gave him."

Anne gazed deep into his eyes. "You asked about a woman. A wife. Is she the one I've been struggling against all these months? I know there's something more than your father's letter binding you to the past—and holding you from any kind of future—"

He was ready to lie to spare her feelings. Then he recalled his pledge to Abraham Ware. He said:

"Yes, she's the one."

"Married to your father's other son. You never told me that part, Philip."

"I saw no need. Anne, I have to go back to the shop. Please don't say a thing to Lumden."

"Of course I wouldn't. But—when you questioned him, your face was as ugly as I've ever seen it. Do you still hate Amberly so?"

"He caused my mother's death! I'd like to kill him."

A weary expression overrode the starkness on his features then. His voice moderated:

"But I've become enough of a realist—like the sergeant—to want to stay alive. Deliberate contact with Roger Amberly would put all the odds on his side, and none on mine. Unless—"A harsh thought changed his face again."—unless a killing was carefully done. The trouble is, in these times—well, I have allegiances to Mr. Edes. And plotting murder's no simple job. At least for me."

"Murder would only make you just what he is!"

He knew she was right. He almost hated her for saying it. "Let's not talk about it, Anne. I said I had to leave—"

"First tell me a little about his wife. Was she beautiful?"

"No, I won't tell you. She's married—and that's the end of it."

"Except inside you."

He whirled away from her, away from the dreadful accuracy with which she'd struck to the heart of his turmoil. He stalked toward the front of the property. When she called his name, he turned in the blue shadows at the side of the house.

Anne was standing in a patch of sunlight outside the barn. Her fists were clenched.

"I'll win against her, Philip. I swear I will!"

He thought he saw tears shining on her summer-ripened cheeks. He turned again and hurried away down Launder Street.

CHAPTER VII

Betrayal

i

A NEW KING, Louis XVI, reigned in France. But some in Boston town proclaimed that they too had been graced with a new monarch, a despot. For although Thomas Gage spoke mildly enough in public, he manipulated the royal troops with a firm purpose from Province House. On the first of September, a few picked companies marched to Cambridge in a surprise raid and seized quantities of powder and muskets belonging to the local militia.

Church bells pealing and small cannon exploding brought Boston citizens to an awareness that something extremely serious had happened. Serious for the colonials—but serious for the British, too, as it turned out.

Response to the raid had been swift, the *Gazette* reported. Clanging bells and couriers on horseback summoned several thousand farmers with their muskets, their scythes—any weapon available—and drew them all toward Charlestown, where Gage's men were busy seizing a second storehouse of powder.

No military clash occurred. The soldiers prudently returned to the city just as the first countrymen came streaming to the site of the expected battle. When they found no enemies, they went home.

But Ben Edes, for one, considered the affair a victory of sorts:

"The general's afraid, Philip. And in fear lies the

capacity for error. Thinking to gobble up arms meant to be used against his men, he practically gave a lesson on how he'll operate if he ever moves in force. You heard how quickly the militiamen rallied?"

"Yes."

"Well, it wasn't quick enough—the raid taught us that. We've got to set up new, faster ways of signaling and mobilizing the countryside. One day Gage will regret being such a generous instructor," Edes chuckled. "Sam Adams is a quick study."

So it proved.

Gage fortified the Roxbury Neck with guard posts during the first week in September. But Adams, Hancock and the other prime movers of the patriot cause came and went—if not unrecognized, at least unmolested. The general continued his policy of not moving openly against the rebel ringleaders, though he kept his regiments busy drilling.

The freedom of movement Gage allowed Adams and the others permitted the Massachusetts House to sit at Salem in early October. In open defiance of the Governor, the House approved formation of a new Committee of Safety, chaired by Hancock, with official power to organize, arm and summon militia contingents to action. Philip began to hear a new term used to identify those select companies now responsible for rallying to an alarm in a very short time. Minute companies, they were called.

Meantime, Abraham Ware's weekly letter to his daughter brought a running account of developments at Carpenters' Hall in Philadelphia.

In response to a set of Massachusetts resolves drafted by Dr. Warren, enacted at a convention in Suffolk County and then sent overland with Revere on horseback, the radicals and the conservatives in the great Congress pulled and hauled against one another, now rejecting Warren's firebrand call for arming the towns and imposing economic sanctions against Britain, now proposing more moderate resolutions opposing the Crown's position.

Finally—"Praise the Almighty as well as those who argue loudest!" Ware declared in one epistle—the Congress adopted a set of ten resolves. Among other things, the resolves declared the exclusive right of the provincial legislatures to regulate matters of internal policy, especially taxation. The resolves also stated that thirteen separate and distinct Parliamentary acts put in force since 1763 were in violation of the colonials' rights to "life, liberty and property." And the radicals won a key point in the form of the sought-for promise of economic reprisals until the Intolerable Acts were repealed.

Ware wrote Anne that the unprecedented assembly hoped to adjourn in late October, after drawing up a petition of grievances specifically addressed to the King. The representatives of the various colonies had already decided to meet again the following year if relief was not obtained.

'*Tis not as much as Sam'l. or Dr. W.—or indeed, myself—would have wished,*" the lawyer said in one of the letters Anne showed Philip. "*On the other hand, there is concert—agreement—and that in itself is fraught with meaning for the future. To see the delegates, foregather at City Tavern at nightfall, and to hear such gentlemen as the very respected Col. Washington of Virginia voice the same concerns as the men of Boston—while we all indulge ourselves in Maderia and great heaps of baked oysters—that, my dearest daughter, is an experience not capable of being fully described, only savored in the proud heart.*

November came. Anne looked forward to her father's return with mixed feelings. She missed him. But she would likewise miss the privacy afforded by his absence, privacy in which she and Philip could be alone in the parlor of an evening. They talked of everything except their own futures, while Daisy and Sergeant Lumden of the Thirty-third laughed and chattered in similar fashion in the kitchen.

The approach of winter made it increasingly apparent that the Port Bill would indeed prove disastrous. Gage interpreted the act as even prohibiting ferryboats from crossing the river. Thus the price of partridges or mutton or cod carted the long way around, by Roxbury Neck, grew astronomically. Decent quantities of firewood and sweet-smelling lamp oil could be afforded only by the very rich—mostly Tories, who were delighted to see the Whigs suffer, and who were not overly concerned when the poor did, either.

Philip, of course, never forgot the presence of Lieutenant Colonel Roger Amberly in Boston.

He questioned Lumden as to where the regiment's commander was domiciled, and learned that it was in a huge house on Beacon Hill, a house whose owner had strong Tory leanings.

Philip loitered outside the house on several different evenings, shivering in the dusk and hoping to catch a glimpse of the man whose death he planned in endless variations. He speculated on ways to arrange what would look like an accident. Other times, he thought of using what little money he'd put by to hire one of the South End mob men to act as executioner.

But luck never gave him so much as one look at his enemy in all the hours he stood in the bitter wind, pondering alternatives.

The answer to one major question still eluded him. Was he actually capable of doing what he told himself he wanted to do? The question unresolved, his plans remained just that.

He finally abandoned the evening spying and let himself be consumed by the routine at Dassett Alley—and

by Anne. Perhaps, he thought more than once, he was
hiding from his own weakness; from a basic inability to
cold-bloodedly kill another human being—

After that first day in August when Lumden revealed
the name of his commander, Anne never raised the subject of Amberly. Nor did she mention Alicia. Philip was
grateful. He finally did admit to himself that he lacked
the will to do deliberate murder.

A part of him cried out for it. But something else,
equally strong, held him back.

ii

"Oh, God, there's going to be war, all right," Sergeant
Lumden declared glumly one night in late December.
"Have you heard the news from New Hamp-
shire—wherever the devil that is?"

"Fort William and Mary," Philip nodded, turning the
tankard of rum punch in his hands to absorb its
warmth. "They're talking of nothing else down at the
Dragon."

Red-haired Daisy hovered by the hearth. Much of her
usual good humor seemed lacking this evening. Philip
wondered why—until he caught up to the fact that she
could scarcely keep her eyes off the mild-spoken British
infantryman with the forehead mole. And she looked
worried.

Philip drank a little, chose his next words carefully:

"In fact, I've even heard gossip that a Boston man,
riding express for five shillings a day, carried a warning
of the expedition to New Hampshire, so the stores could
be carted off."

Gossip was hardly the right word. Philip knew full
well that Revere had done the riding. But he wasn't sure

how far Lumden could be trusted, likable as he might be.

General Gage had intended to strengthen the New Hampshire fort with several boatloads of troops slipped quietly out of Boston late one night. His plan had evidently been picked up by the alert ears of some informer at Province House. It was no secret that each side had its anonymous spies planted on the other.

A patriot named John Sullivan received the warning from Revere. He encircled the fort with a band of men, overcame the small British garrison without so much as a single injury to anyone. Gage's reinforcements arrived to find all the fort's arms and powder gone.

"And I agree with you, Sergeant," Philip finished. "It does bring war that much closer."

Lumden eyed Philip morosely. The latter changed the subject, saying to Daisy, "You've no idea when Mistress Anne and her father will be back?"

"No, sir. They left on some errands." She moved to the table. Philip noted that her breasts rose and fell quickly. Why was she nervous?

The pretty, red-haired cook pulled a stool to the table, sat down and leaned her elbows on the wood. She look intently at Philip.

"But I'm glad you chose to call, sir. Geor—the sergeant has been meaning to speak to you for several days."

Philip shrugged as if to say the sergeant should go ahead. Lumden did, but with difficulty, staring at the open pantry door, at the rime of frost on a window overlooking the backyard—everywhere but at Philip.

"Well, Mr. Kent, the truth is, I—I—"

"Don't hesitate now," Daisy urged. "Tell him!"

Lumden's gray eyes finally met Philip's. "I can speak to you in confidence?"

"Of course."

"I told you that!" Daisy sighed.

Lumden swallowed. "I have been thinking of leaving the army."

"You mean a resignation?"

"No," Daisy answered, clasping her hand over the sergeant's.

All at once Philip understood the girl's tension, the way her eyes lingered on Lumden's face. He recalled how the cook and the soldier had spent many an evening together in the kitchen in recent weeks. Their soft laughter took on a new significance. He said:

"Desertion."

Daisy nodded emphatically. "George and I wish to be married. We have resolved the matter of our different faiths—"

Philip grinned. "That's wonderful! Congratulations to both of you!"

Daisy flushed, prettily this time. Her bright red hair glinted with reflections from the crackling fireplace. Lumden put in quickly:

"I realize desertion's a damned detestable act. Though I hate being stationed here to repress fellow Englishmen, three months ago I would have struck any chap who suggested the possibility that I might run away. But I don't mind admitting my feelings for Daisy have changed my attitude."

Philip said, "George, you're smart enough to appreciate that you've been quartered in a household where sympathies for the Crown are not exactly at a peak—"

"Oh yes, I've picked up a hint or two," Lumden answered with a wry smile.

"So you don't have to apologize. I applaud your decision. I think Mr. Ware will too."

"More and more of the lads are doing it, you know," Lumden said. "Slipping out across the Neck dressed as countrymen. Or rowing from the Charlestown Ferry guard post on the pretext of some official errand—"

"I say bravo to that," Philip told him.

"You must realize it's not cowardice on my part!" Lumden exclaimed. Then he added more softly, "At least not entirely. I doubt if I'd ever have decided to do it, except for—for what I've found in this house. Affection. Tenderness—" He lapsed into silence, turning even redder than Daisy had a moment earlier.

Presently, he managed to go on, "Also, as perhaps I've indicated, I *do* have a liking for the people of Boston—!"

Philip suppressed a smile. "Yes, you indicated that a minute ago, George. You don't need to keep explaining or excusing—"

"In my own heart, I think the King and his ministers are fools, villains or both! They don't realize you colonials are strong-headed. You won't yield easily!"

"We won't yield at all, George."

"Just so! That means action and counteraction—one side against the other—till the fuse ignites *all* the powder, am I correct?"

"I think you are, George."

Lumden banged the table, making the tankards rattle. "But dammit, I've no stomach for going into battle against artisans and farmers whose only crime is holding fast to what rights they feel belong to 'em—and are being taken away!"

"Understood," Philip assured him. "Completely understood. But let's discuss the practical problems—"

"Leaving Boston, you mean?" Daisy asked.

"Yes. It's either the Neck or the river."

"I think it must be the Neck," Lumden said. "A smithy's son gets little chance to become acquainted with water. Been swimming just once in my life. We visited a distant relative's near the River Avon. I only had nerve to wade up to my ankles. Scared to death, I

was! On the voyage across from England, I was sick
nearly the whole time. Y'see?—it's true! I'm a swinishly
bad soldier! Trained for just one thing—like every other
fellow in a British infantry regiment. Trained to be fod-
der for the enemy's muskets and cannon! In the forma-
tions in which we march, a man stands every chance of
being shot down in the opening volley—"

His eyes gazed into some grim distance, seeing the
slaughter he described. Then, as Philip cleared his
throat, Lumden veered the talk back to the subject with
a sharp, distracted gesture.

"I can't chance the river."

"To cross the Neck, you'll need different clothes,"
Philip said.

Daisy put in that she'd already been gathering up
items from serving girls she knew in other houses.
"Discards, mostly. They'll do well enough."

Philip nodded. "But you won't dare speak,
George. Your accent would give you away."

"We have a plan for that as well," Daisy told him.
"All it requires is another person. I've some savings of
my own—do you know a trustworthy lad we could hire
to pose as George's companion? His son—his nephew?
The plan's to work this way—"

She described it in a few sentences. Philip admitted
that, while it contained some risk, it stood a chance of
succeeding, because the British soldiers typically
regarded Massachusetts farmers as oafish types unable
or unwilling to put any kind of check on their consump-
tion of spirits—especially rum.

"I don't know of anyone offhand," he told Lumden.
"I'll make inquiries, though."

"God bless you for that, sir!"

"When do you want to leave?" Philip countered.

"As soon as the arrangements can be completed."

"Where will you go? To that relative of yours you

mentioned? Connecticut, wasn't it?"

Lumden answered, "Eventually I'll go there, yes. For the time being I plan to hide at Daisy's home. A farm beyond Concord. I don't imagine they'll search for me too long."

Philip chuckled. "If they kept up a constant search for every Tommy who's deserted in the past few months, Gage's men wouldn't have time for anything else. And he'd soon run out of men to do the searching! I'd hazard that you'll be safe within a week or two—" A thought occurred to him. "What are you going to do with your uniform and equipment?"

Lumden thought a moment. "Burn the uniform, I 'spose. In that fireplace. As for the Brown Bess—"

"And the blade that fits on the end. The bayonet," Philip prompted. "That's a weapn the colonial troops don't have, and don't know how to use."

The statement was entirely accurate. More than once, Lieutenant Knox of the Boston Grenadier Company had declared that lack of bayonets, as well as lack of training in using same, would put the colonials at a bad disadvantage if they were ever up against British line regiments in a stiff fight. Most of the militiamen tended to scoff. They bragged about their accuracy with a musket, rejected the need for an additional weapon affixed to the muzzle for stabbing and hacking. But Philip respected Knox, and took him at his word. So he tried not to show his eagerness as he asked Lumden:

"What will become of those things?"

"I'll leave them hidden in the barn. Or ditch them in the river. If I tried to haul 'em along with me, they'd be recognized as Crown issue right off. And God save me, I've come to hate all they stand for. Any fighting I have to do, I'll do with my own two hands."

Philip's dark eyes shone with a sudden intensity. "Will you give me the musket and the bayonet?"

Lumden grinned. "In return for finding the reliable lad to help with our plan."

"Done!"

"I prefer not to speculate on what you want with those things," Lumden said. "If the time ever comes when you use 'em against men who might be friends of mine, I hope I'm tilling a field in Connecticut and bouncing a youngster in my lap." He reached over to clasp his pale hand around Daisy O'Brian's.

She stared back with unashamed affection. Philip barely noticed. His mind's eye glowed with an image of the Brown Bess and its shining length of steel. With difficulty, he refocused his thoughts on the reality of the moment.

"One more thing. Who's to know this plan? Mistress Anne, for instance?"

"I have already described our intentions to her," said the girl. "I imagine Mr. Ware will need to be told, too. Beyond that, I've spoken to no one. I haven't sent a letter to my father—and even if I could find someone to write it for me, I won't. If George should be caught—"

"I'd be flogged at the least," Lumden put in. "Or, more likely, shot."

"So I figured it's best my father know nothing of it till George reaches the farm. I hear sending messages out of Boston can be risky these days."

"Agreed," said Philip, rising from the table. There were noises at the front of the house.

Lawyer Ware appeared momentarily, knocking snowflakes from the crown of his tricorn hat.

"Aha, some conspiracy brewing!" he said with a sly smile. "I can tell from the cats' grins you're all wearing." In spite of himself, Ware had taken a liking to Lumden.

Anne entered the kitchen. Philip moved a couple of steps so their hands could touch briefly. With his other hand, he lifted his tankard in mock toast.

"Yes, sir, we're conspirators, all right. We've just recruited a new man to the cause. Or at least subtracted one from the other side. We should celebrate."

"You're mighty free at celebrating with my own supply of spirits, Mr. Kent," Ware said with false seriousness. "What's the nature of this conspiracy?"

As soon as Lumden explained his decision, Ware clapped his hands in delight and demanded that they all drink several festive rounds.

"At my expense," he said with a look at Philip. "This time."

iii

Following the advice of Ben Edes, Philip decided to hire his help at the Green Dragon. Edes said boys who worked there were none too scrupulous about how they earned extra pay.

The boy on duty when Philip dropped in was an unkempt, ragged lad, one Jemmy Thaxter. Recognizing Philip as a friend, the landlord stated confidentially that, yes, Jemmy was willing to do illegal work when sufficiently rewarded.

"But he's been on the streets since he was seven or eight. So drive a sharp bargain. And keep any necessary secrets to yourself."

Philip disliked the fox-eyed twleve-year-old from the start. He especially hated Jemmy's putrid breath and his noxious habit of licking his crooked, yellowing upper teeth.

But Jemmy listened carefully, then said sure, he could come by a rickety cart and a horse in the slums of South Boston where he lived. Some risk to the venture? Never mind—all he cared about was the ten shillings.

Philip didn't ask how the boy intended to acquire the cart and the animal. Steal them, probably. Nor did he outline details of the plan, or its purpose. Those would

be revealed only just before Lumden's departure, when
it would be too late for the boy to betray them.

Jemmy shrugged, apparently unconcerned. "So long's
I'm paid, I'll sup with Old Nick himself. When's this
here cart and nag wanted?"

"When I tell you so and not before. Could be days.
Could be weeks. I'll let you know." The timing, Philip
had been told, was up to Lumden himself.

The whole scheme somehow made him apprehensive.
He charged it off to the worsening mood of the city. The
closed port put hundreds of men out of work at the
shipyards, the sail houses, the ropewalks. Why build a
vessel if she could only be launched to sit in the harbor?
Quarrelsome bands of the unemployed roamed the
streets, harassing Gage's soldiers. Attacks against the
troops became more frequent and more violent. The un-
wary enlisted man or officer who ventured out alone after dark stood the risk of being found the next morning
severely beaten or—in two cases Philip heard about—
dead. The only relief from the general grimness came
during the occasional moments he and Anne managed
to steal for themselves.

On the last night of the old year, he visited Launder
Street exactly as he'd done twelve months earlier. Anne
teasingly suggested they welcome 1775 in the manner
that had pleasured them both a year previously.

Accomplishing the suggestion proved a little harder.
Lawyer Ware yawned and retired well before the clock
chimed eleven. But Daisy and her sergeant kept the
kitchen humming with their claret-primed merriment.
Philip and Anne ultimately had to resort to the pretense
of announcing a short stroll in the wintry air just before
midnight.

Once into Launder Street, they slipped around
through twisting alleys to the sanctuary of the tiny barn,
where they shared each other's embraces with eagerness
and delight. But because of the glow from the kitchen

windows, they didn't dare linger too long. They returned to the house the way they had left, within half an hour after the tolling of the bells.

As the new year opened, food and supplies in the Ware home, as in all of Boston, became more and more limited. The Wares took to burning only a few sticks of kindling in the kitchen hearth at night, and none in the parlor.

And although Philip repeatedly offered Lumden reassurances that the plan would work smoothly, he continued to feel less than certain. Conditions in the city generated that kind of pessimism. Everything seemed to be breaking down.

While the days went by, Lumden grew increasingly fretful. Philip was worried that the man's agitated state would draw suspicion from his senior officers. Almost daily, so Anne reported, the sergeant vowed that he couldn't wait any longer. But he refused to name a day and hour when he would actually desert. Clearly, a violation of military law ran against his principles. Even though he was sustained by Daisy's romantic encouragements, the whole business placed him under a severe strain, Anne said.

Visiting Launder Street the next time, Philip discovered she hadn't exaggerated. Lumden spoke in monosyllables. He paced the Ware kitchen, up and down, up and down, fingering the mole on his forehead. On one of her trips to Dassett Alley, Anne said:

"I think if the poor man delays much longer, he'll suffer some kind of seizure. Or blurt out his guilt to the whole town. Do you suppose we should encourage him to abandon the idea?"

Philip shook his head. "I want that musket."

A somber pleasure brightened Anne's dark eyes. "Papa and I may make a revolutionary of you yet, Philip."

Ignoring the remark, he said, "I agree with you that

Lumden shouldn't keep waiting. Else he may well give the game away. We'll talk to him tonight. Try to force a decision. Speed, after all, is to his advantage. Adams is already predicting that Gage will move in the spring. Go after the militia stores out in the country in earnest. So if our sergeant delays and delays, he may be marching in battle formation whether he likes it or not."

Philip repeated the warning that same evening. The pale infantryman listened in silence. Wintering indoors in the city had turned his cheeks hollow but had added even more weight to his belly.

When Philip finished, Lumden gnawed his lip, said with effort:

"All right—Saturday. Tell the boy Saturday. When it's dark. I'll disappear after evening muster—"

"How soon will you be missed?"

"Not till late Sunday, I shouldn't imagine."

Daisy looked relieved. "I have all the clothing put by."

"Good," Philip said. "Saturday. Seven o'clock."

The next afternoon, Philip asked Ben Edes' permission for half an hour off. He trudged to the Dragon in a thin, sifting snow. He instructed Jemmy Thaxter to bring the cart and horse to Launder Street at the appointed time. Sniffling and wiping his nose on his sleeve, the boy promised he would.

Philip slept badly the two nights prior to Saturday. The day dawned dull gray and unseasonably warm. He had trouble concentrating on his work, the typesetting for Monday's edition of the paper. At closing time he locked the shop and rushed to Launder Street. He found Lumden again pacing the kitchen.

"Well, you do look the picture of a countryman," Philip nodded, taking in the sergeant's attire: a leather hunting shirt with decorative fringe; a flop-brimmed hat and a thick muffler of dark brown wool; dirty trousers that might once have been bottle green; worn boots with flapping sole pieces. Daisy had indeed secured the ultimate castoffs of other households.

"Smear some of that fireplace soot on your neck," Philip instructed. "Under your nails, too." He went to the parlor for a glance at the enameled clock. Nearly six-thirty already.

He lifted one of the draperies, peered into Launder Street. Why was he so damned jumpy? His mind swam with a memory of Jemmy Thaxter's foxy, opaque eyes.

At seven-thirty, standing beside him in the cold, lightless parlor, Anne voiced the fear that had become a certainty to Philip:

"Something's amiss. He's not coming."

"I'd better go find out what's happened—"

"Philip?" He turned on his way out. "Please be careful."

Nodding, he bundled into the surtout he'd purchased a few weeks ago for protection against the damp January winds. He tramped to the Green Dragon, pushed through the doors, blinked against the smoke—and clenched his teeth in fury at the sight of Jemmy Thaxter piling three new logs onto the irons of the blackened hearth.

The boy saw Philip immediately. He bolted for the back.

Philip ran after him, dodging among the startled patrons. "That's Ben Edes' devil!" one exclaimed. "What did Jemmy do this time, sell his sister and give the lad the pox—?"

Philip crashed out through the tavern's rear door, sprinted six steps along the alley, caught Jemmy's collar.

"Leave go!" the boy squealed. Instead, Philip shook him, hard.

"Seven o'clock's come and gone. Where's the horse? Where's the cart?"

Still struggling, Jemmy cried, "I don't want nothin' to do wif' a soldier running away!"

"*Running—?*"

Philip was so astounded, he nearly let the boy go by accident. But he held on. Jemmy coughed, a heavy, wheezing sound. Philip's mouth tightened. His voice dropped, threatening:

"How did you decide that's why the cart was wanted?" He shook Jemmy savagely. "Tell me or I'll break your damn bones!"

"I—I didn't think this was no straight deal from the start. I wanted to see wot I was gettin' into. So I follered you one night. From Edes' place to that house in Launder Street. I peeked in an' saw you talkin' to that lobsterback in the kitchen. He's goin' to ditch, ain't he? That's what I'm 'sposed to do, ain't it, help smuggle him 'cross the Neck? Well, I don't like bloody Tommy any better'n the next. But I ain't mixing in helping somebody from the Thirty-third run away. Ten shillings ain't worth it—nothing's worth it— you git a whip or a musket ball if you're caught—*quit holding me so hard!*"

Something in the boy's darting eyes started suspicion churning inside Philip. But he couldn't quite pin down what was wrong. Especially when his anger was running high, urging him to administer a beating. The frail, dirty boy disgusted him.

"So you haven't got the horse or the cart?" he asked.

Jemmy gulped, admitted it was so. Philip flung him away, cursing.

"Ain't you going to hit me or nothing?"

"Hell, why? The harm's done. But let me warn you, Jemmy. Boy or no boy, breathe a word to a soul and you'll be called on by some gentlemen in liberty caps. They won't spare you because of your age, you sneaking little bastard."

Coughing out a mist of spittle, Jemmy cowered back against the fence opposite the Dragon's rear door. "There won't be a word—nobody knows 'cept me. I

haven't even told the lady, God's truth! I just decided
not to go through with it, is all—"

"Why didn't you tell me that, dammit?"

"I—I was scairt to. I thought you'd beat me."

"Remember that you'll be beaten worse if you don't
keep your mouth closed."

"I will—I swear."

Again Philip felt that sting of suspicion; again he
failed to define the source. It was obvious he'd simply
approached the wrong boy, and now Lumden's whole
escape was in jeopardy. Once more he tried to read
Jemmy's grubby face, darting eyes. He couldn't.

Turning, he sped off up the alley, intending to run all
the way to Launder Street.

At least, he thought as he raced along with the night
air stinging his cheeks, Lumden could return to his unit
for the next muster and not be missed. But Philip also
realized he'd have to call at the Dragon a few more
times, to make certain he'd put sufficient fear into
Jemmy Thaxter to ensure the boy's silence—

A silence which the next moments revealed to be a
fraud.

Philip rounded the corner into the street where
Lawyer Ware's house showed lamplight at its parlor
windows. He stopped in mid-stride, cold dread clawing
his middle.

In front of the house, reins looped and tied to the ring
of the mounting block, a horse fretted and blew out
plumes of vapor.

Philip had seen enough wealthy people riding on the
Common to recognize an expensive saddle. What person
of means was calling on Abraham Ware just at the hour
when Lumden's escape was supposed to be taking
place? It was too damned coincidental for comfort—

Stealing toward the stoop, Philip suddenly recalled
something else. Jemmy had specifically identified Lum-

den's regiment. That was what had been nagging his mind!

Perhaps the boy already knew which regiment wore willow-green facings.

But if not, why would he go to the trouble of finding out? Unless—

Nerves taut, he crept up the front steps, crouched and peered through a slit where drapery and window frame didn't quite meet. Terror soured his throat as he caught a flash of scarlet inside—

An officer's tunic!

Waiting only long enough to confirm that with a second look, Philip whirled and darted back down the steps. The horse neighed, clopped its hoofs. Philip edged away, stole through the passage beside the house and across the tiny yard under the pale stars.

As he approached the closed barn door, his mind seethed with fury. What had happened had become all too evident.

First, he'd blundered, let himself be followed.

And Jemmy had been lying when he claimed he wanted no part of the desertion. The boy's gutter mind had simply recognized a chance for bigger profit. How much had he gotten from the officers of the Thirty-third for informing on the would-be deserter?

Starting to roll back the barn door, Philip again cursed his own foolish mistake. *Who was in the house? What was happening?*

With the door no more than half open, he heard quick movement. Something flashed toward his face. He ducked instinctively, drove his left hand up, battered Lumden's musket aside. A second slower, and the bayonet would have pierced his throat—

"Lumden—hold still!" The terrified sergeant kept trying to wrench his musket loose. *"God damn it, stop! It's me!"*

At last Lumden recognized Philip. He lowered the musket with a trembling hand, whispered:

"Kent—what in the name of Christ went wrong?"

"The boy sold us out. My fault."

"I thought I'd gone stark raving crazy when Daisy spied one of the regimental officers riding up to the front door—"

"Who is it?"

"I don't know, I ran out here to hide. Mistress Anne said she could get rid of him."

Philip prayed Anne's confidence would prove warranted. She, Daisy and Ware had carefully discussed and rehearsed the story they would tell if anyone from Lumden's regiment came searching for him. The story was to be simple and, therefore, easily kept consistent. They would merely state that Lumden had vanished without any explanation.

But though the household had planned on the certainty of an investigation, they had *not* planned on it taking place until Lumden was well out of Boston. To have an officer pounce while the sergeant was still hidden on the premises was a development even the courageous and quick-witted Anne might not be able to handle.

Philip wished her father were home to help. But he knew that Ware, anticipating no difficulty with the departure, had left Launder Street at five, to confer, then dine, at Hancock's.

Chafing his hands against the cold, Philip kept glancing toward the rear of the house. He saw lights but no sign of movement in the kitchen.

He had to trust Anne. Depend on Anne. Her good sense, her bravery—

"Why is the officer here now, Kent? You haven't explained!"

"He's here because that little sod from the Dragon

must have gone to your regimental headquarters. The
boy pretended the plan was too risky. Said he followed
me here, saw you inside, guessed it was a desertion—wanted no part of it at any price. Obviously that's
not true. He saw a chance to get a higher price from
someone else, just for reporting—look, we're wasting
time. Gather up your gear. We'll slip out the back way.
Go to the shop. Anne will be able to turn the officer
away. But he'll probably want to verify any claim that
you're not here—"

"But she may be telling him I *am* here!"

"I doubt it. She knows you'd be questioned. Hard. So
you'd better not be around. Come on, I'll help you—"

He bent in the darkness, fumbled Lumden's pack
straps into his hands—

And went rigid at the sound of a woman crying out in
terror—or pain.

The scream came from the house.

Philip bowled past Lumden, snatched up the
sergeant's musket. He loosened the bayonet from the
muzzle in seconds. With the length of steel glittering in
his hand, he dashed across the yard and up the kitchen
steps as the cry rang out again.

This time he had no doubt that it was Anne's voice.

CHAPTER VIII

Journey to Darkness

i

PHILIP WASTED NO TIME on silence. He kicked the porch door open, sped through the kitchen with barely a glimpse of Daisy O'Brian, round-eyed and uttering small, wordless sounds of terror.

She had good reason to be frightened out of her wits. As he reached the closed parlor doors, he caught the sounds of struggle on the other side.

His breath was a ghostly cloud in the chill darkness. The front hall was illuminated only by the faint light of the January stars through the fanlight. He pressed close to the carved wood of the doors, heard a pained exclamation from Anne—then a voice that dredged up memories of depthless fear and hatred:

"—will not lie to me further, madam! Has he fled or are you concealing him? Come, which is it?"

The familiar voice sounded heavy with sudden exertion. Anne let out another little cry.

"Other commanders may delegate unpleasant business like this, madam. But I punish personally. I punish both those under my direct command and any who abet their treachery—"

Philip pried the doors apart with his free hand and stepped into the parlor's dim lamplight.

He knew the voice—and the man—beyond all doubting. He saw other details only marginally—

Anne's gown disheveled; ripped down the right sleeve, where the officer held her with his left hand—

The man's scarlet tunic, seen from the back. But even from that viewpoint, Philip recognized the additional height, the wider shoulders—

The officer wore his sword in an unusual position. On his right hip.

Because he would have to wield the weapon with a hand that was not crippled—?

Anne glimpsed Philip across the officer's shoulder. She couldn't conceal her reaction. The officer heard Philip's quiet voice even as he started to turn.

"Yes, that would be like you, now that you no longer have to act secretly. Now that your uniform gives you the authority to strike in the open."

Like an image from a half-remembered nightmare, Philip saw the face at last. The features so like his own. The small, cloven U mark near the left brow. For a moment Roger Amberly's expression remained blank. Philip waited at the doorway, bayonet held near his waist.

The stunning recognition hit.

"My God in heaven. *Charboneau?*"

He saw the ruin of his half-brother's hand. The fingers were permanently tightened into a claw, much as Lumden had shown him. The hand had a shrunken, bloodless appearance, as if it had not only locked in its crippled position, but withered from lack of use. It looked tiny, dangling at the end of an otherwise normal arm.

The disfiguring mark turned darker, almost black. Roger Amberly's face became a show of confusion—disbelief and rage mingled as he struggled to comprehend the reality of the man confronting him. The young officer's splendid red coat with its cuffs and lapels of willow green stained the scene with vivid color.

Never taking his eyes from his half-brother, Roger relaxed his grip on Anne's arm. She retreated a step, watching tensely as Philip sought to control the rage in his own mind and heart.

"Charboneau?" Philip repeated. "You're wrong, Colonel. Charboneau died in London. Or was it on the Bristol road? If not one, then the other—as you intended, correct? Charboneau's mother is also dead—because of your harassment. It's a man named Philip Kent you must deal with now." He gestured savagely with the bayonet. "Get outside, so I don't spill your God damn blood in this house!"

To Roger's credit, he stood still, composed. "Philip—what?—Kent?" he said. His mouth took on its familiar, mean twist. "Well, a new name hardly conceals the insufferable bastard boy I met formerly. And I find you in a traitor's house to boot. Oh, yes—" The slight turn of his head was for Anne's benefit "—The dwelling of Mr. Abraham Ware is well known to the general's staff as a place where these so-called patriots hatch treason."

Very slowly, he reached across with his left hand, gripped his sword hilt, suddenly freed the blade with amazing speed. His eyes loomed huge and dark in the shifting flicker of the two lamps. His loathing poured like a torrent through one more sentence he spoke:

"It shall give me considerable pleasure to write my good wife, Alicia—with whom I believe you were briefly acquainted—that circumstances presented me with the opportunity to finally bring about your long-overdue death." Without warning, he ran at Philip, left arm extended, sword reaching out—

Philip had no time to think, only to react in order to save himself. He twisted aside. Roger's sword gouged into one of the doors. For a moment Philip smelled his blood kin: the scented powder in his hair, the damp odor of his woolen coat, the sudden sweaty odor that danger produces in all men. The half brothers stood no more than a foot apart for one frozen instant. Roger's midsection was fully exposed by the force and extension of his lunge. Philip brought his right hand up and stabbed the bayonet into Roger's belly and pulled it out.

Roger's mouth dropped open. His shoulders sagged. He did a peculiar step to the side, his boot heels clicking. Then he stared down at the pierced wool to the left of his brightly polished buttons.

A darker red appeared in the cut in the fabric—and spread, staining. Struggling for breath, Roger let out a labored exclamation.

Now that his initial thoughtless fury had been drained away in the single driving blow of the reddened bayonet, Philip turned cold. Roger was dying on his feet—

It took him a moment to fall. Blurring, his dark eyes seemed to search for Philip, his bravado replaced by a horror-struck look of hurt, by the realization that he might be mortally injured.

Philip felt weak, almost sick. His enemy no longer looked formidable, only helpless. Roger's sword struck the pegged floor to one side of the carpet. With a last, bubbling grunt of pain, he dropped.

Thrusting the bloody bayonet under his left arm, Philip cried, "Help me, Anne!"

She stumbled forward, grabbed Roger's right shoulder. The two turned Roger so that he lay on his back. Mouth open, eyes shut, he gasped like a beached fish. All at once Philip realized the full significance of what had happened—and what had to be done.

"We must get him out. He mustn't bloody the place, because someone will surely come to ask about him. I'll take him through the back. Dispose of the body. You—"He spoke with difficulty; he was still trembling"—you go to the street and untie his horse. Get it going—away from here."

"When—when Daisy announced him," Anne said in

a faint voice, "I could hardly keep my hands still, they were shaking so badly—"

Philip held up one of his own. "Like mine."

"Yes. I knew who he was. But he was in such a fury he didn't notice immediately. How did he get here, Philip? How did he know——?"

"The boy from the Dragon gave us away. Probably took a higher price for telling Lumden's officers he planned to desert. Did you admit anything to Amberly?"

"Nothing. I denied having seen George all day. I denied any knowledge of his desertion. But your brother kept staring at me—he frightened me terribly. I think he knew I was lying. I could tell the first moment he walked in that he was all you'd said, and more."

"Well, we're done with him." The implication of those words still rocked him to the center of his being. "The horse, Anne. But quietly. So none of the neighbors are roused——"

Philip slid Roger's sword back in its scabbard, began to haul the still form by the collar. He dragged the body through the black hallway, seeing Anne limned briefly against the radiance of lamps alight in the house opposite. Then the front door shut.

By the time he reached the kitchen, he thought he heard horseshoes ring on cobblestones. He winced at the loudness.

Daisy rushed to the kitchen door when she heard him coming, looked at the closed eyes, saw the widening stain at the belly of the uniform and ground her knuckles against her mouth. She started those small, incoherent sounds again. Philip realized she might easily become hysterical.

His eyes locked with hers. "Daisy."

"Wh—what?"

"Make no sound or we're undone. I need George's help. I need his help to carry the body so we don't leave blood."

He let go of Roger Amberly's collar. There was a sickening thump when the powdered head struck the floor. Philip drew the bayonet out from under the arm of his surtout, walked by the round-eyed girl, laid the bayonet on the kitchen table.

"Daisy, fetch Lumden. And find me rags to wipe this thing clean. Then burn the ra—*damn you, girl, do what I say!*"

Still dazed, she stumbled out into the darkness. She returned in a few moments with the astonished sergeant.

Staring down at his commanding officer, Lumden seemed pleased—but only for a few seconds. His gray eyes misted with shock. And perhaps pity.

Still struggling against a feeling of numbness, unreality, Philip cleared his throat, said:

"We'll take him through the alleys. Several blocks—as far as we can go without being detected. Then we'll come back here, clean this place and get out."

"We?"

"I'm going with you. That's the only way you'll ever escape Boston now."

"Kent, it's not your affair. I mean—I'm the one wanting to desert—"

"But you can't get across the Neck by yourself. And Amberly must have told someone on his staff what he planned to do. Take his boots, man. Hurry!"

Philip bent, gripped the limp shoulders. He tried to keep his eyes away from the slack lips, the waxy eyelids, the bloodstain that had now spread beneath Roger's jacket to redden his white trousers at the groin and down the inside of his right leg. With a heave, the two men lifted the body, struggled it off the porch and carried it around the barn. After a survey of the crooked alley behind the property, they turned to the right.

They crossed a deserted street, running with their burden. They plunged into another alley. In about two minutes they carried the officer some three squares from Launder Street.

As they were about to dart across one more dark thoroughfare, Philip dropped the body suddenly. Hoofs rang out a couple of blocks away. Wheels creaked. A coach—coming at a good clip.

"We'll leave him here," Philip whispered, shoving the limp form against the wall of a building near the alley mouth. He positioned the body so the head faced the brick wall. The approaching coach thundered—

There was no longer the remotest sense of satisfaction in any of this, only a desperate urgency. He and Lumden backed to the wall, stood elbow to elbow to hide Roger as best they could. Philip prayed the darkness was sufficient concealment—

The two-horse berlin rumbled by, hoofs and iron-shod wheels raising sparks.

As soon as the coach had passed, Philip grabbed Lumden's arm. He shoved the slow-moving man back in the direction of Ware's house.

Rushing along, he tried to organize his tumultuous thoughts. In only a few ticks of time, the present had crumbled—and the future as well. He knew exactly what must be done. There remained the dangerous task of implementing the decision. He cursed Roger Amberly silently as he and Lumden ran along the barn wall and up the porch. Anne and Daisy waited in the kitchen, both of them still pale.

Philip kicked the door shut. On the table lay the bayonet, freshly wiped, free of blood. In the hearth a scrap of rag sent up a curl of smoke.

Well, that was a start toward salvaging the disaster of the past half-hour.

ii

"I'll go to your father's farm," he announced to

Daisy. He was sitting at the table. His head had started
to ache horribly.

Her chestnut hair all a-tangle around her shoulders,
Anne seemed about to offer an argument. Philip prevented it:

"It's the only way Lumden can leave Boston—and he
must leave *tonight*. Where's the rum, Daisy?"

The red-haired cook hurried into the pantry and
brought back the demiflagon set aside earlier to implement the escape. Philip took the jug, placed it on the
table, holding it with both hands to mask the trembling
of his fingers.

"Do you think your father will take us in?" he asked
Daisy.

Wide-eyed, she nodded.

"How do we find the farm? It's out past Concord, you
said—"

"Once you reach the village, you cross North Bridge.
Keep on along the road going west. You'll pass a large
farmhouse. It belongs to Colonel Barrett. About a half-
mile beyond, there's another, not quite so big. That's
my father's."

"All right." He glanced up. Anne was watching him.
She looked exhausted, and far less assured than he had
ever seen her.

"Anne, it will be difficult for you here, so try to prepare yourself. Another officer—perhaps several—will
surely come from Lumden's regiment. Maybe as early as
tomorrow. You did loose the horse—?"

"And saw him gone out of sight."

"We'll just have to trust our luck—which so far
tonight has been very poor indeed. If none of your
neighbors grew overly curious when they heard Amberly's horse arrive—*and* if none of them looked out
their windows to see a British officer walk up to your
door—there will be nothing to link him to this house.
Except his intention to come here. Which he surely

didn't keep to himself back at headquarters. So your story is this: He never arrived. Once we're gone, make sure there's no evidence of it. Check the parlor for blood. For traces of his hair powder—out in the hall too, where I dropped him. Tell your father what happened. Be certain he's ready to deny, as you'll deny—and you, Daisy—any knowledge of the sergeant's plans to desert."

"All right," Anne said.

"You never heard him speak of it, understand? Never."

"Yes."

"He kept to himself except at meals. If he intended to leave his regiment, the secret was his and nobody else's. Now—" Thinking of what he was about to tell them, Philip's eyes grew ugly with frustration. Was there no end to the running? To the destruction of even the smallest hope for a future?

With effort, he mastered the self-pity, went on with what he'd started to say:

"In a day or two, when the danger's past, you must tell two people that I've gone. But only two. You needn't explain why. Just say I was in trouble and had to escape."

"Who must I tell?" Anne asked.

"Ben Edes and Henry Knox. Let them know I'll return to Boston when I can. Ask Edes to give you my sword and my mother's casket."

"And your bottle of tea?" Anne's effort at a smile failed.

"If you wish. I'd feel safer with those things stored here. Edes' shop may go up in flames one day soon—or be closed on order of General Gage."

Again the silent motion of her head agreed to his request. Philip laid his palms on the table, pushed up, feeling incredibly tired but a little less shaky than he had in those first moments when he realized he'd struck

down his mortal enemy—and taken not a fraction of the
pleasure from it that he had anticipated for so long. In
fact, Roger's death had only added a further complica-
tion to an already peril-fraught situation.

George Lumden, who now looked reasonably alert
and had been listening attentively, spoke up:

"Shall I get the musket from the barn, Philip?"

"No, leave it where it is," he answered, reluctantly
handing over the bayonet. "And put this with it. The
weapons and your equipment will help confirm Anne's
story. Anne, be sure to show the musket to anyone from
his regiment—"

"I will."

"If it's not confiscated you can arrange to give it to
Knox for the Grenadier Company."

Philip still wanted the musket himself. But he had
already ruled out taking it along. Possessing a Brown
Bess would virtually guarantee their failure to pass the
guard lines at Roxbury Neck.

He wiped his mouth with the back of his hand. He
glanced from Daisy to Anne, including them both in his
final remarks:

"We'll rely on you to send us word of conditions here.
To notify us somehow if and when it's safe to come
back. George—" He bobbed his head at the red-haired
country girl."—say your goodbyes. But don't be too long
about it. The quicker we head for the Neck, the surer we
can be of getting across."

His words belied his doubt about the ease of the
escape. They had no official papers of passage.
Sometimes the troops let farmers through without
them, sometimes not. They stood an excellent chance of
being turned back.

But he said nothing. Things were bad enough already.

iii

Under the star-glowing fanlight of the front hall, Philip stole a few moments to take Anne in his arms, stroke her hair, whisper his own farewells. With his mouth pressing the warmth of her cheek, and her hands tight at the back of his surtout, he experienced a strange, almost melancholy emotion—

A conviction that not even in their most intimate moments had he ever felt so deeply about her—so concerned, so caring.

Was that love?

Well, whatever the name of the emotion, it brought an unashamed tear to the corner of his eye as they clung to each other in the darkness.

On their way to the front of the house, Anne had shut the parlor doors, as if the act could somehow obliterate what had taken place. But he knew it was not so easy as simply closing a door.

"Anne, I ask you to forgive me."

"For what?"

"For placing you and your father in danger. Danger that may last for days—weeks—perhaps months. I struck Roger without thinking—"

"Because he struck at you!"

"Yes, but that doesn't change—"

The pressure of her fingers against his lips stilled the rest. Her hand was cold, proof she was still very much frightened. But her voice remained calm:

"We'll see it through. The only flaw in everything you suggested is the possibility that someone did see Amberly arrive. I'll coach Daisy to meet that eventuality. She can be prepared to say she received him at the door and reported George gone."

"That's risky. When you're questioned, you may not know whether some of your Tory neighbors have already spoken with the investigators."

"It's a risk we'll have to face—and a situation we'll have to handle as it happens. We'll manage." Again she tried to smile. "Papa's a lawyer, you know. Artful dissembling's not entirely unknown in that profession. Perhaps the men who come won't be clever about their investigation. If we can pick up some hint of whether they've already visited other houses, we can fashion the response accordingly. Either say Amberly did stop, and went on when Daisy reported George gone—or use your story. Amberly never got here at all. Don't worry—women know how to improvise. Constantly fending off men, we have to learn that skill early!"

Her light tone failed to fit the moment. But he knew she was trying to reassure him, a reversal of the scene in the kitchen. He leaned forward to kiss her lips, hesitated as she added quietly:

"In a way, Philip, this night could mark an important turning. I know how the memory of that man ate at you. Now that page of the past is closed. You can go ahead—"

"To being a fugitive?" he said bitterly. "By God, that's not what I planned when I landed on Long Wharf!"

"What did you plan? To grow rich in the printing trade, as you've mentioned? Then go back to England and show them what a fine Tory gentleman you'd become? So you could see that woman again—?"

Her voice had risen. Abruptly, she stopped, averted her head.

"I'm sorry. I admit I've a jealous hatred of her. And a wish that you'll finally discover yourself to be what I think you are."

"It appears I have damned little choice about what I am. Things seem to have a way of getting out of hand these days—"

"The world's always been that way, Philip. There's

something else happening now. Not chance alone destroying the future, but men."

Maybe she was right, he thought, holding her close again. Maybe that was the essential nature of the struggle Adams and Edes and the rest were waging: to free themselves from the capricious dictates of people who would dominate and destroy their lives in a test of wills, a test of an old, creaking system—

Ah, but what the hell good did such idealism—a noble cause—do at a time like this?

The gentle heat of Anne's warming cheek helped soothe away some of his turmoil. She whispered with her lips against his face:

"I'll send word to the farm as quickly as I can. Meanwhile, remember this. I love you." She kissed him with a desperate fierceness.

A noise at the rear of the hallway separated them. It was Daisy and Lumden, the latter lugging the demiflagon of rum.

"I think we'd best go the back way," Philip said.

Feeling alone and not a little afraid, he walked toward the barn with the nervous sergeant at his elbow. The dampness of the January night penetrated even the warm surtout. He turned briefly for a final look at the kitchen's cheery light—and saw Daisy and Anne watching together. Anne's hand lifted in a small gesture of farewell.

He straightened his shoulders and followed Lumden in the darkness. Somewhere the cadence of a regimental drum beating the night's tap-to echoed along the lonely streets.

Their route led them through South Boston, within a block of the Liberty Tree. On its great soughing branches a single, forlorn paper lantern burned. *Shining about as brightly as the hopes of Mr. Edes and friends for peacefully winning their battle,* Philip thought in a moment of deep pessimism.

Even as he watched, a gust of wind blew the lantern out.

iv

On Orange Street, Philip called a halt in the shadow of a ramshackle building. In the distance, beyond the double arch of the town gate, torches winked at the guard post on the Neck.

"Now, George," he announced with a smile that had no substance, "the anointing. And don't forget—not one single, coherent word. You may stumble. You may mutter. But don't let them hear you speak. I'll do the talking."

Tossing away the demiflagon's cork, he poured rum down Lumden's collar, sprinkled some into his hair, then handed him the jug.

"Don't drink. Just take in a good mouthful and hold it a minute, so you'll reek inside as well as out."

The sergeant dutifully tilted the jug, filled his mouth and shut his lips till his cheeks bulged. At last he spat the rum into the gutter. A scraggly dog that had come slinking around the corner caught some of the spray, reacted with a yapping bark. Philip picked up a stone and flung it.

The dog ran off a short distance. But it continued to bark, the noise unnaturally loud in the stillness of the night. Down at the guard post, Philip thought he saw figures moving, aroused by the racket. He swore softly as he slipped his arm beneath Lumden's.

"Lean on me, George. Try to act drunk. Hum a little if you want—but not some Goddamn regimental song!"

They approached the gate and passed through. The moment they did, the wind struck them, whipping across the narrow stretch of land. Philip shivered. Lumden's teeth chattered.

The muddy road out of Boston was rutted from wagon tires, bore countless prints of men and animals. The figures at the barrier ahead took on more definition. Two—no, three British soldiers, one inside the jerrybuilt booth, the others waiting at the horizontal pole.

Philip and the sergeant walked slowly, erratically along the strip of land that connected Boston to the countryside beyond. Ahead, a few lamps in Roxbury burned yellow in the vast darkness. The Charles River lapped on one hand, the harbor on the other, redolent with the tang of the salt sea.

Philip could smell the rum, though. But could Lumden carry off the deception? For that matter, could he?

He had almost, but not entirely, lost the traces of his foreign speech. And if the sergeant accidentally spoke one word, the soldiers would know instantly that he was no Massachusetts man.

As they neared the barrier, Philip said in a loud, complaining voice, "Come on, stand up straight!"

He paused long enough to lob another rock at the dog, still pursuing, still barking. The stone hit the animal's hindquarters, sent him running with a yelp.

Despite the cold night air, Lumden's cheeks shone with sweat. *Damn. Not good,* Philip thought, half-carrying his tangle-footed companion toward the pole.

Two redcoats stood in the snapping glare of torches stuck into the wall of the guard booth. The soldiers brought their muskets up to waist level, bayonets shining. One looked to be no more than fifteen or sixteen. The other was older, a paunchy veteran.

Lumden mumbled and pretended to sag. Philip struggled to prop him up, growling, "Goddamn it, Ned, stand on your pins. I'll not carry you all the way to Roxbury!"

Lumden did a good imitation of drunken blathering

as the heavyset redcoat prodded Philip's chest lightly
with his bayonet.

"No passage to Roxbury till you answer a couple of
questions. What be your names?"

Philip dredged up a last name Knox had mentioned
once, replied, "George Kemble, sir. I farm land outside
Roxbury. My cousin Ned here—Ned Kemble—he's got
a fondness for the town whores. They got him drunk, as
usual. I had to come in and fetch him out of one of the
deadfalls."

The soldier peered into Lumden's face. Lumden affected a moon grin, letting slobber leak over his lower
lip. The soldier looked disgusted.

"Have ye papers to prove your identity?"

"Papers?" Philip feigned a witless look, then a queasy
smile. "Sir, neither Ned or me can write a line. Farm-
ing's what we know. When we sign, it's with a mark.
Listen, I come into Boston at noon without anybody
asking me for papers—"

"Coming in, yes. Going out's a different story.
Bastards like that silver-maker Revere must have papers
'cos they might be on treasonous errands."

"Oh." Tense, Philip tried to look merely unhappy.

"Let go of your cousin, then," said the soldier. "Ye
can't pass without a search."

Philip reluctantly released his burden. Lumden
swayed and clawed at empty air. Philip grabbed him
hastily, causing the sergeant to laugh and spit on the
muddied road.

"Two of the colony's finest! Tell me, Kemble—" He
laid his musket against the pole, started to poke and
probe Philip's surtout."—are you lads members of
these militia companies we hear about? The fine units
they say will take the field against us one day?"

"The Kemble family's loyal to King George, sir,"
Philip said with a toadying smile.

"Ah, yas—"The soldier's quick hand patted down Philip's breeches, squeezed his boots."—every bloody one who comes to the barrier says that. Then we find daggers hid, or cartridges an' ball. 'Course, it really makes no damn difference. If ye ever do have a mind to fight the King's regiments, there's but one thing waiting for you an' the rest who march up an' down with them silly sticks on their shoulders—a grave, Kemble. A grave's waiting for ye. All right. How's the other one, Arch?"

The younger soldier who had been searching Lumden said, "Nothing on him except the smell of dirt an' rum."

Philip seethed at the way the paunchy soldier had spoken with such contempt for the military skills of the colonists. Perhaps if he knew a Henry Knox—!

But he didn't dare let his temper best him now. The paunchy soldier was reaching for the rope that controlled the pole—

The pole creaked as it rose in the wind. The torches snapped and sparked. Philip swallowed, propped Lumden up again, began to urge him forward:

"Walk, Ned, for Christ's sake! All full of drink, you weigh a short ton and you're saggy as a sack of shit besides—"

From the corner of his eye Philip saw the guard booth drop behind. And the pole. Lumden pretended to stumble in the mud. Philip cuffed his ear for effect, cursing even more floridly.

Another step.

Another. The darkness pricked by the lights of Roxbury seemed a reachable haven now.

One more step.

One more—

"Hold up."

Philip clenched his teeth at the sound of the younger soldier's voice. The third redcoat had emerged from the booth to lean on the pole as the boy and his paunchy comrade dodged under and hurried after Philip and Lumden.

The younger soldier grabbed Philip's shoulder roughly. He lost his grip on Lumden. The latter, acting with a vengeance, tumbled face forward into the mud. Harder than he'd expected. A single word burst out explosively—

"Damme!"

We're done, Philip thought as hands jerked his left arm up. The boy soldier said:

"Look there at what you missed! Noticed it when he was walkin' away. That's blood or I ain't never seen it."

"So 'tis, Arch," grumbled the older one, whirling Philip around. Lumden was pushing up from the oozing mud, clambering to his feet. Philip hoped to God that the distraction of the suddenly discovered bloodstain under the arm of his surtout—where he'd gripped the bayonet—might have distracted the soldiers from realizing Lumden had cursed in pure, British English.

"Where'd you come by that, Kemble?" the older one demanded. "Let's have an explanation—and quick."

Philip wriggled free, still maintaining his fawning grin.

"Sirs—didn't I mention already? Ned got mixed up with some real sluts. They damn near clawed me to pieces 'fore I could drag him away. Least I imagine that's how the blood got there. One of the whores had a little knife. I took it away from her and kind of cut her—by accident, y'know?" He winked. "She bled a storm—"

The heavy soldier acted dubious. "Funny place for the blood to land, though."

"Admit it is. Just can't explain it any better. In the fracas I wasn't too particular about keepin' clean. I slipped and fell a couple of times. Maybe there was some of her blood on the floor of the crib, I dunno."

Philip could feel the sweat rivering down the back of his neck. The longer they were detained, the greater the chances they would be detained permanently—turned back. He tried one last, huge grin.

"Guarantee you one thing, though. I fixed that whore just fine. There's one less fluff in Boston to give you a dose of the pox."

That amused the heavy man. "Well, I'd say that's a real service to the Crown. I'm a man who likes his fuckin', but I had that French pox once. It makes you feel like you're bloody well pissin' needles." He stepped back. "Pass on."

"Yes, sir. Thank you, sir."

Supporting Lumden again, Philip fought the urge to run. He forced himself to walk away from the soldiers slowly, his eyes on the wagon-tracked ground ahead of his boots.

The ground grew darker—darker—

At last the periphery of the torchlight was left behind.

The mournful sounds of wind and rolling water filled the night. Roxbury was ahead—and a longer road beyond. Seventeen miles or so stretched between them and Concord village. The darkness began to seem forbidding, hostile.

And well it might, he thought. In order to help Lumden, he'd left Anne behind, her safety, her very freedom uncertain.

All at once Lumden started to blurt out his thanks. Philip hissed at him to keep silent. The thick, gummy mud pulled at their boots with sucking sounds. The night was growing decidedly colder. The wind slashed out of the Atlantic from the northeast.

Philip hardly noticed the string of in-bound carts creaking toward Boston with loads of fish. When the carts were gone, the road again became as empty and bleak as the future to which the disastrous circumstances on Launder Street had led him. Head down, hands deep in the pockets of his surtout, he kept walking into the enormous dark.

Book Four

The Road From Concord Bridge

CHAPTER I

The Letter

i

A COCK CROWED THE morning. The second morning since the two fugitives had crossed Roxbury Neck. Shivering in the chill, his belly growling, Philip crouched in a roadside ditch and peered at the clapboard farmhouse, its weathervane just turning a sulfurous orange in the January dawn.

Behind the farmhouse stood two dilapidated outbuildings. The larger, a barn, was still indistinct in the shadow cast by the frost-whitened hillside immediately behind. Inside the barn, horses whickered. A cow lowed.

They had been watching the O'Brian farmstead for almost ten minutes. Philip said:

"Come on, George, for God's sake! Let's march up and wake him. I'll stand behind your explanation."

The sergeant fingered the mole on his forehead, his habit when in a state of nerves, Philip had observed.

"I wish I'd asked Daisy for some token," Lumden said. "Something her father would recognize as hers—"

Philip jumped the frozen water in the bottom of the ditch, climbed up the bank to the road.

"Well, I'm not waiting any longer. I'm damn near dead from hunger and just about frozen stiff from the wind. What's he going to do, shoot us for redcoats?"

"He might," said Lumden dourly. "I know for a fact Gage has sent out spies disguised as farmers." His teeth

519

started chattering again as he followed Philip to the road.

They'd walked most of two nights and half the intervening day. They had traveled north from Brookline through Cambridge, then northwest to the hamlet of Lexington, and five miles more to larger Concord, which appeared to be a substantial village, perhaps as many as a thousand or fifteen hundred souls. It boasted clusters of prosperous-looking homes, a grist mill situated at one end of a pond of some size, a meeting house and a tavern the creaking signboard identified as Wright's.

On their journey they had gone parallel to the main roads, avoiding the roads themselves, because of the chance that they might be pursued. So the trip had been slow going. Clad only in the fringed leather shirt, Lumden had suffered worst from the winter air.

Passing through Concord village just before first light, they crossed the purling Concord River via a narrow wooden footbridge northwest of town. The land here was different from the flatter country around Lexington. Ridges crested against the skyline. The road Daisy had told them to follow wound between low hills.

They passed the farm she had identified as belonging to someone named Barrett. The next place, poorer than the first, looked bleak in the cold orange glow just touching the eastern ridges.

"George, hurry it up, will you?" Philip grumped now, determined to delay the confrontation no longer.

As they crossed the road and started up the narrow track leading past the house, a figure emerged from the gloom around the barn. Philip and Lumden halted, caught in the open, fully visible in the light brightening the eastern hills.

The figure stood motionless near the barn door, strangely dark, even about the face. A shadow-man.

Philip's heart beat faster. His hand came up, his mouth opened to hail the watcher, let him know they were not thieves—

The figure darted back inside the barn.

Lumden started to ask a worried question. Philip waved him silent, sprinting for the front of the house just in case his fears proved to have foundation.

They did. The shadow-man reappeared, a musket raised to his shoulder.

"Down!" Philip shouted, leaping sideways to tackle Lumden and roll him into the frozen grass as the musket exploded with a puff of smoke.

Philip heard the ball whiz past, strike somewhere out on the road, spent. He shot up a hand, waved.

"Wait! We're friends. Sent here by Daisy O'Brian—"

Already re-loading, the man by the barn hesitated. Within the house, Philip heard cursing.

The man from the barn loped forward, turning his empty musket and grasping it by the barrel, a club. Philip clambered to his feet slowly and drew in a surprised breath. He saw why the man had blended so completely with the barn shadows.

Black hands gripped the musket's muzzle. White teeth glinted between black lips. The Negro was middle-aged, plainly dressed in boots, old trousers, a coarse gray farmer's shirt. But he had a powerful, resilient look about him. Beneath the poll of grizzled hair, his dark eyes were not friendly.

"Honest folks don't come sneakin' into farmyards 'fore the light's up," he said, passing the corner of the house and coming to within a couple of feet of Philip and his companion. "But horse thieves do. Tell me who you be—and right now."

The farmhouse door opened. Behind a plume of breath, Philip glimpsed a short, rotund man in a nightshirt that hung to his bare ankles. The man's eyes and rosy face bore a certain resemblance to Daisy's.

"What the hell you shooting for, Arthur?" the farmer barked.

"Shooting at a couple very strange birds, Mr. O'Brian," said the Negro. "Spotted 'em creepin' across the road."

"We're friends—" Philip began.

"You're a damn liar." O'Brian scrutinized the pair with cold blue eyes. "I never seen either of you before."

"Mr. O'Brian, let me explain," Philip said, taking a single step toward the porch. Arthur tightened his dark hands on the musket muzzle, lifted it back across his right shoulder, ready to strike.

"It's true you don't know us. My name is Kent. This is George Lumden—"

"You still haven't told me anything. Where d'you hail from?"

"Boston. We both know your daughter."

"You do, eh?" A pause. "Which one?"

"The one in Boston of course."

"What's her name?"

"Daisy."

The farmer pondered. Then: "State your business."

"Mr. Lumden's a former soldier of the King's infantry. I helped him escape two nights ago. Daisy sent us here because—"

Well, why not out with it?

"—because Mr. Lumden and your daughter have plans to marry."

Philip thought O'Brian was going to faint. "*Marry*—? You come skulking to the house before the moon's down, and greet me with the news that this one is my future son-in-law? Blessed Mary! These are mad times—but not that mad."

Wary of sudden moves because the big Negro was still poised to attack, Philip slowly reached under his surtout. As he did, O'Brian snorted:

"Arthur, I think I'd best dress and load my squirrel gun. We'll haul these two loonies to Concord and have 'em locked up. Daisy's intended? Sweet God, d'you take me for a total idiot?" He scowled. "I'd wager the truth is more like this. You're King's men. In disguise and hunting military stores!"

"No, sir, that's wrong," Philip said. "Will you look at this? I think it'll help convince you—"

He pulled out the medal on its chain.

O'Brian shook his head. "Wearing a medal from the Mother Church doesn't prove a damn thing. There are plenty of Irish lobsterbacks, I hear tell."

"This isn't a holy medal, Mr. O'Brian. There's a Liberty Tree on it. Won't you look?"

For the first time, O'Brian appeared a shade less skeptical.

"You're one of the Boston band?" he asked.

"I am."

"Let me see."

Philip approached the lower step. O'Brian's thick, gnarled fingers turned the medal, examining both sides before he let go.

" 'Pears real enough. Could be stolen, though."

"But it isn't."

"He's telling the truth, Mr. O'Brian," Lumden said despite his chattering teeth. "I have deserted from the Thirty-third Infantry, in these clothes your daughter found for me."

"You really mean to say that you and my child—? That the two of you—?"

"Yes, sir. I was assigned to quarters at the house where Daisy works. Mr. Ware's house. That's how we met."

Philip waited tensely while O'Brian continued to study them. Then the farmer's features seemed to relax a little.

"Well, I'm damned. I'm waked from sound slumber

by a musket banging and find two beggarly fellows
shivering in my yard—and that's how nuptials are announced these days? Arthur—"

"Sir?"

"What d'you think?"

"It's mighty peculiar, sir."

"It's so goddamn peculiar, there must be a kernel o'
truth to it. Let's fetch 'em inside and hear the whole fancy tale."

Still keeping a watchful eye on Philip and his companion, the Negro followed them through the front door
and the heatless front rooms. In the kitchen, O'Brian
stamped barefoot to the hearth and struck a fire under
some kindling.

"Now," he ordered, "sit yourselves down and let
me hear it from the beginning. Then I'll decide whether
to march you to Concord and the stocks."

Philip decided he liked the crusty old man. He certainly couldn't blame O'Brian for his suspicion. At least
they'd gotten out of the cold. He edged his stool a little
closer to the crackling blaze and joined O'Brian in staring at Lumden.

"One o' you start talking!" O'Brian cried.

Turning red, Lumden said, "What my friend Kent has
told you is gospel truth, Mr. O'Brian—" He got busy
fingering his mole. "I am George Lumden, late of the
Thirty-third. While I lived at the home of the lawyer,
Mr. Abraham Ware, your daughter and I developed—"
He turned redder. "A—a—" He mumbled the rest.

"Louder! Speak up!" O'Brian roared.

"A mutual affection for one another," Lumden said in
a strangled voice. "At the same time, it became clear to
me that I had no stomach for this colonial quarrel with
fellow Englishmen. I say that to you without shame,
sir—I want no part of it! I only desire to marry your
daughter, be a good husband and provide for her for the
rest of our lives."

O'Brian's blue eyes narrowed. "How?"

"Well, sir, in England, my father was a smith. I know something of that trade—"

"God's wonders! I'd say your head's cracked—or mine is!—except you really talk like all this blather is the truth."

"Sir, it is. Daisy and I are—" Scarlet again, Lumden mumbled the rest.

"You expect to marry my child without asking my leave?" O'Brian challenged.

"Indeed not! I—I'm asking it now."

"Well, I ain't giving it! Not yet." The farmer hunched forward. "What's your faith?"

"Church of England, sir."

"Oh, Christ help us—!"

"—but Daisy and I have agreed to marry and raise our offspring in her church!"

O'Brian blinked. "You have?"

"Definitely."

Scratching his chin, the farmer turned to the Negro. "Arthur, what's your opinion now?"

"It's too crazy not to be true, Mr. O'Brian," said the grizzled black. "But I'd like to hear the other one talk some, too."

Before Philip could speak, Lumden said matter-of-factly, "I didn't know men in the colonies asked the opinions of their bond slaves."

Arthur slammed the musket butt on the pegged floor, glaring. For the first time, Philip noticed rings of thickened tissue on the inside of each black wrist. Shackle scars?

O'Brian made a placating gesture. "Arthur, he only speaks out of pagan ignorance." To Lumden: "We don't hold with slavery in the Massachusetts colony. Arthur is a free man of color. He works for his wages and board like anyone else—and can cease to do so and move on whenever he chooses. Bear that in mind when you speak to him."

Lumden flushed still another time. "I meant no offense, certainly. My apologies, Arthur—if I may address you that way."

"Guess so. Only name I got." But the black looked mollified.

Philip felt certain the shackle marks meant the man was a runaway. Perhaps from one of the southern colonies, where the peculiar institution so disapproved by many Boston liberals had long flourished with the assistance of Boston sea captains who brought human cargo from Africa as part of the vastly profitable triangular trade.

O'Brian resumed, "The blessed Lord saw fit to deliver nothing but females from the loins of my sainted, departed wife. Five of my daughters are already wed and living in various towns around the province. Daisy went traipsing off to Boston in the hope of improving her fortunes in similar style—" Another glance askance at Lumden, as if to say he wasn't sure she had. "So there's none but Arthur and me to run the place. If it's sanctuary you're seeking, the price is work."

"We'll gladly pay it," Philip told him. "George plans no return to Boston. And I can't go back for some weeks—if at all. I—" He hesitated only a moment. He felt he could trust the old farmer with at least a portion of the story. "—I encountered some trouble with one of His Majesty's officers. There may be arrest warrants out for me."

"Is Daisy in any danger?" O'Brian asked suddenly.

Philip didn't like lying. But he felt it best to spare the man undue concern.

"I am not aware of any, sir. She and Mistress Ware helped George find clothing for his escape, that's all. Your daughter directed us to come here, and said she'd send a message—"

"About what?"

"Joining us."

"How soon?"

"I don't know, sir."

"But you, the lobsterbacks want to arrest?"

"Possibly, yes."

At that O'Brian broke into his first genuine smile of the morning. "Well, that's a good recommendation!"

Already Philip felt better. The kitchen was warm now, flooded with the gold light of the winter morning breaking across the hillside behind the farm. The Irishman went on:

"And you're in top company. We understand the lives of such men as Sam Adams and Johnny Hancock aren't worth a shilling if they linger in Boston many more days. Fact is, we've been hearing they may seek sanctuary out this way. If you're all you claim, Kent, you'll want an introduction to my neighbor down the road. Jim Barrett—the Colonel. In charge of our Concord militia."

Philip nodded. "Indeed. I've already mustered with the Boston Grenadiers under Captain Pierce."

"Good. Arthur—hang up the porridge pot. Let's feed these scarecrows, and ourselves too. I guess I'd best become acquainted with Tommy here, since it appears I may be stuck with him, like it or not. As soon as they've eaten, you can put 'em to work."

At last the big black managed a grin.

"Mr. O'Brian, I'll keep 'em busy, don't you worry."

ii

Arthur proved a hard but fair taskmaster. He set Martin O'Brian's two unexpected boarders to hammering and sawing from sunup to dark, completing needed repairs on the siding of the rickety barn. Philip was grateful for the labor. It drained his body of strength by day's end, and the exhaustion helped drain his mind of worry about Anne Ware.

But no matter how tired he became from his chores, worry about Anne never escaped him completely. January turned into gray February, and still no message arrived.

During long evenings by the kitchen fire, O'Brian and his prospective son-in-law held lengthy conversations. They exchanged views on the seesaw struggle between Crown and colonies, impressions of British military capability in the event of open warfare. O'Brian was also fairly consistent with questions about the sincerity of Lumden's intent to become a Catholic convert.

O'Brian had by this time taken Philip down the road to the home of leathery Colonel James Barrett, who was readying the Concord militia and minute companies in the event of hostilities. Philip's sincerity and background convinced Barrett that the younger man was a worthy recruit. He drilled in Concord village with men of all ages. Some of the older ones were veterans of Rogers' Rangers in the French and Indian War—the struggle that had been called the Seven Years' War in that lost, dim time in Auvergne. Then, the men had fought on the King's side.

Out in the country, as Philip had heard, equipping the militia with muskets, powder and ball was no problem. The stockpiles had been building up for months. Barrett's smokehouse was a major storage point for arms. Other stores, including half a dozen cannon, were hidden in Concord's meeting house.

But because of the stockpiles, Barrett frequently reminded his companies, their quiet little village in the wooded hills where the Sudbury and Assabet flowed together to form the Concord might well be a major target of an expedition by Gage's soldiers.

Though security at the Neck was now reported tighter

than ever, word of the heightening tensions in Boston reached Wright's Tavern with fair regularity. Patriots managed to row across the Charles by night to carry the news—

Revere had organized a secret company of mechanics to keep track of any sudden troop movements out of the city.

Ships newly arrived from England bore word that America's partisan, old Pitt, the Earl of Chatham, had responded to the declaration of grievances from the Congress. He had laid a plan of conciliation before Parliament. The plan included a provision for withdrawing all royal troops from Boston.

Pitt's plan was defeated. Next, it was rumored that while pretending to draw up a reconciliation program of its own, the North ministry was privately readying even more repressive and economically disastrous measures, including bills to bar New England ships from commerce in any ports save those in Britain and the British West Indies, and to forbid New England fishing vessels from working the North Atlantic banks.

Most ominous of all were reports of another act, already said to be passed in London and awaiting only formal transmittal to Gage. It would authorize the general to use whatever measures he deemed necessary to enforce the various Crown edicts.

As the ice of February thinned under the first onslaught of March winds, the Concord patriots met in dark old Wright's to hear that despite the pleadings of men such as Pitt and Burke, both Lords and Commons had already declared the Massachusetts province "*in rebellion.*" Gage seemed to act accordingly. He sent soldiers to Salem to seize the colonial arms stored there.

The night it happened, loud knocking at O'Brian's door roused Philip from his pallet. He grabbed his musket and ran all the way to Concord.

The provincial alarm system, a combination of mounted couriers and ringing bells in every village steeple, had been perfected now. All the Concord companies were ready to march within a couple of hours.

Then a horseman pounded in to report that the Salem supplies had been moved safely out of reach of the troops—and Gage's officers had chosen not to search and force combat in order to capture them.

But the patriots who made Wright's a rendezvous—Concord's Tory families wisely avoided the tavern—swore that it was only a matter of weeks, or perhaps days, before inevitable bloodshed.

In preparation, the Provincial Congress sitting at Cambridge under the direction of Hancock and Dr. Warren passed a resolve which put the militia companies on notice that any troop movements from Boston *"to the Number of Five Hundred Men"* would be considered grounds for mobilizing to a war-ready state.

Philip supposed he should take a more serious interest in all these dire tidings. But he was too preoccupied with the lack of any communications from Anne. O'Brian was equally worried about his daughter. As was Lumden.

By the second week in March, after discussing the situation with the Irish farmer and the ex-sergeant, Philip decided he would try to re-enter the city.

The very next morning, a cold, rain-spattered day, he was inside the barn preparing to saddle the sway-backed mare O'Brian had offered him. He heard wheels creak, hoofs plopping, looked outside—

The farm wagon appeared on the road at the front of the property. Arthur had driven to Concord for some flour and other staples. There was a second person returning with him. Squinting through the gray rain, Philip detected bright red hair—and shouted to the back of the barn where Lumden was sawing a plank:

"George! Daisy's here!"

Both men went racing through the drizzle as Arthur turned the wagon down the rutted track alongside the house. Laughing and weeping at the same time, Daisy flung herself down into Lumden's arms.

When the embrace ended, she ran to Philip and hugged him impetuously. "Mistress Anne's waiting for you at the tavern in Concord."

"You mean she came with you?"

Daisy nodded. "She and her father have taken rooms there. Adams has fled Boston for good—Mr. Hancock too. Sneaked out like criminals at night."

"The danger's grown that great, then?"

"So everyone says. Only that Dr. Warren stayed behind, Mr. Ware told us."

She glanced around, wiping the joyful tears from her face while Lumden simply stood, his saw forgotten in the mud at his feet. He beamed with almost comical happiness.

"Where's my father?" Daisy asked.

"Gone down the road to speak with Colonel Barrett," Arthur informed her.

She turned to Lumden. "Have you—? That is, will he let us—?"

Lumden just grinned and nodded. Daisy squealed and rushed into his arms again. Philip started for the house to get his surtout. He called over his shoulder:

"Tell Mr. O'Brian I've gone to town to see—"

He stopped suddenly, looking at Daisy.

Holding Lumden's arm, she was staring at him with all trace of happiness momentarily wiped away.

"Daisy, what's wrong?" he asked.

She rushed to him, whispering:

"Mistress Anne will tell you."

"No, you tell me."

"There—there seems to be fairly certain evidence

that the officer—well, the one who came to the house
the night you left isn't—" She couldn't continue.

"Daisy, go on! Isn't what?"

"Isn't dead."

iii

Cold fear, cold and slashing as the March rain,
ravaged him as he swung into the saddle and headed the
mare down the half-thawed road to Concord.

He saw O'Brian's horse tethered outside the colonel's
house but pushed on without stopping. He clattered over
the footbridge and through the center of the village to
Wright's. The mud outside bore marks of the recent arrival of a coach.

Daisy's news had struck him with stunning force. And
yet, reflecting as he dismounted, he realized that it was a
turn of events he might have foreseen. He could not
remember a single second during the haste of that
bloody night on Launder Street when he had paused to
determine whether Roger Amberly was indeed dead.
He had assumed the bayonet stroke to be fatal.

The error could be fatal to him in turn.

Boots dropping clumps of mud, he stalked into the
tavern. The landlord directed him up to the front suite
of rooms. He burst into the gray, chilly parlor to see
Abraham Ware hauling one of three trunks to one of the
bedrooms.

Just throwing off her damp travel cloak, Anne turned.
Her eyes grew wide. "Oh—*Philip!*"

He was not even conscious of crossing the threadbare
carpet to wrap her in his arms and hold her.

"Anne, Anne. I've waited for word—!"

After a moment, they separated. He was alarmed to
notice how wan she was. Despite the joy of the reunion,
she acted oddly ill at ease.

Looking tired and peaked himself, Lawyer Ware harrumphed as he returned from the bedroom.

"Conditions have grown so bad in Boston, there was no way we could prudently communicate with you, Philip," he said. "The couriers do dangerous work—and have enough on their minds without the burden of personal messages."

"I was astonished to hear you were in Concord," Philip told him.

"It took a deal of finagling and some clever forgeries to come up with the papers that got us across the Neck." Ware indicated the trunks. "That's all we were allowed to bring. As to the rest—the house, the furnishings—well, the soldiers or the damn Tories have no doubt looted the place already. But it was run or face possible arrest for my activities. Only Warren insisted on remaining behind, and Revere—to coordinate the spying on the soldiers."

"We've heard Gage is getting ready to move against the towns," Philip said.

"He is. To seize the stores. There's supposed to be an authorization on its way by ship from the Colonial Secretary, Dartmouth."

"We've heard that too." Anne was watching him with a strange, bleak expression he couldn't fathom.

Ware rolled his tongue in his cheek, continued, "Warren will arrange to get Paul and some others out with a warning if Gage moves. That's his plan, anyway. We've come to what Sam Adams wanted all along. Though it may be the only way, God take me, I'm frightened to my bones."

"How is Mr. Edes faring?" Philip asked.

"With difficulty. Distribution of the *Gazette*'s all but forbidden. When Ben and I talked last—two days ago—he was starting to dismantle his press. He hopes to smuggle the pieces and a few fonts of type across the

Charles. Perhaps to Watertown. He and Revere are holding conversations about money—"

Philip frowned, failing ro understand the reference.

"The printing of it!" Ware exclaimed. "Should war come, the colonies will need their own financing. Paul's already drawing designs for the bills. But we've news of more direct concern to you, lad—" His protruding eyes harbored a new respect. "Concerning the officer who met an untimely accident in my parlor. Annie told me everything about it, of course."

"Daisy said there was reason to believe the man didn't die."

"Good reason."

Ware plumped himself on a rickety chair and peered gloomily through the yellowed lace curtains at the rain on the roofs of Concord.

"Thanks to Annie, we were prepared when other officers from the Thirty-third called at Launder Street. My daughter had rehearsed Daisy well. And the officers were careless enough to admit they had questioned some of our neighbors first. They told us Amberly was seen knocking at our door. Daisy lied valiantly. Said Lumden disappeared that morning—I gather he's safe at her father's farm?"

"Yes, he is."

"Daisy told the redcoats she'd shown Amberly the equipment Lumden left in the barn. After which, he went away. She and Annie stuck to the same story although each was questioned twice more. I don't think either of 'em was fully believed—"

"I'm sure of it," Anne put in.

"The only saving factor was, Gage hasn't started torturing suspects for information. As yet! Maybe it's the influence of that American wife of his. The mysterious circumstances surrounding Amberly's whereabouts later might have helped keep us free of trouble, too."

Philip still couldn't fathom that strange, unblinking

look on Anne's face. Her color had faded badly. Gray half-circles of fatigue showed beneath her eyes.

"What mysterious circumstances?" he asked.

Anne replied, "Amberly was apparently found where you left him. Unconscious but not dead. He was removed from Boston a few days later."

"Removed!" Philip exclaimed. "Wasn't he put in a military hospital?"

"He should have been," Ware said. "And he was—at first. But someone interceded on his behalf. To arrange more suitable care."

"Explain what you mean."

"According to a lad on Revere's committee of mechanics whom I asked to keep watch and pick up information, Amberly—still in bad shape, mind—was loaded into a private coach by several men unfamiliar to my informant. Servant types, the boy thought. But not wearing a livery. The coach went out across the Neck with no hindrance."

Ware's mouth turned down, sour. "Evidently it's still possible to purchase special medical privileges, just the way prisoners in England purchase extra food, better quarters—and the way that damned fellow purchased his commission! Someone learned of his plight. Arranged for him to be attended elsewhere than in the military hospital—where he'd more likely die than recover. They're pest houses. The so-called surgeons are no better than butchers. It's all damned curious—"

He gave Philip a challenging look. "But Annie's brought you something whose outward appearance suggests it may serve to explain."

"What is it, Anne?"

"A letter."

"Which we didn't open," Ware advised. "The contents are your affair. Give it to him, Annie. I'm going down to the taproom and try to unfreeze my veins with some flip."

A moment after the door closed, Anne walked to the smallest trunk. She unlatched it, raised the lid. Among the folded articles of clothing Philip saw his mother's casket, Gil's wrapped sword, even the green glass bottle of tea. He was touched by the care with which Anne had obviously packed them.

She produced the letter from the bottom of the trunk, passed it to him.

Sealed with wax but bearing no sigil, it showed signs of much handling. The address, in a delicate, unfamiliar hand, read *Mr. Philip Kent, Esq.*, and was written in care of Ware's home in Launder Street, Boston.

He looked up. "How did you get this, Anne?"

"A private courier brought it to the door. Only hours before we loaded the trunks into the chaise."

"You mean you didn't see my name in the usual list in the paper? You didn't go down to the postal office for it?"

Anne shook her head. Her voice sounded hollow as she said, "Someone spent a great deal of money to hire a messenger and have it delivered faster than the regular service would have."

Somehow, then, Philip had an eerie sense of fate working. The plain room all gray with rainy light suddenly became a place where the gale winds of chance could reach and storm around him. He didn't know why he felt frightened holding the wrinkled letter. But he did.

He broke the wax hesitantly, unfolded the sheets inside. As he began to read the finely-inked lines, a lump congealed in his throat. The room seemed to blur.

The top of the letter bore the words *Philadelphia City,* and a recent date. The salutation was a hand from the past that clawed and held him remorselessly:

My darling Phillipe—

After much difficulty encountered in strenuous

*ocean travel, I have arrived here at the home of my
Aunt and her Husband, Mr. Tobias Trumbull of
Arch Street. I write this to you in secret, by the candle's light. In the next chamber Roger lies abed,
barely conscious and perhaps already in the thrall
of death.*

*Before he took ship from England with his regi-
ment, we had agreed that, in the event military duty
in the colonies resulted in any serious injury, he
would if possible communicate with my cousin by
coach mail or private post rider. No matter their
location in the Empire, the army hospitals are
known to be places where death for the badly
wounded is a virtual certainty, due to unclean conditions, poor physicians, and such like.*

*During a brief wakeful period after he was
discovered   lying   stabb'd   in   some   publick
thoroughfare and conveyed to one such hospital—*

She *knew!* Philip thought, the hand of the past tighter
now, making him breathe hard, and with strain.

*—he managed to pay for a rider to Philadelphia.
From here, my good Aunt Sue dispatched a private
coach northward to bring him back. Many bribes
were necessary to effect this departure. But as funds
are never lacking to Roger, it was accomplished. My
Aunt forwarded the dread news to me on the first fast
packet. I have come to Roger's side, landing in
Philadelphia Harbor only yesterday. Last night my
husband was awake long enough to talk with me a
while. He survived the journey over the rough roads,
though barely, and—*

The next words were underscored with quick slashing
lines.

—he named his assailant. He told me where and how

the act was done.

*He spoke both your new name and the older,
more sweetly familiar one by which I have addressed you. And so, my dearest Phillipe, I come to
write the truth of my heart—I have never forgotten Quarry Hill, nor can I. I tell you from the
depths of my Soul that I want nothing more than
to see you. Speak with you. Be close to you—yes,
I admit without shame—as close as we once were.*

Horror crawled over Philip for a moment. He imagined her bent by a candle in some dark, musty room
that smelled of a suppurating wound.

*I do not know whether my husband also
named you his assailant before he was borne here.
From all I can gather, I do not think so. Perhaps,
in his weakened state, he was first concerned for
his own welfare, and communicating with my Aunt.*

*But I have no assurance. If there is never a
response to this, which I am sending to the Street in
Boston City whose name Roger breathed out last
night, then I will know.*

*Yet if by some miracle this letter finds you, I beg
you come by any swift means to Philadelphia City
so that we may meet and speak. You will be safe
from any reprisals, believe that if you ever loved
me. I only desire your sweet presence again. For
though I may be damn'd eternally for writing it, my
husband is what I knew him to be long ago. A cold,
empty man. To marry him was folly which I have
long since regretted. I beg you to answer my plea,
Phillipe. Take all precautions you deem necessary.
But come even if we may meet only for a day.*

*As token of my good faith and undying love for
you, I close by telling you that I have asked the
doctors attending my husband to make certain he
receives heavy draughts of an opiate to relieve his*

*sufferings—and also to prevent him from again
speaking your name, which I alone heard in the
privacy of his room last night. My Aunt and her
Husband do not know of you, of that much I am
positive. For God's sake come, my darling!*

The letter ended with more savage under-
scorings of the last six words, and a single shattering signature—

Alicia.

Shaken as never before, Philip looked at Anne.

She must have guessed it was something like this, he
thought. Her face was a study in pain as she took the letter from his numbed hand and began to read it.

CHAPTER II

A Death in Philadelphia

i

AT THE END, Anne re-folded the sheets, put them down on a small table, turned to stare out the window. When she spoke, her voice had an edge to it:

"And what will your response be, Philip?"

He couldn't tell whether she spoke in anger or sorrow, probably because he was so unsettled himself. The letter had reached across the years to rouse emotions he hadn't felt so acutely since Quarry Hill.

Anne sensed his uncertainty, spun to face him. He was again aware of how pale she'd grown. Was she ill, refusing to tell him—?

Her suddenly scornful look shocked him out of all such speculation. "She's a proper lady, isn't she? Arranging to meet her lover while her husband lies in the next room—perhaps dying. And she's going to drug him in case he should wake and interrupt the proposed assignation! Oh, yes—a woman of fine principles!"

"Anne—"

"You haven't answered my question. Are you going to run to her, the minute she commands?"

"I don't know."

"My God. You're actually considering it!"

He stood speechless—accused.

"Philip, do you know how far it is to Philadelphia?

Will you travel almost four hundred miles just to let them arrest you?"

"Arrest—? I don't think that's part of her plan."

But he had to admit it well could be. Possibly Roger wasn't in serious condition at all. Perhaps he was recovering, and had prevailed on his wife to help set a trap for the one who had brought him to grief.

Contemptuously, Anne said, "On second thought, I doubt they'll even bother with legal formalities. They'll probably follow their more familiar course. Hire men from some gutter gang—to finish the work your brother started in England. Surely you won't let yourself fall prey to such a transparent plot. You can't be *that* brainless!"

Her voice rang loudly in the dim parlor. As the sound of it faded, the tap of the March rain on the shingled roof counterpointed the strained sibilance of her breathing.

Philip had trouble framing exactly how he wanted to approach a reply. He knew she was struggling against Alicia, as she'd vowed to do months ago. So she'd no doubt exaggerate the dangers inherent in answering Alicia's plea for a meeting.

Yet, the dangers might be entirely real. He said carefully:

"I'll admit everything you suggest is possible. Except for one fact. Alicia had no part in Roger's schemes in England—"

"She certainly didn't try to prevent them!"

"Yes, she did. In Tonbridge, it was only her warning that helped my mother and me escape in time. After that, I'm not even sure she knew what Roger was up to."

"Who are you trying to convince, Philip? Me? Or yourself?"

"Dammit, Anne, listen to reason—!"

"About a woman who wants to take you away from me? No."

"But you're not looking at it clearly—!"

"*Clearly!* That's the pot calling the kettle black! Who said I must, anyway?"

"Anne, if Roger were recovering, I think he'd have already arranged for the kind of men you described to visit Launder Street. To find me or, failing that, force an admission from you about my whereabouts. He wouldn't lure me all the way to Philadelphia."

"You keep saying all that because it's what you want to believe!" Anne cried, tears starting to show at the corners of her eyes.

"I'm trying to think it out!"

"Well, spare me! I've gone through quite enough for your sake these past few weeks. You seem prepared to forget that."

He understood the tactic painfully well, a womanly tactic, springing from her anger. He didn't blame her for the attack on his seeming ingratitude. But neither would he yield to it.

"You were also protecting Daisy and the sergeant. You helped hatch Lumden's plan, remember?"

"The plan never included killing Amberly."

"Or his arrival! Or the boy selling us out!" Philip countered, his voice louder.

"Don't deny the killing wasn't welcome revenge—"

"I will deny it!" He stepped close to her, reached for her arm. "He meant to hurt you. That was what went through my mind first and foremost—"

She flung his hand off, white with rage.

"You're lying! Lying and evading the truth! You've become an expert at it! Does everything that's happened to you in Boston mean nothing? All the work for Edes—was it a dumb-show, without any feeling, any conviction on your part?" Then she lost control completely. "And what passed between us—was that meaningless too?"

No!"

He clenched his fists, regretting the shout. He lowered his voice, but it remained harsh. "But I told you clearly, Anne—I would not be tied—"

"Because you can't decide what you are!" Anne mocked. "A free man, or the trained pet of that—that British whore. Why would you even *consider* going to her?"

"If I tried to explain, you wouldn't—"

"A man of conviction would consign that damned letter to the fire instantly. But maybe I misjudged you. Maybe you really do want to be what she is. Maybe you aren't strong enough to bury all those sick, false dreams your mother poured into you—"

Face darkening, he exploded, *"Don't speak of my mother that way!"*

"I will! Because she's brought you to this—all her rantings about your rightful place as a little lord—"

"Shut your mouth."

"Not till I'm finished. One thing's certain. If you go to Philadelphia, you'll no doubt save yourself from the battle that's coming here. That may be the final proof of what you really are—a cowardly aristocrat like that woman's husband. Well, go and be damned. I'm sorry I ever had hope for you—or let you touch me!"

"I believe, Anne, that decision was *yours*."

His enraged counterattack proved futile. She was trembling on the edge of hysteria. The last faint color had drained from her face. The half-circles of fatigue looked stark beneath her eyes. He wanted to strike her—

He jammed his fists to his sides, tried to speak calmly:

"Anne, you know I care for you—"

"Stop it! We've nothing further to talk about."

"Yes, we do. There's no other way to put the past to rest but to see Alicia one last time."

"Another lie!" she cried, letting the tears come at last.

"No, believe me—"

"You don't belong in Massachusetts, you belong in some stinking, perfumed manor house across the Atlantic. You're going exactly where you want to go—!"

In blind fury she shot a hand toward his throat. He jumped back, startled, as her fingers twisted under his collar, found the chain, tore it savagely.

He felt the chain part, cutting at the back of his neck. She lifted her prize up between them—the broken links, and the medal.

"But don't travel with this, Philip. You're not fit to wear it!"

She flung the medal. He heard it strike the wall, clink to the floor.

Anne looked at him hatefully. Her lips were tight together. Her breasts rose and fell rapidly, taut against her gown. He wanted to take her in his arms, try to make her understand that only by confronting the demon of his past could he reach a final point of decision—

He couldn't put it adequately into words. He tried for a moment, but the result was only incoherent stammering. Anne turned from his outstretched hand.

At last he managed to say, "Just because I go doesn't mean I won't come back."

Her fury changed to sorrowing pity. "And still one more lie. Maybe you can't even recognize the way you lie to yourself any longer. If you go, Philip, I know I'll never see you again."

"By whose choice? Mine or yours?"

"Both!"

Covering her eyes, she ran. The bedroom door crashed shut.

A spatter of rain struck the window. He stalked to the door where she'd disappeared.

"Anne?"

Silence. He wrenched the knob.

Bolted.

Grim-faced, he surveyed the parlor. Saw Alicia's letter on the threadbare carpet, brushed from the small table. He bent slowly, picked up the letter, slipped it into his pocket. He heard soft, anguished crying from the bedroom.

He was angry, ashamed and bitter over the scene just concluded. A weary acceptance dropped over him suddenly. He could be no more and no less than what he was: a man caught in the present but pulled relentlessly toward a past he thought had died.

He lifted Gil's sword, the green glass bottle and his mother's casket from the open trunk. He walked out leaving the liberty medal where it had fallen.

ii

As Philip clattered down the stairs, Lawyer Ware glanced up from his conversation with a group of Concord men in Wright's public room. Philip kept straight on toward the front door.

Ware rushed after the younger man.

"Kent, a word! Anne's been sickly of late. I have a suspicion as to why she—"

But Philip had already stalked out into the rain. He swung up on the mare's back, jerked her head toward the bridge and O'Brian's farm. He heard Ware shout his name, this time angrily. But he did not turn to look.

iii

O'Brian pressed Philip on the reason for the journey. He got noncommittal answers, except for Philip's use of the term "urgent." Finally, O'Brian agreed to let him have use of the mare. But when he heard Philip's destination, he cautioned:

"Some of those Boston express riders claim they've covered the distance in eleven days round trip. Push Nell that hard and she'll die on you. No more than thirty or thirty-five miles a day for her, mind. And rest her often. Or you can't have her."

At that rate, Philip reckoned the trip one way would take more than ten days. But traveling mounted, though slowly, was preferable to the impossible alternative —trying to make it on foot.

"All right, Mr. O'Brian, I promise."

"This is truly a pressing matter?"

"Believe me, it is."

"Then ask Arthur to pack saddlebags for you. Bread and some of the apples from the root cellar. We've an old skin you can fill with the apple wine—"

"Thank you."

"Where will you stay at night?"

"Fields, barns—anywhere. I left what little money I've saved in the hands of Mr. Edes, the printer. God knows what's become of it with things as they are."

"Well," the blue-eyed Irishman said, "I doubt you'll be permitted to sleep in the streets of Philadelphia. I'll advance you a little money—with the proviso you pay it back."

"I appreciate it, sir. Of course I will."

"You do intend to come back soon?"

Philip hesitated a moment. "That's my present plan." He felt guilty about the half-truth. He had no clear idea of the outcome of the journey.

The farmer scratched his nose, scrutinized Philip closely. "Something's happened today—something very strange. I've never seen you so jumpy. Not even when you were dodging Arthur's musket that first morning. I'd still like to know what sudden emergency hauls you off so far."

The truth of it came automatically, and painfully:

"A personal matter I need to settle for good."

"Colonel Barrett won't be happy to lose even one musket man from the Concord company."

"Tell him I have no choice."

He left the farmhouse to search for Arthur in the barn, and say his farewells to Daisy and George Lumden. By early afternoon he was mounted and riding through the drizzle on the road back toward Lexington. Alicia's letter was folded into the pocket of his surtout.

He was still too shaken to know whether what he was doing was right. But he had told O'Brian the complete truth at least once:

He had no choice.

iv

That night, he tried to sleep in the lee of a stable belonging to some Cambridge farmer. He couldn't doze off. He was bedeviled by a sense of his own inadequacy and weakness.

And by guilt.

He'd acted unfeelingly, brutally toward Anne Ware, who had given so much of herself with so little reservation. Excusing himself with the argument that he'd acted in the heat of the moment helped not one whit. And though Anne's accusations still tormented him, he was no longer capable of feeling angry. She'd said what she had because she loved him.

Huddled in the dark with the mare, Nell, standing head down nearby, he fell prey to guilt from another source as well. His own emotions.

He couldn't pretend that he felt no passion for Alicia Parkhurst. The passion had only been submerged out of necessity, and because of Anne's presence. But whether his feelings for the earl's daughter went beyond the physical, he was too weary and confused to decide. Perhaps, during the solitary trip to the city of the curious sect called Quakers, he could sort it all out.

The sorting, he decided, was long overdue.

And so, even though he was thoroughly wet and

miserable, he began to be grateful for the enforced solitude of the post roads waiting to the south.

God forgive me—and you, Anne, if you can, he thought as he sat with his head slumped against the planking of the Cambridge stable. *Excepting a few rare ones like old Adams, it seems the way a man must go is never clear—*

v

The weather improved slightly as he traveled into the Connecticut countryside, following a rutted highway that ran parallel to the river of the same name. Mindful of his pledge to O'Brian, he took care not to push the mare too hard. But though he rode relatively slowly, he ended each day the same way—aching and butt-sore.

In the town of Hartford, he managed to cadge food and a night's rest in the public room of a tavern whose sign still bore a flattering image of round-faced King George. Anxious for news of events in Massachusetts, the landlord and his wife eagerly exchanged great chunks of hot bread and country butter and some deliciously roasted apples for what information Philip could provide. He was allowed to sleep on a bench by the hearth, warm for the first time since his departure.

But he was troubled by dreams in which Alicia's face changed to Anne Ware's, and back again—

By bridge he crossed to the northern end of the wooded island at whose southern extremity rose the thriving city of New York. He spent a morning in its streets, then used one of the shillings O'Brian had loaned him for ferry passage across the Hudson River to the Jersey shore. He pushed on southwestward to the town of Trenton, and paid again to be ferried over the Delaware.

On a late March day livened by a warm breeze hinting

at the end of winter, the old mare set her hoofs on the soil of Pennsylvania. At Frankfort, five miles from Philadelphia, he realized with disappointment that the hoped-for solution to the riddle of his future hadn't materialized during the long ride. His quandry was as deep as ever.

He was also uncomfortably conscious of mounting excitement at the prospect of seeing Alicia.

Of the two women, Anne was by far the more sensible and solid. And no less passionate and giving of herself than the English girl. She'd make any man a fine wife—

But she also represented uncertainty, the peril of this struggling country.

Everyplace he had stopped on the long road south, anxious men had questioned him about the chances of war.

And while he might agree with the principles for which patriots like Adams were struggling, he was still realistic enough to understand that the security—the personal safety—of all who espoused the colonial cause was vastly uncertain.

Alicia, in turn, stood for everything he had been taught to desire during all the years in Auvergne. He knew much of her world was cruelty and sham. It was a world devoted to the ruthless employment of wealth and position and power to acquire more of the same—at the expense of others. Yet even now, a part of him still craved admission to that world.

To shun a chance for entrance had been, to his mother, the greatest crime a man could commit. Sometimes he shared that conviction fervently. Sometimes he was desperately afraid of a long life of poverty, anonymity, and all their attendant dangers.

Once, inspired by the example of the Sholto family, he'd imagined starting a printing enterprise of his own here in America. The craft fired his imagination then,

and still did. He'd seen first hand the power of a paper
like the *Gazette* to move men's minds and hearts on
behalf of a cause—

But with conditions as they were, how could he count
with any sureness on the opportunity to build such a
business?

Ben Edes was being forced to suspend operations,
Ware had said. In the turmoil and disorder of what
seemed an all but certain confrontation, his accumulated
wages held by Edes stood every chance of disappearing
into the patriot coffers. Or of being confiscated if Edes
were arrested. That little bit of money was all he had in
the world. Only a very foolish person would envision a
solid future in that kind of situation, he believed.

Indeed, he thought as he neared Philadelphia, if
America as a whole dared to seek what Sam Adams
openly desired—total independency—she would be, in a
sense, what he had been from the beginning: a bastard
child thrust into a dangerous world alone and un-
protected; a bastard child exposed to countless risks the
more timid and secure would never experience, a
bastard child forced, on occasion, to kill other human
beings in order to survive—

With survival itself completely in doubt.

He wondered in passing whether there would be as
much blood on his hands—and his conscience—if he'd
been born to a higher station. He thought not.

Finally, there remained with him the tantalizing
memory of James Amberly's letter, now stored at
O'Brian's farm. He had long ago abandoned any hope of
ever putting that document to use.

Yet he'd saved it.

Why?

He approached the outskirts of Philadelphia on a road
crowded with market carts. The warm March breeze
blew against his grimy face. Danger might well wait for
him at the home of Alicia's relatives on Arch Street. But

there was still a relief in this coming, at last, to a meeting that had probably been ordained from the beginning. A meeting not so much with Alicia, he thought in another moment of sudden insight, as with himself. The compulsion to find and confront the truth of what he was, and what he wanted, was what had actually driven him onto this long road.

If only he'd been able to explain even a part of that to Anne—!

Phillipe Charboneau, the bastard heir of a nobleman, or Philip Kent, plain printer's helper—which was he?

Time, finally, to know the answer. Perhaps it would happen in that very city rising on the horizon this bright morning.

vi

The city by the Schuylkill River was twice as large as Boston, he learned from a cart driver he caught up with just at the outskirts. The dirt tracks he'd followed from Massachusetts soon changed to smooth brick.

He took pleasure in letting the mare amble for an hour through the wide, tree-lined streets. He was impressed by all the splendid homes, churches and mercantile establishments. He also took note of the numerous street lamps, so unlike the dim, smoke-stained globes of Boston. The Philadelphia design featured four flat panes of glass, topped by a funnel, presumably to let the smoke rise into the air. He asked a stranger whether the lamps were Dr. Franklin's invention. The stranger told him they were.

On all the main thoroughfares, Philip saw well-dressed people. Gentlemen in velvet, with walking sticks. Young ladies with parasols; the most elegant wore vizards to shield their delicate skins from the glare of the noon sun.

Vendors hawked fresh vegetables and something called scrapple on the corners. By the busy wharves, Philip saw trading vessels of every size and description. Though he was exhausted from the trip, the noise and animation of the town buoyed his spirits.

But he remembered the need for caution the minute he began making inquiries about the whereabouts of Arch Street.

He located it near Chestnut, one of the main arteries of the town. This much done, he turned the sweating mare back to the riverfront. He quartered her at a seedy inn called The Ship, securing a small, airless room under the eaves. For one night only.

He waited until dusk on that Tuesday before making his way toward Arch Street on foot. On Chestnut, he spoke to a vendor just throwing a cloth over his half-emptied cabbage cart. The man was familiar with all the well-to-do residents of the area. He directed Philip to a large brick residence fourth down on the right-hand side of Arch.

"Everyone in town knows the Trumbulls," the bearded farmer commented. "The mister owns the biggest ropewalk 'twixt New York and Charleston. And a mighty loyal Tory he is, too. But the household's in mourning—"

Already starting away, Philip turned back swiftly.

"For who?"

The farmer spat on the lamplit bricks. "Why, lad, such fine folk don't confide everything in the likes of me! All I know's what I hear and what any eye can see. Walk up that way—you'll see it too."

Whistling, the old man shuffled off, pushing his cart.

First scanning the block for signs of watchers who might have been posted for his arrival, Philip strode along the walk next to the high black iron fences that protected each house. He was walking on the side of the

street opposite the Trumbull home. When he was in
position to get a clear look, he broke stride and caught
his breath.

All windows in the two-story structure were draped,
barely revealing the hint of lamps glowing inside. On the
imposing downstairs door hung a somber wreath trailing
black crepe ribbons—

For Roger Amberly?

He felt a brief, vicious satisfaction at the possibility.
The emotion shamed him as he hurried on by, and
returned to the rowdy waterfront inn.

Over a tankard of beer at a corner table, he scrawled
a note to *Mrs. Alicia Amberly*, in care of the *Trumbull
Residence, Arch Street*. The message inside was
simple—one sentence long:

*A friend desires to know the cause of the household's
bereavement.*

Then, after chewing the end of the quill a moment, he
signed *P. Charboneau*.

He hired the landlord's boy to carry the note, and
gave him explicit instructions:

"That is to be delivered into the hand of the lady to
whom it's addressed, no other."

"Right, sir."

"And you'll wait for any answer."

"Got it." The lad hurried out.

Philip hitched his chair around so that his back was to
the corner. From that position he could peer through the
smoke and the press of noisy sailors and dock workers
and watch the door. The tavern clock chimed nine.

Philip bought another tankard of beer, drank it all.
He grew drowsy as he rubbed his aching legs. His muscles were still not accustomed to the rigors of days on
horseback.

The beer helped dull the discomfort. It lulled him into
a doze that was suddenly broken by the footsteps of
someone approaching his table.

He opened his eyes, startled by the sight of a tall, cloaked man in a tricorn hat. The man peered down at Philip with ill-concealed disdain.

The tavern boy stood behind the stranger, obviously apprehensive. The man threw his cloak back over his right shoulder far enough to reveal servant's livery—and a brass-chased pistol in his belt.

"Are you the gentleman who sent an inquiry to the Trumbull household?"

Philip's palms started to sweat. He didn't like the way the man's hand rested on the broad belt, so close to the pistol. He tried not to show his concern as he answered:

"I am."

"Charboneau—that's your name?"

"Yes."

"Tomorrow, there will be a room waiting for you at the City Tavern—are you acquainted with it?"

"No, but I'll find it."

The curl of the man's mouth suggested knowledge of some illicit purpose behind the note and its reply. "The lady to whom you addressed your inquiry wishes for me to acknowledge it. You will be contacted at the City Tavern at the proper time. You understand, of course, that it may not be for some days, due to the household's distress—"

"A death—" Philip began, still wondering whether it was all an elaborate ruse—and the servant might suddenly haul out the pistol and shoot him. He slipped his hands to the edge of the table, ready to overturn it as an impromptu shield.

But the man made no menacing moves. In fact, he behaved as if the entire conversation was beneath his dignity. Still regarding Philip with arrogant amusement, he replied:

"A death indeed. The lady's husband, Lieutenant Colonel Amberly."

It could still be a trap; lies. But Philip tried to look sympathetic as he asked:

"When did it happen?"

"This past Sunday. It appears the mourning period for widows is rather more brief than in England."

"If that's any of your affair."

"I wouldn't make the observation to anyone else. But your—association with the lady seems quite—personal, shall we say? Good evening. *Sir.*"

Wheeling, the man stalked through the crowd of noisy seamen and wharf workers. One growled a remark about Tories. The man hesitated, seemed on the point of reaching for his pistol—

His sly eyes moving quickly, the man assessed the numbers against him. He proceeded on toward the door, pausing only for a last, speculative glance at Philip sitting tensely in the corner. Then he went out.

Philip slept badly that night, alert for surreptitious sounds on the stair outside his room. But none came to disturb him. At last he drifted off.

In the morning, he paid for his bed and breakfast, then asked directions to the City Tavern.

The landlord laughed. "You came into a fortune last night, did you? Those are considerably finer quarters than my place. Distinguished gentlemen lodge there—some already gathering to plan the next Congress."

"Just tell me the way," Philip snapped.

The landlord obliged. Philip mounted the mare and set off through the clamor of Philadelphia's market day.

His cheap, travel-stained clothing attracted the same sort of stares from the staff at the City Tavern that he'd gotten from the servant who sought him at The Ship. But he was shown to a large, airy bedroom on the second floor without question. A stable boy took Nell, to rub her down and feed her. In fact it was soon evident that someone had gone to some trouble to finance a comfortable stay. When he inquired about the cost of lodging and meals, he was informed that his bill would be handled by another person—who wished to remain anonymous.

At nightfall a girl brought in a long-handled warming pan to heat the bedclothes. Philip went downstairs.

Excellent though the food was in the busy main room, he found he had no appetite. All around him, he heard nothing but political discussion. He retired to his room at half past eight, settling into a comfortable rocking chair with a prodigious yawn. He didn't mean to fall asleep. But he was still worn out from the eleven-day ride, and he did.

Before he knew it, a sharp sound intruded at the edge of his mind. He lifted his head, listened, picked up only the hum of conversation from below-stairs. After a moment, though, the sound was repeated.

A soft knocking.

He stood up, silently slipped to the window and freed the latch. He had already determined that in the event he was still being drawn into some elaborate trap, the window would serve as a viable escape route. It was a long drop to the brick walk below. But at least it was a way out.

The lamp burning beside the turned-down coverlet cast a grotesque shadow of his head and shoulders as he crept toward the door. He honestly didn't know what to expect; it was possible that he might be confronted by armed men. The backs of his hands itched. His mouth had grown dry.

The knock came again, more insistently. One more step, and he reached out to open the door.

vii

The lamplight raised glints from the brasswork of the pistol in the belt of the tall servant. The knowing smile still quirked the man's mouth—almost as if it were part of a permanent expression.

"I'm to request you to come with me, if you please," the man said.

Wishing for a weapon as he scanned the dark-paneled hall behind the looming figure, Philip asked, "Where?"

The man gestured with a gloved hand. "Down those back stairs. To a coach waiting a few doors from here. It's not possible for the lady who wishes to speak with you to enter a public house by the main door. Especially not this public house. She would be noticed not only because of her mourning black but because of her political associations."

"I don't understand."

"Although the accommodations may be the best in the city, neither Mr. Trumbull nor his good wife would set foot in this viper's pit. As for me, I'd burn this place to the ground—and all within it who are busy hatching treason." The man's muddy brown eyes showed impatience. "Are you coming?"

"Yes. Just a second—"

Philip stepped into the room for his surtout, blew out the lamp.

As he preceded Philip down the creaking back stair, the servant chuckled, a lascivious sound. He didn't both- to hold the door, hurrying ahead through the warm night wind to the end of an alley. There, a high-wheeled coach and team waited, the horses fretting, the driver on the box swearing, one boot on the brake lever.

The servant handed open the coach door and stood aside. Beyond the rectangular opening, Philip could see nothing but darkness.

CHAPTER III

Alícia

i

FOR A MOMENT he was tempted to run. If the Amberly family wished to bait a trap for Roger's slayer, none could be more perfect than this black coach silhouetted against the rooftop chimney pots and the blurred April stars beyond.

The tall servant kept his hand on the open door. But now shadows hid his face. The team whinnied. The driver swore again.

"Step in," the tall man prompted.

Inside, Philip thought he saw a figure stir. He couldn't be certain. From the City Tavern, a fiddle struck up a lively air. Annoyed, the tall man said:

"Sir—if you please!"

Suddenly the figure inside leaned forward just enough to reveal its presence.

"Do, Phillipe. You're safe. And there's little time."

"*Alicia?*"

"Of course."

He climbed the step and plunged into the black interior. He heard soft rustlings just before the servant slammed the door. The coach creaked and swayed as the man climbed a wheel to the box. Alicia rapped the roof. The team started forward.

Philip still couldn't see her. But he could smell a faint,

bitter sweet lemon fragrance—scent or soap—clinging
to her skin. And he could smell claret, strongly.

As the coach swung out from the alley and turned
to pass a row of lighted windows, her face glowed. It
was as if all the time since Quarry Hill had never existed.

She looked at him, too moved to speak. The radiance
of her face was in part due to the contrast with her
widow's weeds: all black, from the skirt to a modish
feminine variation of a man's tricorn. Strands of tawny
hair glinted at the collar of her cape.

In the dim light from the homes going by outside the
slow-paced coach, he saw again the blue eyes that had
once gazed into his with such heat and pain. But the
longer he looked at her, the more aware he became of
subtle changes. A strained set to her mouth. A faint
coarsening of the texture of her skin—too many damaging cosmetics?

And her voice had the ever-so-faint slur of too much
wine:

"Dear God, there are still miracles in this awful
world!" Her cheeks glistened with tears as her black
glove sought his face.

Trying to ignore the changes he'd detected, he slid
closer on the velvet coach seat. His hands circled her
waist while she held his cheeks and brought her mouth
to his, hungrily.

The kiss was long, full of the wine taste of her breath
when she opened her lips to caress his tongue with her
own. At last, laughing in a peculiar fashion—a lilting
laugh, yet one with tears in it—she broke away.

"Hold me. Just hold me a while."

He cradled her against him, her face buried on his
shoulder. Her small gloved hand pressed his arm.

Finally this embrace ended too. She pulled his hands
into her lap, simply staring at him in silent joy as the
coach rattled along. Stark shadows of still-bare elm

branches flickered across the interior. He could now see her clearly. Her black clothing lent her face the quality of a shining cameo. As she ran her right glove down the side of his face, her blue eyes welled with tears again.

"You're not a boy any longer. There are marks on you."

"A long time's gone by, Alicia."

"You're looking at me in such a strange way—"

"I never expected you to come this soon. In fact, I had some doubts you'd come at all. I wondered whether this whole business might be a trap."

"Didn't my letter convince you?" she exclaimed softly.

"To be honest—no, not completely."

"I suppose what I wrote was terribly incoherent. That's how I felt the night Roger spoke your name. The old one. But Philip Kent's a fitting name too, considering who your father was—"

All at once she hugged his hand to her breasts. Even through the layers of her clothing, the touch triggered sensations in his body; a memory of how much he'd loved her.

Did he still?

She started chattering, her delight almost girlish:

"According to the proprieties, I should have waited a week or more before setting one foot outside the Trumbull house. I simply couldn't. And I don't care whether my aunt and her husband are scandalized. Nothing matters except finding you again."

"Where do these relatives of yours think you've gone this evening?"

"For the air. To escape from that stifling house— nothing but the stench of candles burning by Roger's bier. I'll have to take him home for burial. I don't know whether I can endure that—" Her voice broke just a little. "How did you come to bring him down?"

"Must we talk about it?"

"I'm curious, that's all. Roger never explained."

"I'd rather not explain either. Unless it matters greatly to you."

She shook her head. "He never mattered. I knew that the last time I saw you. But I went ahead. The marriage—"

"Children?"

"No, none. Though not for his want of trying. I made a frightful mistake in England, Phillipe—do you mind my calling you by that name?"

"I suppose not."

"I'm glad. I really can't think of you any other way."

"You spoke about a mistake."

"Yes. I should have come with you."

"Why didn't you?"

"Oh, darling, I told you on Quarry Hill—I didn't have the courage. But after you left, I felt nothing for him. Nothing—ever. It may be a mortal sin to say that, with him dead no more than a few days. I can't help it." A pause. Then: "But let's not talk of grim things. I had no idea you'd emigrated. I was astonished when Roger spoke your name. When did you decide on the colonies?"

"When I was in London. It seemed a better choice than crawling back to poverty in France."

"Tell me what's become of you, living in that seditious Boston. Philadelphia's full of talk of armed rebellion—perhaps coming very soon. Have you been caught in that?"

"Some."

"And your mother? How is she?"

"My mother," he said slowly, "died on the voyage to America."

"Oh, I am sorry. How did it happen?"

"Your hus—Roger hired killers to find us. In London, we got away. But they followed us when we took the coach for Bristol. The fear—the running—destroyed my mother's health and sanity."

"What became of the men?"

"There's no need to go into that."

Alicia looked at him, unblinking. "Did you kill them, Phillipe?"

"Let's just say we managed to escape them."

"I heard nothing of any such schemes after the household men lost you that night in Tonbridge."

"I'm sure it's something Roger preferred to keep to himself. I wouldn't doubt Lady Jane knew about it, though. I think she was the one who feared me the most."

"Feared? Perhaps. But she never hated you a tenth as much as Roger did after you ruined his hand."

Philip shrugged: "As you said yourself—why dwell on grim things? It's over. What happened to Roger was the natural consequence of his own desire for revenge. His fault, not mine."

"Ah, you've turned hard," she breathed. "The marks on you aren't only on the surface. Well, I have some of both kinds myself, my dear."

Looking past her, Philip saw that the team had borne them to the riverfront. Warehouses loomed. From the other window, he saw the lights of trading vessels riding at anchor. The tang of the ocean drifted into the coach on the warm April wind.

They sat a few moments in silence. With his leg touching hers, Philip felt the familiar reaction stirring him. He wanted to hold her again. But he made no move.

An open tavern doorway lit her blue eyes briefly. He wasn't sure what he saw in that gaze. Love? Or speculation—an attempt to judge him? For some reason, he was disturbed.

Then he recalled that Alicia Parkhurst was nothing if not deliberate. She had proved that in England, by her decision to remain with Roger even when she professed that she loved only him— A first stir of suspicion came. He asked:

"Can these coachmen of yours be trusted?"

"I would hope so! Else I've squandered several expensive bribes. But I want to hear more about Boston. Have you really become involved with those treasonous people?"

"Wouldn't you suspect that, from what happened to Roger?"

"Yes."

"There's your answer."

"But where do your sentiments lie?" She squeezed his hand. "Not that it's of any great importance, you understand. It's just that so much time has gone by, I can't help wanting to know everything. How have you lived? Have you taken up a trade?"

"I learned a little about printing in London. The experience got me a job in Boston. I worked for a man who publishes a newspaper that—well, is not exactly popular with your General Gage."

"The military governor?"

Philip nodded.

"He's not *my* General Gage! I got fairly sick of Roger's ranting letters. All about the necessity to punish the partisans of the so-called liberty movement—"

"I'd expect that of Lady Jane's son," Philip observed.

"Well, I've no concern for politics—or the past. There will have to be the necessary observance of mourning in England. But when that's done—" She leaned near, a strand of her tawny hair loosening and falling against his skin. "—I can be with you. That's how it should have been after we first met. You remember I thought of it—"

"Of course I remember. But as you said a moment ago—you hadn't the strength."

"Time changes people—"

Stiffening abruptly, she sat back.

"Phillipe, what's wrong?"

The swaying of the coach over the riverfront cobbles filled him with a momentary dizziness, a gut nausea he couldn't control.

"Phillipe—tell me!"

"There is something damnably wicked in all this, Alicia."

"Wicked? Why?"

"Because I killed your husband!"

"And I told you it doesn't matter! Of all people, why would you be guilt-stricken? You told me how many times he struck at you. More than I ever heard of, certainly—"

"Yes, that's true."

"All right, what is it? Did you attack him by surprise? Waylay him?"

"No. We met by accident."

"Then forget him. He's gone! He can no longer hurt you—or claim me. I was a sham wife to him anyway."

"In what sense?"

"The most important one. I took lovers. And every one was you. I'd close my eyes and see your face—always yours. Now that I've found you again, I won't let you go."

"Not unless I'm apprehended," he said with a humorless smile.

"No one here knows who killed Roger! He repeated your name only to me, I'm positive of that. So there's no danger. Provided you weren't detected in Boston—"

"I don't think so."

"So the secret will be buried with him. We're free!"

"Alicia—"

Again he stopped. Shook his head.

"Speak what's really on your mind, Phillipe. I don't believe it's Roger."

With those words, he caught a new, harder note in her

voice. A lantern over the front of a chandler's store highlighted tiny pits in her cheek. His earlier judgment hadn't been wrong. Young as she was, her face was already showing the ravages of the pastes and ointments that had to be worn by ladies of fashion, no matter what the cost. For a moment, her blue eyes looked like agate—

Or so he imagined, as the coach rolled by the chandler's into a gloomier section.

All at once she clapped her black gloves together.

"Dear Lord, I forgot the most obvious question—which in turn gives me the answer." Her smile was the kind of coquetry at which she was so skilled. "You've wed some other woman!"

"No, I haven't."

"Very well—promised yourself. Who is she? Some coarse little merchant's daughter?"

Her mockery angered him. His mouth set. "Anything of that nature, Alicia, has no part in this talk. You say Roger's death can be forgotten. But there's no way of overlooking this. I'm still what I've always been. A commoner. Whatever—" Sarcasm crept in. "—presumptions I may have had at Kentland are gone. I've been forced to make my way without a title, or wealth, and I've done it. Not handsomely. But I haven't starved. Suppose we do feel about each other as we did in England. That doesn't change my circumstances—or my prospects."

"Nothing but excuses!" Alicia breathed, caressing his face with her lips. "I know the truth—you're involved with another woman."

"Alicia, listen—!"

"Do you think I can't make you forget her? I love you, Phillipe Charboneau. I'll love you as Philip Kent, if that's what you want. But I am going to do what I should have done long ago, and that's love you completely—"

Soft and moist, her mouth pressed his face while her gloved hand stroked the back of his neck. He felt the heat of her now. And strangely, he was both excited and appalled.

"I plan to marry you, Phillipe," she whispered. "I'll make you forget any other woman. Every day—and every night—"

Her gloved hand was on his hip, questing. He was aroused.

"—for the rest of our lives."

Alicia's mouth found his, open, hungry. The hand in the glove reached between his legs and closed, holding hard.

Abruptly, he abandoned his hesitation. Reached beneath her cape to feel the warmth and fullness of her breast. She began to moan and twist a little on the seat of the coach, the glove opening and closing, making his arousal almost unbearable.

He had an impulse to take her here, in the coach, with the bribed men riding above. Who gave a damn if they smirked at the sounds they heard in the windy April night? Wealth could buy anything. Their silence, conspiracy to defraud him of the inheritance that was his; murder—

She felt him go limp. She lifted her hand away. He heard rather than saw her rage.

"So it's not the same after all. You've forgotten your own promises back in England."

"Alicia—" He caught her hands again, feeling the tension in her fingers. "When you touch me like that, it's as if nothing's changed. No years have gone by. But I'm still not a rich man like Roger! I have no title, no money to speak of—"

"Surely you have ambitions!"

"Of course. But this plagued war they keep talking about may well ruin them all. Even if it doesn't, there's no way on God's earth I could ever match the wealth you were born to—no way I could buy you the kinds of things you grew up with—and that you take for granted. After six months of a marriage like that, I doubt you'd say any of the things you've said tonight."

She tried teasing him: "Are you so afraid to put me to that test?"

"Alicia, in Boston I lived in a cellar room. A small, grubby cellar room—with one candle for light! That's what you'd have living in America, at least for a few years—"

"You're not thinking clearly, Phillipe. What's to keep us from going back to England? I must take Roger there—surely we can find a ship before the trouble breaks out—"

"And what would your family think of that? I can just see them when you walk in with a printer's devil with one good broadcloth suit to his name."

"I don't *care* what they think, Phillipe! That's what I keep trying to make you understand!"

"But I care. Because eventually, the poverty would destroy everything between us. Suppose I were to become a reasonably successful printer. That would still be meaningless compared to the station of the men who've surrounded you all your life."

She dismissed him with a wave. But her strained smile was clearly visible against other lamps passing outside the oblong of the window.

"England's changing," she said. "My father detests the idea—refuses to admit it's happening—but it is. It's the mercantile class that's coming to power, because they control more and more of the money. Marriages between prosperous businessmen and daughters of peers are becoming commonplace—oh, you don't seem to see it at all! We needn't *go* to England! I'll bury Roger and come back to you here. Nothing is of any importance save one fact—I *love* you!"

She threw her arms around his neck, kissed him—and

he felt himself begin to surrender, his arguments melted by the warmth of her body, the touch of her hands and her hungry mouth. He forgot his suspicion that somewhere, somewhere in this patchwork-puzzle of frenzied emotion, there was an explanation she had not made clear. He forgot—and kissed her again, with passion, while the coach creaked on through the dim Philadelphia streets.

When they separated, she dabbed her eyes. Her laugh sounded both gay and sad.

"How amused they'd be at home. Parkhurst's daughter weeping like some ribbon girl over her swain. I could almost hate you for that, Phillipe—if I didn't love you so much."

Another long, deep kiss. Then, tear-traces gone, she said:

"I do see there's still a battle to be fought."

"With me?"

"Yes! To batter through all those defenses you've raised. Well, I warn you, Phillipe, you'll find me a fierce combatant. Because you and I are going to be husband and wife."

Her directness left him startled and silent. She reached up, rapped the roof twice. The coach began to pick up speed, the heavy iron tires clanking noisily over the bricks.

"However, there are a few proprieties to be observed," she told him. "Can you stay in Philadelphia a few days?"

He came close to saying no. There remained some element that troubled him deeply—and eluded his understanding. Was it Anne? Or feeling like a kept creature at the City Tavern? Damned if he knew—

She touched him. "Phillipe?"

"Yes," he said, "I can stay."

"I'll come to your rooms next time. I can't do it immediately. But I'm sure it can be arranged before too long. Since the burial services must be held in England, I can move about the city making arrangements to transport the body. Aunt Sue's husband feels a new widow should remain indoors, grieving. I shall convince him he's wrong. At least in my case."

She sounds supremely confident, he thought, marveling. It reminded him of the first day he saw her, fresh from the sunshine at Kentland, accompanying the man she was to marry and he was to kill. In his mind he'd called her an elegant whore. A woman who manipulated men to her own ends—

Her remark of a moment ago showed she hadn't entirely changed.

Why, knowing that, had he agreed to stay? He couldn't fully explain it. She had a power to weave spells—wake emotions—that overcame all reason—

She was whispering again:

"I want to be alone with you, Phillipe. I want us to be alone the way we were before. There are years to be wiped out. And more things I want to ask about you than I can begin to think of now."

Her blue eyes picked up the gleam from the leaded windows of the City Tavern. The coach swung past the front of the building, on the way to the alley. She laid a gloved palm on his cheek.

"I'll marry you, Phillipe Charboneau, and God damn what any of the rest of them say."

She brought her face close. The moist tip of her tongue crept into his mouth for one last caress. The coach stopped, swaying. He heard the tall servant grumble something to the driver. Boots crunched on the ground. The door was levered open.

The tall man's eyes, lewdly amused, slid to Philip's face. Philip climbed out. Had the man said a word, Philip would have hit him.

But the servant knew the limits. He mounted to his

place on the box and signed the driver forward.

Philip stood under the April stars, his clubbed hair blowing in the wind. As the coach vanished around a corner, he thought he heard a low, lilting laugh—

A laugh of pleasure. Certainly—

Victory.

God, how easily she manipulated him too! *And yet you don't put a stop to it, do you, my friend?*

Nor could he put a stop to his uneasiness. Its source remained hard to define. Perhaps it *was* Anne—and the vivid image of the liberty medal cast aside. Or the shameful fact that Alicia's husband was not yet even in his grave—

He knew one thing. Only three or four years ago, he would never have raised a quibble about the future Alicia wanted. To have married an earl's daughter would have fulfilled his ambitions completely—

Then.

It was a mark of all the change that time and circumstances had wrought that at this moment, he hesitated—

Remember what she stands for. The same kind of power the Amberlys used against you. How can she give that up?

Of all the questions, that one troubled him most. He knew Alicia too well to believe in miracles of love. Either she had given way completely to passion, and didn't honestly realize the implications of all she'd said tonight—

Or—a return of his earlier suspicion—there was something else he didn't understand.

Instead of going upstairs, he walked around to the main entrance of the City Tavern. At a table in the public room, he drank three tankards of flip, trying to solve the enigma of the night's developments. Failing, he drank one more to get rid of the nagging questionmarks.

He staggered up to his room half-drunk and vaguely ashamed. The landlord had refused money for the drinks. The sum would be added to his bill.

In the darkness, he flung the warming pan out of bed and sprawled, trying to think it through.

Instead, he slipped into sleep—dreaming not of Alicia but of Anne Ware.

ii

A week in Philadelphia's balmy April weather brought him a sense of the pace and mood of the prosperous Quaker city.

On Tuesday evening, the sonorous "butter bells" of Christ Church tolled for the coming of market day on Wednesday. But everywhere, talk concerned itself less with commerce than with the trouble in Massachusetts.

Taking a meal in the tavern's main room of an evening, he found that careful listening provided bits of news that were apparently being relayed by mounted courier to Philadelphia's patriot faction.

Companies of British soldiers, he heard, had once more marched from Boston, this time toward the village of Brookline. Philip assumed the force had numbered fewer than five hundred men. There was no word of hostilities.

But the well-dressed gentlemen who dined and drank and cursed the North ministry under the blackened beams seemed to share the opinion of most everyone Philip talked to: hostilities were now inevitable.

He listened to men at the City Tavern laud some Virginia orator named Henry. In late March, the man had addressed the House of Burgesses and declared that, with war a virtual certainty, he saw only two choices for men of conscience—liberty or death.

The ruffled and powdered gentlemen of the City Tavern also seemed to be among the first to receive overseas news from arriving ships. Yes, the King was determined to force a showdown. The gentlemen banged their sticks on the pegged floor and shouted, "Fie, oh fie!" until the smoky room fairly thundered with the racket of the ferrules.

And when some slightly tipsy patriot rose to quote excerpts of the Henry speech, the sticks thundered with equal ferocity. This time in approval.

Six days passed. Philip was continually worried about Anne Ware and her father. Once he saddled Nell, intending to ride to Arch Street, bid Alicia goodbye and return north.

But with the saddle in place, he unstrapped it again. As he laid it aside, he cursed his own indecision—and Alicia's hypnotic influence on his feelings.

I will see her one more time, he thought. *That will be the end.*

Yet he wasn't sure.

What if, through some strange chemistry of the emotions, she truly *had* decided Roger Amberly's world was not all she had once thought it to be? What if she really did want to be his wife, regardless of his prospects for the future? Time and events had changed him; why couldn't the same thing have happened to her?

As a result of this kind of self-questioning, he remained in Philadelphia—in limbo.

The tavern conversation was full of references to the Second Continental Congress, due to open in early May now that George III refused to give ground. On his seventh afternoon in the city, Philip asked directions to the site of the forthcoming assembly. He strolled through the mild April twilight under the elm trees beginning to show their buds, and reached the imposing brick State House.

In the yard, boots tramped in rhythm. He looked in to watch a local militia unit drilling. Near them, half a dozen splendid saddle horses were tied.

As the militiamen executed a smart countermarch,

Philip was troubled by a memory of Colonel Barrett and the Concord companies—as well as by thoughts of all those who had befriended him, adopted him to their cause—

Ben Edes.

Lawyer Ware.

Anne—

God! he swore silently. *That man was ever born to be torn and troubled by women!*

He absolutely could not stand to wait any longer. He resolved to get a message to Arch Street. Face Alicia, and see whether the encounter would lead to a resolution of the turmoil within him. One moment, he wanted her desperately. The next, he suspected her motives—

Yes, let it be a message to Arch Street! He'd hire another tavern boy and damn the furor it might cause among her relatives.

Vaguely aware of the *clip-clop* of hoofs behind him, he started away from the gate of the yard, determined to force the confrontation before the day was over—

"Sir—a moment. Aren't we acquainted?"

The voice broke Philip's concentration. He turned to see a man on horseback outside the State House gate. A stout, elderly man with spectacles and an all-but-bald pate—

It was Franklin.

The doctor had evidently come out of the State House and mounted one of the horses tied to the ring blocks in the yard. He was gorgeously clad in a suit of deep emerald velvet. White ruffles at the throat matched his white hose. Silver buckles decorated his shoes. Franklin nudged his horse with his knees and rode forward.

The sight of him carried Philip back instantly to Sweet's Lane and Craven Street. Dr. Franklin still wore those glasses with differing thicknesses in the same lens. But the jowly, keen-eyed face appeared to have aged a good deal. The lines were deeper. Franklin's smile as his horse trotted up seemed less natural than before, tinged with a puzzling melancholy—

"Warmest greetings to you, Dr. Franklin," Philip said.

"Mr. Charboneau, isn't it? I remember you distinctly from London."

Philip smiled. "That's mutual, sir. I remember you—and with much appreciation. Your loan of five pounds helped me reach Bristol and the colonies."

"That's splendid, splendid."

"But I've taken an American name here. Philip Kent."

"Capital! I was informed you were forced to leave London in some haste. I trust the list and letter were of assistance in establishing you in the printing trade?" Franklin pushed his spectacles down and peered over the top of the frames. "I mean, sir, I expect the loan to be repaid when your industry makes you rich."

Preferring not to tell Franklin how he'd lost both documents, Philip simply said, "It'll be repaid, you can count on it. I found a very good location with a Mr. Edes in Boston."

"Ben Edes of the *Gazette?* Then you're not set up here in Philadelphia?"

"No, I'm only in the city on—on business."

Gazing down from the expensive saddle of polished leather, Franklin gestured. "Sir, come along! You must let me buy you a mug of coffee or chocolate while you bring me up to date on news from our beleaguered sister city. How recently did you come from there?"

"Close to three weeks ago. I'm afraid any news I have is badly dated."

"Mmm, quite so. However, working with Ben Edes puts you on the proper side, doesn't it, Mr.—Kent, isn't that what you said?"

"Right."

"Good and proper American name. This way —there's a very excellent and popular place just a few steps from here. I insist you let me buy you a refreshment. I want to hear how you've gotten on. After all," Franklin added, still smiling that strangely forced smile, "I had something to do with persuading you to sail to this side of the ocean, I believe."

"You certainly did, sir."

"Perhaps now, with everything in such a catastrophic muddle, you've begun to regret heeding my advice!"

CHAPTER IV

Too Much for the Whistle

i

PHILIP WALKED BESIDE Franklin's horse to their destination, The Sovereign Coffee-House, less than a block distant. The doctor frowned at the sight of several other horses tied up in front. Young black grooms held the reins of two more.

As Franklin swung down with a grace surprising for a man of his years, Philip glanced at the faded sign above the doorway. It bore yet another of those ubiquitous likenesses of the Hanoverian king. But some zealous individual had managed to stain the plump, painted face with what appeared to be dung. The Sovereign's proprietor hadn't bothered to remove it.

"Place looks more crowded than usual," Franklin muttered as he and Philip pushed through the door. "Hope my favorite spot's not taken—damme, it is."

He indicated a deacon's bench under the swirled bottle glass of a window to their left. Franklin scratched his chin while heads turned. There were whispers, pointing fingers. Philip realized he was in the company of a celebrity.

No one in the shop seemed inclined to offer the celebrity a place to sit, however. And Philip saw only one vacant table, a small one in a dingy rear corner.

But Franklin had a sly twinkle in his eye and didn't budge from the entrance. He signaled to the landlord's boy, called sharply:

"Young man! If you please!"

Recognizing his important visitor, the boy rushed forward.

"Very sorry, Doctor, but we've only that back spot open—"

"I suppose we'll have to take it," Franklin shrugged. "By the way, my horse is tied out front, and he's hungry. The big roan—you know the one?"

" 'Course, sir."

"Take him a quart of oysters immediately."

"A quart of *oysters?*"

"You heard me—a quart of oysters!" boomed the older man. More heads turned. Eyes popped and conversations stopped. "You have them this month, don't you?"

"Yes, sir, got plenty."

"Then see to it. My horse craves oysters in the worst way."

Philip threw Franklin a questioning look, but the doctor simply proceeded majestically toward the little table in the back. Philip followed. By the time they reached the table, the boy had returned from the kitchen carrying a small copper pot. Two men rose from a table. Two more. Before a minute had passed, The Sovereign was virtually empty, most of the clientele having followed the boy outside to view the remarkable horse that consumed oysters.

"We can move up front now, Mr. Kent," Franklin said. "My favorite place is vacant."

And so it was. Philip chuckled as Franklin settled on the deacon's bench, remarking, "A little trick I learned when I first took over the postal system years ago. I traveled the routes personally to inspect them. Most country inns where I stopped were crowded of an evening. When I wanted the seat next to the fire and it was taken, I called for oysters for my horse. Never failed. The boy will be back momentarily to take our order."

Franklin's prophecy was correct. The landlord's young helper looked unhappy as he approached, his oyster pot empty. He indicated a red place on his forearm.

"That damn horse won't have a thing to do with oysters, Dr. Franklin! When I tried to feed 'im, he near bit my arm off. I spilled the whole blasted quart."

Franklin looked thoughtful. "Perhaps my horse suddenly lost his appetite."

"And I lost my seat," complained one of the men who had trooped back inside.

"Oh, I thought you'd departed, sir," Franklin said in a bland tone. "Well, there are plenty of other places— boy, two chocolates here. And put the oysters on my bill, of course."

He turned his attention back to Philip, who could hardly control a guffaw as the tricked patrons stampeded through the shop, attempting to regain their former tables. Franklin ignored them. Sunlight through the bottle glass struck fire from his spectacles as he asked whether Philip's mother was satisfied with their new country. Philip told him of her death aboard *Eclipse*.

"Ah, that's tragic news. You have my deepest sympathies. I suffered a bereavement myself only this past December—" The boy arrived with warm mugs of chocolate, left again. "I was still in England when I received word that my dear Joan had died."

"Your wife? Oh, doctor, I'm sorry."

"At least I had my Philadelphia family to come home to—my daughter Sally lives here with her husband, Richard Bache." Philip wondered why Franklin made no mention of his illegitimate son. "And you've found a home too, Mr. Kent—literally, if not philosophically —with Ben Edes?"

"And met Samuel Adams, and Mr. Revere and Dr. Warren and many of the other patriot leaders."

"Excellent men, every one," Franklin nodded, sipping his chocolate. "I'm informed their lives are forfeit if they stay in Boston much longer, though."

"To my knowledge, all but Warren and Revere have gone out into the country. I helped a British soldier find a safe haven there, in fact."

"Helped him desert?"

Philip nodded. "He didn't have any stomach for causing trouble for other Englishmen. I took him to Concord. I've been drilling with one of the militia companies there."

Franklin pulled down his spectacles. "Is it committee business that brings you to Philadelphia?"

Redness colored Philip's cheeks. "No, it's—it's personal. In a way, it was a relief to get out of Massachusetts for a while. Things are so damned confused— Some people want independency, some don't—and most have no opinion but are scared as hell anyway, because everyone's convinced there's going to be trouble."

Sadly, Franklin bobbed his head to agree. "The irony is, just prior to sailing from England—not only in low spirits but in some disgrace, as you may have heard!—I had an audience with one of this country's last good friends. The Earl of Chatham. I told him that in all my years in the colonies, I had never, in any conversation, from any person drunk or sober, encountered a deep and genuine wish for separation. Or the suggestion that such a thing would be of the slightest advantage to America. Yet back on these shores, I find it's being discussed openly. Once, the word was merely whispered —and only by radicals, at that."

The alert eyes pinned him. "Have you a position on

it, Kent? When the second Congress convenes, there'll be much interest in the state of mind of our citizenry. So every opinion's valuable."

Thinking a moment, Philip shook his head in a glum way. "I had unfortunate experiences in England—"

"Yes, you alluded to those when you visited Craven Street. Something to do with a well-placed family, I believe—?"

"That's right. The trouble they caused didn't exactly give me a favorable feeling about the ruling class. On the other hand, all except the most extreme men in Boston—Mr. Adams, for instance—seem to favor some kind of reconciliation."

"Even at this late hour?"

"If it's possible. Maybe it isn't. But with a few exceptions, the soldiers have behaved with restraint. Certainly the Governor has. I mean—elsewhere, I'd guess that a man like Gage would arrest a man like Ben Edes, considering the attacks on the general that the *Gazette's* printed."

"That restraint," Franklin returned, "is one of the reasons Gage's star is already falling in Whitehall. I believe he'll be recalled before too long. The King and his flunkies want decisive action now that they've declared Massachusetts in rebellion."

"I'll admit none of it's pleasant to look forward to—I hoped for a chance to build a future here. Maybe that's why I'm still a little on the fence. I've worn a liberty medal, helped Mr. Edes, things like that. But I haven't supported the cause as completely as I might have. Who wants to see the future go up in musket smoke? And risk dying at the same time?"

"No one who is sane," Franklin said. "But times do come in the affairs of men when such a course can't be avoided. I realize many, many people in America would prefer safety to the perils of war—" Franklin set his chocolate mug down, his voice low, his spectacles like twin fires in the filtered sunlight. "But those who would give up essential liberty to purchase a little temporary safety deserve neither liberty nor safety." A pause. The melancholy look returned. "So we must go ahead, whatever the outcome—though I'm not at all certain a war would succeed."

"Well, that's one view I haven't heard before."

"You hear only the patriot side. Narrow, and admittedly partisan. I try to sound all quarters. I believe only a fraction of our population would support armed hostilities. A fourth, perhaps. A third if we were lucky. We have no army, and who knows how untrained farmers and artisans would behave against regiments that have distinguished themselves on battlefields all over the world? And yet," he went on earnestly after another pause, "I am still persuaded that we're traveling the only road we can. In my opinion there is no greater crime under heaven than for one man to allow another to place him—or his nation—in bondage. However"—He shrugged." "—that's a stand which each must take for himself."

Franklin's words struck Philip like a blow. Struck and drove deep into his mind. An image of Marie Charboneau drifted through his imagination. Her views were certainly in marked contrast to Franklin's. But as a result of the man's quiet, forceful words, Philip found himself agreeing silently.

A sudden, wrenching insight came to him:

What my mother wanted was no less than bondage of another kind. Voluntary bondage to the ways of the Amberlys. Not a fulfilling bondage, as Anne called it. A destructive one. Only my mother never saw that—

Against the murmur of talk that had resumed at nearby tables, Franklin said something else. Philip looked up. The doctor's eyes were hidden by the sunglaring spectacles. Yet Philip had the uncanny feeling that Franklin was looking through him, toward some deep sadness.

"I beg your pardon, Doctor, I didn't hear what you said."

"Oh, I was only thinking of my Billy."

"Your son?"

Franklin nodded, said with faint bitterness, "His Excellency, the Royal Governor of New Jersey. Each man, as I say, takes a stand. Billy's taken his. I helped him obtain his position. Pulled every string I could in London, back in the days when relations with the colonies were more cordial. I wanted Billy to have an important post! But I also thought I'd drilled some sense into him when he was young—"

Franklin's hand clenched, white at the knuckles. "I sailed home only a few weeks ago with the highest hopes. I prayed I'd step off the ship and hear Billy had resigned in protest against the Crown's actions. Well, Mr. Kent, he hadn't. And I'm informed he won't. I love him above any person in this world save my dear departed wife, and I'm not ashamed of that. But, God help me, I love liberty more. Billy, it seems, does not. I hear he's grown extremely fond of the perquisites of his splendid life. It'll drive a wedge between us. Forever, if he persists."

Once more Franklin pulled down his spectacles, and once more Philip saw the sadness. Now he understood another reason for it.

"It's all choice, Mr. Kent," Franklin sighed. "How much are you willing to pay for the whistle?"

"The what, sir?"

"Oh—" A gentle smile. "That's just an old expression of mine. When I was growing up in Boston, a visitor to our house gave me some pocket change. Later that day, in the streets, I met a boy playing a whistle. I'd never heard such a sweet sound. I offered the boy all the money I'd been given—and tooted that whistle mighty proudly when I got home. My brothers and sisters broke out laughing. It came like a thunderclap when they, with my father's corroboration, convinced me I'd paid the lad four times what the whistle was worth. The whistle instantly lost its charm. As soon as I heard my family laughing, and thought of what I'd squandered, I cried with the vexation only the young can summon. Ever since, the incident's stuck in my mind. Whenever I'm tempted toward a comfortable but wrong judgment as opposed to the one that's difficult but right, I say to myself, 'Franklin, do not give too much for the whistle.' That's what Billy's done, you see. I—" Franklin seemed to speak with great effort then. "—I will very likely never see him again unless he resigns. And I don't think he'll have the courage. He's still enchanted with the whistle for which he's paid too dear a price."

Philip stared at his own hands. After a moment, the doctor let out a long sigh. "Well, that's all beside the point—we were talking of broader matters. I really wish I know where all the turmoil will end. We're a powerful people here in America. Unique in many ways. Should the ministers decide to test us to the limit, I think they will be mightily astonished—at first, anyway. In a long war—" A doubtful lift of the shoulder. "I've expressed my views on that."

"Do you think the ministers will test us, Doctor?"

"Given George's determination—yes, I believe it will happen. His Majesty's not an evil man. But he's a bad, misguided king. And there's not a person in his administration who'll gainsay him. Not North, not Dartmouth, not Kentland, not—"

Franklin stopped, clacked down his mug.

"What's wrong, Mr. Kent? You're white as ashes."

"You spoke a name—I'm not sure I understood —Kentland?"

Franklin nodded. "Aye, James Amberly, the Duke of Kentland. A member of the little clique known as the King's Friends. He's an assistant secretary for overseas affairs, in Lord Dartmouth's department." The jowly man peered over his spectacles. "You're acquainted with him?"

"I—I heard the name at Sholto's," Philip said quickly. "They said he was highly placed—but I also heard that he had died. Could there be two noblemen with that name?"

"There is one hereditary Duke of Kentland and only one, Mr. Kent. Come to think of it, though, I do recall that Amberly was gravely ill a few years ago. For months, he never left his country seat. He did recover eventually. Came up to the town and took a place in the government. That, I believe, had been his plan before an old war wound caused the illness."

"He's alive? Today?"

"I can't speak for today. But I conversed with the Duke outside the House of Lords a fortnight before I sailed. A wise, humane man in all respects—save for his blind loyalty to King George. His wife's another case entirely. A regal bitch, with the emphasis on the latter. I'll admit Amberly didn't look too healthy when we spoke. But he's certainly able to get about and assist Dartmouth in the execution of foreign policy. I also understand his only son is serving in the military somewhere in these very col—*good heavens!*"

Philip had stood up suddenly, nearly overturning the table. His face was stark with the disbelief hammering in his mind.

They said he died. *They told us he died.*

The implications of the treachery left him in a cold fury, shaking. He could barely speak:

"Dr. Franklin—you'll pardon me—there's something I must do—"

"Wait, Kent! I remember what you told me in Craven Street—your father not married to your mother—*was Amberly*—?"

Leaving the doctor's question unanswered, Philip tore out of The Sovereign and broke into a run. He under-

stood some if not all of it. But most important—the
knowledge was like a white iron searing him—he
thought he understood Alicia.

There would indeed be a confrontation now. One that
would rattle the Tory teeth of the whole Trumbull
family!

He ran through the streets to the City Tavern, dashed
across the public room toward the stairs. First his
surtout and saddlebags. Then his horse. Then Arch
Street—

The landlord stopped him at the foot of the stairs:

"Mr. Kent, you've a visitor upstairs. Came
in the back way, just after dark." The man's smirk
widened. "The same benefactress, I believe, who's
handling your bills while you're here. I'm not anxious to
be known as a man who takes a lot of Tory money. But
when a woman's as fair, and as rich, as the one who—"

Philip was gone up the stairs.

He found the door to his room locked. He pounded
the wood till Alicia freed the latch to admit him.

ii

Her shoulders shone golden in the glow of the single
candle burning beside a pewter tray. The tray held two
goblets and a decanter of shimmering claret.

Alicia stepped back to let him enter. Her tawny hair,
unbound, hung down over her shoulders. She clutched a
woolen coverlet she'd wrapped around herself, holding
it at her breasts. But not so high that he couldn't see the
pronounced shadow at her cleavage. One raking glance
at the room revealed all the details she'd so prettily—and carefully—arranged.

The bed was turned back. The shutters were closed
against the spring dark. Her clothes were a lacy spill in
one corner.

Her bare feet whispered on the floor as she glided

toward him. The sudden way he slammed the door banished the heated glow from her eyes.

Her mouth went round. She started to frame a question. He was faster:

"Why didn't you tell me Lord Kentland is still alive in England?"

"What?"

The woolen coverlet slipped, showing her right breast. He closed his fingers on her forearm.

"Why didn't you tell me my father never died?"

The aroused pink tip of her breast shriveled. She seemed unable to speak. His voice savaged her:

"Why, Alicia?"

"I meant to when the moment was right—" She struggled, backing away. His grip held her. His fingers left livid white marks on her skin. "Who told you?" she breathed.

"A gentleman recently arrived from England—if that matters. My father wasn't dead when my mother and I were turned away from Kentland. It was all a fraud, a hoax! The mourning servants, the pretended grief—good Christ, how stupid they must have thought us! Peasant clods from France. Willing to eat whole any story they fed us!"

"Phillipe, let me explain—"

"They were right, weren't they? Who arranged it, Alicia?"

"If you'll stop hurting me—"

He bent her wrist. "Tell me, God damn it."

"Please, Phillipe—" She was almost whimpering. "Let go."

When he didn't, she bent her head, the tawny hair spilling across her forehead. She tried to press her mouth to his hand, kiss it, even as she brought her other hand up to stroke his arm.

"Please. Please don't hurt me, darling—"

He shoved her, hard.

Stumbling, Alicia collided with the bed. She shot out one hand to cushion her fall. The coverlet had dropped to her feet. By the gleam of the candle she was like some carved figure, nipples and belly and triangle of tawny hair sculpted and shadowed by the light—

She started to get up from the edge of the bed. She looked at his face, thought better of it. Her quick, breathy speech revealed her terror:

"Lady Jane hatched the scheme. She never stopped fearing you and your mother and that letter the Duke wrote. When—when it became evident you wouldn't leave until you saw your father, Lady Jane decided to arrange things so you'd have no further reason to stay. No hope of a meeting—"

"And it was easy for her to buy black wreaths for the door of Kentland. Easy to buy the mournful looks of the servants. Pay them enough and they'd go through any mummery—Lady Jane can buy anything or anyone, can't she? With money or with threats. Wealth and station—that's all it takes to create a little show to fool the stupid French boy and his mother."

"She was *afraid!* She knew her husband would acknowledge you publicly as his son if he ever met you face to face. She realized she had to use desperate means to get rid of you—"

"Meantime letting Roger pursue his own preventive measures!" Philip said, acid in his voice. "After she'd convinced us Amberly was dead and we'd run to London, she let Roger make sure we never walked out of the city alive. I never realized I had such power over her! Oh, my mother claimed there was great value in the letter. But I don't think I ever understood the full value until today."

He walked toward her slowly. Still huddled on the bed, she seemed to grow smaller.

"What I found out today also explains several other cloudy issues. Up in London, we could never pick up

any word of Amberly's death." His dark eyes narrowed
as he remembered the willow grove beside the Medway.
"And when you warned me about Roger, just before
my mother and I fled from Tonbridge, you said something that struck me as very odd. Something about
preparations for the burial. They could wait, you said.
While Roger finished his business with us. Yes, of
course they could wait."

He dug his fingers into the scented skin of her shoulder. Her breasts shook as she tried to writhe away,
crying out softly. He refused to let her go.

"You knew then that my father wasn't dead. You had
courage enough to warn me about Roger—but not
enough to tell all the truth. I thought you were hiding
something. I never guessed what it was."

Tears flooded her cheeks. In an almost hysterical
voice, she begged him to release her. He did. But it was
an effort to keep his hands off her throat.

She wept softly as he walked to the shutters, thrust
them open a little way. He fixed his eyes on the April
stars. He was fearful that he might do her physical
harm.

Soft footfalls. Hands slipped around his waist, clinging. Her breasts, her thighs were fierce against his back
and buttocks.

"Don't hate me too much. I tried to tell you about
your father but I couldn't bring myself to it. I'm no more
than what I was raised and taught to be. If you'd
stayed—if you'd discovered the hoax—I was sure you'd
meet Roger another time. Perhaps be killed—"

He seized her hands, broke the hold, whirled on her.

"Or kill him? And ruin your precious future? Lady
Jane wasn't the only one who wanted me gone!"

"Phillipe, I love you—and I loved you then. Only the
other night, I told you I'd made the wrong choice. It
took years of living with Roger for me to appreciate

that. I know I should have given you all the truth before.
I couldn't because, in my own way, I was as fearful as
Lady Jane. Yes, your accusation's true. But that's over.
That's the past, sweetheart—"

She slipped her arm around his neck, brought her
mouth near his, whispering:

"You're the only one I care about!"

Wildly, her mouth pressed against his. Her breathing
was strident as she kissed him, then again, moving her
body so the points of her breasts rubbed against him—

"Lie with me, Phillipe. Now—on that bed. Let me
show you the past doesn't count any longer. Roger's
gone—your father is alive—we've found each
other—*please, Phillipe. The bed*—"

A final, icy comprehension spread through him. Once
more he shoved her away.

"I think, Alicia, the past counts very much in your
case. Especially the way it's linked to the change in your
circumstances. Roger's dead. The Duke is living
in England. And I'm his only heir."

"That's your strength! Your advantage!" she cried, a
false joy on her face, an enthusiasm too bright, too in-
sistent. "If you return to London secretly—if you lo-
cate your father before Lady Jane gets word of it—and
show him the letter—Phillipe, you do still have the letter?"

He noticed a sheen of perspiration on her upper lip.
She no longer looked soft in her nakedness.

He said, "What if I answered no? Suppose I sent it
down to the sea with my mother's body?"

"*Tell me the truth!*" Alicia cried, running at him, one
small fist raised to strike.

A half-step away, she checked, sensing that she'd
betrayed herself. Her tone turned pleading. "Don't twist
words and make sport, Phillipe. Not when that letter can
mean a whole new world for you—"

"And you."

"You said you wanted to be what your father was! It's within your reach!"

"I realize that."

And it was a grievous burden.

A lifetime of longing—of being turned aside—of being wounded and counted no more than a cipher—all that could be erased. Canceled forever. His pledge to Marie could be fulfilled. And his savored dream of seeing England again, this time as a man of property—

No, more than that. A man of property and *title*.

It was all possible.

To such fulfillment could be added the bounty of this sleek, golden-breasted girl. A woman to teach him. To counsel him, and smooth his passage into the courts and the salons where his mother said he truly belonged.

If all that was his, *why in the name of Almighty God did something in him turn aside?*

As if in answer, the fragmented past leaped to mind—

He thought of Girard and his promise of the new winds that would blow away the tottering structure of a society gone corrupt, a hierarchy past its time.

He thought of plain Ben Edes and the power of his clattering wood press, of the meaning of so many of the pieces by Patriot and the others that he and Edes had labored long into the night to set and proof and print.

He thought of the liberty medal, and the night of tea sifting into Boston Harbor.

And he thought of all Benjamin Franklin had said only an hour ago.

Philip stared at Alicia, his eyes remote, strange. She was beautiful. *Beautiful.* But in his mind, a voice mocked—

And how much are you willing to pay for the whistle, my friend?

Alicia crept back to the bed, abruptly conscious of her nakedness. She covered her breasts and her pubis with the coverlet, her shoulders prickled with goosebumps. Philip smiled an odd smile. The spring air drifting through the half-open shutters was not all that chilly.

In the silence of his mind he said to Marie, *You were wrong. The greatest crime a man can commit is not bowing to poverty and obscurity but bowing to slavery. Allowing another to put you in ruinous bondage. Bondage of the body. Or bondage of the soul. Forgive me, if you can.*

Weight seemed to lift from him, a vast, encrusted weight of doubts, sometime hopes, vengeful yearnings. The weight broke and crumbled and he knew what Alicia was—

A creature exactly like the Amberlys.

How long, then, before he was transformed himself? Enslaved—and enslaving others in turn?

Slowly, he repeated the thought of moments ago:

"I do realize what's in reach, Alicia. But for some peculiar reason, I have a small doubt. One tiny doubt—"

He approached the bed. With one swift motion he stripped the cover from her body, hooked his hand down between her thighs, holding the hair of her, and the lips of flesh, for what they were—a marketable commodity.

"The doubt tells me you wouldn't offer this unless I had the letter. You wouldn't offer this, or all your endearments, or your vow that nothing else matters but our being married—"

She wrenched away, tumbled off the bed, fell to her knees. She was weeping again, this time in desperation:

"I love you, Phillipe. God as my witness—"

He extricated himself from the frenzied play of her hands.

"Forgive me if I don't believe that. Maybe you loved me a little in England. But never enough to tell me I was deceived. Never enough to leave Roger. You didn't love me enough to offer yourself until you were certain Roger was dying—and you realized I might, just might, still have a paper with monetary value. I never knew James Amberly. Perhaps he's not the same as the rest of you. But I intend to pass up the opportunity to find out."

"You incredible fool!" she cried, kneeling on the bed, her bare belly heaving, her embarrassment forgotten. "To walk out on riches—position—because I made one mistake—"

"Alicia, you made many more than one. At Kentland. On Quarry Hill and by the river. In the coach the other night—many more than one."

She screamed, "That letter is everything you wanted!"

"Once. Now, I don't want anything it can buy, including you. The price for using that letter is too high, you see."

"Price? What price? Phillipe—dear God, answer me!"

I must go, he thought. *Now—quickly—because I'm liable to kill her if I don't.*

Studying his own flexing hands, he avoided the sight of her kneeling on the bed. The tawny hair was a tangle around her shoulders. Her blue eyes were stunned and full of fear. Her shadow, cast by the guttering candle, was misshapen, hideous on the beamed ceiling—

Abruptly, he crossed to the corner where he'd left his saddlebags. He picked them up, still without looking at her. He walked toward the door.

"The letter can give you everything," she wept, rocking back and forth, small fists beating on her bare thighs. The mounting note of hysteria in her voice disgusted and saddened him. He kept on. Only four paces to the door—

"With the word of the Duke to verify your claim, you'll have what thousands of men dream of with never a hope—Phillipe? *Don't go—!*"

"Goodbye, Alicia."

"I'll go mad if you leave me—I'll kill myself—"

"Nonsense. You'll be married to another rich man within a year."

"I won't! I love *you!*"

"But not enough."

"Yes, now enough—more than enough—!"

"Goodbye, Alicia."

Screaming his name, she leaped from the bed, flung herself at him. She lost her footing, sprawled. Struggling up, she wrapped her arms around one of his boots.

Looking down at the tawny head, he felt pity. And a sense of walking through a dark, hostile valley where faint sunrise at last showed the path ahead. His urge to harm her physically drained away.

"You can't leave. I can't survive if you leave. *Phillipe—!*"

He was prying her fingers loose one by one. He didn't enjoy the sight of her agony, because he saw in her eyes the madness that can come of a lustful dream destroyed.

"Alicia, you've forgotten something," he said gently. "My name is Philip Kent. I'm not the man you wanted. I'm a Boston printer. The man who owned the letter—he died."

Lifting the latch, he went out quietly into the darkness of the corridor.

iii

Past ten o'clock, pushing the mare as hard as he dared, he reached the Delaware and roused the old ferryman in his shanty. With a lantern hung from a pole at the prow, the barge put out.

The river was flowing swiftly. The April night had turned cool. Philip stood with one hand on Nell's muzzle, staring at the black of the far shore while, behind him, the old fellow grumbled at the tiller.

The deed's done, he thought. Done in haste, perhaps. Done in anger, too. And—yes—still done with some guilt, because of Marie.

He wished the purling water would carry the barge faster. *I must bury that guilt now,* he said to himself. *The guilt must go down to its death because I have lived her life too long—*

He had no illusions about the existence of a hereafter, the kind of which divines were fond of speaking. Yet in some silent, mystic way, he hoped that the change which had taken place in him tonight would be understood by the woman who had given him life—along with another gift he could no longer claim.

The barge coasted toward the Jersey shore, where the dim lights of isolated farms showed in the wind-soughing dark. He admitted privately that many a man would call him crazy for what he'd done.

Slowly, though, he took a new perspective on it. With Alicia, he had only spoken aloud the final resolution that had been building for months and months. He didn't want what the parchment in Marie's casket could obtain for him if it meant becoming like the Amberlys and their kind. Users of others. Masters of others—by decree, or tax, or deceit, or secret assassination. He despised them. He had become a different sort of man.

Looking back, he couldn't mark the hour when he had changed. But he felt that the outcome of the night-marish scene with Alicia had probably been foreordained. Only his conscious mind hadn't known it until it happened.

The barge bumped against the rickety dock among the reeds. The old man tied lines, then hauled down the lantern. He had ruined yellow stumps for teeth, foul breath. But there was a certain sprightly gleam in his eye as he held the lantern aloft.

"Ye speak like a New England man, sir. Be ye riding home that way?"

"A New England—?" Taken aback, Philip smiled. When had the very sound of his voice altered?

He nodded in a friendly way. "Yes, I am. Out of Boston. I'm going there now."

"There's much talk o' fighting soon. Will ye be part of it? Or are ye Tory?"

"No, sir. I guess I'm what they call a Whig. I'll be on the fighting side."

" 'Tis a horrible thing—bloodshed. Battle. I lost a son on the Plains of Abraham, y'see—"

"I'm sorry to hear that."

"—even so, we can't give in to that fat old German farmer, can we, eh?"

"No, sir, that we can't."

Philip swung up on horseback, stepping the mare on-to the splintered planks of the swaying dock. Hoofs thudded, hollow. Then the horse was on soft shore ground. Philip turned her head north under the April stars. Behind him, the old ferryman waved the lantern and cried Godspeed.

Philip kneed the mare's flanks, absolved, at peace with Marie. His only worry was one that reached into the bottom of his heart—

He must find Anne. Now, above all, he must find Anne.

What if she'd gone from Concord with her father? What if hostilities had already started, and in the chaos of men mustering, he lost all chance to see her again?

What if she no longer wanted to see him? Because of the way he'd left her, he wouldn't blame her—

Against all the advice of O'Brian, he urged the mare to greater speed. He soon had her galloping at the limit of her strength.

CHAPTER V

Alarm at Midnight

i

AFTER THE RISING of the spring moon, Philip began to recognize familiar countryside.

The night was warm. The balmy spell had followed him all the way north from Philadelphia. Ideal weather, nothing worse than a couple of short rain squalls while he slept in the open. Tonight was no exception. Even so, he felt no lift in his spirits when he realized that he was less than ten miles from Concord.

He'd been riding ten days—or was it eleven? His skin was gritty. He'd washed his face and hands at spring-fed wells along the way—that is, he had whenever he'd been able to find a farmer who didn't mind a bedraggled stranger stopping on his property. Several times he'd been run off with threats and, once, with a blast of a musket.

As a result, he carried most of the grime of his journey with him—all over. His body ached from the up-and-down jolts of the ride. He'd long ago decided he would never be a good horseman, any more than he'd be a good sailor. He was a landsman, through and through.

Knowing it wasn't far now to the little village where, with luck, he might find Anne, he still couldn't throw off his lethargy. He slumped in the saddle, offended by his own sour smell. His senses were uniformly dulled.

The moon bleached the surrounding pastures dead

white. Ahead, he glimpsed the houses in tiny Lexington. More than a few showed lamps. That was odd. Surely the time was close to midnight—

He yawned. All at once he blinked. He noticed miniature, moon-touched figures on the neat central green of the village. The figures, some with lanterns, seemed to be scurrying every which way.

Immediately he suspected some kind of trouble. A British foray, perhaps. A raiding party on the way, hunting military stores.

Or perhaps they'd already arrived. He decided to forego satisfying his curiosity. Tugging the mare's rein, he cut across a pasture, intending to bypass the village.

As he rode, another peculiar fact struck him. Once north of Boston, he'd observed a great many countrymen on the roads this evening. Most had hailed him cordially, receiving a tired hail in return. He really hadn't paid much attention, or wondered about it at the time. But now, thinking of the running figures in Lexington, he began to ask himself why so many people were abroad. Was this some special occasion? A holiday?

Actually, he didn't even know the exact date. April seventeenth? The eighteenth, maybe. He'd lost track. But he wasn't familiar with any holidays around that time. Perhaps the fine weather had brought people out. Sent friends to gather at the taverns. And young men to court at neighboring towns and farms—

Soon Lexington lay behind him. He located a break in one of the low stone walls that flanked the level road to Concord. Less than five miles now. He yawned again. Stretched. The insides of his legs were nearly raw under his breeches.

Almost drowsing, he suddenly sat bolt upright. He heard a racket on the road ahead. Someone whacking on wood—

He peered under overhanging trees, made out a farm-

house set back from the left side of the road, where the
stone wall ended. He slowed Nell's pace, riding more
cautiously. The night was redolent with the smell of
spring earth. He discerned a horseman—

No, two.

Wrong again. There were three, sitting restless
mounts in front of the house.

One of the men hallooed and once more whacked the
porch post with a crop.

A door opened. A candle gleamed. The householder
wakened by the noise appeared as a blur on his
doorstep. Reining the mare to a stop by the end of the
stone wall, Philip sat dead still. He couldn't tell whether
the mounted men wore uniforms.

"Curse ye for raising such a noise at twelve o'clock!"
the farmer complained. "Who are ye? What do ye
want?"

The tallest rider maneuvered his horse forward so the
farmer's candle lit his profile and tricorn hat.

"You'll recognize me, Mr. Hunnicutt. Dr. Prescott
of Concord—?"

"Oh, aye. But I don't know those two with you."

"Express riders out of Boston. I met them near
Munroe's Tavern in Lexington. They came to alert the
Clarke household, where Hancock and Adams have
been staying. I told them that since I reside in Concord,
I'd best ride along and verify their identities."

"All right, but why waken sober folk at midnight,
Doctor?"

"Because, sir—" Philip stiffened, recognizing the
new voice instantly. "—after arranging for sexton
Newman to hang warning lanterns in his steeple at
Christ's Church tonight, Mr. Dawes and I came out of
town—he by the Neck, myself across the Charles in a
rowboat with wrapped oars—to alarm the countryside."

"Alarm?" the farmer repeated, sounding fully awake.

"Yes, sir. The regulars are coming out."

Philip's hand tightened on the reins as Revere went on:

"I fear you'll have noise a-plenty in a very few hours. The British are moving across the Charles in boats."

"My God! Ye can't be mistaken?"

"No. They're coming. No less than five hundred and perhaps as many as fifteen hundred. Dr. Warren's intelligence said their destination is Concord."

"No doubt they're after what military stores are left there," said the man identified as Dr. Prescott.

"Arm yourself accordingly." Revere added.

With a touch of his tricorn, the silversmith wheeled his horse and started out of the yard. Philip nudged the mare forward as Prescott said to the farmer:

"One more thing, Mr. Hunnicutt. A patrol of at least nine British officers passed through Lexington a while ago. They appeared to be bound this way—advance scouts, perhaps. Did you by any chance hear them pass?"

Hunnicutt said he hadn't. He'd been sleeping soundly.

"Well, they still may be ahead of us," Prescott said. "Good night, Hunnicutt." He rode out beneath the trees where Revere and his companion waited, both turning now as Philip's horse approached.

Hunnicutt vanished indoors. His voice sounded loudly, shouting to his wife. Philip was too tired to feel fear over the grim news he'd heard. He clattered up to the trio barring his way in the road, saw steel wink—a dagger or hunting knife—in the hand of Dawes. The lanky man was a Boston cordwainer. Philip had seen him once or twice with Revere at the Dragon.

"Who is it?" Revere called sharply as Philip reined in a few yards from them.

"It's Kent, Mr. Revere. Philip Kent, from Ben Edes' shop."

The silversmith gigged his horse into an open,

moonlit place in the road. "Come forward so I can see your face."

Philip did. Revere relaxed, saying:

"Edes told me you'd left the city. Where are you bound?"

"The same place as you. I've just come from Philadelphia."

Dawes slipped his knife out of sight. An owl hooted in a dark grove farther down the road. Young Dr. Prescott stepped his horse in closer to study the new arrival, asked Revere:

"You know and can vouch for this man?"

"Yes. He's a high Son of Liberty." Revere managed a tired smile. "Not to mention one of my dental patients."

"Then come along," Prescott said. "Time's running short."

With Dawes and Dr. Prescott riding abreast ahead, Revere fell in next to Philip, who said, "So the regulars are coming out at last?"

"In force." With cynicism, he added, "Are you surprised?"

"No, I guess not. But as I said, I've been away a while. I've no idea of what's happened in town—"

"Something's been afoot for several days. Officers combing the countryside, some in disguise, some not. Tonight our mechanics' committee detected the beginnings of a most peculiar activity. Light infantrymen and grenadiers of various regiments started turning out of their quarters and slipping off to boats that were recently moved to the Back Bay shore. There's been a lot of talk about a major troop movement. But no one knew exactly when it might come. This evening, we got our answer. One of my lads saw two mongrels lying bayoneted in the street."

Philip shook his head. "I don't understand."

"They're killing the dogs to prevent their barking. To

conceal all signs of what's supposed to be a secret expedition."

"I rode around Lexington," Philip told him. "I saw lanterns—men running on the green—"

"The minute companies are being called out. Hancock and his whole retinue—plus Mr. Adams—are packing to leave. They'll have their necks in ropes if the soldiers catch 'em—"

Abruptly, Revere reined in, responding to the upraised hand of Dawes farther up the road.

Philip inhaled the soft scents of the spring countryside, heard the gentle nickering of the horses—and drew a deep breath, his lethargy shattered. In this mild night, all silver and peaceful, the dreaded confrontation was in the making.

The night should be wracked with storms, he thought. *Rains, lightnings, thunder-peals—somehow, it's all wrong in such pleasant weather—*

He heard a whisper from Dawes, who was pointing down the road to Concord:

"Two men riding, Paul. I thought I saw metal trappings. Could be some of those officers."

"If there are just two, then the nine have split into teams. Let's see what they're up to—"

Dr. Prescott started to object. But Revere was already spurring his horse forward between Dawes and the physician. The two followed, Philip bringing up the rear.

Momentarily, he caught the sound of hoofbeats ahead. He couldn't see the riders. Trees arched thick over the road here, weakening the moonlight. The distant ridges around Concord further solidified the darkness of the background.

All at once, Philip heard what sounded like a voice in the woods on his left. He turned his head as twigs crackled. Suddenly three mounted figures broke from the shadows. Philip stood in the saddle, shouted:

"*Revere—!*"

"Keep your horse standing where it is," said the foremost rider. His cloak was thrown back, making his scarlet jacket dimly visible. In his right hand he held a military pistol at full cock.

The two officers with him were similarly armed. One chuckled in a humorless way:

"A nice bag of rustics, eh? It's well we took different sides of the road. Where are the rest?"

"Seizing the two ahead," replied the first officer.

Shouts rang out. Philip's belly tightened as he saw four more British officers ride from the thickets on the right side of the road. They filed their horses one by one through a gap in the stone wall, surrounding the others. Two more officers returned along the road to join them. One of the group called out:

"Major Mitchell? A catch here—"

"Good work!" answered the officer covering Philip with the glinting pistol.

Within moments, Revere, Dawes and Prescott had been driven back to where Philip sat captive. The four of them were ringed by the muzzles of nine side arms. Major Mitchell addressed the silversmith in clipped, proper English:

"May I crave your name, sir? And those of your companions?"

"I am Paul Revere of Boston."

"Revere! Gentlemen, we've made a fortunate catch." To the silversmith: "Who are your friends?"

"The others may speak or not, as they choose."

"They'll damned well speak or we'll blow their God damn heads off," another officer growled.

Mitchell raised his free hand. Then:

"What are you doing on this road, Mr. Revere? Riding express, perhaps?"

"I esteem myself a man of truth, sir. So to that, I can only answer yes." With audacity that astounded Philip, the silversmith went on, "May I ask the nature of your mission?"

Major Mitchell chuckled, genuinely amused. Philip couldn't help being surprised at the civility of it all. These redcoats were the enemy! Perhaps it was a measure of the reluctance of those on both sides to bring matters into open conflict that Mitchell deigned to answer at all.

"Why, Mr. Revere, we're out chasing deserters." His tone implied that he didn't expect Revere to believe the statement. He added, "And that's as much information as you'll get. But I expect a good deal more—"

He pointed his pistol at Revere's forehead, his voice less affable.

"I am going to ask you some questions, sir. If your replies are not truthful, I'll shoot you down."

Another of the men said, "There's moonlight back in the pasture, Major. We can get a better look at them there."

"Very well," Mitchell agreed. He indicated the prisoners. "Turn your horses about. Ride through that break in the stone fence beyond the trees."

Philip tugged the reins, fell in next to Dr. Prescott. The physician leaned over quickly to whisper something Philip couldn't catch. An officer thwacked Prescott's shoulder with the muzzle of his pistol.

"No talking!"

The young doctor swore under his breath.

As the four prisoners and their nine captors proceeded back along the road to the gap in the wall, another of the officers behind Philip exclaimed:

"By God, Mr. Revere, we've all heard of your riding. You will take your hands off those reins and let your horse walk."

The first officers reached the stone wall. They positioned their mounts to either side of the opening, waiting for Prescott to go through. With a yell, the doctor dug in his spurs. His horse leaped the wall.

A pistol exploded. Men cursed. Another gun went off, streaking the night with a bright powder flash. Then a half-dozen things seemed to happen at once.

Revere jumped to the ground, dodged between the startled officers and vaulted the stone wall on the other side of the road. Dawes, with an almost jovial shout, turned full about and spurred past Major Mitchell, clouting him with a fist as he raced by.

The major reeled in the saddle. His pistol discharged in the air. Smoke and the fumes of powder swirled. The officers' horses neighed and reared.

Philip saw the gap in the wall standing open. He kicked the mare forward, sighting on Dr. Prescott. Man and mount were a blur of silver out in the pasture, racing away from the stone wall.

Philip's horse plunged through the opening. He sensed rather than saw a pistol whip up on his left; an officer fought to control his horse and aim at the same time—

The mare almost stumbled in brambles as she cleared the wall. The pistol crashed, the orange glare blinding Philip momentarily. He felt the air stir behind his head where the ball passed. Bent over the mare's neck, he shouted to her for speed.

She escaped the brambles, sped across the loamy earth of the pasture, Philip still bending forward from the waist to present the smallest possible target. Another pistol exploded.

On the road—dwindling—sounds of confusion. Oaths. Commands bawled by one officer, then another. Revere had run off one way, Dawes had escaped another. They seemed to be the quarry Major Mitchell's party wanted most. At least, glancing over his shoulder, Philip saw no immediate signs of pursuit.

The ground swept by beneath the mare as she tried to respond to Philip's hammering boot heels. He could already feel her flagging. Ahead, where the pasture ended and a grove rose against the moon, Dr. Prescott had already disappeared.

Philip looked back again. One of the British officers was galloping after him, cloak streaming—

The mare reached the safety of the trees. Philip reined in. The pursuing officer stopped in the middle of the pasture, cursing loudly.

New shouts rang from the Lexington road. The officer in the pasture abandoned Philip for the more important fugitives, and cantered back toward the stone wall.

ii

After twenty minutes of walking the mare through the wood, Philip finally picked up the road to Concord again. He surveyed it in both directions from the screen of trees. Then he bore left toward the village cupped among the hills.

The brilliantly white April evening was still warm and sweet. But he was cold. Pistol fire and Mr. Revere's news—*The regulars are coming out*—had at last struck a heavy note of dread. Well before he rode into visual range of Concord, he heard the church bell begin to toll.

The alarm echoed from ridge to ridge, to wake the sleeping farmers, bring them hurrying into town. Philip recalled Dr. Franklin's grim reservations about the ability of country folk to stand against crack British regiments.

Clang and *clang,* the Concord bell pealed in the April stillness. He rode into the village to see a repetition of the sight glimpsed from the outskirts of Lexington. Men criss-crossed the street near Wright's Tavern, lanterns bobbing. Doors opened as young men and old turned out—with muskets. Dr. Prescott, then, had gotten through ahead of him.

In the confusion outside Wright's, he saw two boys on

farm ponies start in the direction of the South Bridge. Sent to summon militia companies from the neighboring towns, undoubtedly. Philip had seen it all rehearsed before. Heard it planned at the militia musters. Yet tonight, as men bawled questions, orders and milled uncertainly near the tavern, he could sense a difference. Voices were hoarse with strain. This was no rehearsal. Tonight—*clang* and *clang*—the regulars were coming out.

He hauled his aching frame down from the mare, pushed into the crowd. By a lantern's glare, he saw Dr. Prescott trying to answer a dozen questions at once:

"Yes, I think Mr. Revere is captured. Yes, he personally saw the regulars on the move. No, I don't know how many. More than five hundred, he was sure of that—what? No, not complete regiments. Flanker companies from different regiments. The light infantry, the grenadiers—"

That information produced a murmur of apprehension from the Concord men, perhaps fifty strong by now. Most had muskets. They understood the implication of Prescott's news. If General Gage had dispatched light infantry and grenadiers into the countryside, he was in deadly earnest. The flanker companies were the toughest, bravest fighters, the soldiers most accustomed to the heaviest combat—

A stocky man Philip recognized as Major John Buttrick, Colonel Barrett's second in command, fought his way to the stoop of Wright's. He raised his hand for silence. Gradually, the crowd quieted. Buttrick said:

"All those already armed remain here. Those not yet equipped, get your muskets and reassemble as quickly as you can. We have stores still to be moved here in town—we'll need every hand."

"Are we getting any help?" someone shouted.

"Yes! We've already sent to Lincoln for their minute

companies. We should be in good force if the lobster-backs get this far."

No one appeared encouraged by Buttrick's words. Everyone from stripling to graybeard knew full well that even several companies of militia could probably not stand for long against thoroughly trained British troops. But no one voiced the fear openly.

Buttrick continued to issue orders. Philip's attention was distracted. In the lantern light around Wright's stoop, hostile eyes locked with his.

Lawyer Ware.

His nightshirt was carelessly stuffed into his trousers. His thin hair blew in the breeze. The protruding eyes that could look so comical now looked anything but that.

At Buttrick's command, the crowd broke. Philip started for the tavern. Despite Ware's threatening expression, he intended to find Anne. Ware stood on the stoop, waiting. Never had the little man looked so formidable—or so full of wrath.

Philip had gone half the distance to the glowering lawyer when Buttrick caught his arm.

"You're Kent, aren't you? From O'Brian's place?"

"That's right."

"When you go to fetch your musket, make sure Barrett's heard the bell. Sometimes," he added with an empty smile, "Jim's fond of the rum jug and sleeps too deeply."

Then Buttrick was gone into the confusion of lanterns and shadow. Men were scattering to the various houses that held caches of supplies.

Lawyer Ware continued to stand on the step of Wright's. As Philip approached, the little man barked:

"Gone to Philadelphia, were you?"

"Yes, sir."

"Well, you've come back at a most inauspicious time. I'm sure you regret it."

"Regret it? Why?"

"I presumed you wanted to flee from danger—and your shameful actions."

Philip didn't fully understand Ware's scathing words. They angered him. A vein stood out on his forehead as he shot back:

"I went on necessary private business, Mr. Ware. Is Anne inside?"

"Whether she is or isn't makes no difference. I warned you in Boston, boy. I said I wouldn't have her hurt. What you did—and what you must have said when you left—have brought her such grief as I've never seen before. I pressed her, but she refused to give me any details—except to say there was nothing more between the two of you. Go carry out your commander's orders. And don't try to see her again."

"Mr. Ware—"

"Don't. Ever."

"Mr. Ware, listen! Anne understood I had to leave. Had to settle one matter before—"

"*Understood?* No, she didn't!"

Caught in the impulsive falsehood, Philip turned scarlet. He began:

"If you'll let me explain—"

"I want none of your damned explanations! Neither does she. Annie risked her life for you when the British investigated the death of that officer. And your repayment was to leave her and give her grief. I warned you against it!" he repeated, his frail shoulders trembling.

"Let Anne be the one to say she doesn't want to see me!" Philip said, reaching out to shove Ware aside. The lawyer's veined hand darted for a trousers pocket—

And Philip was staring into the round black circle of a gun muzzle.

The beautifully worked silver scrolling of the pocket pistol flashed in the lamplight. The lawyer's hand shook so badly that Philip expected the pistol might go off any second. Ware had it cocked. At close range, the ball could tear half his head away.

"I've kept this for emergencies," Ware said. "Thinking that if I was ever caught by redcoats wanting to arrest me, I'd use it on them. I'll use it on you if you don't leave. Don't ever let me see your filthy face again."

"Damn it, Mr. Ware, I don't understand why—"

"You don't' eh? Then you're stupid! Wanting to protect you in some misguided way, Annie's hid the truth. But she can't hide the white look of her face. The spells of weakness that come on her more and more—"

Against the mournful tolling of the bell, Philip's thoughts flashed to the last time he'd seen her. He recalled the strange, unnatural pallor very well.

Ware said, "I will make you one last promise, Kent. If my daughter is, as I suspect, carrying a child—"

"A *child!*"

"—and if the child's yours, I'll find you, wherever you are. And I'll kill you. Don't make the mistake of doubting me."

He spun and walked up to the door of Wright's, wispy hair blowing back and forth across his forehead, the pocket pistol still shaking in his hand.

Stunned, Philip considered trying to lunge, disarm the little lawyer. At all costs, he needed to see Anne—

A voice bawled behind him, "Kent, damn you, get going to Barrett's! That's an order!"

Buttrick ran on. The door of Wright's slammed. The bell shattered the night, *clang* and *clang*—

Philip stumbled toward the mare. As he hoisted himself to the saddle, he glimpsed Abraham Ware peering from one of the front windows of the tavern, frail, yet somehow almost Biblical in his wrath.

A child, Philip's mind kept repeating, as if that would help him comprehend the astonishing fact. *Our child?*

He tried to recollect when it might have happened. Surely it had to be the night before New Year's. He had to see Anne! Suppose she and her father fled before morning. He might never find her again—

He almost turned the mare's head back. But he encountered Buttrick once more. Again the major yelled for him to hurry. So he kept on toward North Bridge, past silent, hard-breathing men rolling flour barrels to a new hiding place.

As the mare clattered over the plank bridge, the church bell finally stopped its wild pealing. One thought thundered in Philip's mind, so compelling he almost wept.

She knew the day I left her. She knew but she wouldn't use it to hold me—

And now, with the regulars marching somewhere beneath the paling stars, it might be too late. If the British came as far as Concord, men could die—

Philip Kent among them.

iii

At Colonel Barrett's farm, lanterns burned in the barn. Philip found the militia commander assembling his gear. A bit addled and still smelling of rum, he had nevertheless wakened to the bell.

"Did Buttrick think I wouldn't, for God's sake?" Barrett belched. "That's one tocsin I'd hear even if I were down in hell. I'm glad you're back, Kent. Some said you'd gone for good. To the Tory side, maybe."

"I couldn't ever stand on the Tory side, Colonel."

"Good. Because we'll need every man if they're sending fifteen hundred to strip this farm of all we've hidden away. Good black powder in the attic with feather ticking over it. Cannon buried in the furrows of the back field—and d'you know how much is left in Concord?"

"I saw flour barrels being moved—"

"That's a fraction! There's nearly ten tons of musket balls and cartridges. Thirty-five half-barrels of powder.

Gun carriages and tents and salt fish and beef and harness and spades and—well, plenty to make it worth Gage's while to search it out, I'll tell you. Worth our while to defend, too. A couple of days ago there was a rumor this raid might be coming. So some of the stuff's been hauled to towns west of here. But by no means all. Here, I'm talking too much—get going!"

iv

Not many minutes later, Philip turned the mare into the yard of O'Brian's. He found the whole household— the Irish farmer, Daisy, Lumden and Arthur—awake and wondering at the exact meaning of the alarm.

Because of the tense situation, Philip's sudden appearance elicited only momentary surprise, and the briefest of greetings. They all wanted to know why the bell rang. Philip explained. Arthur finished rounding up the arms for him and for O'Brian: a musket apiece and shoulder-strap cartouches packed with lead ball and paper-wrapped powder charges.

O'Brian hummed a military tune, checking his supplies with a sprightliness more appropriate to a man half his age. Lumden voiced the wish that a spare musket could be found. He felt obliged to be ready to defend O'Brian's house.

Arthur's teeth showed in a hard smile. "Don' fret, Sergeant George. Tommy comes this far, there's sickles and scythes in the barn. And a loft where you can drop down on 'em by surprise."

"By God, you can count on it."

Philip found a moment to draw Daisy aside.

"I tried to see Mistress Anne in the village. Her father wouldn't permit it. I don't want to put you in danger, Daisy, but is there any way you can get to her? Slip in and give her a message and then get out before there's trouble?"

Daisy didn't hesitate. "Of course I can."

"Then tell her—" A lump seemed to congeal in his throat. Already the musket felt dead heavy in his right hand. "Tell her she has my love. In case I don't see her again."

"All right," the red-haired girl whispered, awed by his stark look.

"And tell her I'm sorry I caused her any—"

"Kent! Let's move out!" came O'Brian's hail from the front of the house.

Nodding wearily, Philip started away. A thought crossed his mind. He called, "One moment more, sir—" He turned back to the girl, who was already pulling a shawl around her shoulders. "Daisy, are my things still stored in the clothes press?"

"Your sword and the tea bottle—?"

"And the box."

She nodded.

He leaned his musket against the wall, went to the clothes press, knelt and rummaged in the bottom until he located the leather-covered casket. He opened the lid, drew out the document on top, replaced the casket, shut the press doors and walked swiftly back past Daisy to the kitchen, where Arthur had already kindled a fire.

He stared at his father's witnessed letter for a few seconds. Then he put it in the flames. He retrieved his musket and left the house by the front door.

He drew a deep breath of the sweet morning air as he joined O'Brian out by the road. Behind the ridge, the eastern sky was already growing light.

CHAPTER VI

"God Damn It, They Are Firing Ball!"

i

THE HOT MORNING sun beat against Philip's neck as he obeyed the command to load.

He braced the musket's butt on the ground. He tore one of the paper cartridges with his teeth, poured its contents down the muzzle, then dropped the ball in after it. Three twisting strokes of the ramrod and the load was seated.

He was conscious of sweat on his palms, the nervous expressions of the men around him. Several hundred by now. The Concord companies had been reinforced with units that had marched in from Lincoln, Acton, Bedford. And there were young and old men who belonged to no company at all, but who had brought their ancient squirrel guns, even a few pistols, in response to the couriers and the tolling bells that had spread the dreadful tidings across the countryside—

The regulars are coming out.

From the slant of the sun, Philip judged the time to be near eleven o'clock. He stood next to O'Brian on the Muster Field, a high hilltop place well back from the north side of the road that led west from the river bridge.

As the mounted officers resumed their conference, he wiped his sweating forehead. Squinted at the white clouds sailing calm and stately overhead. His mouth was

613

dry, with a metallic taste. Was this how it felt when a man faced death in battle?

Because there was no longer any doubt that the stage was set for conflict. Just down the hillside, invisible from the Muster Field to which the militiamen had retreated, British units in their brilliant, blazing red had crossed the bridge to the west side—

It still seemed unreal.

So did the whole morning. Since first light, he'd lived through a terrifyingly swift sequence of events. Events far different from any his wildest imagination had ever conjured in Auvergne. Or London or Boston, for that matter.

Through it all, he'd searched for Anne. He hadn't seen her—nor her father, thank God.

Perhaps he'd only missed her by moments. But that was no comfort. Not now.

ii

He and O'Brian had arrived in Concord at dawn. People were everywhere: armed men tramping in from the hills, others still moving stores to new hiding places. In dooryards, women gathered with their sleepy children, whispering, their faces drawn.

About six o'clock, a scout brought news from Lexington.

Many companies of British soldiers were indeed on the march. At Lexington green, the arriving redcoats and Captain Parker's minutemen had exchanged shots. The scout had spurred his horse away at the first sounds of firing. Thus, he couldn't answer what seemed to be everyone's question—including O'Brian's:

Were the British firing ball or only noisy powder?

The scout swiped at his mouth. "I do not know. But I think it probable they were using ball."

The man could offer no more definite information as

to who had fired first, the Crown soldiers or some hot-tempered colonial. But the stunning truth spread throughout the village in a few minutes, casting a new pall—

Shots exchanged.

A war of words had turned to a war in fact.

The Concord companies formed up and marched out toward Lexington before seven, to probe the enemy's strength.

A slender country fellow Philip knew as Hosmer beat time on his drum as they trudged east in the steadily brightening light. At that hour, the column comprised not many more than a hundred men, drab in their plain shirts, their farm-muddied boots and trousers.

Someone let out a yell, pointed. Away in the east, Philip and the others spied the head of what seemed a great red serpent crawling along the level road to meet them—

Several hundred grenadiers and light infantrymen at least. Preceded by their musicians thudding drums and tootling fifes. Bayonets glittered in the rising sun. Ornamental plates on the tall black caps of the grenadiers winked like mirrors. Crossbelts and pipe-clayed breeches showed brilliant white. The music and the sound of their coming filled the countryside.

Colonel Barrett reined in, scowling. A moment later he ordered his companies to turn about and countermarch. The men in the colorfully faced red uniforms pouring along the road far outnumbered Barrett's force. There might be as many as five hundred or a thousand approaching, their brave music louder by the moment.

So on Barrett's order, the Concord companies preceded their enemies back to the village, keeping in surprisingly good formation and showing no panic. But their own riffling drum and single fife were all but drowned out by the massed instruments behind them.

A strange procession indeed, Philip thought as he

tramped back into town. He and his companions marched—even joked—as if that immense scarlet serpent didn't exist—

The officers spurred ahead to warn the women and old men to retreat to their homes. The flood of armed redcoats would be sweeping into Concord before another hour was up—!

The militiamen kept in their ranks and halted on command. Philip again searched the scurrying clusters of townspeople for a glimpse of Anne. He didn't see her.

He reflected with a grim amusement that the colonials had almost behaved like a sort of advance honor guard for their foes—music competing against music in the warmth of the April morning. Toward the end, Hosmer had actually picked up and matched the cadence of the British drums.

As the British tattoo grew still louder, officers and townsmen argued briefly. Some, the Reverend Emerson for one, wanted an immediate confrontation right in the village. Barrett finally overruled the hotter tempers. The supplies in town had now been reasonably well hidden, he said. No one as yet had a clear indication of how thorough—or how violent—the British search would be.

"And if it does come to battle, the longer we wait, the better. We'll have more men from the neighboring towns."

Many questioned Barrett's decision loudly and angrily. But no one disobeyed when he gave the order for the men to march.

They headed up the road in the direction of North Bridge and the high ground of the Muster Field. On the way, scouts reported that the British bandsmen had broken formation. Retreated to the rear of the column. Some light infantry companies were leaving the road, scaling the ridge on their right to search for hostile forces—

Once across the bridge, Barrett ordered his officers to clear the hillside of a considerable number of townsmen and farm families who had waded the river to watch any forthcoming action. Looking back during the ascent to the Muster Field, Philip saw red and white uniforms through the trees lining the road from Concord.

Six or seven companies of light infantry, it looked like. Moving westward—no doubt to find the supplies at Barrett's farm.

The colonel left Major Buttrick in command as the country soldiers reached the hilltop. Barrett galloped off to his farm for a last-minute check of the hidden stores.

The sun grew hotter.

The British companies advanced across the bridge. Three deployed on the river's west bank. The other four marched on toward Barrett's, to the steady thumping of the drums.

Soon Barrett came riding back, having circled wide to elude the searchers. He dismounted on the brow of the hill and surveyed the situation down at the bridge.

All the time, more men arrived. From the south, from the north, they flowed in singly and in groups. The sun kept climbing toward the zenith.

Philip and the others fidgeted while Barrett spoke with his officers. The morning wind blew warm across the hilltop.

Word circulated that Barrett was gambling on the main thrust of search and seizure being aimed at his farm. Perhaps all that the redcoats left in town wanted to do was show their authority—by means of their presence.

Before long, however, he was proved wrong. About ten, a man slipped across the river. He reported that the leader of the expeditionary force, a Lieutenant Colonel Smith, had established a command post at Wright's. His soldiers were scouring the town for stores.

With restraint, the spy said. The townspeople were not being abused—or even touched. But sacks of bullets and barrels of flour were being pitched gleefully into the millpond by the redcoats. That remained the extent of the damage to the moment—

The whole action seemed hesitant, Philip thought. It was as if the British still hoped to bring the colonists to heel without violence. Could the report from Lexington have been exaggerated? The possibility helped him breathe a little easier—

Especially about Anne. Wherever she might be in town, her safety seemed more certain than it had a few hours ago.

Then, just before eleven, the black plume of smoke climbed into the sky.

From the Muster Field, it wasn't possible to see what buildings were afire. But the meaning of the smoke column seemed unmistakable. One of Barrett's adjutants confronted him angrily:

"Damn it, sir, will you let them burn the town down?"

A few moments later, Barrett gave the command to load with ball.

iii

Hosmer struck up his drumbeat again. In a column of twos, the country soldiers marched to the edge of the hill and started down.

From his position alongside Martin O'Brian, Philip saw the Irish farmer grin a hard grin. And realized Barrett's strategy had been sound. The double file trailing away ahead and behind surely must total five hundred by now. The three British companies on this side of the bridge appeared to number no more than a hundred or a hundred and twenty at most.

Barrett sat his horse at the crest of the hillside. As

Philip and the others trudged past, he kept repeating a stern command:

"Don't fire first. If there's to be shooting, don't fire first!"

Philip's heart beat hard, almost matching the rhythm of Hosmer's drum. Below him, the head of the column reached level ground, turned in the direction of the bridge. The whole proceedings still did not seem quite real—

Except for that black pillar of smoke over the treetops that screened out all sight of the village.

"Hah, look! They're scurrying back!" O'Brian rasped cheerfully.

As the British officers shouted commands, the three companies hastily formed up and faced about. In a moment, their cadenced marching hammered the planks of the bridge. Hosmer's drum beat furiously in answer.

Barrett spurred down the hillside to the head of the column, his eyes narrowed against the April sun. Philip and O'Brian reached the road, turned left after the men ahead of them. Across the murmuring river, Philip could see little except a rush and flash of scarlet-clad forms. The light infantry companies were dividing, one moving to each flank of the third company, which now faced toward the far end of the bridge.

The men of this company were drawn up in street-fighting formation—three ranks, one behind the other. The sun shone on the brown barrels of their muskets, flashed from their bayonets as the first rank knelt. The second rank moved up close behind.

Barrett shouted, "Faster cadence, drummer!"

Boldly, the colonel headed his horse out ahead of the double file. The first in line were men from the town of Acton, Philip believed.

Barrett rode to within shouting distance of the bridge as half a dozen redcoats frantically started trying to rip up the planks on the far side.

"Leave the bridge alone!" Barrett bawled in a threatening voice.

Philip heard no order given. But suddenly the muskets of the kneeling front rank of the central British company exploded.

Smoke—spurts of fire—

At the head of the militia column, the captain of the Acton contingent pitched over.

Hosmer's drumming stopped in mid-beat as he toppled. Blood from his throat spilled red over his drumhead—

Barrett's horse screamed and shied from the thunderous volley. Somewhere Buttrick's voice rang out:

"Fire, for God's sake—*fire!*"

Drawn up two by two in the long column, only the foremost militiamen had a clear shot. But seconds after the British fired, and without any specific command, the men in the rear of the column broke for both sides of the road.

Philip ran to the right, O'Brian the other way. Over the racketing of the muskets, Philip heard the Irishman's enraged yell:

"God damn it, they are firing ball!"

Philip dropped to one knee in the marsh grass. He hit the musket's muzzle to send powder through the touchhole, braced the piece against his shoulder—and for one awful instant amid the shouting, the rattling fire from the militiamen, the confused yells and orders, the blowing smoke, his very will seemed frozen—

Across the narrow bridge, he saw an officer down. Another fell. The kneeling front ranks scrambled up, dropped behind to permit the second rank an unobstructed aim. Finally, Philip's finger tightened—

Tightened—

Taking an eternity, it seemed.

It had come.

In the cries of pain, the corpses of the drummer and the Acton captain, he heard and saw the end of the settled world he'd hoped for—

Gone. All gone this April morning—

He fired.

He reeled back against the musket's kick, saw a light infantryman at the far end of the bridge spin and sprawl on his face. Whether Philip's own ball had scored the hit, or a ball fired from another of the crackling muskets, he did not know for certain.

But he knew an era had ended and another had begun, for himself and for all the shouting, cursing Americans who leveled their weapons and continued firing on the King's soldiers across the river.

iv

The colonials never fully understood the reason for what happened next.

Over the long months in which the conflict had been building to this climax, many who had openly predicted that war would come had, at the same time, reminded their listeners of one more fact. Haphazardly drilled, poorly equipped Massachusetts farmers would be no match for regimental troops that had fought honorably all over the world—and won.

And yet, with his own eyes, Philip witnessed the astounding aftermath of the exchange of volleys—one from each side.

Even as he crouched in the long grass and frantically rammed home his next load, he saw the crack British light infantrymen break ranks. Carrying or dragging their dead and wounded, they plunged back up the road to Concord.

Not in formation. Running—like a mob in panic.

Their passage raised clouds of dust.

No one could explain the frantic retreat. Was it caused by the surprising courage of the double file that had marched down the hillside to confrontation without cover? Was it produced by the American musket fire, a thunder more intimidating in its noise than its accuracy? Or was it the result of the British simply never expecting any resistance at all?

Whatever the reason, the redcoats fled. Without plan and without pattern, they fled—while Barrett rallied his men, Philip among them.

The colonel led his troops over the bridge. At the east end, a young, tow-haired redcoat lay on his face, shot through the back. Caught by a ball when the front rank moved away so the second could fire? Who would ever know?

Philip trudged by the fallen soldier. The boy's shoulders moved slightly. He was still alive. One of the Americans spat on him. But no one touched him.

The militiamen followed Barrett, moving in ragged formation. Some three hundred yards from the bridge, the colonel led them up a hillside. On command, they sprawled in the long meadow grass behind a low stone wall, to await orders or the next action.

In the distance, Philip spied companies of grenadiers in their tall, glossy black caps moving out from the blowing smoke that still hid most of the village. The grenadiers—reinforcements for the bridge—met the noisy, panic-stricken light infantrymen running the other way. Perhaps there was some plan to re-form the entire force, return and confront the enemy. It never materialized. In a few minutes, all the troops had disappeared back into the smoke.

Philip lay with the grass tickling his cheek. He was still stunned by the significance of the brief battle. *They had fired on the King's troops.*

The other men resting behind the wall were equally stunned—and equally quiet. After their first triumphant yells at the bridge, a strange silence had settled on them. It continued as the tramp of more marching feet sounded from the direction of the river.

Philip raised on one elbow, caught sight of the companies that had marched to Barrett's re-crossing the bridge at quick-step. He glanced down the line of the wall, searched for an officer. But Barrett, Buttrick and the others in charge had disappeared.

He asked about them. A man four places down said they'd crept away along the ridge to survey the town at closer range. There was no one to issue a command to fire as the four companies tramped by along the road directly below—well within musket range.

Not a shot rang out. Barely a mumbled curse could be heard from the men crouched behind the stone wall. Did they all feel what he felt? Dread? One skirmish did not make a successful revolution—

The noise of the returning companies gradually died away. A jay circled in the hot, still air above the watching farmers. The bird shrilled at them.

By noon, the British expeditionary force had taken the road back to Lexington. Concord lay quiet in the April light.

v

Everywhere, it seemed, men were running again. Excited now, jubilant. Making bawdy, contemptuous jokes about the Crown soldiers.

The hilltops around Concord were black with running figures—musket-armed countrymen still pouring in from all points of the compass. Many marched in across South Bridge.

Receiving hasty orders in the village street, they hurried out again to climb and move along the ridges that overlooked the highway back to Lexington and Boston.

When the fact of the British departure was certain, Philip and the rest had descended the hillside and raced back to the village. There, along with other chagrined officers and men, they discovered the cause of the smoke that had precipitated the march from the Muster Field, and the subsequent volleys.

Far from burning the town, grenadiers under Smith's command had simply found several gun carriages among the stores cached in Concord's meeting house. They had dragged the carriages into the open and set them alight. Philip stared ruefully at the charred, smoldering remains. He shook his head with a dour amusement. So easily did war begin. By a mistake, a wrong judgment—

All around him, men with muskets kept moving out toward the east. North of the village he saw them thick on the ridges. Someone in the crowd seized his arm.

He whirled, recognized O'Brian, his blue eyes fierce.

"Come along, come along, Philip! We're to give chase. We'll chivy them all the way back to Boston, damned if we won't!"

"Pack of strutting peacocks!" another man yelled. "Marching with their God damn fifes and drums—we showed 'em, I'll say!"

"Aye," a third agreed. "They fired ball and they'll get ball in return—from now on."

The trio, including O'Brian, disappeared in the dust and commotion.

Philip wiped his forehead. Sweat trickled beneath his shirt. He searched the faces of the excited people clustering outside their homes and near the meeting house—where the remains of the gun carriages finally collapsed into ash.

No sign of her. Not anywhere. With a weary sigh, he started for the east edge of town.

"Philip?"

He turned, blinking into the smoke and glare. He was afraid in the depths of his soul that his ears had played him false. And false hope was worse than none—

A patch of smoke cleared. He saw her.

Her plain gray dress was stained, torn at the sleeves, wet all around the hem. Her chestnut hair was tangled. Something seemed to turn and break inside of him. Tears welled in his eyes as he shouldered the musket and ran toward her.

She ran too, closing the distance between them with amazing speed. Dropping the musket, he swept his arms around her, kissing her tear-stained cheek, kissing her unashamedly in the smoky sunlight.

"Anne," was all he could say at first. "Oh, Annie, oh my God, Annie—I thought I'd never see you again. Your father turned me away from Wright's last night—"

"And told me about how he threatened you," she said, half-laughing, half-crying as she wiped her eyes.

"Did Daisy find you? I sent a message—"

"Yes, she brought it. That's why I've been searching for you all morning. Were you at the bridge?"

"I was. But I only got to fire one round before the redcoats ran."

Her hands seemed all over his face, his arms. Squeezing, touching.

"You're not hurt—?"

"No, no. Only two or three died on our side."

"I'm such a sight—I look so terrible—" Her face was still wet with tears. She spoke in short, almost incoherent gasps. "We've been at the millpond, pulling out the flour barrels. The poor grenadiers—they were so polite. They neglected to crack the barrels open. The flour around the lids sealed them shut. So most of the flour is good as new. Philip, that fat, frightened puppy—" Her laugh was ragged. "—Smith, the commander—he paid for wagons and chaises to carry his wounded back along the retreat route. *Paid* for them! Gentlemen to the end!"

"Some of those gentlemen are shot down dead," Philip told her. "I'm supposed to go up the road and find Barrett's companies again. We're to follow the redcoats and harry them, Mr. O'Brian said—"

"Smith ranted about the delay of the reinforcements he sent for. There may be many more troops marching out from Boston—"

"Annie, forget the troops." He touched the freckles on her cheek, barely able to speak. "Last night, your father said—he told me—"

"That I'm going to bear a child? It's true."

"Why didn't you speak of it before I left for Philadelphia? You knew it then, you must have!"

She answered quietly, "Of course I did. But I wouldn't have used that to hold you—"

"Just what I suspected!"

"I'd have no man without love, Philip. And I want no man except you—" Her voice broke. She brushed at her tear-streaked face, embarrassed. "Truly, I never thought you'd come back. What—what happened in Philadelphia?"

A peculiar smile pulled up the corners of his mouth. "I almost bought a whistle. But it cost too much."

"A whistle? Whatever are you talking about?"

"It's not important," he said, still smiling that strange smile.

"But the woman, Philip. What about her?"

He thought a moment, then said, "I'll tell you one day. When we're old and our child's grown up, maybe. All you need to know now is that it's done—and I know what I want and what I am."

"What I hoped and prayed you'd turn out to be!" she whispered joyfully, hugging him.

"Annie, there's nothing I can offer you—Christ, not even the certainty I'll come back today. Who knows what kind of fighting there'll be if we chase the British? But if I can come back, Annie, I want to marry you—"

"Not because you think you must," she said with a shake of her head. "Not because of my father. Or for any other reason except—"

"That I love you," he finished, kissing her.

Some passing men jeered and called him a yellow shirker, and why didn't he get a move on? He paid no attention, his hands fierce against Anne's back, holding her, feeling the warmth of her through the stained dress—and the trembling, too, as she wept her happiness.

She wrapped her arms around his waist, buried her face against his shoulder. "We'll raise good strong sons, Philip. You'll start a fine printing firm of your own and be a rich man—we'll have a splendid house—"

"Annie, Annie—" He lifted her chin, caressed tears from her eyes. "That's a good dream. But not a certain one. The fire's broken out. Right here in Concord this morning. And in Lexington, they said—"

"Yes, eight or nine of Captain Parker's best were shot down on the green. But you saw how the people rose up in the countryside—came to fight—"

"Still, it's a terrible thing to think of what can lie ahead. The colonies locked in war with the strongest nation on earth—God knows what sort of future any man will have—"

"*I* know!" she exclaimed, her face shining. "I know—now that you've chosen your side. You'll live, and we'll take what comes—and we'll still be together when it's done, you'll see. What Sam Adams wants will happen now, it must—"

"You mean independency?"

"Yes—maybe declared by that very Congress meet-

ing in May. Philip, it has to come! A new country. Free
of the old bonds just like you're free of them. But we'll
weather everything—and turn the Kent family into
something strong and fine."

He let himself smile a little, saying:

"Provided your father doesn't put a ball through me
first. Where is he?"

"Down at the pond hauling out the flour barrels." She
laughed. "I told him I felt an attack of female dizziness
coming on. He's utterly confounded by such things. I
said I was going back to Wright's to rest—but I was
really coming to hunt for you again. By the time you
return, I'll see that he's properly tamed—since you've
decided to do the decent thing," she finished, teasing.

He kissed her for another long, sweet moment.

"Somehow, I think you're right, Anne."

"About what?"

He pressed her hand. "I think the Kents will turn out
to be a very fine family indeed."

He retrieved his fallen musket and, after one final
wave, started walking east.

vi

Philip headed out of Concord in company with other
men. A great many sang. Some recounted the fight at the
bridge second or third hand, or continued making
obscene jokes at the expense of the royal troops. Philip's
belly growled. How long was it since he'd eaten or slept?
It seemed an age.

Yet there was a spring in his stride; a fresh sense of
direction. Despite the uncertainties and dangers ahead,
he was, for a few moments, completely happy.

The euphoria didn't last long.

How would England react now? he wondered. With

armed might, surely. Unrestricted and unrestrained. Only in that way could the King hope to put down this rebellion in the cause of freedom—

No matter. He'd follow the road from Concord wherever it led. And come back to Anne, and see their baby born. The first one, then many more—

Dirty, weary, he still hummed a little as he left the highway and started to climb the hillside toward the ridge, where he thought he'd glimpsed some of the Concord contingent. The higher he climbed, the hotter the sun seemed to burn. Almost like a fire on his face.

He climbed toward the blue sky and the free air at the crest of the ridge and caught up with three men he recognized. He was soon out of sight of Concord, lost among the other Americans streaming east to fight.

Philip Kent, patriot soldier . . . Judson Fletcher, disgraced aristocrat: the battle for the new nation's survival weaves their fates in a pattern that will forever taint the Kent family with "the Fletcher blood" in

The Rebels

Volume II

of

The American Bicentennial Series

Afterword

Several people deserve a generous share of thanks for their contributions to this book.

First, Lyle Engel, whose concept of the series provided the canvas for this panoramic picture of our beginnings as a nation.

Marla Ray merits special mention for her editorial help and continuing encouragement.

Norman Goldfind, vice-president and editorial director of Pyramid Books, who developed the concept with Mr. Engel, has lavished the kind of interest and attention on the project that, all too often, an author finds missing.

And Norman and Ann Kearns, senior editor at Pyramid, must be thanked for a host of perceptive suggestions that helped strengthen the final work immeasurably.

Finally, I must tender appreciation to my family, who collectively endured months of three different typewriters clacking at strange times, small mountains of research books cluttering up the otherwise orderly premises and periods of authorial gloom and doom alternating with nonstop monologues about Paul Revere's dentistry or Dr. Franklin's air baths that monopolized dinner-table conversations. My wife especially was patience personified when I kept the lights on and the coffee kettle whistling in more predawn hours than I'm sure she cares to count.

I often think that far too many Americans today do not know how and why this country came into being—and, more tragic, do not care. Perhaps in some small way, these novels will help remedy that unhappy situation—and prove, at the same time, as entertaining as only an epic adventure of the spirit can be.

To all those people named, who have been instrumental in my own personal rediscovery of our heritage—a rediscovery that has been, if I may be allowed to use the word in this cynical age, inspiring—I owe a lasting debt.

And Don—thank you for that very first phone call.

JOHN JAKES

ABOUT THE AUTHOR

John Jakes was born in Chicago. He is a graduate of DePauw University, and took his M.A. in literature at Ohio State. He sold his first short story during his second year of college, and his first book twelve months later. Since then, he has published more than 200 short stories and over 50 books—chiefly suspense, nonfiction for young people and, most recently, science fiction. He has also authored six popular historical novels under his Jay Scotland pseudonym. His books have appeared in translation from Europe to Japan. Originally intending to be an actor, Mr. Jakes' continuing interest in theater has manifested itself in four plays and the books and lyrics for five musicals, all of which are currently in print and being performed by stock and amateur groups around the United States. The author is married, is the father of four children, and lists among his organizations the Authors Guild, the Dramatists Guild, and Science Fiction Writers of America.

ON SALE WHEREVER PAPERBACKS ARE SOLD
— or use this coupon to order directly from the publisher.

MYSTERY & SUSPENSE

IF YOU ENJOYED THIS BOOK, HERE ARE MORE PAPERBACKS JUST RIGHT FOR YOU . . .

Ngaio Marsh

N2986	A Man Lay Dead 95¢ £	
V3353	Overture To Death $1.25 £	
N2994	The Nursing Home Murder 95¢ £	
V3017	Vintage Murder 1.25 £	
V3081	Tied Up In Tinsel £ $1.25	
N3158	Hand In Glove 95¢ ·	
N3184	Death of A Fool 95¢ £	
N3265	Death In A White Tie 95¢ £	
N3321	Night At The Vulcan 95¢ £	
V3384	Singing In The Shrouds $1.25 £	

Rex Stout

ADVENTURES OF NERO WOLFE:

N3269	Black Orchids 95¢
N2891	The Broken Vase 95¢
N2774	Fer De Lance 95¢
N2691	Too Many Cooks 95¢
N3187	Rubber Band 95¢
N2739	Some Buried Caesar 95¢ ‡
N2639	Not Quite Dead Enough 95¢ ‡
N2968	Over My Dead Body 95¢ ‡

Send to: PYRAMID PUBLICATIONS,
Dept. M.O., 9 Garden Street, Moonachie, N.J. 07074

NAME

ADDRESS

CITY

STATE   ZIP

I enclose $_____, which includes the total price of all books ordered plus 50¢ per book postage and handling for the first book and 25¢ for each additional. If my total order is $10.00 or more, I understand that Pyramid will pay all postage and handling.
No COD's or stamps. Please allow three to four weeks for delivery.
Prices subject to change.   P-48